DEMON
ROAD

ALSO BY
DEREK LANDY

DEMON ROAD

Limited Signed Edition

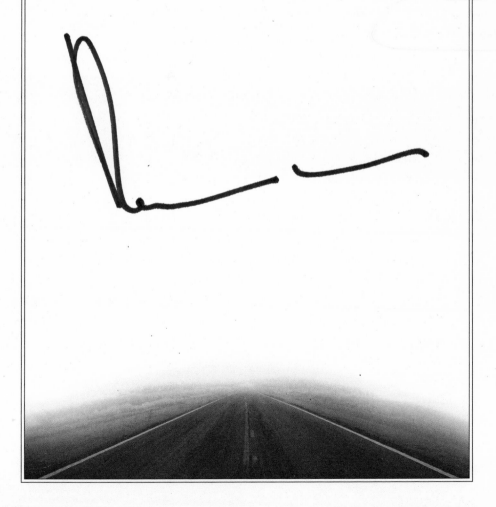

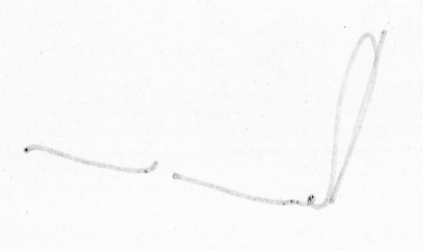

DEREK LANDY

DEMON
ROAD

HarperCollins *Children's Books*

First published in hardback in Great Britain by HarperCollins Children's Books 2015
HarperCollins Children's Books is a division of
HarperCollinsPublishers Ltd
1 London Bridge Street, London SE1 9GF

Visit us on the web at www.harpercollins.co.uk

Derek Landy blogs under duress at www.dereklandy.blogspot.com

1

HB ISBN: 978-00-0-814081-6
TPB ISBN: 978-00-0-814086-1
Limited Edition ISBN: 978-0-00-816050-0

Typeset in Joanna MT Std by Palimpsest Book Production Ltd,
Falkirk, Stirlingshire

Printed and bound in England by
Clays Ltd, St Ives plc

MIX
Paper from
responsible sources
FSC
www.fsc.org
FSC C007454

FSC™ is a non-profit international organisation established to promote
the responsible management of the world's forests. Products carrying the
FSC label are independently certified to assure consumers that they come
from forests that are managed to meet the social, economic and
ecological needs of present and future generations,
and other controlled sources.

Find out more about HarperCollins and the environment at
www.harpercollins.co.uk/green

Laura J –

I introduced you to scary movies, the books of Stephen King, and the myriad delights of horror.

You introduced me to StarKid.

I have still not forgiven you.

1

TWELVE HOURS BEFORE AMBER LAMONT'S parents tried to kill her, she was sitting between them in the principal's office, her hands in her lap, stifling all the things she wanted to say.

"We don't stand for troublemakers in this school," said Mrs Cobb. She was a fleshy woman in her fifties who wore a necklace so tight that when her neck quivered and her face went red, Amber expected her head to just pop off, maybe bounce on the floor and go rolling underneath her massively imposing desk. That would have been nice.

"There is a reason we have been placed in the top three educational facilities in the great state of Florida," Cobb continued, "and do you know what that is? It's because we run a tight ship."

She paused for effect, as if what she'd said needed to be absorbed rather than merely tolerated.

Cobb inclined her head slightly to one side. "Mr and Mrs Lamont, I don't know you very well. In previous years, there has been no reason to summon you here. In previous years, Amber's behaviour has been perfectly adequate. But your daughter has been sent to my office three times in the past month for altercations with other students. *Three times.* That is, I'm sure you'll agree, beyond the pale. Speaking plainly, as I feel I must, her behaviour this semester has worsened to such a degree that I am, regrettably, forced to wonder if there might have been some drastic change in her home circumstances."

Amber's mother nodded sympathetically. "How terrible for you."

Her parents were, as expected, completely calm in the face of overwhelming stupidity. That specific type of calm – detached, patient but at-times-veering-into-condescension – was pretty much their default setting. Amber was used to it. Cobb was not.

Betty Lamont sat in her chair with perfect posture and perfect hair, dressed smartly yet demurely. Bill Lamont sat with his legs crossed, hands resting on the understated buckle of his Italian belt, his fingers intertwined and his shoes gleaming. Both of them good-looking people, tall, healthy and trim. Amber had more in common with Mrs Cobb than she did with her own parents – Cobb could, in fact, have been Amber in forty years' time, if she never found the discipline to go on that diet she'd been promising herself. The only thing she seemed to have inherited from her folks' combined gene pool was her brown hair. Sometimes Amber let herself wonder where it all went wrong with her – but she didn't ponder that mystery for very long. Such pondering led to the cold and darker places of her mind.

"It gets worse," Cobb said. "The parents of the other girl in this... *fracas*, we'll call it, have intimated that they will report the incident to the local newspaper if we do not take appropriate measures. I, for one, refuse to see this school's good name dragged through the mud because of the actions of one troublesome student." At that, Cobb glared at Amber, just to make sure everyone present knew to whom she was referring.

"Can I say something?" Amber asked.

"No, you may not."

"Saffron's the one who started it. She picks on anyone who isn't as pretty and perfect as her and her friends."

"Be quiet," Cobb said sharply.

"I'm just saying, if you want to blame someone, then blame—"

"You may not speak!"

Amber answered her glare with one of her own. "Then why am I here?"

"You are here to sit and be quiet and let me talk to your parents."

"But I could let you talk to my parents from somewhere else," Amber said.

Cobb's face flushed and her neck quivered. Amber waited for the pop.

"Young lady, you will be quiet when I tell you to be quiet. You will respect my authority and do as you are told. Do you understand?"

"So I'm not allowed to speak up for—"

"Do you understand?"

Her mother patted Amber's leg. "Come on now, sweetie, let the nice old woman speak."

Cobb's eyes widened. "Well, I think I have identified the source of the problem. If this is how Amber has been raised, I am not surprised that she has no respect for authority."

"Naturally," Bill said, as composed as ever. "What's so great about authority, anyway? It takes itself far too seriously, if you want my opinion. You have a little problem that you blow all out of proportion, drag Betty and myself across town for a meeting we're obviously supposed to dread, and here you sit at your ridiculously large desk like a mini-despot, assuming you wield some sinister power over us. Betty, are you feeling intimidated yet?"

"Not yet," Betty said kindly, "but I'm sure it will kick in soon."

Amber did her best not to squirm in her seat. She'd seen this enough times to know what was coming next, and it always made her uncomfortable. Her parents had only so much tolerance for people they viewed as irritations, and the level of punishment they doled out depended entirely on how they were feeling on any particular occasion. The only thing Amber didn't know was how far they intended to take it today.

Cobb's unremarkable eyes narrowed. "Obviously, the apple hasn't fallen far from the tree. I can see where your daughter gets her attitude."

Mrs Cobb was now little more than a lame wildebeest, the kind Amber had seen on nature documentaries. Her parents were the lions, moving through the long grass, closing in on both sides. Cobb didn't know she was the wildebeest, of course. She didn't know she was lame, either. She thought she was the lion, the one with the power. She had no idea what was coming.

"You've just said, essentially, the same thing twice," Bill pointed out to her. "Added to this, you seem to talk entirely in clichés. And we've been entrusting you to educate our daughter? We may have to reconsider."

"Let me assure you, Mr Lamont," Mrs Cobb said, sitting

straighter and smoothing down her blouse, "you will not have to worry about that any longer."

"Oh, excellent," Betty said happily. "So you'll be leaving the school, then?"

"No, Mrs Lamont, it is your *daughter* who will be leaving."

Betty laughed politely. "Oh no, I don't think so. Bill?"

Bill took out his phone – what he half-jokingly referred to as the most powerful phone in Florida – and dialled a number.

"We do not allow cellphones in the Principal's Office," Cobb said.

Bill ignored her. "Grant," he said, smiling when the call was picked up. "Sorry to be calling in the middle of the day. No, no, nothing like that. Not yet, anyway. No, I'd like you to do me a favour, if you would. The principal of Amber's school, you know her? That's the one. I'd like her fired, please."

Faint fingers of a headache began to tap on the inside of Amber's skull. So this was how far they were willing to take things today. All the way to the end.

"Thank you," said Bill. "Say hi to Kirsty for me."

Bill hung up, and looked at Cobb. "You should be receiving a call any moment now."

Cobb sighed. "This isn't amusing, Mr Lamont."

"Don't worry, it's about to get decidedly funnier."

"I have made my decision. There is no arguing—"

Bill held up a finger for quiet.

Cobb was obedient for all of four seconds before speaking again. "If you're not going to talk rationally about this, then I have nothing more to say to you. It is unfortunate we could not work out our—"

"Please," said Betty. "Give it a moment."

Cobb shook her head, and then her phone rang. She actually jumped.

"I'd answer it," Betty advised her gently. "It's for you."

Cobb hesitated. The phone rang twice more before she picked it up. "Hello? Yes, yes, sir, I'm just... what? But you can't do that." She turned her face away. She was pale now, and her voice was hushed. "Please. You can't do that. I didn't—"

Amber heard the dial tone from where she was sitting. Cobb sat frozen. Then her shoulders began to jerk, and Amber realised she was crying.

Amber felt queasy. "Bill," she said, "maybe we don't really have to get her fired, do we?"

Bill ignored her and stood up. "Right then," he said. "Amber, we'll let you get back to class. You're working at the diner later, aren't you? Try not to eat anything – we're having duck tonight."

Her folks headed for the door, and Amber looked back at Cobb, who stood up quickly.

"Please," Cobb said, wiping the tears from her eyes. "I'm sorry. You're obviously very important people and... and Amber is obviously a very special girl."

"Very special," said Bill, one foot already out of the office.

"I'm sorry I didn't recognise that," Cobb said, hurrying out from behind her desk. "Special students deserve special treatment. Latitude. They deserve latitude and... and under-standing. Leeway."

"Leeway, latitude and understanding," Betty said, nodding. "They've always been our touchstones for a happy life."

"Please," Cobb said. "Don't have me fired."

"Well, I don't know," said Betty. "It's really up to Amber. Amber, do you think Mrs Cobb should keep her job?"

There was some part of Amber, some sly and distant part, that wanted to say no, that wanted to punish her principal for her shrillness, her pettiness — but this was a part that wasn't thinking of Cobb as a person. No matter how much Amber may have disliked the woman, she was not prepared to ruin her life just to teach her a lesson.

"Uh yeah, she can keep it," Amber said.

"Thank you," Cobb said, her whole body sagging. "Thank you."

"Wait a second," Bill said, stepping back into the office. "Mrs Cobb, you accused us of being bad parents. If you want your job back, you're going to have to do more than just apologise."

"Oh yes," Betty said, clapping her hands in delight. "You should beg for it."

Amber stared at her parents in shocked disbelief, and Cobb frowned.

"I'm sorry?"

Betty's smile vanished. "Beg, I said."

Amber had been wrong. She thought she had known the full extent of her parents' punishments, but this was a level beyond. This was vindictive, like they were running out of patience on some scale no one else could see. This was something entirely new.

Cobb shot a quick glance at Amber, then looked back at Bill and Betty. "Uh... please," she said quietly. "Please can I keep my job? I... I beg of you."

Bill shrugged. "Yeah, okay." He swept his arm towards the door. "Shall we?"

They left the office, left Mrs Cobb standing there with tears running down her face, and walked the length of the corridor without speaking. Right before her parents turned right, for the parking lot, and Amber turned left, for the classrooms, Bill looked at her.

"This girl you had the 'fracas' with," he said, "Saffron, right? Wasn't she a friend of yours?"

"When we were kids," said Amber, her voice soft.

He nodded, considered it, then walked away.

Her mother patted Amber's shoulder and looked sympathetic. "Children can be so cruel," she said, and followed her husband.

2

THE HEADACHE THAT HAD been building since lunch finally struck by the end of school, driving thin needles of pain deep into Amber's temples. She popped a couple of Tylenol and, by the time her shift at the diner was half over, the pain had faded to a dull throb somewhere at the back of her skull.

"My folks are getting weirder," she said.

Sally looked up from the magazine she was reading. "Sorry?"

"My folks," Amber repeated as she wiped the table. She did her best to sound casual. "They're getting weirder."

"Is that possible?"

"I didn't think so. But do you know what they did today? They were called into my school and they made my principal cry. She literally shed tears. She was begging and everything. They... they traumatised her. It was so messed up."

Sally shifted position, leaned back on the countertop in her red and yellow Firebird Diner T-shirt, and looked thoughtful. "That," she said eventually, "is awesome. I would have loved my folks to have made my principal cry when I was a teenager. When my two start high school, I want to make their principal cry. I hated mine. I hated all my teachers. They always said I'd never amount to anything. But look at me now, eh? Thirty-three years old, no qualifications, and a waitress in a crappy diner with a neon Elvis on the wall."

Amber gave her the thumbs up. "Living the dream, Sally."

"Damn right," Sally said. "And hey, at least your parents are taking an interest for once, right? Isn't that something?"

"I… I guess."

"Listen to me. Just stick it out for another few years and then you can go off to college somewhere and build a life for yourself."

Amber nodded. New York, she figured, or Boston. Somewhere cooler than Florida, where the air alone wouldn't make her sweat.

"My point is," Sally continued, "wherever and whenever you decide to start your own family, you can do it right." She gave a little grin. "Okay?"

Amber could never resist one of Sally's grins. "Yeah," she said. "Okay."

"Attagirl."

Customers came in, and Sally put a spring in her step as she walked to greet them. "Hi there!" she said brightly. "Welcome to the Firebird! Can I show you to your booth?"

Amber watched her, marvelling at how natural her sudden cheerfulness seemed. A smile from Sally could turn a bad mood on its head – it was a phenomenon that Amber had witnessed on multiple occasions, and it rarely failed. The customers smiled back and they exchanged a few words and Sally led them to a booth by the window. Even though the Firebird was the third most successful fifties-themed diner franchise in the state – and Amber had no idea where that statistic had sprouted from – Wednesday afternoons were always slow. On slow days, it was policy to sit as many patrons by the window as possible in order to entice people in. Hungry people liked eating with other hungry people, it seemed. Amber had never been able to understand that. For as long as she could remember, she had always hated people watching her eat. She didn't even like eating meals with her parents.

Although, if she was to be honest with herself – and if she couldn't be honest with herself, then who could she be honest with? – their inherent weirdness might have had something to do with that.

Her parents were odd. Amber had known that for quite some time. Ever since she could remember, it was like they shared a private joke that she'd never been let in on. She loved them, of course she did, but she'd always felt like an appendage. She didn't complete the family because the family didn't need her to be complete. Bill and Betty Lamont were so perfect for each other that there were no gaps left for Amber to fill.

Two guys walked into the diner, both in their late teens. Joking and chatting, they stood at the PLEASE WAIT TO BE SEATED sign and only looked at Amber when she smiled and said "Hi!" in her perkiest voice. "Welcome to the Firebird. Can I show you to your booth?"

"Don't see why not," said the first guy.

She smiled again and turned on her heel, making sure to keep the smile in place. She wasn't pretty like Sally, wasn't tall like Sally, wasn't captivating like Sally and certainly did not look as good in her yellow shorts as Sally did, but, even so, there were so many mirrors in the diner that to lose a smile at any point could mean a drastic loss in tips. She stood by the booth in the corner and her two customers slid in on opposite sides of the table.

"My name's Amber," she said, taking her notepad from her back pocket, "and I'll be your waitress this evening."

"Hi, Amber," the first guy said. "My name's Dan, this is Brandon, and we'll be your customers."

Amber gave a little laugh. "What can I get you?"

"We're keeping it simple today. We'll take your cheeseburger deals. The whole shebang."

Amber marked the orders down. "Two cheeseburgers with the works, two fries. No problem at all. And to drink?"

"Coke," said Dan.

"Coke it is."

"Actually, no," said Dan, "I'll have a strawberry milkshake instead."

"One strawberry milkshake, gotcha. And for you?"

Brandon didn't look up from the menu. "Do you have 7-Up?"

"We have Sprite," Amber said.

"That's nice," Brandon said, raising his eyes to her slowly, "but I didn't ask if you had Sprite. I asked if you had 7-Up."

Amber's headache started to spike again, but she kept her smile and smothered her words. She needed this job. The Dark Places convention was in a few months and tickets were not cheap.

"I'm really sorry, we don't have 7-Up," she said brightly, like she'd just been told she'd won a bunny in a raffle. "Would you like Sprite instead?"

Brandon took off his glasses and cleaned them. "If I had wanted Sprite, I'd have asked for Sprite, now wouldn't I?"

"Please excuse Brandon," Dan said, grinning. "He's in one of his moods. Brandon, out of all of the drinks that they have here, which one do you want?"

Brandon let out a heavy sigh. "I suppose I'll have a milkshake."

"Okay then," Amber said, pencil at the ready. "What flavour?"

"Well, I don't know. What flavour do you recommend?"

"I've always loved chocolate."

"Then I'll have vanilla," Brandon said, and put his glasses back on.

Dan was trying not to laugh at the antics of his buddy. Amber stood there and smiled. "Sure thing," she said. "Can I get you guys anything else?"

"If we think of anything," said Dan, "we'll be sure to ask."

Amber smiled and left them, fighting a swirling tide of nausea. She got through the swinging doors to the kitchen and leaned against the wall for a moment, waiting for the feeling to subside. When she was sure that she wasn't going to pass out or puke, she gave in the order and stood beside Sally, both of them making milkshakes.

"What are your guys like?" Amber asked, ignoring her surging headache.

"Two businessmen," Sally said, "slumming it, flirting really badly with me and destined to end up with sauce splattered down their shirts. What about yours? The one in the glasses looks cute."

"He's a tool."

"But not that cute," Sally said quickly. "In fact, if you had let me finish before interrupting, you would have heard me say he looks cute, but, on closer inspection, he's obviously a tool."

Amber grinned. "You were going to say that?"

Sally nodded. "If you had just let me finish, instead of babbling on like you always do."

"I am a babbler."

"Yes, you are."

Amber placed the milkshakes on a tray, took a deep breath, and went back out.

Brandon watched her walk over, and Amber tried for a smile. It wasn't convincing, but it'd do. She didn't care about the tip anymore – all she wanted was for these two guys to leave, to take their bad vibes with them, and allow her to wallow in whatever sickly unpleasantness had been threatening to engulf her all day.

"Now then—" she started, but the headache sent fresh needles of pain straight to the back of her eyes and she winced, and the tray overbalanced and the milkshakes slid sideways, toppling off the edge and smashing to the ground.

The sound of breaking glass swept the headache away, and as Amber's vision cleared she could see that the milkshakes had gone everywhere. They'd drenched her sneakers and splattered the cuffs of Brandon's jeans.

Dan howled with laughter, but Brandon glared at her, heat rising in his face.

"Oh my God," Amber said. "I am so sorry. I am so incredibly sorry."

"You…"

"I'll get this cleaned up. I am so sorry."

"You stupid fat pig."

Amber froze.

"You clumsy, ugly little troll," Brandon said. "You did that on purpose."

"I didn't, I swear—"

"You dumped it over me on purpose."

"It was an accident."

Sally hurried over, mop already in hand. "It's okay, no big deal, we'll get this—"

Brandon jabbed a finger at Amber. "She did it on purpose."

Sally laughed. "I'm sure it was just—"

"I want her fired."

Sally stopped mopping, and her laugh turned to a bemused smile. "She's not going to be fired for dropping a tray, all right? It happens all the time. How about this? Your meal is on the house."

"Our meal is on the floor," Brandon said. "Where's the manager? I want to speak to the manager. I want this fat pig fired."

Sally's face turned to stone. "Get out," she said. "Both of you. Out. You're not welcome here."

Dan held up his hands in mock-innocence. "I didn't do anything," he said. "I was just sitting here. What did I do wrong?"

"You picked the wrong friend," said Sally. "Go on. Out."

Brandon kept his gaze fixed on Amber. His face had gone pale and rigid, like he was about to dive at her. Dan had to practically drag him to the door.

Sally stood there with her hands on her hips. "Wow," she said when they had gone. "What a couple of tools. You okay, honey?"

"I'm fine."

Sally patted her shoulder. "They're morons. Don't listen to a word they say."

Sally helped Amber clean up the mess. The two businessmen sneaked glances whenever they could, and Amber couldn't blame them. Even mopping the floor, Sally was pretty. She didn't get red-faced with the exertion like Amber did, and her hair didn't fall out of its ponytail, like Amber's did. She even looked good in the Firebird T-shirt.

Amber tried her very best not to look at her own reflection in the mirrors, though. She was in a bad enough mood already.

The rest of her shift dragged by. When it ended, she pulled on a fresh T-shirt and shorts that weren't yellow, said goodbye to the cook and to Sally, and stepped out on to the sidewalk. It was already getting dark, but the heat was waiting for her, and her forehead prickled with sweat as her lungs filled with warm air. She'd spent her whole life in Florida, been born and raised in Orlando, and she still reacted to the heat like a tourist. It was why, despite having a big, two-storey house to call home, her bedroom was on the first floor, where the air was fractionally cooler, especially on a day like today, when the clouds were gathering. Rain was on its way. Lightning, too, most likely.

Amber had a fifteen-minute walk home. Other kids would probably have been able to call Mom or Dad for a ride, but Bill and Betty had very firm ideas about what independence meant. Amber was used to it by now. If she was lucky, she'd get to the front door before she got drenched.

She crossed the street and slipped down the narrow lane that led to the dance studio she had hated as a child. Too uncoordinated, that was her problem. That and the fact that the dance teacher had hated her with startling venom. Amber was never going to be as pretty as the pretty girls or as graceful as the graceful girls, and she had come to terms with that, even as a kid. Her dance teacher, however, seemed to take issue with it.

Amber got to the badly painted sign of the ballerina and the curiously eighties hip-hop dancer, and Dan and Brandon turned the corner in front of her.

They were talking about something – Dan was chiding Brandon and Brandon was looking pissed off – but when they saw Amber they went quiet. Amber stood there, her legs stiff and suddenly uncooperative, and another headache started somewhere behind her eyes.

Brandon grinned. There was nothing friendly in it.

Amber forced her legs to work again, and she took the lane to her left. They walked after her. She quickened her pace through the growing gloom.

"Oink, oink, little piggy," Brandon said from behind her.

Amber broke into a run.

They laughed, and gave chase.

She plunged out of the lane and cut across the road, slipping between the back of a laundromat and an attorney's office. Immediately, Amber realised this was a mistake. She should have headed towards the pizzeria where there would have been people, and light, and noise. Instead, she was running across an empty lot and finding herself out of breath. A hand closed around her jacket and she cried out, twisted, got tangled in Dan's legs, and they both went down.

She landed heavily, painfully, with Dan sprawling over her.

"Oww," he laughed, rolling over. "Owww, that hurt."

Amber got up and backed off, rubbing her hands where she had skinned them as she fell. The headache was a thunder cloud inside her skull. Goosebumps rippled. Her stomach churned.

Dan stood, panting, and Brandon jogged up to them, taking his time.

"This isn't funny," Amber said.

"It's not meant to be," said Brandon.

"Why'd you run?" Dan chuckled. "We wouldn't have run if you hadn't run. Why'd you run?"

"Let me go," said Amber.

Dan swept his arm wide. "We're not stopping you from going anywhere. Go right ahead."

Amber hesitated, then stepped between them. They loomed over her on either side. She took another step, started walking away, but the moment her back was turned Dan was right behind her, on her heels.

She spun, her vision blurring for a moment. "Stop following me."

"You can't tell me where to go and where not to go," Dan said, suddenly angry. "This is America. Land of the free. Don't you know that?"

She could taste copper in the back of her mouth. "Leave me alone," she said dully.

"We're not doing anything!" Dan yelled, right in her face. She flinched away from him.

"Admit what you did, little piggy," said Brandon, circling her. "Admit that you spilled that milkshake on me on purpose."

"I swear, it was an accident."

"If you admit that you did it on purpose," said Dan, the reasonable one once again, "then we'll go away."

He was right in front of her as he spoke, but he sounded a

hundred miles away. She had to end this now, at once, before the blackness at the edge of her vision overpowered her and she collapsed.

"Okay," Amber said, "okay, I did it on purpose."

They nodded, like they had known all along. But they didn't leave.

"You made me look like a liar," said Brandon.

Amber tried focusing on Dan. "You said you'd go away."

"Jesus," he said, making a face. "Don't be so frikkin' rude."

"Okay," she said, "I shouldn't have done it. I'm sorry. It was stupid. I'm very sorry. Please let me go home."

"For the last time," said Dan, "*we're not stopping you. We're not stopping you from doing anything.* Why is that so hard for you to *understand*? Are you really that *dumb*? Are you really that *stupid*? Stop treating us like we're the *bad guys* here, okay? You're the one who threw that milkshake on my friend. You're the one who got us kicked out. You're the one who ran. You're the one who made me fall over. My knee is *bleeding*, did you know that? But am I *complaining* about it? Am I making a *fuss*? No, I am *not*. But *you*? You won't stop turning this whole thing into some big frikkin' *drama*."

"I don't..."

"What? What was that?"

"I don't feel well."

Her knees started to buckle and she reached out to steady herself, grabbing the front of Dan's shirt. He grimaced and pushed her hand away and she stumbled, and then Brandon was there, grabbing her, straightening her up—

—and then he hit her.

The pain was nothing compared to the violent storm in

her head, but his fist rocked her, sharpened her, and she saw him look at his own knuckles, like he was surprised that he had done it, and then everything was moving very quickly and when she felt a hand on her face she bit down hard and heard a howl.

Her vision cleared. Brandon's horrified face swam into view. She hit him back, as hard as she could, and his jaw came apart around her fist.

A moment stretched to eternity.

She watched her fist.

It was weird – in this gloom, her skin almost looked red.

A deeper red than the blood, though, the blood that exploded in glorious slow motion from the wreckage that had been Brandon's face. Was *she* doing this? Was this happening? In that moment, that luxurious moment, Amber found the time to wonder if she was imagining this part. Surely this was some sort of bizarre hallucination, brought about by adrenaline and those increasingly painful headaches.

There was no headache now, though. There was no pain of any sort. Instead, she felt… wonderful. She felt free. She felt…

Powerful.

Time started to speed up again. Blood splattered her T-shirt and Brandon hit the ground and, now that she could perceive normal sound once more, Amber registered his gargled screaming. Both hands were at his face and he was crawling frantically away, leaving a trail of blood as he went. Dan backed off, staring at her, his face white and his eyes wide and utterly, utterly terrified.

She had done that. The blood and the screaming and the

shattered bones. It had been no hallucination. She had done that.

She raised her blood-speckled hand. Normal skin again. That was good. Normal was good.

Something in her mouth. Something that tasted of copper. She spat. Brandon's finger hit the ground.

Amber turned and ran.

3

THERE WAS BLOOD ON HER HANDS.

Not in a metaphorical, figurative sense, although of course there was that, too, but in an actual, physical sense, there was actual blood on her actual hands, and it was proving surprisingly difficult to wash off. Amber scrubbed furiously, looked at the result, and then scrubbed again. It occurred to her, not for the first time, that her hands were quite small. If the rest of her body could have been in proportion with her hands, then maybe she wouldn't have been such a target. These were the thoughts that occurred to her as she was scrubbing the blood away.

"Amber?" came her mother's voice from beyond the bathroom door.

Amber looked up at herself in the mirror above the sink — wild-eyed and panicked. "Yes?" she called, keeping her voice as steady as possible.

"Is everything okay?"

"Everything's fine," Amber said. "I'll be out in a minute."

Amber listened to her mother hesitate, then walk away down the hall.

She turned off the faucet and examined her hands. For one ridiculous moment, she thought they were still bloodstained, but then she closed her eyes and shook her head. The frantic scrubbing had turned them both red-raw, that's all it was. No need for her imagination to be going into overdrive on this one. There was enough to freak out about as it was.

She put the toilet seat down and sat, taking deep breaths, and examined the facts. Yes, she had seriously injured that guy, but she had been acting in self-defence and she had been outnumbered. She really couldn't see how the cops wouldn't be on her side about this – if only she hadn't injured him quite so dramatically.

Amber frowned. What was his name? The name of the guy whose face she'd destroyed?

Brandon, that was it. She was glad she remembered it. For some reason, it felt important that she remember his name after what she'd done to him.

She hadn't meant to do it, and she hadn't a clue how it had happened. She'd heard stories about adrenaline, about what it could do to the human body. Mothers lifting cars off toddlers and stuff. It was, she supposed, *possible* that adrenaline had granted her the sheer strength to shatter bones on contact, and anyway how much strength would it *really* take to bite through a finger?

The very thought made her want to throw up again.

She stood, and examined herself in the mirror. Her skin was pale and blotchy and her hair was a tangled, frizzy mess. Her eyes – hazel, with flecks of gold, and the only part of herself she didn't hate – were red-rimmed from crying.

She went to her room, changed her blood-splattered T-shirt

for a top that the lady in the store had said would flatter her figure. Amber wasn't so sure she believed her, but it was a nice top, even if it didn't look especially good on her. She realised her hands were trembling.

She sat on the edge of the bed. Of course they were trembling. She was in shock. She needed help. Advice. Comfort.

For the first time since she was a kid, she needed her parents.

"Ah hell," she muttered. It was worth a try.

She heard them in the kitchen, putting the finishing touches to dinner. Amber crossed the hall, walking with heavy, leaden feet. The house was filled with the aroma of duck, cooked to perfection, and usually this would have her belly rumbling. But the only thing her belly was doing now was housing a whole load of fluttering butterflies. She tried to remember the last time she'd talked to her parents about anything important. Or the last time she'd talked to them about *anything*.

She couldn't.

Her mouth dry, she stepped into the kitchen. Bill was checking the duck in the oven. No sign of Betty. Amber could feel her courage begin to falter. She needed both of them in the room at the same time. She couldn't do this with only one. Could she? Or was this a condition she was setting for herself purely to have an excuse to back out?

And, just like that, her courage deserted her.

Relief sapped the rigidity from her joints and she sagged, stepped backwards without Bill even realising she'd been standing there. She walked back to her room. Maybe she could bring it up over dinner, provided there was a lull in the conversation. The *two-way* conversation, of course, as

Amber was only rarely asked to contribute an opinion. There probably wouldn't be a lull, though, but even if there was this was hardly an appropriate topic. After dinner, then, or later tonight, or—

Amber stepped into her room but Betty was already in here, the blood-splattered T-shirt in her hands.

"Whose blood is this?" her mother asked.

Amber searched for an answer that wouldn't come.

Betty dropped the T-shirt on the bed, crossed over to her, and took hold of Amber's arms. "Are you hurt?" she asked. "Did someone hurt you?"

Amber shook her head.

"What happened?" Betty asked. "Tell me, Amber."

"I'm fine," Amber managed to say.

Her mother looked deep into her eyes, like she'd find the truth locked away in there.

"It's not my blood," said Amber quietly.

"Whose is it?"

"At the Firebird. Some guys."

Betty let go of her and stepped back. "How many?"

"Two. They followed me. They *attacked* me."

Betty had a funny look on her face. "Amber, sweetheart, what did you do?"

"I did nothing," Amber said, her words suddenly rushing out. "I defended myself. I did nothing wrong. They were abusive customers. We asked them to leave. I saw them when I was walking home and they chased me. They attacked *me*, Betty. Two against one."

"You defended yourself? Are you okay?"

"I'm… I'm fine. Really."

"And how are *they*?"

Now Amber squirmed. "Um, I don't... I don't know. One of them, I... I think I broke his jaw. And bit his finger off."

"You bit his finger?"

"I bit his finger off."

"Oh, sweetheart," Betty said, taking Amber into her arms. Amber stiffened. She didn't know when her mother's arms had last embraced her. "And you're sure you're not hurt?"

"I'm sure. The adrenaline just... I'm fine."

"Has this happened before? This surge of strength?"

"No," Amber said, wondering how long she had to stay like this. "First time."

"How are you apart from that? How are you feeling? Headaches? Nausea?"

"A... a little. How did you know?"

Betty broke off the hug, and looked at her daughter with actual tears in her eyes.

"Betty?" Amber said. "Mom? Are you feeling all right?"

Betty laughed, a nervous laugh that she cut off sharply. "I'm fine, Amber. I'm just... You've been through a traumatic experience and I'm... I'm relieved you're okay."

"Are you going to tell Bill?"

"Of course." Betty smiled, then, the most beautiful smile Amber had ever seen her wear. "Don't you worry. He's going to want to hear about this. So are the rest of them."

Amber frowned. "The others? Betty, no, please, I don't want anyone to—"

"Nonsense," said Betty, waving Amber's objections away with one hand while the other took her phone from her pocket. Her slim fingers danced lightly over the keys and in mere moments a group text had been sent.

They sat on the bed while they waited for the others to arrive. Betty asked Amber about school, about her friends, about her job at the Firebird, and she listened as Amber spoke. It was a new sensation for Amber, talking about these things to her own mother. For the first time since Amber could recall, Betty seemed actually interested in her and the life she was leading. She nodded and smiled, probed deeper where needed, and, when they heard the first car pull into the driveway, Betty came forward and kissed the top of her head.

"You make me so proud," she said softly.

Tears came to Amber's eyes, unbidden, like a burglar breaking into her home, and proved just as shocking.

"You let the others in," said Betty. "I'll help Bill with dinner. Good thing we chose a big duck."

Amber waited until Betty had left before rubbing her eyes. Her knuckles came away wet. There was a curious tightness in her chest that made her breathe funny. She stood up, took a moment to calm herself. She couldn't be sure, but she suspected that this was what it meant to have a loving parent. It was proving to be an unsettling experience.

The doorbell rang and she answered it. Two of her parents' closest friends, Grant and Kirsty Van der Valk, lived only five minutes away, so she wasn't surprised to see them arrive first. What did surprise her was the smile that Grant wore, which was as broad as his chest.

"Hey, kiddo," he said, giving Amber a hug. He'd never called her kiddo before. Never hugged her before, either. He smelled of expensive aftershave, applied with restraint.

He stepped back, still smiling. He had hair that had always reminded Amber of Elvis Presley's in his later years – though the sideburns were not quite as ridiculous. "How'd it go with that principal of yours today? Your dad told me you spared her job. You're a better person than me, you know that?"

"That was never in any doubt," said Kirsty, taking her turn for a hug. If Grant was Elvis, then Kirsty was Pricilla – beautiful, red-headed and so wonderfully *vivacious*. Today that vivaciousness was directed solely at Amber. "How are you?" Kirsty asked softly, like this was a conversation just between them. "Are you feeling okay? How long have you been having the headaches?"

"Not too long," Amber mumbled, starting to get a little freaked out by all this. Did she have a brain tumour that everyone knew about but her?

Then Kirsty's eyes widened. "Good God, that smells amazing. Did you help them cook?"

Amber tried a smile. "They don't let me near the oven," she said, and led them into the living room, where they were soon joined by Bill. As they chatted, he stood by Amber's side with his arm round her shoulder like the proud parents she'd seen on TV.

Then the doorbell rang again, and Amber excused herself. Neither of her parents had any family, so this tight group of friends had long since become a substitute. She supposed, in a way, they were her aunts and uncles, though they treated her with the same cool detachment she'd grown used to.

She opened the door and was immediately swept off her feet.

"Hello, beautiful!" growled Alastair.

Amber didn't know how to react to this. Her feet dangled.

Alastair laughed and set her back on the ground. Like her

parents and the Van der Valks, Alastair Modine was older than he looked. He had an easy, smiling face behind all those bristles, and was more casual than the others, preferring jeans to suits and rolled-up shirtsleeves to a collar and tie.

"Heard you got in trouble at school," he said, whispering it as though it was a secret. "I knew you were a troublemaker from the first moment I saw you. You were only a few hours old, but I knew. I knew." He took a moment to look at her. "You look more and more like your mom every day."

Amber smiled politely, even though she knew this was an outright lie. Betty was beautiful. Amber was plain. Betty was statuesque. Amber was not. These things she knew.

A third and final car pulled up in the driveway. "The others are in the living room," she said.

Alastair glanced back at the car, then gave Amber another smile and went to join his friends.

Amber stood in the doorway, watching Imelda walk up as the rain started to fall. Her blonde hair was styled and immaculate. Her clothes were perfectly coordinated. Her make-up was flawless. This was all to be expected. Imelda Montgomery was a living, breathing example of a woman who had every box ticked. All except for the smile. Imelda had a pretty face that begged to smile – and yet Amber had never seen her genuinely happy. Not even when she'd been married to Alastair.

"Amber," Imelda said as she stepped inside.

"Hi," Amber said, and that was the extent of their conversation. It was all Amber expected. Imelda made even her parents look affectionate.

They moved into the dining room, and Amber ate dinner

with her parents and their friends. They drank wine and she drank Coke. The last time she'd eaten with them had been three months earlier, on her sixteenth birthday. Until tonight, she'd never seen them in such a good mood. Well, apart from Imelda who, in fact, had looked even grumpier than usual. But that was Imelda. She was a special case.

Amber hadn't invited any of her friends to her birthday. Her true friends, her *real* friends, were all online anyway, on fansite messageboards and forums. She didn't need to meet any of them in the flesh. Online, she could pretend to be popular and funny and interesting, and she didn't have to worry about disappointing anyone when her smile didn't light up the room. Online, nobody cared about the wattage.

She endured questions about the possibility of boyfriends and the casual drudgery of school and she was just beginning to enjoy herself when she remembered the taste of that boy's blood in her mouth. Her appetite vanished abruptly, and she pushed the food around on her plate while the others talked on. Despite what Betty had said earlier, they didn't discuss the burst of violence that had darkened Amber's day. She was grateful for this.

"You look tired," Betty said, leaning across to her.

Amber nodded. "I think I'm going to have an early night, if that's okay."

"Of course it is," said Bill. "Leave your plate – we'll clean up. You get to bed – you've had a big day."

"The biggest," said Grant.

The others nodded and smiled their understanding – only Imelda appeared annoyed. More than annoyed, actually. Practically agitated.

Amber was too tired to care about that now. She stood, noticing for the first time that no one else had even touched their dinner, and smiled and said, "Goodnight."

She got a hearty chorus in response, and she went to her room, closing the door behind her.

Rain pelted the window like machine-gun bullets. Outside it was hot and wet, but here it was air-conditioned cool, just the way she liked it. She wanted to go straight to bed, even though it was just after ten, but she also needed to talk about what had happened to her today. She logged on to the In The Dark Places messageboard.

The Dark Princess said...
Hello? Anyone on?

Mad Hatter99 said...
Princess! Where u BEEN, girl?
snuggles up closer for a hug

The Dark Princess said...
Been busy with school n stuff. Having a REALLY strange day.
You seen BAC recently?

Mad Hatter99 said...
Me too! U missed the convo yesterday. What u think of Tuesday's ep?
She was on earlier. Had some role-play stuff going on. Y?

The Dark Princess said...
Just need to talk to her. Nvr mind. Too sleepy to wait up. Nite nite x

Mad Hatter99 said...
Nooooooo! Don't leave me!

Amber logged out of the messageboard and lay back on her bed. Taking off her clothes was far too much effort. Brushing her teeth seemed a ridiculous waste of energy. She could barely keep her eyes open. She heard her parents and the others talking, but couldn't make out the words. There was laughter. Excitement.

Her phone rang, buzzing against her hip. With numb fingers, she pulled it from her pocket and held it to her ear.

"It's me," said Sally. "Just got a call from Frank. Two cops came into the Firebird ten minutes ago asking about you."

Faint alarm bells rang in Amber's head. "What'd they want?" she asked groggily.

"You," said Sally. "They said you attacked those guys from earlier. Did you? They said one of them's in the hospital."

Groaning, Amber sat up. "Did Frank tell them my name?"

"Of course he did, Amber. They're cops. What happened?"

The doorbell rang. Amber hung up, slipped her phone into her pocket while she stood. The room spun for a moment. When she was sure she wasn't going to fall over, she walked with Frankenstein feet to the window.

There was a patrol car in the driveway.

4

THE CHATTER IN THE house died away, replaced by a new, unfamiliar voice. A man's voice. Official-sounding. Amber wished she wasn't so tired. If she could only get her brain in gear, she'd be able to explain herself. She was sure she'd be able to make the cops understand. She took a few deep breaths to clear her head, and walked unsteadily to her door. She opened it. If they wanted her to emerge with her hands up, they were going to be disappointed. She was far too tired to lift her arms.

From the sounds of things, the others had stayed in the dining room, and Bill and Betty had taken the cops into the living room to talk. Amber stayed close to the wall as she moved, in case she needed the support. She got to the family photo in the hallway – the only framed photograph of the three of them – and stopped. From here, she could look across the corridor, through the open door.

Two officers of the law stood there in full uniform, talking to her parents. The cops were saying something, but Amber couldn't focus enough to make out the words. She didn't know why she felt so tired. They all stood in the centre of the room, watching each other. Amber shuffled her shoulder along the wall, then stopped again, concentrated on what the cop was saying.

"…just need to speak to her, that's all."

"Amber's not feeling well at the moment," Bill said. "Maybe if you come back tomorrow she'll be strong enough."

"Mr Lamont," the cop said, "I understand what you're doing. Please don't think I don't. Your daughter may be in trouble and you want to protect her. I get that. I do. But you're doing her no favours if you don't let us speak to her."

Despite her drowsiness, Amber felt her insides go cold.

"My husband isn't lying," Betty said, sounding upset. "If you'd just call Chief Gilmore, I know he'll vouch for us and for Amber. Whatever you think happened I just know didn't happen."

"We're not calling the Police Chief, we're not even calling this in, until we've had a chance to speak with Amber," the cop said. "We have two young men who swear that she assaulted them."

"One sixteen-year-old girl assaulted two men?" Bill said. "And you're taking them seriously? You're actually wasting your time with this nonsense?"

"We'll get this whole thing cleared up if you'll just let us speak to her."

Bill put his hands on his hips and shook his head despairingly. Betty looked at him.

"You are such a perfectionist," she said. The upset she'd briefly displayed had disappeared.

"I just like it when things are neat," said Bill. "This… would not be neat."

"I'm sorry, what wouldn't be neat?" one of the cops asked. But Bill and Betty ignored him.

"This is a special day," Betty said. "A wonderful day. For sixteen years, we have waited for this day. What's happening now is a minor inconvenience. That's all it is."

"Mrs Lamont," one of the cops began, but Bill talked over him.

"It's already in the system," he said to his wife. "Already logged."

"No, it isn't," Betty answered. "That one said they haven't even called it in yet. Gilmore will make it go away. He's done it before, and for the money we're paying him he'll certainly do it again. You might have to drive their car into the marshes later on tonight, just to confuse their colleagues, but why not?"

The officers glanced at each other.

Bill looked at his wife and smiled. "You're serious, aren't you? You really want to do this?"

"Yes," said Betty. "I really do." She took a coat from the back of the couch and put it on, pulling the sleeve down past her wrist and wrapping it around her hand.

"Uh, excuse me?" said the cop.

"So which one do you want?" asked Bill.

Betty nodded to the cop closest to her. "That one."

"Fair enough," Bill said, shrugging. "I'll kill the ugly one."

"Hey," said the big cop, but his next words were muffled by Bill's hand covering his face.

Only it wasn't Bill's hand. It was red, and tipped with black talons. Bill's face was red, too, but different, altered, and he was bigger, taller, suddenly towering over the cop, a red-skinned monster with black horns curling from his forehead, like a ram's horns.

The demon that had taken Bill's place slammed the cop's head against the wall. The head crumpled like an empty soda can.

The cop's partner jumped back in shock, scrabbled at his holster for his gun, then remembered Betty and turned just as she changed. One moment Betty. The next a monster. Tall. Red. Horned. Her fist went right through his chest, popping out the other side in a spray of blood. The cop gurgled something that Amber couldn't make out. Betty opened her hand, letting go of the sleeve, and withdrew her arm from both her coat and the cop's torso.

Amber ducked back as the dead cop collapsed.

"Well," she heard Bill say, "that's done it."

Betty laughed. It was her laugh, all right, but it was coming from the mouth of a demon.

The door between the living room and the dining room opened, and Amber inched forward again to watch Grant lead the others in. They stared in shock at the carnage.

Kirsty covered her mouth with her hand.

Bill turned to them. "We can explain."

Kirsty rushed forward. "That's my coat! What the hell, Betty?"

Amber's knees went weak.

"Can we talk about your coat later?" said Grant. "Right now can we talk about the two dead cops on the carpet?"

"I'll call Gilmore," said Bill. "We'll get it all smoothed over. This is not a big deal."

"They're cops!"

Bill-the-demon waved a hand. "We got a bit carried away. We shouldn't have done it. Happy? It's low key for Betty and me for the rest of the night, we promise. We kill Amber, and that's it. No more killing for the *week*."

Amber's stomach lurched and suddenly she was cold, colder than she'd ever been.

"I really am sorry about your coat," Betty said to Kirsty. "I'll buy you a new one."

Kirsty shook her head. "It was limited edition. You can't get them anymore."

Amber slid sideways, forgetting how to walk, forgetting how to breathe. Her feet were heavy, made of stone, dragging themselves across the floor towards her bedroom while the rest of her body did its best to stay upright. She fell through her doorway, down to her knees, turned and reached out, numb fingers tipping the door closed. Her mouth was dry and her tongue was thick. Something was happening in her belly and she fell forward on to her hands and knees, throwing up on the rug she'd had for years. She didn't make a sound, though. She heaved and retched, but didn't make a sound.

Her parents were monsters. They had grown horns. They'd *killed cops*. Her parents – and their friends – were going to kill *her*.

Betty had drugged her. That's what she'd done. A sedative or something, served up in the food. No, the Coke. Amber looked at the mess on her rug and wondered how much of the drug was congealing down there.

She reached out, hand closing round the bedpost, using it to pull herself up, steady herself, stop herself from toppling sideways. She had to get out. She had to run. She started for the window and the room tilted crazily and she was stumbling towards it. She threw herself to one side before she smashed through the glass, instead banging her elbow against the wall. It hurt, but it didn't bring her parents running. She was so thirsty. There was a bottle of water on her nightstand, but it was all the way across the room.

Dumb, numb fingers fumbled at the window. Stupid, dumb thumb jammed against the latch. Dull teeth bit down, drawing blood from her lip. The pain was sharp, sharpened her for a moment, and her thick, stupid, unresponsive fingers did what they were supposed to do. The latch squeaked, moved, and she braced her forearm against the sash of the window and pressed in and up, using her whole body to slide the window open. Then her legs gave out and she fell, cracked her head against the sill on the way down.

Amber lay with her eyes closed, blood pounding in her ears like drumbeats, like footsteps, like knuckles on a door.

"Amber?"

Eyes opened.

"Amber?" Betty said from the hall. "Are you okay?"

No answer would mean the door opening, Betty looking in.

An answer, then. An answer.

"Yeah," came the word, awkwardly, from Amber's mouth. More followed. "Tired. Sleeping." Each one clumsy on her tongue.

The door. The handle. The handle turning, the door opening. Bill's voice from somewhere else. "Where do we keep the stain remover?"

The door, closing, and then Betty's footsteps, walking away.

Amber turned on to her side, then got on her hands and knees. Stayed there, breathing, gathering her strength. Without raising her head, she reached for the sill. Grabbed it. Hauled herself up until she got an arm out. Grabbed the sill on the other side. Pulled herself up off her knees, got her head out of the window, into the heat and the air and the rain.

Amber fell to the grass, her legs banging off the window frame. They'd find her like this. She hadn't escaped. She couldn't rest, not like this. She had to get away. Had to keep moving.

Amber was crawling now, along the wet grass, through the dappled shadows of the trees. She had to get away. She had to crawl faster. Had to get to the road. Get to the road, get into a car, drive away. Escape.

The ground beneath her changed, got harder. Not grass. Not anymore. Darker. Harder. Smoother. The road.

Approaching footsteps, hurrying through the rain. They'd found her. They'd found her already. Her arms were weak, no strength left. Her body lay down. Her mind… her mind… where was her mind?

Shoes. High-heeled shoes on a wet road, right in front of her. A voice. A woman's voice. She knew that woman's voice.

"Hello, Amber," said Imelda.

5

AMBER AWOKE IN A room that was not her own. Clean lines and no clutter. Heavy curtains kept the dark from escaping into the morning light. Moving slowly, she pulled the covers off and stood. She was in her underwear. Her clothes were neatly folded on the dresser. Clean and dry. She crept to the window, parted the curtains, and looked out over Lake Eola. She frowned. An apartment in the city overlooking Lake Eola. She didn't know where the hell she was.

But she was alive. That was something, at least.

Amber grabbed her clothes, put them on. Her phone was gone. She started to reach for the glass of water by her bed, but stopped, remembering the Coke. There was a bathroom, clean and polished, looking like it had never been used, and she drank from the faucet and wiped her mouth. Then she went to the door, put her ear against it, heard nothing.

She opened it, hesitated, and stepped out.

The apartment was vast, impressive, and utterly devoid of personality. It looked like the penthouse suite of a hotel. Everything was clean and in place. Every colour matched, every curve and line complemented the curves and lines around it.

It had all been designed to cohere, to fit, to belong. There was a designer kitchen to her left, all gleaming metal with a huge breakfast island, and a balcony to her right, a view of the city beyond, all glass and palm trees, and ahead of her was the way out.

She was halfway to the door when she noticed Imelda standing in the living room, her back to her. She was on the phone, listening while someone spoke.

Amber reached the apartment door, opened it silently, and stepped out into the corridor. White walls. She moved up to the corner, and peered round.

At the end of the corridor was the elevator, the door to the stairwell, and a window. Standing at that window, looking out over the skyline, was a tall man in blue jeans, black T-shirt and battered cowboy boots. On the side table behind him there was a mirror, a bowl of potpourri and a shotgun.

Amber stared at the shotgun.

She pressed herself back against the wall and closed her eyes. She was breathing too loud. She was breathing too loud and he'd hear her, she knew he would. She peeked out again. He was still looking out of the window. The shotgun was still there.

She had no choice. She couldn't go back, and she couldn't stay where she was. She had to do something. She had to move forward.

Fighting the urge to break into a sprint, Amber took small, slow steps. She got to the side table without making a sound, then picked up the shotgun. It clinked slightly on the table and the man turned from the window. He was good-looking, somewhere in his mid-forties. His black hair had hints of grey. His narrow eyes were calm.

"You should put that down before it goes off," he said.

"Get out of my way. Get out of my way or I'll… I'll shoot you."

"Your hands are trembling," he said. "Give it to me." He reached his left hand forward slowly and Amber took a single step back and then there was somehow a pistol in his other hand, and he was aiming it right at her head. "Now you're really scared," he said. "Now you want to run screaming. That's perfectly understandable. But I'm not going to move. You're not getting past me."

"Please," she said, the shotgun shaking badly in her grip now. "They're trying to kill me."

"Then why aren't you dead?" he asked. "Put the shotgun back on the table and go back inside the apartment."

Tears ran down her face. "Please don't make me."

"Put down the shotgun."

"I don't understand what's going on."

"I'm not the one who's going to explain it to you. Either shoot me or put down the shotgun."

Amber shook her head, but found herself putting the weapon on the side table, anyway. The man slid his pistol into a holster on his belt before picking up the shotgun.

"Probably wasn't even loaded," she said quietly.

"No, it was," the man responded. "You would have cut me in two if you'd pulled that trigger. Go back inside, Amber. Talk to Imelda."

She didn't have much of a choice. Amber walked back the way she'd come, hesitated at the apartment door, and then walked in.

Imelda saw her, held up a finger for Amber to wait.

"We're keeping tabs on all of her friends, aren't we?" she said into the phone pressed to her ear. "Exactly. I wouldn't worry about this, Kirsty. We'll find her. It's only a matter of time. Okay, I've got to go. I want to check out the principal of her school." She listened. "Because after that wonderful display yesterday, she knows for certain that the principal isn't in league with us. Yes, I am clever. I'll call you if I hear anything. Bye now."

Imelda hung up. "Want some breakfast?" she asked, walking to the kitchen. She poured orange juice into a tall glass and placed it beside an assortment of croissants and pastries. Then she looked back at Amber and waited.

"What's happening?" Amber said.

"It really is a long story," Imelda said.

"There's a man outside with a gun."

"That's a friend of mine, Milo Sebastian. You don't have to worry about him. You have to worry about your parents."

"What's wrong with them?"

Imelda managed a smile. "You think they're behaving oddly? That's just because you don't know them very well."

"They're demons. Monsters."

"Oh, Amber... We're all monsters. Metaphorically, I mean. The whole human race. We hate, we kill, we do terrible things to each other and to the planet. But we are also, in our case, actual monsters. With horns."

"I really don't understand any of this," said Amber. "Please just tell me what's happening."

"I'm going to explain everything. But to start with I'll have to show you. I'm going to change now, all right? I'm going to turn into... well, into a monster, just like your parents. And I want you to remain calm. Can you do that?"

Amber swallowed, and nodded.

"I'm not going to hurt you. I just want to show you."

"Okay."

"You're sure?"

"Yes."

"Okay. Once again, I want you to remain calm. You're perfectly safe."

Imelda's skin turned red and her teeth grew sharp and she had black horns and it all took less than a heartbeat.

Amber screamed, picked up a potted plant and threw it, but it fell short and smashed to the floor.

"You killed Henry," Imelda said, dismayed.

"*Help me!*" Amber screamed.

"You're panicking," said Imelda.

"*You're a monster!*" Amber screeched.

"This is not news to me."

Amber sprinted for the door.

"You tried that, remember?"

A wave of pain swept through Amber, making her stagger but not fall. She pushed herself away from the door and ran for the window.

"What, you're going to jump?" Imelda asked. "Really? We're on the thirty-fifth floor."

Amber grabbed a cushion off the couch and held it out with both hands.

"I'm not entirely sure what you mean to do with that," Imelda admitted.

"You're a monster," Amber said, her voice cracking.

"Yes," said Imelda. "And I hate to break it to you, sweetie, but so are you."

Amber looked at her hands. Looked at how red they were. Looked at the black nails that had pierced the cushion she held.

"Oh my God," she said, feeling how her tongue brushed against teeth that were somehow longer than they had been a moment earlier. Her head swam. She raised her hands, felt horns. "Oh God. Help me. Please…"

Imelda the Monster walked forward slowly. "Amber, I need you to calm down…"

Amber backed away unsteadily, leaving a trail of floating feathers in her wake. She began to cry.

"Stay away from me."

"You asked me to help you. I'm helping you."

"Stay back," said Amber, voice breaking.

"Okay."

"Help me."

"Make up your mind," said Imelda with a faint smile.

"Please, just… why do I have horns?"

"Because you're like me," said Imelda. "You're like your parents, and Grant and Kirsty and Alastair. You're a demon, sweetie."

The word stuck in Amber's mind like a bone in her throat, so that she barely registered Imelda darting towards her until it was too late to do anything about it.

"Sorry about this," Imelda said, and punched her into unconsciousness.

6

Amber stirred from her dreamless sleep, waking without opening her eyes. She snuggled down deeper into the pillow, slowly drifting off again, and then she remembered where she was and what had happened and she sat up so fast she almost fell out of bed.

Back in the bedroom in Imelda's apartment. The curtains were open now. The day was bright and warm. She examined her reflection in the mirror on the wall. She looked normal. Her hair was a mess, but that was the full extent of the damage.

It had been real. She knew it had been real. She'd had horns. She'd grown them as her skin had turned red and her nails had turned black – just like she had before she'd pulverised Brandon's jaw with a single punch. She'd grown them just like Imelda had grown them. Just like her parents had grown them.

But no. No, that couldn't be right. There had to be an explanation. A reasonable, logical, real-world explanation.

She stood. She was fully dressed, in T-shirt and shorts and sneakers. That was good. She left the bedroom. The man with the guns sat on the couch, his long legs crossed, reading a tattered paperback. Milo Sebastian, she remembered. He looked up at her, then went back to reading.

"Where's Imelda?" Amber asked.

"Out," he said.

She waited for him to furnish her with more information, but apparently he wasn't much of a talker.

"Out where?" she pressed.

"Out with the others."

A wave of alarm rushed through Amber's veins. "My parents? What's she doing with them?"

"Pretending to look for you." Keeping a finger on the page he'd been reading, he folded the book closed and raised his eyes. "You can wait for her here. She shouldn't be too much longer."

Amber hesitated, then took a few steps further into the room. "Don't suppose you'd let me go, would you?"

"You've got nowhere to go to," Milo replied. "The cops can't help you. Chief Gilmore can only afford his luxury condo with the money they pay him. Your parents, and their friends, are very powerful people. You must know this."

Amber didn't reply. She didn't mention the ease with which they'd had her principal fired.

She went to the couch across from where Milo was sitting, and sat on the edge, knees together and hands in her lap. "Do you know what's going on?"

"I'm not the one to talk to about this."

"So you do know. You know they're monsters, right? You know Imelda is a monster? And it doesn't bother you?"

"Does it bother you that you're just like her?"

Amber shook her head. "I'm not. I'm... I don't know what

happened or what drug she gave me, but I'm not like her. I'm not like them. They're monsters. I'm normal. I mean, I think I'd know if I were a monster, right?"

He looked at her, didn't say anything.

"Why do you have all those guns?" she asked.

"Your parents might start suspecting that Imelda isn't being honest with them. She asked me to make sure no harm comes to you."

"You're here to protect me?" Amber stood up suddenly. "So I could walk out of here and you couldn't stop me?"

Milo opened the paperback again, without fuss, and resumed reading. "Try it and see."

Whatever rebellious fire had flared inside her sputtered and died at his tone, and Amber sat back down. "Do you know where my phone is?"

"Destroyed."

Her eyes widened. "I'm sorry?"

He kept reading. "It's the easiest way to track you."

"But that was my *phone*."

"Best not to make calls. Or send emails. Those are the kind of things that would lead your parents straight to you."

"And how do you expect me to... to... to do *anything*? I need my phone, for God's sake. I need..." She faltered. She needed her phone to go online, to talk to her friends. She needed that now more than ever.

Milo didn't seem to care. He had gone back to reading his book. A western, judging by the cover. Amber had never read a western. She couldn't imagine they were any good. There were surely only so many stories you could tell about cowboys and shooting and horses before it all got boring, even for those who liked such things. How many times could you describe a saddle, or a saloon, or a desert plain?

Still, it was something. He liked books and she liked books. There was common ground there.

"Ever read *In The Dark Places?*" she asked.

Milo didn't look up. "No."

"It's a really good series. It's been adapted into a TV show. They're on Season Three right now. You should read them. They're all about these star-crossed lovers, Balthazar and Tempest. She's a Dark Faerie and he's an Eternal. That's, uh, that's what they're called. He's got an evil brother and her parents are nuts and she's just been possessed by the ghost of her ex-boyfriend. It's set in Montana. They sometimes have horses on the show."

"Horses are nice," Milo said, in a voice that indicated he wasn't paying her the slightest bit of attention.

Amber glowered and stopped trying to make conversation.

They sat in silence for another ten minutes, and then Milo's phone buzzed. He checked it, and stood.

"She's back," he said, tucking the western into his back pocket and picking up the shotgun. He left the apartment, and Amber immediately leaped up, scanning her surroundings for an escape route.

After a few moments, she sat back down.

She heard the faint ping of the elevator arriving, and then low voices as Imelda and Milo exchanged whatever they had that passed for pleasantries. Thirty seconds later, Imelda came in.

Amber sat back into the couch, her arms folded.

"I'm sorry," was the first thing Imelda said.

"You hit me."

"You were screaming."

"Not when you hit me."

"If it makes a difference, I'm pretty sure you were going to faint, anyway."

"So why didn't you let me faint?"

Imelda hesitated. "I should have let you faint. I'm sorry." Her apology apparently over with, Imelda walked into the kitchen. "Have you had anything to eat?"

Amber didn't answer. She was starving, and thirsty, but to respond was to forgive, and she wasn't prepared to do that yet.

Imelda made herself a cappuccino without trying to engage her again in chit-chat. When she was done, she came over, sat where Milo had been sitting. She took a sip, placed the delicate cup on the delicate saucer on the delicate coffee table, and sat back. "You need to eat something," she said. "I can hear your stomach rumbling from here."

"That's not hunger. That's anger."

"Your belly rumbles when you're angry? I didn't know that about you."

"There's a lot you don't know about me."

"Well," said Imelda, "that's not strictly true."

"You've barely ever *spoken* to me."

"That doesn't mean I don't know you. Your parents kept us all very well informed – and they know you a lot better than you think."

Amber looked at her in silence for a moment. "What did you do to me earlier? My skin and... What was that?"

"You know what that was."

Amber shook her head. "No. I'm not like you. I'm not a monster like you. What did you do to me?"

"I didn't do anything. You were born that way."

"I wasn't born with red skin, Imelda. I wasn't born with frikkin' *horns*."

"No, but it was inside you."

Amber glared. "Show me, then. Go on. Change. Transform. Go demony. I want to see it again."

"Amber, I don't think—"

"Go on," said Amber. "I wasn't really expecting it the first time. Now I'm ready. Let's see you in all your glory."

Imelda sighed. "Fine," she said, and stood, and her skin reddened and her features sharpened and her horns grew, and Amber shrank back instinctively.

There was something about the very shape of Imelda now, the way the horns curved, the way her face – once a pretty face, now a beautiful face – caught the sunlight, there was something about all of it that sent a shiver down Amber's back. This was the shape that nightmares took, deep in the darkest parts of her subconscious.

"You can do this, too," Imelda said. Her teeth were pointed. She was taller. Her shoulders were broader. Her clothes were tighter. Her top had come untucked. "You just decide you want to shift, and you shift."

"Is that what you call it?"

"Shift, change, transform. You can come up with your own name for it, if you want."

"I don't want. I don't want to shift. I don't want to be a monster." Amber realised she was shaking.

"It's really not that bad," said Imelda. "You get powerful. You get stronger and faster and you feel something inside you just… alter. It's like you're becoming the person you were always meant to be."

"Not person. Monster."

The smile on Imelda's face faded. "Monster," she said. "Yes." She reverted to her normal state, and tucked in her top. She looked almost embarrassed as she sat back down. "Well, there you go, anyway. That's how it's done. If you're ready to listen, I'll tell you how it started."

"You're not going to let me leave, are you? So go ahead."

Imelda took another sip from her cup. "I've known your parents since I was your age."

"I know," said Amber.

"No, you don't. I met your parents when I was sixteen years old. They were already courting."

"Courting?"

"That's the old word for dating. Which is probably an old word for whatever it is you call it now. We met Grant a year later. Bill befriended Alastair at Harvard, and Kirsty was added to the group after Bill and Betty got married."

"Bill didn't go to Harvard."

"I think it's safe to say that you don't really know your parents, Amber. Is it safe to say that?"

A strange feeling overtook Amber, a feeling of being adrift, cut off from everything she had thought she knew. "Yes," she admitted softly.

"I'm telling you this so that you'll know that we were all friends by the time the world welcomed in the New Year... of eighteen hundred and ninety."

"I'm sorry?"

"I'm one hundred forty-six years old, Amber, and your parents are three years older than me."

Amber didn't have anything to say to that.

"Bill and Alastair met some interesting people at Harvard," Imelda continued. "There were all kinds of clubs and societies back then: curious people looking to expand their horizons. They started out by merely dabbling in the occult, Bill and Alastair. And they drew the rest of us in."

"What do you mean by occult?" Amber asked. "You mean like black magic?"

"I mean *all* magic. Or as much magic as we could do, anyway. There were limits to the levels to which we could rise. I... I have no excuses for the things I've done. I let myself be swept along, but Bill and Betty... This was *all* they thought about. Early on, Bill came to us with a story he'd heard, of a deal with a being called the Shining Demon. In exchange for a tribute, this Demon would grant power, strength, magic and, if you obeyed the rules, eternal life."

"By turning you into demons yourselves?"

"You're skipping ahead," said Imelda, "but yes."

"Why would you want to be turned into demons?"

"Did you not hear what I said? About the power and the strength and the eternal life?"

"But you'd be *monsters*."

Imelda gave her a soft smile. "Look at me. Do I look like a monster? We can hide. We're very good at it. But you interrupted me. Bill came to us with this story he'd heard. We got interested. We wanted to know if it was true, and if so how we could get a deal like that for ourselves. It took us years, piecing together the different clues, following every lead..."

"And then you met the Shining Demon."

"We were told about a book. *The Blood-dimmed King*, it was called. We tracked it down to this magician in Boston, and we stole it. The Blood-dimmed King is a devil, or *the* Devil, or the King of Demons or... something. He goes by many names, and he has these Demons who interact with people here on Earth – Demons with a capital D. The Shining Demon is one of them. The book detailed how we could make contact."

"How did you?"

"It was a ritual. It took months to prepare. So many requirements to meet, things to arrange. We couldn't eat for four days beforehand. Couldn't drink for two. It was hard, arranging everything. Almost impossible. But we did it. We managed it. And we made contact."

"Did it look like you?" Amber asked. "You know, monster– you?"

Imelda shook her head. "He was... he was something else. But the book said that one of the most important rules was not to look at him. You avert your eyes. I only caught glimpses. The first thing I noticed was the smell. We were in a basement. Dark. Cold. And then there was this smell of sulphur. It got stronger and stronger until... One moment we were down there, just the six of us, the next this light started to burn, right in front of us, and he kind of grew out of that light. We all looked away immediately."

"And you didn't sneak a peek?"

"All I can tell you was that he glowed. He shone." There was a strange look in Imelda's eye. Almost wistful.

"And he offered you a deal," Amber said, a little louder than necessary.

Imelda snapped out of it. "Yes. He offered us power. Power enough for seven people."

"But there were only six of you."

Imelda went quiet for a moment. "That's right. He told us

what we'd have to do. The terms and conditions were...
unexpected. Half of us – Kirsty and Grant and myself – wanted
to walk out right there and then. But in doing so we'd break
the circle and... well. He would tear us apart. So we stayed.
And we listened. And, in the end, we agreed."

"To what?"

She cleared her throat. "The Shining Demon would give us
power enough for seven people. So two of us would have to
have a child. That child would grow up, and their power would
manifest at some stage in their sixteenth year. They'd become
as strong as we were. Just like you."

"Okay," said Amber. "And then there'd be seven of you. What
was wrong with that?"

"It was what was expected in return, Amber. Some Demons
want souls. The more they have, the stronger they get. The
stronger they get, the stronger the Blood-dimmed King
becomes. But the Shining Demon didn't want souls from us.
He wanted a jar of blood from each of us. Our blood, which
had magic in it already, spiced with... more magic."

"And how did you spice your blood?"

Imelda's eyes locked on Amber's.

Seconds passed.

"You're looking at me like you're expecting me to figure
something out," Amber said, "but I have no idea what it is
you're hoping for."

Imelda held her gaze. "Your parents had a son."

Amber's eyebrows rose. "I have a brother?" She'd dreamed
of having a brother or a sister, someone to talk to, to share
with, to alleviate that awful feeling of loneliness that would
creep up on her whenever the house got too quiet.

"Your parents had a son," Imelda repeated. With emphasis on the *had*. "He reached his sixteenth birthday. A few months later, he started having headaches, started feeling sick, and then his power manifested."

"Yes? And?"

"And we killed him."

Amber paled. "What?"

"The Shining Demon explained it all to us, down in that cellar. He told us how we'd have to absorb the seventh's power, how that would make our blood more potent, how that would be a suitable tribute."

"You killed my brother?"

"We killed him," Imelda said. "And then we ate him."

7

THE WORLD DULLED.

"No," said Amber in a soft, soft voice.

"Our demon forms made it easy. Made it far too easy."

Amber shook her head. "You can't have done that. Please, Imelda, tell me you didn't do that."

"We could never let the children reach the stage where they'd realise what they were. It was too dangerous. Too unpredictable. We got stronger with each child we consumed, but each one was born with a strength to rival our own. You're the only one I've seen actually get a chance to shift."

"Was... was I going to be eaten, too?" Amber was suddenly standing. "They were going to eat me? They were going to kill me and eat me? My own frikkin' *parents*?"

"Please sit down."

"I don't think so!"

"Fine," Imelda said, sounding tired.

"So go on! Tell me what you did to my *brother*."

"We killed him and we ate him, and he made us stronger," Imelda said. "We each gave a pint of our blood, which was practically sizzling with power by that stage, and by then Kirsty and Grant were expecting."

"No," Amber said. "No, you can't. None of that happened. That's sick."

Imelda didn't meet her eyes. "Once their son reached his sixteenth year, once we'd eaten him, it was my turn, with Alastair, and we ate my child when she turned sixteen, and then it was back to Bill and Betty."

"You took turns? What was it this time? Another brother? Maybe a sister?"

"It was a girl."

Tears rolled down Amber's cheeks. "I had a sister. I had a sister and you killed her."

"Yes, we did," Imelda said, pulling at a tiny loose thread on her sleeve. "Every sixteen years, the seventh's power was recycled through us, making us stronger, and then the surplus was available again for the next child."

"So that's what you've been doing?" Amber asked. "For, what, the last hundred years?"

"We make it a point not to grow too attached to our children. It's the only way to stay sane."

Amber laughed. "Sane? You think this is sane? This is the most insane thing I have ever heard! This is nuts! It's sick and it's wrong! It's evil! You're saying my parents are—"

"Psychopaths," said Imelda, looking up at her. "Yes. Pure psychopaths. The others, they *became* psychopaths. They let the power corrupt them, eat away at their consciences. But Bill and Betty, they were born that way. They just hid it until they didn't need to any longer."

"So everyone's a psycho except you," said Amber. Her

fingernails – still ordinary fingernails, thank God – were digging into her palms. "That's what you want me to believe now?"

"If I'm a psychopath," said Imelda. "why haven't I killed you? The others aren't around. If I killed you now… ate you… I'd absorb all of your power. I wouldn't have to share it with anyone. So, if you really do think I'm the same as your parents, why are you still alive?"

"I don't know," Amber said. "Maybe you're trying to talk me to death. Or maybe, because the Shining Demon demands a jar of blood from each of you, having me all to yourself would break the terms of your deal."

Imelda smiled. "I'm breaking the terms already by keeping you alive. But I admire your logic. You're always thinking, aren't you? That's what I've always loved about you, Amber."

"You've never loved *anything* about me," Amber said. "Before this, you barely spoke to me."

"I couldn't do it anymore," said Imelda. "I couldn't pretend anymore. Not like the others."

"So how come you're different?"

Imelda hesitated. "The last time I had a child, something went wrong. I'd tried to remain detached from her, but I couldn't. The moment I held my newborn baby in my arms I knew… I knew I wasn't supposed to feel this way."

"You loved her."

"Yes."

"But you still killed her."

"*Alastair* killed her. I tried to run. I tried to take my daughter and escape, but Alastair knew what I was planning. He promised me that if I returned he wouldn't tell the others. I was scared. Confused. Weak."

"So you brought your daughter back to be killed."

"Yes."

"And let me guess – you felt bad about it."

Imelda looked up. "This stops here. With you. I've spent the last ten years building up my courage. I'm sorry I was never kind to you, but it was too risky. I was afraid the others would see what I was planning. Alastair, especially. He knows me the best. But now I'm going to break the cycle. You're going to leave with Milo. Tonight. I'll be joining you as soon as I can, but you have one chance to get out of this alive, and Milo knows where to start."

"You're sending me away? But you can't. This is my *home*."

"Is it? What exactly do you have here, Amber? Friends? Really? Are you going to stay because of school? Because of your job at the diner? These things are enough to make you stay?"

Amber swallowed. "Then where am I going?"

"Milo knows. I don't."

"Why wouldn't you know where I'm going?"

"Because if your parents figure out that I'm helping you," said Imelda, "they will torture me until I tell them everything. If I don't know where you are, I can't betray you."

Amber stared. "But... but then what'll happen to you?"

Imelda hesitated. "Your parents are very ruthless people, sweetie, and they're not going to pass up the opportunity to absorb more power."

"They'd eat you?"

"And if I'm very, very lucky? They'd kill me first."

8

MILO CAME IN AND Imelda talked to him at the far side of the apartment in a low voice Amber couldn't make out. He nodded occasionally and replied, and barely even glanced Amber's way.

She busied herself with looking through the bag Imelda had given her. A few items of clothing and underwear, everything in her size. She dug a little deeper, found a bag of toiletries. Dug deeper. Found a bag of money.

Tens, twenties and fifties in tightly packed rolls. Her eyes widened. There must have been thousands in there. Tens of thousands. A hundred thousand?

All the essentials that anyone would need to go on the run.

Milo and Imelda came over, and Amber stood to face them.

"It's time to go," Imelda said.

"I don't want to," Amber announced.

"I understand that," said Imelda, "but it really is for the best. Milo will keep you as safe as he can and keep you out of sight as much as possible. We're paying him for this – ten thousand a week. Take it from the money I gave you."

"You're not listening to me. I don't want to go."

"I am listening to you, but you've got to listen to me, too. I know what your parents are capable of."

"You can hide me here."

"They'll check here," Imelda said. "Alastair is already looking at me strangely. He's got his suspicions. It's only a matter of time before he stops by for an unannounced visit."

"Maybe he doesn't want to hurt me, either. Have you thought of that? Maybe he's like you. Maybe he's sick of it."

Imelda shook her head. "I wish that were true."

"Ask him!" Amber said. "Talk to him! Talk to my parents! Maybe they'd change their minds if you talk to them!"

"Sweetie, no…"

"Have you tried?"

"I haven't," Imelda admitted.

"Then you don't know, do you? You want to send me away when I might not even have to go. I know my parents, too, all right? I know what they're like. Talk to them. They're weird, but they're practical. All you need to do is reason with them."

"Amber, Bill and Betty aren't going to change their minds," said Imelda. "They're furious. They're desperate. They haven't slept. They haven't stopped searching."

"They're worried about me."

"They're worried you've escaped. Sweetie, you saw them. You heard what they said. If they find you, they will kill you. You have to trust me on this."

"So that's it? You think you can hand me a bag of clothes and a bag of money and send me off somewhere? I don't even know where you're sending me. I'm not going, you understand? I am not going and you can't make me!"

Imelda glanced at Milo. "She's not usually like this."

"And who the hell is *he*?" Amber almost shouted. "You're sending me off with a strange man I don't even know? How is that a good idea?"

"I trust him."

"He was going to shoot me earlier! And you want me to get in a car with this guy? For how long? How long will all this take?"

Imelda hesitated. "I don't know. Maybe… two weeks?"

"*Two weeks?*"

"Or three."

"*What?*"

"It's the only safe way. You'll have to get yourself some more clothes and things, but that bag will do for now."

"We really need to get going," said Milo. "I want to be on the road before dark."

Amber held up her hands. "Okay, okay, listen to me. Just listen, all right? That's your idea. That's the plan you came up with. So now I have a plan. Milo here goes home. He goes home and he plays with his guns and he's happy. And, while he's being happy, you and me get in a car and we drive somewhere nice and we never look back."

Imelda shook her head. "I told you, I can't go with you."

"Why? Why can't you come with me? Jesus Christ, you're the only person I know who isn't trying to kill me."

"It's better for you if I stay, honey. I can keep an eye on what they're doing. If they're close to finding you, I can steer them away."

"You just don't want to be around me."

"That's not true."

"Of course it is. The only reason you're helping me is because you feel guilty. You don't give a crap about me – if you did, you wouldn't be handing me over to him."

Imelda shook her head. "That's not true."

"Well, there we have it – we have two plans. Your stupid plan where I go with some lunatic called Milo, and my good plan, where you and me go somewhere far away, with mountains and trees and maybe a log cabin. We'll go to Montana. It's cool in Montana. We won't have to live in this constant *heat*."

"Let's have a vote," said Milo. "I vote for the stupid plan and so does Imelda."

Amber glared at him, then redirected the glare at Imelda. "Why him? Who is he? What does he have to do with all this?"

"I have my own history with Demons," Milo said. "I'm as qualified for this job as anyone possibly could be."

"So you've made a deal, just like my parents did? Bad people make deals with Demons – bad people who like to eat their children. Have you ever murdered anyone, Milo?"

"Amber, that's enough," said Imelda.

"You want me to get in a car with this guy—"

"Yes," Imelda snapped. "I do. Because I can't be there and he's the only one I know who'll be able to protect you. He's also the only one I know who'd be *willing* to protect you. Amber, this is messed up. Don't you think I know that? And don't you think this is breaking my heart, sending you away? I've finally been able to tell you the truth, after years of being too afraid, and instead of showing you all of the love I have for you, love that I've had for you since the day you were born, I have to send you away and pretend to be just like the others. I have to pretend to care nothing for you, Amber. I have to pretend to see you as nothing more than our next power boost.

This is breaking me, sweetheart. This is ripping me up inside and I don't know how the hell I'm not falling to the floor in tears, but I'm not. Because I have to be strong. For you. And you have to be strong for me. Because you're the only person in this world that I love, and if anything happens to you I'll... I'll..."

"I'm sorry," Amber said quietly.

"Oh, honey," Imelda said, pulling her into an embrace. Amber didn't know what to do for a moment. This wasn't the quick hug of Grant or Kirsty, or the picked-up-off-the-ground hug of Alastair. This was something else. This was genuine, and Amber found herself lost as to how to respond.

But she gradually wrapped her arms round Imelda and hugged her back, and she didn't even notice the tears that were spilling off her cheeks and soaking through Imelda's blouse. She felt Imelda cry, and realised she was crying herself. This one hug was the warmest, most sincere physical contact she had ever experienced, and she didn't want it to ever end.

9

Rain mingled with the tears on her face as Amber got into the SUV.

Milo had parked it round the back of Imelda's apartment building. They didn't want Amber in plain view. They didn't want her walking across the sidewalk for a few seconds because that was a risk they couldn't afford to take. Their paranoia was affecting Amber. She waited until Milo had the back door open, and then she ran through the heat and the rain, practically dived in. Milo threw a blanket over her and closed the door.

He got in the front, started the engine, and as the SUV was pulling out on to the street Amber realised she hadn't said goodbye to Imelda, and a sliver of anguish pierced her heart.

She made sure she wasn't about to cry, and then pulled the blanket back.

The SUV's exterior may have needed a wash, but the interior was clean and smelled of polish. Milo struck her as the type to maintain his vehicle in perfect running order, and she realised that she wouldn't have been surprised to learn that the dirt and the dust on the outside were nothing more than camouflage.

They drove without speaking for five minutes. Amber resisted the urge to speak. She wanted Milo to get uncomfortable in the silence. When the clock on the dash showed 8pm, she sat up, but kept the blanket wrapped round her head like a shawl. To her irritation, he looked perfectly comfortable.

"So where are we going?"

Milo moved into another lane. "We're going to see a friend of mine. He might be able to help."

"Help how?"

"We're hoping he'll have some ideas on how to evade your parents."

"You're *hoping*? Imelda said there was a plan. Hoping for ideas does not sound like a plan. Who is he, this friend of yours?"

"His name's Edgar Spurrier," Milo said as they slowed at the lights. "He used to be a journalist. His investigations took him deeper and darker than any respectable news agency was willing to delve, so now he's a freelance... something."

"So he's unemployed, basically."

They started driving again. "He prefers the term 'freelance something'."

She frowned. "Was that a joke?"

Milo shrugged.

"Where does he live?"

"Miami."

"That's, like, three or four hours away. Why aren't you more organised? Why isn't he here? Or why can't you call him? I'd loan you my phone only, oh yeah, you *destroyed* it."

"No phone calls, if we can help it," said Milo, totally missing Amber's subtle jibe.

"I have a new plan," she said, sitting forward. "Turn around.

Take me to Montana. That's where they film *In The Dark Places*, so I'd be able to just hang out, watch them film, and I have plenty of money now so I could afford to rent a cabin there until all this dies down."

Milo glanced at her in the rear-view. "This isn't going to die down."

"No, I know that, I just—"

"I don't think you do," said Milo. "This isn't a problem that's going to go away, Amber. Your parents aren't going to change their minds. Your life, as you knew it, is over. You have to leave behind your friends and family. There's no going back."

"I *know* that," she insisted, though even she was aware how unconvincing she sounded.

An accident on the turnpike delayed them, forced them into a slow-moving convoy that crawled through Miami's sprawl of Art-Deco architecture. The rain was heavier here. Neon lights bounced off the wet blackness of the asphalt. It would have been beautiful if Amber hadn't shrunk away from every car that passed them, just waiting to see her parents' faces staring out at her.

By the time they pulled up outside Edgar Spurrier's crappy condo, it was past twelve and fully dark. The humidity closed in on Amber the moment she left the confines of the SUV. The rain eased off slightly, but the clouds were still heavy. Lightning flickered like a badly placed bulb and in the distance she heard thunder.

Edgar's condo was not air-conditioned. A large fan hung from the ceiling and threatened to move the warm air around, but couldn't work up the energy to do so with any degree of conviction.

Edgar himself was a tubby guy with blond hair that hung limply to his shoulders. He had an easy smile and nice twinkling eyes, and beneath his shorts his legs were surprisingly hairless. He handed Amber and Milo a glass of iced tea and took one for himself, then they all sat in his mess of a living room. Books and papers competed for space with notepads bursting with scribbles. No pizza boxes or empty beer bottles, though. Edgar may have been disorganised, but he was no slob.

"Milo has already briefed me on your situation," Edgar said, settling back into his chair. "You've got yourself into what we in the trade call a pickle, Amber. Milo could have taken you to a dozen so-called occult experts around the country and they would have sent you away with useless advice and a headful of mumbo jumbo. Instead, he brought you to me, where deals with the Devil are something of a specialty. The Shining Demon is one of my particular areas of interest."

He paused, and Amber felt the overwhelming need to fill the silence.

"Okay," she said.

That seemed to satisfy him. "Now then," Edgar continued, "your particular quandary is that running isn't going to work."

A bead of perspiration trickled down Amber's spine. "It isn't?"

"It isn't," said Edgar. "Your parents will eventually find you. It's inevitable. I'm sure Milo will explain this to you later. They will find you and they will kill you. So you need to be proactive, am I right? You need to take the fight to your parents."

Amber hesitated. "Uh yeah, except, I mean, I don't want to *actually* fight them."

"No, no," said Edgar, "you don't want to physically take

them on, not at all. I'm not suggesting that for a minute. But you want to take the *figurative* fight to them, agreed?"

"I guess."

"You can't spend the rest of your life *running*. You can't spend the rest of your life *hiding*. Because, if you do, the rest of your life will be very short indeed. So you need an alternative. If I were in your position, what would I do? I've given this a lot of thought since Milo approached me. A lot of thought. But only this morning did the obvious course of action occur to me." He sat forward. "Amber, what you're going to need to do is talk to the Shining Demon *yourself*."

She blinked. "I'm sorry?"

"Not going to happen," said Milo.

Edgar held up a hand. "Hear me out."

"Not going to happen, Edgar."

"Just hear me out, buddy, okay? Keep an open mind about this. There's nothing we can do to stop her folks from wanting to eat her. There just isn't. Consuming her flesh is the only way they can grow stronger, and the only way they can pay the tribute they owe. Because, don't forget, they *do* owe that tribute."

"We haven't forgotten," said Milo.

"So there's nothing we can do there," Edgar said, leaning back in his chair. "If you don't want to talk to the Shining Demon, what does that leave us with? You could go after them. Take them out. Kill them before they kill you."

"I don't want to kill my *parents*," Amber said, aghast.

"They want to kill *you*," said Edgar. "You're going to have to reconcile yourself with the facts here, Amber. This is life or death we're talking about. It's kill or be killed."

"She doesn't want to kill her parents," Milo said. "So we're not killing her parents."

"I figured as much," said Edgar. "I'm a pretty smart guy, remember? You may have thought I was sitting here looking pretty, but what I was actually doing was going through all the options and throwing out those that were a no-go. I threw out everything except the one I started with – Amber here summoning the Shining Demon, sitting him down and having a chat."

Amber glanced at Milo. He wasn't saying anything, but he didn't look happy.

"So that's my idea," said Edgar, talking straight to Amber now. "You explain how unfair all of this is. You didn't ask for it, after all. You are an innocent party, caught up in your parents' diabolical machinations."

"Why would he care?" she asked.

Edgar chuckled. "Good question. And of course you're right. The Shining Demon isn't going to give one whit about any of that. He's a capital D Demon, after all. He likes it when innocent people suffer. That's kind of his thing." Edgar sat forward. "But you, my dear girl, hold a special appeal. The Shining Demon is notoriously picky about who he appears to. He'll only do a deal with someone if they pique his curiosity. But here's the thing. You, Amber, are enough to pique *anyone's* curiosity."

She suddenly felt uncomfortable. "Why?"

"You're the demon offspring of demon parents," Edgar said. "But whereas your folks are demons by circumstance, you are demon by birth. That makes you, technically, a purer form of monster – if you'll forgive the description. You have also, by virtue of being alive right now, potentially compromised their original deal, which will certainly have got his attention."

"So summon the Shining Demon and say what?" Amber asked. "'Hey there, please could you change the terms of my parents' deal?'"

Edgar shook his head. "The terms are unbreakable, there's no getting around that. But he could make it so that your parents and their friends never find you. He could make it impossible for them to hurt you. He could do a hundred things that would ruin your parents' plans and make eating you redundant."

"What would I have to do in return?"

Edgar shrugged. "Seeing as how your parents and their friends were going to eat you and then give him their supercharged blood, it stands to reason that he'd want to get that same energy some other way. Sending you out to harvest souls is a very common method of payment."

"I'm not killing anyone. I'm not doing that."

"Very well. If those are the terms of the deal he offers, you just say no. No harm, no foul. But he might not want you to kill. There might be something else."

Amber raised her eyebrows. "Could I offer him my demon side? Is that possible?"

"Even if it were, I doubt that would entice him."

"I'm not going to give him my soul," she said, a little sharply. "It's mine and he's not getting it."

"Sounds reasonable," said Edgar. "Not to worry, however – I do have a suggestion of my own. You're unique enough to summon him and, if you offer him something equally as unique, you might just find yourself with a deal."

"What do you have in mind?" Milo asked.

"The one that got away," Edgar said. "It's a story I was told by a very dangerous man, name of Dacre Shanks. You heard of him?"

Milo shook his head. Amber didn't bother.

"Dacre Shanks was a particularly nasty serial killer back in the late sixties, early seventies. This small-town Sheriff's Department eventually tracked him down, in 1974 I think, and went in all guns blazing. Shanks fell in a hail of bullets. Couldn't have happened to a nicer guy. Anyway, I met him a few years ago, and he told—"

"Wait," said Amber. "You just said he died in 1974."

"He did," Edgar said, nodding. "But before the cops closed in on him, he'd already made his deal with the Shining Demon."

"He's still alive?"

"Technically? No. But he's still around. Last I heard he was in his hometown of Springton, Wisconsin, happily killing a bunch of teenagers, but that was fifteen or so years ago. If you can find him, he might be able to help you."

"You want us to ask a serial killer for help?"

Edgar shrugged. "It's a scary world – you got to be prepared to meet scary people. Dacre Shanks qualifies as a scary person. He's up there with Elias Mauk and Leighton Utt... maybe even the Narrow Man. Outwardly, charming as all heck, but... well. Serial killer, you know? I met him through a mutual acquaintance and arranged an interview of sorts. The man just wanted someone to talk to, and he talked a lot. I got some very graphic descriptions of what he'd done to his victims, some very disturbing insights into his mind... We talked about death, about how it felt when those bullets riddled his body, about what happened after. Milo knows what I'm talking about, right?"

Milo said nothing, and Amber frowned.

"And we talked about the deal he'd made with the Shining Demon," Edgar continued. "How he summoned him, what the terms were, how he found out about him in the first place. And he told me a story I'd never heard before, and I thought I'd heard all the stories about our shining friend. He told me about a man who'd made a deal — I don't know the circumstances surrounding it, but it was a deal like any other — and then welched on it. The Shining Demon granted him whatever he wanted, but, instead of paying him back in the agreed-upon fashion, this guy skips town, and the Shining Demon loses him. And the Shining Demon *never* loses a mark."

"What does this have to do with me?" Amber asked.

Edgar smiled. "If you can find this guy, you can offer his location to the Shining Demon in exchange for getting your parents off your back."

"You know where he is?"

"Haven't a clue," Edgar said, almost happily. "Shanks wanted to talk, sure, but he was pretty cagey with the things he had to say. You'd have to ask him yourself. You might like him. He's got some pretty funny stories. They'll give you nightmares, but they're still pretty funny."

"Uh," said Amber, "I don't really want to talk to a serial killer."

Edgar chuckled. "You'll be perfectly safe. Milo here will look after you."

Amber glanced at Milo. Just how dangerous *was* this guy?

"Why don't you come with us?" Milo asked. "You know him, he knows you, you can make the introductions."

"I'd love to," said Edgar, "but he said he'd kill me if he ever saw me again."

"Why?"

Edgar shrugged. "The conversation turned sour — what can I say? Serial killer, you know?"

10

EDGAR WENT TO FETCH the paraphernalia Amber would need to summon the Shining Demon, and the moment he was out of the room Amber looked over at Milo.

"I'm doing it *now?*"

Milo shrugged.

"Imelda said it took days of fasting and loads of preparation."

"There's more than one way to summon the Shining Demon," said Milo. "Sometimes you don't even have to summon him – he'll appear right when you're at your most vulnerable."

"Milo, I don't know…"

"If you don't want to do this, say so. We'll find some other way."

"Is there another way?"

Milo didn't answer.

Amber slowly clasped her face in her hands and dragged her fingers down her cheeks.

Then she sat forward. "So what do I say? How do I greet the Shining Demon? Do I call him sir, or lord, or master?"

"He's not your lord and not your master, so you don't have to call him anything. Relax, okay? You don't have to be so nervous. Talk to him like you'd talk to me, but don't agree to anything other than the terms *you* want. Ignore everything he says that isn't on topic. He'll try to trick you. Listen to *every* word he uses, because he uses them for a reason."

"You're not making me any less nervous."

"Sorry."

"Do you think this is a good idea?"

"It's the best one we have."

"That's not saying a lot, though, is it?"

"No, it's not."

Amber sat back. Her insides were in knots. "What do you think Imelda will do when she finds out I actually *met* the Shining Demon?"

"That all depends on whether this plan works."

"How do you know her, anyway?" she asked.

"How does anyone know anyone?"

"I don't know. They meet?"

"There you go," said Milo. "We met."

Edgar came back in. Amber didn't know quite what she had been expecting – maybe a robe, or a ceremonial dagger, or a box full of candles with pentagrams moulded on to their sides. She wasn't expecting a large leather pouch, shaped like a deflated balloon.

"It's a gunpowder flask," Edgar said proudly, handing it over with something approaching reverence. It was heavy, filled to its leather stopper with what felt like sand. "Persian, nineteenth century, made from a camel crotch."

"Ew."

Edgar chuckled. "Don't worry, the camel's long dead."

"Still ew."

"See those engravings on the hide? Those intricate little engravings? I don't know what they are. Pretty, though, aren't they?"

"There's gunpowder in here?" she asked.

He shook his head. "Something far more powerful. Far more valuable, too. The only reason I'm letting you use it is because I couldn't get it to work myself."

Milo frowned. "You tried summoning the Shining Demon?"

"Everyone wants something," Edgar said, a little sadly, "but I just wasn't interesting enough for him to bother with. Story of my life, huh? But, if this will work for anyone, it'll work for Amber, and then I can finally find out if it was worth the money I paid for it, or if I was scammed. Y'know, *again*."

"How do I use it?" she asked, handing the flask back.

Edgar cleared a space on the coffee table and laid it down, then sat. "You pour the powder in a circle around you, making sure there are no gaps. You put a match to it. It catches fire. That's it."

"It's that easy? And then the Shining Demon will appear?"

Edgar hesitated.

"What?" Milo asked, suspicion in his voice.

"The Shining Demon doesn't do that anymore," Edgar said. "Appearing, I mean. You can't make him come to you. Instead, you go to him."

Amber went cold. "I what?"

Milo frowned. "She what?"

"I couldn't get it to work, so I just have to go by what the guy who sold it to me said, all right? You put a match to the circle, and when it's lit you... arrive."

"Where?" said Milo.

"Wherever the Shining Demon is," said Edgar.

"Hell?" Amber asked, her voice small.

"Maybe. But don't look so scared. It's absolutely fine. You'll be perfectly safe."

"It doesn't sound perfectly safe," Milo said.

"It is, though. She'll be in no danger whatsoever. As long as she doesn't step outside the circle."

"I don't like this," Amber murmured. "Will you both be with me, at least?"

Edgar made a face. "We'll have to stay here, I'm afraid. Them's the rules. But you don't have to worry about a thing. You'll meet the Shining Demon. You'll explain your situation. You'll offer him the guy who welched on the deal in exchange for a way to protect you from your parents and their friends."

"And only that," said Milo. "Do not deviate from the script."

"That's a good point," said Edgar. "The Shining Demon likes to talk, by all accounts, and he might try to get you to agree to something you really shouldn't be agreeing to. Keep it simple. If he likes the terms, he'll accept them. If he doesn't, douse the flames and you'll come straight back. Do not step out of the circle. I cannot stress that enough."

"What if he pulls me out?"

"He won't be able to touch you so long as you stay where you are. Also, for your own wellbeing, it's probably advisable not to look directly at him." Edgar got to his feet. "There. I think that's everything."

Amber looked up at him. "I still have, like, a billion questions."

"A little knowledge is a dangerous thing," said Edgar. "You'll be fine. Come on, you can do it in the backyard."

He took the powder flask and walked out to the kitchen. Milo got up, helped Amber stand. Her legs felt weak.

"Am I actually going to do this?" she asked.

"You can change your mind at any time."

She expelled a long breath. "I can't believe I'm going to actually do this..."

They went out back. The dark yard was modest, with a small pool that needed a serious skimming. Whether the sweat on Amber's face was from the humidity or the trepidation, she couldn't be sure. The rain had stopped, which allowed the cicadas to start singing again. Edgar led Amber to a patch of crabgrass and handed her the powder flask and a battered matchbook with a picture of a staircase on the front.

"All set," he said.

She looked to Milo for instruction, but he just stood there, cool in the heat. Expecting either of them to correct her at any moment, she undid the stopper on the flask, crouched down, and began to pour.

The opening was small, and the fine black powder came out in a thin, steady stream. The warm breeze made the grasses ripple, but the powder flowed straight down like it was a perfectly still night. Amber turned 360 degrees, making sure not to leave any gaps, and when she finished she stood in the small circle and plugged the flask with the stopper. She held it out to Edgar, but he waved it away.

"Hang on to it until you're done," he said, and she hung the strap over her shoulder so that it dropped diagonally across her chest.

She took a match from the matchbook and crouched again.

Her mouth was dry. Her hands were shaking. She needed to pee. She looked up at Milo.

"See you when you get back," he said.

Amber ran the head of the match across the sandpaper strip. The match flared, and with shaking hands she put the flame to the powder. It lit instantly, expelling a stench so violent it made her head turn. The fire spread from the point of contact in both directions, and she stood and watched it surround her. When the flames met and the circle was complete, the flames turned blue and she was indoors now, in a castle, its vast walls constructed of hewn stone, its ceiling too high to see, its thick wooden rafters swallowed by shadows.

In front of her were five arched doorways with corridors like the fingers of a splayed hand. Tapestries hung on the walls, depicting various acts of depravity, their shock value immediately shamed by the even more gruesome images captured in the stained glass of the long windows that sliced through the wall above.

It was cold here. The sweat that had layered her body in the Miami heat was now making her shiver. Her breath crystallised in small clouds. She thought she was alone until she heard the giggle.

Someone was standing in the dark area between the doorways. Lurking.

"Hello?" she called. Her voice didn't sound like her own. It sounded like the voice of a scared child. "I... I see you. I can see you. Hello?"

The shape didn't move.

From somewhere, from elsewhere, came the sound of

screaming, a chorus of pain carried to her on the wind. It was gone almost before it had registered.

"Hello," said the shape.

It came forward, into the light. Tall and thin, a genderless thing, wearing a patchwork robe that may have been a gown. Heavy make-up, black and badly applied, rimmed its eyes, while its thin mouth was smeared with red lipstick. The foundation it used covered the entirety of its bald head in a thick grey-white that may have been ash.

"Are you the Shining Demon?" asked Amber.

The curious thing gave a high-pitched titter, covering its mouth with long-fingered hands.

"No, no, no," it said in its curious voice. "No, no. But he knows you're here."

"Where am I?"

Another titter. "In his castle."

"Is this hell?"

"To some. What's your name?"

"Amber."

"Hi, Amber. I'm Fool."

"Hi, Fool."

"Do you want to play with me?" Fool asked. "I know lots of games. Do you want to play Who Can Scream the Loudest? I'm very good at that. Or maybe Who Can Bleed the Most? I bet you'd win. I'll give you a head start, if you'd like."

"I don't think so."

"Step out of the circle, Amber."

"I'm sorry, I can't."

"Sure you can," said Fool, moving closer. "Step out of the circle."

Fool smiled. Its teeth were small shards of coloured glass sticking out from bloody gums.

It turned its head suddenly, its eyes narrowing. From one of the corridors came a glow.

"He's here," Fool whispered, and without giving Amber another glance it sprinted from the room.

Amber fought the urge to run, even though every instinct in her body was screaming at her. She watched as the glow got brighter, then turned, lowering her head while her hands shielded her eyes. The room was suddenly lit up. From behind her, the light tread of bare feet.

"You seek an audience with me," came a voice. Male. Hushed.

"Yes," she croaked out, closing her eyes. "I'm... I..."

"I know who you are, child. I know why you're here. You seek protection from those who would harm you."

She nodded. Her mouth was so, so dry. "My parents. And their friends."

"I know them, too," the Shining Demon said. "So eager. So ruthless." His brightness soaked through her eyelids. It hurt. "You are the first to have escaped their platter. The first to find your way to me."

"I need your help."

"But of course," said the Shining Demon, and she could hear the smile in his voice. "I am the only one who could possibly help you. I am your only hope, am I not? Come, Amber, let me show you my castle."

"I... I was told to stay in the circle."

"Mmmm. Yes. Wise, I suppose."

"Where are we?" she asked. "Is this hell?"

"Questions, questions," said the Shining Demon. "Such an inquisitive species, the living. The dead have no need for questions. The dead are quite content in their gentle ignorance." He was walking now, circling the circle in which she stood. Amber didn't speak. She had the feeling he wasn't finished.

"This is his kingdom," the Shining Demon continued. "The one known by many names. My dark and terrible master."

"The Blood-dimmed King," Amber said.

"One of his names, yes," said the Shining Demon. "This is his kingdom, but we are in my castle. You are my guest, Amber. I assure you, no harm will befall you if you take one simple step…"

She turned away from the sound of his voice. "I'm… I'm sorry, I can't. I'm just here to make a deal."

Silence. And then, "Pity."

She licked the dryness from her lips. "Can you help me? Can you take back the power you gave them?"

The Shining Demon came to a stop somewhere to her left. "Your parents, their friends, they have ideas above their station. Ambitions. Some might say blasphemies. But a deal is a deal – I cannot break my part any more than they can break theirs. I cannot take back their power, or alter the terms of the bargain I made with them. But there may still be a way for me to help you. What are you willing to give in return?"

She swallowed. "There's someone you made a deal with, years ago. He cheated you."

"Nobody cheats me, child."

"This one did. You gave him what he wanted and then he ran. He never held up his end of the bargain. Do you remember him?"

90

The Shining Demon paused for a moment. "I know the one you speak of."

"I can find him. I can find him for you."

"Do you know where he is?"

"No, but I can find out. I think I can find out."

"Interesting," he said.

"Do we have a deal?"

"If you do find him, Amber, then we will talk of deals." Bare feet on stone. He was walking away.

"No," she said.

A sound, like the sharp intake of breath, whistled through the room.

"No?" he echoed.

She had the feeling she had just committed a serious breach of demonic etiquette, but carried on regardless. "I want your word that we'll have a deal if I bring him to you."

"Is that what you want? Truly?"

"Yes," she said, with what she hoped was steely resolve.

He moved closer. "A time limit, then," he said. "How long will you need?"

"Uh… six weeks?" she said, doubling what Imelda had suggested.

"You have three," said the Shining Demon, and Amber did her best not to grimace. "Twenty-one days. Five hundred and four hours."

"And… and then you'll protect me from my parents?"

He was standing right in front of her now. "I cannot alter the terms of the deal I struck with them, but, if you bring me this man in the time allotted, I will alter you, Amber. Your blood will be poison. To consume you would mean death."

"But I'll be all right, yes?"

That smile, appearing again in his voice. "Your blood will be poison to everyone but you. You have my word. Do I have yours?"

"I… I guess. What's his name? The man who cheated you?"

"I can give you no more help. I am extending my hand to you – shake it, and we will have a deal."

"I… I can't reach out of the circle," Amber said.

"Come now," the Shining Demon responded. "Tradition must be upheld or the bargain is not binding."

"I was told not to leave the circle."

"You are still standing in it, are you not?"

Amber bit her lip, then slowly reached her hand out.

The Shining Demon grabbed her hand and twisted, and Amber cried out and screwed her eyes shut tighter as he pressed a fingertip into her wrist. It burned.

"Five hundred and four hours," said the Shining Demon as he moved his finger. "If you fail to bring this man to me in the allotted time, your soul is forfeit."

"No!" Amber cried, trying to pull away. "I didn't agree to that!"

"Those are the terms," the Shining Demon said, and released her so suddenly that she nearly stumbled out of the circle.

She turned away from him, clutching her right hand as she cracked her eyes open. The number 504 was burned into the inside of her wrist, a mark, a brand that was already hardening into a scar. The pain faded quickly. "I didn't agree to this," she said. "I didn't—"

A wind rushed in from all five corridors, a dank wind that

brought with it hints of rot and sickly perfume and overripe fruit and human waste, and the wind extinguished the circle of fire and Amber was outside again, in Miami, and Milo was rushing forward to catch her as she fell.

11

MILO WOKE AMBER BEFORE five, stirring her from a fitful sleep. She had dreamed of demons and horns and the castles of hell, and she had dreamed of her parents chasing her. She had dreamed of herself as a monster, drenched in blood.

She turned over in her cot and cried silently.

When she had showered and dressed, she joined Milo in the kitchen. He'd made himself a coffee, and poured a juice for her. They drank in silence, listening to the soft sounds of snoring that drifted from Edgar's bedroom. He had gone to sleep like an excited schoolboy after quizzing Amber about everything she had seen and heard. Her entire experience was now on paper, told through the crazy scribbles and hieroglyphics that was Edgar's handwriting.

Everything except the time limit, the number that was now burned into her wrist. She wasn't going to embark on this journey with Milo already viewing her as a screw-up. If she could come away with only one thing from all this craziness, it was going to be the respect of the people around her.

Her wrist ached slightly, and she glanced at it. The numbers now read 500.

Four hours gone already.

Amber pulled her sleeve down quickly to cover it, as Milo laid the map he was perusing on the countertop. "Wisconsin," he said, tapping the old, creased paper. "And right here is Springton, Dacre Shanks's old hunting ground. It's about fifteen hundred miles from here. We'll be taking I-75 for some of it, but we're going to be doing our best to stay away from traffic. Your folks will be pulling out all the stops by now, and we don't want to be spotted by any of their people."

"How long will it take?"

"Twenty hours of driving, maybe twenty-two, if we were taking the quickest route. But because we're not... I don't know. Add another six hours on at the least. Twenty-eight hours on the road, driving eight hours a day, is a little over three days."

"We can drive more than eight hours a day," said Amber. "I've got my learner's permit: we can alternate."

"We won't be alternating."

"Why not?"

"Because I'm the driver," said Milo, in a tone that suggested finality, "and we're taking my car, and, while I'll be able to travel longer at the start, it's going to quickly average out at eight hours a day of driving time. You don't have to know why. You just have to know that those are the rules."

"Whatever," she muttered. Three days to get there, maybe a day to find Shanks and talk to him, which would leave her with seventeen days to find the man they was looking for and deliver him to the Shining Demon. Plenty of time.

"We'll need to change vehicles before we leave Miami, though," Milo said.

Amber frowned. "You think my parents know what we're driving already?"

"It's not that," Milo said, shaking his head. "For a trip like this, we need a special kind of car." He took her empty glass, and washed it and his mug in the sink. "I'm also going to need an advance on the money, by the way."

"How much?"

"Five grand ought to do it."

"Right…"

He looked back at her. "You think I'm going to abscond with it?"

"No," she said quickly. "No, not at all, it's just—"

"You don't know me," said Milo, putting the mug and glass down to drain. "Imelda does, but you don't. You don't know if I'm trustworthy."

"She trusts you."

"But you don't. And why would you? I've done nothing to earn your trust. Handing over five grand to a guy you've just met and whom you don't yet trust would seem to be a stupid thing to do."

"So I shouldn't give you the money?"

"No, you should," he said. "I'm just pointing out the corner you've been backed into. Trust me or not trust me, you're going to give me the money because you don't have a choice."

"I'm confused," said Amber. "Is this a life lesson I should be making a note of?"

"Something like that."

"I don't suppose you're going to tell me what that lesson is, are you?"

"You'll never learn it if I just tell you," Milo said. "Ready to go?"

"Uh yeah, OK," she said. "Should we say goodbye to Edgar?"

He frowned. "Why?"

"Because that's what people do. They say hello, how are you, goodbye, and they say thanks for your help."

"Edgar doesn't need any of that." Milo folded the map, and Amber watched how it shrank into a neat little packet. She'd never have been able to do that so cleanly.

It had stopped raining. They got into the SUV, and she passed him a money roll. He flicked through it, counting the five thousand, and nodded. She lay across the back seat, the blanket over her once again. Milo turned on the headlights and they got back on the turnpike. The roads were still quiet.

It was warm under the blanket. Amber yawned, closed her eyes. She wasn't going to sleep. Sleep meant bad dreams. Sleep meant monsters. But when she opened her eyes and sat up they were pulling up outside a dark house somewhere in outer suburbia, the sky only just beginning to lighten, birdsong threading the pale air.

"Grab your stuff," Milo said.

They got out and took their bags from the back. Amber stood holding hers while she watched Milo go round to the passenger side. He opened up the glove compartment, took out a gun, and clipped the holster on to his belt. Then he closed the door, pressed the fob, and the SUV beeped and locked.

"Are you a cop, or something?" she asked.

"No," he said.

He walked into the darkness between two houses. He didn't tell her to follow him or to stay, so she hoisted her bag over her shoulder and she followed. They came to the side door of a garage. Milo took out his wallet, searched inside it for a moment, and came out with a key. He opened the door and went inside. Amber waited a few seconds, then followed.

He shut the door after her, and locked it. Amber stood in complete darkness. The window had been boarded up. Milo moved around her.

"Is there a light in here?" she asked.

"No," he answered.

She dug into her shorts, came out with the matchbook that Edgar had given her. She struck one and light flared.

A long table against one wall contained all manner of tools and engine parts. She could suddenly smell oil, like the curiously sweet aroma had been holding itself back until she could see what she was smelling. A car covered by a tarp took up most of the space in the garage.

"You took his matches, huh?" Milo said, putting his bag on the table.

"Oh. Uh yeah. I forgot to give them back. I didn't think it'd be a big deal."

"Don't worry about it," Milo said. "I took the powder flask."

Her eyes widened. "He paid a lot of money for that. Isn't he going to be mad when he finds out?"

"Don't see why he would be," said Milo, moving to the tarp. "It works for you and you're going to need it again, with any luck. Why would he be mad about that?"

"Because it's not mine."

"Edgar doesn't care about things like ownership. He doesn't even own the condo he's living in."

"He's renting it?"

"He's stolen it."

Amber frowned. "How can you steal a condo?"

"By pretending to be the son of the elderly owner so that you can ship her off to a home for the infirm."

She gaped. "That's horrible!"

"Not really," said Milo. "The owner used to be a nurse who mistreated her patients. Edgar made sure everyone in the home knew about it, too."

"Oh," said Amber. "Well, I guess that's okay, then."

Milo pulled back the tarp, revealing a black car, an old one, the kind Amber had seen in movies, with a long hood and a sloping back.

"Nice," she said.

He looked at her sharply. "Nice?"

She hesitated. "It's pretty. What is it?"

"It's a 1970 Dodge Charger, and it is a *she*."

"Right," said Amber. "She's very nice, then."

Milo walked round the car, looking at it lovingly.

"The reason we can only travel eight hours a day," said Amber, "is it because your car will fall apart if we go longer?"

"You see any rust?" Milo asked, not rising to the bait. "Storing an old car in this humidity is not generally a good idea, not for any length of time, let alone twelve years. But she's different. She is pristine. Under the hood there she's got the 440 Six Pack, three two-barrel carburettors and 390 horses. She's a beast."

"Yeah. Words. Cool."

His hand hovered over the roof, like he was unsure as to whether or not he should actually touch it. Then he did, and his eyes closed and Amber wondered if she should leave him to it.

"You, uh, really love this car, huh?"

"She was my life," he said softly.

"Yeah. This is getting weird."

He opened the door, paused, and slid in. Sitting behind the wheel, his face in shadow, he looked for a moment like just another part of the car. She heard the keys jangle and she backed away from the hood. If the car really hadn't been started in twelve years, she doubted anything was going to happen, but she didn't want to be standing there if it suddenly blew up.

And yet, when Milo turned the key in the ignition, the garage reverberated with a deep and throaty growl that rose through the soles of Amber's feet and quickened her pulse. It was impressive, she had to admit that.

Milo flicked the headlights on and they shone blood-red for a moment, before fading to a strong yellow.

"Cool," she whispered, and this time she meant it.

12

THEY STUCK TO RESIDENTIAL roads as much as they could on their way out of Florida, staying off the expressway and I-95. Like she'd done in the SUV, Amber had to lie on the back seat, covered. She closed her eyes, but didn't sleep – not at first. Instead, she listened to the Charger. It creaked when it turned. It seemed *heavy*. There was no confusing it with its modern counterparts, cars that acted as cocoons against the world around them. To ride in a modern car was to ride in a deprivation tank – to ride in the Charger was to ride in a streamlined behemoth of black metal. *A beast*, as Milo called it.

Amber examined her hand, tried to remember what her claws had looked like. She was a beast, too, of course. A monster. Not a monster like her parents, though. They were predators – heartless and lethal. No, Amber was the prey, all innocence and vulnerability – except when she had her claws out.

The way she had punched that boy – Brandon, his name was Brandon – hadn't been weak. She probably would have killed him if she'd hit him any harder. She wondered if she *could* have hit him harder. She wondered how strong she was. She wondered what she looked like. Imelda was more beautiful as a demon than as a person. Her parents, too, had been taller and stronger and more beautiful. Amber wondered if the transformation would have the same effect on her, and found herself wondering what she'd look like taller, and slimmer, and prettier. She hoped her eyes didn't change, though. She liked her eyes.

She woke when they reached Homerville, across the state line in Georgia. Milo gave her a baseball cap and told her she could sit up front if she pulled the cap low over her brow. The further they got from Miami, he said, the safer she'd be. It was midday now. They passed through Pearson, and then Hazlehurst, and then Soperton – all brown grass and tall trees and identical houses with mailboxes by the road – and not one word was spoken the whole time.

"Thanks for doing this," Amber said to fill the silence.

Milo nodded, didn't say anything.

"I know I'm paying you, and this is just a job, but I didn't thank you earlier. I should have."

He didn't say anything to that, either.

A few minutes passed before she said, "Is this what it's going to be like the whole way?"

He didn't take his eyes off the road. "What is this like?"

"You know," said Amber, "the silence. The awkward, heavy, awkward silence."

"You used awkward twice."

"It's very awkward."

"I like to drive in silence. It lets you think."

"What do you do when you're done thinking? Or if you've got nothing to think about? Does the radio work? Maybe we could put on some music."

"But then we wouldn't be in silence."

She sighed. "You're really not listening to me."

"I like to drive in silence," said Milo again. "You're paying me, but this is my car and, since I like to drive in silence, we drive in silence. That's just the way it is."

"Even though it makes me uncomfortable?"

He shrugged. "If you can't stand to be alone with your thoughts, maybe there's something wrong with your thoughts."

"Of course there's something wrong with my thoughts. I'm going through a very tough time."

"We all go through tough times."

"My parents are trying to kill me."

"We all have issues."

"Maybe I'm suffering from post-traumatic stress. Did you think of that? Did Imelda? No. She just offloaded me on to you and now here we are. I probably need major psychiatric attention and you won't even let me listen to calm, soothing music. I could have a breakdown at any moment."

"You seem fine to me," said Milo, not taking his eyes off the road. The endless, straight, monotonous grey road.

"I'm a demon," she said.

"Like I said, we all have issues."

Amber glared. "Talking to you is like talking to a... a... Whatever."

She folded her arms and directed her glare out of the window. She didn't intend to go to sleep.

She woke to farmland and trees, a full bladder and a rumbling stomach. "Where are we?"

"Outside Atlanta," said Milo. "You can go back to sleep if you like."

She sat up straighter, pulled her cap off. "No. If I sleep any more, I won't be able to sleep tonight." The thought struck her. "Where *are* we sleeping tonight?"

"We'll find a motel."

"It better be a nice one. I've seen motels on TV and they look horrible." They approached a gas station. "Can we stop here? I'm starving. And thirsty."

"There's a bottle of water in the glove box," said Milo, and didn't slow down.

She gaped as they drove by. "*Seriously?* Why didn't you stop? I need food!"

"We're going to be stopping in an hour or so to fill the tank – you can eat then. It's going to be the first full tank she's had in twelve years."

"Is that so? Well, isn't that lovely? I am really, really happy for your *car*, Milo, but what about me?"

"Your parents and their friends, with all their vast resources, are searching for you. I'm not going to stop this car unless I absolutely have to. Now drink your water."

She punched the release for the glove box. It popped open and a bottle of water rolled off the stack of maps into her hand. She looked at the gun in its holster, sitting quietly in the light cast by the small bulb, and closed it up.

"I also have to pee," she said, twisting the cap off.

"Hold it in."

Right before she took a swig of water, she scowled. "I'm not sure I like you."

Milo shrugged. That annoyed her even more.

The water soothed her parched throat, but she didn't drink much of it – her bladder was full enough as it was. "We must have driven more than eight hours by now, right?" she asked. "We've been on the road since before seven. It's almost five now. That's, like... ten hours."

"It took you a disturbingly long while to add that up."

"Whatever. So why can you only drive for eight hours?"

"On average."

Amber sighed. "Why can you only drive for eight hours *on average*?"

"Because that's my rule."

She looked at him. "You're not a sharer, are you? Okay, fine, let's keep this professional. Let's keep this employer and employee. Let's talk about, like, the mission. What do you know about this Dacre Shanks guy?"

"Just what Edgar told us."

"What do you think he'll be like? Do you think he'll be nice?"

"There are no nice serial killers."

"Well, I know *that*," said Amber, "but he's not going to kill us on sight or anything, is he?"

"Don't know." Milo took a small iPad from his jacket. "Look him up."

She grabbed it off him. "*You're* allowed to have internet access, but *I'm* not? How is that fair?"

"Because your parents have no idea who I am, whereas they've undoubtedly got their eyes on your email account."

"Oh," she said. "Oh yeah."

She tapped on the screen for the search engine and put in Shanks's name.

"Dacre Shanks," she read, "the serial killer known as the Family Man. Oh God, do you know what he did? He kidnapped people that looked alike to make up a perfect family. Then he killed them all and started again. Says here he killed over three dozen people before he was shot to death, most of them in and around Springton, Wisconsin. We're actually going to try to talk to this guy?"

"All we need him to do is give us the name of the man who cheated the Shining Demon."

"And why should he give it to us when he didn't give it to Edgar?"

"Because Edgar posed no threat," Milo said. "Whereas we do."

"Do we? He's a serial killer who, like, came back from the grave. I know you've got your guns and you're really good at being horrible to people, but do you seriously think you can threaten him?"

Milo frowned. "I'm not horrible to people."

"Really? You really don't think you're horrible to people?"

"No," he said, a little defensively. "I'm nice. Everyone says it."

"Oh man," said Amber. "People have lied to you. Like, a lot. But even if we could threaten him – is that a good idea, to threaten a serial killer who's come back from the dead?"

"I've threatened worse."

"Worse how?"

"Just worse."

She sighed. "Fine. Don't elaborate. How are we supposed to find him, anyway? What if he isn't in Springton anymore?"

"We'll find him," said Milo. "We're on the blackroads now."

"The what?"

"Guy I knew once called them the blackroads – roads connecting points of darkness, criss-crossing America. Stay on the blackroads and you'll eventually meet every unholy horror the country has to offer. It's a network. Some people call it the Dark Highway, or the Demon Road. It's never the same route twice and there are no maps to guide the way."

"Then how do you know we're on it?"

"I've travelled it before. So has this car. You get the feeling for it."

Amber looked at him for a quiet moment. "Sometimes I think you just make stuff up."

13

MILO PULLED THE CHARGER up to a pump at a truck stop and Amber was allowed out. She stepped on to the forecourt and stretched, arching her spine and feeling it crack. The afternoon wasn't much cooler than the afternoons she'd endured in Orlando. It was hot and the sun was bright and the air was laden with moisture. A truck roared by on the road, rustling the trees on the far side and kicking up mini-tornadoes of dust that danced around Amber's bare calves.

The place was pretty run-down. Desperate blades of grass surged from cracks in the ground like drowning men in a sea of concrete. A long building with a sagging roof and dirty windows identified itself as a Family Restaurant. The letter E was missing from the sign outside, turning EAT HERE into EAT HER. Amber turned her back on it.

Beyond the fence there was corn, miles of it, and a clump of sorry-looking forest behind the truck stop itself. An old Coca-Cola billboard was rusting and peeling on a metal strut.

"Hey," said Milo, and she turned and he tossed her the baseball cap over the roof of the car. "Head down at all times.

Just because you can't see a CCTV camera doesn't mean it can't see you."

She pulled the cap low. "You really think my parents would be able to find me here? In Florida, okay, they probably have cops and officials doing whatever they want, but we're not in Florida anymore."

"Your folks have been around for over a hundred years," Milo said, sliding the nozzle in. "Let's not underestimate how far their reach spreads."

The gas started pumping and Amber headed round the side of the station, following the sign for the restroom. The clerk, a bored-looking guy in his fifties, didn't even glance up as she passed his window.

The restroom was empty and relatively clean. The early evening sun came in through the three windows up near the ceiling. Amber chose the only cubicle with a toilet seat, and when she was done she washed her hands in the sink. The mirror was dirty but intact, and she took off her cap and looked at her reflection. Butterflies fluttered deep in her belly.

You just decide you want to shift, and you shift, Imelda had said. Amber decided she wanted to shift, but her body ignored her. She tried again. She tried to remember how it had happened in Imelda's apartment, how it had happened when she'd bitten that finger off, but she couldn't even come close to replicating those feelings.

Did she even want to? What if she shifted and she couldn't shift back? What if she became stuck as a demon, unable to revert? No matter how much she tried to cover up, someone was bound to see, and then word would reach her parents and they'd come after her, the predators after their prey.

Amber looked into her own eyes. She hated being the prey. She commanded her body to change and this time it obeyed.

The pain blossomed and she cried out, and even as she was doing so she was watching her reflection. Her skin darkened to a glorious red in the time it would have taken her to blush. Her bones creaked and throbbed and her body lengthened – her legs, her torso, her arms. Her feet jammed tight in her sneakers. She was suddenly tall, suddenly slim. Her face was longer, her jawline defined, her cheekbones raised and sharpened. It was still her face, but her features were altered. Her lips were plumper. Her brown hair was black now, and longer, the tangles straightened.

Dizziness, an astonishing wave of vertigo, nearly took her to the ground. She gripped the edge of the sink, kept herself standing, unable and unwilling to look away from the beautiful demon in the mirror.

And she was beautiful. Her skin, though red, was flawless. Her teeth – pointed now, and sharp like fangs – were white and straight. Her raised cheekbones changed everything. Only her eyes had stayed the same. She was glad about that.

And, of course, there were her horns. Black horns, like ribbed ebony, curling out from her forehead and sweeping back. Breathtaking to behold.

Although her shorts looked shorter on her longer legs, they were now baggier, and threatened to slip off her hips. She pulled the neckline of her T-shirt to either side, revealing hard black scales that travelled across her shoulders.

She looked at her hands. They were small no more. They were good hands, strong hands, not small and weak like they had always been. Her fingernails were black, but there was

110

something else, an itch in her fingertips. She curled her right hand and her nails lengthened to claws so suddenly it actually frightened her. She gripped her right wrist with her other hand, not trusting this new and alien appendage not to suddenly attack her. She concentrated, and the claws retracted at her command.

"Awesome," she whispered. This was how it was meant to feel, she was sure. Shifting was supposed to make her feel strong, and powerful, and confident. Not scared, not like she'd been in Imelda's apartment. Not panicked, like she'd been when she'd smashed that boy's jaw.

Brandon, she reminded herself. *His name was Brandon.*

Then the door opened, and a broad woman in a trucker's cap barged in, making it halfway to the cubicles before she even noticed there was somebody else there.

Frozen, they looked at each other with wide eyes. Then the trucker spun on her heel. Spun to flee. Spun to call the cops. And with the cops would come her parents.

"No, wait!" Amber said, lunging after her. She caught the woman before she reached the door, pushed her a little harder than she'd intended. The trucker slammed into the wall.

"Sorry," said Amber, "sorry, but—"

The trucker took something from her belt. A clasp knife. She flicked it open and Amber held up her hands.

"No, wait, I'm sorry, please—"

But the trucker was too scared, too adrenalised, to listen. She rushed forward and Amber backpedalled, losing track of the knife. Immediately, she felt her skin tighten. Her hip hit the sink and the trucker stabbed her right in the belly.

Amber gasped, more from shock than pain. She expected the pain to follow. The trucker stabbed again, and again.

Still nothing.

Amber got her hand up, dug her fingertips into the trucker's face, and forced her back. Her other hand grabbed the woman's knife hand, gripping the wrist, keeping the blade away from her. It suddenly became clear to Amber that all she had was strength. She had no idea what to do next.

The trucker was more streetwise. She slammed her free arm on to Amber's elbow and punched her. It wasn't a particularly strong punch – she was obviously right-handed and she'd been forced to punch with her left – but her fist still connected with Amber's nose and tears still came to Amber's eyes. Anger flared, and she pulled the trucker in and threw a punch of her own. Her fist, which had grown black scales across the knuckles, collided with the trucker's jaw and sent her spinning into the far wall. The knife fell as the trucker hit the hand-dryer, its roar filling the room.

The trucker regained her balance, her eyes focusing once more. Amber stood across from her, only dimly aware that she was snarling. The woman broke for the door.

"I said don't!" Amber shouted. The trucker got to the handle and was pulling the door open when Amber reached her. She got a hand to the woman's head and bounced it off the door, slamming it closed. Amber pulled her back like the trucker weighed no more than a child, and threw her against the cubicle wall. It caved in under her weight and the woman crumpled to the floor. The hand-dryer deactivated.

Amber stood over the trucker to make sure she wasn't getting up. After a moment, Amber frowned, and knelt by her. She felt for a pulse. Couldn't find one. Alarmed, she rolled the woman on to her back, only then noticing the steady rise and fall of her chest. Amber checked the pulse again, searching for a few seconds until she found it.

She stood, and lifted her shirt as she turned to the mirror. Her belly was covered in those black scales, like armour. Even as she watched, though, they were retracting.

The trucker moaned.

Amber bolted into the sunlight. A car passed on the road and she dropped to her knees behind a pallet of chopped wood wrapped in plastic. When the car was gone, she was up, running bent over, making for the shelter of a parked truck, then the trees beyond.

She plunged into the shade and kept going, the trees quickly becoming a wood. Her horns bounced off a few low-lying branches and she ducked her head as she continued, following the sounds of water. She walked for a minute or two, and then light dazzled her eyes. For a heart-stopping moment, she thought the Shining Demon had come for her, but it was only the sun glinting off the surface of a slow-moving river.

Amber looked back. Listened. No sounds of pursuit. No cries of alarm.

She lifted her T-shirt again. The black scales were gone. Her belly was flat, toned, and uninjured.

She pulled off her clothes, left them in a pile and examined herself. Her arms, though red, were devoid of any black scales. She could see her muscles now, rolling beneath her skin. She held her right arm up and curled it, popped her bicep, and laughed out loud. She was strong. She was seriously strong. She had a strength that belied even her new and impressive muscles.

When she'd punched the trucker, scales had grown up over her knuckles. That time, their growth had been natural, instinctive. This time, she closed her fist and concentrated. The skin around her knuckles tightened, and black scales pushed their way, painlessly, to the surface. She focused on her hand now, and felt the skin tighten and watched the scales spread.

She held both hands out. Black scales grew, covering her hands and forearms. She looked down at herself. Her feet were now encased in them. Then her legs. Her belly and her chest. Her neck. Amber took a breath and closed her eyes and felt her face tighten, and the scales grew to cover her head.

She opened her eyes. Her eyelids hadn't grown scales, and neither, thankfully, had her nostrils or mouth – though when she tried opening her mouth wide she found she couldn't. She tapped her fingers between her horns and along her scalp, feeling the scales that had flattened her hair.

She walked to the river and gazed at her own rippling image.

Clad in her armour, she smiled.

She turned her fingers into claws, taking a moment to appreciate just how big, and how monstrous, her normally small hands had become. Then she went to the nearest tree, hesitated, and drew her fingernails across the trunk, leaving four deep grooves in her wake.

She did it again, faster this time. Then again. And then she slashed at the tree, carving out narrow chunks. If she could do that to a tree, what could she do to a person?

The thought disturbed her, threatened to dim her smile. But she shook it off, stepped back and leaped, her hands digging into the tree, and she climbed like she was born to do it. The tree swayed outwards and she went with it, until she was hanging over the river. Practically upside down. Amber laughed, exhilarated. Even her feet seemed to be digging in. Then she made the mistake of glancing at them.

Her feet were misshapen things, her toes as long as her new fingers, and every one of them curled around the tree.

The shock, the panic, the idea that she had deformed herself beyond repair, shot through her and her feet returned to normal and so did her hands. She fell, crying out, twisting in mid-air and then landing in the water.

The scales retracted as soon as she was submerged. When she'd regained her wits, she powered to the surface, already calming. She trod water for a bit, waiting for her heart to stop hammering so hard, then lengthened out and swam for the far side, marvelling at how effortless it all was. A few strokes and she was there. She turned, swam underwater the whole way back. Her fingers brushed silt along the riverbed.

Amber spent another few minutes just swimming. Skinny-dipping. She laughed as she did the backstroke. She'd never been skinny-dipping in her life. She'd never thought she'd ever get the chance. She never thought she'd ever have the confidence. And now here she was, in all her red splendour, in a river somewhere in Georgia. Were they still in Georgia? She wasn't even sure. That just made her laugh more.

The laugh died when she got the feeling that she was being watched.

She looked around. She could see no one in the woods on either side of the river, but the feeling didn't go away. She swam back, hesitating before pulling herself out of the water, then moved up on to the grassy bank towards her clothes.

She was halfway up when she saw the face staring at her through the foliage.

14

AMBER DARTED BEHIND A tree, as much to hide her nakedness as her black horns. Behind cover, she cursed silently, and immediately started looking around for an escape route. There was no way she could get away without being seen. Her only hope was that the person, whoever it was, would be freaked out enough to run away, but not freaked out enough to report the sighting.

She saw the face again in her mind. Shaggy hair – light brown. A boy. No, a young man. Maybe eighteen or nineteen.

"Hello?"

Amber stiffened.

"Hello? Miss?"

She shut her eyes and didn't reply. Silence, she decided, was her best option at this point.

"I know you're there," the boy said. He had an accent. English? Scottish? "I saw you run behind the tree. You know I saw you. I don't get why you're pretending you're not there."

No. Irish. That was it.

"This is getting a little bit silly," he continued. "This is like when my little cousins play hide-and-seek and they close their eyes because they think that makes them invisible. You... You're not closing your eyes, are you?"

Amber hesitated, then opened her eyes, and cursed silently again.

"I didn't mean to peek," he said. "My name's Glen. Glen Morrison. I was just passing, and... Well, no, that's not strictly true. Sorry, I don't want to start off on a lie, you know? The truth is, I've been sleeping here for the past few nights. In these woods. I'm temporarily between abodes, and my financial situation is not what one might call robust. I don't want you to get the wrong idea, though. I'm not lazy. I didn't come over to your country to scam the system or anything like that. I do have prospects. Well, I *had* prospects. It's a very long story, and I wouldn't want to trouble you with—"

"Glen," Amber said.

There was a pause, and then, "You're talking!"

"I am," said Amber. "Glen, I'm naked."

She could practically hear him nod. "I noticed. I mean, oh God, I mean I couldn't help but notice that you were... that you had no... that you were, uh... oh man, what's the word?"

"Naked," Amber prompted.

"Yes, thank you. Naked. You are naked, yes."

"And since I'm naked, Glen, I find having a conversation with a complete stranger a little weird. You know?"

"Oh, I do," Glen said, with an assurance that made it sound like it was a situation he found himself in regularly.

"I'm not sure that you do, Glen."

"Probably not," he admitted. "But, if it makes you feel any better, you don't have anything to feel embarrassed about."

"You're not helping, Glen."

"Sorry. I like your horns, though. Is that rude? Can I say that?"

"Glen... would you please go away?"

"Oh," he said. "Oh. But... Yeah. I mean... right. Sure. Of course. You're naked. You want to be alone. I come along, you feel self-conscious. Obviously. That's natural. That's perfectly natural. I'm intruding upon your special me time."

"And when you go away," Amber said, "could you please not tell anyone about this? About me?"

"Sure," he said, sounding disappointed. "Okay. Well, I suppose I'll just... head off, then."

"Thank you," Amber called.

She waited to hear his retreating footsteps, then waited a bit longer.

"Glen," she said, "are you still there?"

"Yeah," he answered. "Listen, I don't want you to think any less of me, all right? But... but I may need to check your clothes and steal any money you might have."

Amber's eyes snapped wide. "What?"

"I just don't want this to make things weird between us," he said, and then came the sound of rustling fabric as her shorts were lifted off the ground.

"Do not rob me," she called.

"I'm really sorry."

"Do not frikkin' rob me, you little creep!"

"I feel really bad about this."

She pictured him rifling through her pockets, his grubby little hand closing around the roll of cash she'd put in there. She concentrated on growing those scales again, and felt her skin begin to tighten. Then she heard a sharp intake of breath. Glen had found the money.

The scales didn't cover her entire body but they did enough to protect her modesty. Anger boiling, she lunged out from behind the tree, but her horns got tangled in the branches and her feet flew from under her, and she crashed heavily to the ground. She felt some of the scales retract. Glen stared down at her, open-mouthed.

"Wow," he whispered.

She snarled, showing him her fangs, and his eyes went wide. He dropped the money and spun, but Amber was right behind him, faster than he could ever hope to be. She grabbed the collar of his jacket and he shrieked as he was launched backwards.

"Do you know what I've just done?" she growled as she stalked after him. "I've just broken some poor woman's bones in the gas station. I threw her around like she was nothing and then I went for a goddamn swim. You think I'd hesitate for even one moment before I ripped your throat out for robbing me?"

Glen scrambled back on all fours. "Please, I didn't mean anything!"

"You meant to steal from me."

"I'm starving!"

She leaped, landing on top of him in a crouch, her right hand closing round his neck and pinning him to the ground. "Not my problem."

He looked up at her, tears in his eyes, and those tears just made her angrier. She wanted nothing more than to grow talons, to feel them slice into the soft meat, to sink her teeth in, to feel that warm blood flow down her...

She blinked. Wait, what?

She loosened her grip. The impulse to tear his throat open was rapidly receding.

"Are you going to kill me?" he whispered.

"No," she said dully, and stood. "No, I'm… I'm not going to kill you. I wanted to. I was going to. But…"

"I wouldn't worry about it," he said. "Something's going to kill me sooner or later. Most likely sooner, to be honest. If I had a choice, I'd prefer it to be you."

Amber took a few steps back, then turned, walked to her clothes. She let her scales retract fully as she pulled them on, ignoring the uncomfortable feeling of dry fabric on wet skin. Still frowning to herself, she sat on a log to wipe the soles of her feet before putting on her socks and sneakers.

"Your clothes don't fit you, y'know," Glen said.

He was tall and skinny, scruffy but not bad-looking. He bent to pick up her roll of money and she bared her teeth. He walked over slowly and held out his hand.

Amber finished tying her laces and stood, taking her money without a word and stuffing it back into her pocket.

"You should probably invest in a wallet," he said.

"Shut up, Glen," said Amber.

He nodded. "Yeah. That's fair."

She turned away from him, hiked her shorts up to her waist, and started walking back towards the gas station.

He caught up to her. "Can I ask a question, though? What are you?"

"What do I look like?"

"Honestly? A demon."

"Then there you have it."

He nodded. "You'd think that'd shock me, right? Meeting a

demon? A few weeks ago, it would have, but my life has taken a pretty weird turn lately, so I've adopted a policy of complete and utter credulity in all things. It saves everyone a lot of time. These days I don't ask for proof or reasons or anything. I just accept. That doesn't mean I'm not curious, of course. I'm very curious. I mean, look at you. A real live demon, just walking around. Do you live down here?"

"Down where?"

"Here. In the woods."

She frowned. "Are you stupid? Why would I live in the woods?"

"Well, I just thought, y'know…"

"Stop following me."

"Okay. Right. But can I ask another question? Why do you have money? How do you buy stuff?"

She stopped walking and turned to him. "How do you think I buy stuff? I walk into a store and say I want something and I pay for it."

He frowned. "You walk into a shop like that?"

She remembered her appearance. "Oh," she said. "No. This is new. I'm still getting used to it. I keep forgetting I have horns."

"They are magnificent," he breathed, staring at them.

"Eyes down here, Glen."

"Yes, sorry." He blushed. "You're… Sorry. You're just the most beautiful girl I've ever seen. Like, prettier than most actresses and models, even."

Amber grunted, and started walking again. "This isn't the real me."

"No, it is," Glen said, matching her pace. "Like, you're

beautiful in a way that I've never seen before. Everything about you, your face, your horns, your amazing teeth, your skin that's my favourite shade of red, your legs, your body, your—"

"You can stop anytime now."

"I'm not scared," he said. "You might think I'm scared of you because you're a demon and most people would be scared of demons, and that's why you put up this wall, to reject others before they reject you, but I'm really not scared. You're not scary. You're beautiful, not ugly. And I've seen some ugly things. I mean, I really have. Back in Ireland, I was attacked by this, by this *creature*, you know? It passed something on to me, the Deathmark. Wanna see it?"

"Not really."

He held out his right hand, proudly showing her his palm. Just below the surface of his skin, a tendril of darkness circled like a fish in a bowl. "Isn't it freaky? Ever since it happened, I've been meeting the oddest people. I met this guy in Dublin, this real weird guy, knows all about monsters and stuff. He said this thing will kill me in forty days if I don't pass it on to its intended target. That was, like, thirty-two days ago."

"You're going to die in eight days?" said Amber, frowning.

He nodded, and seemed oddly unbothered about it. "Unless I pass this mark on to a woman called Abigail. Apparently, she's a bad person. Like, really bad. Killed a lot of people, that kind of bad. I'll be doing the world a favour by passing this on to her. That's what I was told. She's supposed to be in a bar here in America that I haven't been able to find – The Dark Stair. You know it?"

"Sorry."

"Yeah, me neither. I looked it up online and nothing. I don't even know what state it's in. Maybe I'll find it, maybe I won't, but I'm here now, y'know? If I die, I want to die *here*. I want to see bigger things before I go, better things than the creature that attacked me. I want to see proper monsters. American monsters. I didn't think I'd see anything as beautiful as you, though."

"Right," said Amber. "Well, I better get going."

"Where are you off to?"

"Oh, uh, Springton. It's in Wisconsin. We have to find someone."

"We? Who's we? You and your boyfriend?"

"No, no. He's a… he's a guide, I guess."

"A guide to what?"

"Um…"

Glen's eyes widened. "Are you on the Demon Road?"

She hesitated. "No."

"You are!"

"We're not."

Glen was practically dancing in excitement. "I'm on the Demon Road, too! The guy, the weird guy, he said I should get on the Demon Road while I still had the chance, to see all the horrors the world had to offer. We're on the same road! What are the chances? Do you have a car?"

"No," Amber said automatically. Then, "I mean, I don't, personally. My friend does."

"Yeah? Do you think he'd let me tag along, like?"

"I… I don't mean to offend you or anything, but probably not. He doesn't know you and you *did* try to steal my money."

"I gave it back, though."

"Only after I caught you."

"That's true. But don't you think this is meant to be? I mean, what are the chances, really, of us meeting like this? Two people like us, cursed by darkness, meeting on the Demon Road?"

"According to my guide, they're actually pretty good."

"Oh. Really? Oh. Well, could you still ask him if there's room for one more?"

"Glen, you tried to rob me."

"Which turned out to be a mistake."

"And we're on a very dangerous journey, to be honest. We've got people coming after us and we're probably headed straight into even more danger, so I think it'd work out better for you if we just say goodbye here and now."

"But I don't have any other friends."

"You and me aren't friends, Glen."

He looked dismayed. "So I have no friends?"

"I have to get going."

She started walking again.

"I could help," he called after her. "And I wouldn't be a burden. I'd carry things, and I'd sit in the back and I wouldn't say anything, unless you needed me to say something, in which case I obviously would. Does your radio work? I could sing if it doesn't. I know a lot of songs. I don't have the best voice in the world and I might not remember every single one of the lyrics, or sing them in the right order, but I can carry a tune and I'll just make up the bits I forget. My dad used to do that all the time. It was like a gift he had, you know? Only he wasn't very good at it. I'm much better."

His voice eventually started to fade, and Amber left him behind. As she neared the edge of the woods, she focused on shifting back. What had Imelda called it? Reverting, that was it. She concentrated on her breathing, on calming down, on becoming her again, and, just when she thought it wasn't going to happen, an explosion of pain rocked her, made her stumble.

She put her shoulder to a tree and stayed there, blinking, her brown hair falling across her brow. She looked at her hand and noted the normal skin. She looked down and noted that her clothes fitted her once again. So that was normal, too, then.

Great.

15

A TANGLE OF BRIARS scraped across Amber's bare shin and she grimaced, bent down to rub it, then continued on. Moving through this little patch of forest had been easier as a demon – her red skin, even without the scales, was a lot hardier than the pale flesh she usually wore.

She felt the damp unpleasantness of her clothes more acutely now, too, as she did the embarrassment over a stranger seeing her naked. Both these sensations were washed away when she remembered what she'd done to that woman in the restroom. She could have killed her. She had *wanted* to kill Glen.

Amber forced herself to move on.

Emerging from the treeline further up from where she went in, she walked along the road back towards the truck stop. She kept her head down, really wishing she'd thought to grab the baseball cap as she ran from the restroom.

The throaty growl of the Charger's engine caught her by surprise, and she turned to watch it pull in sharply behind her.

Milo got out. He looked mad. She walked to the passenger side and he threw her the baseball cap. "Found this in the restroom," he said. "It was lying next to a woman who swore blind she'd been attacked by the Devil."

Amber put it on. "Um. Thanks."

They looked at each other over the roof of the car.

"I got you a sandwich," he said. "You can eat while we drive."

"It wasn't my fault," Amber said as Milo ducked to get in. "I shifted and she walked in. She pulled a knife, for God's sake!"

Milo straightened up. "She's fine, by the way."

Amber winced.

"A few nasty bruises. A dislocated shoulder. Maybe a fractured cheek. Definitely a concussion. But your concern over her wellbeing is touching."

"I get it, okay? You can stop now. I feel guilty enough as it is."

"I'm sure you do," said Milo. "But it isn't all bad. She's going to have a great story to tell, about the time she was attacked by a genuine, bona fide devil. A red-skinned devil with horns, no less. She's going to get some mileage out of that one. The cops have already been called, don't you worry."

Amber glared. "I just wanted to see what I looked like in a mirror. Is that so bad?"

"Not at all," said Milo. "Doing that in your bedroom mirror behind a locked door, no problem at all. Doing it in a truck-stop restroom, however…"

"Can we just go? Can we? Before the cops get here?"

"Sure." He hesitated, then looked at her again. "But I need you to understand something, Amber. This will catch the attention of your parents."

She blinked. "I'd… I'd…"

"You hadn't even considered that, had you?"

She frowned. "No. But I should have. What the *hell*?"

The expression on Milo's face softened. "What did Imelda tell you? Your demon side is more confident. You can take that to mean arrogant. And you can take *that* to mean self-centred. You're not going to be thinking too much of the consequences of your actions when you've got your horns on. That's what makes it so dangerous."

"Do you think they'll come here themselves?"

"I would, if I were them." A van passed on the road beside them. "We've lost our advantage. Up till now, they didn't know you were running; they just thought you were hiding. Now that they know, they'll be coming after you."

"I'm sorry," she said. "I'm so sorry."

He shrugged. "Come on, the sooner we get away, the better. At least no one here knows where we're headed."

Amber winced, and Milo froze.

"What?" he asked.

Dammit. Dammit, dammit, *dammit*. "Someone might know where we're going," she said.

Milo blinked at her. "I don't understand. Who did you find to talk to around here?"

"A guy. His name's Glen. I met him in the woods," she said. Then she added, "He's Irish."

"Oh well, he's Irish," said Milo. "That's okay, then. The Irish are renowned for how tight-lipped they are. What the *hell*, Amber?"

"I'm sorry, all right? I wasn't thinking."

"Some random guy in the woods?"

"He's not random," she responded, a little hotly. "He's like us. He's, you know... cursed by darkness."

Milo actually laughed. "He's what?"

"They're the words he used," she said, scowling. "And they're not too far away from what you said about the blackroads connecting points of darkness, whatever the hell *that* means. And, y'know, he's dying, actually. Glen. He's got the Deathmark."

"What's a Deathmark?"

"I... I thought you'd know."

"Edgar's the occult expert, not me."

"Well, the Deathmark is this thing that he has that's killing him, and he's on the Demon Road, too. He wants to see some real American monsters before he dies."

Milo rubbed a hand over his face. "He's going to get his chance."

"What do you mean?"

Milo folded his arms on the car roof and leaned on it. "People travelling the blackroads tend to meet, Amber. I told you that. Whether they're drawn to each other by some unconscious radar or it's all down to recurring coincidence or part of some grand scheme straight from hell, the fact is travellers tend to meet. That's why I'm confident of finding Dacre Shanks. But think who *else* is going to be on the blackroads. If your parents come here, and they will, and your new friend is still in the neighbourhood, the chances are they'll find him. And if he knows where we're going..."

"So... what do we do?"

Milo sagged. "We have two options."

Her eyes widened. "The first is killing him, isn't it? We're not doing that. We're not killing someone just because I made a mistake and said something I wasn't supposed to. What's the second option?"

"Convince him to come with us," Milo said. "Go get him. We'll take him as far as Springton and let him out there. If we have to tie him up and throw him in the back seat, we'll do that, too."

"I don't think convincing him will be a problem," said Amber. She turned, and started walking for the woods again.

"You have five minutes," said Milo. Amber didn't respond.

She retraced her steps until she found him. He was sitting on the same log she'd been sitting on, his elbows on his knees and his head down.

"Glen?"

He looked up quickly, but his hopeful smile vanished. "How do you know my name?"

She walked forward a few steps, and took off her cap. He regarded her suspiciously. Moments passed. His frown deepened, and then his eyebrows rose.

"You?"

"My name's Amber."

He jumped up. "But... but where's... what happened to you?"

"I told you, the skin and the horns are new. This is what I look like without them."

He couldn't take his eyes off her, but for entirely different reasons than before. "But what happened?" he asked. The look on his face was pure dismay.

Amber flushed with embarrassment and hurt. "I changed back," she said, putting the cap on again. "It doesn't matter. If you want to come with us, you can."

If she had asked him that while she was tall and red and beautiful, she knew he would have leaped for joy at the offer. As it was...

"Where are you going?" he asked doubtfully.

"Springton, Wisconsin," she said. "I told you."

He shrugged. "I'm terrible at place names. I forgot it the moment you said it. Couldn't have remembered it at gunpoint."

Amber stared at him. "Seriously?"

"I won't forget it again, though. Springton, Wisconsin. Springton, Wisconsin. Okay, it's embedded. Why are you going there?"

Anger coiled. "Because we are, okay? We're on the Demon Road, you're on the Demon Road, the Demon Road is taking us to Wisconsin, and we thought we'd be nice and offer you a lift that far. But hey, if you're inundated with other offers..."

She turned, started walking away, and after a moment she heard his running footsteps behind her, hurrying to catch up.

16

"THIS IS REALLY COOL OF YOU," said Glen from the back seat for the fourth time.

Milo nodded, and Amber felt him glance sideways at her. She didn't respond. She kept her eyes on the road as they drove past endless fields of white cotton pods, bursting like tiny puffs of cloud from all that green.

"So Amber tells me you're her guide," Glen continued. "You've travelled the Demon Road before, then?"

"We try not to talk about it," said Milo.

"Talk about what?"

Milo sighed. "When you're on the Demon Road, you don't really talk about the Demon Road. It's considered... crass. You can mention it, explain it, all that's fine... but just don't talk about it. And don't call it that, either."

"What, Demon Road?"

"Yeah. Try to be, you know... a little cooler about it."

"Oh," said Glen. "Yeah, sure. Blasé, like? Yeah, no problem. Kind of a nudge nudge, wink wink kind of thing, right? If you have to ask, you'll never know. First rule of Fight Club, that sort of vibe? Yeah, that's cool. I can do that."

"Good."

"So how long have you been on it?"

Amber turned in her seat. "He just said we don't talk about it."

"But how am I supposed to ask questions if I'm not allowed to talk about it?"

"Don't ask questions, then."

"But how am I supposed to learn?"

Amber went back to glaring out of the window.

Milo sighed again. "I haven't travelled these roads in years."

"Why not?"

"I didn't need to."

"Do you know them well?" Glen asked.

"I did. Once upon a time."

"So what are you?"

"What do you mean?"

"Well, Amber can transform into this beautiful demon girl, I'm dying of some monster's creepy Deathmark... how come you're here? What did you do or what was done to you?"

Milo didn't answer.

Glen leaned forward. "Could you not hear me?"

"He's ignoring you," said Amber.

"Why? What'd I say?"

"You're asking a whole lot of questions," said Milo. "I like to drive in silence."

"So do I," said Amber.

"You do?" said Glen. "I hate driving in silence. I always have to have the radio on, even if it's country music or something horrible like that. God, I hate country music. And I don't mean the country music you have here in America, I mean the stuff we have in Ireland. Country singers here sound like they've been in a few bar-room brawls, you know? Back home they're just blokes who walk around in woolly jumpers."

"Woolly what?"

"Sweaters," Milo said.

"Oh," said Amber.

"My dad was a country-music fan," said Glen. "At his funeral, they played all his favourite songs. It was awful. I wanted to walk out, y'know? Only I didn't because, well, I've never been one to walk out of places. Well, no, I mean, I walk out of places all the time, obviously, or else I'd never leave anywhere, but I've never walked out of somewhere on principle. I can't even walk out of a bad movie. My dad used to say I was just too polite for my own good. Suppose he was right." He quietened down for a moment, his cheerfulness dimming, then looked up again, smile renewed. "So, Milo, how'd you get to be a guide? What qualifies you? Do you have, like, a dark and tormented history or something? Are you a demon, too? What's your angle?"

"You writing a book?" Milo asked.

"Uh no. Just making conversation."

They lapsed into a short-lived silence.

"You know what this car reminds me of?" Glen asked. "You ever hear of the Ghost of the Highway?"

Milo was done talking, so Amber took up the reins. "No," she said. "Never have."

"It was this guy who drove around, years ago, with his headlights off," Glen said. "He'd drive up and down all these dark American roads at night, looking for his next victim."

"That's an urban legend," Amber said. "When someone passes

the other way and flicks their lights at him, he runs them off the road. We've all heard it."

"No, but this is real," said Glen. "Or, well, okay, maybe sort of real, but he *did* kill a few people back in the nineties. I looked it up. There are a load of websites about him."

"There are websites about everything."

"Yeah, I suppose. But it was a seventies muscle car he drove, I remember that much. Black, too. I think it was a Charger. Or a Challenger. So cool. Is this a Charger?"

Amber's gaze drifted to the window again. "Yeah," she said, hoping he'd shut the hell up now.

"There were a few survivors because he didn't, like, get out of the car to finish them off, or anything. All he was interested in was bashing them off the road. Though he did run a few down, but, if you ask me, anyone who thinks they're gonna sprint faster than a car kind of deserves to be run down, am I right? Ever since I heard about the Ghost of the Highway, I've wanted a car like that. And now I'm in one!"

"A dream come true," Amber muttered.

"Just to drive in something that cool... We don't have anything this awesome in Ireland. There are a few petrolheads who'll import the odd Mustang or whatever, but you wouldn't be able to drive around without people going, *Who does your man think he is?* – you know? But here you can drive a car like this and people won't automatically think you're a tool. People are more accepting here, y'know? But those police reports, in the victims' own words, describing what it was like to be chased down by this terrifying black beast of a car... One moment they're driving along fine, the road pitch-black behind them, the next these red headlights suddenly open up in their rear-view mirror..."

Amber stopped gazing out of the window, and looked at Milo out of the corner of her eye. His expression remained calm, but his hands gripped the wheel with such force that his knuckles had turned white. She suddenly had a knot in her belly.

"It was things like that, y'know?" Glen continued, oblivious. "Things like that that made me fall in love with America. A country so big you can do something as crazy as that as a *hobby* and never get caught... wow. I'm not saying I *want* to do something like that, but I appreciate the fact that I *could*. Land of the free, right? Home of the brave."

Glen settled back, lost in his own overwhelming sense of wonder, and Milo didn't speak again for another two hours.

By the time they stopped off at a Budget Inn in Jasper, Georgia, Milo looked a lot paler than he should have. His face was gaunt, his eyes distant. He got out of the Charger slowly, almost like it didn't want him to leave, and only when they had left it behind them in the parking lot did he regain a little of his spirit. He told Glen to shut up three times as they checked in.

For his own reasons, Glen attempted an American accent that sounded like a cross between John Wayne and John Wayne's idiot brother. Amber thought that the woman behind the desk would ask her for proof of age, but the woman seemingly couldn't have cared less. Amber went to her room with a small bag containing necessities, a vending-machine sandwich, and a lukewarm can of Coke. The water in her shower took forever to heat up, but eventually she stood under the spray and closed her eyes. She worked a full mini-bottle of shampoo and conditioner into her hair, which had dried out in knots and tangles following her dip in the river, and when she was done she stood in front of the bathroom mirror naked.

Unimpressed with what she saw, she resisted the urge to shift. She didn't see the point of feeling even worse about herself.

She turned on the TV. Every second channel had a preacher in an expensive suit talking about God and the Devil. She watched for a bit, hoping in vain to hear some words of comfort, but all she got was fear and greed. She flicked over to a horror movie, but that failed to distract her, so she turned the TV off, and all the lights, and climbed into bed. The mattress was uncomfortable and unfamiliar. The pillows were simultaneously too thin and too soft. She lay in the darkness. Voices came through the walls. TV sets played. Toilets flushed.

She thought about Milo and Glen and Imelda, and the trucker and Brandon. She thought about the Ghost of the Highway, and she thought of her parents, and how they were probably coming after her even as she lay there.

She got up, dragged a chair in front of the door, and jammed it up against the handle like she'd seen people do in movies.

She went back to bed. Sleep was a long time coming.

17

THEY SET OFF EARLY the next morning. Milo looked healthy and strong again, and he must have been up for a while because the Charger was gleaming when they got in. Glen told them all about his night. It wasn't very interesting.

When he realised nobody was answering him, Glen dozed for an hour in the back seat before checking on their location on his phone. "Ooh!" he said. "We're going to be passing Nashville! Can we stop?"

"No," Amber and Milo both said.

Glen looked hurt. "But... but this might be my last chance to see it. I'm dying, remember?"

"You haven't mentioned it," Milo said, making it the second joke he'd told since Amber had met him.

"Can't we even just drive through?" Glen asked. "You don't even have to go slow. Come on, please? Elvis started out in Nashville – it's where he recorded his first record. *Elvis!*"

"He did that in Memphis," Milo said.

Glen frowned. "Isn't Nashville in Memphis?"

"Nashville and Memphis are both in Tennessee. Which is where we are."

"Oh. Are we going to be passing through Memphis?"

"No."

"But I'm dying. Why are you in such a rush, anyway? Isn't it time you told me what's really going on? We're friends. We're on this trip together. That bonds people, y'know. We're bonded now. We're inseparable. We should have no secrets from each other. I've got no secrets from you. I told you all about the monster who attacked me and gave me the Deathmark and my quest to find The Dark Stair. What's your quest?"

"Don't call it a quest."

"But what is it?"

Amber turned to him. "We're dropping you off in Wisconsin. That's as far as you're going with us. Believe me, it's safer for you not to know anything beyond that."

He blinked at her. "But... but we're inseparable."

Amber turned back. "Not nearly as inseparable as you think."

Glen went quiet. A few minutes later, he was tapping away at his phone again.

He chuckled. "They have a Toledo in Ohio," he said. "Hey, do you think that's where the phrase Holy Toledo comes from? Do you? Hello?"

"There's also a Toledo in Spain," said Milo with dull exasperation. "It's a holy city."

"So that's where it came from?"

"I don't know, Glen."

"Makes you wonder, though, doesn't it?"

"I guess."

Glen nodded, went back to tapping.

*

They found a Walmart in Knoxville and pulled in.

"What're we doing here?" Glen asked.

"Need to buy some clothes," said Amber.

"Need help?"

She frowned at him. "No."

She ignored his look of disappointment, and got out. She pulled her cap down lower and turned her face from the security cameras on her approach. Once inside, she scanned the signs for the clothing section, and picked up a few toiletries on the way over. She added some fresh underwear to her basket and followed that with a pair of jeans a little longer than she usually wore. She grabbed a belt, a new top, a few cheap bracelets, and went looking for a light jacket. When she had everything she wanted, she took them to the dressing rooms.

Once inside the cubicle, she tried on the clothes, looped the belt through the jeans, and turned to the mirror. The jeans were comfortable around her waist but gathered at the ankles. She looked like a girl wearing her big sister's pants. Then she shifted, and her glorious red-skinned reflection grinned back at her. She tightened the belt, noting how the jeans were now the perfect length, how her T-shirt was now flatter around the belly and fuller around the bust. She added the jacket, turned and admired herself, imagining for a moment strolling back through Walmart like this, and wondering if the cries of alarm would dent her confidence. She doubted it.

But discretion, as ever, was called for, and she unbuckled her belt and reverted, and the jeans gathered at her ankles and her belly swelled to its usual proportions. Sighing, she changed back into her own clothes, put everything else into the basket, and left the cubicle, the cap once again pulled low.

She waited in line behind a woman who smelled really bad, and when she was gone the Hispanic boy at the till gave her a smile.

"Hi there," he said.

"Hi," she responded.

He started passing her items over the scanner – one at a time, slowly. "I like your eyes," he said.

Amber blinked at him. "What?"

"Your eyes," he repeated. "I like them."

She blinked. "These?"

He laughed. "You have any others I should know about?"

"No," she said, and blushed. He wasn't the best-looking boy in the world, but he wasn't bad, and he had a confidence that she could only manage when she was demonified. It was attractive. Hugely so. His name tag identified him as Eugenio.

"This is the part where you tell me you like my eyes, too," he said, in a mock whisper.

"Oh, sorry," said Amber. "I like your eyes, too." She did. She really did. They were brown like chocolate.

"How nice of you to say so," he said, giving her another smile. "So does a nice girl like you have a boyfriend? I only ask because if you say yes I will spiral into a bottomless pit of despair and loneliness, and you wouldn't want that, would you?"

"No, I wouldn't," she said. "And I don't have a, you know… a boyfriend."

"That seems highly unlikely. Are you sure?"

Before she knew what she was doing, she giggled. Dear Lord, she giggled.

"I'm sure," she said.

"Well then, how about we meet up later, if you're free? Do you live around here?"

"Ah, sorry, I don't. I'm just passing through."

"Oh no," Eugenio said, losing his smile and widening his eyes. If anything, that made him even cuter. "So I'll never see you again? Is that what you're saying?"

"Probably."

The last item to scan was a pair of socks. He held them to his chest. "So the moment I put these through and you pay, you're going to just walk out of here, walk out of my life, and never look back? But what if I don't scan these socks? Will you stay?"

"I'm afraid not," said Amber, packing the other stuff into flimsy plastic bags. "I'll just have to do without the socks."

He gasped. "But how can you do without socks? They are an integral part of any civilised society. A sockless person is no kind of person, that's what my father always says."

"He always says that?"

"He's not a very good conversationalist."

Amber laughed.

"Hey, Juan," said an unshaven guy standing behind Amber, "would you stop flirting with ugly chicks and do your damn job?"

Amber went cold with mortification even as her face flushed bright red. Eugenio lost his good humour in an instant.

"My name is not Juan," he said, "and be careful what you say about ladies, sir. You don't want to be rude."

The unshaven man had incredibly soft-looking curly hair, entirely at odds with the hardness of his face. "You wanna know what's rude, Pedro? Making paying customers stand in line while you try to get into this girl's pants."

Eugenio's jaw clenched. He dragged his eyes away from the man only when Amber held out her money. "I apologise," he said to her.

"It's okay," she said quietly.

He handed over her change. The rude man was now ignoring her as he dumped the last of his stuff on to the conveyor belt. Amber gathered up her things and walked away, eyes that were filling with tears firmly fixed on the floor.

By the time she reached the Charger, she was back in control again. She slipped the bracelets on over the numbers on her wrist, concealing them, then put the bags in the trunk and got in.

"I'm hungry," she announced, keeping her words curt, afraid that anything else might result in the others hearing her voice tremble. The topic of food set Glen off on some random tangent. Amber didn't listen. She replayed the scene in her head, only this time as she stood in the checkout lane she shifted, horns bursting from her forehead, fingernails turning to talons, and in her mind she watched herself tear the rude man's face off.

They passed into Kentucky, and by the time they stopped at a roadside diner with a startling view of the Daniel Boone National Forest, her embarrassment had been replaced with anger. And anger faded faster than embarrassment. She got out of the Charger and closed her eyes to the breeze. It was still hot, but the air was better out here. It moved through the great slabs of lush forest on either side of the road, brought with it all manner of freshness.

"Big trees," said Glen, and she had to agree with him. They were indeed big trees.

Inside the diner, the freshness was replaced by the smell of hamburger fat. There was a broken jukebox in the corner that played 'Here I Go Again' by Whitesnake on a loop. They sat at a plastic-covered table, and Amber ran her finger along the top, expecting to leave a trail in grease. The fact that it was perfectly clean disappointed her slightly.

They ate their burgers without speaking a whole lot. She could tell this was driving Glen insane, and it provided her with a glimmer of quiet amusement. He took some pamphlets from the stack beside the register and perused them while they ate.

"Did you know that the forest has one of the world's largest concentration of caves?" he asked.

"Yes," Amber answered, even though she knew no such thing, and cared even less.

Glen put that pamphlet aside, picked up another. "Hey, this is where Kentucky Fried Chicken was invented! Corbin, that is, not this diner. We should get some KFC! You want some?"

Amber loved KFC. "I hate KFC," she said.

Glen looked glum. Amber beamed inside.

Amber and Milo shared the bill, and Glen looked embarrassed. She actually had some sympathy for him, the way he sat there, all pathetic and grateful. She was about to say something nice to him when he shrugged, looked up and said brightly, "Well, I'm off for a wee!"

He practically skipped to the restroom.

"Curious boy," Milo muttered.

He led the way out of the diner, humming the Whitesnake song which was now firmly lodged in Amber's head, too. She was not looking forward to another half a day on the road. She wouldn't have minded staying here for a while, looking at the forest, enjoying the air. Apart from anything else, she liked the fact that Kentucky had mountains. Florida suddenly seemed way too flat for her liking.

A car pulled up, parking on the other side of a battered truck, and Amber glimpsed the occupants.

Terror stabbed her heart and she dived behind the Charger.

Milo stiffened. All at once his gun was out of its holster and held down by his leg.

Amber heard the car doors open and close. The *beep* as it locked. Footsteps on loose gravel.

And then her mother's voice. "Excuse me, we're looking for our daughter. Have you seen this girl?"

The driver of the truck. She could picture him in her head. Hispanic. Short. Wearing jeans and a T-shirt. He'd been eating at the counter when they'd ordered. Had he looked up? Had he noticed her?

"Sorry," she heard him say. "Can't help you."

The truck started, reversed all the way round the back of the Charger, and the driver happened to glance her way. She shook her head, mouthing the words *please, no*.

He hesitated, then pulled out on to the road and drove off.

"Hi," she heard her dad say, from the other side of the car.

"Hi there," Milo answered. He holstered his gun.

"We're looking for this girl," Bill said. "Would you have seen her, by any chance?"

His voice moved round the car. Milo opened the door, shielding Amber from view, keeping his feet planted to hide her own. He took off his jacket and threw it in.

She heard Bill and Betty stop walking suddenly. For a moment, she thought she'd been spotted.

"That's a nice weapon," said Bill. "What is it, a Glock?"

"Glock 21," said Milo. "You cops? I've got a concealed carry permit."

Betty had a smile in her voice. "No, we're not police. We're just looking for our daughter. Have you seen her?"

There was a moment while they showed Milo a photograph.

"Sorry," Milo said. "Don't think I've—"

The door to the diner opened and Glen came out. His eyes flickered over Amber and rested on her parents.

"Hi," he said, puncturing the silence. "Did we do something wrong?"

Betty laughed politely, with just the right amount of sadness. "No, we're not police officers. We're just looking for this girl. Have you seen her?"

Glen walked out of Amber's view. She shrank back against the Charger. If she had to trust in Glen's acting prowess, she wouldn't be hiding for very much longer. She got ready to shift. If she shifted before they did, maybe she could outrun them in the forest.

"Yeah," said Glen, "I've seen her."

Amber screwed her eyes shut. *No, you idiot.*

"You have?" said Betty, excited.

"You have?" said Milo. "Are you sure?"

"Sure I'm sure," Glen said. "They were at the table behind us when we got here. You'll have to excuse Milo – he doesn't notice a whole lot when Whitesnake is playing. I'm the brains of the operation. Name's Glen. How do you do."

"Hello, Glen," said Betty. "I'm Betty, and this is Bill. You've seen our daughter? You're sure it was her?"

"I think so," said Glen. "I didn't get a good look at her face, but I'm pretty sure. She was with a woman, a small woman with grey hair. They had a map out."

"When was this?"

"Milo?" said Glen. "When did we get here?"

"About an hour ago," said Milo, clearly resenting his role in this.

"Did they say where they were going?" Bill asked.

Glen hesitated. "Uh, listen, I'm sure you're good people, but if your daughter's run away, she probably has her reasons. No offence, but for all I know you might lock her in the cellar or something."

"We love our daughter," Betty said. "All we want is for her to be safe. That woman she's with, she's part of a cult. We have to get her back before we lose her for good."

"A cult?" Glen echoed. "Oh wow. Yeah, absolutely. My cousin went off and joined a cult years ago, so I know what that's like. It was a UFO cult. I hope your daughter's not in a UFO cult − they're the worst. I heard the woman say they were going to Toledo. I'm usually terrible with place names, but I remember that because, y'know, the phrase 'Holy Toledo'. Hey, you think that's where the phrase comes from?"

"Either that or the holy city of Toledo in Spain," said Bill. "Did you happen to see what they were driving?"

"A white van," said Glen, "in dire need of a wash. I didn't notice any UFO bumper stickers or anything, so you might be in luck. Like I said, they left about an hour ago."

"Thank you, Glen," Betty said, and Amber listened to their retreating footsteps.

"Hope you find her," Glen called.

Their car beeped and they got in, and Amber crawled on

her hands and knees to the front of the Charger as her parents'
car pulled out on to the road and accelerated fast.

She stood.

"So," Glen said, "your parents, huh?"

18

THEY SPENT THE NIGHT at a Motel 6 somewhere in Indiana. Amber barricaded her door again, and she tossed and turned, but didn't fall asleep until a half-hour before Milo knocked. She didn't eat any breakfast and she kept her head down and her cap on while walking out to the Charger. It gleamed, the dust and dirt of the previous day's travel washed away like it had never happened.

If only that was true.

As they were bypassing Chicago, Amber relented and told Glen about Shanks. He'd earned the right to sit at the table with the cool kids, she reckoned. They drove through an endless suburban sprawl of strip malls and chain restaurants, the parking lots and signs repeating as if copied and pasted, and got into Springton, Wisconsin a little before three that afternoon. The day had dulled, become cold, and sporadic showers of rain splattered the windshield. They passed the high school, a building of red brick set a dozen steps above street level, and carried on to the town square. The library sat on one side, and opposite it, on the south side, sat the Mayor's Office – white, with pillars outside denoting its obvious importance. The buildings to the east and west housed various businesses and eateries.

They got out. Stretched. It was maybe ten degrees cooler than when they'd started their journey, and Amber was wearing jeans now. They felt weird on her legs. She pulled on a jacket and made sure her cap was secure.

"What do we do now?" she asked.

"We ask about Dacre Shanks," said Glen before Milo could answer. "We split up. We'll cover more ground that way. The sooner we get to him, the better, am I right? We've got your parents on our tail, Amber. I may have been able to throw them off the scent yesterday, but that won't stop them for long. Here, that guy looks like he might know something."

Glen strode towards an old man walking his dog.

Amber looked at Milo. "He's trying really hard."

Milo nodded. "You notice how quiet he was this morning? He didn't make one single stupid comment."

"And he *was* very useful yesterday."

Milo hesitated, then shook his head. "Doesn't make one bit of difference. This is where we cut him loose, *before* we talk to Shanks. The less he knows..." He trailed off.

Amber frowned. "What?"

"Nothing."

"What, Milo?"

Milo sighed. "Your parents know him now. If we leave him here and they find him, they might..."

"Do you think they'd kill him?"

"They killed those cops without a second thought, didn't they?"

They both looked at Glen, who was now arguing with the old man while the dog yapped and nipped at his legs.

"So," Milo said, "should we leave him, or...?"

They looked at each other and burst out laughing.

Glen jogged back. "What? What are you laughing about?"

"Nothing," said Amber, trying to contain herself. "Did you learn anything?"

"No," said Glen. "Turns out that old guy is German and doesn't speak a word of English."

"Then what were you arguing about?"

Glen looked puzzled. "How should I know?"

This set Amber and Milo off again. Glen tried to laugh along with them, then gave up and went for a walk.

A full third of the library was given over to computers, the bookcases crammed together in the space left. Amber walked the labyrinth until she found a section marked Local History. It was a single shelf with five books on it – four of them the same book. She flicked through the fifth – *Springton: A Legacy*, by a local author with a bad photo. She learned that Springton was established in 1829, and got its name from its wondrous spring-water reserve. She learned that the industry that built up around it polluted that reserve so much that the water became virtually undrinkable. The author called that 'ironic'.

Amber flicked through the rest of it, then checked the index. No mention of Dacre Shanks.

She replaced the book and wandered out of the stacks. Glen found her.

"They have a *Springton Gazette*," he said. "I asked the librarian if I could see the old editions, y'know, to read the articles on Shanks as they were printed? She said they're only available on microfiche."

"What's microfiche?"

"I don't know. Some kind of small fish, presumably."

Amber frowned. "Where's Milo?"

"Chatting up the other librarian. The cute one."

Amber looked around. Milo stood in that slouchy way of his, giving a smile she hadn't imagined he possessed to an attractive woman in her forties. She had brown hair with a streak of silver running through it. The librarian laughed and Milo's smile widened.

"I could do that," said Glen. "I just picked the wrong librarian to charm, that's all. I picked the old one. I thought she'd be the one to ask. If I'd known there was a younger one, I'd have called dibs."

"She's twice your age."

"Older women find me intensely attractive."

"Well, that's good, because younger women certainly don't."

Glen stopped glaring across at Milo, and switched his attention to Amber. "Oh, is that so? So you're telling me that you feel no attraction to me whatsoever?"

She blinked at him. "What? Where has this come from? No. None. None at all."

"Yeah," he said, laughing. "Right."

"Seriously."

"There have been studies carried out that say the Irish accent is the sexiest in the world."

"Who carried it out? Irish people?"

His smile faltered for a moment. "Maybe," he said, and then it was back. "I could charm you. You know I could charm you. The only thing stopping me is your age. You're too young for me. I prefer girls in their twenties."

"I will have to live with that crushing disappointment."

"Of course," he said, moving closer, "I could make an exception."

"Please don't."

"I could overlook the age thing if... you know."

Amber frowned. "What?"

"If you transformed," he whispered.

She lost all good humour. "Drop dead, Glen."

She made for the exit. He followed.

"Oh, go on! Just transform once for me. You're amazing when you transform. You're astonishing. Those horns are just the most beautiful—"

She spun round to face him. "Stop calling it that. Stop calling it transforming. You make me sound like an Autobot."

"Well, what's it called?"

"I don't know. Shifting. There isn't really an official term for it."

A slow grin spread across his face. "I've got one. Do you want to hear it?"

She walked away. "No."

"It's a good one," he said from right behind her.

"I don't care."

"You'll love it," he said. "I promise you, you'll love it."

They reached the exit. Milo was walking towards them. Amber couldn't help herself.

"Fine," she said. "What? What would you call it when I change?"

Glen's grin was immense. "Getting horny."

"Oh, I hate you so much."

Milo joined them. "She's hiding something," he said. "The moment she guessed where I was steering the conversation she closed down. You find anything?"

"Just a new level of annoyance," said Amber.

"She wants to join me in my utter hilarity," said Glen. "You can see it in her face, can't you? She wants to joke around. Give in to it, Amber. Give in."

She sighed. "Are you finished yet?"

Glen grinned, and turned to Milo. "What's microfiche?"

"Microfilm."

"Ohhh. So it's not a small fish."

"Come on," said Amber, "let's get something to eat. I'm starving."

They had lunch sitting in the window of one of the cafes on the square. They watched the high-school kids pass on their way home. A bunch of younger kids came into the cafe, and Amber looked at Milo with her eyebrows raised. He shrugged, and nodded, and she turned on her stool.

"Hi," she said, keeping her voice down. "I was wondering if you could help me? Have any of you heard of a man called Dacre Shanks?"

The name made the kids draw back in suspicion.

"Ask someone else," one of them said.

"So you've heard of him?"

"We're not talking about that."

"Why not?"

"Cos they're scared," said the smallest kid, black, with adorably huge eyes. "They're afraid their allowance might be taken away."

"Whatever," the other one said, and got up and walked out, followed by his friends. All except the little kid.

"You've heard of Shanks?" said Amber.

"Course," the kid said.

"And the others – they won't talk because they're scared of him?"

The kid laughed. "Scared of who? The boogie man? Naw, they're scared cos last year a bunch of us trashed two of those dollhouses they got up in the school, and when people found out they beat the hell out of us. I'm talking grown-ups here, y'know? Punching and kicking me while I'm all curled up on the floor, crying for my momma. Disgraceful behaviour, know what I'm saying?"

"I'm sorry, dollhouses?"

"I know, right? *Dollhouses*. This town's obsessed with them."

"What's your name? I'm Amber."

"Name's Walter," said the kid. "Walter S. Bryant. The S stands for Samuel. Had a teacher once, said my destiny was to become a poet with a name like that. But he didn't know what the hell he was talking about. I can barely spell, and most of the words I know don't even rhyme with each other."

"Walter, what's so important about a few dollhouses?"

"Where you from?"

"Florida."

"Florida," he repeated. "Wait, you mean with Disney World and all?"

"Yep, we have Disney World."

"You ever been?"

"A few times," she said. Always with friends, though – never with her parents.

"Aw man," said Walter. "Disney World. I'd like that, walking around and everything looking like it's out of a cartoon or something. Ever meet Mickey Mouse?"

"I have."

Walter laughed. "That's cool. You met Mickey Mouse. That's cool."

"I'm from Ireland," said Glen.

"I don't care," said Walter.

"Can you tell me about the dollhouses?" Amber asked.

"Oh yeah," said Walter. "I knew you weren't from around here, cos if you were you'd know already. There's this dumb story everyone's been telling us our entire lives, and they all expect us to believe it, y'know? Dacre Shanks. He *was* a real person, back in the 1970s, cos I looked him up. He was a toymaker, right? He had a little store down beside where the arcade once was, but he only made crappy toys like dolls and model railways and stuff. Nothing cool. But what nobody knew was that he was also this serial killer, and he killed a ton of people before the cops figured out who he was and came and shot him."

"I looked him up, too," said Amber. "I didn't see any mention of dollhouses."

"Course not," said Walter, "cos that's the part they made up, isn't it? The story is, he came back from the dead, right, ten years later, and kept killing and he, like, shrank his victims or something and put them in these dollhouses he made."

Amber frowned. "He shrank them?"

"How stupid is that, right? Not only do they have him come back from the dead, but they have him shrinking people, too. Anyway, the school had three dollhouses that supposedly held these shrunken victims – although officially they're just normal dollhouses with nothing weird about them at all. Cos every school has a few dollhouses in a huge glass cabinet right inside the door, don't they? I mean, *that* part's totally normal.

Nothing weird about that. Ask any of the teachers; they all say the story's a load of crap, but they say it in a way that's supposed to make you think they're lying. We had to pass those dollhouses every single day. I'm not stupid. I know why they were there. It was a message, wasn't it? *Stay in school. Keep your head down. Don't question authority. Or Dacre Shanks will get you.*

"Well, practically everyone else in my school were cool about going along with it, but me and a couple of others, and you just met them a few minutes ago, got talking one day and figured hey, we were getting a little tired of being treated like fools."

"So you trashed the dollhouses."

Walter nodded. "Stomped two of them to splinters before we were caught."

"What happened then?"

"Aw, everyone went insane. I knew the school would be mad and all, but they were threatening to expel us. It was crazy. Only reason they didn't is cos they didn't want the State Board to know about their dumb stories. But everyone, like, the whole entire town, was against us. Everyone except the old people. They didn't see what the fuss was about. But our folks, some of our older brothers and sisters, they just... I didn't know they'd take it so seriously."

"Is that when you were beaten up?"

"Yeah," Walter said, with an impressive amount of bitterness. "Broad daylight. Had to stay indoors the whole summer after that. People in this town are nuts, and they all worship that Medina chick."

"Who?"

"Heather Medina. She's the one who stopped Dacre Shanks from killing any more kids. According to the story."

"Does she still live around here?"

"Yeah, lives over on Pine Street. Works in the library."

"Brown hair?" asked Milo. "Silver in it?"

Walter nodded. "That's her. She won't even mention his name, though, so good luck trying to get anything out of her. She looks perfectly normal, but she's as crazy as the rest of them. That's why her husband left her, I heard. They expected us to believe a story like that, and then they were actually angry when we didn't. Moment I'm old enough to drive I am out of here. I may not be able to spell or rhyme, but I'm pretty smart. Smarter than everyone in this town, anyway."

"Definitely looks like it," said Amber. "Thank you so much for your help."

"Don't worry about it," the kid replied. "I'm assuming you'll take care of this?"

He held up his bag of doughnuts so the teller could see it, and Amber smiled. "Sure thing, Walter. See you around."

"Stay frosty," Walter said, and walked out.

Amber paid for the doughnuts, and rejoined Milo and Glen as they were putting on their jackets.

"You think you'll be able to get back in the librarian's good books?" Amber asked.

"Don't know," admitted Milo. "Women have a tendency to learn fast around me."

"Told you I should have talked to her first," Glen said.

They left the cafe and walked back to the Charger, where a stocky man in his late sixties stood admiring her. He gave them a quick smile as they approached, and when Amber saw the star on his shirt her own smile faded.

"Now this is a damn fine automobile," the man said. His

moustache was a deeper shade of grey than his hair. "A friend of mine had one, back in my youth. Light gold, it was. A thing of beauty. He crashed it not far from here, going too fast, and he just lost control. That's all there was to it. Nobody else was hurt, thank God, but my friend, he was killed instantly. I don't know, ever since then, I see one of these cars and I just think… death." He gave a little smile and a little shrug.

"Well, that is a story with a sad ending," said Milo.

"Isn't it just?" The man smiled at them, for real this time, though there wasn't much friendliness in it. "How are you folks? My name is Theodore Roosevelt, no relation to the big man, I'm afraid. You can call me Teddy. As you can probably tell by the badge, I'm the sheriff 'round these parts. If no one has bothered to do it, I bid you welcome to Springton. Now what brings you nice people to our little town, I wonder?"

"Just passing through."

"Ah, that old staple. Just passing through. It's hard to make new friends when everyone's just passing through, that ever strike you as a truism? I'm collecting them – truisms, that is. Collecting them, coming up with them, going to put them all into a book when I'm done, try and get it published some day. Kind of going for a homespun sort of feel, you know? Going to call it *Words of Wisdom*, something hokey like that. Hokiness sells."

"That another truism?"

Teddy smiled. "I guess it is. Might not include it in the collection, though. So is this a family trip?"

"That's what it is," said Milo.

"You and the kids, on a family trip. Your wife not come with you?"

160

"I'm afraid she's not with us anymore."

"Oh, I am sorry to hear that, Mr Sebastian. I am truly sorry." The air went quiet around them.

"You checked the plates, huh?" said Milo.

"One of the perks of being the sheriff," Teddy answered. "Funny, your details mention nothing about you having a family."

Milo nodded. "The kids were born out of wedlock. They're very self-conscious about it."

"Very," said Glen.

"Your kids don't look a whole lot like you," Teddy said. "Also, from what I hear from a certain elderly librarian, your son is Irish." He hooked his thumbs into his belt loops. "We get people like you passing through all the time. Oh, and by 'people like you', I don't mean the Irish. I mean gawkers. What I like to call bloodhounds. They hear about our town, hear we used to have a serial killer, and they come sniffing around, thinking how exciting it all is, how fun. But the wounds that man made still haven't closed over, and you walking around asking clumsy questions is just going to get people's backs up."

"It's my fault," said Glen, his shoulders drooping. "I'm not his son, I'm his nephew. Yes, I'm from Ireland. But I'm dying. I don't have long left."

"That so?"

"It is. I came over here to see America before I... before I pass on. And yeah, you're right, I asked to come to Springton because of the serial killer. I've always been fascinated with that stuff. A kind of morbid curiosity, I suppose. But I never intended to upset anyone, Sheriff. I'm really sorry."

"What's your name, son?"

"Glen, sir."

"Well, Glen, I'm sorry to hear of your ill-health. What have you got, if you don't mind me asking?"

"Lupus," said Glen.

Teddy frowned. "Is that fatal?"

"Oh yes," said Glen. "Very."

"You sure? I don't think it is."

"It's not always fatal," Glen said quickly. "If you get treatment for it, no, it's not fatal. Rarely fatal. But I have a rare form of lupus that is very fatal."

"Glen, forgive me for asking this, but do you know what lupus is? A friend of mine has lupus, a reverend. His joints get all swollen up, he gets rashes, he's tired all the time, and his hair even fell out."

Glen nodded. "I have the other kind of lupus."

"The kind that has none of those symptoms?"

Glen bit his lip for a moment. "I get the feeling you're not believing me."

Teddy sighed. "You're not too bright, son, and that's okay. There's no law against being stupid. There's also no law against being a bloodhound, but I'm going to have to ask you to stop pestering people with questions – especially my daughter."

"Your daughter?"

Teddy nodded. "She works in the library. She's the librarian who is not elderly."

"Ah," said Milo. "Heather called you."

"She may have mentioned it during one of our regular father-daughter chats."

"So are you going to run us out of town?"

Teddy chuckled. "I don't think I have to do anything quite so dramatic, do you? Quite the opposite, in fact. It's getting late

162

in the day and, as you folks aren't from around here, I'd like to invite you to stay overnight in our little town."

"That's mighty Christian of you."

"And to save you some money, you'll be staying with us, my wife and I. Have a good home-cooked meal. That sound good?"

"We really couldn't impose," said Milo.

"It is not an imposition, I assure you," said Teddy. "I insist on you staying with us. That okay with you?"

Milo glanced at Amber, and nodded. "Sure," he said. "That'd be great."

"Excellent," Teddy said, beaming. "I'll tell her to make up the rooms. Our bed-and-breakfast rates are quite competitive, just so you know."

19

SHERIFF ROOSEVELT'S PLACE WAS a neat little house out on the edge of town. It had pebbles instead of grass in the front yard, and a path of cobblelock paving. Mrs Roosevelt – Ella-May – was a handsome woman who struck Amber as someone playing at running a B&B. She had a way about her, a way of asking questions and getting answers, that suggested a whipsmart mind, even in her advancing years. Running a B&B seemed a rather tame endeavour for someone like her.

The house looked like a picture-perfect amalgamation of various local tourism brochures. Everything was pretty, with a restrained, folksy charm. Milo and Glen had to share the twin beds in the double room, but Amber got a room all to herself. It had a small TV in the corner, the very opposite of a flatscreen.

Dinner was at eight. Amber had a bath to pass the time, and as she lay in all those bubbles she tried not to look at the countdown on her wrist.

438, it said now. Three days gone out of her twenty-one. Lots of time left. Plenty of time. Providing they find Dacre Shanks.

When eight rolled around, she was dressed and hungry. She went downstairs, following the aroma.

Teddy sat at one end of the table. Amber and Glen sat to his right, and Milo to his left. Glen kept his hand curled, hiding the Deathmark from sight in the same way that Amber's bracelets hid her scar. When Ella-May was finished serving the food, she sat opposite her husband.

Teddy interlocked his fingers and closed his eyes. "Lord, thank you for this meal we are about to enjoy. Thank you for our guests – after some initial frostiness, they have proven themselves to be nice enough people, and they've paid in advance, which I always take as a sign of good manners. Thank you for no dead bodies today and no real crime at all, to be fair. Thank you for my beautiful wife, my wonderful daughter, and for the continuing wellbeing of my town. Amen."

"Amen," Amber muttered, along with Glen. Milo and Ella-May remained silent.

"So, Milo," Teddy said as he reached for the potatoes, "what do you do for a living?"

"I get by."

"That it? That's all you do?"

Milo smiled like he was a normal, good-natured kind of guy. "I make ends meet, how about that?"

Teddy shrugged. "That's fair enough. A man who doesn't want to talk about his business shouldn't have to talk about his business. Where you from, originally?"

"Kentucky," Milo said.

"Aha," said Teddy. "The Bluegrass State."

"That's what they call it."

"You a farm boy, Milo?"

"Yes, sir."

"Pigs? Cattle?"

"Some." Milo's smile was easy and his tone was relaxed. He was like a different person. "Ella-May, this is one humdinger of a dinner."

Ella-May smiled. "Why, thank you, Milo. Humdinger, eh? Never heard my cooking called that before."

Milo actually chuckled. "How long you two been married?"

"I was nineteen," said Ella-May, "he was twenty-three. We were married in the summer. My father, who was sheriff, could not let his future son-in-law waste his natural gifts in an aluminum factory, so he made him a deputy and started him on the road to becoming the fine, upstanding law-enforcement official you see before you with gravy dripping down his chin."

"Goddamn it," Teddy said, dabbing at himself with his napkin.

"We were so in love."

Teddy winked at Amber. "She was besotted."

"Yeah," said Ella-May, "I was the one going all moon-eyed. I was the one blushing and stammering and falling over bushes…"

Teddy pointed his fork at her. "Hey. I fell over *one* bush."

"But it was a big one."

"Damn near broke my neck," Teddy muttered.

"I swear, my husband is brighter than he lets on."

"I'd have to be," said Teddy.

"Was your dad sheriff when Dacre Shanks was killing people?" Glen asked Ella-May.

Milo's smile vanished. "Damn it, Glen."

"What?"

"Boy, you have got to be the most tactless person I have met that I haven't punched yet," said Teddy.

Glen looked confused. "We were talking about cops and sheriffs and stuff. I'd have thought that'd be a natural segue into, y'know…"

"We don't talk about that man at the table," Ella-May said.

"Right. Um, sorry."

She nodded. Teddy shoved another forkful of food into his mouth and chewed. Milo looked pissed. Thirty seconds passed where no one said anything. Amber's wrist burned. She parted the bracelets and took another peek: 436 hours.

"We're looking for him," she said quietly.

"Looking for who?" Ella-May asked.

"Shanks," she said. "We need to find him."

Milo watched her, but didn't say anything. Glen shot her a glare and kicked her under the table. She kicked him back harder.

"Ow! God!"

"We lied to you," she said. Teddy put down his knife and fork and listened. "My life is in danger. I'm not going to tell you how or why or who is coming after me because, I'm sorry, but you're safer not knowing. And I'm safer with you not knowing. We lied. We're not family. We didn't even know each other until a few days ago."

"I'm not her cousin," Glen said, rubbing his shin.

"They don't care about that," said Milo.

"But I am dying," Glen added. "It's just I'm not dying of lupus. I'm not even sure what that is. I've got the Deathmark, see, and—"

"They don't care about any of that, either," said Milo.

"Dacre Shanks is dead," said Teddy. "Shot him myself. Me and three other deputies. One of the bullets caught him in the head. We never bothered figuring out who fired that one. But it took off the top of his skull."

"We know he's dead," Amber said carefully. "But we also know there's more to it than that."

"You've been listening to too many ghost stories," Ella-May said, getting up from the table.

"No," said Amber, "but I have seen too many monsters."

Amber went to bed and had a bad dream. Her demon-self was crouched over Ella-May's dead body, and she was scooping out and eating the woman's insides. Standing behind her were her parents, scooping out Amber's own guts from a gaping cavity in her back.

She woke up and cried for a bit. When she stopped, she heard a creaking – slow and regular. She got up, looked out of the window, saw an ember glowing in the dark. She put on jeans and a sweatshirt, went out on to the back porch.

"Did I wake you?" Teddy asked from his rocking chair.

She shook her head. "I haven't been sleeping too well, that's all. I've never known anyone who smoked a pipe before."

He smiled. "I didn't used to. Took this up in my forties when my hair started going grey. Thought it'd make me look wise and somewhat distinguished. Does it?"

"Somewhat."

He nodded, and puffed away.

"I'm sorry for the upset we've caused," said Amber.

"Ah, you seem like you're going through a lot, so I'm not going to hold it against you. Ella-May isn't, either, despite her silence earlier. That man has been a plague on our family, so we don't especially like talking about him at the dinner table."

"You knew him?" she asked.

Teddy nodded. "Everyone knew him. Nobody knew him well. Probably how he got away with it for so long."

"How did you find him? How did you figure out what he was doing?"

Teddy tapped the stem of his pipe against the chair, and put it back between his lips. "We didn't," he said. "Ella-May did. I'm a smart enough fella. I was a good deputy and I make a good sheriff. But Ella-May is my secret weapon. She paid attention to the little things, the little details. She added things together. She made enquiries. All under the radar. Not even her father suspecting for one moment that what she was doing was gathering evidence.

"Then her dad passed away. Nothing dramatic. He wasn't killed in the line of duty or anything like that. His heart just gave out one sunny afternoon while driving back to the station. He pulled over to the side of the road and had his heart attack and died. Responsible to the last. His replacement was not a particularly intelligent man. I brought Ella-May to him and she gave him all her evidence, told him her conclusions, and he ignored it all. He didn't want to imagine that a town like Springton could hold a horror like that. Dacre Shanks was a creepy little guy in a creepy little toystore. Sheriff Gunther, that was his name, was content with that. Creepy was fine. He could understand creepy. But serial killer? That was beyond him.

"So I started an unofficial investigation. My fellow deputies trusted me, and they trusted Ella-May. All the work she'd done meant we hit the ground running. We quickly had enough so that we could call in the Feds. Gunther found out, was not happy, threatened to fire us all. He called the FBI, told them it was all a big misunderstanding. That same night we got word that someone else had gone missing, a boy who fit the profile of some of Shanks's other victims. We convinced the judge to get us a search warrant – without Gunther's help – and we raided that toystore."

"Did you save the boy?" Amber asked.

"No, we did not." Teddy puffed on the pipe, but it had gone out. He didn't seem to notice. "We ran in on Shanks standing over him, though. All four of us opened fire. You know the rest. Gunther lost his job after that and I was elected in his place. For some reason, the folks around here have been electing me ever since. I don't think they're too smart."

"And what about after? There were other murders, weren't there? Ten years later, something like that?"

"Feds came to investigate. Thought there was a copycat. But, by the time they got here, the killings had stopped."

"Did your daughter have anything to do with that?"

Teddy struck a match, lit his pipe again. Gave it a few puffs. "The world is full of bad men, Amber. Bad women, too, I guess. Some of them hide in plain sight, and some of them don't. Some of them wear masks, and some of them wear smiles. I thought I'd seen the full extent of evil when we burst in on Dacre Shanks. Turns out I was wrong. There's another evil, a whole other layer of evil that I'd only read about in the Bible. I believe you know what I'm talking about."

She nodded.

"I've glimpsed impossible things," Teddy said. "I haven't seen them fully because I honestly don't think I'm able. But

I've seen enough to know that whatever path you're on, it's something I can't help you with."

"I understand."

"You get back to bed now, Amber. And you have good dreams, you hear me? The world's just about full up of the other kind."

20

Sheriff Roosevelt had already left for work when Amber got up the next morning. She joined Milo and Glen at the table and Ella-May served them breakfast, but didn't eat with them. Amber ate in silence and Milo didn't say a word. Even Glen seemed subdued.

They threw their bags in the Charger and went back inside to pay. Ella-May gave Milo a handwritten receipt and walked them to the door and they stood there, waiting for someone to say something.

Ella-May was the one to puncture the quiet. "I'm not going to ask about your business," she said. "I'm not going to ask why you're interested in a man who has killed so many people, or how you know what you know. There's a dark underbelly to this country and I am well aware that there are people who have to walk through it – oftentimes through no fault of their own. If you're on that path... well, I'd pray for you if I prayed."

Amber gave her a small, pained smile.

Ella-May nodded brusquely. "I've called Heather. I told her to speak to you if she's in the mood. That's no guarantee that she will, mind you. My daughter is her own woman. The library opens late today, so she'll be at work at two. You could call in then, see if she's feeling talkative. Good day to you, now."

She closed the door.

At ten minutes past two, they walked into the library and found Heather Medina restocking shelves in the Self-help section. Up close, she was an attractive woman with plump, soft lips but hard eyes. There was a thin scar on her neck that disappeared behind the collar of her blouse. Everything about her, from her manner to the shoes that she wore – practical, like she was ready to run or fight at any given moment – screamed survivor. Amber liked her instantly.

"Your mother sent us," Milo said.

Heather nodded, and kept sliding books on to the shelves. "She told me you're a curious bunch, with a particular interest in our town's recent history. I told her I'd already been speaking to you. I told her you're not exactly subtle."

"She said you'd talk to us if you were in a talkative mood," Amber said.

"And you're wondering what kind of mood I'm currently in?" asked Heather. "It's Amber, right? And Glen? I used to have a boyfriend called Glen. Really good guy. I guess he was my first love. My high-school sweetheart. Dacre Shanks came back from the dead and killed him when I was sixteen."

She said it so matter-of-factly that Amber didn't notice the words sliding down her spine until they made her shiver. "It's true, then? Everything we've heard?"

"Well, I don't know," said Heather. "It all depends on what you've heard, doesn't it?"

The elderly librarian passed, gave them all a suspicious look, and Heather smiled, keeping her eyes locked on her until she'd moved out of earshot.

"When I was a kid, we all knew who Dacre Shanks was," said Heather. "I grew up hearing about the things he'd done and how my mother had been the one to figure it all out. In the playground, my friends used to re-enact the night he died. They'd take turns to be my dad and the other deputies, and they'd go in, guns blazing, and whoever was playing Shanks would howl and scream and whirl around and around as the bullets hit him. It was town history that quickly became town legend. My sister, Christina, she was older than me, looked just like my mom, so, even though my mother wasn't actually there the night Shanks died, the kids decided it'd be neater, more *satisfying*, if she were. Christina was in great demand during recess."

Heather smiled sadly, then shook the smile away.

"Christina went missing when she was sixteen," she continued. "The ten-year anniversary of Shanks's death, to the hour. She vanished, right out of her bedroom. Over the next few weeks, four others disappeared too – a man, a woman, a fourteen-year-old boy and a three-year-old girl."

"I'm sorry," Amber said quietly.

"It tore us apart for a while, my family. But my parents... I don't know. They're stronger than most, maybe. Then, exactly a year later, another five people went missing. Man, woman and three kids. Year after that, another five... They wouldn't be related, the five people, but they would all look vaguely alike in some way. It's what Shanks used to do. He'd make his grotesque little families."

"And everyone thought it was a copycat killer," said Milo.

"Everyone but me," said Heather. She rolled the cart of books to the Cooking section, started transferring them to the shelves. "Even my mom couldn't see what was happening. She has an amazing mind, but believing that a killer had returned from the dead was a stretch too far for her. I was sixteen years old and Shanks came after me – chased me through the old theatre where we used to hold our recitals. I ran straight into the janitor and we went flying, but, when I looked up, Shanks was gone. Me and a few friends broke into his old store and found a secret room that my dad and the other cops hadn't even looked for. There were all these dollhouses. They were fully furnished, but only half of them had any figures in them. These little people, like porcelain or something, sitting at the table or watching TV or playing with tiny, tiny toys on the carpet. I recognised my sister immediately. She was sitting on a bed upstairs, reading a book with a big smile on her face."

"Figurines of his victims," Glen said. "Creepy."

Heather shook her head. "You're not getting it. Shanks made the house, the furniture, all that stuff. But he didn't make the figures. He caught them."

Milo frowned. "Sorry?"

Heather made sure the elderly librarian wasn't within range, and she leaned in. "The figures *were* his victims. That was my sister sitting on the toy bed. My *actual* sister. He'd got her smile wrong, though. Christina always had this lopsided smile. He got that wrong."

"But you said the figures were made of porcelain," said Amber.

"That's what it looked like," Heather replied. "But I saw what he did to their bodies, when they were dead. He embalmed them. The cellar of his toyshop was one big embalming room. Then he dressed them and... and posed them. He'd stitch expressions on to their faces and arrange their arms this way or that... When he had them the way he wanted, he'd cover them with a kind of resin to hold them in place, and put them in the dollhouse."

"Yeah, no, still not getting it," said Glen. "Because the figures in dollhouses are tiny. It *sounds* like what you're telling us is that he killed them, embalmed them, and then shrank them, but you're a normal, sane lady so that can't be what you're actually saying."

"He didn't shrink them," said Heather. "Not really. Shanks called it doorway magic. He had this key, this special key, which acted as a tunnel, I guess, from one door to *any* other, whichever one he wanted. That's how he took people. That's how they vanished.

"When he took Glen – my boyfriend – he told him about it. Glen wrote it all down. I found it when I went looking for him, a scrap of paper soaked in his blood. Shanks was linking a normal door to the dollhouse doors – when you passed through, you became smaller. Shanks would work on the bodies here, get them into the proper poses, and then put them through into the dollhouse, where they'd be the size of figurines."

"I really don't mean any offence by this," Amber said, "but I hope you realise how nuts that sounds."

Heather smiled sadly. "I know."

"Because it really sounds nuts."

"And it is," Heather said. "But it's also what happened. People know it, too. Well – everyone of my generation. They've all heard the stories. They were there when Shanks started coming after me and my friends. They might not believe the story anymore, they may have come up with more rational explanations or dismissed the whole thing as nonsense, but a part of them still believes."

"That's why they beat up those kids last year," said Milo.

"Poor little Walter," Heather said, nodding. "I've heard his theory, that this is all some plot to get kids to behave themselves. If I were him, I'd probably think the same. But keeping the dollhouses at the school was our way of honouring Shanks's victims – remembering them even if we couldn't come right out and tell everyone what had really happened. The people who beat up those kids probably didn't even understand why they were so angry – not consciously, at least. But this entire town has been scarred by Dacre Shanks, and he still haunts us."

"How did you stop him?" Amber asked.

"First thing I did was steal his key. Then I trapped him. I managed to fool him into trapping himself, actually, in the fourth dollhouse. I was the only one of my friends to survive, and I barely did that."

She lifted her top to show them a jagged scar across her belly.

"Cool," breathed Glen.

Amber watched as Heather cast a furtive glance at Milo and then, almost like she'd just realised what she'd done, she blushed, and busied herself with tucking in her shirt.

"Where's the dollhouse now?" Amber asked.

"Why?"

"We… we need to talk to Dacre Shanks."

Heather stopped what she was doing. Thirty seconds passed in which nothing was said. Even Glen stayed quiet.

"Who are you?" Heather finally asked.

"We just need to ask him something," Amber said. "Just one thing and then we'll be gone."

"Who are you?"

Amber tried figuring out the best way to say what she had to say. "Some people want to kill me. They're monsters, I guess. Like Shanks. They won't stop until I'm dead. My only hope is to find this guy we're looking for and Shanks is the only one who knows his name."

"They're like Shanks?"

Amber nodded. "And there's five of them. Please, Heather, all I want is to ask him this guy's name."

"I'd like to help," Heather said. "I really would. But no one talks to Shanks. No one. Any opportunity to get free, he'll take it."

"We won't do anything to risk—"

"I'm sorry," said Heather. "He's killed too many people already. I've kept him trapped by not letting anyone know he's there, and certainly not letting anyone talk to him. You're just going to have to find another way to get what you need."

"There is no other way," said Milo.

"Then I'm sorry. I truly am. But if Shanks gets free it won't be you he goes after. It'll be me. It'll be people from this town. Springton will go back to being his hunting ground."

"Maybe we can help," said Amber. "He's trapped in a dollhouse – but how secure can that be? Those kids easily trashed two of the dollhouses kept at the school. He will eventually be found."

"And I suppose you have a better way?"

"We'll take the dollhouse away from here," Milo said. "Destroy it, bury it, burn it, whatever."

"Too risky. Sorry, but I'm not going to change my mind. My mom suggested I talk to you, and I've talked to you. If I had known you wanted to actually communicate with him, I'd never have agreed to it. If my mom had known that, I doubt she'd have even mentioned you to me. I can't help you, and I won't help you. I'm sorry about that, I really am. But I have to ask you to leave the library."

Amber had no argument left, and so she found herself walking out into the sunshine with Glen and Milo at her heels.

"Huh," she said. "I didn't think she'd actually say no. I mean, I should have but I didn't. We can't *make* her tell us where she's keeping Shanks, can we? I'm… I have no idea what to do now. What do we do?"

Glen shrugged. "How about we break into her house?"

Amber frowned. "Seriously?"

"Of course. This is life or death, right? You need to speak to this guy, so let's search her place and find him, then get the hell out of here before her dad comes after us with his gun. Do we know where she lives?"

"Pine Street," said Milo.

"There you go," Glen said, clapping his hands. "That's our plan, right?"

Amber looked at Milo.

"Sure," said Milo. "That's our plan."

Pine Street was a picket-fence affair: neat lawns and trimmed hedges and not one oil stain on a single driveway. They found the Medina house without a problem, passed it and drove down to the corner. Amber and Glen walked back, rang the doorbell and waited. They chatted about nothing, but they did so loudly and with much false cheer. A neighbour walking her dog glanced at them. They smiled politely, and rang the doorbell again.

The door opened, and Milo let them in.

While they searched, Milo did his best to patch up the window he had broken. He left money on the table for the damage. The dollhouse wasn't in any of the rooms. The attic was empty. The cellar was bare.

The dollhouse wasn't there.

They got back to the Charger.

"Okay," said Glen, "I'm out of ideas."

"It's in the library," Amber said. "It is, isn't it? Big old place like that probably has a hundred rooms that aren't being used. I bet they have big old locks on the doors, too."

"If the dollhouse is not where she lives," said Milo, "then it's probably where she works."

Glen sounded grumpy in the back seat. "It'll take ages to search that place."

Milo started the car. "Then I guess we'll have to do it at night."

21

THE LIBRARY WAS CREEPY when it got dark.

The staff turned out the lights and locked up. Heather Medina was the last to leave. When the silence had settled and ten minutes had passed, Amber and the others emerged from the restroom where they'd been hiding. The occasional bright sweep of headlights from the street outside was the only illumination they were granted as they made their way through the maze of bookcases. Those lights sent shadows dancing and flitting from floor to wall to ceiling, and each one set Amber's heart to drumming.

They split up, their task made easier when Glen found a set of keys lying in the office inbox. Locked doors swung open and revealed storage spaces, boxes of books and plaster busts gathering dust. They found desks piled on top of each other and a room full of broken chairs.

Finally, they found a door at the end of a dark and windowless corridor for which they had no key. Milo knelt and proceeded to pick the lock. It took a lot longer than Amber expected.

When the last tumbler slid into place, Milo pulled on the

handle and pushed. The door opened to a small room with a single table at its centre, and upon that table was a dollhouse.

Amber stepped in. They were deep enough in the library that she felt confident in turning on a light. The single bulb brightened slowly, its radiance dimmed by dust.

The dollhouse was magnificent. Front opening, with two stories and an attic space. It was the kind of thing Amber would have loved as a little girl, if only her parents had paid more attention to her subtle hints. If only her parents hadn't been planning to murder her from the day she was conceived.

She peered through the little windows, saw furniture. Beds and dressers. Downstairs, there was a hall with a staircase, and a kitchen.

"Can you see anything?" Glen whispered from beside her.

Something moved past the window and Amber recoiled sharply.

There was a moment, while she stood there, the hair on her neck prickling and every instinct urging her to run, when she genuinely considered just calling up her parents and imploring them to rethink their plans and let her come home. She was ready, in that moment, to forgive them, to carry on with her life as if nothing had happened.

The moment passed.

She cleared her throat. "Hello?" she said. She peered closer, but it was dark in there. "Are you there? Dacre Shanks, can you hear me?"

No answer. At least none that she could hear.

Glen hunkered down to look through the side windows. "Maybe he's sleeping," he said, then knocked heavily on the roof. "Hey, wake up in there!"

Milo took hold of Glen's wrist. "Please don't do that to the serial killer."

Glen took his hand back. "What? He lives in a dollhouse. He's the size of Thumbelina, for God's sake. You think he scares me?"

"It's not about whether or not he scares you," said Milo, "it's the principle of the thing. Wherever possible, you do not antagonise serial killers. That's just a general rule of life."

"I don't think it applies to serial killers you could fit in your pocket."

"Quiet," said Amber, leaning closer to the large upstairs window, the one looking on to the landing. Someone was standing there, very still. Someone who hadn't been there a moment earlier.

"Hello? Mr Shanks?"

Then she heard it. They all heard it. A man's voice. Quiet.

"Hello," it said, from inside the dollhouse.

If a voice could crawl, this one did. It crawled over Amber's face to her ears, scuttled in and burrowed its way into her brain. She could feel its legs, cold and frenzied. "You have my attention."

Her mouth was dry. Her mouth was so dry. "Mr Shanks, my name is Amber. I need—"

"Pleased to meet you, Amber."

For a moment, she couldn't talk. "Yeah," she said, feeling stupid and scared and childish. She was so very afraid. "I need your help. We've come—"

"And who are your companions?" Dacre Shanks asked in that creepy-crawly voice of his.

"Um, this is Milo and that's Glen."

"Hi," said Glen. Even he sounded scared.

"Mr Shanks," said Amber, "I'm here because I've been told you know of a man who tricked the Shining Demon – did a deal with him, then went on the run."

There was a pause. "Ah yes," came the voice from the window. "Indeed I do. I met him many years ago. Interesting fellow."

"Do you happen to remember his name, or where I might find him?"

"I remember his name, yes, and I also know the town in which he was born. Would that be of any use to you in tracking him down?"

"Yes," said Amber. "Very much so."

There was a moment of silence from inside the dollhouse. "How nice," said Shanks.

"Are you really tiny?" Glen asked suddenly, his curiosity overcoming his fear. "Can I see you?"

Milo put his hand on Glen's shoulder to shut him up.

Amber glared, grateful to Glen for allowing her to focus on something she could scorn. Reluctantly, she looked back through the window.

"Sorry about that," she said. "This man, could you tell me his name?"

Shanks said, "Forgive me for asking... Amber, wasn't it? Forgive me for asking, Amber, and forgive me for being so crude, but what exactly is in it for me?"

She frowned. "I'm sorry?"

"If I tell you what you came here to learn, what do I get out of it?"

"I... I don't know. What do you want? We can't release you."

"Why not?"

"Because you'll kill people."

"And?" said Shanks.

"And it'll be my fault."

"And this would upset you?"

"Well, yes."

"You are a curious girl. Tell me this – why do you want the man you seek?"

"I just want to talk to him," said Amber, aware how pathetic this sounded.

"About the Shining Demon?"

"Yes."

The man in the window moved slightly, and the light almost hit his face. He was wearing a short-sleeved shirt and a tie. "You want to make a deal? Or you've already made one and you're having second thoughts? Maybe I can help you. Release me and I'll speak to the Shining Demon on your behalf."

"I'm sorry, Mr Shanks, but you're not getting out."

"Then what else do you have to offer me? I am trapped in a dollhouse – what, apart from freedom, do you think I require? A pet?"

"We could get you a cute little convertible," said Glen. "Maybe throw in a Barbie if you're feeling lonely?"

Amber froze, awaiting Shanks's response.

"Your friend is very rude," he said eventually.

"I'm sorry," she responded. "And he's not my friend. Mr Shanks, you're absolutely right, there is nothing I can offer you. We're not releasing you. You've killed innocent people before and you will do it again. I can't allow that to happen."

"Then we are at an impasse."

"I guess we are." She bit her lip. "So why not just tell me?

You're not getting out, right? So we're not going to be making a deal here. If we're not going to make a deal, there's nothing you have to gain from this situation. And, if you have no chance of gaining anything, then you won't have anything to lose by telling me what I want to know, will you?"

A low chuckle. "I see your logic. Cleverly done, young lady."

"Thank you."

"But you're wrong about me not having anything to gain. You see, I've been stuck here for... I actually don't know how long."

"Thirty-one years," said Glen.

"Really? Well now... thirty-one years. Imagine that. In that case, I've been stuck here for thirty-one years. I can't go insane and I can't kill myself because I'm already dead. So I've been sitting here for thirty-one years, and I only rise out of my bored stupor when that door opens and little Heather Roosevelt pokes her pretty head in to make sure everything is still in place. Oh, but she's not a Roosevelt anymore, is she? She got married. She won't tell me to whom, but I saw the wedding ring – for as long as it was there. She's getting old, though, isn't she? Every time I see her, she is less and less like the troublesome teenager who trapped me in here in the first place.

"But here I sit. Bored. I don't need to eat or sleep. I don't age. I feel each and every one of those seconds as they drag by, too many to count, too many to keep track of. I haven't spoken to anyone in all that time. I talk only to myself these days, just because I like the sound of my own voice – as you've probably guessed. I haven't talked to anyone and I haven't interacted with anyone until you three walked in here.

"Your problem, as I have said, stems from the mistaken presumption that I have nothing to gain by not telling you what you want to know. The fact is, though, I do. I haven't spoken to anyone until you. I haven't interacted with anyone until you. But you know what else I haven't done? I haven't hurt anyone... until you. You need this information and you need it badly, or else you wouldn't be here talking to someone like me, but I'm not going to tell you simply because it makes me happy to disappoint you."

"Wow," said Glen. "You're a dick."

"I suppose I am, Glen, yes," said Shanks. "I take my pleasures where I can – small and petty as they may be."

Glen sneered through the window. "Well, why don't I just reach in there and smush your head?"

"Please do."

"Glen," said Amber.

He stepped back. "What? Am I the only one here who is aware of the fact that the big, bad, scary man we're talking to is, like, three inches tall? Am I the only one amused by that?"

"If you reach in there," said Amber, "you'll be opening the dollhouse. He can escape."

"Where to? A cartoon mouse hole in the skirting board? He'll still be only three inches tall."

"Are you sure about that?" Milo asked. "We don't know how this doorway magic works. You open that dollhouse and he might return to normal size."

"Don't listen to them, Glen," said Shanks from the window. "Reach in here and teach me a lesson."

Glen faltered. "Uh... no. No, I don't think so, if it's all the same to you."

"Are you a coward, Glen?"

"Only when threatened."

"Such a shame. My first impression of you was that you possessed a spark your companions lacked. But you have revealed your true nature, and your true nature, I am afraid to say, is a crushing disappointment."

Glen shrugged. "You're actually not the first person to say that."

"You are a coward and a dullard, just like the rest of your countrymen."

"Ah now, here," said Glen, "don't you go insulting my countrymen."

"What is Ireland but a land of mongrels, wastrels and whelps?"

"Ah, that's a bit strong…"

"Drunken buffoons stumbling through their maudlin lives, violent and thuggish and self-pitying, a nation of ungrateful—"

Glen laughed. "I'm sorry, pal, I don't care what you say. You're three inches tall. My mickey is bigger than you. And that was a pretty blatant attempt to provoke me, but what you're failing to realise is that Ireland is the greatest country in the world, you dope."

"Then why are you in America?"

Glen leaned down to grin straight into the window. "Because America has the best monsters."

There was a moment of silence, and then, amazingly, laughter.

"I like you," Shanks announced. "I like all three of you. And I will answer your question, Amber – but only to you. Not to your friends."

"We're not leaving," said Milo.

"That is my only condition," Shanks said.

"Why?" Amber asked. "Why not tell all of us?"

A chuckle. "Because I am tricky. Because I like pushing buttons. Glen may be a delightful buffoon, but Milo here is obviously your protector, and as such he takes things a lot more seriously. Since I am acquiescing to your request, I need to find some way of satisfying my quiet need to torture. Making your companions leave the room is a small triumph, but, as it has been pointed out, I am a small man."

Amber deliberated, then looked at Milo. He grunted, and left the room. Glen went with him.

Amber shut the door, and moved back to the dollhouse. "Yes?"

"Heather doesn't know you're here, does she?" Shanks asked.

"Why does it matter?"

"She has kept this dollhouse in this room for thirty–one years. My prison has many windows, but all I see are walls. She even took the other dollhouses to the local school, so I couldn't gaze at them for solace."

"And if I ask her to move it somewhere else? Somewhere with a view, maybe? If you give me the name of the man I'm looking for and the town he grew up in, I'll ask her. You have my word." Amber frowned. "Hello? Mr Shanks? Are you still there?"

"A view?" he said, even quieter than before. "You offer me a view?"

"Well, what do you want, Mr Shanks?"

"To be free."

"I told you, I'm not releasing you."

"There is more than one way to be free, Amber." Shanks

stood with his hands clasped at his chest, his face still in darkness. "I'll give you the name of the man you seek. I'll tell you where to find him."

Amber frowned. "And in return?"

A hesitation. "In return, you find a way to kill me."

She had to be honest – she hadn't been expecting that. "I'm sorry?"

"I'm never getting out of here," said Shanks. "Don't you think that's unnecessarily cruel? I know I've done bad things, evil things, but surely you understand that nobody deserves an eternity of this? Heather would gladly kill me if she could."

"I'm... I'm not killing anyone."

"Then get your protector to do it. He looks like he'd even enjoy the opportunity."

"This isn't why we came here."

"But you'd be doing the world a favour!" Shanks said. "What if I escape? The first thing I'm going to do if I ever get out of here is kill Heather Roosevelt. Then I'm going to kill her parents, and all of her friends. Then this entire town. So do the right thing, Amber. Find a way to finish me off now, while I'm vulnerable."

She shook her head. "We're not killers. We're not like you."

"Please," said Shanks. "You'd be putting me out of my misery."

"You've murdered innocent people," said Amber. "You deserve your misery."

"Then I'll give you something more!" Shanks said. "I'll give you his name, his address, and I'll even tell you how to get to him tonight."

Her heart beat faster. "He lives close?"

"No. He lives in Oregon. But distance doesn't mean a thing when you've got my key. It's on the wall behind you. See it?"

There was a single nail in the wall, and hanging from that nail was an ornate brass key. Amber took it down, tracing her fingers over the intricate etchings along its side. The head of the key was shaped like a lock.

"Heather hung it there to taunt me," said Shanks. "Always in sight, always out of reach. But that key can get you where you want to go instantly. Do we have a deal?"

Amber looked back at the dollhouse. "I'm not going to kill you, Mr Shanks."

"Then get Buxton to do it! He might even know how!"

"Buxton?"

"Gregory Buxton," said Shanks. "I first met him in the town of his birth, a bland little place called Cascade Falls. That's who you're looking for, and that's where you want to go."

"How do I know you're telling the truth?"

"See for yourself! Put the key in the lock of the door there. Turn it twice, but keep saying his name in your head, his name and the name of his town."

"Gregory Buxton," she said, turning to the door, "Cascade Falls."

"Try it," said Shanks. "Keep saying that, turn the key, open the door and walk through. That's all the proof you'll need. But then, once you've spoken to him, promise me you'll do as I ask."

"I'll... I'll talk to Milo about it."

"We had a deal!" Shanks shouted from behind her.

Amber didn't turn. "I didn't agree to anything." She put the key in the lock, repeating Buxton's name and the name of his town over and over in her head. She twisted the key and heard the door lock, then turned it again, heard the tumblers slide and settle. Then she opened the door and stepped through, but at the last moment the corridor became a dimly lit hall with a grand staircase and long shadows. The door shut behind her with a crash that reverberated through the floor itself. She spun. The door was now white and it didn't have a handle. She pounded on it. It was thin wood that shook under her fist.

And then Shanks's voice came drifting down from upstairs.

"I told you I was tricky."

22

AMBER LURCHED SIDEWAYS, a fast-moving terror spreading outwards from the back of her neck to her fingertips and toes. She ran from the hall, seeing now how fake it all was, how flimsy the walls were. She skidded into the kitchen, with its table and chairs and stove and fridge, and her foot caught on something and she went stumbling, nearly falling over a sofa. The architecture was crazy. It made no sense. One half of this room was a kitchen, the other a living room.

She heard Dacre Shanks coming down the stairs.

"I fibbed," he called. "I tricked you. You can use the key, but only I control where it leads. I admit it, I played you for a fool. In my defence, though, you were an easy target."

Amber ran quietly into another room, a room with floor-to-ceiling shelves. Upon those shelves were rows of cardboard painted with the spines of anonymous books. This was the library, and it was also a utility room with a washing machine and a plastic bed for the dog.

She caught her foot again. A crack ran in a perfectly straight line between the dual rooms. It took her adrenalised brain another moment to piece it together. This was a dollhouse, after all. The front was a façade that split somewhere near the middle, and opened up like uneven wings, like the covers of a book, revealing the interior with its collection of half-rooms. Closed up like this, nothing made sense, and everything was folded together at an unnatural angle.

"Amber," Shanks called in a sing-song voice.

She ducked down in the dark behind a washing machine. Her hands were shaking.

"You're being silly," he continued. He was still in the hall, probably trying to figure out which way she'd run. "I'm not going to hurt you. You're the first person I'll be able to talk to, eye to eye, in all the time I've been here. Come out. Come on. You know I'm going to find you eventually."

She shuffled forward a little, and peeked round the edge of a bookcase. She glimpsed him, just enough to see the knife he held as he moved away. He was checking the other side of the house first. She'd been given a moment, a chance to think, to put her thoughts in order.

When he didn't find her over there, he'd come over here, and he'd find her within seconds. So she had to move. Upstairs. That was the way to go. Upstairs would have multiple bedrooms, which meant more places to hide. She gripped the bookcase, getting ready to pull herself up on to her quaking, trembling legs, but her gaze caught on her hand, and she looked at how soft and pink it was.

She'd almost forgotten.

She shifted. She felt that pain again, that peculiar kind of pain as the strength flooded through her and her limbs lengthened and her body reshaped itself. She had horns now, and her hands were long-fingered and tipped with black nails.

She forced the fear down and got up off her knees. She crept quickly and quietly back through the kitchen-living room, keeping her eyes locked on the darkness at the other side of the hall.

She reached the staircase. From a few steps away, the banisters had seemed ornate, but as she ascended she could feel the chips and inconsistencies in the wood beneath her hand. The steps didn't creak, though, and for this she was thankful. She sank into darkness and then plunged into light, a harsh light that cascaded through the circular window and bathed the second-floor landing in hellish reds and fiery oranges.

Amber moved to the side, into the shadow, and crouched, looking through the wooden railing and down into the hall. Seconds passed, then Dacre Shanks walked into view, crossing from one side of the hall to the other. She watched her enemy, marvelling at how easily the hunter can become the prey. All it takes is a new perspective.

To her right, a half-wall with a doorway leading into a bedroom, the wallpaper a dark colour, a blue or something like it. Maybe a green. Pressed against it, in the closed wing of the front of the house, another bedroom of a lighter colour. It was hard to tell in all this gloom, but it was probably pink.

To her left, the main bedroom and a bathroom with a Jacuzzi and a tub. No shower, though. There was also a toilet and a sink with a framed piece of reflective plastic that acted as a mirror.

Dacre Shanks strolled back into the hall, and raised his head. He was a narrow man, with dark hair turning grey and receding fast from his temples like it was afraid of his face. His face was something to fear. A long nose and a thin mouth and eyes in shadow. "Are you up there, Amber? Did you sneak by me? Oh, aren't you a clever one? Aren't you a sneaky one? But you know what you are, most of all? You are fun. You are a fun one. So come on down, Amber. You win our little game of hide-and-seek. I give up."

He raised his hands in surrender and chuckled.

"I'm waiting," said Amber.

Shanks swivelled his head to where she was crouched. He couldn't see her, though. His eyes passed over her.

"What was that?" he called. "I'm afraid I didn't quite hear you. Old age, you see. I'm not as young as I used to—"

"I said, I'm waiting."

Shanks zeroed in on her position, and gave her a smile that opened like a wound. "Waiting for me?"

"I'm not like the others you've killed," Amber said. "I'm not going to scream and run away."

"Ooooh," said Shanks, and laughed. "A fighter, are we? Heather was a fighter, back in her teenage years."

"And she beat you," said Amber. "So now I'm going to beat you."

"Wrong," said Shanks, a flicker of irritation crossing his features for the first time. "She tricked me. She didn't beat me, she tricked me into doing this to myself."

"So not only are you weak," Amber said, "you're also an idiot?"

Shanks made a sound she couldn't identify, and started up the stairs. "I've been doing this a very long time, young lady. I've hunted all kinds of people."

Amber stood as he approached. "You've never hunted anyone quite like me."

He reached the top, came towards her, and she stepped out of the shadows and smiled, giving him a flash of her fangs.

He froze, stared at her, and then his eyes narrowed. "You are a girl full of surprises, aren't you?" he said, starting to move to the side. Circling her. That knife in his hand. "So that's why you want Buxton. You have your power and now you want more. Funny the effect power has on a person."

"I suppose it is," she said, turning with him as he circled.

"Has it changed you, Amber? Apart from physically, I mean. Are you a different person now?"

"Like you wouldn't believe."

Shanks smiled. "I bet. I saw you and I thought to myself, *easy target*. Now look at you. Suddenly I feel very silly indeed."

"How did you get me in here?"

Shanks's chuckle was dry, and lacking good cheer. "You don't have to worry about that," he said. "You're never going to leave."

He lunged, jabbing low and then slashing high. Amber dodged backwards, barely avoiding the blade that whistled by her throat. Shanks didn't stop moving, however. In an instant, he was on her, pushing her back against the banister. She grabbed at his knife hand, fingers closing round his wrist. He was stronger than she'd expected. Not as strong as her but close enough. He headbutted her and pain flashed outwards from her nose. His other hand was on her throat and he was pushing her back, over the banister. She grew talons and raked his arm.

Howling, Shanks released his grip. They stumbled, locked

together. Blood ran from Shanks's forearm, but he ignored it and reached up for her horns. He suddenly stepped back and yanked downwards and Amber cried out, her knees hitting the floor. He kicked her, the toe of his shoe connecting with her chin, and Amber sprawled.

"You're all strength," Shanks said, kneeling on her throat, "but no finesse. No style."

"Amber!" came Milo's voice from all around them. "Amber, someone's coming. We must have set off an alarm. Amber?"

Through the window behind Shanks, she could see out into the room as Milo stepped in. He was a giant.

"Amber?" he said, his voice astonishingly loud.

Shanks smiled down at her. "Hush now. Don't spoil the surprise." He pulled her up, holding the knife against her throat, and moved her to the window.

Glen came in after Milo, closing the door. He noticed the key. "Where is she?" he asked, fiddling with it. The key twisted as he fiddled, locking the door.

"Oh my," whispered Shanks. "This will be even easier than I thought."

Milo came closer to the dollhouse, peering through the windows. "Shanks. I'd like a word."

Behind him, Glen turned the key in the other direction, and opened the door.

Shanks shoved Amber away, and ran for the stairs.

Amber toppled, still woozy from the kick to the head. She looked down through the banisters, saw Shanks sprinting for the front door. He vanished right before he hit it and she snapped her head up—

—as he smashed into Glen, throwing him violently off his

feet, then rebounded, went stumbling towards Milo as Milo turned. As the door slammed shut behind him, Shanks hit Milo with a wild swing boosted by his momentum, and Milo twisted and went down. Shanks got his feet under him, looked around and then through the dollhouse window, and a smile broke across his features.

Amber stood up, fresh terror mounting.

She heard footsteps, running footsteps from beyond the closed door.

"Get out of there!" came Heather's voice.

Shanks's face took on an expression of pure joy, and he darted behind the door.

"Heather, no!" Amber screamed, stumbling to the window. "Don't come in!"

Heather didn't hear her. She threw the door open and ran in and Shanks grabbed her, pushed her back against the wall and plunged his knife into her and Amber went cold.

Heather stared into Shanks's eyes, her mouth open, but no sound coming out.

"I told you," Shanks snarled as he dragged the blade across her belly. "I told you I'd kill you, you interfering little bitch."

He gave the knife another twist and Heather made a sound halfway between a sigh and a gag, and then a series of explosions filled Amber's ears. Shanks went stumbling, letting Heather fall as he scrambled out of the door. A moment later, Milo rose into view, his gun in his hand.

He helped Glen back to his feet, then tore the jacket off him. He crouched by Heather, pressing the jacket against her wound. "Keep applying pressure," he said. "Glen! Call an ambulance!"

Heather grabbed his arm. "Stop Shanks," she said, her voice weak. "Stop him."

Milo hesitated, then stood. "Glen, stay with her. When help comes, find Amber."

Then he was gone.

23

AMBER RAN FOR THE banister, leaped over it, and dropped to the floor below. The impact juddered from her feet to her hips, but she sprang for the white door the way Shanks had... and smashed straight into it.

She staggered back, landed on her ass.

She got up, hurried to the closest window. From there, she could see the huge figure of Glen pressing his jacket against Heather's wound as he talked on the phone, giving the address. There was blood everywhere. Amber looked past them, to the door, to the brass key still in the lock.

"Glen!" she yelled.

Glen looked around. "Amber?"

"Glen!"

He took Heather's hands, laid them on the jacket. "Hold this," he said, and hurried over, checking the windows. "Amber! You in there?"

She waved until she caught his attention. His face filled the window.

"Amber! You're red again!"

She stopped waving. "I'm also trapped in here."

"Yes," Glen said quickly. "Of course. How do I get you back to normal size?"

"The door. Close it and lock it, then unlock it and open it. Don't walk through."

Glen frowned. His eyebrows were massive and hairy. "Why?"

"The key! It's the key Heather told us about, the one that let Shanks travel between doorways!"

"Ohhh," said Glen. "Okay, cool. Hey, Amber? What does it look like when someone is dying? I think Heather might be dying."

"The door, Glen!"

"Right," he said, then hunkered down to peer in. "And listen, if this doesn't work, you can live in my pocket. I won't mind."

"The door!" she shouted.

Glen hurried to the door, stepping over Heather's outstretched legs as he did so. He locked it, unlocked it and opened it, and Amber ran forward, and right before she slammed into the dollhouse door it turned into the room outside, and she stumbled into Glen, who shrieked and spun as the door slammed shut behind her.

"Amber!" he gasped.

Relief washed over her, but then Heather raised her head, her eyes widened and she screamed.

"No, no, it's okay!" Glen said. "It's Amber! She's with us! She won't hurt you!"

Despite her wound, Heather scrambled away from them both, leaving a bloody smear on the ground.

"Glen, it's okay," Amber said. "I'm leaving. I'm going after Shanks."

"Well then, I'm going with you."

"No, you stay with her."

"I'm going with you," he insisted. "Heather's fine. Heather, aren't you fine? The ambulance will be here shortly, and all I'll be doing is soaking up blood. I'm going with you."

"Fine," Amber muttered, taking the brass key from the lock and pocketing it. She opened the door. The corridor looked perfectly normal.

"If you disappear again, I'll rescue you," Glen said from beside her.

She patted his shoulder, and then shoved him out into the corridor. He tripped, went sprawling, but at least he didn't disappear. She ran, jumped over him and kept going.

He did his best to keep up. "I don't mind that you did that," he called.

Amber ignored him.

She burst out into the night air just as Milo came striding back to the Charger, his gun held down by his leg.

"Amber! Where the hell were you?"

"Never mind that," she said. "Any sign of him?"

"No," Milo said as he opened the car door. "Get in. He's probably headed to the toystore."

"Maybe not," she said. "He mentioned the other dollhouses – he might be going there, instead. You check the toystore, I'll check the school."

"We're not splitting up," said Milo. "It's too dangerous."

"It's my fault he's out!" she shouted. "If he hurts anyone else, that's on me! I'll be fine – I'm a goddamn demon, okay? Go!"

Milo hesitated, then tucked his gun into his waistband and jumped in behind the wheel. Glen hurried up behind her as the Charger was speeding away.

"Come on," said Amber.

Glen panted and wheezed as they ran the block to the school, whereas she ran easily, giving a wide berth to every darkened doorway while Glen staggered by, oblivious to the threat Shanks posed. They got to the corner and paused, peering out across the street.

"It doesn't look like he's here," Glen whispered, still panting.

"Let's get closer."

Glen grabbed her arm. He could barely fit his hand around her bicep. "Maybe we should wait for Milo. He has the gun, right? I mean, you've got claws and you're amazing, but a gun's a gun."

"If we delay, he might hurt someone."

"So? Do you really care?"

She snapped her head round to him. "What?"

He held up his hands. "Hey, sorry. I just... You didn't exactly force me to stay with Heather, you know?"

She snarled. "You said she'd be fine."

"Well, yeah, but what do I know? I just said that so I could come along."

She leaned in. "Of course I care about Shanks hurting people."

"Right. Okay. I thought maybe you didn't really give a crap about that stuff. My mistake."

Amber wanted to hit him, wanted to take out her anger and frustration on his stupid face, but right before she made a move an alarm rang out, drawing her attention back to the school.

"Looks like we're the lucky ones," she said.

"I'll call Milo."

"You do that. I'm going to— damn it."

She ducked back as a police cruiser swept in, hopping the kerb and stopping right at the foot of the steps.

"Wow," said Glen. "Response time here is *fast*."

They watched Sheriff Roosevelt get out, and Dacre Shanks walk down the steps towards him.

Amber couldn't hear what Teddy was saying over the noise of the alarm, but Shanks kept on coming with his head down. Teddy backed away, his hand resting on the butt of his holstered gun.

Amber broke from cover, sprinting towards them, Glen at her heels.

She was halfway across the street when Shanks got close enough for Teddy to recognise him. Teddy jerked back, went for his gun, but Shanks took three quick steps and plunged his knife into the sheriff's throat.

Amber roared and Shanks turned to her, Teddy's gun in his outstretched hand.

She pulled up, stumbling a little. Glen ran into the back of her.

Shanks smiled at her. "Where's your friend?"

Amber hissed as Teddy sank slowly to the ground.

This just made Shanks smile wider. "He's a dangerous one. I could tell just by looking at him. Do me a favour, would you? Call out to him? Tell him to join us, and to leave his gun behind?"

"He's not here," said Amber.

"But he'll be here shortly," Glen added.

"Well then, I had better be ready for him, hadn't I?" said Shanks. "You are both going to accompany me into the school, if you please. Oh, and young lady, if you would do me the courtesy of changing from this beautiful red-skinned creature back to the dull little girl you really are, that would be simply marvellous."

She didn't want to. What she wanted to do was take her chances and dive at him. Maybe he'd shoot her, maybe he wouldn't. Maybe he'd miss. But she wouldn't miss. She'd carve his face up. Rip out his eyes. Tear his throat out with her teeth.

The gun in his hand didn't waver. Amber swallowed her anger, and reverted to normal.

"There," said Shanks. "Isn't that better?"

24

THE ALARM WOULDN'T STOP WAILING. It howled through the high school's wide corridors, an unrelenting assault on Amber's eardrums, and escaped through the open door that led out into the night.

Glen sat with one hand cuffed to the radiator. Amber herself was on her knees, both hands cuffed behind her back. She watched as Shanks opened the glass cabinet, and trailed a long finger over the contours of the dollhouse within, the last surviving dollhouse that contained so many of his victims.

He looked back at her, and smiled.

"This is my life's work," he said, his voice barely audible over the alarm. "This is everything that has ever given my existence meaning. What is *your* meaning, Amber? What is *your* purpose?"

Amber didn't say anything.

"Do you even know?" Shanks continued. "Do you have any idea? You probably don't. Very few do. I didn't – not when I was alive. I needed to die before I could see why I needed to live. The Shining Demon helped me. He granted me my new life, and he gave me the key that made everything so much *easier*. Do you have it, by the way? Did you bring it with you?"

"He wants you to help me," Amber said.

"Sorry? What was that?"

"The Shining Demon," she said, louder this time. "He wants you to help me."

Shanks laughed. "I don't think so, Amber. He plays games, as is his right as a Duke of Hell, but that is not a game he is interested in playing. He would rather we scurry about on our own, fumbling blindly in the dark. We arouse his curiosity only rarely, I'm afraid."

She shook her head. "I'm special. He said it himself. If you hurt me, if you harm me or my friends, he'll be—"

He hit her. It was a slap, an open palm, but it struck so fast and so suddenly that it rocked her, sent the world tilting and the floor rushing up to crack against her skull.

She lay on her side, the alarm in her head, tasting blood. Then she felt Shanks's hands on her as he pulled her back to kneeling position.

"My apologies," he said. "I don't like it when people lie to me. I shouldn't have lost my temper. That was rude. But try not to lie again, all right? It brings out my ugly side."

"Every side is your ugly side," Glen said.

"Do you really think it wise to taunt the man with the gun?"

"You think I'm scared of you?"

"Yes," answered Shanks. "You said as much, not fifteen minutes ago."

"That was then," Glen said. "This is now. You know what I think? I think you're the coward. You're a big man with the gun and the knife, but take those away, and you're a pathetic little loser."

Shanks said, in a bored voice that the alarm nearly drowned out, "You do realise I don't need you, yes? All I need is Amber here. You are quite disposable."

Glen laughed. "Of course I'm disposable. I've got four days to live. I'm practically dead already. Four days or right now – what difference does it make? Shoot me, or take these cuffs off and we'll settle this like men."

Amber watched them, waiting for her moment.

"I think I'll shoot you," said Shanks. "It'll be funnier." He raised the gun.

There.

A brief wave of pain washed over Amber as she shifted into her demonic form, and she charged into him, her shoulder catching him in the middle of the back and one of her horns scraping his neck. Shanks went down and she fell on top of him. She tried to snap the handcuffs that bound her wrists behind her – she felt the links strain – but her demon strength wasn't up to the task. Instead, she knelt on his hand and he let go of the gun, and she twisted and fell back, managing to kick the weapon. It skittered across the polished floor towards Glen. He reached for it with his free hand, but it stopped just short of his splayed fingers.

Shanks pushed her off. She got to her knees while he leaped to his feet. He darted for the gun and she threw herself at his legs. He fell sideways, smashing through the glass of the cabinet, narrowly avoiding the dollhouse inside.

Roaring, he clambered out, glass covering him in a thousand crystals. He grabbed Amber by the throat and threw her backwards, then reached down for the gun. In his fury, his clumsy attempt to snatch it up merely pushed it a few inches further away. Glen closed his hand around it, brought it up and fired three times, point-blank, into Shanks's chest.

The alarm cut off.

Shanks straightened up and kept going, toppling over backwards. He landed in a bed of glass and didn't move.

Amber stood up. Glen stared at the gun in his hand. The air carried a whine in the sudden silence.

"You okay?" Glen asked, his voice dull.

She nodded. "You did it."

"I did," said Glen. "I killed—"

Shanks sat up so suddenly it actually made Amber cry out in surprise. Glen tried to get another shot off, but Shanks tore the gun from his grip and pressed the barrel into his jaw.

Amber froze.

"You can't kill what's already dead," said Shanks. "Haven't you ever heard that?"

"I've always wanted to test that theory," said Milo from the door.

Shanks leaped up, grabbed Amber and put the gun to her temple. She felt her scales harden, but she doubted they'd be able to stop a bullet.

Milo walked slowly into the school, holding his gun in both hands, his head cocked slightly, aiming down the sights.

"Take one more step and I'll shoot," said Shanks. "Amber won't look so beautiful with half her face missing, now will she?"

Milo didn't lower the gun and didn't stop moving forward. "We're not letting you leave."

Shanks laughed. "Oh, Milo, I doubt that is your decision to make."

"You and me aren't on a first-name basis, Shanks. Let her go and I won't blow your head off. You remember what that feels like, don't you?"

Shanks's grip tightened. "I do indeed. But you may have noticed the last person to do that is now lying on the sidewalk outside with his life leaking away along with all that blood."

Milo gave a little smile. "I noticed, all right."

"Put the gun down. You know it can't hurt me."

"That's not exactly true, though, is it?" said Milo. "It can't kill you, no, but it can hurt you. Might even put you down long enough for us to take those cuffs off of Amber's wrists and put them on to yours."

"One more step," Shanks said. The cold steel pressed harder into Amber's head. "Take one more step."

Milo stopped walking.

"Good doggy," said Shanks. "Now toss the gun."

"Can't do that, I'm afraid. Against my upbringing."

"Toss it or your ridiculous Irish friend dies first."

"Glen is not my friend," said Milo. "And the moment that gun moves away from Amber's head, I pull my trigger. I'm a pretty good shot, I have to warn you."

"Then Amber will be the first to die."

"You kill her, I pull my trigger. Whatever you do, this trigger gets pulled."

"Unless I give up," said Shanks, "in which case you still put me back in that prison. You think you're giving me options, but they all end the same way. The only difference is how many of you I get to kill. Well, Milo? Which one will I start with? The rude Irish boy, or the red-skinned demon girl?"

Milo didn't answer for a moment, and then he spread his arms, taking his finger from the trigger. "You got me," he said. "Don't hurt either of them. I'm putting my gun down."

He laid his pistol on the floor and straightened up, his hands in the air.

Shanks shook his head. "I'm actually disappointed," he said. "I thought we were headed for a showdown."

Milo cracked a smile. "Like in *High Noon*, you mean?"

Shanks pushed Amber to her knees beside Glen, but kept his gun trained on Milo. "Something like that."

Milo didn't seem particularly worried. He was so casual, he shrugged. "Ah, I was always partial to *The Wild Bunch*, myself."

"Me too," said a voice behind them.

Shanks turned to see a shotgun levelled at his chest, and then Ella-May blasted him off his feet.

Shanks hit the ground, the front of his shirt obliterated. He rolled like a rag doll.

Milo holstered his pistol and ran to Amber, the handcuff key in his hand. She reverted to normal instantly, but Ella-May wasn't even looking at her.

Shanks chuckled, and stood.

Ella-May racked the shotgun's slide and blasted him again. And again. Each blast threw him further back, turned his clothes to rags, mutilated his flesh. But, every time he stood up, his skin was unmarked.

The fourth blast hurled him backwards through the door. Ella-May followed him out, and Milo, Amber and Glen followed.

Shanks got up, smiling. "You can shoot me all you want,"

he said, "you're not going to kill me. It's not going to change anything. Look at you. Ella-May Roosevelt. You got old."

"Maybe a few grey hairs here and there," Ella-May said.

"You look like them, you know. Your daughters. The ones I killed. Just like I killed your husband. You're not so smart now, are you, Ella-May? You led them to me all those years ago when you had your whole life ahead of you... and now look. You're old, with your life behind you, and I've taken every last one of your family from you."

"You took Christina," said Ella-May. "But that's all you're going to take from me."

Shanks narrowed his eyes and looked down at the street, where a blood-drenched Heather was helping a blood-drenched Teddy into the back of the cruiser.

"We Roosevelts are a hardy lot," Ella-May said, and blasted Shanks in the back.

For a moment, he flew, his spine arched and his arms flung wide. Then gravity found him, gripped him, yanked him down, hard, into the concrete steps. He bounced and twisted and tumbled and finally flipped, hitting the sidewalk with his head turned the wrong way round.

Milo walked down the steps after him, and calmly cuffed his hands behind his back as he lay there, unmoving.

A car pulled up and a man leaped out, carrying a black bag.

"Doc," Ella-May said in greeting as she handed the shotgun to Amber, "good of you to come so quickly. I need you to see to my husband and daughter while I drive us to Waukesha Memorial."

The doctor stared at the scene. "What the hell happened?"

"Heather has a stab wound to the abdomen," said Ella-May. "As far as I can tell, it missed the major organs. Teddy has had his throat cut. No arterial damage. Both have lost a lot of blood."

The doctor glanced down at Shanks. "What about this man?"

"He doesn't need your help," Ella-May said. She hurried down the steps and guided Heather into the passenger seat.

"Dad first," Heather said. She was corpse-pale and covered in sweat. "His pulse is barely there."

The doctor didn't ask any more questions. He climbed in the back and Ella-May got behind the wheel. She reversed away from the sidewalk and swung round.

"Guess you'll all be gone by the time I get back," she said through the open window.

"We will," said Amber.

"Good," said Ella-May, and she floored it, the cruiser's lights flashing.

Milo watched her go. "Passed her and Heather on my way here," he said. "Figured if she was half as tough as her daughter, giving her the shotgun might not be a bad idea."

Shanks moaned. His bones cracked and his neck straightened.

"Welcome back," said Milo, hauling him to his feet.

The streets were quiet in Springton. This didn't surprise Amber, not after the stories she'd been told. Tomorrow the townspeople would discuss the gunshots and the alarms and all this blood, and they'd let the theories settle in beside the legends and the myths they'd already stored up. She wondered what Walter S. Bryant would make of it all.

"What do we do with him?" asked Glen, keeping a respectful distance from Shanks as Milo forced him to walk.

"We're taking him with us," Milo said.

Shanks grunted out a laugh. "Are you inviting me to join your motley crew? I'll say yes, but only if I can be leader."

"Safest option," Milo said, ignoring Shanks and talking to Amber as they neared the Charger. "We can't leave him here, not after everything that's happened."

"We could chop him up," said Glen. "Or, I mean, you could chop him up. Bury him, maybe?"

"Maybe," said Milo. "But there'd always be the risk of someone digging him up by accident."

"I do have a tendency to return when you least expect it," said Shanks, chuckling.

They stopped at the rear of the Charger and Milo turned him so that Shanks's back was to the car. Amber noticed that all of their bags had been taken out of the trunk and were now in a pile on the ground.

The trunk opened silently, red light spilling out.

"So we'll take him with us," Milo said. "It'll be inconvenient for a few weeks, but the car will eventually digest him."

"What?" said Shanks, his face going slack, and then Milo shoved him backwards.

Amber's eyes played a trick on her then. For one crazy instant, it looked like Shanks was sucked into the trunk as the trunk itself *enveloped* him, the lid slamming closed like a great black jaw. Shanks kicked and battered and yelled from inside, and then all that noise turned down, like the Charger was slowly muting him.

Amber blinked. "Whoa."

Glen was frowning. "Did you see that? Did I see that? What the hell was that?"

Amber looked at Milo. "Were you serious? About the car digesting him?"

Milo trailed a hand lovingly over the Charger's contours. "She's a beast," he said.

25

THEY DROVE OUT OF SPRINGTON, parked behind a billboard, and Milo took out the maps while Amber examined Shanks's brass key.

"Could we use that?" Glen asked, now sharing the back seat with their bags. "It took Shanks wherever he wanted to go, right? Can we use it?"

"He said only he controls where it leads," Amber said, trying to read the tiny writing along its side. She gave up. "I doubt he'd want to help us." She tossed it into the glove compartment and took out the iPad, started tapping.

Glen let a few moments go by before speaking again.

"I don't mean to whinge," he said, "but I am really uncomfortable with there being a serial killer in the boot."

"In the what?" said Amber.

"Trunk," Milo translated.

"Can he get me?" Glen asked. "What's separating me from him? Is it this seat? Upholstery and foam? What if he still has his knife? Does he have his knife? We didn't take it from him, did we? He might be burrowing through to me right now."

"You're safe," said Milo absently. "The car will take care of him."

"And that's another thing I'm uncomfortable with," Glen began, but Amber interrupted.

"Cascade Falls," she said, list on the screen. "There's one in Virginia, one in Michigan…" She frowned. "No, wait, those are waterfalls. I think. Well, they might be waterfalls *and* towns. What one do you think Shanks was talking about?"

"Found it," said Milo, laying the map across the steering wheel. "Cascade Falls, Oregon."

"How do you know that's the one Gregory Buxton grew up in?"

"It feels right."

She raised an eyebrow. "*That's* what we're going on?"

"You're on the blackroads, Amber. You've got to learn to trust your instincts."

"If you're sure…" A moment later, she had called up images of a sleepy little town beside a lake. "The town of Cascade Falls. Less than ten thousand people. How long will it take us to get there?"

"Don't know," said Milo, folding away the map. "Two thousand miles… Four days, maybe. Get there some time on Saturday."

Amber adjusted the bracelets on her wrist, sneaking a peek at the scars there: 406 hours left. Take four days away from that, and it would leave her with…

She scrunched up her face.

"What's wrong?" Milo asked.

"Nothing," she mumbled. "Doing math."

Three hundred and ten hours. Which was… thirteen days,

or thereabouts. Just under two weeks. Fully aware that time was slipping away from her, and equally aware that there was nothing she could do about it, Amber nodded. "Okay then, we better get going. Unless you want to find somewhere to sleep?"

She was quietly pleased when Milo shook his head. "Too wired after all that drama. I'll drive until morning, then we'll pull in somewhere for a few hours. That okay with you?"

"That's cool."

"I'll be dead by Oregon," Glen said quietly from the back seat.

She turned, but his face was in shadow. "Aw, listen, Glen…"

"Maybe I should go somewhere fun for my last few days, and let you go on without me." She could see the edge of a sad smile. "You've been to Disney World, Amber – do you think that'd be a good place to die?"

"I've… never really thought about it."

"Maybe on one of the rollercoasters," Glen said. "Or on that other ride, what's the really annoying one?"

"It's a Small World."

"That's it. Go in alive, come out dead. That'd be something, wouldn't it? I wonder how many people die in theme parks every year."

"I don't know," said Amber. "But I do know that the chances of someone actually getting injured in the Orlando parks is, like, one in nine million or something."

"Wow. That's not bad. So someone dying on It's a Small World would be pretty rare, then?"

"Well, yeah… You're moving very slow and not a whole lot happens. Are you sure that's where you want to spend your last few days, though? Isn't it a bit…"

"Tacky?" said Milo.

"That wasn't what I was going to say. I was just wondering if it'd be better for you to spend time with your family."

"My family hates me," Glen said. "Why do you think I wanted to come here so badly?"

"I'm sure they don't *hate* you," said Amber.

"They might," said Milo.

Amber ignored him. "My parents want to kill me," she said. "I'm sure your parents aren't nearly as bad as *that*."

"Well, maybe not," said Glen, and he laughed, and Amber laughed, and then they remembered what they were laughing about and they both stopped.

"You two are a pair of idiots," said Milo, and he pulled out on to the road and drove.

They took the interstate west for a few hours, then slipped off on to the back roads. They drove through Sigourney, then Delta, and passed a sign for a town called What Cheer. Farmland and electricity pylons flashing by almost hypnotically. Amber started taking a mental note of the populations listed on each sign, testing her dreadful maths skills by adding them up in her head – 2,059, 328, 646... By the time they were in sight of Knoxville, Iowa, she was going to tell Milo that in the last hour they had passed 15,568 people, then she decided not to. It just wasn't that interesting.

They had breakfast at the Downtown Diner, then slept for a bit in the car. Exhaustion pulled Amber down deep into a dreamless sleep. Even her subconscious was too tired to play.

When she awoke, she cracked one eye open. Milo sat behind the wheel, looking through the windshield, unmoving. He wasn't blinking. His face was slack. She wondered if he slept with his eyes open, like a shark. She moved slightly and he turned to her, and that blank expression was wiped away like it had never really been there. He nodded to her, and started the car, and Glen sat up suddenly in the back.

"What?" He blinked. "Oh. Sorry. We're off again, then." When neither Amber nor Milo answered, he nodded to himself. "Another few hours closer to my death."

"Glen—"

"No, Amber. No. Don't try to comfort me. I'm beyond comfort. There's nothing you can do, nothing you can say, which would ease the weight I feel on my soul. It's heavy. It's so heavy. How much does a life weigh? Can you answer me that? No, I don't think you can. So thank you for your effort, Amber, and I truly mean that. But you won't see a smile from me today."

Amber felt bad. She had been about to tell him to shut up.

"You're not going to die," said Milo.

"Death is tapping me on the shoulder as I sit here."

"Nothing's tapping you anywhere. You're not going to die because we're going to stop off at The Dark Stair and you can deliver the Deathmark to this Abigail, whoever she may be, and then you can leave us alone."

Amber frowned. "You know where it is?"

Glen shoved his head between them. "You know where The Dark Stair is? You knew where it was all this time and you didn't tell me?"

Milo pulled out on to the road and started driving. "I wasn't sure if it'd be on our way. As it turns out, it is."

"Where is it?" asked Amber.

"Salt Lake City," said Milo. "It's a bar for people like... well, like us, I guess. People on the blackroads."

"Wait, wait, *wait*," said Glen. "If it *wasn't* in the direction you happen to be heading, would you have told me? Or would you have just let me die?"

"I'd have told you."

Glen gaped. "You'd have let me die!"

"I'd have told you," Milo said again. "I couldn't tell you before now because Amber's parents might have found you if you went off alone."

"I have less than four days to live, Milo! What if Shanks had told us that Gregory Buxton lived east instead of west? What then?"

"Then I'd have put you on a Greyhound."

Glen glanced at Amber. "A dog?"

"A bus."

He turned to Milo again. "And what if that Greyhound got a flat tyre? Or was in an accident? Or I got delayed somehow? I get lost *very* easily, I'll have you know! If you'd told me where The Dark Stair was at the very beginning, I'd have already delivered the Deathmark and I wouldn't be dying right now! Admit it! You don't care if I live or die, do you?"

Milo thought about it for a few seconds. "Not really," he said.

Glen gasped again.

They drove for another ten minutes without anyone saying a word, but Amber had to ask. She just had to.

"This isn't going to throw us off schedule too much, is it?"

"Ohh!" cried Glen, and Amber winced. "Oh, I'm *sorry* if my *impending doom* is throwing you off schedule, Amber! I'm sorry if my *imminent demise* is inconveniencing you! Tell you what, you let me out here. I'll roll over by the side of the road and die quietly without *causing anyone too much bother!*"

Milo waited until he had finished, then answered. "It shouldn't," he said.

"Are you still talking about this?" Glen cried.

"Salt Lake City is that weird place, isn't it?" said Amber. "Run by the Amish, or something."

"Founded by Mormons," said Milo. "And yeah, they're pretty strict with their liquor laws and they don't look too kindly on public profanity, but we're going to be well-behaved and we're not going to drink, now are we? Besides, The Dark Stair isn't exactly typical of Salt Lake City. It isn't typical of anywhere, for that matter."

"Do you know it well?"

Milo shook his head. "Been in there twice, for no more than half an hour apiece. There's a lot of kids running around. I remember thinking how weird that was. We'll spend tonight in Nebraska somewhere, get to Salt Lake City tomorrow afternoon or thereabouts. From there it's another eight hundred miles to Buxton's home town. It's Tuesday now — we're still on track to get to Cascade Falls by Saturday."

Amber nodded. "Okay. Yeah, okay."

"Bet if I died back here you wouldn't even notice," Glen muttered, but they ignored him.

They drove on flat roads through flat lands. A few trees here and there, though paltry things, and lonesome. Telegraph poles linked hands over green fields and brown, and carried on into the wide, never-ending distance. A train on the tracks, its carriages the colour of rust and wine, names and slogans painted on the side in indecipherable graffiti.

They stopped at an Amoco gas station outside of a town called McCook, and Amber and Glen went in to use the restrooms and get sandwiches while Milo waited in the Charger. It was just after two and it was warm. The smell of gasoline was on the air.

"How much do you know about Milo?" Glen asked while they were waiting to pay for the food. The old man in front of them was having trouble pulling his wallet from his sagging pants.

Amber shrugged. "I know I'm paying him a lot of money to get me where I need to go."

"So you don't know anything about him?"

She sighed. "No, Glen, I don't."

The old man got his wallet halfway out before it snagged on the corner of his pocket. Amber watched, with an interest that surprised her, the tug of war that followed.

"Remember that story I told you," Glen said, "about the Ghost of the Highway?"

"I don't want to talk about this."

He nodded, satisfied. "Then you suspect it, too."

"I don't suspect anything."

"Milo's the Ghost."

"Glen, seriously, drop it, okay? We've been driving for hours and I am sore and cranky."

"He's a serial killer, Amber."

"Don't be ridiculous."

The old man turned slowly, looked at them with frowning eyes. Amber gave him a pleasant smile, and waited for him to turn back round.

"What's ridiculous about it?" Glen asked softly. "He uses a car instead of a knife, but he's still a serial killer. And that isn't any ordinary car. You know it isn't. It's…" He leaned in closer, and his voice became a whisper. "It's possessed."

224

"Glen, you sound so dumb right now."

"You saw what it did. It swallowed Shanks. That wasn't my imagination running away with me, no matter how much I try to convince myself. It swallowed him. It's possessed."

The old man finally paid and moved off, and they stepped up to the cash register.

"Any gas?" the bored girl asked.

"Nope," said Amber, and paid.

They walked outside, looked across the forecourt to the Charger.

"We're at a gas station and he's not even filling the tank," said Glen. "How many times has he had to stop for petrol? Twice? Three times? Travelling all this way, he's had to stop for petrol three times? Do you know how much fuel a car like that burns?"

"So this car has good fuel economics. So what?"

"Aren't you wondering what else it runs on? He said it'll digest Shanks. How many other people has it digested? And look how clean it is. It's always clean and I've never seen him wash it. It's like it cleans itself. And what's the deal with him only being able to drive it eight hours a day?"

"On *average*," said Amber. "He's driven it longer."

"But what's the deal? Why that rule? Why eight hours? Because it's road safe? Or maybe it's got something to do with him not wanting to push his car too hard or else it'll get *tired*."

She turned to him. "Fine, Glen, I'll play this game. What does it mean? Huh? What does it all add up to?"

He hesitated before answering. "I think the Charger's alive."

"Oh my God..."

"Don't look at me like that. It's not just a car, is it? It's more than that. You know it is. You got him a sandwich, right? What's the betting he's not going to eat it?"

"And what will that prove? He's not hungry?"

"He doesn't eat when he's driving," said Glen. "I don't think he sleeps when he's behind the wheel, either. Did he sleep this morning? Did you see him sleep? I didn't."

She rubbed her eyes. "I was sleeping myself, okay? I didn't see much of anything."

"What about going to the toilet? We needed to pee – why didn't Milo?"

"Dude, I'm really not going to talk about anyone's bathroom habits."

"We've asked him to pull over so that *we* could pee, like, twenty times so far."

"You've got a bladder problem."

"I pee, you pee, he doesn't pee. Have you seen him pee?"

"No, Glen, I have not seen Milo pee. What the *hell* are you talking about?"

"I think the Charger sustains him. I think it takes his… y'know, his waste—"

"Ew."

"—and uses it, and when he's behind the wheel his body doesn't need to function the way our bodies do."

"That is disgusting. And stupid."

"He said the Charger would digest Shanks. That means some part of it is organic."

"He was being metaphorical, you idiot."

"Are you sure? He's the Ghost, Amber. He's a serial killer, and he's bonded to the Charger. Maybe he doesn't do it anymore, maybe he's reformed, I don't know. But you said he took it out of storage for the first time in twelve years? What if it's like an addiction? He's stayed away from it for all this time and he hasn't needed to kill. But now he's back using it again. How long before it takes him over? How long before he becomes the Ghost of the Highway?"

"This is a stupid conversation and it is ending right now."

She walked across the forecourt, black asphalt hot even through the soles of her shoes. Glen kept up.

"It swallowed Shanks. It's alive. You know what I think? I think the reason he doesn't turn on the radio is because he's scared of what the car might *say*."

She spun round to him. "If you're not happy with our mode of transport, you don't have to travel with us. No one's asking you to."

Glen looked her dead in the eye. "I'm not leaving you alone with him."

"He's not going to hurt me."

"You don't know him."

"Neither do you," she said, and stalked back to the Charger.

She got in, slamming the door. After a moment, she got out again, held the door open while Glen got in the back. Then she retook her seat and slammed the door a second time.

"Everything all right?" Milo asked.

"Fine," said Amber. "Here's your sandwich."

He took it. "Thanks. I'll have it later."

He turned the key and the Charger roared to life. It rolled smoothly across the loose gravel to the road as an eighteen-wheeler thundered by. Milo watched it go. While he was distracted, Amber reached for the radio.

Her fingers hovered over the dial. One turn. One turn, one

twist, and music would fill the car, or static, or someone complaining about something, or commercials, or preaching… or a voice. A voice unlike any she'd ever heard. The voice of the car. The dark voice of the dark car.

She dropped her hand, and the Charger pulled out on to the road, and they drove on.

26

They got to Salt Lake City the next day. Glen stared out at the snow-capped mountains that rose up behind the gleaming buildings like the backdrop of some insane science-fiction movie.

"They're *massive*," he breathed. "Are those the Rockies?"

"Yeah," Amber replied sarcastically, "because every mountain range in America is the Rockies."

"They actually *are* part of the Rockies," said Milo, and Amber glowered. "That's the Wasatch Range there."

"We don't have anything like this in Ireland," Glen said. "Like, we have some awesome mountains, like the Sugar Loaf, and MacGillycuddy's Reeks, and the Giant's Causeway up north, but... but that's less of a mountain and more of a... bit of rock. Are we anywhere near the Grand Canyon?"

Amber was pretty sure she knew this. "No," she said, with a slight hesitation in her voice.

Milo gave her a nod, and she relaxed.

Glen lost interest in the mountains pretty fast, and started paying attention to the streets. "This place doesn't seem that weird," he said. "Apart from their remarkably straight roads, that is. What did you say they were? Scientologists?"

"Mormons," said Milo.

"Which ones believe in the aliens?"

"Scientologists," said Amber.

"I'd love to have been a Scientologist," Glen said, "but I was never that good at science. I'll say one thing for the Mormons, though – they love their straight roads, don't they? I doubt Scientologists would have been able to build roads as straight as these, what with believing in aliens and all. Theirs would be all bendy."

Amber frowned. "Why?"

"Well, because they'd be looking up all the time, wouldn't they? Or maybe they'd try to build their cities around alien symbols, like crop circles, y'know? That'd be cool. Wouldn't be straight, though, and it'd be hell getting from one place to the other if all their roads were circular. The Mormons had it right, I think. Straight lines. That's the way to go. Who are the people with the beards?"

"Muslims?"

"No, the beards and the funny hats and building barns and stuff."

"The Amish," said Amber.

"And where do they control?"

"Nowhere. I mean, they have their communities, but they don't build cities or anything."

"They'd probably be better known if they built cities."

"Yeah. I'll mention that to them."

A few minutes later, they pulled in across the street from a run-down bar with a faded sign out front that showed a picture of a staircase. They crossed, and Milo pushed open the door. The place was as quiet as it was empty. By the looks of things, no one had been in here in years.

Milo didn't say anything, though, so Amber kept her mouth shut, and for once Glen wasn't yattering on about something. They came to a set of stairs and started down them.

Within moments, they were slowly sinking into ever-increasing gloom, and still no music or voices, no clink of glasses or sounds of laughter. They went further down, and further, and, just when Amber thought they couldn't possibly go any further, the wooden stairs turned to stone, and still they went down.

It was cold now, and pitch dark. The wall that Amber brushed against occasionally was now stone like the steps, cold and hard and wet. And then suddenly it wasn't there anymore, and when Amber went to touch it she reached too far and nearly toppled. Glen grabbed her, pulled her back from the edge.

All three of them stopped.

"We should go back," she said, though her voice sounded small and distant, like they were in some enormous cavern.

"Just a little further," Milo said. "Put your hand on my shoulder."

She did that, and Glen put his hand on hers, and they resumed their descent.

Gradually, Amber became aware of the darkness lightening to gloom again. Then a colour. Red. A hazy red. She heard music. And voices.

There was a wall beside her again. She could see it. It was painted a dark yellow, almost gold, and it blocked off the cold. Her fingers trailed over old fliers for old singers and old bands, her nails riding the bumps and the tears.

The stairs were wooden again, a dark wood, worn smooth by footfall. The music was fast – piano and trumpet music, the kind they used to dance to back in the 1930s or 1940s. The ceiling was low, and Milo and Glen had to duck their heads. Amber didn't. She kept her head up and her eyes open, as the bar was laid bare before her.

The place was packed. People drank and smoked and talked, danced and sang. The bar itself took up the centre of the room, the beating heart of the establishment.

"I'm too young to be in here," Amber said.

Glen looked nervous. "I think I am, too. Hey, no, look – they have children in here, like Milo said."

Amber counted maybe half a dozen kids wandering around.

"Should people even be smoking in a room that has children?" Glen asked. "I don't know if they should be doing that. They shouldn't even be smoking, anyway. Aren't they breaking the law?"

"Stay behind me and say nothing," said Milo, and led the way to the bar. The man serving was big, with a beard that spread from clavicle to just under his eyes. The sleeves of his white shirt were rolled back over strangely hairless forearms. "Hey," Milo said in greeting.

The big man looked up at Milo, then at Glen, and then at Amber, much as she tried to hide. But, instead of ordering her out or asking for ID, he said, "Three beers, then. Take a seat."

Glen beamed, and went immediately to a free table. Milo shrugged at Amber, and she followed him to a table near the back wall. Glen frowned, and joined them.

"What was wrong with my table?" he asked. Milo didn't answer.

The barmaid came over with their drinks on a tray. Amber

was pretty sure they weren't called barmaids anymore, but she couldn't for the life of her think what they *were* called. Besides, barmaid suited this place.

"Here you go," the barmaid said, setting their drinks down.

"Thank you," said Milo, putting a note on the tray. "I wonder if you can help us find someone. Our travelling companion—"

"Friend," Glen cut in.

"—is looking for someone. Abigail. If you can point her out to us, the tip's all yours."

The barmaid smiled. "Oh, no need, sir. Abigail's already found you."

Amber frowned. "She has?"

The barmaid walked away, and out of the crowd a little blonde girl in a pretty dress appeared.

"Hello."

"Hi," Amber said, forcing a confused smile on to her face. "What's your name?"

"I'm Abigail," said the girl, smiling back. "I'm the owner of the bar."

Glen paled. "*You're* Abigail?"

Milo frowned. "You're the *owner*?"

"Yep." She giggled. "Yeah, everyone has that look on their face when they find out. It's a funny look." She smiled again at Amber. "By the way, I *love* your horns."

Shock surging in her chest, Amber's hands went immediately to her head. No horns. Everything was normal.

Abigail looked at Milo, looked at him with eyes that saw more than what was there, and she smiled again. Amber wondered what she could see.

Lastly, Abigail looked at Glen. "You've got the Deathmark."

"Uh," said Glen.

"You're here to kill me, are you?"

Glen swallowed thickly. "No?"

Abigail nodded. "That's what I thought."

"I'm sorry," said Glen, "I didn't know you were a... a kid. Now I feel bad. I feel, like, really bad. I was told you'd killed people. Aw man. Now what do I do?"

"I can help you, if you want," said Abigail.

Glen brightened. "You can remove it?"

"Oh yes," the little girl replied. "It's quite easy."

She tilted her head, and the people around them surged, slamming Glen's head down on the table while they pressed a knife to Amber's throat. She froze.

Someone else had a knife to Milo's throat. "He really isn't a friend of ours," he said.

They gripped Glen's arm, straightening it out on the table, and a big man walked up, holding a butcher's cleaver.

"No!" Glen screamed. "No, no, please!"

"Don't be so silly!" Abigail giggled. "He's only going to cut your hand off. It's not like you're going to lose your entire arm!"

The cold blade pressed deeper into Amber's throat, like its wielder knew how much she wanted to shift into demon form.

"Please don't do this," said Glen, trying to sound reasonable. "I didn't know. I didn't know you were Abigail. If I'd known you were a little girl, I would have said no."

The big man tapped the cleaver on Glen's wrist a few times to test his aim, and then raised the cleaver high above his head.

Glen abandoned all attempts at appearing reasonable and started screaming again. "Oh God please don't do this please

234

don't cut my hand off I need it I didn't know I didn't know the old man didn't tell me!"

Abigail held up a finger, and the man with the cleaver paused. She leaned closer. "What old man?"

Glen gasped. "The… the old man who passed the Deathmark on to me. He just said this was intended for someone who deserved to die. Said you'd killed people. Lots of people."

Abigail pursed her lips. "Did you ask his name?"

"No," said Glen.

Abigail shrugged. "Pity." She looked at the big man with the cleaver, was about to issue an order when Glen continued.

"But he had grey hair! And he was small! And Spanish! And he had a big grey beard!"

Abigail laughed. "*Lautaro Soto* asked you to kill me? That is so cute! He's not Spanish, though, he's Mexican. Or he *was*. He's dead now, right?"

Glen nodded. "Died as soon as he passed the Deathmark to me."

"He always was a sneaky one," said Abigail. "Hey, guys, you can let him up now."

Abigail's people released their grip. The guy with the cleaver looked disappointed. The knife was taken from Amber's throat and, like this happened every day, people around them went back to whatever they had been doing.

"Are you still going to chop my hand off?" Glen asked meekly.

Abigail laughed again. "No, you ninny! Everything has changed! This isn't the work of my enemies – this is Lautaro, one of my oldest, dearest, most recently departed friends."

"So… so you'll let me go?"

"Absolutely. So long as you deliver that Deathmark to someone else instead."

Glen's eyes narrowed. "But... but I thought it'd only work on you."

"Nope, it'll work on anyone."

"So I could have just given this away at any stage up until now?" Glen said, his voice rising. "Why didn't anyone tell me that? Why didn't the old man tell me that?"

"Lautaro probably didn't want you wasting it on some random person on the street," Abigail said. "But the guy I want you to pass it on to, he really deserves it. His name's Ralphie. He's a complete meanie, Glen, he really is. Him and his brother. Ralphie and Ossie. Oh, they are meanies. Drug dealers, too, and they have been known to kill a person for money. They're in on this for sure – they did everything Lautaro told them to. Make sure you kill Ralphie, though. He's the smart one." She paused. "Admittedly that's not saying a lot."

"Why did they want to kill you?" Amber asked.

Abigail shrugged. "Why does anyone want to kill anyone? It's just a thought that occurs, isn't it? Things happen and the thought occurs. They used to work for me, ages ago. Then they did something stupid, and I said things I regretted, but by then it was too late. They went and found God – I imagine He was between the sofa cushions, I'm always losing things there – and they hooked up with Lautaro. He was a preacher – he'd been after me for years. He was convinced I was the spawn of the Devil, which is just rude. Lautaro was the kind to look the other way when it came to Ralphie and Ossie dealing drugs and killing people, but still believe he was fighting the good fight when it came to me. Together they must have come to the conclusion that it would be a neat idea to kill me."

"So how did the old man end up in Ireland?" Glen asked.

"Educated guess?" said Abigail. "They figured out the Deathmark would be the only thing that could kill me, but making one isn't like reaching into a box of cereal and pulling out the cheap plastic toy, you know? Real, actual work is involved. Lautaro must have known someone in Ireland with the skill to do it, so over he goes, they make the Deathmark, and Lautaro intends to carry it back to America with him. Only he's an old man, and old men are frail, and the Deathmark can wear you down and wear you out if you're old and frail." She shrugged. "They miscalculated. It happens. So, right before he dies, he finds a healthy young man like you, Glen, and he gets you to agree to carry it over the ocean and use it to kill me. To kill... *me*."

Abigail's voice went very cold and very quiet.

Then that happy smiled returned. "But look at us! We're taking those meanies' plan and we're turning it back on them! How surprised are they going to be when you turn up on their doorstep, Glen? Can you imagine the look on their faces?"

"I... I don't know if I'm up to this," said Glen.

"Not on your own," Milo said. "But with our help you can do it. We'll make sure."

Glen blinked. "You'd... you'd do that for me?"

"Of course."

Glen started to smile, then stopped. "It's because you want me to go away, isn't it?"

"Of course."

Scowling, Glen turned back to Abigail. "I don't think I can do this. I can't kill someone. I thought I could, I thought I'd just pass it on to you, but... I can't. A few days ago, I shot someone – a bad man. For a moment, I thought I'd killed him. It was dreadful. He was a serial killer, but I felt dreadful, anyway.

I'm sorry, I just don't have it in me. But you have lots of people here that work for you, right? I can pass the Deathmark on to them and they can kill your friend for you."

Abigail shook her head. "The Deathmark can be passed on once, and no more. Lautaro Soto passed it to you. Whoever you pass it to next – they die. No loopholes. No exceptions. And, by the looks of it, Glen, you don't have an awful lot of time left."

Glen looked at his hand, at the black trail that was swirling faster. "I know."

"But, lucky for you, Ralphie and Ossie don't live far. Isn't that lucky?"

Glen stood up, clutching his hand. "We have to go! We have to go now!"

"Sit down, sit down," said Abigail. "I don't know where they'd be this early in the evening. I know where they'll be tonight, though."

"We can't wait that long," Glen said.

"Of course you can. You stay here and I'll be back when I know more. This is a busy bar and I am a busy lady. Enjoy the atmosphere."

She gave them another smile, swung her feet off the chair, and hopped off and walked away.

Glen hesitated, then sat back down, and Milo leaned in. "You *accepted* the Deathmark?"

"Did I?" said Glen. "Oh right, yeah. Yeah, the old guy may have said something about… uh, what was it? *In order to pass the Deathmark to another person, that other person has to willingly accept it. Or* something."

Amber glared at Glen. "You said you were *attacked*."

Glen looked hurt. "I was!"

"You said you were attacked by a *creature*."

Glen nodded. "Or a creature-like person, yes."

"I'm sorry? What? What's a creature-like person?"

"It's a, I mean, it's a person that looks like a creature, obviously. Like a, y'know… an old person."

"You said *creature*."

"I *meant* old person."

"And you accepted the Mark?" said Milo.

"I didn't know what it was!" Glen said. "This old guy comes out of the shadows and attacks me—"

"Attacks you?"

"—or talks to me, or whatever, and he says he's about to die, will I take this Mark of Death to its intended target, a terrible person called Abigail who's been hiding in this bar in America… What am I supposed to say? No?"

"Yes," said Amber. "You're supposed to say no."

"Well, I'd say no *now*," said Glen. "Obviously, I'd say no *now*. I'm in possession of all the facts *now*. But back then I wasn't. And he seemed so harmless and he… he reminded me a little of my granddad."

"Oh, for God's sake."

"What? My granddad was very important to me growing up."

"So just because he reminded you of your dearly departed grandfather—"

"Oh no, granddad's not dead. He's just living in Cork."

Amber glared. "He told you to kill someone in America and you said yes."

"My granddad?"

"*Soto.*"

Glen paused. "I suppose I did say yes, yeah. But I'd never

been to America and I'd always wanted to go. This seemed like the perfect opportunity."

"You," said Milo, "are an incredibly stupid person."

Glen slumped in his seat. "Whatever."

Amber stood, and Glen's mouth dropped open.

"You're abandoning me?"

"I'm going to the restroom."

"Oh. Uh. Carry on."

Sighing, she walked away from the table. She found the restroom, which turned out to be delightfully clean, and on her return trip she passed the dance floor. She saw Abigail, flanked by two burly members of staff, pointing to a woman doing her best to avoid eye contact. The staff members walked up either side of the woman, said a few words. The woman shook her head stiffly. The people she'd been talking to, her friends, took their drinks and moved away. She watched them go, pleading with her eyes.

The staff members took a firm grip of her elbows, led her to a room in the back. They nudged her gently through the open door and she immediately turned, tried to leave, tried to talk, but she was crying too much to get the words out.

Abigail was joined by the other children. The way they smiled sent actual shivers down Amber's spine. Six of them, six beautiful little children, walking for the room now. The staff members moved away. The woman stepped back, hands up to keep the children at a distance. Her knees buckled. She was in hysterics now. The little boys took thin knives from their pockets and the little girls took thin knives from their purses, and they went into that room and the woman started screaming and the door closed.

Amber hurried back to their table. "The kids are killers," she said, interrupting whatever Glen was saying to Milo. "The kids," she said again. "The children. Abigail. I just saw them go after a woman with knives in their hands."

Glen frowned. "Seriously?"

"Yes, Glen. Seriously."

"They're actual killers, like? Actual murderers?" The moment he said it, panic set in. "We have to get out of here. We have to leave. Don't we? Who goes first? We can't make it obvious that we're leaving."

"We're not going anywhere," said Milo.

"Did you not hear what she said?"

"We're waiting for Abigail's instructions. What she does here in the privacy of her own bar is her own business. It's got nothing to do with us."

"You don't seem surprised," Amber said to Milo. "About the killer kids."

"Of course not," he replied. "I recognised her the moment I saw her."

"You know her?"

"I've read about her. She's Abigail Gateling. Killed her entire family when she was eight years old. She was shipped off to an insane asylum while the authorities were figuring out what to do with her. She escaped the asylum and knocked on the first door she came to. She was found the next morning, drenched in blood."

Glen gaped. "And she's loose?"

"She's dead," said Milo. "This all happened in 1932."

Amber stared at him. Glen started crying. It kind of ruined the moment.

27

THE CHARGER WAS WAITING for them when they emerged from the bar. Night had fallen.

Milo took one of the maps from the glove compartment, planning their route from the directions Abigail had given them. When he was satisfied, he folded the map and passed it to Amber, and they started driving.

Glen sat in the back and didn't say much. If everything went according to plan, he would be free of the Deathmark by the end of the night. If everything went according to plan, he would be responsible for somebody's death.

The further they moved from the city, the wider the spaces became. Houses had room to breathe, and they drew in big, deep breaths. Thirsty lawns became crabgrass and scrub bush. The landscape exploded outwards, rearing up into mountains that loomed dark against the night sky. The roads became wide trails of dust.

They drove for another half an hour, until they had left all trace of civilisation behind, and Milo pulled over. Leaving the engine running, he opened up a map.

"Are we lost?" Glen asked.

"No, we are not," said Milo. "Just figuring out where to go. They should be around here somewhere, I just can't—"

Headlights lit them up from behind and something rammed into them. Glen screamed and so did Amber, and Milo thrust the map at her and while the creased paper filled her vision the Charger was already leaping forward, roaring. The light from behind was blinding and all Amber could hear was the growl of engines, and Milo twisted the wheel and the car spun, and something thundered by, clipping the driver's side mirror.

The Charger spun full circle and came to a stop, trembling with suppressed violence. Amber shoved the map down to her feet and only then did she become aware of Glen's curses. On the dusty road ahead of them, a dark-coloured pickup truck circled round, catching them with all of its many spotlights. Amber squinted.

"Seat belts on," Milo said in a quiet voice.

Amber knew hers was already fastened, but she checked anyway.

"There are no seat belts back here," Glen said, panicking. "Why are there no seat belts?"

"Lie on the floor," Milo said.

Glen whimpered, and slithered out of sight. He pulled the bags down on top of him.

The pickup shot forward and Milo kicked the Charger into reverse. Amber held on. The pickup's lights filled the windshield. Milo drove with one hand on the wheel, the other on Amber's seat, looking over his shoulder.

He braked suddenly, yanked the wheel, and the Charger spun again, throwing Amber against the door, but the pickup clipped them and the whole car jolted sideways. Milo's hand worked the gears and his boot stomped on the gas, and the Charger spat up dirt and dust and it was back under control and back on the road, the pickup right behind it.

"Who the hell is that?" Glen screeched from beneath all the bags.

Amber braced one hand against the dash and pressed herself back into her seat. To look behind was to be blinded, so she kept her eyes on the road ahead, the dirt trail almost indistinguishable at this speed from the land through which it cut. The pickup hit them and the Charger jumped and Milo fought to keep it under control. They were hit again and Milo hissed under his breath and the rear of the car started to slide sideways. The pickup slammed into Amber's side. She screamed, the scream barely audible over the roar of the engines and the shriek of twisting metal.

The Charger spun to a rocking stop. The engine cut out.

In the relative silence, Amber could hear Dacre Shanks, shouting from the trunk. His shouts were slowly muted.

The pickup looped round. For some reason, that loop seemed so casual, so playful, that it made Amber's anger rise in her throat.

Milo turned the key. The Charger spluttered.

"Oh God," Glen said.

The pickup came back at them, picking up speed.

The Charger spluttered again.

Amber pulled at the door handle, but the lock came down, sealing her inside.

She whipped her head round to Milo as he turned the key

a third time. The Charger roared, its headlights burning a devilish, hellish red.

It lunged out of the pickup's path a moment before impact, turned with a spray of pebbles and sand, and now they were speeding behind the pickup, closing in to slam into its tail lights. The pickup wobbled, almost hit a lonely tree, and Milo put his foot down. The Charger came up on the truck's right side. The pickup swerved into it. Milo responded in kind. The two vehicles battered at each other for a quarter of a mile or more, and then the pickup pulled away in front as the trail narrowed between two hills.

Milo commanded the Charger like he was a part of it. It was hard to see in the darkness and the quick bursts of light, but he seemed to be almost smiling. He looked darker, like the colour of the steering wheel was soaking into his hands and spreading through his skin. His jaw seemed more angular. The pickup's tail lights somehow reflected in his eyes, making them glow red. And were those horns beginning to protrude through his hair?

The pickup tried to get away and the Charger rammed into it once again. Milo's smile broadened and, when he opened his mouth, red light shone out between his white teeth.

Something bright arced in the sky. Amber tried to shout a warning, but it was too late, and the brightness exploded across the hood and flames covered the windshield.

Milo twisted the wheel and there was a new noise, a rapid popping, like fireworks. It took Amber a moment to realise they were being shot at. The bullets punctured the side of the car and cracked the rear windshield and Milo grunted, twisted in his seat. The Charger hit something and bounced and suddenly the sound of the road beneath them vanished, and they dropped, and Amber screamed and Glen screamed, and they were nothing but a fireball dropping into darkness—

—and then they crunched into the slope and Milo wrenched the wheel, using the brakes and gas pedal to propel them, slalom-like, round the trees and boulders that dotted the hillside.

The slope flattened out and the Charger crunched into the scrub and the earth and then rolled to a stop on a narrow little road. The last of the flames died on the hood.

Milo turned his head to Amber. The red glow faded from his eyes, as whatever was lighting him from within slowly extinguished. She stared at him. Didn't say anything.

"Glen," he said gruffly. "You okay?"

"No," said Glen, clambering slowly up. "Is it over? What happened?"

"We were led into an ambush."

"They knew we were coming?" he asked, and peered out. "Are we safe?"

Milo got out without answering. Amber unlocked her door, but had to lean back and kick it to get it open.

The Charger was wrecked. The hood, where the Molotov cocktail had hit, was a blistered mess of crumpled metal. Both doors were badly dented, the frame on the passenger side buckled. The rear windshield had two bullet holes in it. The driver's side had plenty more.

"Sorry about your car," Amber said dully.

Milo circled it, limping. The left leg of his jeans was soaked in something dark.

"You've been shot," said Amber. Then, louder, "Oh my God, you've been shot!"

"Just a graze," Milo responded. "I'll be all right by morning."

She ran over to him. "You've been shot, Milo! Look at the blood! You're leaving bloody footprints behind you!"

"I'll be all right by morning," he repeated, removed his arm from her grip, and got back behind the wheel.

Amber would have stayed where she was, but the adrenaline was wearing off and now she was feeling the cold. She got back in the car.

"What do we do now?" Glen asked.

"Get the blankets out," said Milo. "We're spending the night here."

"What if they come for us? They have machine guns."

"The car's not going anywhere," said Milo, "and neither are we. If they come for us, they come for us."

"And you expect us to *sleep*?"

"You do what you want," said Milo. "But me, I'm tired, and I want to close my eyes."

And, for the first time since Amber had known him, Milo did just that behind the wheel of his car.

There were moments, in the time it took her to fall asleep, where she thought death had claimed Milo without her noticing, and each time she'd freeze, coldness spreading from her heart until she heard, very faintly, the sound of his breathing.

Very faintly.

28

WHEN SHE WOKE, it was morning, and the sun was doing its best to get rid of the chill that the night had brought. Milo was outside, walking in a circle. He was wearing new jeans, and his limp was barely noticeable.

Keeping the blanket wrapped round her, Amber pulled the handle of the door. It swung open smoothly. She got out, stretched.

"How's the leg?" she asked.

Milo stopped walking. "Good," he answered. "It was just a graze, like I said."

He looked normal. Normal eyes, normal mouth, normal skin. No horns. He was lying, though, and, by the way he was looking at her, he was daring her to call him on it. But she didn't. He was entitled to his secrets. He'd earned that much from her.

She turned to get back into the car, and actually took a step back in surprise. "Jesus."

The Charger's hood was unblemished. Its dents were gone. No bullet holes and no scratches. It gleamed in the morning sun, not even a trace of dust on its glorious blackness.

"Turns out the damage wasn't that bad," said Milo.

Amber grunted as Glen sat up in the back and yawned. Milo got in, slid the key into the ignition and twisted.

The Charger woke immediately with a deep and healthy rumble.

It took half an hour, but they found their way back to the road they'd been on, and fifteen minutes after that they crested a dusty hill, and stopped. Below them stood a ramshackle house that looked like it had been built in stages by very different builders who only had a crooked eye in common. Parked outside was a badly damaged pickup truck.

"That's them!" Glen said needlessly.

Milo shared a look with Amber, and inched the Charger forward. He put it in neutral and turned off the engine. They rolled down the gentle hill, accompanied only by the crunch of wheels on dirt. They got to the bottom and Milo steered them behind the pickup, and stopped.

He got out with his gun in his hand, and as he attached his holster to his belt Amber and Glen climbed out after him. Amber kept low, remembering the sound of the machine gun from last night. Glen kept even lower.

They moved quickly but quietly to the house. Milo peered through the window for a few moments. Satisfied, he went to the door and got ready to kick. Something in his face changed, though, and instead he leaned forward, tried the handle. It turned, and the door opened, and he shrugged. Straightening, he holstered his gun and walked in, Amber and Glen at his heels.

The living room was barely habitable. An old TV sat huddled on a crate, cornered by a dirty couch and a filthy armchair.

They walked straight through to the kitchen, where two men sat eating cereal. Ralphie and Ossie, presumably. The brothers looked at them, frowning, like their arrival just didn't compute. The spoon in the bigger one's hand hovered halfway to his waiting mouth. He was a tall, stout man, his curly hair cut tight, fully dressed in jeans and an oil-stained T-shirt. The smaller one had his arm jammed inside the cereal box. He had a beard and a stupid Mohawk, and he only wore an old pair of boxers.

"Boys," said Milo, nodding at them.

The smaller man looked at all of them, one at a time. At no stage did comprehension dawn on his overfed face.

"You're the people from last night," said the bigger guy.

"Yes, we are," said Milo. "You're Ralphie, am I right? We were told you were the smart one." He turned to the smaller man, the one still wearing the look of dumb confusion. "And that makes you Ossie. So which one of you was in the pickup, and which one of you had the gun?"

"I don't know what you're talking about," said Ralphie, putting his spoon back in the bowl.

"That pickup outside says otherwise."

"That ain't ours. You can't prove nothing."

"Then it's a good thing we're not law enforcement, isn't it? Want to know what I think? I think you had the gun and the Molotov. I think Ossie here is the driver of the family. Would I be right, Ossie?"

Ossie glared at his brother. "Told you we should've finished them off."

"I thought they were dead," Ralphie replied.

"Who tipped you off?" Milo asked. "It doesn't matter to me

one way or the other, but I'm sure Abigail would like to know who betrayed her."

"Abigail is the Devil," said Ossie.

"She looks like a little girl."

"Looks are deceiving!" Ossie said, standing.

Milo's hand went to rest on the butt of his gun. "I'm going to have to ask you to sit back down, Ossie."

"She looks like a little girl, but she ain't!" Ossie crowed. "She's the Devil and we're the only ones brave enough to tell it like it is!"

"Be brave while seated, what do you say?"

"You don't scare me. I have seen with my own eyes the true face of evil, and it is that little girl. 'And the great dragon was cast out, that old serpent, called the Devil, and Satan, which... which...'" Ossie looked at Ralphie for help.

"Uh," said Ralphie, "'which... deceiveth'."

"'Which deceiveth the whole world!'" said Ossie. "'He was cast... he was...'"

He looked to Ralphie, who frowned and looked down, trying to remember.

Milo sighed. "'He was cast out into the earth, and his angels were cast out with him'. You fellas need to brush up on your Bible studies. Besides which, you used to work right alongside Abigail, did you not?"

Ralphie narrowed his eyes. "We were wayward, yes. But we were shown the true path."

"By the old man, right? Lautaro Soto? That the true path you're talking about? The one that allowed you to continue dealing drugs and killing people for money?"

Ralphie had nothing to say to that, so Ossie answered for him.

"She's still the Devil."

"Be that as it may, we came here to deliver something to Ralphie and, once that's done, we're going to drive away and hopefully never cross paths with you again. That sound good to you?"

The brothers shared a look of suspicion. "What've you got?" asked Ralphie.

Glen cleared his throat, and stepped forward. "I'm the one who has it, actually. The old man, he gave it to me, and now I suppose I'm returning it to you." He held up his hand and they saw the Deathmark.

Ralphie jumped to his feet.

"I'm really not happy with the number of people standing up right now," said Milo.

Ralphie jabbed a finger at Glen. "That is for her! You deliver that to Abigail! How did you even get that? Lautaro was supposed to—"

"Lautaro is dead," said Amber. "We get that you were trying to kill someone you think is evil. I believe you when you say she is. But you two are every bit as bad."

Ossie shook his head. "We'll kill you dead, but we won't damn your immortal soul."

"Dead's dead," said Milo. "Ralphie, you're going to stand there and let Glen lay his hand on you."

"You ain't touching my brother," Ossie said through gritted teeth.

Glen tried a smile. "Listen, I really don't want to hurt anyone, and this really isn't personal, but if I don't pass it on to you, Ralphie, it'll kill me."

"So die," said Ralphie.

"Well now, that's not really fair, is it? I don't have anything to do with any of this. So let's all be grown-ups here and do what has to be done," Glen said, stepping towards Ralphie.

What happened next happened way too fast and also way too slow. One moment Ossie was standing there, seething and tense, and the next he had the biggest hunting knife Amber had ever seen in his hand. Before she'd even asked herself where the hell he'd been hiding it, he was taking his first lunging step towards them. By this time, Milo's gun was already out of its holster. He fired twice, the gunshots loud in Amber's ears, and Ossie jerked as two small holes appeared in his chest, really close together. Even as he tumbled gracelessly to the ground – and here Amber realised he'd never even had a chance to complete that first step – Ralphie was bolting to the bedroom.

Glen yelled and ran in after him and time returned to normal, and then Glen came sprinting out of the bedroom, yelling even louder. The sound of that machine gun filled the house. Bullets peppered the walls in a shower of splinters. Milo dived, Glen dived, and Amber ducked and stumbled, and before she knew it her skin was red and she had horns again.

Ralphie strode from the bedroom door beside her, swinging the machine gun from side to side, firing the whole time, yelling and cursing and not noticing her as she straightened. She yanked the weapon from his hands, grabbed him by the throat, and lifted him off his feet. Ralphie dangled there for a moment, gurgling and struggling, finally registering who and what had a hold on him, and then Amber swung him up over her head and flipped him. He hit the floor and she raised her foot to turn his head to bloody splinters.

"Amber!" Glen cried, stumbling into view. "Amber, stop! What are you doing?"

Glen's stupid face sapped some of the rage from behind her eyes, and she froze, startled by both the depth of her viciousness and the suddenness with which it had overtaken her.

She threw the machine gun into the bedroom. "Whatever," she said.

Glen smiled at her, nodding like a lovesick idiot. She pointed a taloned finger at the man on the floor who was gasping for breath. "You going to do what we came here to do?"

"Oh yeah," Glen said, and crouched. "I'm really sorry." He pressed his hand to Ralphie's arm.

The blackness swarmed under Ralphie's skin, quickly spreading through his whole arm.

Glen straightened, checked his hand, and smiled in relief. "It's gone," he said. "I'm going to be okay. Hear that, Amber? I'm going to live!"

"Oh joy," she muttered.

Ralphie's breathing, already laboured, became a rattling wheeze.

"You okay?" Milo said to Amber.

She frowned at him. "Why shouldn't I be?"

He shrugged. "It's just, you haven't shifted back yet."

"So? What's wrong with staying like this for a while?"

"Exactly!" said Glen. "She's got nothing to be ashamed of! Look at her! She's beautiful! She's magnificent!"

"Yeah, Milo, I'm magnificent." She walked by Glen, heading to the door. "It's like breaking in a new pair of shoes, you know? You've got to give it the time it needs."

"Um…" said Glen. "I am really sorry about this."

She turned. Glen stood perfectly still, Ralphie behind him, holding that big hunting knife to his throat. Ralphie was sweating badly.

"Easy now," said Milo.

Ralphie started moving Glen around them, heading to the door.

"There was nothing personal here," Milo continued. "You get that, right? Your brother came at us. I had to put him down. There was no malice to it."

Amber resisted the urge to run at Ralphie and tear his face off. She was chock-full of malice.

"Gun down," Ralphie said, his voice sounding strangled. Inky tendrils of tattoo were writhing on his skin.

"Can't do it," said Milo.

Ralphie stopped with his back to the door, and spat out a mouthful of black phlegm. "I'll kill him."

"Then I'll shoot you."

Ralphie blinked quickly, and black liquid began streaming from the corners of his eyes. He said something unintelligible, then tried again. "Keys."

Milo hesitated, then took out his car keys. He tossed them and, when Ralphie reached out to catch, Glen slipped from his grasp. In an instant, Milo's gun was in his hand, but Glen came stumbling towards him and Ralphie ran out of the house.

"You didn't shoot me!" Glen cried, amazed. "We really are friends!"

Milo ignored him and walked for the door. Outside, the Charger roared to life.

Amber ran, beating Milo outside as Ralphie steered the Charger up the dusty hill. Milo strolled out after her, looking entirely too calm. He put his gun back in its holster, and started walking up the hill as the clouds of dust settled.

"You don't seem too upset," she said, walking beside him as Glen followed along behind, checking himself for injuries.

"Why should I be upset?" Milo asked.

She glared. "He's got your car."

"No," said Milo. "My car has him."

They walked up the slope. Glancing at her shadow on the ground and noting how cool her horns looked, Amber matched his pace, slow and leisurely, all the way up the hill – even though her entire body wanted to sprint and run and leap and fight. She wanted to tear faces off and bite through throats and pull out hearts. She wanted to rip and tear and decapitate and disembowel. She wanted violence. She wanted to kill.

They got to the top of the hill. The Charger was just ahead of them, one wheel up on a gentle mound of dirt, its engine still running.

As they neared, the door sprang open and grey smoke billowed into the open air. Ralphie threw himself out, coughing violently. He hit the ground and started dragging himself along by his elbows.

"She's got a tricky tailpipe," said Milo. "If you're not careful, it'll back up on you."

Once he was far enough away from the car that had almost killed him, Ralphie got to his hands and knees, still coughing, black spittle dripping from swollen lips. He spat. There was at least one tooth in all that dark phlegm. He got the coughing under control and, breathing loudly, he stood, swaying. He took the hunting knife from his belt. He looked sick.

"You want," said Milo, "I can shoot you now, put you out of your misery."

Ralphie gargled out a laugh, then pointed the knife at Amber. Grunts were all he could utter. She knew what he wanted, and she obliged. He wanted his chance to take out a demon before he went. There was something admirable in that, she supposed. She walked forward, and heard Milo sigh.

"Uh," said Glen, "should we be letting her do that?"

"She's not a kid," Milo answered. "She's dumb, but she's not a kid. She can do whatever the hell she wants."

Ralphie grinned at her. His lips were so swollen they looked like they might burst.

Even though he was dribbling blackness, Ralphie held that knife like he knew what he was doing. Excitement fluttered in Amber's belly. She didn't know how to fight, but she was being given a chance to prove herself by a man who was going to die, anyway. She had nothing to lose.

He darted at her and she jumped back. He came at her again and she slipped sideways. He was unsteady on his feet and he nearly toppled, but after coughing up a lungful of black ink he turned to continue.

She moved in close and he swiped. The blade skittered across the scales that were suddenly covering her forearm, and she hit him. It was a bad punch, but her fist sank into his soft side, and it hurt him nonetheless. Blackness began to seep into his T-shirt where she had broken the skin. He was rotting from the inside out.

He lunged but she moved and he missed. He stumbled and fell to his knees. Coughed. Spat. Got back up. Lunged at her again. Repeated the process.

He was done. Disappointingly, it was over before it had even begun.

He struggled to his feet and Amber ran forward and jumped. Powerful muscles launched her into the air faster than she'd expected, propelling her across the space between them just as Ralphie was turning to her. Her knee struck his chest and they went down, Amber on top. The knife clattered against a stone somewhere.

Beneath her, Ralphie's eyes were wide and blinking. He was trying to suck in air through his open mouth. Amber was kneeling on him. No, not on him. In him. She stood, removing her knee from the hole in his chest. Trails of blood and ink and rotten insides stretched between them like lines of spittle. She could feel it soaking through her jeans.

She reverted to normal without meaning to, and the cold realisation of what she had done washed over her. Milo and Glen were at her side now. The blackness was rising through Ralphie's skin, leaking from his pores. It weakened his flesh, turned it mushy. His arms and legs lost their form, like the bones themselves had dissolved. His ruined ribcage fell in on itself. A stench rose. Human waste and rotting meat. Then his face caved in. In another few moments, all that was left of Ralphie McGarry were his soaking, black-drenched clothes.

29

THEY GOT BACK TO The Dark Stair a little before noon. The place was empty apart from Abigail, who sat on the bar with her legs swinging. Amber hadn't said anything on the ride over. She'd changed her jeans, though.

"It's done," said Milo.

"Never doubted you for a moment," said Abigail. "Did you encounter any difficulties?"

Milo took a moment. "You tipped them off."

Abigail's big eyes widened. "Me?"

"You led us right into an ambush."

She giggled. "You got me! You see right through me! I just thought, hey, wouldn't it be funny if Ralphie and Ossie got the drop on Milo Sebastian and his pals?"

"I don't remember giving you my name."

"I don't remember needing it." Abigail smiled. "I'm a huge fan of your work. I hope this doesn't mean we're not friends, though. I think we could all be great friends. Don't you?"

Milo didn't say anything. He just turned, walked for the stairs. Glen hesitated, then bowed to Abigail and followed.

But Amber stayed where she was. "What was his last name?" she asked. "Ralphie's?"

Abigail fixed her big blue eyes on her. "McGarry. Why? You like to know the name of your victims?"

Amber went cold. "He's not my... I just needed to know..."

"Oh, I didn't mean anything by it," Abigail said happily. "Are we going to be friends, Amber? I do hope so. From everything I've heard, you don't have many friends left."

"What... what have you heard?"

"Oh, sweetie, I know it all. I know all about your mean, mean parents. I know they're looking for you. I know they got halfway to Toledo, of all places, before they began to suspect that someone had lied to them. They're not very popular in places like this, with people like us, but they do have people who owe them, and people who are scared of them. They're coming for you, Amber."

"Are you going to tell them I was here?"

"I won't have to," said Abigail sadly. "Someone else will. It's inevitable. They're already looking for your car. A black Dodge Charger. That's a car that sticks in the memory."

"Can you help me?"

Abigail's smile was impish. "Help you how?"

"Could you... could you stop them for me?"

"You mean... kill them? You want me to kill your parents and their friends? But... but I'm just a little girl. What could I possibly do against big, bad monsters like that?"

"I don't want to kill them, I don't, I just... I want..."

"I'm not in the monster-stopping business, I'm afraid. But I will do you one favour. When they ask where you've gone, I'll pretend I don't know."

260

Amber frowned. "But you *don't* know."

That smile again. "Oh, Amber, I know everything."

Amber left The Dark Stair, found Milo and Glen waiting outside.

"She says my parents are back on our trail, and they know the car."

Milo nodded. "To be expected. Come on, then. No more detours."

"So," Glen said, chewing his lip, "here is where we part ways, huh?"

Milo said, "Bye," and walked to the Charger.

"Bye?" said Glen. "*Bye?* That's all I get, after everything we've been through?"

"Yep," said Milo.

Glen turned to Amber. "What if there *is* no bye? What if I didn't have to go?"

"But you do," said Amber. "You don't have the Deathmark anymore. You can go home."

"I don't have a home," said Glen. "My dad is dead. Everyone else despises me."

"Then explore America."

"I want to," he said. "With you."

"Glen..."

"Now just wait, Amber, okay? Yeah, there are times when we've butted heads, all three of us, but that's what makes us a great team. We each contribute. You're the brain. Milo's the muscle. Me? I'm the heart."

"No, you're not."

"Then I'm the soul."

"You're not the soul."

He frowned. "Then what am I? I'll be anything."

"You can be the appendix," said Milo.

"Then I'll be the appendix!"

"The appendix is a completely useless part of the colon."

"Whatever!" Glen cried. "I'll be the nose! I'll be the nose of this team! But I *do* contribute, you can't deny that. I helped against Shanks, didn't I?"

"Kind of," said Amber. "But Milo and me, we *have* to continue on this road. You don't. You can stop."

"I don't want to stop. I want to help. Please, Amber. I've never belonged anywhere before. Let me belong."

She looked over his shoulder at Milo.

"Don't look at him," said Glen. "He'll only shake his head. He's probably shaking his head right now, isn't he?"

She paused. "He's not *not* shaking it."

"I know you're shaking your head, Milo!"

"I want you to know that," Milo responded, sounding bored.

"Amber, please," said Glen. "We have something, don't we?"

"I'm sorry?"

"You and me. We have a connection. You feel it, too, I know you do. Especially... especially when you change. Especially when you get horny."

"Do *not* call it that."

"You can't abandon me," said Glen. "Ever think that maybe when we met it was meant to be? Fate has thrown us together, Amber. The universe has decided that we are to be a part of each other's lives from this moment on."

"But why does the universe hate me?"

"Amber, I'm asking you to let me help you on your quest. Let me help you stay ahead of your parents. If anything happened to you, Amber, anything that I could have prevented, I'd never be able to live with myself."

"Now you know how we feel," said Milo.

Glen ignored him. "You need all the help you can get. Don't try to deny it. I don't know why you're even listening to Milo's opinion. You're *paying* him to be here, but me? I'm here for *free*. I'm here because I care. We are a well-oiled machine, and do you know what we've been built for? Stopping you from being eaten. That's it. That's our purpose. That's my purpose. Don't deny me my purpose, Amber. Don't do it."

She sighed. "Fine."

His eyes widened. "Really?"

"Sure."

"Thank you! You will not regret it!"

"I better not."

"What was it that changed your mind? The team bit? The part about the well-oiled machine?"

"Mostly it was how pathetic you sounded."

"That'll work for me!"

"But don't call it a quest."

"Absolutely." He turned. "Hear that, Milo? I'm coming with you."

Milo ignored him and got in the car.

30

THEY LEFT SALT LAKE CITY and drove through a wide expanse of nothing. Mailboxes stood at the mouths of dirt trails that branched off from the road, trails that led to not much more than the rusted corpses of propane tanks and farm machinery. They passed a three-storey house that rose above the scattering of trailer homes around it, and a construction yard that had become a cemetery for old cars.

They drove until the flatness developed some hills. Amber preferred that. There was something so vastly empty about a featureless horizon, like they could drive and drive and the horizon would just fall away. There were moments when the earth seemed flat, and they were hurtling right to the nearest edge. Hills were good. Even the smallest and slightest of hills blocked her view of whatever lay beyond the next bend, allowing her some degree of hope. There was a certain kind of comfort in ignorance.

They got to a truck stop outside of Boise, Idaho, and Amber had a grilled ham and cheese sandwich and fries. She endured Glen talking about how everything in America came with fries – even when you didn't order them – and then they drove on for another two hours. They reached a small motel in Baker City with only two free rooms available. Milo decided to spend the night in the car and wouldn't change his mind, and they were on the road again before seven the next morning.

A little after midday on Saturday, their destination crept up on them. First there was nothing but trees rising up on either side, Douglas firs and red cedars mostly. The valley deepened, and there was a flower bed on a grass shoulder with a circular sign informing them that they were now entering Cascade Falls, and that the population was 9,243. A smaller sign beside that told them this was a Tree City USA. The first building they passed on their right was a nice-looking bar and restaurant – the first on their left was an Econ-o-Wash. They passed a feed and supply store, a used car lot, a drugstore, the Cascade Falls Heritage Centre, and a grand old hotel that stood tall and proud, looking out over the town.

"We'll stay here tonight," said Amber.

Milo nodded. His face was lined with tiredness, even though his eyes were bright. They parked in the front lot and got out. Amber and Glen eased the stiffness from their spines. Milo didn't have to.

They passed through the stone archway into the foyer. Lots of dark wood and old paintings. The woman behind the desk smiled. "Welcome to the Varga Hotel. My name is Ingrid. Do you have reservations?"

"We don't," said Milo. "Is that all right? Would you have three rooms for us?"

"You may be in luck." The smile stayed in place, like fresh flowers at a graveside, while Ingrid checked the outdated computer before her. "You're in luck," she said. "We do indeed have three rooms available. How long will you be requiring them for?"

"Tonight to start with," said Amber. "We may need them tomorrow night, but hopefully not."

Ingrid nodded. "Very well. But please do let us know at your earliest convenience, to make sure we can keep them for you if there's a sudden rush. Please fill out these forms." She slid them each a card and provided them with pens. "Have you been to Cascade Falls before?"

"First time."

"Oh, I'm sure you'll love it," Ingrid said as they wrote and lied. "We have a surprisingly diverse community. I know the town looks white bread through and through, but we have so many different cultures and people – it's a real American town, that's what my grandmother used to say. I was born here, you know."

"That so?" Milo asked.

"Born and raised," said Ingrid. "I moved away when I was twenty, got married and started a family in Boston. I liked it well enough, but I came back here for a weekend to visit my folks and realised I never wanted to leave again. I let go of my husband and my kids and all my stuff. I didn't need it. Didn't need any of it. Everything I needed was right here. This is a wonderful town. The people are lovely. Wait till you meet Mr Varga. He owns the hotel. You'll love him. Everyone does."

Her eyes had glazed over while she was talking, and her smile had stretched so wide Amber thought her skin might tear.

"We're actually looking for someone," Amber said, her voice cutting through whatever daze Ingrid was sinking into. "Gregory Buxton. Do you know him?"

Ingrid blinked, took a moment to process the question, then shook her head. "Sorry, I don't. I know an Althea Buxton, though. She's a nice old lady. Maybe she's related?"

"Maybe," said Milo. "She live around here?"

"Over on Bleeker Street. My mom and her used to be friends. Then she got all religious. Or maybe she was always religious. Althea, I'm talking about, not my mom. You'd never find my mom in church. She never had any time for organised religion, said it was all a big scam. Of course, she was visiting psychics every week and forking over most of her disability allowance, and if anything is a scam it's those crooks. She passed away two years ago. My mom, that is, not Althea."

"I'm sorry to hear that," said Milo.

"Thank you. Taken before her time, that's what everyone said. The Saturday after she died, one of the psychics she saw regularly called the house and asked why she'd missed her appointment. I said you can't be a very good psychic if you didn't see this coming. Know what she did? She offered her services as a medium at a reduced rate. I told her to go to hell, and hung up the phone."

"Nothing but vultures," said Milo.

Ingrid nodded. "That's what I said. I told Mr Varga about it and that's the exact word I used. I said she was a vulture. Mr Varga agreed with me. He's a very smart man, and he's been around the world, not just to Boston, like me. He knows a thing or two."

By this time, they'd all slid their cards back to her, and she scooped them up and placed then carefully into a narrow wooden box. She took three keys from the board behind her and handed them over.

"You're all on the second floor," she said. "Dinner is served from seven till ten, but, if you aim to be in the dining room at eight, you might even get a visit from Mr Varga himself."

"Well, that'd be lovely," said Milo, and smiled.

They dropped their bags in their rooms – Amber's had a four-poster bed and a heavy dresser with a huge mirror – and got back into the Charger. They drove to Bleeker Street, a pleasant road in a pleasant neighbourhood, up the hill slightly from a church. They found the house with Buxton on the mailbox and knocked on the door.

An elderly black woman answered, dressed in a bathrobe and slippers with a cross around her neck.

Amber smiled. "Althea Buxton?"

"Who are you?"

"Mrs Buxton, my name is—"

"What do you want?"

"We were hoping to—"

"What's this about? Who sent you?"

"Uh, no one sent us."

"I'm not going to invite you in."

"That's quite all right," said Amber. "We're looking for your son, actually. Is he around?"

"My son passed away."

Amber frowned. "It is *Gregory* Buxton we're looking for."

"I know who my son is," Althea snapped. "I only had one of them, and he passed, ten years or more. He's gone now and that's that. I can't help you."

She stepped back, and closed the door firmly, the sound coinciding perfectly with the plummeting of Amber's heart.

"That's it, then," she said dully. "It's over. He's dead. I have nothing to offer the Shining Demon. My parents will keep chasing me until they... they..."

Milo walked back to the car. "He's not dead," he said.

Amber looked up. "What?" She hurried after him. Glen followed. "How do you know he's not dead?"

"The Shining Demon would have known it," Milo said, leaning on the hood. "That old lady is scared."

"Of us?"

Milo looked back at the house. "Of someone."

They parked in the courtyard at the back of the hotel, and Amber took Milo's iPad to her room, using the free Wi-Fi to log on to the *In The Dark Places* messageboards. The very idea that she suddenly had some time to herself, plus an internet connection, filled her with such a feeling of warmth that it actually brought a tear to her eye. She refused to cry, though – to cry for something as silly as the ability to chat online would cheapen somewhat the things she genuinely had to cry about. Which were many. And dreadful. She didn't mind the tear in her eye, though. That didn't count.

She skimmed the users chatting, and her heart lifted when she saw names she recognised. This was a world she understood.

This was a community where she belonged, a place where she wasn't a monster. Wasn't a killer.

She shook her head, like the movement itself would be enough to shake the memory from her mind. Ralphie McGarry was dying, anyway. Glen had seen to that. She'd just helped him on his way, that's all. It had been a mercy killing. It had been the right thing to do. She wasn't to blame for any of it. She wasn't to blame for the circumstance she'd found herself in, nor the action she had taken. She wasn't even to blame for the brief flash of pleasure she had derived from killing him.

"Not me," she said aloud. "That wasn't me."

She pushed down the arguments brewing behind her words and instead focused on the words in front of her.

The Dark Princess said...
Hi BAC.

Balthazar's-Arm-Candy said...
Well hey there, stranger! Been a while! Y u no respond 2 my emails???

The Dark Princess said...
Been really busy, sorry. Family stuff.

Balthazar's-Arm-Candy said...
Problems?

The Dark Princess said...
You could say that.

Balthazar's-Arm-Candy said...
That's why we come here, right? To escape the
parental units and their insanity.
Hey, u hear that the full cast has
been confirmed for the con? 1st time EVER!

The Dark Princess said...
Doubt I'll be going actually. Plans have changed.

Balthazar's-Arm-Candy said...
Seriously?
U wanna talk about it?

The Dark Princess said...
It's nothing anyone can help me with.
Wow, that sounds dramatic! I'm doing OK, though.
Everything is messed up but I'm making new friends.
Kind of.

Balthazar's-Arm-Candy said...
Online or irl?

The Dark Princess said...
Real life. Weird, I know.

Balthazar's-Arm-Candy said...
Tres weird.

The Dark Princess said...
World's gone all upside down. Not able to email cuz

of reasons. Some pretty scary stuff happening.

Balthazar's-Arm-Candy said...
Sounds intense.

The Dark Princess said...
It is. Didn't want you worrying, that's all.

Balthazar's-Arm-Candy said...
Well I wasn't. I am NOW though.

Sith0Dude said...
OMG! Laurie killed Stryker! What the HELL?????

Balthazar's-Arm-Candy said...
Private convo, Sith0Dude.
(BTW spoiler warnings – heard of them??)

Sith0Dude said...
U shouldn't be having private convos in public forums.
How am I sposed to know?

(There's a spoiler warning at the start of this thread!)

The Dark Princess said...
Go away Sith0Dude.

Sith0Dude said...
U guys suck.

Balthazar's-Arm-Candy said...
You sound weird, Princess. Worryingly weird.

The Dark Princess said...
I'm sorry. Just wanted to log on, talk to you, get some normality back.

Balthazar's-Arm-Candy said...
Am I helping?

The Dark Princess said...
You always help.

Balthazar's-Arm-Candy said...
Wish I was with you. Why is Australia so far away? Wish I could just hop on a plane to Florida.

The Dark Princess said...
Not in Florida anymore.

Balthazar's-Arm-Candy said...
Gone travelling?

The Dark Princess said...
Yep.

Balthazar's-Arm-Candy said...
Where?

Amber hesitated. It was practically inconceivable for her parents to check these boards. They didn't know she chatted here, didn't know what her user name was… but even so. Even so they scared her so much that she wasn't about to take that chance.

The Dark Princess said…
Not far. Damn, have to go.

Balthazar's-Arm-Candy said…
Something I said?

The Dark Princess said…
Course not. It's late though. Need sleep. Early start tomorrow.

Balthazar's-Arm-Candy said…
Take care of yourself, OK? And check in regularly. U got me worried now!

The Dark Princess said…
Sorry! TTYL

Balthazar's-Arm-Candy said…
Peace.

Amber logged out, turned off the iPad, and let it drop on to the bed. Little by little, they were robbing her of every last semblance of normality, stripping her of every last link to her old life. She didn't even know who she was anymore. Everything her personality had been built on was a lie, and the more she examined it, the more it crumbled beneath her gaze.

If she wasn't a beloved daughter, and if she wasn't an only child, then who was she? Ten days ago, Amber Lamont had been a good person. But now she was someone who'd bitten off a finger. Now she was someone with a pair of jeans soaked in the black blood of a man whose chest she'd caved in.

Now she didn't know who she was.

31

W<small>HEN</small> A<small>MBER</small> <small>CAME</small> <small>DOWN</small> for dinner, her place was set at a large, long table, next to Glen's and across from Milo's. Another guest was joining them, an attractive, dark-haired woman in her thirties.

"Company!" the woman said, clearly delighted. "I haven't had company while eating for ages! Are you staying long?"

"Probably not," said Amber. "We're on a family road trip. This is my cousin Glen, my dad Milo, and I'm Amber."

"Very pleased to meet you," said the woman. "I'm Veronica. Have you travelled far?"

"We've been on the road for a few days," Milo said. "What about you?"

Veronica gave them all quite a beautiful smile. "I actually live here. Not in the hotel, but Cascade Falls. Well, I did. I thought I'd bought a place but it fell through at the last minute, and I've already sold my old house, so here I am, destitute. Destitute in a lovely hotel, but still... destitute."

"Why are you moving?" Amber asked. "It's such a beautiful place."

"It is," said Veronica, "it really is. And I'm going to miss it, but sometimes you just have to –" she fluttered her fingers – "leave."

"I noticed some closed-down stores," Milo said. "Does that have anything to do with it?"

Veronica shrugged. "Maybe. A few of my friends have moved away recently, a few more are about to follow them... No single reason, though. It's still a great place to live. We just... I don't know. We want somewhere new. So where are you from?"

"Georgia," said Milo. "My wife and I split up, and this trip is our father-daughter time."

"Father-daughter and cousin," said Glen quickly.

"How nice," Veronica said. "And your wife was okay with taking Amber out of school for this?"

Milo hesitated for just a moment too long, and Amber jumped in. "When he says they split up, what he means is, Mom passed away last year. Visiting all her favourite places is our way of saying goodbye."

"Oh no," said Veronica. "Oh, I'm so sorry."

"Not at all," said Milo, shooting a look at Amber.

"I'm from Ireland," said Glen.

Veronica nodded and smiled, and didn't say anything to that.

Glen looked mystified. He started to speak again – probably to repeat what he'd just said in the hope of a different reaction – when the doors opened and a man entered. Tall, astonishingly so, with broad shoulders and narrow hips, accentuated by the grey fitted coat he wore – tight around the midsection, then flowing to the floor. His trousers were black, his legs long, his arms long, even his fingers were long. He was handsome, had the complexion of a man who spent his time indoors, and his black hair was swept off his high forehead in an exaggerated widow's peak. He had a long nose, cheekbones like knife cuts, and twinkling dark eyes under a heavy brow.

"Miss Cartwright," he said, smiling. His accent was foreign, and unfamiliar to Amber. "It is a pleasure to see you, as always. And our newest guests – my deepest apologies for not being here to greet you upon your arrival. My name is Johann Varga, the owner of this hotel. I trust your time with us so far has been pleasant?"

"It has," said Milo. "Thank you."

"Have you travelled far?" Varga asked.

"It doesn't seem like it," said Milo, sounding genuinely friendly. "We've only been here a few hours, but even we can see that a town like Cascade Falls really rejuvenates a person, body and soul."

"Doesn't it?" Varga said. "A most peaceful place we have here. We are all quite rightly proud."

"You should be," Milo said, smiling.

Varga nodded his appreciation. "Alas, I have business to attend to. I hope to talk to you all again. For now, I bid you goodnight."

Amber joined the polite chorus that responded, and Varga left, drawing the doors closed behind him.

"Lovely man," said Veronica. "He does a lot for the town. It wouldn't be what it is today without him, and he never asks for anything in return. Sometimes I wonder what it must be like to be that selfless…"

"I like to do charity work," said Glen.

Veronica took her eyes away from Milo, and smiled like she was interested. "What kind?"

Glen shrugged. "It varies. I volunteer at homeless shelters

and animal rescue places, mostly. Cancer research. That sort of thing."

"You have no particular charity that's close to your heart?"

Glen adjusted his sitting position. "Well, I mean, yeah, I do. The main one, the main charity I do work for, is oil spills. Y'know when you see all those people in waterproofs cleaning seagulls and wildlife? That's me. I've always loved wildlife and I live near the sea back in Dublin, so it's pretty handy."

"Do you get a lot of oil spills in Dublin?"

"Uh, well, not really, no. But I'm always there if a whale gets beached, or whatever."

"Oh? What do you do when that happens?"

"Well, I... I push it back into the sea."

Veronica nodded, and waited for him to say more. When it became clear that he had nothing else to add, she turned back to Milo, and Glen frowned and sank a little lower in his chair.

After dinner, Amber took a shower in the bathroom down the hall from her room. It was a quaint affair and while, on the whole, she much preferred hotels that had bathrooms, it was still better than some of the motels they'd had to stay in so far.

She dried herself off, dressed in pyjamas, and bundled up her clothes, balancing her shoes on top. The carpet was soft under her bare feet as she walked to her room. Rounding the corner, she heard voices, and Milo and Veronica came into view, headed for Milo's room. They saw her and stopped. She blinked.

Eventually she said, "Just had a shower."

Milo nodded. "Good."

"How was the water?" Veronica asked.

"Hot," said Amber.

Milo nodded again, like this was an important piece of information he needed to file away. "Okay, well, see you in the morning."

"Yes, you will," Amber replied. "Goodnight."

Veronica gave her a beautiful smile, and Amber watched them both disappear into Milo's room.

She got to her own room and locked the door, then put her clothes on the chair. Then she stood in the middle of the room and frowned.

She had to admit, it was weird seeing Milo and Veronica... together. She found herself actually surprised, probably because the kind of things she associated with Milo were danger and fear and, to a possibly worrying degree, death. It had never occurred to her that he might have normal feelings behind all that alert coolness. She was even disappointed, in a way. She would have thought that someone like Veronica, as undeniably sexy as she was, would have had no effect on him. Amber had expected him to be above that sort of thing.

She laughed to herself at how prudish she sounded. He was a grown man, and he was allowed to do whatever he wanted, and it had nothing whatsoever to do with her.

She crossed to her bed, pulled the covers back, and slipped between them. The sheets were crisp, and she smiled. Nothing better than a freshly made bed. The pillow was cool, and she sank back into it. Not too soft, not too firm. Just right, as Goldilocks had said. She looked up at the ceiling, an off-white without any cracks.

Her smile faded.

She thought about Dacre Shanks, being digested in the trunk of the Charger. She thought about the Charger itself, and what manner of beast it was. She thought about Heather Medina and her father, wondered how they were. She thought of Gregory Buxton's mother, and what they were going to do if they couldn't convince her to help them. And she thought of her parents.

Most of all, she thought of her parents.

When tears came to her eyes, she rubbed them away and turned out the light. She dozed, then woke and lay there, changing position every few minutes.

Finally, she rolled on to her back again and listened to the hotel. It creaked softly. Groaned. Doors opened and closed. She heard muted footsteps. Muted voices. A dimmed world beyond these four walls, a world that was not about her, a world that didn't concern itself with her fears or her troubles. A world that would not mourn her passing, yet neither would it celebrate. An indifferent world. Uncaring. A world that reduced her to a speck.

Amber sat up. "Well, that's depressing," she muttered aloud.

She turned on the light and got up. She drew back the curtains, then opened the window and leaned out, breathing in the night air. She liked how cool it was. The air actually made her shiver. She allowed herself a smile, let herself enjoy the sensation.

There was movement below her – a window opening. Amber watched with mild amusement as someone else leaned out to experience the night in the same way as her. All she could see was the top of the guest's head. Maybe this was a thing people felt compelled to do here – look out across town and contemplate life.

Another window opened, and another head poked out. Then another, and the top of yet another guest's head. Amber stifled a giggle, remembering clips she'd seen from an old game show called Hollywood Squares. She resisted the urge to call out to them, let them share in the joke. But her smile faded when she watched the guests climb out of the windows, clinging to the wall, face down, before they let themselves drop into the darkness below.

Something blurred by to her left – someone dropping from a window above. She turned, looked up, straight into the face of Varga himself as he clung to the brickwork, his coat billowing behind him, his eyes wild and boring into hers. Then he released his hold on the wall and plummeted towards her.

32

AMBER SHRIEKED AND WHIPPED her head back, and Varga fell past her window.

She shut it quickly, backed away, then left the room, running to Milo's.

She slammed her fist against the door. "Milo, open up! Milo!"

Glen emerged from his room. "Amber? What's going on?"

"We have to leave. Varga's... I don't know what he is. But there's others like him, and we have to get out of here before they... do something."

Glen nodded. "You're not making a whole lot of sense, you know."

Amber ignored him, twisting the handle of Milo's door. To her surprise, it opened, and she ran in. The room was empty. The bed hadn't been slept in.

Amber's fingers curled in her hair. "Did you see him?"

"See who?" asked Glen.

"Milo! Who else? Did you see him?"

"Since dinner? No. Did you?"

"I saw him heading in here, with her."

"Her who?"

"The woman, Veronica."

Glen looked dismayed. "She went off with Milo? Aw man. She was giving me the eye all evening."

"She barely looked at you."

"That's called being coy."

Amber brushed past him, ran back to her room. Glen tried coming in after her, but she pushed him out.

"I'm getting dressed," she said. "Wait there. Tell me if you see anyone."

She slammed the door, ripped off her pyjamas and pulled on her clothes. When she was done, she left the room and hurried down the stairs.

"Can you please tell me what's going on?" Glen asked, right behind her.

Amber put a finger to her lips, and he scowled and shut up.

She crept through the hotel, noting for the first time how quiet it suddenly was, like it was holding its breath. There was no one at the front desk. She turned to share a look with Glen, but he was completely oblivious to how creepy it all was.

"Can I talk now?" he asked.

She hissed, and hit him, and he scowled again and rubbed his arm.

She led the way to the rear of the hotel. By now, even Glen had noticed how unnatural the silence was.

"Where is everyone?" he whispered.

Amber didn't answer.

They got to the small door leading to the parking area in the courtyard. The few feeble lights outside did little to dispel the encroaching darkness, but Amber really had no choice. She counted to three, then lunged from the hotel. Nothing jumped out at her, thank God. She ran to the hedge and stopped, her feet kicking up a shower of little stones. Glen almost bumped into her.

"Oops, sorry," he said. "What's wrong? Why— Hey, where's the car?"

"He's gone," Amber said softly.

Glen walked to the middle of the courtyard, like that would give him a vantage point from which to see the missing Charger. "Where? Where's he gone? Do you think he has Veronica with him? We should have a rule in future. The I saw her first rule. Y'know, it would have been me, but I'm too much of a gentleman to make a move so soon."

From overhead, a fluttering.

Amber looked up. The lights in the courtyard made the darkness above an impenetrable shroud of starless black.

She turned her head, following the fluttering as it moved from right to left. Then another, from in front to behind. More fluttering, getting closer and closer and then swooping up and away.

The fluttering not of feathers, or of wings, but of clothes.

"Glen," Amber whispered.

Glen stood there with his hands on his hips. "Milo knew I liked her. It was obvious. Maybe it's an Irish thing, but guys do not do that to each other. That is uncool."

"Glen."

"When he gets back, we're going to have a talk. Man to man."

"Glen, get inside," Amber said, her voice flat.

From above, a giggle.

Glen looked round. "You hear that?"

"Get inside, Glen."

Frowning, he watched her as she backed up to the door. The darkness was alive around them. On either side, a dreadful whispering, gleeful and mocking, while above, that fluttering. Always the fluttering.

Amber stepped backwards into the hotel, holding the door open for Glen as he came after her. He was frowning as he walked, kept turning his head. The darkness rippled above him. She saw shapes moving. The whispering got louder. Louder. There was laughter now – cruel and malicious laughter. Glen stopped looking around and fixed his eyes on Amber. He was terrified. His face trembled, like he was holding in a scream, like he was getting ready to bolt.

On either side of him, people were stepping from the shadows. An old man with white hair. A middle-aged woman with a pearl necklace. A young man with acne. More and more. They all wore identical smiles.

Then the shadows moved and something reached down from above and Amber grabbed Glen and yanked him inside, slammed the door and pressed her back to it.

Instant silence.

Except for Glen.

"Ohhhh my God! Holy crap! Would you look at my arms? See the goosebumps? What the hell was that? That was creepy! Oh *yikes*, y'know?"

He rubbed his arms and the back of his neck and laughed. "This place gets to you after a while, doesn't it?"

Amber stared at him. "Did you not see them?"

"See who?"

"The people."

"Where?"

"Out there! We were surrounded!"

"Uh, we were the only two out there, Amber…"

"They were about to grab you!"

"Who were?"

"The people! You heard them!"

"That was the wind. It was all creepy and spooky and scary and, y'know… The wind."

"That was voices. That was people whispering and laughing."

"It *did* sound like laughing."

"And what about the people flying?"

"Flying? What?"

"They were going to grab you!"

Glen put both hands on her shoulders, and said with an irritatingly soothing tone, "Amber, we're freaked out. The hotel is empty and Milo has taken off and we haven't a clue what the hell's going on, but we have to try to remain calm. If we let our imaginations run away with us, then we're—"

"Screw you," said Amber, walking past him.

"I didn't mean anything bad," Glen said, following. "Where are you going?"

"To my room. I'm going to barricade the door and wait till morning."

"Yeah, a good night's sleep is probably best."

"Shut up, Glen."

She climbed the stairs.

"Hey, I get it," he said. "You're scared. I get it, I do. Maybe if you change into your, y'know, other self, you mightn't be so freaked out. You might be able to calm down."

"Calming down is not a good idea when we're in danger. We have to stay frightened and alert."

"I agree," said Glen. "And I believe you. I believe that we're in danger. So I think we should go to your room, barricade the door, you should change into your other self, and we'll wait until morning."

Amber glared at him. "We?"

"I'm in danger, too, right?"

She sighed. "Yeah."

"Well then," he said, and walked into her room.

Gritting her teeth, Amber followed, and locked her door.

"I'll take first watch if you want," said Glen, moving to the open window. "You can change any time now."

Amber felt the blood drain from her face. "I shut that before I left," she whispered.

Glen rested his hands on the sill. "Hey," he said, "you can see Althea's house from here."

And then he was snatched away.

Amber screamed, found herself red-skinned before she knew what was happening. She ran to the window, looked out, saw nothing but heard laughter. She shut the window again, made sure the latch was secure, and closed the curtains. She pushed the dresser in front of the door. Finally, she dragged the bedclothes into the corner and sat, the duvet held tightly to her chin.

Something scraped against her door. Fingernails.

Someone whispered through the keyhole.

Amber waited for morning.

33

She didn't sleep.

She was tired and her eyes wanted to close, but she didn't sleep, not with Glen having been snatched away, not with Milo missing, not with those... *people* out there. Nor did she change back. She kept her horns and fangs and talons, as much of a comfort to her as a gun to a soldier.

A half-hour before dawn, the silence left the hotel. Amber heard footsteps in the room above. She heard a window close in the room below. They were returning.

When dawn broke the darkness, the curtains let through a few weak strands of early morning sunlight. Gradually, she heard the sounds of normality seep through the floorboards. Doors opening and closing. Voices bidding each other good morning.

She waited until seven, until the sun was up and the day had properly begun. She got up. Opened the curtains. Cascade Falls lay fresh-faced before her.

She pushed the dresser back into place, and unlocked her door. When nobody came rushing in, she took a deep breath, and felt her horns retract.

She stepped out, careful to move as quietly as possible. She crept to Milo's room, reached for the handle, but the door opened before she touched it.

Amber yelped, and Milo jumped back.

"Jesus," he breathed, scowling at her.

She pushed by him, into the room.

"Where were you?" she whispered.

He looked at the open door, then at her, and then he closed it. "I'm sorry?"

"Last night, you disappeared. You took the car."

He nodded. "Veronica wanted to go for a ride. She'd never been in a Charger before. Why?"

"They took Glen."

"Who did?"

"Varga," she said. "Varga and the others took Glen."

"I'm not sure I understand."

"They were flying around last night and they dragged him right out the window!"

Milo looked at her.

She glared. "Don't you dare say I imagined it all."

"I wasn't about to," he murmured. He went to the bed, pulled his bag out from underneath, and removed his gun and holster from a side pocket. He clipped the holster to his belt and slid it out of sight. Then he put his jacket on over it.

He led the way out, and over to Glen's room. He listened at the door for a moment, then pushed it open. Glen's gentle snoring was the first thing to greet them.

Milo parted the curtains and Glen woke, turned over, gazing at them both blearily.

"What are you doing in my room?" he asked, his voice thick.

"What *happened*?" Amber asked.

"Sorry?"

"Last night," said Milo. "Amber, start from the beginning."

"I couldn't sleep," she said, "so I opened the window. I saw Varga and maybe five or six others climbing down the wall. No ropes, no gear, they were *sticking* to the bricks. Then they... then they let go and they *flew*."

Glen frowned. "They flew?"

"Yes," she snapped, then ignored him and turned back to Milo. "Then I went to get you, but you were gone. Glen came out, and we went outside to look for the car."

"That was gone, too," said Glen unhelpfully.

"But there were people out there with us," Amber said, "and I could hear more of them flying overhead. They almost got Glen, but we got back inside, went to my room... I'd closed the window before I left, but it was open, and Glen went over to it and he was pulled out."

Glen frowned. "I was?"

She whirled. "You were pulled out the window, Glen."

He processed the information. "Ohhh," he said. "That's what happened."

Amber was ready to kill him. "*What?*"

"I woke up on the ground," said Glen. "I must have fallen out."

"You didn't fall. You were pulled! If you had fallen, half your bones would be broken!"

He shook his head. "Not necessarily. If my body had been completely limp on the way down, I'd stand a good chance of—"

"Shut up, Glen! How can you *not* remember?"

"I must have blacked out. I remember everything you said,

except the bits I didn't see, like, and I remember getting to your room and then waking up outside. I went back in, knocked on your door, but you were asleep—"

"I was not asleep."

"Well, then you didn't hear me, so I just went back to bed."

"And, if that was you, you did not knock. You scraped."

Glen's frown deepened. "Why would I do that?"

"Amber," said Milo, "you saw Varga, right? You're sure it was him?"

"Positive."

"Then we'll go have a talk with our gracious host."

She nodded. "Right. Good. Yeah."

"I have a question," said Glen. "What kind of a world is it we live in when a man will step between another man and the woman he obviously shares a deep connection and intense physical attraction with?"

"Are you talking about Veronica?" Milo asked, sounding genuinely puzzled.

"Yes, Milo, yes, I am."

"She doesn't like you, Glen."

"That is a lie."

"She said you reminded her of a startled meerkat."

Glen went quiet for a moment. Then he responded with, "That makes very little sense."

"Get up and get dressed," said Amber, leaving the room. "And bring your bag down with you. We're not staying here tonight."

Glen grumbled, but when he was dressed Amber led the way downstairs.

"Well, hello there," Ingrid said brightly when she saw them. Her eyes dipped to their bags. "Are you leaving us so soon? Did you have a good night?"

"Some of us had a better night than others," said Glen, strolling over.

Ingrid looked concerned. "Oh, that's a shame for some of you, then. Anything I can do to persuade you to stay?"

"Dunno," said Glen. "Do you have a younger sister?"

Milo stepped sharply in front of him. "Could we speak with Mr Varga, please?"

Ingrid gave another one of her smiles. "I'm sorry, Mr Varga is out on business for the day. We're expecting him back tonight, though, if that's any use to you?"

"Sure," said Milo. "We'll talk to him then."

"Wonderful," said Ingrid. "Is there anything else I can help you with?"

"No, thank you," said Milo, handing over his key.

Amber and Glen did the same, and they walked out to the Charger without saying another word. They got in.

"I don't like this town," Amber said. "We're leaving as soon as we get Gregory Buxton's location."

Glen nodded. "So we interrogate his mum. Force her to tell us where he is."

She turned to him. "What?"

He blinked. "We... we don't interrogate his mum?"

"She's, like, a hundred!"

"She's religious," said Milo, starting the car. "Today's Sunday. She'll most likely be going to church. Which means she'll be out of the house."

"We break in!" said Glen. "We're good at breaking into

places! Although technically we didn't break into the Springton Library, we just hid in the toilets, but the end result is the same."

"Shut up," Milo said calmly. "I'll break in, search through her stuff. There has to be a postcard or a letter or an address book or something."

"What'll we do?" Glen asked.

"We'll follow her," said Amber. "Make sure she doesn't come back early. If she does, we'll delay her."

"How?"

"You said that older women find you irresistible, right?"

Glen blanched. "You want me to... seduce her?"

Amber shrugged. "Only if you have to."

They parked a few streets away from Althea Buxton's house, and went walking. On their third time passing her street, they saw her emerging. Milo disappeared behind her house, and Amber and Glen followed her on the five-minute walk to the church.

Right before Amber stepped through the door, she wondered if she'd burst into flames the moment her foot touched the ground.

Thankfully, she didn't.

They chose a space on a pew near the back, where they could keep an eye on Althea. Amber tried to remember the last time she'd been in a church. Had she *ever* been in one? Her parents had never bothered with it – surprise, surprise – and her school was pretty secular. Maybe all she'd seen of the inside of churches had been from movies and TV. She looked up at a statue of Christ on the cross, noting how much he must have worked out to get abs like that, and thought for the first time about praying.

Was God the answer? Up until recently, she'd never had to think about it before, but having been faced with the stark reality of demons and devils – she only had to look in the mirror for proof of that – maybe now was the time to start.

Would it help if she got down on her knees and prayed? She contemplated, for a moment, the idea of praying for her parents, praying that they'd see sense, that they'd recover from whatever madness had gripped them. But she dismissed the idea almost as quickly. She might as well wish for a happy childhood where they hadn't ignored her.

"I don't feel well," Glen whispered. "I think I've got internal injuries."

Would a priest be able to absolve her of her sins? Amber wondered what this priest would make of her horns. If she stepped into a confessional box and she told him the truth, the whole truth, and revealed herself in all her red-skinned glory, what would his reaction be? Would it shatter his faith, shake it loose, or renew it? Would he have an answer for her, or would he cast her from this holy place, cursing her existence and damning her in the eyes of his Lord?

Was she *already* damned in the eyes of his Lord?

Jesus looked down at her, all rippling muscles and skimpy loincloth, and he didn't give a whole lot away. A sneaky one, that Jesus.

"My friends," the priest said. He was young and, even from where she was sitting, Amber could see the bags under his eyes like dark rings. He needed sleep. She could relate.

"Today brings us troubling times," he continued. "We turn on the news and we see civilisation crumble around the world. War and crime and terrorism and hatred. Poverty. Injustice. Everywhere we look, warning signs of evil. It is taking hold. It is taking root. But, you ask, why would I need to turn on the news to see evidence of this? Why would I need to open a newspaper, or go online? Have not the seeds of evil already taken root here in our very own town?"

A ripple of murmurings through the churchgoers, and Amber sat up a little straighter.

"I have God on my side," said the priest. "He is my shepherd. He guides me. He protects me. But, even so, I am afraid. I am beginning to doubt. Not God, however. He is as strong as He has ever been. No, my friends, I doubt myself. For my flesh is weak. And my heart is weak. Two weeks ago, we buried our great friend, Father Taylor, and suddenly I am standing up here alone. I find myself missing his comforting presence. I miss his words, his counsel. Most of all, though, I miss his bravery."

The priest glanced briefly to one side, and Amber noticed for the first time a large photograph, propped up on an easel. It showed a smiling, white-haired old man.

"He knew, you see," the priest continued. "He felt it. I denied it. And now it's too late."

"The man in the picture," Amber whispered to Glen.

"What about him?"

"I saw him," said Amber. "I saw him last night outside the hotel."

And then someone started singing. With a low voice, a quiet voice.

"Down in the willow garden, where me and my love did meet."

Disquiet spread softly.

"As we sat a-courtin', my love fell off to sleep."

Amber could see him now, the man who was singing. He sat with his head down.

"I had a bottle of Burgundy wine. My love, she did not know. So I poisoned that dear little girl, on the banks below."

The people on either side of him started to shuffle away.
He continued to sing. And then a female voice joined him.

"I drew a sabre through her, it was a bloody knife."

A third voice now, and more shuffling away, and the singing got a little stronger.

"I threw her in the river, which was a dreadful sign."

Another person joined the song, singing with his head down, and a fifth, and a sixth, and now people were getting up, their pushes becoming shoves in their attempts to create distance, and the panic was rising with the singing voices, and a seventh and an eighth person joined the song and the priest backed away with a look of horror on his face and people were crying now and running for the exit.

Amber saw Althea, pushed from behind and falling to her

knees. Amber sprang off the pew, barged into the surging crowd and was nearly knocked off her feet herself. But she made it, and she gripped Althea's arm and pulled her up, and now Glen was in front, clearing the way to the door.

"*My race is run, beneath the sun. The scaffold waits for me.*"

Amber looked back, saw ten or twelve people now standing, but still with their heads down, and still singing.

"*For I did murder that dear little girl, whose name was Rose Connelly.*"

And, just as Althea fainted and her whole bodyweight collapsed into Amber's arms, they burst out into the sun.

34

Between herself and Glen they half walked, half carried Althea up the hill and back to her house.

She was, despite her modest height, quite a heavy woman, and the journey was slow and difficult. Althea came out of her faint twice, started muttering, then succumbed to it once again, the cross around her neck dangling beneath her chin. They got to the house and Amber knocked, calling Milo's name. A few moments later, the door opened and he let them in. On their way upstairs, they filled him in on what had happened, then laid Althea carefully on her bed. All at once the muttering stopped and Althea was sleeping deeply.

Milo and Glen shared a glance, then left the room. Amber frowned until she realised that she was expected to take care of the undressing.

Ten minutes later, she joined them both in the living room.

"Next time an old person needs to be readied for bed," she said, "one of you is going to do it."

The living room was modest, with a low-hanging faux-chandelier and wallpaper that hadn't even been in style when it was made. Rugs lay atop the carpet and the curtains were heavy and old. A sofa and an armchair huddled round the cold fireplace, the armchair facing a TV so stocky it would have crushed the old lady if it had fallen on her. Beside the window there was a small, circular table covered with a tablecloth. Framed photographs stood like privates in a parade. There was a painting of Jesus over the mantelpiece.

"I've been to church," said Glen, standing at the window and peeking out from behind the blinds. "That is not supposed to happen. That was creepy. It was more than creepy. It was... it was very creepy."

Milo was flicking through an address book, but paused long enough to glance at Amber. "Think it's got anything to do with what you saw last night?"

"Probably," she said. "The priest was talking about how the seeds of evil have already taken root here. I'm pretty sure those were some of the seeds he was talking about. Did you find anything?"

"Not yet," Milo replied. "But maybe Althea will be more willing to talk to us after this."

"She'll probably need one of us to be with her when she wakes, though," said Glen. "Just to make sure she doesn't freak out. I'll take first watch."

"Wait," said Amber. "You think waking up to find a strange Irishman in her bedroom will reassure her?"

Glen frowned. "What's wrong with that?"

Amber didn't bother answering. She just went back upstairs. She sat in an armchair, watching Althea sleep. After a few minutes, she closed her eyes. Just for a moment. Just to rest them.

*

When Amber awoke, the sunlight had a red tinge to it, like drops of blood in bathwater. She yawned, sitting up straighter in her chair. Mid-yawn, she froze. The bed was empty.

Alarmed, she hurried downstairs to find Althea sitting in the living room with Glen.

"Amber," said Glen, smiling broadly, "you're finally awake!"

"I didn't have the nerve to disturb you," Althea said. "You looked exhausted, so I thought to myself I'll let this poor girl sleep."

"Uh, thank you," said Amber. "I hope I didn't frighten you, or anything."

Althea smiled ruefully. "Takes more than a young girl to frighten me, let me tell you."

Milo came in, holding a saucer with a delicate cup of steaming tea. "Here you go, Althea," he said, passing it over.

"A saint, that's what you are," Althea said, taking it from him and sipping.

"Not too strong this time?"

Althea chuckled. "No, dear, it's perfect, thank you."

Milo sat in the armchair and looked at Amber. "Althea was just telling us who those people in church were. Some of them have been ill recently."

"That's right," said Althea. "I know Tom Prendergast hasn't been in work since Monday, and Rachel Faulkner didn't show up for her shift in the cafe yesterday or the day before. She didn't even call in sick. And I'm not one to listen to gossip, but that Stevens boy hasn't been well all week. They say he's got an infection."

She nodded when she said it, like Amber would know what kind of infection she meant.

"Do you think they were all sick with the same thing?" Amber asked.

Althea took another sip from her cup. "I'm sure I don't know. But it would appear so, wouldn't it? They were all complaining of weakness, and everyone who saw them remarked on how pale they looked. Then there were the…"

She trailed off.

"Then there were the what?" Milo prompted.

But Althea only smiled. "Nothing, dear. Worried people, that's all it is."

"You said something earlier about strange deaths?" Glen said.

"Oh heavens, no," Althea responded, her small eyes glittering. "Such talk is nothing more than salacious gossip, and I for one do not partake. But we have had a very odd year, a very unsettling year. People have died in mysterious circumstances and others have claimed to see them days or even weeks later, walking the streets. Always at night, though. Always at night. And it all began with that poor family."

"Tell us," said Glen. "Please."

The tip of Althea's tongue popped out from between her lips as she considered the request, and then vanished. She put her cup and saucer on the coffee table and sat forward on the sofa. Milo and Glen leaned in. Amber perched on the arm of Milo's chair and did the same.

"The Mastersons," Althea said. "Lovely family. The mother was a lawyer, her husband was a teacher. Mathematics, I think. They had two beautiful children. The boy was the youngest. A prodigy, they said. Sit him at a piano and he could play like Mozart. Hand him a violin and he could play like Vivaldi. The daughter, though, Rosalie, she was the one you'd remember. I daresay you'd have fallen in love with her at first sight, Glen. Beautiful and kind, intelligent and funny. She was the flower of Cascade Falls. She had many would-be suitors and, from what I've heard, they were remarkably well-behaved around her. No inappropriateness of any sort. Until Caleb Tylk.

"Caleb was a troubled boy," she went on. "Fights. Suspended from school three times. Vandalism. But, like every boy his age, he was in love with Rosalie Masterson. She was polite to him, which is testament enough to her character, wouldn't you say? But that was Rosalie. A girl much too lovely for this world."

"So I'm guessing something really bad happened," said Amber.

Althea nodded gravely. She reached for her cup, took a sip, and replaced it on its saucer. "Caleb Tylk's attentions were wildly, grotesquely inappropriate. He mistook her kindness for something more, and she was forced to reject his advances. He didn't take it well. They said he hanged himself on the old tree beside the Varga Hotel."

"They *said?*" Glen echoed. "They didn't know for sure?"

"My friend, Sally-Ann Deaton, insists that she saw him hanging there, but, by the time the authorities came, the body was gone."

"What happened to it?" asked Amber.

"Nobody knows," said Althea. "But three nights later, cruel and bloody murder paid a visit to the Masterson house. The mother had her head cut off. The father had his heart ripped out. The son, that poor boy, was torn limb from limb. And Rosalie was taken."

"You think Caleb did it," said Milo.

"Oh yes," said Althea. "Rosalie's bedroom door had been

broken down. On the wall beside the open window was *Caleb Tylk loves Rosalie Masterson*, written in Rosalie's own blood."

Silence followed her words. She took her saucer in her hand and had another sip of tea.

"Since then, things have gotten bad, and are getting worse. People are dying, and rising again. Oh, come now, wipe those looks off your faces. You know. I can tell. There's something out there… something evil. You can feel it, too. He is not of this world."

"He?"

"Varga," she said. "It's all centred around him."

"Why don't you leave?" Glen asked.

"I would've been out of here last week if my car hadn't broken down," Althea said with a chuckle. "At first, I was stubborn. I have lived in Cascade Falls my entire life and I was determined not to let any unholy creatures force me from my home. But then, well, my mind was changed. Vampires can do that to a person."

Glen blinked. "Vampires?"

"Well, of course," said Althea. "What did you think we were talking about?"

"I… have no idea," said Glen. "But vampires? Really?"

Althea nodded. "That's why I carry a crucifix with me wherever I go, and it's why I never invite anyone into my house after dark. Those people singing in church today were the vampires' human familiars – people who have been enslaved, but who have not yet been drained completely. I know my stuff, you best believe it."

"Are we seriously talking about Dracula-style vampires here?" asked Glen, an excited grin starting to spread.

"Of course we are," said Althea. "If you'd looked close, you would have seen that they all share two puncture wounds on their necks."

"Wow…" said Glen.

Althea looked at him sadly. "Just like yours."

35

GLEN'S SMILE FADED. "I'm sorry?"

"Your bitemark, dear," said Althea, tapping her collar.

Glen frowned, and his hand went to his own neck. His eyes widened. "*What?*"

He leaped to his feet, spinning so that Amber and Milo could see the puncture wounds.

Amber stood, almost stumbled. "Oh hell."

"What does it mean? *What does it mean?*" Glen wailed. "Oh God, am I a vampire? Does this mean I'm a vampire?"

"You're not a vampire," said Milo. "But you are marked."

"Not again! I can't be! I've already been marked! I had the Deathmark! I can't be marked again!"

"What does marked *mean?*" Amber asked.

"It means the vampire who bit Glen can find him anytime he or she wishes," said Althea, and then shrugged. "I've done my homework."

"*I'm marked,*" Glen breathed, his eyes wide.

"There's no need to make a big deal out of it," said Milo, but Glen was already moving towards the front door.

"I need to walk," he said. "I need to... I need to be *free!*"

And then he was gone, the door swinging closed behind him.

"What a dramatic young man," said Althea.

But, before the door had clicked shut, Glen was barging back through.

"They're here!" he cried, slamming the door and scuttling to the window.

Amber frowned. "The vampires?"

Glen looked back at her, real fear on his face. "Your *parents*."

She ran to the window before she knew what she was doing, in time to see her parents' car vanish round the corner. She went cold.

"Did they see you?" Milo asked, hauling Glen up by his collar. "They know your face. Did they see you?"

"No," Glen said. "No, they didn't."

Milo turned to Althea. "How many ways out of town?"

"Just two, I'm afraid," she answered. "The road to the east and the bridge to the west."

"They'll have them covered. Two on each, and the last two searching the town. We have to move."

"Wait," said Amber. It was all too much. All too fast. She needed things to slow down; she needed to be able to think. "They... they don't know why we're here, do they? I mean, they may have tracked us to this town, but they clearly haven't spoken to Shanks. They don't know about Althea or her son, and they don't know about the vampires. In a few hours, Cascade Falls will be crawling with the things, right, Althea?"

Althea nodded. "And every night it gets worse."

"There you go," said Amber. "That'll keep them busy. All we have to do is lie low until morning, then we'll just sneak past them. Althea, we'll take you with us. We'll pack your bags while we're waiting."

"That's a plan," said Milo. "But, if they've followed us this far, they know what kind of car we're driving. I'll have to hide it."

"There's a small barn just before the bridge," said Althea. "There's nothing inside and it's never locked."

"That's it, then," said Milo. "I'll get the car under cover and come back as soon as I can. Do not open the door to anyone. Vampires can't enter a property unless they're invited, am I right about that, Althea?"

"Yes, you are, Milo."

Milo turned to Glen. "What about you? Can I trust you not to do anything stupid?"

"I am a creature of the night," Glen whispered.

"That'll have to do," said Milo, and hurried out.

Amber locked the door behind him.

When Althea's bags were packed and sitting in the hall, Amber took her upstairs so she could get some rest. When she was gently snoring, Amber came back down and found Glen standing at the window, looking out.

"Have you seen them again?" she asked. "Glen? *Glen.*"

He looked round, startled. "What? Sorry?"

"My parents," she said. "Have you seen them again?"

"Oh," he said. "No. Haven't seen them."

She nodded, and stood beside him. His gaze was once again on the town beyond the glass. He looked tired. Worn out. First the Deathmark and now this… Despite how much he annoyed her, she couldn't help but feel sorry for him.

"*There*," he said. "Did you hear it?"

She pushed down her worries about her parents, shoved them deep into a dark, dark hole, and made a big show of listening. "Uh no. I don't think so. Hear what?"

He frowned. "Nothing. Never mind."

"How are you feeling?" she asked gently.

He didn't look at her. "Feeling is something only the living do."

"Oh yeah?" Amber said, and punched his shoulder. "Feel that?"

"Ow!" He rubbed his arm. "How can you hit so hard with such small hands? God!"

She gave him a grin. "Don't be so dramatic."

"I think I'm entitled to be dramatic, actually," he said, glaring. "I'm the one bitten. I'm the one with the mark of the vampire upon his skin."

"*Upon his skin?*" she mocked.

He looked out of the window again. "You don't know what it's like for people like me."

"What, the Irish?"

"The damned. The doomed. Those with the vampire's kiss upon our lips."

"The vampire kissed you?"

"It's a metaphor."

"Barely."

His eyes widened. "There it is again!"

Amber frowned. "There what is?"

"A whisper," he said. "Or a… not a whisper, a call. But it's… it's soft. You're sure you don't hear it?"

"I'm pretty sure. Where's it coming from?"

"Out there," he said. He bit his lip. "Amber, would you promise me something?"

"Depends…"

"You… you won't let me die alone, will you?"

He looked at her, and all the pain he had ever felt was right there in his eyes.

"You're not going to die," she said. "You've been bitten. That means a vampire fed on you. You haven't been turned."

"I know, I know that, but… but you wouldn't let me die alone, right? We're friends, aren't we?"

"Yeah. I guess. Sort of."

"Well, even sort-of friends don't let each die alone, do they?"

She sighed, and took his hand. "No, they don't. You're going to be fine, Glen. We're going to wait till morning, and then we're going to leave. Easy as pie."

"Yeah," said Glen. "Yeah. Sorry. I've never really had much of a family before, except for my dad. He was like me, y'know? Sensitive. My mam, she used to slag him about it. Make fun of him, like. Then he lost his job and it was like all she ever did was slag him."

"How did he die?" Amber asked softly.

Glen hesitated. "Alone," he said.

"Do you have any brothers or sisters?"

"A brother. He's a dick."

"I had a brother," said Amber. "A long, long time ago. A sister, too. Never knew them. I always wanted a brother when I was growing up. A brother would beat up anyone who laughed at me or called me names."

"My brother was the one who laughed at me," said Glen. "He was the one who called me names."

"I don't think my brother would have been like that," Amber said. "I think he would have been nice. So you wouldn't go back to Ireland? Back to your mom?"

He smiled sadly. "She doesn't want me. Never did, I suppose. I wasn't the happiest kid growing up so I kind of... pretended I was? I got on her nerves a lot. Were you happy as a kid?"

"I thought I was," said Amber. "I mean, I knew my parents were different. They didn't hold my hand, they didn't play with me... I thought it was something I'd done, maybe something I was doing wrong. So I tried to act more like the other kids, but that didn't work, so I tried to act more like my parents, but that didn't work, either... It's only now that I can look back and realise they never noticed. All of my little efforts to please them or make them proud, anytime I changed my behaviour to get some kind of reaction out of them, they just... never noticed. Because they didn't care."

"So we were both sad kids," said Glen.

"I guess. The more I think about these things, the clearer I see what my life was really like."

"Scary, isn't it?"

"It is."

They smiled at each other, and she gave his hand a squeeze and went to let go, but he held on. His eyes found hers, and they softened, and he leaned in.

"I swear to God," she said, "do not try to kiss me."

He faltered. A moment passed, and then he hugged her arm and let it drop.

Another moment passed.

"That was so awkward," said Amber.

"I was just about to say that."

"That was weird and unsettling."

He nodded. "It was an ill-advised move, it's true."

"Were you seriously going to kiss me?"

"Apparently."

"Your eyes went funny."

"I've been told that happens."

"I thought you only liked me when I was all demony."

"You really think I'm that superficial?"

"Yes."

"You could be right," said Glen. "But isn't it possible that I might have grown as a person in the last few days? After all my brushes with death and everything?"

"I guess," she said.

"I think I might have," he went on. "I'm probably realising that, when it comes to beauty, it's what's inside that counts. Or maybe beauty is what my eye, y'know, beholds it to be? I think I might have turned a significant corner in, like, sorting out what's hot and what's not. This is a big moment for me. But I didn't mean to make things awkward between us. I just think you're really awesome and I thought we were having a moment and I made a mistake. I'm sorry."

"Listen, Glen, I want you to know—"

"I value your friendship, too."

"—that I am in no way attracted to you at all in the slightest."

He blinked. "I'm sorry?"

She winced. "I should have said what you said, about the valuing friendship stuff. Dammit. Can I go back and change my answer?"

"You don't think I'm cute?"

"I think you're reasonably good-looking, sure. But that doesn't mean I'm attracted to you."

"Why not?"

"It just doesn't."

"Are you sure that makes sense, though?"

She patted his shoulder. "I'm going to check on Althea. Maybe she'll be ready to talk about her son now. When I come back, we can hopefully pretend this never happened."

"Yeah," he said. "Okay."

She walked upstairs, feeling weird.

Althea was sitting up in bed. "Is Milo back yet?" she asked.

"No. But don't worry about him," said Amber. "Milo can take care of himself. How are you doing?"

Althea smiled. "I'm old, and I need a lot of rest, but apart from that I am as fine as I ever was. Or so I like to think." She chuckled. "Old age has a tendency to creep up on a person when they're not looking. It's sneaky like that." She sat back, folding her hands over her belly. "You wanted to know about Gregory, didn't you?"

"Yes," said Amber. "If you'll tell me. He's still alive, isn't he?"

Althea smiled sadly. "As far as I know. I don't know where he is, but maybe I can help you find him. How much do you know already?"

"We know he made a deal with the Devil."

"A lot of people would have trouble even uttering those words, but I think you've seen more of the truth of this world than you'd like. Would I be right?"

"I guess so."

"Figured," said Althea. "Gregory... Well. I understand why he did what he did, but that does not make it right. Not in the eyes of the Lord."

"Why did he do it?"

"Oh, it wasn't about greed or lust or power, if that's what you're thinking. My son isn't perfect, but he's a good man. It was because of my grandson, you see. Gregory made that deal out of love. And love is God's weapon. It's because of this that I pray, every night, that he finds his way back to the Lord, and I pray the Lord is willing to receive him. I'll add you to my prayers, if you like."

"Thank you," said Amber, oddly touched. "It'd be nice to have someone praying for me. What's your grandson's name?"

"Jacob," said Althea. "He had the cancer from a young age. By the time he was ten, his home was a hospital bed. He had tubes coming out of him and tubes going into him and then he needed help to breathe and then he couldn't see... Science failed him. It did its best, but it wasn't up to the job. I was praying, every day I was praying, but it seemed likely that God's plan was to kill that little boy and take his soul up to heaven. A fine plan, I supposed, in the overall scheme, though I couldn't for the life of me figure out why God was putting him through so much pain. I couldn't really see the point of that, to torture a little boy who'd never done nothing to nobody. If God had felt the need to torture, why not torture those folks who were just scraping into heaven, just barely? Maybe by making them suffer, they'd actually prove worthy of an afterlife? But by putting all that cancer into such a small boy, well... It just seemed cruel.

"But the Devil, you see, the Devil has no time for God's plans. The Devil and that Shining Demon of his are there to stir things up. Gregory made that deal and I'm glad he did it, because poor Jacob did not deserve what God was doing to him. I'm glad my son did what he did, even though he damned himself by doing it."

"What did the Shining Demon want in return?"

"Souls," said Althea. "What does he ever want? Souls, souls and more souls — the more innocent, the better. But my son is smarter than the Shining Demon. Jacob was healed, and Gregory disappeared without having to shed one single drop of blood. The Shining Demon doesn't know where to even look. So I doubt you'll be able to find him, if you don't mind me saying."

"You don't have any idea where he is?"

"I don't," said Althea. "Gregory probably thinks it's safer that way — safer for him and safer for me."

"What about your grandson?"

Althea shook her head. "Jacob doesn't know. Don't think he does, anyway."

"Could we talk to him?"

"I don't have a phone number for him, I'm afraid. He lives in Cricket Hill, that's in Colorado. Burkitt Road, I think. I might be wrong."

"He doesn't stay in touch?"

Althea smiled. "Young people have their own lives to lead, as you well know. No one has any responsibility to call me, or even write. Do you call your grandparents?"

"I, um, I never had any."

Althea patted her hand. "That's a shame. I have a feeling you'd have made a good granddaughter. What about your friend?"

"Glen? No, his family isn't anything to brag about, either."

"Well then," said Althea, "it's a good thing he has you and Milo, isn't it?"

"I guess."

Althea smiled. "Go on, now. Let an old woman get her rest."

Amber left the room, closing the door gently. She went to the bathroom, then made herself a sandwich in the kitchen. She made one for Glen, too, and took it to him. The living room was empty.

"Glen?" she called.

She searched the house, growing more and more panicked. Finally, she went to the window, looked in the direction Glen had been looking when he'd heard those whispers calling to him. In a darkened area across town, a single house was lit up.

Taking a heavy crucifix from Althea's wall, Amber followed him out into the night.

36

AMBER WALKED QUICKLY, sticking to the shadows, the crucifix clutched tightly in her hand. The streets were unnaturally quiet, the entire town of Cascade Falls holding its breath for morning. But morning was a long way off.

Halfway across town, Amber saw her first moving car of the night. She ducked behind a fence, scampered sideways, peering out through the leaves of a manicured hedge.

The car passed slowly, and so close that Amber got a good look at both Grant and Kirsty.

Her breath caught in her throat.

No demon horns for her parents' old friends. They looked perfectly normal, sitting there, scanning their surroundings like hawks, searching for prey. Amber had an irrational urge to stand up, let them see her.

She resisted.

The car moved on and Amber thought about what she'd seen. She thought about their faces. Calm but eager. Patient but excited. They knew she was close and they knew they were closing in. The urge to stand up faded quickly, replaced by a hatred so deep she now had to stop herself from screaming curses at them. Her heart pounded ever harder in her chest and she shifted without meaning to. This time there was no pain to accompany the transformation.

When the car had turned the corner, Amber moved on, still in her demon form, crossing the road quickly and slipping into shadow once again.

She got to the Varga Hotel without encountering anyone else, and skirted it. An image flashed into her head of vampires crawling all over the outside walls like flies on a rotting piece of meat, but so far there was nothing unusual – or unnatural – to be seen. She carried on through the darkened neighbourhood, to the only house with lights on.

Keeping to the shadows, she circled it, then crossed the road, and ducked down behind some bushes. She waited, making sure she hadn't been seen, then peeked back across the road at the front door, which gaped open like a hungry mouth.

Something bad had happened.

She bit her lip, feeling her sharp teeth. If there were vampires in there, she had the crucifix. If her parents were in there, the crucifix wouldn't make a damn bit of difference and she'd be walking to her death.

But she didn't have a choice. Glen was in that house, she just knew it, and she wasn't going to leave him behind – not if she could help it.

Keeping low, she jogged back across the road, straightening up as she approached the door. At the last moment, she reverted to her normal appearance – if she was wrong and everything was fine, she didn't want to give the owner of the house a heart attack.

Amber climbed the two small steps, pushed the door open the rest of the way, and, holding the crucifix out before her, she walked in.

The hall corridor was long and narrow, at the end of which was a door with a large partition of clouded glass. A doorway to her left led into a living room that was well maintained but barely lived in. Another doorway to her right opened on to a neat, bookshelf-lined study. She passed a small table on which sat a type of phone she'd only seen pictures of, the kind with a rotary dial. There was a bedroom on her left. A bathroom on her right.

The house was quiet and well lit. No shadows moved beyond the clouded glass ahead.

Amber stopped and listened. She counted to ten and, when she still didn't hear anything, she turned the handle and nudged the door. It swung open gently into a second living room, one that showed definite signs of having being lived in. The TV set in the corner, the logs beside the fireplace, the magazines and books scattered around on the various items of furniture – this was the room the owner of the house spent most of his time in.

He'd spent his last few moments in here as well.

His body lay crumpled beside the old sofa, his head twisted all the way round. His death had been quick – or at least it looked that way. Small mercies. Amber wondered if there would be anyone left in this town to gossip about it after tonight.

The living room connected to the kitchen. Amber crossed the carpeted floor silently. She got to the doorway and peeked inside, and a mournful weight dropped from her chest to her belly. Glen lay on the table, arms and legs flung wide, his eyes open and blinking. Dozens of small wounds punctured his body in perfect sets of two, and from those wounds trickled what little blood he had left. His skin was so pale. He looked empty. On the cusp of death.

His eyes flickered to her. He opened his mouth to moan, and all that escaped was a breath. A finger moved, and that's all he could manage.

A vampire stepped into the kitchen from the utility room ahead. She was middle-aged and as pale as Glen. She smiled at Amber, revealing her fangs.

Amber moved backwards out of the kitchen. The doors connecting the living room to the two main bedrooms were now open. Vampires stood there, watching her hungrily.

She backed up to the door with the clouded glass. They followed. Eight of them. She held up the crucifix. A look of physical pain passed over the vampires' faces. One of them actually recoiled, as if from a great heat. They hissed in anger.

The middle-aged woman was the bravest. With every step she took, Amber shrank back. The woman's eyes were astonishing. They blazed. Amber couldn't look away.

"Put down the cross," the woman said.

Her voice melted in Amber's head. The words sang. They tugged at every small corner of her mind, and brought with them a pleasing, numbing warmth.

Amber's arm dipped.

"Put it down," said the woman. "We won't hurt you."

Amber wanted to. She wanted to so badly. She didn't like holding the crucifix like this. She didn't want to hurt the woman's feelings. But the other vampires, she didn't like them. They scared her. Especially the way they were moving closer, their smiles spreading. In a matter of moments, one of them would be close enough to bat her arm down, maybe knock the crucifix from her hand altogether.

Would that be so bad? Maybe not. Maybe she should let them.

The woman's blazing eyes flickered briefly to the lowering crucifix, and Amber could think clearly again.

She bared her teeth, which became fangs, and her skin turned red and her muscles got bigger and her limbs lengthened and her horns grew and now it was the vampires who shrank back, their eyes wide as she stood before them, beautiful and terrible and snarling.

The middle-aged woman gaped. "What are you?"

Amber simply snarled, and stepped backwards into the corridor. Her free hand closed round the handle, and she slowly shut the door between them.

She backed off faster along the hallway. Shadows moved into the light beyond the clouded glass and bunched up, forming a solid mass. Amber reached the front door, put her foot out on to the first step.

The clouded glass shattered as the vampires came through. Amber spun, leaped off the steps and ran. They came after her, a cackling, spitting mass of bodies. She got to the street as a hand grabbed her shoulder and she shoved the crucifix behind her and heard a scream and the hand fell away as she ran on. They were in the air now, dark shapes flitting through the night sky. One of them swooped for her and she ducked, went stumbling. She jumped a low fence and ran through a backyard. The sudden fluttering of clothes from above and she felt a hand grasping at her hair, barely missing as it passed.

She ran to the next house, didn't slow down as she neared the front door. There was a whoosh of air behind her, and she just *knew* it was the middle-aged woman, the one with the honeyed voice. She leaped, putting her shoulder to the door, and it splintered and she went sprawling inside. She scrambled up. The door hung off its hinges, but the doorway itself was clear. They couldn't come in without an invitation.

She turned, saw a figure on the stairs, saw something glinting in the dark, and she dived to the ground as the shotgun blast filled the house. Then she was up, snatching the gun from the hands of its owner.

"What the hell?" she screamed.

The owner, a chunky guy in his forties with a bathrobe tied loosely over his boxers and T-shirt, held up his hands immediately. "Please!" he cried. "Don't hurt us! Just leave! God, please!"

"I'm not going to hurt you," she snapped.

He got a good look at her, he must have, because his face went slack. "Oh God... you're the Devil..."

"I'm not the Devil," she said. "My name's Amber. I'm not going to hurt you."

"Please," he sobbed. "Spare my family."

"I'm not going to hurt you," she repeated, louder this time. "You know what's going on, right? You know about all this craziness?"

He nodded quickly. "The... the things. The..."

"Go on. You can say it."

He swallowed thickly. "The vampires."

"There you go," said Amber. "Cascade Falls is overrun by vampires, right? Do I look like a vampire to you?"

"You look like the Devil."

"Still not a vampire, though. And I'm not going to hurt you or your family. Listen, they can't get in unless you invite them, all right? So you're perfectly safe."

"Are you going to eat us?"

"No," she said irritably. "I'm not going to eat you. Just do what I say and you'll live, got it?"

He nodded slowly. His eyes were moving now, darting to the front door as his thought processes came back online.

She handed him back his shotgun. "I'm going to trust *you* not to shoot me, okay?"

He hesitated, then took the weapon. "Thank you."

"I'm going to leave the first chance I get," she said. "If I can, I'll draw them away from you and your family. You want my advice? Get out of town first thing tomorrow."

"Yeah," he said shakily. "Yeah."

"I'm going to check the back," she said, "and see if I can get out there. Anyone even approaches that door, you blast them, understood?"

He nodded, and she patted his shoulder.

"You're all going to be okay," she said. "I promise."

She hurried into the dark kitchen, found the back door with the key still in the lock. She opened it, but didn't step out. She leaned, looking upwards. No sign of them.

She heard voices elsewhere in the house. She didn't want to freak out the guy's wife, but she really had no choice. She went back into the hallway.

He wasn't talking to his wife. He was talking to a vampire,

standing just outside the front door. The shotgun dangled in his hand. From here, Amber could see the vampire's blazing eyes.

The owner of the house stepped back. "Please," he said dully, "come in."

37

THE VAMPIRE WAS ON the man in an instant, mouth clamped round his jugular, and the other vampires poured in through the door. They half ran, half flew up the stairs, giggling in their anticipation. The screams of the family shook Amber out of her paralysis.

She turned and ran.

The town was a dark, jangled blur. She jumped walls and plunged through bushes. She trampled flowers and ducked under branches. She ran on road and lawn and sidewalk. The more she ran, the faster she ran. The oxygen she sucked in added fuel to her legs. She jumped over the hood of a parked car without touching it and smashed through a fence without feeling it.

She had reached Althea's house before she even looked back to see if they were following. They weren't.

She reverted to normal and nearly collapsed. Her muscles burned and she gasped for breath. Althea's door opened and Milo hurried out, took her arm and dragged her inside.

"Where the hell *were* you?" he asked as he closed the door behind her.

Veronica stood up from the sofa when she saw Amber. She was pale, and her clothes were dirty and her knee was bleeding.

But Amber didn't care about her. "Glen," she said. "They've got Glen."

Milo hesitated, and Amber sank into his chest and he hugged her.

She cried.

38

AMBER SLEPT AND DREAMED of dead things.

She awoke to sunlight and faint voices, coming from somewhere in the house. Calm voices. Quiet. She got up, and dressed by the window. From her vantage point on the hill, she had a pretty good view over the town. From here, Cascade Falls looked peaceful, the kind of peaceful only found in graveyards.

A car moved a few streets over, slipping in and out of view at a leisurely pace. Then it was gone.

She knew that car. She had travelled in it practically every day for the last three years, ever since her parents had bought it.

There was more movement, from another part of town. Two people walking. She squinted. Alastair she recognised immediately. The other person was momentarily obscured by a tree. Imelda emerged and Amber bit her lip to stop the sob from escaping.

She watched them walk up to a house. They shifted, their red skin and horns impressive even from this distance. Alastair kicked down the front door, and they strolled in.

Amber stood at the window, frowning.

Finally, there was movement, Alastair dragging someone out

of the house. He turned and threw the body on to the front lawn, and the moment sunlight hit him the man burst into flames. Amber couldn't hear his screams, but she could see Alastair laughing as he flailed. Imelda walked by Alastair and the burning vampire without looking at either of them, and went to the next house. Alastair reluctantly followed.

The burning vampire finally lay still, and the fire consumed him, flaring so brightly Amber had to look away. When the flames died, there were no remains left behind.

Imelda kicked in the door of the next house, and led the way in.

Door to door, killing the vampires that lay inside, searching for Amber. At the rate they were moving it'd take them until the afternoon to reach the hill – but they were coming.

Althea got the hell out of Cascade Falls by midday. They loaded up Veronica's car with her belongings and Veronica got behind the wheel. She hadn't said much the previous night. Amber knew that she had been running from vampires when Milo found her, and that was it. She had a look in her eyes, though – haunted. She was a different person from the woman who'd sat with them at dinner. Milo kissed her, and they said goodbye, and Althea waved at Amber as they drove quickly away.

"You liked her, huh?" said Amber to Milo.

He looked at her, and didn't answer.

"Thanks," she said.

Milo shrugged, and went back inside. Amber followed.

They watched from a window as Alastair and Imelda dragged vampires out into the sun. They were getting close.

Amber's parents passed the house. Amber started to duck down, but Milo grabbed her, held her in place.

"Movement attracts the eye," he said.

Her parents drove by without noticing them.

They couldn't see where Grant and Kirsty were.

"We have to leave," said Milo. "We go now and we have a few hours' head start. Maybe even a full day. Amber? What do you think?"

"We're going to leave Glen?" she asked quietly.

"There's nothing we can do for him now."

"We don't know that he's dead."

"You said he looked—"

"I know what I said," she snapped. "But I don't know for sure, do I?"

Milo let the silence settle for a few moments.

"We're not vampire killers," he said.

"I didn't say anything about—"

"You want to stop them. You want revenge. I can see it in your face."

"And along the way we can save the lives of whoever else is stupid enough to still be in this town."

He looked her dead in the eye. "What do you think we are? We're not the cavalry. This isn't our job or our responsibility."

"We stopped Shanks."

"Because we had no choice," Milo said. "Here, we have a choice. We get to the car and leave. Let your parents and their friends kill the vampires. They might actually do some good, for a change. Amber, you need to think about this. Jacob Buxton is a two-day drive away, and who knows how far we'll have to travel to get to his father after that?"

"Milo, I got an entire family killed last night."

"That wasn't your fault."

"How can it not be? I led the vampires right to their *house*. We have to do *something*. We stopped Dacre Shanks. We can stop these, too."

"Dacre Shanks was one guy with one trick," Milo said. "We don't know how many vampires there are – could be two dozen, could be a hundred, could be most of the town – but even one of them has the potential to kill both of us without thinking twice."

"So we do what Imelda's doing," said Amber. "We hit him now, during the day."

"Hit who?"

"Johann Varga," she said. "He'll be asleep, right? We get to the house I was in last night. If Glen isn't there, we go to the hotel, find Varga's coffin or whatever, and we stake him. It works, right? Staking them?"

"According to Althea's theory," said Milo.

"We stake Varga and, if Glen is there, we take him with us. If he's dead, we give him some kind of funeral. We're not going to just abandon him, Milo. I should have been here with him. I shouldn't have let him out of my sight. The moment he mentioned hearing voices I should have realised what it was and tied him to a chair or something."

"You didn't know."

"I should have. And now I owe him."

Milo looked at her, sighed, and walked from the room. A minute later, he was back, holding a hammer in one hand and a broken baseball bat in the other, the bat's broken end sharpened to a point. "This is what I was doing last night

330

while I was waiting for the coast to clear," he said. "This is our stake."

"That'll work?"

"It should. To be extra sure, we'll take a detour to the church, douse it in holy water. The hammer, too. We'll need to travel by foot, and take it slow. Amber, are you positive you want to do this? We'll be walking right into the vampires' nest, somewhere your folks are going to end up at, sooner or later. This is hugely, insanely risky."

"I know."

"You're not going to change your mind?"

"I can't, Milo."

He nodded. "In that case, bring the crucifix. We're going to need it."

By the time they got across town, the sun was dipping dangerously low in the sky. The body of the owner of the house was still in the living room, but Glen was gone. Amber knew he would be. They searched the house quickly, then moved on to the Varga Hotel. The only car Amber recognised in the lot was Imelda's. They went in through the rear door. There was no one around, not even Ingrid at the front desk.

"Where do we go?" Amber asked, her whisper oddly loud in the absolute quiet.

"Basement," said Milo.

They found the heavy door leading down. It got much too cold much too fast as they descended the stone steps. Milo went first, the stake and hammer in his hands, even though Amber was in full demon mode behind him. The very air down here made her want to turn round and run screaming, and never look back. There was a sense of something bad, something waiting for them beyond the wine racks. Something lurking.

They got to another door. Milo pulled his hand back from the handle.

"Cold," he whispered. He wrapped his sleeve round his hand and opened the door. A weak light flickered down another set of stairs.

Fear wrapped its fingers round the corners of Amber's mind and started to tug. She grew talons and bared her teeth, but that did nothing to bolster her courage.

The room below the basement was small, but even so the single light bulb had difficulty chasing the darkness away. Chained to the floor directly under the light bulb was a dried-out husk of a corpse, arranged in a cross-legged position with its head down. It wore rags and its hair was long. The sight of it was distressing, but it wasn't the source of Amber's fear. That came from something else.

The corpse looked up and Amber saw fangs.

The corpse, the vampire, didn't seem particularly surprised to see them, but his eyebrows rose as Amber stepped into the light.

"Huh," he said. His voice cracked. "And what are you supposed to be? The Devil? Has the Devil come to drive a stake through my heart after all this time?"

Milo approached him warily while Amber hung back.

"Hello, Caleb," said Milo.

Caleb Tylk managed a half-smile. "You've heard of me."

"We heard what you did to the Masterson family."

Caleb's smile soured. His skin was dry like parchment, and it flaked with every new expression. "And who are you?" he asked. "And why are you visiting me?"

"We're not here for you," said Amber. "We're here for your master. Where is Varga?"

"Varga's no master of mine," Caleb said. "He's kept me chained up here for two years. *Two years*. He won't let me sleep in a coffin, won't even let me sleep in the ground. Look around you. Concrete. Is that any way to treat your own kind?"

"What did you do?"

Caleb smiled. "Step closer so I can see you."

Talking in a normal voice soothed Amber's nerves, and she walked forward.

"Ohhh," said Caleb. "You're *wonderful*. A little closer, please."

"I don't think so."

"Just a little closer…"

Amber gave him a beautiful smile, and took another few steps. Then she slammed her right foot into his chest and knocked him on to his back. She kept her foot where it was, pinning him to the floor.

"What did you do," she said, smiling, "for Varga to chain you up like this?"

Caleb tried to push her foot off, but she ignored his feeble efforts.

"I broke his rule," he said at last. "I broke his sacred rule. I mean, what did he expect? That I'd wake up and be magically able to put my human life behind me without any second thoughts? He knew. He must have known. He's too old, you see. He forgets what it was like."

Amber put her weight on to her right foot. She heard one of Caleb's ribs crack. "What rule did you break?"

He snarled against the pain. "I didn't go elsewhere. I fed in the town where we lived." He paused. "Also, I don't know, something about being gauche, whatever that means…"

"You created more vampires than he could control," said Milo.

"Exactly," Caleb said. "It's all about control for him. He has to control everything and everyone. Well, I am not going to be controlled."

"You slaughtered an entire family."

"They had it coming."

Milo frowned. "How, exactly, did they have it coming?"

"I'd see them walking around town like they were too good for the likes of me. The parents, they never liked me. I called at the house one day and they looked at me like I was something they'd thrown up. And that kid, that annoying little brat—"

Amber twisted her foot in a semi-circle and Caleb grunted. "What about Rosalie?"

"What about her?" he fired back. "She was the worst of them. The biggest hypocrite of a family of hypocrites. She'd give it up for anyone with a bit of money, but the moment she realises I'm not going to be buying her diamond earrings, that's it. I'm shut out. Not all the way, of course. What fun would that be? No, no, she takes pleasure teasing me, promising me things and acting like she'll eventually give me a treat if I keep following her around like a little puppy…"

"So you killed her," said Amber.

"I should have," said Caleb.

"You turned her, didn't you?" Milo asked.

Caleb's lip, that dry, thin thing, curled. "She was supposed to be mine. I turned her for me. After all those years of her teasing me, laughing at me behind my back, leading me on…

I was going to be her master until the end of time. You want to know why? This is the truly funny part. Because, no matter what she'd done to me, I still loved her. Ain't that a riot? Even after everything she'd done."

"After everything *she* had done?" Amber said, her anger rising.

Caleb didn't notice. "But no. The moment Varga saw her, that was it. He took her from me. He said it was to punish me further, but he has me down here because he's afraid that Rosalie will choose me over him. I hear them together sometimes. He has no idea. She's using him, the same way she used me. It's pathetic is what it is. Let me out. Let me out of these chains and let me get my strength back and then I'll take care of Varga for you. I'll kill him myself, you understand? He fears me. He fears what I can do."

"Caleb," said Amber, "you're a pathetic loser and you're never getting out of those chains."

He glared at her. "I'll kill you," he said.

She moved her foot up to his throat, and pressed down. "Where is Varga?"

He gurgled, eyes blazing. Finally, he pointed to the wall beside Milo. She left her foot where it was while Milo examined the brickwork.

"Found something," he said, and a moment later a door in the wall swung open.

Once again, that terrible, freezing dread came over her, prying at her mind, and once again she wanted to run screaming from the cellar.

"Jesus," she whispered.

"Yeah," said Milo, and that's all he said.

Amber stepped off Caleb's throat and followed Milo into the corridor beyond. It got even colder. Even the light was cold. Milo turned the corner and stopped. Amber hesitated, then stepped out after him.

In front of them was a door. A big, thick, metal door, just like the ones they had in banks.

Amber stared. "Seriously?"

Milo examined the box on the wall beside it. "A time lock," he said. "Set to open when the sun goes down."

"How are we supposed to stake him when he sleeps in a frikkin' *vault*?"

"It does seem really unfair." Milo looked at her. "What do you want to do?"

"They must have Glen somewhere in this hotel," she said. "We have to find him. If he's alive, we take him with us. Any vampire we find along the way, you hammer that stake into their heart."

He nodded. "That I can do."

39

THEY STARTED AT THE room at the very top of the hotel.

Amber put her shoulder to the door. After three tries, she broke it down. The room was dark, the window boarded up from the inside. In place of a bed there was a coffin. Around it, flowers and framed photographs of a beautiful blonde girl. Rosalie Masterson. It had to be.

At Milo's nod, Amber lifted the coffin lid. Rosalie lay within, her head resting delicately on a satin pillow. Her perfect skin was pale. Her lips, plump and bow-shaped, were red. Her chest did not rise with her breathing. No pulse was noticeable in her throat. She looked dead and yet wonderfully, fantastically alive, like she was going to wake at any moment and break into a smile.

Milo pressed the tip of the stake over her heart. It sizzled against her skin, and Rosalie frowned in her death sleep. He raised the hammer, and hesitated. Amber had the irrational urge to leap forward, to stop him from doing what they'd come here to do, but her feet were stuck to the ground and she could only watch as he brought the hammer down.

The stake pierced Rosalie's chest with a sudden spurt of blood and her eyes snapped open and she screamed. Her eyes burning with hatred, yet clouded by confusion, she tried to grab the stake, tried to pull it out, but Milo hammered it down again and that was the one that did it. All tension fled from Rosalie's body and her arms fell by her sides and her legs stopped kicking and her skin puckered and burst and the stench of violent decomposition sent Milo reeling and Amber gagging. When Amber looked back, the beautiful girl had become little more than a skeleton, slick with its own blood.

Milo retrieved the stake, and they left the room and went into the next one. Room by room they went, coffin by coffin. Some vampires turned to skeletons, some to putrefying corpses, and some to dust. They all died with that same wide-eyed horror, though, that same look of disbelief on their faces.

The sun was dipping below the horizon and, just as they were about to abandon their search, Amber noticed a small door, tucked away in the eastern corner of the hotel. The key was still in the lock. Milo turned it, pushed the door open.

Glen lay on the bed inside. He was corpse-pale and his eyes were closed.

"Is he dead?" Amber asked softly.

Milo stepped in, and felt for a pulse. "Not yet," he said. "He's weak but alive."

Relief burst inside her, almost making her gasp, and she walked forward, shook Glen roughly. He muttered in his sleep but didn't wake.

"We have to leave now," said Milo. "We'll carry him out."

"I'll do it," Amber said, and hauled Glen to a sitting position. She ducked down, careful not to skewer him on her horns, and then straightened, Glen draped across her shoulders like a stole.

"You're smiling," said Milo.

"You're not," said Amber, "but don't pretend you weren't worried about him. He grew on you, didn't he?"

Without bothering to answer, Milo stepped out of the room and Amber heard Ingrid from the front desk say, "What... what are you doing?"

Milo looked at the hammer and stake in his hands, at his blood-splattered clothes, and before he could answer Amber stepped out to join him.

Ingrid cursed when she saw the horns, and bolted. Even with Glen on her back, Amber caught up to her easily. She kicked at her ankles and Ingrid yelped and went tumbling. She hit the stairs and rolled and spun and went flying again, finally sprawling on to the foyer floor below. Crying in pain, she started crawling. Her left leg appeared to be broken.

Amber and Milo walked down after her. Ingrid crawled by the front desk.

"You're not even one of them," Amber said. "You're still human. How could you do this?"

Ingrid turned on to her back. "The Master will kill you!" she screeched. "The Master will use you as—"

Amber kicked her in the face and Ingrid rolled over and shut the hell up.

Then a cold feeling came over Amber, slithering up her spine to tingle at the base of her skull. She turned, as did Milo, and they watched Varga sweep into the room. In a few quick strides, he had crossed to Milo, knocked the stake from his hand and pitched him over the desk. Next he turned to Amber, his eyes shining.

"You have the blood of my children on you," he said. Fury danced in his eyes. "You have the blood of my Rosalie on you."

Glen slipped off Amber's shoulders, fell in an unconscious heap. A series of nonsense words surged in her throat, jammed and wouldn't come out. She wanted to apologise, to threaten, to beg and to scream; she wanted to make noise and stay quiet. Instead, all she could do was raise her crucifix. Varga's lips curled back over his long, sharp teeth.

"Put that down," he commanded, and Amber recognised the authority in his voice, and she wanted so desperately to obey. Yet she was still thinking clearly enough to keep her trembling arm in place.

"This town is my town," Varga said. "You come here and you kill my children, my *Rosalie*, and you desecrate my home by bringing that," he sneered as he said it, and his eyes locked on to the crucifix in Amber's hand, "over the threshold. You have offended me in a great many ways, you foolish creature. Do you really expect to leave here alive?"

"You attacked my friend," Amber said, forcing the words out.

"I didn't touch a single hair on his singular head," said Varga. "In truth, I do not know who did. There are too many of us. We are best when we are few."

"Then we... we did you a favour. We—"

"You have murdered my children!" Varga boomed, and Amber stumbled back.

"The ones in this hotel were mine," he said, his voice calm once more. "The ones out there are... insubordinate things, never meant to be. The boy's doing. But they are no less my children."

Amber was so fixated on Varga that she didn't even notice Milo running at him. Varga did, however, and he spun, dodging the stake that was aimed at his back.

340

"Run!" Milo cried.

She did. She didn't think she would but she did. She ran, leaving Milo to face Varga alone. The moment she was out of the foyer, however, the fear drained away and she stopped, looked back. What the hell was she doing?

She turned back to see Milo slam into the wall. He dropped in a crumpled heap, the stake and hammer clattering to the ground nearby.

And then a familiar voice. "I hate vampires."

Fear surged once again, but this was not the supernatural terror that emanated from Varga's very pores – this was a fear much closer to her own heart. Her father's voice. Not even her demon form could keep that fear from infecting her. Now she really did want to run. She wanted to run and just keep running.

She made herself move up to the corner and peer round.

Bill and Betty led the demons into the foyer – tall and glorious with their red skin and horns. Alastair was the biggest of them – he had to duck when he came through, his horns scraping the top of the stone archway. Grant was the broadest, though – his jacket stretched tightly across his chest – and Kirsty's red hair had darkened to match the red of her skin. Imelda came last, eyes narrowed and focused on Varga.

"More mongrels," Varga said, distaste curling his lip. "You are not welcome here."

Bill smiled. "Unlike you, we don't need an invitation to walk in. That was always the problem with your particular breed, you know – you're just too polite."

"Ah," said Varga. "You think you have encountered my kind before."

"We have."

"No. If you had, you would be running right now. But my business is not with you. Leave here and I will forgive the transgressions you have made against my family."

"Family?" said Kirsty. "Oh, you mean all those nasty little vamps we've been dragging out into the sun all day? That family? That's a big family. You must get around."

Varga watched her without speaking as they slowly, casually, surrounded him.

"We'll leave," said Betty. "We'll walk out of here right this second, providing you tell us what we want to know. We're looking for a girl called Amber. She would have come in a black car. Do you know her?"

"I have seen the girl."

"You have? That's wonderful. Where is she?"

Amber prepared to run, but Varga smiled, and didn't say anything.

The demons raised their crosses, and Varga hissed.

"Where is she?" asked Bill, stepping closer.

Varga tried to back away, but the circle was too tight. His skin began to smoke. "All who have spilled the blood of my family are mine to kill," he said, his voice pained. "The girl. Her companion. And all of you."

Alastair laughed. "I'd like to see you try, bloodsucker."

Varga said something that Amber didn't catch and turned to him, locking eyes. Alastair swayed slightly, and his hand dipped.

That was all Varga needed.

He dived on Alastair impossibly, ridiculously fast, powering him backwards out of the circle. Next he tossed him as if he was a baby, hurling him with such force into Grant and Imelda that all three went down. Kirsty lunged, the crucifix held before her, and Varga turned to a man of smoke that burst apart when the cross passed through him.

Kirsty spun, sudden fear in her eyes, black scales beginning to spread across her skin as the smoke swirled and coalesced behind her. Varga's long-fingered hand closed round the back of her neck and he slammed her face-first into the wall.

He turned as Bill and Betty stepped closer together, their crucifixes up.

"You vampires and your magic tricks," said Betty. "The smoke, the bats, the hypnosis... You're like a bad vaudeville magician. You belong in a top hat on a crummy stage with a bored assistant, and instead here you are, bothering good, decent folk like us."

"Where is our daughter?" Bill asked.

"You will die first," said Varga. "Your mate will watch and cry for you, and only when grief has overtaken her heart will I end her life."

"You bore me," said Bill.

"And I have a name," said Betty.

"You are insects to me," said Varga.

"So rude," said Betty, just as Amber saw something in her other hand, a water bottle, and she flicked it and the water hit Varga and sizzled like acid against his face.

He recoiled, hissing in pain, and Bill was upon him in an instant. With black scales covering the fist that held the crucifix, Bill hit him, a right cross that sent the vampire stumbling over Glen's sleeping form. Bill ran at him, hit him again, and now Betty was there, pressing her crucifix to the side of Varga's head. They worked as a team, dividing the vampire's wrath between them, denying him focus and constantly driving him back. Betty squeezed the remains of the water bottle right into his face and Varga howled, hands over his eyes, and Bill's hands turned to talons that slashed at Varga's neck.

The swipe would probably have taken his head if he hadn't turned to smoke before it landed.

Varga solidified behind them, his skin already healed of the holy water's effects, his eyes burning with hatred.

He seized Bill and leaped upwards in a blur. The back of Bill's head hit the ceiling and he plummeted to the ground while Varga stayed up there. Betty moved instantly to stand over her husband, composure gone from her face for the first time, keeping the crucifix raised, and Amber realised with a sickening certainty that her mother had never shown her that protective instinct.

Varga scuttled across the ceiling and was lost to Amber's sight, but she was able to track his movements by the way Betty was keeping the crucifix between them. When Betty lowered the cross, Amber knew Varga had dropped to the floor. But, when Betty lowered her cross slightly again, she had no idea what was happening until she heard the growl.

Amber inched forward, searching for the source of the sound. Whatever the dog was and wherever it had come from, it was big, and it had shocked Betty so much she had almost taken a step backwards. But to move back was to abandon her husband, and Betty wasn't prepared to do that.

Amber moved slightly again, until she could see the animal. She'd been wrong. It wasn't a dog. It was a wolf. Huge and grey, it came slowly across the floor towards Betty, growling, its hackles raised and its teeth bared.

It barked once, sharply, and Amber flinched at the sound, and she saw her mother swallow and adjust her hold on the crucifix, and the wolf suddenly leaped. It burst into smoke before it hit the crucifix and hands reached from inside that smoke, knocking the cross from Betty's grip. She spun but the smoke had become Varga, and he had her, and he threw her into the wall.

She stumbled back and grew talons, but Varga moved so fast they were useless against him. He struck her with a lazy swipe across the ribs and she gasped, and he grabbed her round the throat. Betty clutched at his wrist as he tightened his hold. She sank to her knees, unable to breathe.

If Varga killed Betty, he'd kill the others just as quick. He'd kill Milo and Glen and then he'd come after Amber. She wouldn't have a chance of stopping him. The only chance she possibly had was to run right now, while his focus was elsewhere. Her parents would die. Milo and Glen would die, but she would get away. She'd be free.

It all made sense. It was logical. Practical. But logic wasn't why she crept forward, or why she picked up the hammer and stake. It wasn't logic that was burning at the very core of her being. It was anger. It was fury.

He was hurting her mom.

40

"Do you feel that?" Varga asked Betty, his voice soft. "Do you feel your vertebrae beginning to snap? How does it compare, do you think, to burning in sunlight? How does it compare to the deaths you have subjected my family to? Eh?" He leaned in closer. "When I take your head, little demon, I will mount it on my wall."

Amber charged and Varga heard her and spun, too late to stop the stake from piercing his chest. His back hit the wall and Amber swung the hammer, but he grabbed the wrist of the hand holding the stake and it barely moved. He smiled at her, showing his teeth.

She smiled back, showing hers.

She slammed the hammer into his face. He hissed in pain – the impact leaving a circle on his skin that sizzled like she'd just hit it with a clothes iron – and then she hammered the stake through his ribcage.

Varga stiffened, his eyes widening and his mouth opening. No blood, though.

She hammered again, and his surprise was overtaken by fury. He closed both hands round the stake, but could do nothing to stop her from hammering it in deeper, and deeper, and then she hit the stake so hard the head flew off the hammer. She dropped it, pounded at the stake with her fist, and now Varga was screaming and writhing, and she hit it one more time and a torrent of dark blood gushed from the wound, hit her full in the face, and drove her backwards. It blinded her, got in her mouth, got up her nose, and it covered the floor and she slipped, fell, spitting and coughing and wiping her eyes, and there was blood all over her, drenching her, flattening her hair to her scalp.

And then the torrent weakened, and shortened, and Amber blinked madly and looked up as the last of Varga's blood, which had turned black and thick, like tar, dripped slowly from his wound. He was nothing but a shell now, a dried-out husk, as grey as ash. He dropped to his knees and they cracked beneath him and his whole body crumpled, his suit flattening like a sail suddenly becalmed. His skull toppled, too heavy for his spine to support, and when it hit the ground it exploded into dust and fragments.

"Amber."

The voice, the tone, made her revert instantly, and she turned to see her mother – with her mother's face – struggling to her feet. She clutched her side like her ribs were broken. Or worse.

"You saved me," Betty said, her voice weak. "After everything that's happened, you saved me."

Amber stood, covered in blood, and couldn't find anything to say.

"We made a mistake," said Betty, leaning on the front desk for support. "We did. We have made such a huge mistake. But we're here now."

"I know what you want," Amber said.

Betty shook her head. "Not anymore. Whatever you've heard, things have changed. We changed them. Give us a chance, sweetheart. Let us explain."

"You'll just lie again."

"That's over with," Betty said, with a conviction in her eyes that made Amber believe her. "It's all over with. We've been doing this a long time, baby, and we're sick of it. We want something different."

"How many of my brothers and sisters have you killed?"

It was funny, but witnessing the hurt on her mother's face was almost enough to make Amber run to her.

"We're bad people," Betty said finally. "But we're trying not to be. Please, Amber, come back to us. We can start again. As a family."

Betty took a step towards her and her knee buckled, but before she hit the ground Amber was there, helping her hobble back to the desk.

"Thank you," Betty said, gritting her teeth against the pain. "Oh, sweetheart, you have no idea what we've been through. We thought we'd lost you."

"Can you stand?"

Betty managed a small laugh. "Always so considerate, aren't you? You didn't get that from your father, let me tell you. Didn't get it from me, either, I'm afraid."

Amber suddenly realised how vulnerable she was, but Betty released her hold of her as soon as she could balance on her own. Amber had gotten some of Varga's blood on her mother's top. It was an expensive top. Betty didn't even seem to notice.

"Do you know who you've always reminded me of?" Betty continued. "My mother. Your grandmother. I've never told you about her, have I?"

"You've never told me anything."

"Well, that ends today. From this moment on, no secrets between us. Deal?"

"Betty, you can't just—"

"Mom."

Amber frowned. "What?"

"I think I'd like you to call me Mom from now on," Betty said. "Do you think you could do that?"

"I... I don't know..."

Betty shook her head. "I'm going too fast, aren't I? I'm sorry, sweetheart. One step at a time, that's how we get our family back together."

"Betty... Mom... I don't know if I can believe you."

Betty's eyes glistened with sudden tears. "Right," she said. "Of course. I mean... obviously. We've put you through a lot and we have to... we have to earn back your trust. I get that. I do. But you have to see it from our perspective, Amber. You are our daughter and we love you above all else. Your safety and wellbeing are all we care about. You don't have to forgive us, sweetheart, not yet, but this family is not going to be split up anymore. We love you, baby."

Tears sprang to Amber's eyes and her mother pulled her in for a hug. She held her close and Amber sobbed, and when the sobbing was over Amber just closed her eyes for a few moments.

Just a few. That's all she needed for now.

"Go home," Amber said, moving back a little. She'd left a blood smear on Betty's chin. "I've got something to do and, when it's done, I'll go home, too, and we can go back to being a family."

"Wherever you go, we go," said Betty. "We are not leaving your side."

"I'll only be gone a few more days. I've started something and I need to finish it. But I'll see you at home, Mom. You and Dad."

Amber kissed her cheek, started to pull away.

Betty held on to her wrist. "What do you have to do?"

"Just something."

Betty's grip tightened.

"Mom, you're hurting me."

"Families stay together."

"Mom, please let go."

"We'll just ask your father, what do you say?"

And then Milo pressed the muzzle of his gun to the side of Betty's head and said, in a soft voice, "Let her go."

Betty's eyes widened slightly. Amber said nothing. Betty released her.

Keeping his gun aimed squarely at Betty's head, Milo moved to stand beside Amber.

"And just who exactly are you?" Betty inquired.

"I think you know who I am," said Milo. "I think you've already run a check on my car."

Betty half smiled. "Indeed we did, Mr Sebastian, but we could find precious little about you. Aren't you a bit old to be hanging around with sixteen-year-old girls?"

"And you're suddenly a concerned parent? You expect us to believe that?"

"So you're the one poisoning our daughter against us."

"No, you did that when she overheard you planning to kill her."

Betty stood straighter. Her ribs didn't seem to be bothering her as much anymore. "Amber, I've known men like him my whole life. He's nothing but trouble. You can't listen to a word he says. He doesn't know the facts. He doesn't know us."

"I... I trust him," said Amber.

"You can't," said Betty. "He's been lying to you this whole time. He's brainwashing you, can't you see that? He's turning you against us." She fixed her glare on Milo. "This is kidnapping. What you've done is kidnapping."

"Amber saved your life tonight," said Milo. "I'd remember that, if I were you."

"You don't matter," said Betty. "You don't matter to us. Amber, I forbid you to go anywhere with this man."

Milo picked Glen off the floor in a fireman's lift, and walked towards the door. Amber hesitated, then followed.

"Amber!" Betty said sharply, taking a few steps in pursuit. "Amber, you stay right here, young lady!"

Amber shook her head. "I have to—"

"You will stay with your family!"

Amber shifted, felt the power and the strength surge through her, and she snarled. "You're lucky I don't rip your head off, Mom. You think I believe a word you say? Do you?"

Betty met her glare with one of her own. "This is your one chance. The only chance you'll get. If you walk away, we'll come after you, and I personally will eat your heart, young lady."

Amber backed out of the door. "Love you, too," she said, and ran.

41

THEY DROVE FOR FIFTEEN HOURS. Every mile they clocked took a little something more from Milo. He was gaunt. He looked thinner. Amber didn't say anything. Glen slept. There were times when his breathing got so soft she thought he'd died. She didn't say anything about that, either. All she cared about was getting as far away from Cascade Falls as she could. They stopped four times in those fifteen hours. She'd been able to scrub her face and change her clothes, find her sunglasses and pee twice, and that was it. No time to do any more. No time to waste.

When they got to Death Valley National Park, it was past midday and the Nevada sun was a merciless thing. The asphalt stretched further than Amber could see and straighter than she could fathom. Heat rose in thick, hazy waves that shimmered and glimmered, but in the Charger it was cool. The air-conditioner was never on, but in the Charger it was always cool.

"How far are we from Colorado?" she asked.

"We're not going to Colorado," said Milo.

Amber frowned. "What?"

"Your parents expect us to run straight to wherever we're

headed next, now that we know they're right behind us. But we're going to meander. They're the ones in the hurry, not us. Let them overshoot us. We don't have a deadline."

Amber said nothing to this. They drove and she sat there. Her body was still, but her mind was whirling. In her head, arguments raged. Up until now, the one little secret she'd been keeping from Milo hadn't seemed like a big deal. It was the kind of thing she'd been planning to tell him once it was all over, the kind of thing she expected him to raise an eyebrow at, maybe shake his head in mild exasperation. But the events of the last few days had cleared her vision. She could see now that little details could have far-reaching consequences. She could see now that she didn't have the luxury of keeping secrets.

"What if we did have a deadline?" she asked softly.

"Sorry?" said Milo.

She took off her sunglasses. He kept his on. "You said my parents are in a hurry, not us. You said we don't have a deadline. But what if we did?"

Milo glanced at her. "Something you're not telling me, Amber?"

She looked away. "I… It seems silly now, but I didn't want you to think I was stupid."

The Charger slowed. "What are you talking about?"

"I'd just met you," said Amber. "I didn't know you, I didn't know Edgar. You gave me all these instructions for what not to do when talking to the Shining Demon and I followed them, I followed them all. But then he started talking about a deadline…"

Milo braked so suddenly she cried out and Glen slid off the back seat and into the footwell.

When he spoke, Milo's voice was barely above a whisper. "What did you agree to?"

She hesitated, then took off her bracelets and showed him her wrist.

He frowned. "A number?"

"A countdown."

"What the hell?" he said, voice raised. In the confines of the Charger, it sounded like a shout. "Why didn't you tell me? Why the hell didn't you tell me?"

"I'm sorry," she said, "I just—"

"Why did you keep this from me? You've had this since Miami and you're only telling me about it now? *Why?* You didn't want me to think you were stupid?" There was something going on behind his sunglasses, like his eyes were glowing. "Good going, Amber, because now I *know* you're stupid."

Suddenly the car felt too small. Too cramped. The cool air nipped at her face and crept down her collar.

Amber threw open the door and jumped out into the heat. She walked over cracked and dry ground, her legs stiff, her arms rigid by her sides, her shoes kicking stones. She started to think about her parents again, and she walked faster, but the thoughts kept up. She broke into a run, tears blurring her vision. When she was out of breath, she shifted into her demon form and ran on. In her demon form, she could run forever. In her demon form, she never had to worry about crying.

A racking sob took her by surprise and Amber stumbled, fell to her hands and knees. Tears dropped to the ground and the ground soaked them up thirstily. Not even her demon form could shield her.

She tried to get up but couldn't. She rocked back on her

haunches. Her eyes fixed on a spot on the ground and held it. It took her a good long moment to figure out that she was looking at her shadow. The way her shadow was, all bunched up like that, it made her horns look like Mickey Mouse ears, except thinner, and sharper. If Micky Mouse was a demon's shadow, she decided it'd be an exact match.

Walter S. Bryant, the kid back at Springton, had wanted to go to Disney World. She wondered if he ever would. He stood a good chance, she thought. At least Springton was still standing. How long did Cascade Falls have, now that the vampires were free to drain it dry? She wondered if it would rise from the dead, like so many of its other victims, but then decided not. Whatever it would be in the future, it would no longer be Cascade Falls, just like this shadow she cast was not Amber.

She reverted. Immediately, she began to sweat. The sun burned at her scalp. If she stayed here, the sun would eventually fry every last inch of her, she was sure. Fry her to nothing. Rob her of all liquids. Maybe she'd end up looking like Varga, right before he crumpled. She still had his blood on her. It was matted into her hair. She needed a serious shower before she'd be free of him. She'd need mouthwash, too. She could still taste it.

She stood, looked to the road. She'd run a long way. Her eyes dry now, she walked back to the Charger. Milo got out as she neared, looked at her over the roof. He took his sunglasses off, had to squint against the glare. His eyes looked tired, but perfectly normal.

"Sorry," he said.

"No, you're right. I was being stupid."

"You're allowed to be stupid. You're in a unique situation. There is no correct way to handle things."

"I still should have told you."

"How long do you have left?"

She looked at her wrist. "Two hundred and forty hours."

"Ten days," said Milo. "It'll take maybe fifteen hours of driving to get to Colorado. If Jacob Buxton can tell us exactly where his father is, we won't have a problem."

"Are you okay?" she asked.

"What do you mean?"

"You don't look well. You look sick. And your eyes…"

"I'm fine," he said.

"We're way above the eight-hours-a-day rule. Let me drive."

He shook his head. "I can keep going. I'm not tired. Remember, it's eight hours a day on *average*. I can handle a little more."

"We've been driving for double that."

"I can handle it, Amber. Besides, we're on a schedule. Now get in."

She hesitated, but he was already behind the wheel. She slid into her seat and buckled her belt, and the Charger ate up the endless road, the asphalt vanishing under its wheels.

42

When they were on the Beltway and making good time, Glen woke, and Amber bounced a crucifix off his head just to make sure he was still human.

"Ow," he said.

She examined him, then sat back and buckled her seat belt once more. "No burning or scarring," she said. "You're not a vampire."

She glanced at Milo, but he was staring straight ahead. Just like he had been for the last few hours.

Glen struggled to sit up. He was astonishingly pale, and every movement was slow and lethargic. When he was sitting up straight, he asked, "Where are we?"

"Nevada," said Amber. "How are you feeling?"

Glen licked his lips and worked his tongue around his mouth for a few moments. When he spoke again, his voice was clearer. "Awful," he said. "Really, really bad, like. Should I be in hospital? I feel like I should be in a hospital of some description."

"You're fine," said Amber. "You've just lost some blood."

"Oh," he said. "Oh yeah."

"How much do you remember?"

"Uh… bits. I remember being in Althea's house, and someone calling to me, and I went out—"

"You didn't think that was odd?" Amber asked.

"Sorry?"

"Someone calling to you from the other side of town," she said. "That didn't strike you as unusual at all?"

He frowned. "I didn't really think about it, to be honest. I just… went. Walked right into a house and there were loads of them, just waiting there. They were laughing at me. Then they…"

His frown deepened. After a moment of staring at nothing, he shook his head and looked up. "And you're sure I'm not going to turn into one of them?"

"Not according to Althea," she said. "You'll only turn after a vampire bite kills you. You're not dead, are you? So you're not one of them. But I'll throw the cross at you again if you want."

He held up a hand weakly. "No, no, you're fine, thanks. How did we get away?"

"We were outnumbered," she said, "and then you ran in and saved us."

His eyes widened. "I did?"

"No. You were asleep for the whole thing. Milo and I got us out."

Glen sighed. "So it was me being my typical useless self, then, was it?"

The look on his face robbed Amber of the joy of teasing him. "You're not useless," she said. "You were just bitten. It could have happened to any one of us."

"Yeah, except it happened to me." He rubbed a hand over his face. "Listen, can we stop for food, or something? I'm starving."

"We got you some nuts," said Amber, passing him a small bag.

He stared at it. "Nuts? Seriously?"

Amber glanced at Milo for help, but his face was set and he was looking straight ahead.

She gave Glen a smile. "Your body needs to make more blood. Nuts are a good way of doing that. When we stop, you can have fruit and meat and milk and whatever else you need."

Clearly unconvinced, Glen did his best to open the bag. Amber took it from him, opened it, and handed it back.

"Thanks," he mumbled, and started eating. After a moment of chewing, he looked up. "Nevada is where Las Vegas is, right? Are we going to be anywhere near it?"

"We're in Las Vegas now, dummy."

Glen brightened immediately and looked around, saw nothing but freeway. "Uh... where is it?"

"That way," she said, pointing.

They both looked out at the concrete border that separated the roads as they sped by.

"I can't see much beyond the, y'know, wall," said Glen.

"Yeah," said Amber.

"Are we going to see the Strip?"

"No."

"The hotels? Any of the casinos?"

"Probably not."

"Are we just... are we just driving round the city?"

"Yes."

"And we're not going to see anything of the city itself?"

"Yes."

"We are?"

"No, I mean, yes, we're not."

"So, after all these years of hearing about Las Vegas, and seeing it in movies and TV, I finally get here and... and all I get to see is a wall?" Tears sprang to his eyes.

Amber frowned. "Are you crying?"

"Am I?" Glen said, and sobbed loudly. "Dear Jesus, I am. Why am I crying? I'm not even that sad." He wiped tears from his cheeks like they were pesky insects. "It's just I really wanted to see Las Vegas."

"You've lost a lot of blood," said Amber. "You're very emotional."

"Apparently."

"I'm going to turn round now, and pretend you're not crying, because I don't know how to deal with that."

He nodded as he wept. "Sounds fair."

She turned round and looked out of the windshield and after a few minutes Glen stopped crying and fell asleep.

They carried on into Utah. By this stage, Amber had had enough of Milo's deteriorating condition. His skin was getting greyer by the mile. She demanded that he stop and he reluctantly obliged, and they stayed at a Super 8 in Green River. Amber slept like the dead that night. In the morning, Glen had some colour in his cheeks and Milo was back to normal and the Charger gleamed. As she got in, Amber was overcome by the feeling that it had been waiting for them.

She looked at her brand, not even hiding it now: 221 hours left.

They got to Cricket Hill, Colorado, a little after two that afternoon, then spent another hour trying to find Burkitt Road. It led them into the tree-covered hills, the way getting narrower the further they went. The road turned to a trail and the trail petered out, and they had to leave the Charger and continue on foot. A light rain fell, but the trees protected them for the most part and Glen didn't complain, despite the fact that he was obviously still very weak.

"Gregory Buxton doesn't sound like the kind of man I expected," Amber said, breaking the silence.

Milo glanced at her. "Meaning?"

"Meaning he's a good guy," said Amber. "From what Althea said, anyway. He made that deal to save his son, and he hasn't hurt anyone. He's not like Dacre Shanks or... or my folks. How can we offer him to the Shining Demon now that we know all that?"

Milo's strides were annoyingly long. "Offering him up is your best chance at survival," he said.

She hurried along beside him, leaving Glen struggling to catch up. "There has to be something else. There has to."

"So what now? You want to turn around?"

"No," she said. "I want to find him. He's managed to cheat the Shining Demon and stay alive for all this time. He sounds like someone who can help me."

"If Jacob will tell us where he is," Milo said.

"What do we do if he won't help?"

"Let's find him first," said Milo. "Whatever happens after that happens after that."

They followed the trail to a cabin. It may have been sturdy once, may have been proud and strong, may have stood in this clearing and proclaimed its toughness to all the trees that surrounded it, but time and circumstance had worn it down. It sagged like an old man now. The window to the right of the narrow door drooped sadly, and weeds burst from the rotten boards on the porch. A battered motorcycle was parked outside, its tyres flat, joining the cabin in its moroseness.

Amber and Glen stepped over a curving line of moss-covered stones, half buried in leaves, and followed Milo up to the door. The porch creaked dangerously under their weight. The door opened before Milo could even knock.

"What do you want?" Jacob Buxton asked. He was about forty, and skinny, only a little taller than Amber, and he needed a shave. He needed a good night's sleep, too. He looked awful. His eyes were bloodshot and his dark skin was irritated just under his jaw. He scratched at it absently with dirty fingernails.

"My name's Milo Sebastian, and this is Amber and that's Glen," said Milo. "You're Jacob, right?"

"I'm not interested in whatever you're selling," Jacob said. "Do yourselves a favour and go away."

He started to shut the door.

"We're looking for your father," said Amber.

Jacob paused, thought for a moment, then said, "Good luck with that."

"I'm in trouble."

"You will be if you don't leave," he said, threatening words that didn't sound like a threat.

"Please," said Amber. "Your father's the only one who can help me."

An expression passed over Jacob's face that may, on anyone else, have been mistaken for amusement. "You expect him to help? You've obviously never met him."

"No, but we were told about him."

He allowed the door to open a little wider, just so he could brace himself idly against the frame. "Believe me, the legend doesn't begin to even approach the man."

"Can you tell us where he might be?" Milo asked.

Jacob looked at them both. "Seriously?"

Amber frowned. "You're talking like you expect us to know something I don't think we know."

"Well then, let me enlighten you. I don't know where my father is," said Jacob. "That's why I'm here. That's kind of the whole point."

"Could I possibly use your bathroom?" Glen asked.

"No," said Jacob.

"Mr Buxton," said Milo, "we've travelled a very long way to talk to you. If you could just be straight with us, we'll move on and we won't bother you again. Those rocks we stepped over to get here – I'm assuming they go right around your property, yes? What do you need with a protective circle?"

Jacob examined him, then switched his gaze to Amber. She tried to look as knowledgeable as Milo.

"The girl doesn't know what you're talking about," Jacob said.

"She's new," said Milo.

"I'm learning," said Amber. "And I know more than Glen."

"I literally know nothing," Glen offered up happily.

"When you say protective circle," Amber said to Milo, "do you mean like the other one? The one I was in? So it's an occult thing, right?" She switched her focus to Jacob. "What's it for? What's it keeping out?"

"The witch," said Jacob.

Amber glanced at Milo to make sure he wasn't smiling. No smile, which meant no joke. She looked back at Jacob.

"There are witches?"

"There are."

"And why is she after you?"

Jacob ignored the question. "Who told you about me?"

"Your grandmother."

"She's still alive, then?"

"You don't know?"

"We had a falling out. She tends to skip over the unpleasant realities of our little family drama. Lovely woman, but stubborn as hell." Jacob started suddenly, like he'd seen something in the trees behind them. Amber glanced back, saw nothing but woodland.

"Listen," said Jacob, once his focus returned, "you want to know where my father is? I don't know. I'm sorry about that, but there it is. I don't know where he is and there's nothing you can do to *make* me know." He looked at Milo. "That's what you're planning, isn't it? Sorry, my friend. You look like you can dish it out, but I just don't have the information you're looking for. This is a dead end. You may as well go back to where you came from before you draw its attention."

"The witch," said Milo.

Jacob nodded.

"We're not going anywhere."

"I'm serious," said Jacob. "If it sees you, it'll go after you."

"Then you better invite us in."

Jacob sighed. "Whatever. Enjoy your walk back."

He closed the door.

Amber started to ask a question, but Milo held up a hand. She clamped her mouth shut and looked around. She wondered if it was a witch like the one in The Wizard of Oz or like the ones in that Roald Dahl book. She'd hoped it was a witch like the ones in *Harry Potter*, but she doubted it.

The cabin door opened and Jacob stood there, looking thoroughly pissed off.

"Get in, quick," he said.

43

THE CABIN WAS CLUTTERED with books and magazines and tied-off trashbags. Despite this, it was neat, to a degree, though a smell definitely lingered in the air.

"The witch is trapping you here?" Amber asked. "What happens if you try to leave?"

"It chases me back," Jacob answered, closing the door behind them. "It doesn't want to kill me. It just wants to plague me. It took me a few years to figure that out. It doesn't make things any better. Doesn't make it any easier to escape."

"The bathroom?" Glen asked.

Jacob sighed, and gestured to a door. Glen smiled his gratitude, and hurried in.

"How long have you been here?" Milo asked.

"Living here? Ten years," said Jacob. "Trapped in this cabin? Seven months. Stay away from the windows, please." He frowned. "You know, I can't remember the last time I had visitors. That says something, doesn't it? If I can't remember that? I'm not sure what it is I'm supposed to do now, though. Do people still apologise for the mess? I guess they do. In that case, excuse the state of things. My trash isn't picked up anymore. I do my best to recycle, but what I'd really like is to take all this junk outside and burn it. But like any Boy Scout I am well aware of the dangers of open fires in wooded areas. So tell me who you are or I'll kill you all with an axe."

Amber must have taken on a funny look, because Jacob gave her a smile.

"Not really. The axe is out back, and I've never killed anyone with it. But I am mighty curious as to who the hell you are and what you want with my father."

"We just want to talk to him," Amber said. "Your grandmother told us you might be able to help."

Jacob scratched his neck. "What else did she say?"

"She told us that when you were a kid you had cancer. Your father made a deal with the Shining Demon to cure you, but, when your dad was supposed to start repaying his debt, he ran, and the Shining Demon couldn't find him."

Jacob nodded. "She tell you what my dad had to do in return for saving my life?"

"She said he was supposed to harvest souls. But he never had to, because he ran."

Jacob looked to Milo. "You're a man of the world. You believe that?"

Milo hesitated. "Some of it has the ring of truth."

"And what part strikes that one bum note?"

"The fact that he never had to hurt anyone. I find that hard to accept."

"That's because it's not true," said Jacob. "When I was sick, my grandmother would pray by my bed almost every evening. She wasn't there to talk, wasn't there to chat, she wouldn't bring me any comic books or grapes, or *Get Well Soon* cards... It was like she wasn't even there for me. She was there to speak to God. She prayed so long and so hard, with the muttering and the clasped hands and the tears in the eyes, that she actually scared me. She was just so… fervent. Every night after she'd left, I'd lie there, hooked up to all those machines, terrified that right there, in that silence, when I was alone… God would answer. And I'd be the only one to hear it.

"Althea may have come to terms with one part of what my father did, but not the whole thing – not the parts that threaten her idea of who her son is. See, she was prepared to accept that what he did was necessary, but it only worked for her if he remained a saint. Anything other than that would have ruined everything."

"So your dad isn't a saint," Amber said. She had some experience of that.

"His intentions were good," Jacob replied. "I was dying. He was willing to do anything to save me. *Anything*. And he did. If he hadn't made that deal, I'd have been dead by the age of eleven."

"Where was the deal struck?" Milo asked.

"In my hospital room," Jacob answered. "My father and the Shining Demon, standing over my bed. The light was everywhere. There were no shadows. None. At first, I thought it was God, you know? I thought maybe He'd heard my grandmother and here He was to cure me. But then they started talking about the deal, and about what my father would have to do. Pretty soon the Demon didn't sound like God anymore. But my dad didn't sound like who I thought he was, either. He was talking to this Demon and he was negotiating the terms like he knew all the ins and outs. One thing I can say about my father, he is

368

a smart man, and he likes to read. If a subject interests him, he'll read enough to make himself an expert, or as close to one as it's possible to get. And that's how he was talking to the Shining Demon – like an expert. I didn't know it at the time – how could I? – but he was negotiating a loophole in the agreement that not even the Shining Demon noticed."

Amber looked round as Glen walked in. "I think I broke your toilet," he said.

Amber closed her eyes.

"It has a difficult flush," said Jacob. "Wait until the water stops gurgling, and try again."

Glen responded to Amber's glare with a helpless shrug, then nodded and left.

Jacob moved into the kitchen – a lacklustre affair with a stove and a table. He boiled some water as he talked. "If you're going to ask me what that loophole was, don't bother. I don't know. But, after my dad had shaken the Shining Demon's hand, the Shining Demon reached down to me and his fingers – I remember them being long, long fingers – passed into my stomach. They didn't break the skin or anything, they just passed right through, and they hurt. I mean, they hurt like hell. My dad had his hand clamped over my mouth to stop me from screaming – we didn't want to alert the nurses – but I was thrashing and kicking and then I opened my eyes again and the Shining Demon was holding this grey lump of sludge and tissue. That was my cancer. The pain was gone; the sickness was gone. He just took it all away from me. I looked to my dad and for a moment, just the briefest of moments, I saw what the Demon had done to him. His skin was grey – the same grey as my cancer – but it was hard, and his eyes glowed, and he had fangs, and he had these two amazing, massive wings, like giant bat wings, growing from his shoulder blades. Just a glimpse is all I got of this, this *winged beast*, and then he was back to normal, but I'll never forget it. Never."

"Wings?" Amber pressed. "No horns?"

"Protrusions," said Jacob. "My dad had a headful of hair, but in that moment he was bald, and he had these short protrusions all the way around his head, like a crown. I suppose you could call them horns. Small horns. But big wings."

"What was the harvest schedule?" Milo asked.

"Three souls a year," said Jacob as he set about making four mugs of coffee. "For the first three years, he delivered. That's the part that Althea likes to forget. But then the excuses started. The Shining Demon sent out his representative, and Dad assured him he'd get back on track. But, while he was telling the representative that he found it difficult to go out three times a year, I was watching him go out every other *week*. There were people disappearing from all over our neighbourhood. The cops even came to speak to him. It got so bad, we had to move. He didn't have to tell me what was happening. I knew. He was harvesting a lot more souls than agreed upon, but he wasn't giving any of them to the Shining Demon. He had found a way, in all his research, to feed off those souls himself. He was making himself stronger."

"He'd planned to disappear all along," said Milo.

Glen joined them in the kitchen. "Sorry," he said, smiling, "would you happen to have a plunger available?"

Jacob frowned at him, then took one out from under the sink and handed it over.

"Any chance you'd have something bigger?" Glen asked.

"No," said Jacob.

"This'll do fine, then," Glen said, and left.

Jacob took a moment to look concerned, then handed Milo and Amber a coffee. Amber didn't like coffee.

"When I was seventeen," Jacob said, "my dad called me into the living room and sat me down and told me he was leaving. He said the representative had made it quite clear that unless he started making up for lost harvests, his own soul would be forfeit. He said if he told me where he was going, the Shining Demon would know, and he'd torture it out of me. He told me I was out of it. Obviously, he lied about that part." He sipped his coffee, leaning against the stove.

"So my dad left, and Althea took me in for a few years until I found a job and could manage on my own. I'd get the occasional postcard, but that was it. The representative started coming to see me, but, for all his threats, the cancer never came back."

"The Shining Demon must have been furious," said Amber.

Jacob shrugged. "He wasn't happy about it, no. But he knew that I didn't know where my dad was. Funny thing about Demons – and I mean proper Demons – they don't let anything cloud the subject at hand. He could have had me killed a thousand times over, just to appease his own irritation, but he kept his eyes on the prize. I think my dad knew that. I hope he did.

"Anyway, about fifteen years ago, the representative knocked on my door to tell me that this would be his last visit. He said he had better things to do with his time than trying to track down a cheat. Silly me, I took this for good news.

"Few weeks after that, I got the feeling I was being watched. Couldn't shake it. I was convinced someone – something – was following me. I started glimpsing it out of the corner of my eye. The witch. It started with some destruction of property. No big deal. Then it killed my neighbour's dog. Then it killed my neighbour. I moved. Had to move three times. The cops were getting interested, just like they'd been interested in my dad. It always found me. There's no way to stop it. I bought this place, where I didn't have any neighbours, and set up the perimeter to keep it out. I did learn *some* tricks from my old man. I used to drive into town every week, stock up on groceries and whatnot, but that got too dangerous, so now I get it all delivered."

"This has been going on for fifteen years?" Amber asked. "And the Shining Demon is hoping you'll wake up one day and, what, decide you've had enough? Tell him where your dad is?"

"I don't *know* where he is," Jacob said. "I keep telling you. The Shining Demon understands this. He didn't send the witch to get me to *talk*, but to *torment* − to try to get my dad to come to my rescue. Which, obviously, has not happened."

"Is there anyone who *would* know?" Milo asked.

"No one I'm familiar with. Why do you need to find him, anyway?"

"My parents made a deal with the Shining Demon that involves me," said Amber. "I'm trying to get out of it. I was hoping your dad might be able to help."

Jacob sighed. "For what it's worth, I believe you. And I'm sorry that I'm not able to tell you what you want to know."

"If you did know where he was," said Milo, "would you have told the Shining Demon?"

Jacob hesitated, then gave a grim smile. "Probably not."

"That's what I figured."

Glen walked in. They looked at him.

"The toilet is fine," he announced.

Milo sighed, and held out his hand to Jacob. "Thanks for talking to us."

Jacob shook Milo's hand, then Amber's. "Sorry I haven't been of any use to you."

"Thanks, anyway," she said.

Glen held out his hand to shake. Jacob gave him a nod instead. "Nice to meet you."

He led the way to the door, opened it, and they walked out. The light rain had stopped, though the sky was still overcast.

"Good luck," said Jacob. "Genuinely."

He closed the door, and they walked back towards the car.

"I broke his toilet," Glen said the moment they were back on the trail.

Amber ignored him, and looked at Milo. "Do you believe him when he says he doesn't know where his dad is?"

Milo sighed. "Yes, actually, I do. I wish I didn't."

"So what do we do now?"

"I... I don't know."

"We can't just stop. After all this, we can't just stop. There has to be some way of finding out where Jacob's dad is. What about the whole *winged beast* thing?"

Glen frowned. "Winged beast? There's a winged beast?"

"Surely someone has seen him flying around and posted it on some weird forum somewhere," Amber continued. "The internet would eat up something like this."

"You were talking about winged beasts? Seriously?"

"You're assuming Buxton is still harvesting souls," said Milo.

"Well, yeah," Amber responded. "I mean, why wouldn't he be?"

"Maybe he decided that killing innocent people is not something he wanted to continue doing."

"Guys, come on, stop walking so fast," Glen said. "I'm still weak."

"Or maybe he likes it," said Amber. "He killed who knows how many people in order to get strong enough to leave. I can't see how he'd be willing to lose that strength, can you? I'd say he'd want to get even stronger."

"I guess," Milo said slowly. "Especially if he thought the Shining Demon could turn up at any moment..."

"See, that's what I think," said Amber, snapping her fingers. "I think he hasn't stopped killing. Maybe it's not every other week, like Jacob said, but I bet it's still significant."

"Can you please slow down?" Glen said from behind them. "When Jacob finds out what I did to his toilet, he'll be coming after me and I'm too weak to defend myself. Also I don't know how."

"There's probably nothing about it online," said Amber, ignoring him. "Or, if there is, it's hidden away in some remote part of the web that we'd never find."

"Maybe not us," said Milo, "but someone who does this kind of thing for a living... Maybe."

Milo took out his phone and dialled a number. He waited till the call was answered.

"Edgar, old buddy," he said, smiling. "Looks like we're in need of your services yet again." His smile dropped slightly. "I'm not sure what you... oh, you mean the *powder flask*. Yeah, I think we may have accidentally taken that with us..."

Amber grinned, left Milo to explain himself, and carried on back down the trail to the car. Within moments, Milo and Glen were lost from sight. Another few seconds, and she could see the Charger.

Then a sound from somewhere to her left. The snapping of a twig.

Amber stopped walking, her eyes flickering from tree to tree. Nothing there. Nothing hiding, lurking, creeping… Nothing waiting.

And yet…

She walked off the trail a few steps, her feet crunching on dry twigs. Awareness prickled at the base of her skull.

She was being watched.

There were eyes on her, she was sure of that, and there was ill intent behind those eyes. Something out here wished her harm, and every step she was taking was one step closer to it, whatever it was.

But there was nothing there. Even in this failing light, she could still see clearly enough to know that. She took another step. The primal side of her, the unthinking lizard brain, would have commanded her body to spin and sprint at that moment, such was the spike of fear that shot through her. But she overrode it. Of course she did. There was nothing there. Nothing but trees.

Snap.

The sound, another twig breaking directly in front of her, turned her hands to talons, but she fought the change. The demon part of her was too confident, too assured. To start relying on it would be a mistake. She got herself back under control, and her reddening skin returned to normal. A twig had broken. That's all. No big deal. She glared at a tree as she approached, daring it to try and scare her again. It was just a stupid tree with stupid branches, with knots in its trunk that looked like a screaming face, eye sockets that gaped in hollow darkness.

The eyes opened.

Amber cursed, stepped back, her ankle buckling. Twigs cracked like bones as the tree untwisted, every sharp movement revealing another part of its body – a head, an arm, a hand, a leg. Not a tree but a thing, a thing of rough skin and knots, of bark and running sap and hair like twigs and leaves. A thing that stood and waited, straight and tall, but bent as it moved, its crippled spine curling gratefully, its long limbs reaching for Amber even as she scrambled backwards. Its mouth remained open, locked in a frozen scream, and a sound escaped like chattering teeth.

The witch.

It darted towards her and Amber fell back, hit the ground, and rolled desperately. When she looked up, she was alone.

She got up and went home, said goodnight to her parents and went to sleep. In her dreams, she was still in the woods, walking behind the witch, her senses dull. When she woke up, she went to school and sat in class. Her thoughts wandered back to the woods, where she was still walking. It seemed so real, in a way. After school, she worked her shift in the Firebird, then went home and went straight to bed. She dreamed of the gutted remains of an old house in the middle of the woods, and being led down into the basement.

In her dream, she went to sleep. In her sleep, she dreamed.

And in the morning she woke.

44

THE BASEMENT WAS STONE and cold. The ground was hard-packed dirt. Morning light sneaked in through the gaps in the wooden ceiling and the narrow window, set high on the eastern wall. The window didn't have any glass, but it did have metal bars, just like the cast-iron gate that was used as a door to the corridor beyond. Just like a prison cell. Amber sat up.

Five women looked back at her.

They were filthy. Their clothes had become dull rags. Their hair was long, unkempt. They looked like wild women, feral and dangerous, but they sat round her like they were waiting for a bus.

"Don't be afraid," one of them said.

Another one snorted a laugh.

"Fine," the first one said. "Do be afraid. But don't be afraid of us. We're not going to hurt you." She was in her forties, but her long hair was already grey. Down here, access to good hair dye was obviously limited. "I'm Deborah. You can call me Deb. This is Juliana, Honor, Faith and Iseul. What's your name?"

Amber put her back to the wall, and drew her legs in. "Amber," she said. "Where are we?"

"Somewhere we won't be found," said Juliana, the one who'd laughed. She was a little younger than Deb, with blonde hair that was once curly and was now merely knotted. Her face was hard but not unkind. "Do you have anything on you? A phone, something like that?"

Amber shook her head.

Honor, a girl in her early twenties with flawless ebony skin and a mouth full of metal braces, sat forward. "Does anyone know where you are? When it took you, were you close by?"

"I don't know how long I was walking, but I have friends who'll be looking for me," Amber replied.

"They won't find us," said Juliana. She got up, went to the barred gate, stood leaning against it. "You don't think people searched for us? Iseul over there is the niece of one of the richest men in the state – you don't think he had tracker dogs and helicopters looking for her?"

"My friends are different," said Amber. "This is the kind of thing they specialise in. One of them, anyway."

"I wouldn't get your hopes up," said Deb, her voice suddenly lifeless. "I don't think *anyone* specialises in this stuff."

Amber held her gaze. "What," she said, "witches?"

The other women frowned.

"Witches?" said Honor.

The Korean woman, Iseul, tossed a twig into the centre of the room. "The thing that brought me here was no witch," she said. "It was a tree-monster."

"And what's a tree-monster?" Amber asked.

378

"It's what took us," said Juliana. "It took you too, right? Looks like a tree until it opens its eyes? We don't know the technical term for it, but what it is, is a tree-monster."

"She's a witch," said Amber. "That's just how she looks."

"How would you know?" asked Deb.

"Because that's what she is. She was sent after a guy who lives in these woods, Jacob Buxton."

"Gretchen was right!" the fifth woman, Faith, suddenly exclaimed as she jumped to her feet. "She told us! The one person we all had contact with in the week before we woke up here! Gretchen knew he was in on it!"

"Who's Gretchen?" Amber asked.

Deb hesitated. "She was down here with us. Then she was taken away, and we haven't seen her since. There have been others, too. We were all that was left until you turned up."

By the looks on their faces, Amber knew that none of them harboured any hopes that Gretchen was still alive.

"Jacob's not responsible," said Amber.

"Bull!" cried Faith. "You don't think we've talked about every single possible thing that links us? Jacob Buxton is someone both Honor and I made deliveries to. Juliana called by his cabin to talk about the local elections. Iseul spoke to him outside her store. Deb went on two dates with him, for God's sake! We all spoke to him and, a few days later, we end up here!"

"Jacob wasn't the only thing we had in common," said Deb, sounding like they'd had this conversation a hundred times before. "There were six other people, there were eight locations... We live in a small town, Faith."

Faith jabbed a finger in Amber's direction. "But now she's saying Jacob Buxton is involved!"

"He's involved," said Amber, "but he's not responsible. He probably doesn't even know that you're missing. How long have you been here?"

"Gretchen was the first," said Deb, "a few weeks before me. It's April now, right? So I've been here ten months. Nearly eleven."

"I've been here four," said Honor. "I was the newbie, until you."

"How do you know all this about witches?" asked Juliana.

"The witch," said Amber, "because that's what she is, was sent by someone, it doesn't matter who, to basically make Jacob's life hell. The cabin is the only place he's safe from it."

"But why were we attacked?" Honor asked.

"I don't know," said Amber.

"Who are you? How do you know so much about this?"

"I needed to speak to Jacob. I didn't know him before yesterday. But does it matter? The only thing that matters right now is getting out of here."

"These walls are solid stone," said Honor. "The floor is hard-packed. We can't dig our way out, if that's what you're asking."

"And the shawl-women only ever let us out one at a time to use the bathroom," said Iseul.

Juliana smirked from the gate. "I love it that you still call it the bathroom."

Iseul grinned back. "I'm a civilised lady, what can I say? *Hole in the ground* doesn't have quite the same sense of grandeur."

"Who are the shawl-women?" Amber asked.

"They work for the tree-monster," said Juliana. "Or the witch, whatever. We've never seen their faces. They never talk. They bring us game that we have to skin and cook ourselves."

"How many of them are there?"

"At least five."

"Have you ever tried overpowering them?"

"Yeah," said Juliana, wincing at a painful memory. "I wouldn't advise it. Maybe if we all jumped on one of them at the same time… but they're never alone. We've never had the chance."

"Well, don't worry," said Amber. "You've got me now."

The sunlight glinted off the metalwork in Honor's smile. "I like this girl already," she said. "She's funny."

Amber stood, fighting a wave of dizziness that passed as quickly as it arrived.

"You're going to be woozy for a few minutes," said Deb. "We've all been there."

"What did she do to me?"

"It has a stinger," said Faith. "You've been poisoned. It doesn't last, don't worry. That's how it got all of us."

"And why is she keeping us alive?"

"Ah," said Iseul, "we're back on that cheery topic, are we?"

"We don't know," said Deb. "Why did it take Gretchen? Why did it take the others? Why not us? Why doesn't it just kill us and get it over with? Why doesn't it let us go? If we knew why we were here in the first place, we might be able to figure out an answer or two."

"Shawl-woman," said Juliana, backing away from the gate, and everyone who had been sitting got to their feet.

The shawl-woman came shuffling out of the darkness of the corridor, and Amber could see how the name had come about. Her clothes seemed to consist entirely of shawls, filthy, dirty and ragged, stitched together with twine, of varying fabrics and lengths. Her hands were lost in huge sleeves, and her face was hidden. A flick of her wrists and two skinny rabbits were tossed between the bars.

Juliana scooped them up, gave them a cursory examination, and called out after the shawl-woman as she shuffled back where she'd come from. "These are rabbits. I distinctly asked for duck!"

"She did!" said Iseul. "I remember!"

The shawl-woman didn't respond and didn't turn round.

Juliana held the rabbits out to Amber. "Dungeon tradition – the new arrival skins and cooks breakfast."

Amber's eyes widened. "Uh…"

"She's joking," said Deb.

"Oh, thank God."

"You guys are no fun," Juliana grumbled.

Amber watched as the women skinned and cooked the rabbits over a fire. They sat in a circle and ate, sharing cups of rainwater, collected in a bucket under a small hole in the ceiling. The rabbit was chewy. She did her best not to gag on the gristle. It occurred to her that her demon teeth would have no problem shearing through her meal, but thought it best not to shift in front of these women – not unless she had to, at least.

"Tell us about yourself, Amber," said Deb. "Where are you from?"

"Florida."

"And how come you know so much?"

Amber crunched on something. She pulled a bone from between her teeth, and swallowed the rest. "Me and my friend, we're looking for Jacob Buxton's father. My friend is the expert in all this."

"How does a teenaged girl from Florida fit in?" Juliana asked.

"I'm, uh, I'm in trouble. There are some people after me."

"Witches?"

"No. No, these are... different things. But they're after me, and that's why we came to Colorado, and that's why I'm here now."

"What kind of trouble are you in?" Deb asked.

"The bad kind."

Deb looked at her, gave a little shrug, and didn't ask any more. Amber got the feeling the real interrogation was yet to begin.

"I need to use the bathroom," she announced.

"You mean the hole in the ground," said Honor. "You sure? You'll be alone with the shawl-women. They won't hurt you if you don't try anything, but they're pretty creepy for someone who's just arrived."

"I really have to go," said Amber.

"A girl's gotta go, a girl's gotta go," said Deb, getting up and walking to the gate. She drank the last of her water, and rattled her cup against the bars. "Bathroom break!" she hollered. "Call of nature!"

She stayed where she was for a moment, looking out into the corridor, then she turned to Amber. "They're coming. Two of them. One's gonna walk in front, one behind. They'll take you straight to our luxurious hole in the ground, and when you're done they'll take you right back. You want my advice? Don't try to escape. They'll be expecting it, especially with someone new."

Amber stood, and nodded. "Thank you."

The shawl-women shuffled up. Without a word, the women went to the far wall, and stood with their foreheads pressed against the stone. The gate creaked heavily, and the shawl-women beckoned Amber out. Nerves sparking in her belly, Amber slipped out, and the gate was closed and locked behind her.

The shawl-women smelled of leaves and earth. They didn't say anything as they walked the length of the corridor, Amber between them. She tried to peek at their faces, but their hoods were too low. The darkness was punctuated by slivers of daylight. The wooden ceiling had been blackened by the blaze that had felled the rest of the house.

They passed the turn into another corridor, and Amber was brought to a small chamber. When they passed through the doorway, she was dismayed to discover that the hole in the ground was an actual hole in the actual ground.

The shawl-women stood in the door, waiting.

Amber hovered beside the hole. "Uh, would you mind turning around?"

The shawl-women didn't move.

Amber blushed as she manoeuvred herself into position. It took her half a minute to relax enough to pee. When she was done, she straightened up, careful not to fall into the hole, and pulled up her jeans. The shawl-women parted and they escorted her back the way they'd come, one in front and one behind.

When they passed the junction to the other corridor, however, Amber slowed to a stop. "What's down there?"

Neither of the shawl-women responded.

She did her best to keep it friendly. "Hello? Can you talk? I think I'm supposed to go down that way. Do you mind?"

She tried to step out of their little procession, but the shawl-woman behind blocked her way with one arm, while the shawl-woman in front turned.

384

"Please," said Amber. "I'm only sixteen. I'm a kid. All the others are women. Can't you let me go? Please? I promise I won't tell."

The shawl-women didn't respond.

Amber smiled. "I really tried to be nice," she said, and shifted, feeling the power flood her.

They grabbed at her, but she shoved them away, running down the other corridor. It widened to a room and she ran in and the smell hit her, made her stagger back.

The room was filled with flayed bodies. Here and there she saw animal carcasses, rotten and decaying, but it was the human remains that made her scream. They hung from the wooden beams, held in place by twisted and rusted nails. Their insides, the guts and organs, the meat and the bones, were nothing more than blackened heaps on the ground, long since picked over by rats and birds and maggots. It was the skins that the witch obviously valued, as shredded as they were.

No other door in here. No way out.

She turned and the shawl-women came at her. She swung, her talons digging into the first shawl-woman's chest. Panic biting her nerve endings, she ripped the shawls away, snarling into the face beneath. She was prepared for a human face, she was prepared for a monster's face, she was prepared for any face – as long as there was one. But instead of a face, instead of flesh and blood, she was greeted by a mass of tightly twisting sticks that writhed under her grip.

Something lurched in Amber's mind and her thoughts jammed for a long, desperate moment, and then the second shawl-woman wrapped an arm round her throat and pulled her backwards.

She grabbed at the arm, feeling nothing but more sticks through the fabric. The stick-thing in front of her reached out, those twigs lengthening, working their way around Amber's body, scratching and cutting her skin, tightening round her ribs. It was hard to breathe. Hard to stay upright. Her black scales did their best to protect her as thin branches wrapped around her head like vines, forcing her eyes closed. They were in her hair, coiling around her horns. Her arms were trapped, her claws useless. She wanted to shriek, but couldn't draw the breath that would let her. She wanted to shout, wanted to give up, wanted it to be over, but she didn't have a voice and there was no one to listen. She was going to die. They were going to kill her.

She fought against her own fear, fought the wave of panic that threatened to wash all rational thought away. A notion flashed through her mind – that of a Chinese finger puzzle, where the more you struggle, the faster you're caught. She focused on one thing. Just one thing.

She reverted.

The branches around her midsection tightened, but everywhere else they loosened, and she sucked in a breath. Amber resisted the urge to struggle and instead went limp, and gradually the pressure eased.

The branches moved from her face and she opened her eyes, just in time to see the witch enter the room.

45

THE WITCH APPROACHED LIKE a curious cat, her head tilted to one side. Even though her spine was curved, she loomed over Amber, her knotted hair almost touching the low ceiling. There was something behind her eyes as she examined Amber, a kind of intelligence, her long, sharp fingers poking and prodding. The shawl-women's branches moved subtly to clear a space in anticipation of every poke. No words were spoken, no obvious communication passed between them. The shawl-women moved independently of the witch but also with her, as if they were all part of the same body.

The witch peered closer. She scraped her fingers through Amber's hair, searching, Amber realised, for the horns that had just been there.

Her curiosity far from satisfied, the witch scratched and scraped deeper and harder, and Amber gritted her teeth against the pain.

There was a voice now, coming closer. One of the women from the cellar.

"Where are you taking me? Please. Please, let me go back to the others. Oh God, please..."

Faith came into the room, dragged by two more shawl-women. She saw the witch and shrank back, but was unable to stop the shawl-women from dragging her to Amber's side. She finally fell silent.

The witch reached out, her coarse fingers turning Amber's head one way and then the other. Dirty fingernails pried open her mouth, and Amber had to resist the urge to bite down. She nearly gagged as the witch explored. All of a sudden, the witch switched her attention to Faith, went through the same routine, and then came back to Amber, fingers prodding her chest and belly.

"What's it doing?" Faith whispered.

"Examining us," Amber said.

The witch snapped her head up and Amber shut her mouth.

Tears flowed down Faith's cheeks, but her soft voice was surprisingly steady. "Our Father, who art in heaven, hallowed be Thy name..."

The witch left Amber and moved to Faith, started squeezing and poking her body the way she had Amber's, but Faith didn't stop her prayer.

"Thy kingdom come, Thy will be done, on earth as it is in heaven, give us this day our daily bread, and forgive us our trespasses, as we forgive those who—"

All at once the witch stopped, and stepped back, and for one crazy moment Amber though the prayer was working. But then she knew. The witch had made her decision.

Tree roots burst from the dirt at Faith's feet and tore through her tattered jeans, burrowing into her legs. Faith screamed, nearly pulled free of the shawl-women, but they clung on and the roots kept coming. Amber cursed, cried out, tried to help and then tried to pull away, but there was nothing she could do but stand and watch as Faith's agony reached new heights, dragging her screams along with it. Branches bulged under her skin and twigs poked through, spraying blood, opening up gashes and wounds, from which fell her steaming innards. And then the screams were cut short and Faith made one last gagging sound and died.

Her chin dropped to her chest, but she didn't fall and she didn't stop moving. The roots continued to fill her, discarding the organs and the bones and the meaty essence of her body at her feet. The skin at her neck bulged, and a moment later she raised her head.

Amber stared.

The thing that had once been Faith took a step, breaking free of the roots that had pinned it to the ground. It dragged its other leg behind it. That one wasn't working right.

The witch examined the Faith-thing, inspecting her handiwork. As she did so, her mouth moved, like she was talking to herself. Then the Faith-thing's mouth started moving, a perfect mirror to the shapes formed by the witch. There were no words, however. Instead, a series of sounds became audible – a hollow rush of air and a distant creaking.

The witch turned her head towards Amber, and the Faith-thing mimicked the movement exactly. The witch raised her left arm and its new puppet did the same.

But the movement caused a tear in the skin along the underside of the Faith-thing's upper arm, a tear that joined with another rip and became a gaping hole from which sharp twigs protruded. The Faith-thing tried to hold itself together, but the rips were appearing all over now, and every tear led to two more, and in seconds the Faith-thing fell apart, the sticks tumbling to the floor.

The witch gazed down at her failed puppet, and the shawl-women dragged Amber backwards. She didn't resist as she was taken back to the basement. They flung her inside, then closed the gate behind her.

The other women rushed forward.

"What happened?" asked Deb. "Did you see Faith? They came in here and took her and then we heard screaming."

"She's... she's dead," said Amber. "I'm sorry."

There were no gasps and no arguments and no tears. The women just stood there, the reality settling upon their shoulders, almost too heavy to withstand.

"What happened?" Deb asked again.

"She examined us," Amber said dully. "The witch. She examined us both and then made her choice."

"What did it do to Faith?" Juliana pressed.

"Filled her with branches," said Amber. "Roots and twigs and branches. Filled her up. I found a room full of... full of that stuff."

"Gretchen?" said Deb.

"I don't know," Amber answered. "Probably. She's been doing this for a while. Experimenting. Trying to get it right."

"I don't get it," said Honor. "Filled her with branches? What does that mean?"

"The branches are alive," Amber said. "The witch controls them, or they're part of her or something. The shawl-women aren't women, they aren't people. They're just sticks. They're all extensions of her, I think. When she was finished with Faith, it was just Faith's skin, her face and her skin, filled with branches, doing whatever the witch was doing."

"But that's insane," said Iseul.

Amber nodded. "I think she wants to – the witch – I think she wants to be… us."

"Why?"

"I don't know."

"Why'd she let you live, and not Faith?"

Amber hesitated.

Juliana seized her arm. "What are you hiding?"

"Juliana," said Deb.

"No!" Juliana shouted. "She'd hiding something. Look at her. She's not even denying it."

Amber shook her head. "I don't know why—"

"Liar!"

The force of the word made Amber step back. The others looked at her.

"Why did the witch spare you?" Iseul asked.

"I don't know," said Amber. "I swear."

"Faith's been with us for months," Honor said. She had tears in her eyes, but her voice was steady. "Then you come in, and suddenly Faith gets killed? Why? Are we next? Am I next?"

"Why did that thing let you live?" asked Juliana. "Are you working with it? Are you? Answer me!"

Amber looked at them, saw the grim determination in their eyes, and knew she wasn't going to be able to talk her way out of this.

"I want you to be calm," she said.

"Just answer the question!" Juliana shouted.

Amber held up her hands. "I will. I'm about to. But I'm going to ask you to remain calm. I'm trapped here, the same as you. My life is in danger, the same as yours. We're on the same side. I'm not going to hurt you."

"Hurt us?" Deb said. "What do you—?"

Amber shifted, and the basement erupted in screams and shouts and curses.

"I'm not going to hurt you!" Amber said as they all scrambled back.

"Stay away from us!" Juliana screeched.

"I am!" said Amber, backing up to the far wall. "Look! I am! I'm not going to hurt you!"

They stared at her, and she did her best to appear non-threatening. She tried smiling.

"Look at her teeth!" Iseul whimpered, and Amber stopped smiling.

"Who are you?" asked Deb.

"I told you, my name's Amber."

"You're a devil!" said Honor.

"No, I am not. This doesn't mean anything. The horns, the skin, it doesn't change who I am. Not really. Not who I am inside. I'm still a good person, I swear to you!"

"You're working with the witch! That's how you know so much about it!"

Amber shook her head. "No, I'm not. And the only reason I know so much is because, well, this is the kind of thing I've been doing for the past two weeks."

Deb frowned. "You've been a devil for two weeks?"

"Please stop calling me a devil. It's a long story, how I got like this, but two weeks ago I thought I was totally normal and I didn't know anything like this even existed. Now here I am, and I'm doing my best to deal with what's being thrown at me, and I think I'm doing a pretty good job of it, actually, and I'm not a bad guy and I'm not a devil, and I don't want to hurt anyone except maybe the witch because of what she's done to Faith, and what she's doing to us, and... and I don't know what else to say."

They stared.

"So you're not a devil?" Juliana asked.

"No. My parents are kind of demons, though, and I inherited that from them, and now they're trying to kill me."

A few moments passed.

"Harsh," said Honor.

"Yes, it is," Amber responded. "Listen to me: I'm in at the deep end. I know this is freaky, I know this is terrifying, and it's very hard to believe someone when they have red skin and horns, but I'm not the bad guy. I'm really not."

Deb was the first one to take a step closer. "But this is why the witch chose you over Faith?"

"I think so," said Amber. "When I'm like this, I'm bigger, stronger... My skin might even be tough enough to stay in one piece if she takes me over. I'd be a better... vessel, maybe."

"If it wants to take you over," said Iseul, "then why didn't it?"

Amber relaxed a little more. "Like I said, she's been experimenting. She's been testing herself. It hasn't been going well for her."

"But now that you're here," said Iseul, "it might have found the vessel it's been waiting for."

"Yeah," said Amber. "Now she's ready to put all her experiments to use."

"So what happens to us?" Honor asked. "Do you think it'll let us go?"

"Hey," said Deb. "Hey. Before we start cheering too loud, let's figure out if we can help Amber, all right?"

Amber frowned. "You want to help me?"

"If we can."

"Thank you. Sincerely, thank you. But I don't know if you can do anything. The witch on her own is powerful, but add in those shawl-women and there's not a whole lot anyone could do."

"But what does it do, then?" Juliana asked. "Okay, it takes Amber's skin, takes her face, but so what? Now it looks like a devil – no offence, Amber – and so where can it go? What the hell does it want?"

"Oh my God," said Honor, practically running up to Amber. "When you're like this, and again no offence, yeah, you look evil and all, but you're also... I mean, you're beautiful. She's beautiful, right, guys?"

The other women nodded.

"Maybe that's why the witch chose you over Faith," Honor continued. "Not only because you're bigger and stronger and a more likely vessel, but also because you're better-looking."

"Uh," said Amber, "okay... I don't really know where you're going with this, though..."

"The one thing we never understood is what all this has to do with Jacob Buxton. You said the witch was sent to make his life hell, right? But none of this has any effect on him in the slightest. Amber, how long has the witch been doing this?"

"Killing people? I don't know. But she's been tormenting him for fifteen years."

"Fifteen years," said Honor, "this ugly old tree-monster witch-thing is making Jacob Buxton's life a misery. Fifteen years and it never stops. It never leaves. It doesn't go on vacation and it doesn't go home to its witch-husband and their little witch-kids. It's a single lady in an all-consuming job, and all it does – *all it does* – is watch over this one man. My brother was in the army; he worked in a sniper team. They had to stay in one place for days, watching their targets. He said the longer they watched, the harder it was to pull the trigger. Because they'd got to know the targets, they'd developed almost a fondness for them..."

"Holy crap," said Deb. "It's in love with him."

Honor snapped her fingers. "Exactly! He's all hidden away in his cabin and he doesn't talk to many people, does he? But every woman who has had contact with him, no matter how briefly, is snatched away and hidden in a dungeon."

"She's jealous," said Amber. "She wants her rivals out of the way and now she wants to take the form of one of us so that she can be with Jacob."

"B I N G and O," said Honor.

Juliana looked at them like they were nuts. "Seriously? The tree-monster's in love? That's our theory?"

"It's a good one," said Iseul.

"It's a tree-monster! What does it know about love?"

"More than some people," said Amber.

"Okay, okay," Deb said, "so we have a possible motive. If we were trying to solve a crime, this would be an important moment for us all. But it changes nothing. The lovestruck witch is still probably gonna take over Amber and then kill the rest of us. Knowing it has a softer side will not help us in the slightest."

"Wow," said Honor. "I know we've been living in a dungeon and all, and we're all in danger, but you are surprisingly depressing."

46

AMBER SLEPT ON A bed of leaves. It was exactly as uncomfortable as she'd expected.

In the morning, she woke to the sound of the gate opening. Two shawl-women stood there. Two more lurked beyond it. Their intentions were obvious.

Amber got up slowly. The other women stood beside her. It was a touching show of solidarity, but they couldn't help her. They couldn't stop what was about to happen.

"Don't change," said Deb. "If it's your red skin it wants, stay like you are."

Amber nodded, and passed through the gate, and it creaked shut behind her. The shawl-women brought her back to the room with all the carcasses, where the witch was waiting.

A long, gnarled finger reached out, poked Amber's shoulder. It poked again, and prodded her chest, but Amber didn't shift. The witch must have sensed her resolve, because she regarded her anew. After a moment, the shawl-women released their hold, and the witch struck her.

The force of the blow rattled Amber's skull and made her stumble, but she didn't fall. Holding one hand to her stinging cheek, she looked up at the witch and said, "I'm not going to change."

The witch hit her again, in the belly this time, doubling her over. Amber gasped and groaned, and fell to her knees. After a few panicked moments, she sucked in a breath, and the shawl-women hauled her up.

The witch was going easy on her. She couldn't afford to damage her vessel.

"I don't care what you do," Amber wheezed. "I am not going to change."

The witch observed her. Amber didn't like that. She could almost see the gears move behind those eyes.

She heard shouts of protests and curses, and Amber's heart plummeted. The shawl-women dragged Juliana in first, then Deb and Honor and Iseul. Despite their struggles, the captives were lined up along the wall.

"What's it want?" Honor asked, trying to free herself of a shawl-woman's grip. "It's not going to practise on me. No way am I letting that happen."

Amber sagged. "She doesn't want to practise," she said.

At Juliana's feet, roots cracked the hard-packed dirt, started twisting round her shoes. Juliana screamed, tried kicking, but Amber knew full well what was going to happen next.

"Okay!" she said. "Okay, just stop! You hear me? Stop."

The witch observed her a moment longer, and the roots retreated.

"They go free," Amber continued. "You let them go right now. That's the deal. Let them go, don't hurt them and don't go after them, and I'll change. You can... you can use my skin."

The witch considered the proposal for a moment, and then pointed at her. Amber hesitated, then shifted into her demon form. At once, the shawl-women released their captives.

The women shared a look of uncertainty, like they were expecting to be grabbed again the moment they started believing they were free. Iseul was the first to move to the corridor. No shawl-woman went to stop her. The witch didn't even look round.

Iseul ran.

Deb and the others started edging out.

"Up here!" Iseul yelled. "The way out is up here! Follow my voice!"

Honor hesitated. She looked at Amber, looked at the witch, and hurried out. Juliana went next.

"Thank you," Deb said to Amber, then she followed the others.

Amber waited to hear screams or shouts that would indicate they'd been recaptured. When that didn't happen, she looked back at the witch. "Seems we have a deal."

The witch stepped forward, and reached for her.

Amber's hand encircled her wrist. "I'm sorry," she said, black scales spreading across her skin, "you weren't expecting me to go without a fight, were you?"

She wrenched the witch towards her and slashed at her face. The witch howled, an unearthly sound that made Amber's bones quiver, and then they went tumbling. Roots sprouted from the ground, trying to hold Amber in place, but she was on her feet and moving, still tangled up with the witch as they crashed into the wall.

The witch's hair came alive and Amber shut her eyes against

a hundred stabbing splinters that scraped across her scales. She felt her way up from the witch's shoulder, found her neck and got two hands on it as they stumbled round the room. She started squeezing, then grew her talons and sank them into the witch's flesh. It didn't make any discernible difference.

There were shawl-women on her now, pulling her away, and Amber cracked her eyes open to find a target. When she found one, she swiped, and the shawls ripped cleanly and the branches underneath came apart. The clothes collapsed to the sound of falling sticks, but even as that happened another figure rose on the far side of the room. It wasn't even attempting to look like a person this time – the stick-thing joined the shawl-women and wrenched Amber's arms behind her back. They forced her to her knees, and she looked up as the witch stepped into view.

Amber's snarl turned to an angry, defiant roar.

The witch turned her head, and through that tangle of hair Amber saw an expression flash across her face—

Fear.

Amber smelled smoke moments before she noticed the flickering light. A fire. There was a fire raging, spreading fast. The shawl-women were loosening their grip as the witch's attention was diverted.

Amber heard shouting. The women. At first, she thought their voices were raised in panic – then she realised they were voices raised in challenge.

"Come get us!" she heard Deb shout. "Come get us, you monstrous bitch!"

Amber tore free and the shawl-women and the stick-things fell to the floor, nothing more than scattering branches. She launched herself at the witch and they fell back, hit the table and rolled off. Amber ignored the witch's long limbs and held her close. She bit down on an ear, tore a chunk out of it, and the witch shrieked and bucked wildly. Amber lost her grip, went tumbling, and only managed to get to her knees before the witch had scuttled round behind her. Hands gripped her. The world tilted and blurred and Amber hit the far wall and dropped.

The ceiling was on fire.

A beam dropped and the witch jumped back. Amber sat up, watching her panic, and a curious sense of victory took hold. Then she remembered that she was here as well, and the feeling vanished.

The witch ran.

Amber scrambled up and followed her, surging into billowing clouds of smoke that seared her lungs and burned her eyes. She groped blindly for the walls, letting them guide her, tripping on roots and banging her horns. She felt cool air on her skin and staggered towards that, before doubling over as coughs racked her body. She forced herself up, forced herself to focus on that cool air, and then she stumbled against steps. She climbed them on her hands and knees, felt more hands on her, dragging her up, and she emerged into fresh air and light.

The hands released her and she heard Deb and Honor, and she curled up, coughing, and dug her knuckles into her streaming eyes. She looked up, blinked against the sunlight. Juliana peered at her.

"Amber? You okay?"

She nodded, and coughed, and nodded again.

"People!" Iseul yelled. "Look!"

Amber looked to where Iseul was pointing, saw a dark figure move through the trees.

"Amber!" Milo shouted.

She forced herself up, wiped her eyes again, tried to answer, but coughed instead, made do with waving. Milo broke into a run, holding an axe in both hands. Something moved ahead of him.

Deb yelled a warning as a coughing fit bent Amber double and the witch sprang from cover. Milo went down, losing the axe, the witch all over him. She lifted him, threw him against a tree. He smacked into it horribly and spun and hit the ground. The witch moved in to finish him off, but Glen and Jacob Buxton were already there to help him to his feet.

The witch froze when she saw Jacob.

Amber sucked in a breath, broke free of Juliana's grip, and scrambled into a run. She scooped the fallen axe off the ground, jumped to a tree stump and leaped high. She swung, the axe cutting deep into the witch's neck and lodging there, and Amber landed empty-handed and went stumbling. The witch shrieked, arched her back and twisted, yellow blood spraying from her wound like sap. She found the handle, yanked it free and let it fall, but her head rolled to one side and she toppled, like she'd lost all sense of balance.

Amber ran back for the axe, but the witch caught her with a desperate swipe of her arm and Amber went rolling. She looked up to see the witch snatch up Jacob and run.

Amber grabbed the axe and took off in pursuit. The witch was easy to lose in the trees, but she caught flashes of Jacob's clothes and kept up. Her seared lungs burned.

She tripped on a log and stumbled and smacked her horns

off a branch and fell, cursing. She got up, ran to the last place she'd seen Jacob, ran on, shouting his name.

Then she slowed. The witch was on the ground, bent over on her knees with her arms out in front, like she was praying. Her head was turned sideways, with yellow blood slowly leaking from her wound. Jacob stood just out of her reach, looking down at her.

"She's dead," he said. His voice was oddly dull. "She was running and getting weaker, and stumbling, and then she put me down... and just sort of... sank to her knees."

He looked up, looked at Amber.

"Milo told me you were a demon," he said. "You don't look anything like the way my father did."

Amber reverted, and Jacob looked back at the witch.

"She was almost *gentle*," he said, sounding surprised.

47

THREE MINUTES. THAT WAS how long Milo gave her to say her goodbyes. Any lead they'd had on Amber's parents had been eaten up by the witch. Her brand read 168 hours. They couldn't afford to waste any more time. Amber knew this. She agreed with it. And yet, as she was being ushered to the car, she realised that she didn't want to go. The women who had been held captive in that dungeon had welcomed her into their group even when she'd revealed the truth about herself. They'd accepted her. She'd belonged. They'd formed a family down there, formed bonds that would never be broken, and she'd been so close to being a part of that. Now they were standing there by Jacob's cabin, watching her go, their questions unanswered, her questions unasked.

Then she was in the Charger and she was leaving them behind.

"You okay?" Milo asked as they were driving away from Cricket Hill.

"I'd liked to have stayed a while," Amber said.

He nodded. "You understand why we had to get out fast, though, right?"

"My parents."

"Them," said Milo, "and we want to be far away from here when those women return home. The cops are going to be all over this. We can't afford to be delayed any longer than we already have been."

"Yeah," she said, looking out of the window. "I know. Where are we going?"

"New York!" Glen said excitedly from the back.

Milo sighed. "It didn't take Edgar long to find mentions of a winged beast. He found eleven in all, on obscure websites on something called the Dark Web. One sighting in Louisville, two in Baltimore, and the rest in New York."

"Is that where Gregory Buxton is?" Amber asked.

"We think so," said Glen, nodding seriously.

A flicker of annoyance crossed Milo's features. He'd had to deal with Glen for an entire night without Amber there to act as a buffer, and it was clearly taking its toll. "Edgar will be meeting us in Brooklyn," he said. "He'll get there ahead of us, snoop around, and hopefully by the time we get there he'll have something more solid."

"Okay," said Amber. "Good."

"Something else bothering you?"

She glanced at him. "Since when are you so eager to chat?"

"He was worried about you," said Glen.

Amber raised an eyebrow. "Really?"

"Don't know why you're so astonished," Milo said. "I looked away for one moment, and you were gone. I didn't know if you'd got lost, if the witch had grabbed you, or if your parents had tracked us down faster than I'd anticipated."

"We searched all night," said Glen. "Well, Milo did. I tried, but, until I've regained all my strength, I'm more hindrance than boon. At least that's what Milo said."

Amber suppressed a smile. "How did you find the witch's house?"

The road widened to become a highway, and Milo piled on the speed. "I knew we were in the right area when there were no more birds singing, but we could have been wandering for days if Glen hadn't seen the smoke from the fire those women lit."

"It was nothing," Glen said bashfully. "I shouldn't be called a hero just because I saw some smoke."

"No one's calling you a hero," Milo said.

"They're not? Really? But I saw the smoke."

Amber settled back and let Glen prattle on until his strength left him and he fell asleep. It was funny — when he wasn't talking, there seemed to be something missing, a vital element they'd left behind. She almost wanted to wake him and set him off again, like a wind-up toy, but she decided against it. He'd been through just as much as she had, and so she let him rest.

They stopped at a gas station for food and Amber and Milo got out, leaving Glen to snore gently in the Charger. As they were walking back across the forecourt, Milo said, "One of the women said you were there when the witch killed someone. Faith — was that her name?"

Amber nodded.

"I'm sorry you had to see that."

"Me too."

"We can talk about it, if you want."

The Charger stood before them, waiting to hear her story. She imagined her confession filling it like fuel, and she slowed.

"I killed her," said Amber.

Milo frowned. "Faith?"

"The witch," she said. "I killed her, just like I killed Varga."

"They were monsters."

She looked at him. "They were still living things. Almost living, anyway. One moment they could think and have opinions and do things, and the next... they couldn't. Because I killed them."

"They had both killed plenty of innocent people. You stopped them from killing more."

"I ended their lives."

"Yes, you did. And you have to live with that. But better you end theirs than they end yours."

"Have you killed people?"

Milo didn't answer for the longest time.

"Sorry," said Amber. "I didn't mean to—"

"My earliest memory is of murder," he said.

She looked at him. Didn't say anything.

"I woke up one morning in a motel with no idea who I was. I didn't know my name, didn't know where I was from... My life was a blank. The only memories I had were flashes of being in that car, driving at night. The only faces I could remember were the faces of the people I'd killed."

"Glen was right," Amber said softly. "You're the Ghost of the Highway."

"That's what some of the newspapers called me, yeah. I didn't know it, not when I was in that motel room that morning. I remembered everything about the world, but nothing about my place in it. I went outside, though, and I saw the Charger waiting for me. I could've walked away, I guess. Left it behind.

But I was terrified. I was alone, and lost. I didn't know what had happened, why I couldn't remember... But I knew, even then, that the car was a part of me. That I'm only complete when I'm sitting behind the wheel.

"I must have stood there for an hour, maybe longer, just looking at it. I knew what I was. I was a killer. More than that, I was a monster. I remembered fragments about a deal – vague fragments, from years before – and I remembered the Demon who spoke to me... Couldn't remember the words, though. Couldn't remember the terms, or even the reason why I'd summoned him in the first place."

"Is your name even Milo?" Amber asked. "Are you even from Kentucky?"

He gave a small smile. "According to the ID in my wallet. As far as I can tell, though, it's a false identity. Why I needed one, I don't know. But it was the only one I had, so I clung to it."

"What did you do? Did you get in the Charger?"

"I did," he said. "It was fine for the first few hours. I just drove. I was outside of Miami, so I headed for a hospital. Couldn't remember one thing about my life before the deal, but I remembered streets, oh yes. I remembered where everything was. But the more I drove, the more I began to slip away. I didn't notice it at first, how calm I was getting. How content. And then, just like that–" he clicked his fingers – "I knew that if I didn't get out of that car that I'd be gone again. So that's what I did.

"I stored the Charger, took a bus to the hospital. They couldn't find any head trauma. I went to shrinks, hypnotists... Hypnotists helped, actually. I started to remember more – but it was all about my time in the car, travelling the blackroads, choosing victims... Nothing about me. Nothing about my life before all that. I got in touch with Edgar to try to figure out more about the deal I'd done, or even just find out which Demon I'd done it with. It didn't work. I gradually accepted that my old life had been wiped away and there was no getting it back."

"You still don't remember anything?"

He shook his head.

"Jacob said the Shining Demon sent out a representative when his dad stopped harvesting souls. Did anyone like that ever come to you?"

"No. I'd have welcomed it, actually. Finally, I'd have some answers."

In the Charger ahead, Glen woke up. Amber saw him look around in sleepy befuddlement. He spotted her and waved.

"That was twelve years ago," said Milo. "Every few months I'd go by the garage, take the cover off and just... look at her. But I wouldn't touch. Wouldn't get in."

"Until I made you."

He looked at her, frowning, like he'd just remembered she was there. "You didn't make me do anything."

"You needed the car to take me on the blackroads."

"That was my choice," said Milo. "Besides, enough time has passed. I don't feel the same need as I did back then. I wouldn't have been able to handle the Charger before. I'd have been in danger of slipping right back into my old habits."

"And now you're not?"

"Of course not. It doesn't take me over like it used to."

"Sometimes it does."

"What?"

"When you've been driving too long, you kind of... You get weird. You look thinner."

Milo shrugged. "It can be a strain, sure. But I'm in control."

"You don't quit an addiction by going back to it."

"I'm in control, all right? Trust me."

"So... it really is alive? The car?"

"In a way."

"Can it hear us? Can it understand us?"

"Of course."

She looked over at the Charger, noticing how still it seemed, like a cat about to pounce.

Milo smiled. "She's not going to hurt you."

"How do you know?"

"Because I know when she doesn't like someone."

"It talks to you?"

"Sort of. Relax, Amber, okay? Things are different now. I'm older and stronger. I'm in control now, not the Charger. When you're in this car, you've got nothing to worry about, okay? It's everyone else out there," he said. "They're the ones who have to worry."

48

THEY STAYED IN KANSAS that night, and were gone by eight the next morning. Amber watched the landscape rise, flat land developing hills the further east they drove. They passed through Missouri and Illinois and got back into Indiana at five that afternoon. Tomorrow, Milo said, they'd be in New York.

They found a motel just like half a dozen others they'd stayed at, L-shaped, the rooms opening directly on to the parking lot. Amber got a room at the upper half of the L, Glen got one in the middle, and Milo got one nearer the corner.

They ate at a nearby diner and Milo and Glen went to their rooms. Amber took the iPad to hers, used MapQuest to work out that they had twelve hours of driving ahead of them. She really, really hoped that'd be the end of it. She couldn't handle any more.

At seven, she got so bored she went for a walk. She didn't know the name of the town they were in, but it was pretty big. Maybe it even qualified for city status. She got something to eat in a McDonald's, even though she wasn't hungry. Eating was something to do to pass the time.

When she was finished, she dumped the remains of her meal in the trash, slid the tray on to the stack, and walked out on to the sidewalk, nearly colliding with a pretty blonde girl who was passing. They smiled at each other, did that awkward dance where one moves round the other, and the girl walked on. Amber was going the same way, but she delayed for a moment, just to make it clear that she wasn't following this girl, and then she walked after her.

There was a guy up ahead in a crappy suit, slurping on a smoothie. He watched the blonde girl approach, then put the smoothie on top of a trash can and brought his hands together in an appreciative clap.

"Now that is how you fill a T-shirt," he said, grinning, as he fell into step beside her. "Hey there, baby, how're you doing today?"

The girl didn't answer, just kept walking.

Amber stayed a few paces behind.

"You are looking mighty fine, princess. Where you headed?"

"I'm in a hurry, sorry," the girl said.

"Where you rushing off to? Why don't you stay a while, talk with me?"

She shook her head, walked faster.

He kept pace. "I'm a nice guy, I'm a good guy. Ask anyone, they'll tell you." When she didn't answer, he lost his good cheer. "I'm just being friendly. Can't a fella be friendly these days? I'm paying you a compliment, for Christ's sake. Least you can do is say thank you."

The words left Amber's mouth before she realised what she was saying. "Leave her alone."

The guy swung round, his forehead creased in a frown, while the blonde girl took the opportunity to speed-walk away.

He gave Amber the once-over, and was not impressed. "What'd you say?"

Amber looked up at him and tried to keep the tremor out of her voice. "She didn't ask for the compliment. You gave it and she didn't ask for it or want it. She shouldn't have to say thank you for something she didn't want in the first place."

The guy stared at her, and laughed. "What the hell are you talking about? What does this have to do with you? We were just having a conversation." He turned, like he expected the blonde girl to still be there. "Aw man..."

He looked back at Amber. "What were you saying?"

"Nothing," said Amber, and walked by him.

He followed her. "You jealous, that it? Bet you never had someone come up to you out of the blue and compliment you, now did you? No. You know why? Because you are fugly. You are fug-ly."

"All right," Amber said.

He stopped following her, content to have the last word. "Next time, mind your own goddamn business, you goddamn troll-looking bitch."

Troll. That was it. That was the word that guy had used, back in the Firebird. Troll. What had his name been? Brian? Ben? Brandon.

Amber turned. The guy was just about to walk away, but when he saw Amber looking at him he squared up, eyebrow raised.

"We got a problem?"

"I get it," she said. "I'm short. I could do with losing a few pounds. I'm not as pretty as some other girls."

"And you look like a troll."

People passed them by, not giving them anything more than a cursory glance.

"So what?" Amber asked. "What if I do look like a troll? I don't think I do, personally, but let's say that I did – so what? What's it got to do with you?"

"Hey, you're the one started this," the guy said.

"That's right," she said, nodding. "I started this when you started hassling that girl."

"I complimented her!" he said. Almost shouted.

"She didn't want your attention."

The guy took a big step towards her. "Well, that's her problem, now isn't it? I compliment a girl, that's what it is. Not my problem if she takes it wrong."

Amber looked up at him calmly. "But you have eyes, right? You saw how quick she was walking? You saw how uncomfortable she was? So, even if your intention was to be nice, why didn't you back off when you noticed how uneasy you were making her?"

"So a man's not allowed to compliment a woman anymore, is that what you're saying? I swear, there's just no talking to people like you."

He stepped back, done, but she wasn't going to let him get away that easy. She just couldn't.

She grabbed his shirt, both hands bunching at his chest, and powered forward. He stumbled at first, too surprised to react, and then started laughing. Amused, he let himself get pushed into a narrow alley, then planted his feet and twisted. Amber lost her grip and tripped over his leg and fell to her knees. The ground was cold and wet.

"I'm not exactly sure what the hell is happening," he said,

"but it looked like you were trying to hurt me. Which is goddamn *hilarious*."

Amber stood, and met his gaze. "Just thought I'd give you what you're after."

"Ohhh, you mean with *you*? Not a chance, little girl. I like 'em tall and stacked, know what I'm saying?"

"I know," she said, and shifted into a tall, stacked, red-skinned demon. "So how do you like me now?"

His eyes widened and his mouth opened, but before he could yell she grabbed him, yanked him off his feet, and threw him deeper into the alley. He went rolling through a puddle and scrambled up and she shoved him back.

"Am I pretty enough now?" she said, smiling and showing her fangs. "Am I sexy enough now?"

She hit him, a backhanded swipe that sent him spinning, and stalked after him. "I've wanted to do this my whole life, you know that?"

"Get away from me!" he screeched.

He tried to run past her, but she caught him, of course she did, and she slammed his head into a set of filthy pipes running down the wall. He wobbled and fell, but his arms were still working and he started dragging himself away.

She lifted him off the ground by his ankle, swinging him into the wall. There was an awful crunching sound, and he landed heavily.

"What's wrong?" she asked. "All out of compliments?"

Her hand closed round his throat and she straightened, taking him with her. She held him off the ground with an ease that delighted her.

"Don't worry," she said, "I'm not going to kill you. I'm

going to let you go. But you're never going to forget this, are you? And so whenever you see a pretty girl walking down the street – or even a not-so-pretty girl – you're going to have to wonder to yourself – is she a demon? Because you wanna know a secret? There are a lot more than me out there. There are *thousands* of us, but you're not going to know who's who until it's too late."

"I'm... sorry," he gurgled.

"Shhh. It's almost over. I just want to leave you with something." Her free hand grew talons. "I'm just going to carve the word troll on your forehead."

He kicked, flailed, and she ignored him, and her smile grew wider as the tip of her nail touched his skin. She flicked downwards and he screamed and the scream pierced her calm like she'd been cut herself.

Amber dropped him in alarm and stepped back, and he curled into a ball with both hands pressed to his forehead. Blood flowed freely.

She looked at her hand, and watched as her talons retracted and her skin returned to normal and she was Amber again, the girl, the human, not the demon, and her thoughts were her own and all she wanted to do was puke.

She didn't, though. She swallowed thickly and stepped back. She hurried from the alley, keeping her head down, and half ran back to the motel.

Amber sat on the edge of her bed. A few minutes later, she realised she was shaking. She took a shower, dressed in pyjama bottoms and a T-shirt, and went back to where she'd been sitting.

"What the hell?" she whispered to the empty room.

She turned on the small TV to get her thoughts on to something else, and began flicking through the channels. She bypassed a *Two and a Half Men* marathon and found an old TV show where a man in a suit, tie and mask was fighting a werewolf. It wasn't very good, but it was better than *Two and a Half Men*. She watched it until she got bored, then flicked over and caught the end of a *Dark Places* rerun.

Her smile faded before it had even begun – the first time she'd seen this episode she had been at home, with her parents. It was the one where Balthazar was being stalked through an empty town by a trio of hunters. Bill had walked in just when they were explaining how they'd been tracking him. She remembered, with perfect clarity, the look on her father's face as he itched to tell her how ridiculous that explanation was.

To his credit, though, he had kept his opinions to himself. But then, she supposed, he always did. She tried to remember a time when he had criticised a favourite book or show, and wasn't surprised when she came up empty. In some ways, he'd actually been a good father.

Amber turned off the TV. It was dark now, almost eleven. She should sleep, or at least try. Instead, she picked up the iPad and logged on to the *Dark Places* forum. Nobody she liked was chatting so she skimmed the conversations and the GIFs. She looked into Balthazar's ice-blue eyes and found a piece of that old comfort, that sense of familiarity. She started to well up, and laughed at herself, but it was a laugh without humour. She dropped the iPad on the bed and went to the window, pressed her forehead against the glass. She watched a man walk from one of the rooms towards the street.

Bill had been right, of course. The scepticism on his face was entirely justified. The way the hunters had been tracking Balthazar was indeed stupid. She was just thankful that her parents had no such things as subdermal locators. The only way they could track her was by searching for the Charger – but looking for one car in all of America was an almost impossible task, even with their resources. Still, the car was a possibility, no matter how unlikely, but the people within the car were mere ghosts – Amber hadn't sent emails, she hadn't posted anything that could be traced back to her, Milo didn't use a credit card, and Glen didn't even *have* a credit card.

The man passed through a patch of darkness and she waited for him to emerge. When he didn't, she looked closer, trying to pick him out in the gloom. A bus's headlights swept the area, revealing its emptiness. She found herself looking up, like the guy was a vampire who had just lifted into the air and flown away instead of turning left or right or walking off down some lane she couldn't see. This was what she had been reduced to – seeing the supernatural when she should have been seeing the ordinary. In that direction, craziness lay.

Of course, the only way anyone could *possibly* track them was – according to Althea Buxton – if one of the vampires who had bitten Glen decided to come after him, but why the hell would they have done that? Why go after Glen, of all people? What was so important about him? The only reason she could think of, in all her wild imaginings, would be if her parents had noticed he'd been bitten. Then the smart move would be to either force or coerce the vampire who'd done it to lead them to him and, as a result, her. That'd be the smart move. That'd be the sneaky, unexpected thing that they'd probably think of.

Amber took her head away from the glass as her body very slowly turned cold. She felt sick and weak and she didn't want to move, but she went to her bag, took out the crucifix. Her hands were shaking.

She opened the door and stepped out. The parking lot was half full and still, lit by a street lamp that sprouted from a half-hearted flower bed along the sidewalk. Cars passed on the street beyond, but not many. The night was dark and it was quiet. It was holding a secret.

On bare feet Amber walked from her room, passing window and door, window and door, window and door.

She was paranoid. Of course she was. She was letting her imagination take over. This was natural. She was going to knock on Glen's door and he'd answer and she'd hand him the crucifix and the next morning he'd insist that she'd been sleepwalking, that he was irresistible to her, and she'd ignore him and they'd drive on and that would be the end of it.

Amber got to his room. His door was open. She stepped in.

The room was dark. Glen lay across the bed in his boxers. There was blood still dripping from his neck and his eyes were open but unseeing.

Amber dropped the crucifix and both hands went to her mouth as her knees gave out and she sagged against the wall. A whine escaped her lips that she quickly bit back before it became a scream.

He thought he'd got away from them. They all did. But Glen had been killed that first night in Cascade Falls – it had just taken this long for it to register.

She turned on to her hands and knees, finding it difficult to breathe. She needed to get out. Get Milo. Get in the car and drive. The vampire had found them, and if the vampire was here…

She looked up. From where she was, she could see through the open door, all the way across the parking lot, to where her parents and their friends were standing.

49

AMBER CLAMPED A HAND over her mouth to keep from crying out. Her father emerged from the manager's office, talked with the others. Grant and Kirsty started walking towards Milo's room. She couldn't be sure, but it looked like they had guns in their hands.

Her parents and Imelda went left, headed for Amber's room. Alastair hung back, keeping an eye out. Amber left the door to Glen's room open – she didn't want anything to draw them to her – and forced herself to her feet. She stumbled to the window. Once her parents realised that her room was empty, they'd come straight here. Imelda would probably try to distract them, but she only had moments.

Alastair approached the Charger, running his hand over the bodywork admiringly. From where she was, Amber could see the trunk as it clicked open, spilling red light. Alastair frowned, moved closer.

Dacre Shanks lunged out at him.

They went down and there were shouts and curses and Amber backed away from the window, nearly falling over the bed, nearly falling over Glen's body. She caught a glimpse of herself in the mirror as she turned red and grew horns. She may have looked fierce, even in her pyjama bottoms and little T-shirt, but she didn't feel it. Outside in that parking lot right now was no mercy and certain death. The idea that she should stand and fight passed so fleetingly it was like it was never there. Which left only one course of action.

She hurried into the bathroom, shut the door and, as an afterthought, locked it. She stepped to the wall as her hands grew talons. Her first slash was pitiful — it barely scraped the plaster. But her second took some of that ridiculously light wood with it. She slashed again, and kicked, her bare foot smashing through to the other side. Another few slashes to weaken it further and then she took three steps back.

She heard gunshots. Grant and Kirsty had found Milo.

She charged, hit the wall with her shoulder, and exploded into the bathroom on the other side in a shower of splinters and cheap plaster. She stumbled a little but stayed upright, yanked the door open and hurried through. The room's occupant, a startled man with an alarming beard, was already on his feet, clutching a pillow to his chest. She backhanded him on her way past and he flew into the corner, crumpling into an unconscious heap. For his own good. Her parents would most likely kill any witness they came across.

Right before she left the man's room, she heard her father's voice somewhere behind her.

She ran out. Gaudy green neon lit up the small swimming pool in which dead bugs swam with cigarette butts. She jumped the railing. On the road ahead a patrol car was swerving into a U-turn, its siren suddenly blaring, coming back to investigate the sound of gunfire. For one crazy moment, Amber thought they could help her, but of course they couldn't. No one could.

She stuck to the darkness, running along the embankment beside the railing, keeping the motel on her left. The patrol car braked sharply and she looked back. Betty stood in the middle of the road, entirely calm in the headlights. The cops got out, yelled at her to put her hands up, and Bill landed on the car roof. He yanked the first cop off his feet and the second cop started shouting and then a shadow lunged at Amber and she went sliding down the embankment, tangled in arms and legs, catching the glint of a knife in the corner of her eye.

She hit the ground – cold, hard concrete – and Dacre Shanks squirmed on top of her. She grabbed his wrist, keeping the blade at bay. He hissed at her, trying to scratch through her scales with his other hand. He was thinner. His cheeks were sunken and his skin was pallid. The Charger had drained him and it showed. He looked ill, the kind of ill you don't recover from.

Amber rolled, shoved him off, let go of his wrist and kicked him away from her. He got up, slashing, and she kept back, out of range, her talons out and her fangs bared.

She would have spoken to him, would have told him to run now, while he still could, but there was something in his eyes that told her he wasn't going to listen. A madness. The reasoning side of Shanks's brain had shut down at some stage in that trunk and this was all that was left.

He came at her and the blade slid off the scales that had formed round her ribs. She hit him, a punch that lifted him sideways, that cracked his fragile bones. He gasped and she brought her fist down on his forearm. His fingers sprang open and his knife fell and he staggered back, clutching his hand and tilting to one side. She glanced behind her, making sure she was out of her parents' line of sight, and, when she looked back, Shanks was coming for her again.

She slashed at him, her talons gouging furrows into his cheek. He stumbled past, hands at his face, his bottom lip flapping against his chin. Moaning words she couldn't understand, Shanks tried reaching for her, but Amber grabbed him, took him off his feet. She slammed him against the wall and his head smacked wetly against concrete. Then she let go, and he dropped.

He tried to crawl, but that was all his body could take. With catastrophic speed, he came apart as she watched. His arms folded beneath him like they were made of rubber, and his face hit the ground, shattering his jaw. His eyes rolled up so he was looking at her when his flesh caved in. His hair, his scalp, his skin slid from his skull, and blood and bile and a dozen other noxious fluids sluiced from his pores. His eyes clouded and melted, dripped from their sockets while his face peeled back like the skin of a grape and his clothes flattened, soaked in the juices of all that remained of Dacre Shanks.

"What a way to go," Alastair said from behind her, and she spun.

In demon form, Alastair was seven feet tall, his shirt stretching to contain his mass. His beard was longer, and pointed. Behind it he smiled. "I don't know who he was, or why he was locked in the trunk of that car, but to die by melting? That is quite something."

Her mouth was dry. She'd never be able to outrun him. She didn't have a hope of overpowering him, either.

424

"You've led us on quite the chase, young lady," he continued. "I've got to admit – I didn't think you had it in you. Honestly. You've surprised me. Hell, you've impressed me. But it all ends here, I'm afraid."

She only had once chance – attack him now, while he least expected it. Attack him, put him on his back, and run. Sprint. Hide.

"Alastair," she said, "please don't hurt me."

He smiled, stepped forward, about to say something else, and she slammed into him. He grunted and she went for his eyes. When he grabbed her wrists, she tried to knee him in the groin, but he shifted position, took the knee on his hip, and a simple push sent her tumbling head over heels across the ground.

"It takes a while to get used to, doesn't it?" he asked. "The strength, I mean. It takes a while longer to stop relying on it, though."

She ran at him and he ripped a metal pipe from the wall and swung it into her jaw. The impact rattled her skull, and when her brain came back online she was lying face down on the ground.

"See what I mean?" Alastair said, standing over her. "You've got all this strength and so you figure hey, all I need to do is land a few punches, am I right? And then before you know it you've run headlong into a metal pipe and it's lights out."

Amber started to get to her hands and knees.

"I think it'd be a nice thing to tell you that I liked you most of all, out of all our children that we've killed. But that'd be a lie." He stomped on her back and her face hit the ground. "But you're a sweet girl, there's no denying it, and I hope you feel like you've had a good life."

"I'm sure she does," said Imelda, walking up to join them.

Alastair chuckled, picked Amber up by the scruff of the neck. "Look what I found."

"Doesn't she look beautiful?" Imelda said, sauntering closer. "Red suits you, sweetie."

She picked up the fallen metal pipe. "You hit her with this?"

"Indeed I did," said Alastair.

"And she's still conscious?"

"As it turns out, our little Amber is a bit of a tough cookie."

"Yes, she is," said Imelda, and swung the pipe into Alastair's face.

Amber dropped as Alastair staggered back. Imelda hit him three more times – once to get him on the ground, and twice more to keep him there – and then hurried back to help Amber to her feet.

"We have to run now," she said, and they ran.

They got a few streets over, reverting to normal, but still sticking to the shadows. They found a small park, the grass easier on Amber's bare feet than the sidewalks, and hurried to the group of trees at its centre.

"Milo," said Amber. "Where's Milo? I heard gunshots."

Imelda hesitated. "Me too."

"You think they... you think they got him?"

"I don't know, sweetie. We can't think about Milo right now."

"What? We can't just leave him. Glen's dead but Milo, Milo might still be alive."

"It's you they want, Amber, not Milo. The best thing we can do is get you as far away from here as possible."

"You're coming with me?"

"Well, I can hardly stick around after beating up my ex-husband, now can I?" Imelda said, and glanced behind them. She hissed, dragged Amber into the trees and ducked down. "They're behind us," she whispered.

"So we run."

Imelda bit her lip.

"Imelda, we run."

"They're faster than us," Imelda said. "We'd never make it."

"Then we hide," said Amber. "We stay here and we don't make a sound."

"They'll find us."

"Then what do we do? Do we fight?"

Imelda peeked out, and a soft moan of panic escaped her. Finally, she looked Amber dead in the eyes. "You're going to have to run."

Amber frowned. "You said you were coming with me."

"I know, sweetie, and I'm sorry, but I'll hold them off, all right? You get as far away from here as—"

"No," said Amber. "No. I am not leaving you. I'm not leaving Milo and I'm not leaving you. I already had to leave Glen and I'm not doing that again. I need you to come with me."

Imelda gripped Amber's shoulders. "Amber, please. All I care about in this world is you. Your safety is the only thing that matters to me. I have done awful, terrible, unforgivable things in my life, things I can't walk away from. All that bad stuff has finally caught up to me. Tonight is the night I pay for all the evil I've done. No, no, I'm okay with that. Do you understand? I'm okay with it. I deserve it. I... I think I even need it. But please, I am begging you, let the last thing I do be counted as a good thing. Let me help you escape."

"But I don't want you to die."

"I love you, Amber. I love you, sweetheart. I need you to live. I need you to be the one that lives. I couldn't do that for my own children. I can do it for you. That's what a parent is for. That's what it means. When you're older, you'll understand. When you have children of your own, you'll see. You're all that matters. You're all that *should* matter. You replace us. You carry on. You have to carry on, Amber."

And then a familiar roar, and the Charger screeched to a halt on the street ahead. The passenger door swung open and Milo pulled the seat forward.

"Move!" he yelled.

Amber glanced at Imelda, and Imelda grinned. "Of course, I'd like to carry on as well."

They started running.

Amber glanced behind her. The others were in pursuit, with Bill way out in front. He was moving so fast he'd be on them in seconds.

Milo revved the engine, like that would make them run faster.

When they were in throwing distance of the Charger, Amber heard a gunshot. Imelda grunted, lost her rhythm and stumbled, and Amber tried to stop, but Imelda shoved her on.

"Run!" Imelda snapped, and fell.

Amber ran. Milo pushed the seat back and she jumped in. Behind her, Imelda lunged at Bill as he tried to sprint by her. They went down in a snarling, snapping tumble. The Charger's wheels spun as Milo accelerated, but Amber twisted in her seat as the others descended on Imelda, claws slashing and fangs tearing.

428

"Go back," Amber said. "We have to go back!"

"They'd kill us," said Milo.

"I'll pay you! I'll pay you everything I have!"

"I can't," he said. "I'm so sorry."

She turned to argue with him, to scream at him, and only then did she notice how pale he was, how much he was sweating. He steered with his left hand while his right was pressed into his side. Blood darkened his T-shirt.

His head dipped and his hand dropped from the wheel and the Charger started to swerve off the road. Amber reached over, tried to correct their course, shouting for Milo to wake up.

The Charger hit the lamppost and Amber slammed her head against the dash.

50

THE SUDDEN PEACE AND quiet was unnatural, and it brought Amber back from the brink of unconsciousness.

She opened her eyes, sat up, looked around. A few seconds. She'd only lost a few seconds.

In the distance, she heard sirens.

She got out of the car, made sure her parents weren't anywhere in sight, and reached back in, pulling Milo on to the passenger seat and trying to ignore the amount of blood he was losing. When he was strapped in, she hurried round to the driver's side. As she reached for the handle, she had a sudden fear that the Charger would lock her out, but the door opened under her touch and she slid in.

Her horns scraped the car ceiling, and she reluctantly reverted to give herself more room.

She adjusted her seat, buckled her belt, and put the Charger into gear. They lurched on to the road and she hissed, wrenched the wheel, managed to get them going straight. This wasn't like the car she'd driven in Driver's Ed. This was a monstrosity, a heavy metal beast, and she was fully aware that any moment it could surge out of her control. She slowed at a

Stop sign, signalled, and turned on to a larger road. A larger road with other cars moving.

"Please don't let me crash, please don't let me crash," she muttered, not entirely sure if this was a prayer she was offering to God, to the Devil, or to the Charger itself.

An hour later, she pulled over, reached into her bag on the back seat, and pulled out some clothes. She put on socks and shoes and wrapped herself in a coat. The temperature in the car had plummeted. She covered Milo with a blanket, and drove on.

It took another hour and a half to get to Dayton, Ohio. She wasn't taking the smaller roads, like Milo had. She stayed on I-70 and just kept heading east. By now, her parents would have searched her motel room, found the iPad, found the MapQuest search. They knew where she was headed, so there was nothing to be gained now by sneaking. It was a straight blast towards New York.

She kept glancing at Milo as she drove. He slumped, pale and sweating, unconscious. Unconscious but not dead. Amber was okay with that. She trusted the car to heal him.

She picked up speed after Dayton, got to Columbus in an hour, picked up more speed, then had to pull into a gas station as the tank was verging on empty. This worried her, but she filled it carefully, with reverence, almost like it was a blood transfusion. Then they got back on the road and made it as far as Pittsburgh before sunrise, and morning traffic started to clog the lanes.

At eight, Milo woke.

Amber took an off-ramp, drove through a few quiet streets until she came to a parking lot behind a crappy-looking gym. She helped Milo out of the Charger and he stood in his bare feet, straightening up slowly. His blood had drenched the passenger seat.

"How're you feeling?" she asked.

"Bad," he muttered. "But I've been worse." He prodded the bullet hole in his ruined T-shirt, wincing every time. "I'll be okay in a day or two. Maybe even a few hours." He frowned, and looked around. "Where are we?"

"Somewhere in Pennsylvania," she said. "We passed Pittsburgh, like, an hour ago. Maybe more."

"You've been driving all night?"

"I wasn't exactly going to be able to sleep."

"No," Milo said, "I guess not. Okay, this is good. We should we in New York in another five hours. I'll drive."

"You're too weak."

"I'll be fine. Your turn to get some rest. Do me a favour — reach in there and grab my bag, would you? Get your own as well."

Amber passed him his bag and found his boots tossed on to the back seat. She walked beside him as he limped to the gym, and watched him bribe the guy inside. Milo headed off to the men's locker room, and she went to the women's. She showered, brushed her teeth, and put on the jeans that were too long for her. She turned the ends up, pulled on a fresh T-shirt and a jacket, and went outside to wait by the car. Milo joined her a few minutes later. He was moving easier now, dressed in clean jeans and a jacket over a dark plaid shirt.

"Glen's dead," Amber said when he reached the car. Blurted, really.

Milo hesitated. "Yeah," he said. "I figured."

"A vampire did it. It's how they tracked us."

He nodded, and she looked away.

"Do you think she got away?" Amber asked. "Imelda, I mean. She could have escaped, right?"

Milo put his bag in the trunk. "She wasn't getting away from that, Amber."

She glared. "We should have gone back for her."

"Then we'd both be dead, and my death would have been a lot quicker than yours. Keys?"

She handed them over. "Shanks is dead, too. The Charger let him out, you know."

"I know. If it wasn't for that, I would have been asleep when your parents' buddies kicked down my door. Get in, Amber. We can't afford to lose any more time."

She opened the passenger door. There was no blood on the seat. The car had soaked it all up. Absorbed it.

She got in. Milo lowered himself, carefully, behind the wheel.

And they drove to New York. The car felt empty without Glen.

Amber felt empty, too.

She woke to a yellow cab blasting its horn at a bike messenger who was giving it the finger. Sitting up straighter, she wiped the drool from her chin and watched the brownstones tick by in a rhythm she could hear only in her head. The afternoon sun glinted off stained-glass windows and she checked the scars on her wrist: 122 hours left. Five days.

She yawned.

"You were having a bad dream," said Milo.

"Was I? I don't remember." Plumes of steam poured out from orange and white pipes, twice the height of the people that passed them. This was the New York of the movies – not the gleaming skyscrapers of Manhattan, but scaffolding and cracked sidewalks, health-food stores and cafes and bricks and mortar the colour of chocolate. This was Brooklyn.

"Ever been to New York before?" Milo asked.

"Twice," said Amber. "When I was eight and then again when I was twelve. We all went. Imelda took me up the Empire State Building and we saw the Statue of Liberty and we went to see The Lion King on Broadway. I don't remember what my parents or the others were doing. Huh."

"What?"

"Before all this, I thought Imelda didn't like me all that much. But she was the only one who ever did anything with me."

Milo looked at her. "If she's still alive, and if it's at all possible, we'll get her back."

They found a place to park – which wasn't easy – and walked a few blocks to a pizzeria on Park Slope. Edgar Spurrier grinned when he saw them, half of his pizza topping spilling over and dripping on to his tie.

"Ah goddammit," he said when he noticed. As he dabbed himself with napkins, Amber and Milo slid into the booth.

"You two," said Edgar, dumping the napkins on the table beside him, "have been busy. Oh, I have been hearing about you and your adventures."

Amber frowned. "From who?"

"From the folks in the know," said Edgar. "Tittle-tattle. Scuttlebutt. The black Charger and the demon girl. This partnership of yours is garnering quite the reputation – and I've been sitting back and basking in the reflected glory of it all." His smile left him. "And you stole my powder flask."

"I meant to apologise about that," said Milo.

"Did you? Did you really?"

"I thought we might have need of it before you would."

"And you didn't think to ask? You didn't think that I would have gladly loaned you my powder flask, for which I paid more than a pretty penny, out of the goodness of my own heart?"

"Not really, no."

"Yeah, you're probably right," Edgar said, and shoved the rest of the slice into his mouth. Chewing, he said, "Do you still have it? You haven't lost it, have you?"

"We still have it."

"Good." He chewed on, and swallowed. "Amber, how are your parent troubles?"

"They still want to kill me, if that's what you mean."

"They haven't changed their minds about that, huh? A damn shame. My parents wanted to kill me when I was your age, too, but for entirely different reasons."

"Have you had any luck finding Gregory Buxton?" she asked, but a waitress came over before Edgar could answer. They ordered a few slices and she walked off, taking Edgar's crumpled-up napkins with her. Edgar leaned forward.

"I've been narrowing it down," he said. "I not only have the neighbourhood, I have the apartment building, and I'm pretty sure I even have the apartment. Buxton's been living under an assumed name – which I have naturally found out. All we have to do is stake the place out until he comes home."

"I'm impressed," Milo said.

Edgar shrugged. "I just do what I do. It's no big thing. I mean, you couldn't do it, and nobody you know could have done it, but I did it because I'm me, and I'm just that smart."

"And insufferable."

"That goes hand in hand with genius, my friend. I'm coming with you, by the way."

"Ah, Edgar, I don't know about that…"

Edgar dropped his pizza slice. "You are not leaving me out of this. You're about to go hunting a winged beast. *A winged beast*, for God's sake. How many people get to say that in their lifetime?"

"Probably not very many."

"*Exactly*. I've been studying this stuff for most of my adult life. Sure, I've tried to do things, practical things, every now and then, but none of them have met with any success. But this? Hunting a winged beast? This would be me *doing* something, instead of just reading about it. There are a multitude of untold horrors that lurk in America's shadows, and I want to start *stalking* them."

"You rehearsed that," said Milo.

"Did not," said Edgar. "It all came to me just then. Milo, come on – have I ever asked you for anything?"

Milo sighed. "No."

"And Amber, do you owe me for all my help?"

"I guess."

"Then it's settled," he said, and grinned wider.

"You," said Amber, "are a very strange man."

"I know," said Edgar. "And I love it."

51

GREGORY BUXTON'S APARTMENT BUILDING was right beside the East
River. The other buildings on the street were redbrick, but this
one was brown, the colour of dirt. The wall closest to the river
was armoured with rusted scaffolding, and it was flanked by
an auto-rental place on one side and the Kent Sugar Refinery
on the other. The auto-rental place was devoid of any actual
autos, and the Sugar Refinery was a flattened wasteland enclosed
by barbed-wire fences.

Milo pulled over to the kerb on the corner. Night was falling,
and New York was lighting up like a great beast opening its
countless eyes. They crossed the street, took the stairs to the top
floor. They knocked on Buxton's door, and when nobody
answered they moved away to wait. A little under an hour later,
a black man in his sixties came up the stairs, went straight to
the door and slid a key in. They walked up behind him.

"Gregory Buxton?" Milo asked.

The old man froze. Amber thought for a moment that he
might make a break for it, but he surprised her by turning.
He was tall, looked strong, with broad shoulders and thick
forearms. His white hair was cropped short, and his face was

heavily lined. She could see the remains of a handsome man beneath all that wear and tear. His mouth had settled over the years into a calm, straight line, and his eyes, while wary, were not unfriendly.

"Nobody's called me that in years," he said. "Come on in."

He turned back to his door, opened it and walked inside. The door swung halfway shut, hiding him from view.

Milo took out his gun and they moved quickly but cautiously. Milo opened the door the rest of the way, and Amber watched Buxton leaning into his refrigerator.

"Got no beers, I'm afraid," he said. "I used to drink, then decided it wasn't worth the hassle. Got some juice and some soft drinks, though, if that tickles your fancy."

He straightened up, saw Milo's gun, and didn't react one way or the other as they walked in. It was a drab apartment, but neat, and well maintained.

"I'll have a juice," said Amber.

He poured her a glass, left it for her on the table, and sank into his armchair, enjoyed the comfort for a moment with his eyes closed, and then looked up. "So who might you be?"

Amber stepped forward. "My name is Amber Lamont. This is Milo, and that's Edgar Spurrier. They're helping me."

"Helping you do what, Amber?"

"My parents and four of their friends made a deal with the Shining Demon."

"Aha," said Buxton. "They're the children-eaters, huh? Yeah, I heard about them. Tough break."

"The Shining Demon said he'd renegotiate that deal so that I get to live… if I give him something he wants."

"Me."

"Yes."

"And this is why you're here? To ask if I'll go peacefully?"

"I'm pretty sure you won't."

"I'm pretty sure you're right. How did you find me anyway?"

"We just needed to know what to look for, and your son told us that."

For the first time, Buxton looked interested. "You talked to Jacob?"

"We did more than that," said Milo. "Amber took care of his witch problem."

"No kidding? That thing's been driving him nuts. How is he? He okay?"

"He's good," said Amber. "And so's your mom."

"You *have* been getting around. I do my best to check up on them from time to time, but there's only so much I can do from all the way over here. I guess I owe you my thanks."

Milo shrugged.

"How have you managed it?" Edgar asked. "Staying invisible for so long?"

"I did my research," said Buxton. "I know all the tricks, all the little symbols you've got to scratch and the words you've got to recite. It's limiting, though, I admit. I'm not as free as I'd like to be. Every move I make I've got to think of the possible ramifications. I've got to worry about stepping out of the shadows. One slip-up, just one, and the Shining Demon would be able to latch on to me and he'd never, ever let me go. I've stayed one step ahead of him all this time because I've been playing it patient and playing it smart. It's not much of a life, but I'd be willing to bet that it's better than death."

"You haven't stopped killing," said Amber.

Buxton fixed her with a look. "No, young lady, I guess I haven't. I didn't plan on killing anyone, not at the start. I thought I'd get him to cure Jacob and then I'd take my son and vanish. But I had to be sure the cure was permanent, which meant Jake had to go through all these tests, and suddenly I was sticking around for a lot longer than originally intended. So I harvested souls, just like I said I would.

"Eventually I came to the conclusion that Jacob would be better off without me. The refrain of the deadbeat dad, huh? Yeah, I'm aware, but that doesn't make it any less true. So I took off. All my tricks worked and the Shining Demon never came close to finding me. But, see, in order for my tricks to work, I needed some degree of… well, I guess you could call it mojo. And the only way I could get my mojo was to keep harvesting souls – only instead of passing them on to the Shining Demon's grumpy old representative, I kept them for myself. The more I kept, the stronger I got, and the stronger I got, the more I harvested."

"Then you must be pretty strong by now," said Amber.

Buxton gave her a small nod. "Strong enough," he said. "I try to harvest the guilty. Criminals, gangsters, corrupt officials, people like that… Their souls aren't as potent as the innocent, but they'll do the job. I've slipped up now and then – I ain't proclaiming to be some sort of saint – but I do all right."

Amber looked at him, sitting in his chair like he was chatting with his buddies. "How are you so calm?" she asked.

"Why wouldn't I be?"

"Because we've come to your door and told you we want to hand you over to the Shining Demon. If I were in your shoes, I'd be furious."

"What good would that do?" Buxton asked. "You haven't

handed me over yet, have you? And you haven't told the Shining Demon you know where I am or else he'd be here already. I figure I've got breathing space."

"And if we said we were going to summon him right now," said Edgar, "how would you feel then?"

Buxton shrugged. "Guess you'll have to try to summon him to find out."

Milo took his gun out again, and rested it on his knee. "You're planning to kill us," he said.

"I am," said Buxton.

Edgar went pale. "But there's three of us," he said. "And we've got a gun."

"I'll manage," said Buxton.

Milo gave a soft smile. "I'm pretty fast and pretty good."

"You'll have to be."

"If we don't hand you over," Amber said, talking quickly before the situation spiralled, "do you have any way to help me? If you know all the tricks, is there something we missed?"

Buxton took his eyes off Milo, and looked at her. "You've got two choices from what I know of your situation. You either keep running and hope they stop hunting you after a dozen or so years, or you hunt them. Personally, I'd hunt them down and kill them before they kill you."

"I don't want to kill anyone."

"You killed that witch, didn't you?"

"Well, yeah, but…"

"You don't think that witch was a living being? Sure, she might have been different from me and you, but she had a heartbeat. She drew breath. She had a life and you ended it. You've already killed, Amber."

"I know that," she said, a little too loudly. "I know."

Buxton shrugged. "So killing a few more is surely no big deal."

"What if she hides?" Milo asked. "You've stayed invisible to the Shining Demon for all this time – is there a way for Amber to do the same?"

"Sure," said Buxton. "There wouldn't be much mojo involved in that one. You'd just have to pick a small town, somewhere out of the way, somewhere off the Demon Road, and blend in. Spend the rest of your life there in this small, out-of-the-way place, never excelling in anything, never making a mark, never causing a fuss or creating a stir... Think you can do that, Amber? Think you can live a life of perfect ordinariness?"

She hesitated.

Buxton smiled. "Of course you can't agree to that. I don't care if you're the most boring person on the planet – nobody's going to choose a life of mediocrity."

"I just want my parents to stop."

"Then kill them."

"I can't do that."

"Then they're going to win."

"Isn't there *anything* I could do?"

Buxton sighed. "You could go to Desolation Hill."

"Where's that?"

"Alaska. I don't know the whys and wherefores, but that's the one place you'd be invisible to the Shining Demon and anyone he'd send after you. When I was starting out, I thought I could hide there for a few months, maybe even a few years – but I only lasted a week. I wouldn't advise making the journey."

"Mr Buxton, I was really hoping you'd be able to come up with some way to help me."

"Yeah, I get that. But, seeing as how my advice would be to kill your folks and their friends the first chance you get, I don't think you're going to be paying me too much heed. Which leaves us in an awkward situation."

"Uh," said Edgar, "what would that be?"

"Mr Spurrier, wasn't it? Mr Spurrier, what Milo and Amber here have decided in the last few minutes, quite independently of one another, is to hand me over to the Shining Demon. Milo doesn't really care what happens to me one way or the other, and Amber figures I've killed plenty of people already, so maybe I deserve to pay for my sins. To her credit, it wasn't an easy decision to make, was it, Amber?"

"I... Mr Buxton, I'm sorry."

Buxton waved away her apology. "Nonsense. And you may have a point. An argument could be made that I've done more harm than good in my—"

He moved without warning, kicking the coffee table into Milo's leg and knocking the gun from his knee. Milo's hand flashed and he caught the pistol before it hit the ground, but Buxton was on his feet now, slamming another kick into Milo's chest, driving him back and toppling his chair. In the three seconds it took Amber to grow horns, Buxton hurled her into Edgar, sending them both over the back of the couch.

Milo reached for his fallen gun, but Buxton kicked it away. He grabbed the back of Milo's jacket and threw him against the wall.

Amber ran at him, claws out. He dodged her swipe and kicked her feet from under her. He picked up the chair Milo

444

had been sitting on and broke it across her shoulders. Amber dropped, struggling to stay conscious.

She heard Buxton grunt, saw Milo driving him backwards. They knocked over a lamp and hit the kitchen table, shifting it sideways. Buxton threw a punch and Milo covered up, moved in, responded with a headbutt and then an elbow to the bridge of the nose. Blood spurted. Buxton took an unsteady step. Milo kicked at his knee and spun him, got him in a chokehold, but Buxton powered backwards, slammed Milo into the wall. Milo didn't let go. Buxton's face was turning purple.

Buxton staggered to the middle of the room, to where Milo's gun had come to rest.

Amber cursed, tried to get up, but her legs were still shaky. She wobbled and fell as Buxton dropped to his knees. He stopped trying to break the chokehold and his fingers closed around the gun. He lifted it, but instead of aiming over his shoulder to shoot Milo, he aimed right at Amber.

Black scales rose on her skin. She doubted they'd do any good at this range.

Milo released the hold immediately and stepped back, leaving Buxton to suck in lungfuls of air.

"Is it over?" Edgar asked from behind the couch. "Did we win?" He peeked out. "Aw hell."

Scales retracting a little, Amber got to her feet slowly. Buxton did the same, moving so that he had all three of them covered. He wiped some of the blood from his nose.

"Hard luck," he said. "You almost got me."

He backed up to the door, opened it, gave them one last look, and ran.

Amber hesitated. She looked at Milo, and he looked at her, and together they sprinted for the door.

"But he's still got the gun!" Edgar shouted after them.

They burst out on to the landing, caught a glimpse of Buxton running up the stairs. They followed. Halfway up, Buxton dropped the gun. Milo scooped it up without slowing.

Amber reached the door to the roof before Milo and she charged through. Buxton was running for the edge. Milo fired a warning shot into the night sky, but Buxton didn't slow down. Amber piled on the speed. There was nowhere for Buxton to run.

But, of course, he had no intention of running.

He changed suddenly, from tall, broad-shouldered old man to taller, broader-shouldered demon. Wings, massive wings, split the back of his shirt. His dark skin turned grey. He reached the edge of the rooftop and those wings unfurled and he dived upwards, wings beating the air. Amber stopped running and watched, her mouth open. Buxton twisted, looked down at her. His grey face looked like it had been carved from granite. He had a crown of small horns circling his skull, just like Jacob had described.

Milo ran up beside her, fired two more shots as Buxton's wings closed over and he plummeted. Just before he fell out of sight, his wings opened and he swooped, disappearing into the darkness.

"What do we do?" Edgar asked.

"We chase," said Amber.

She ran to the roof's edge and leaped.

52

EDGAR CRIED OUT AND Milo called her name, but then rushing air filled Amber's ears and she slammed into the fire escape of the auto-rental building across the alley, her strong fingers wrapping around the wrought-iron railing. She turned, braced her feet, and flung herself back to the other side, dropping lower as she did so. She flipped, curled her body, hit the bricks with her feet, and once again she powered back to the fire escape. Down she went, clinging to the railing one side and bounding off the other, until she dropped to the alley floor. Someone cursed in the darkness, a homeless woman huddled in a sleeping bag, and Amber jumped over her and sprinted for the street. A car passed, didn't see her, and Amber ran out, eyes on the sky.

There.

She took off in pursuit, reverting when she approached people and shifting when she was clear. She cut across streets and alleys and car lots and barged through dogwalkers and couples out for a late-night stroll. She kept Buxton in view.

Then she lost him. Of course she did. She knew she had to, she knew she couldn't keep this up, but even so it stoked her anger, made her run faster, made her more determined to catch sight of him again.

She caught glimpses that sent her hurtling in different directions. The more she ran, the less inclined she was to revert. As plain old Amber, she slowed down, she got out of breath, she puffed and panted and wheezed – but as the demon, she was relentless, her muscles were strong, and she never weakened.

Let the people of New York wonder about her. Let them wonder if this was just another weirdo New Yorker going to some costume party or a real-life demon running through their streets. She didn't care. The only thing she cared about was tracking down Buxton and tearing his goddamn wings off.

Light behind her and her shadow lengthened and she whirled as the Charger braked. Edgar was already in the back seat. She jumped in and they took off. Amber had to duck her head so that her horns fitted.

"You were running around in public," said Milo as they turned a corner, drifting slightly. "What the hell were you thinking?"

"I'm thinking, if we let him get away, I'm dead," she answered. "That's what I'm thinking."

Milo craned his head out of the window. "You were seen."

"I'd rather be seen than be dead."

"Hold on," said Milo.

He turned the wheel sharply and they spun 180 degrees, the seat belt biting into Amber's shoulder. She could see Buxton's dark silhouette, barely visible beyond the street lights. The Charger pursued.

"I'd just like to take this moment to apologise," Edgar said from the back. "I know I was not the best use back there. Violence has never been my thing."

Amber lost sight of Buxton.

"It's fine, Edgar," said Milo through gritted teeth.

Edgar continued. "I just want to assure you that, were we to find ourselves in a similar situation again, I would do my very best to be a good source of backup."

Neither Amber nor Milo responded this time. They were too busy trying to spot Buxton.

"It's just," Edgar went on, "I've never been that athletic. Even in high school, I was always considered to be on the slower side of fast. I preferred books and TV to going out and doing stuff. I blame my parents, to be honest. They rarely encouraged me, and when they did it was lacklustre and, I felt, disingenuous."

Amber pointed. "There!"

Milo swerved, almost hitting a yellow cab coming the other way. Amber locked her eyes on Buxton's beating wings. The beating was getting slower. He was tiring. Then he vanished.

Amber frowned. "Where's he gone?"

"He dropped," said Milo. He gunned the engine. "I'm going after him on foot. Edgar, you drive. Circle round the block, make sure he doesn't slip away."

"Uh," said Edgar, "you want me to drive this car?"

"She won't hurt you," Milo said. "She likes Amber."

"What does she think of me?" Edgar asked.

"You don't want to know."

Edgar looked dismayed. "Rejected by an automobile. A new low."

"I'll come with you," said Amber as Milo undid his seat belt.

"You stay with Edgar."

"No, I'm coming with—"

"I can't have you running around looking like that," Milo said. "Stay in the damn car and I'll chase Buxton towards you."

Amber stared at him, but Milo was already turning the wheel. He braked, then leaped out and ran between two buildings, his gun in his hand. She forced herself to remain in the car.

It was a good plan. Despite her anger, despite her sudden fury, it was a good plan.

Edgar grunted as he climbed out of the back seat and got behind the wheel. "Okay then," he said. "Off we go."

The Charger moved away from the kerb slowly, and didn't pick up a whole lot of speed.

"Faster!" Amber snapped.

"Driving a car is like riding a horse," Edgar said patiently. "You've got to get to know her over time, figure out her—"

Amber snarled at him. "Faster."

Edgar swallowed thickly, and put his foot down.

They were just rounding the block when Edgar glanced up, hissed and wrenched the wheel in the opposite direction.

Amber's horns knocked heavily against the ceiling. "What the hell, Edgar?"

They were speeding along now, Edgar spending more time looking out of the window than he was looking at the road ahead. "Buxton," he said. "He's got Milo."

"He's what?"

They turned on to a busier street.

"You didn't see? He's carrying him," Edgar said. "Milo looks unconscious. Oh God, you don't think Buxton's going to drop him, do you?"

Amber ignored the question. "Where are they? I can't see them."

"Straight ahead of us," said Edgar, swerving round traffic. "See them? Straight… oh hell. Where are they? They were right there, they were – *aha*!"

Another wrench of the wheel and once again Amber's horns scraped the ceiling. "Little bit of warning," she said, growing angrier.

"Sorry," said Edgar. "They're over my side. Can you see them?"

"I'll take your word for it."

Edgar's driving was attracting a lot of attention. Car horns blasted them when they passed, and Edgar shouted an apology to each one.

"Stop doing that," Amber said.

"Driving?"

"Apologising."

"Oh," said Edgar. "Sorry. But this is exciting, isn't it? I mean, if he doesn't drop Milo, it'll be exciting. If he drops Milo, it'll be tragic and terrible, but right now it's exciting. Can you feel it? Can you feel the excitement?"

"I can feel it," Amber said, wanting to kill him.

"Look at me," Edgar continued, "driving a demon car, hunting a winged beast… Danger is all around, but do I turn and flee? Does my courage fail me? It does not."

"Are you *still* talking?"

"I talk when I'm nervous. I guess I talk when I hunt demons, too. This is my first time hunting a demon, and I'm talking, so I guess I must talk when I hunt demons. Ha! These are my demon-hunting pants. I always wear them when I'm hunting demons."

She wanted to tear out his throat, but didn't. If she tore out his throat, he might crash.

"This car is something magnificent, isn't it?" he asked. "You hear people talking about how engines growl – well, this one actually does, doesn't it? You can hear it, right? That growl. That power. This car is alive. Hey, I wonder if I'll be affected. You know, because of... uh..."

"Because Milo is the Ghost of the Highway and this car is possessed?"

"Oooh," Edgar said, "he told you, cool. Yeah, I wonder if I'll suddenly get all possessed and dark and stuff."

"I doubt it."

"Yeah, you're probably right." Keeping track of Buxton and Milo through the open window, Edgar swept round a corner. Less traffic here. More closed-up businesses and art galleries. A hell of a lot of art galleries. They were heading towards the harbour. "It would be quite something, though. To feel that kind of power. When you're like this, Amber, in this form, what's it like? If you don't mind me asking, of course."

She gave up trying to spot Buxton. "I'm better. Stronger. Faster."

"Beautiful."

She glared at him.

"Sorry," he mumbled. A moment later, he slowed.

Amber tensed. "What?"

"They're landing," he said. He turned another corner. No cars here now. No pedestrians. Boarded-up businesses and warehouses. He killed the headlights and they cruised slowly through an open gate.

They passed cargo containers, stacked high like building blocks, and massive cranes that loomed over temporary offices.

Edgar drove so close to a pyramid of broken pipes that their jagged ends almost scraped the Charger's bodywork. They crept by it all, to the warehouse on the yard's east side, and Edgar cut the engine and looked at Amber nervously. She sighed, and got out. She could smell the sea.

Beyond the yard's high walls, New York rattled and hummed. But within them it was quiet.

"I think they're in there," Edgar whispered, eyes on the warehouse ahead.

Amber nodded, started walking towards the door.

"I'd feel better if I had a weapon," Edgar whispered beside her. "I should get a weapon. Maybe there's a gun store nearby that's still open."

"Get a weapon," Amber responded, "don't get a weapon, it's all the same to me. I'm going in."

Edgar puffed out his chest. "And I'm going in with you." He looked around, and picked up a rusted crowbar. "And I'm going in armed."

Amber shrugged. She really didn't care.

With Edgar on her heels, she passed through the door. There was a small corridor with stairs leading up. She skirted them, made straight for the door at the other end. It creaked slightly when she opened it. Beyond it was the warehouse proper. It was empty, apart from an engine block in the middle of the floor.

"They're not here," she whispered.

Edgar nodded. "Might be upstairs. Might be on the roof. I can't go on the roof. I'm afraid of..."

His voice trailed off.

She followed his gaze to the engine block. The light from

a street lamp came in through the high windows, and glinted off something shiny amid all that rust. She walked closer. Were they handcuffs?

She turned, and Edgar swung the crowbar into her head.

53

THE WORLD TILTED.

Amber was aware – somehow – of being dragged. Unconsciousness pulled at her, but instead of going down, instead of sinking into its depths, she managed to stay afloat, managed to keep her head above the waterline. Something cold encircled her wrist. Something metal. Then her eyes were flickering open, and Edgar was walking away and she lay back, looking up at long bars of brightness. She wanted to rest. Staying awake was so hard. And it hurt. Her head hurt, where Edgar had... where he had... what had he done?

Hit her with a goddamn crowbar, that was it.

Amber frowned. The pain was already receding. Her thoughts were beginning to clear. The bars of brightness above became strip lights hanging from the warehouse ceiling. The coldness on her wrist became a handcuff. She listened to a curious hissing and waited for her brain to sort itself out.

She ran her tongue against her fangs and bit down, letting the pain sharpen her further. Then she sat up. Slowly.

Edgar had cuffed her to the engine block. Of course he had. She didn't know how much an engine block weighed, but it was a hell of a lot more than she could lift, even in her current state.

She looked over at him. The hissing sound was the fine black powder being poured from the powder flask. Edgar moved sideways, close to joining up the large circle he was making around her.

"You're working for my parents," Amber said.

He glanced up, just long enough to smile and shake his head, then went back to work. "Nope. I understand why you'd think that, but I've never even met your folks. Don't think I'd want to, either. What kind of people would eat their own children? I swear, there are some sick and twisted individuals in the world, are there not?"

He moved sideways again, close to completing the circle.

"Then what are you doing?" she asked, standing.

"Hold on for just one moment," he said distractedly. "Need to get this just right... There. Done."

The circle complete, he straightened up, a hand on his back. "Not as young as I used to be," he chuckled, and stoppered the flask. "Amber, I really hope you understand that none of this is personal. It's not that I don't like you. I do, I really do. I think you're a smart, interesting person. To go through the stuff you're going through and still remain so positive and good-natured? That's a rare gift you have, Amber. Value it. Truly."

"What are you doing? What's the circle about?"

"Come now," he said. "You're not stupid. You know what this is."

"You're going to summon the Shining Demon?"

"Finally, we're on the same page."

"But we were going to do that, anyway."

"This isn't for you, Amber. This has never been for you. Despite everything, you're still just a teenager, yes? You think the world revolves around you. Sorry to disappoint you, kiddo, but this is for me. I've tried to summon the Shining Demon in the past, but I guess I'm just not interesting enough for someone like him. But this time I think he'll appear. I think he'll be willing to deal once he sees what I intend to offer as a blood sacrifice." He stepped over the circle and came towards her. "It's a shame, really. Getting a good look at you like this, even I'm hesitating. Killing you is going to be like killing something on the endangered species list, a tiger or leopard or something." He moved a little closer. "You truly are magnificent."

Amber lunged. The handcuff held her, but Edgar flinched back anyway, then laughed.

"Look at those fangs!" he said. "Look at that snarl! You, Amber, are a truly scary girl, if you don't mind me saying. But beautiful, too. Undeniably beautiful. How does it feel, to know that the monster version of you is the beautiful one? That skin. Those horns..." He pursed his lips. "I wonder how much I'd get for them..."

"Edgar, please..."

He waved her words away. "Don't bother, Amber. This has been a dream of mine ever since I heard about our bright and shiny friend. I see people like you, people like Milo and Buxton, and I wonder – why not me? What's so wrong with me that I don't get to share in all this wonderful, unholy power? I don't even want anything, that's the funny part. I'm not asking him for anything – all I want is the power to harvest him some souls."

"You're going to kill me?"

Edgar nodded. "Blood sacrifice. The clue's in the name."

"You think he'll want to talk to you after you've killed one of his demons?"

Edgar laughed. "Oh, so now you *are* one of his demons, eh? You changed that particular tune pretty darn quick."

"Edgar, you need to think about this," said Amber. "In the past few weeks, I've made mistakes and people have died. I killed—"

Edgar laughed. "It's really touching to see how concerned you are for my conscience, but you're hardly the first girl I've killed. Oh dear, I'm sorry, did you think that you were? Oh Lord, no. I've been killing lovely young ladies for a long time now. Some of them in situations like this, as a blood sacrifice. Some of them because they deserved it. Some of them just because I felt like it. America's monsters don't all have horns, you know. Some of them are just ordinary people. Like me."

"Milo will find you."

"I'll deal with Milo."

"He'll kill you," Amber said, through clenched teeth.

"I have his car. Separate Milo from his car for any length of time, and what is he? He's just a man. But me? I'll be a demon."

He slid a knife from his jacket.

She forced a snarl on to her face. "You think he's not on his way here right now?"

"He's busy tracking Buxton. Besides, he doesn't know where we are."

"He's the Ghost of the Highway," she said. "He's linked to that car. It's a part of him. Wherever it is, he's able to find it."

For the first time, she saw a brief flicker of doubt in Edgar's eyes.

"You kill me," she said, "and it works, and you arrive in the

Shining Demon's castle and he gives you what you want, you know what's going to happen then? You're going to arrive back here and Milo will be waiting. And he's not going to give you even a moment to test out your brand-new demonic powers. He's just going to shoot you right in the face. You think you stand a chance? You think he's going to miss?"

Edgar didn't say anything.

"He's a good shot," said Amber. "And you've got a big frikkin' head."

Edgar put the knife away. "Then I'll just move the car down the street," he said. "You don't go anywhere, you hear?"

She watched him walk out, keeping the snarl on her face, but the moment he was gone she reverted. The handcuff didn't get any looser around her wrist, but her hands, those small hands of hers...

She gritted her teeth against the pain and started to pull her hand out. For a moment, it felt like her bones were going to pop, or she was about to scrape all her skin off, but then her hand moved, and she bit her lip to stop from crying out. It was working. It was going to work.

Headlights moved across the walls, but the engine she heard didn't belong to the Charger. The idea flashed into her head that maybe Milo had found her, that everything she'd said about him being able to track down his car was true.

She redoubled her efforts to free herself. She was not going to let him rescue her. She'd never hear the end of it.

With a hiss of pain, Amber pulled her hand free and immediately shifted to get rid of the pain. Picking up Edgar's crowbar, she ran to the door, just as her father called her name.

54

AMBER THREW HERSELF DOWN, scrambling behind cover.

"We know you're there, Amber!" Bill shouted. "We know you're listening!"

She took a peek. Two cars, engines off but the headlights still on, and Bill and Betty walking into the blinding glare, taking centre stage in full demon form.

"Come on out, honey!" Bill shouted, his long shadow dancing around the yard. "We'll make it quick and painless, I promise!"

Amber moved slightly so she could see the Charger. She glimpsed Edgar, cowering in the darkness behind it.

"It's me, Amber," said Betty, clasping her hands and holding them over her heart. "It's Mommy. We are so sorry for scaring you. We really are. And we feel so, so bad for everything that's happened – but you know why we had to do it, don't you? You understand. I know you do."

"Come on out, honey." Bill wrapped his arm round his wife, and she rested her head against his shoulder. He kissed her horn. "You won't feel a thing, and then it'll all be over."

Amber moved backwards, and took the stairs up. Even there, she could hear their voices.

"It's the Shining Demon," Betty said. "The deal we made with him, the things we've had to do to fulfil our end of the bargain… None of this is what we wanted, Amber. None of it."

Amber emerged into a large, empty space that smelled of sawdust. Windows lined each side, and she crossed to the nearest one, peeking out. In the darkness behind the headlights, she saw Alastair and the others, but the gloom was too pervasive to make anyone out clearly.

"We didn't want to scare you," Betty continued, "or chase you. We didn't want to drive you to associate with the… the people you've been associating with. We just wanted our baby, in her short life, to be happy. To be loved. This has all gone so wrong." Betty turned, buried her head in Bill's shoulder.

He patted her back. "It's okay, sweetheart. Amber understands. Amber, you understand, don't you? Come out here right now. The life we gave you is ours to take away. It doesn't belong to you."

"Please, baby," Betty cried. "Don't make this any harder on me."

Anger boiled in Amber's throat as she watched her parents look at each other sadly.

No one's buying this, she wanted to shout. *No one's believing this. Why are you bothering to pretend?*

But she kept quiet.

Bill turned slightly, beckoned with a finger, and the others came forward out of the darkness.

Amber stiffened as Imelda was shoved into the light.

Imelda fell. Her hands were bound behind her and she had a gag over her mouth. Her clothes were torn and, even from where she sat, Amber could see the bloodstains. Most distressing of all was that the tip of one of Imelda's horns had been snapped off.

Bill dragged her through the dirt. They got to the pyramid of broken pipes and he held her face mere inches away from a jagged piece of metal. "If you don't come forward right now, young lady, we're going to kill your dear Auntie Imelda. She had us fooled, she really did. I genuinely thought she despised you from the moment you were born. We all did. But we couldn't see into her nasty, treacherous little heart."

"Does Imelda deserve to die?" Betty asked, walking with her hands out, imploring the entire dockyard. "Yes, she does. But does she deserve to die tonight? Does she deserve to die in your place, in unbelievable pain? Well, that is something only you can answer, Amber. What do you think?"

"We're going to count down from ten," Bill shouted. "Nine. Eight."

Amber couldn't let it happen. She just couldn't. Imelda was the only person in the world who loved her. She thought she'd lost her before – she couldn't handle losing her again.

Amber ran back down the steps. They didn't see her running towards them until she dropped the crowbar and stepped into the light. Bill stopped at the count of three.

"I'm here," said Amber.

"Well now," said Kirsty, "don't you scrub up well?"

"I told you she was beautiful," said Betty.

"My daughter," said Bill. "Who would have thought it?"

"Let her go," Amber said. "Let Imelda go and you can have me."

Bill smiled, pulled Imelda to her feet, and led her back to the group. From this close, Amber got a good look at the beating they'd given her.

"Wait," said Alastair, stepping forward. "Bill, Betty... I have an alternative. We don't have to kill Amber. You hear that, Amber? You don't have to die. You impressed me, back in Indiana. You're strong. Fierce, even. You're someone to be admired. You're like us."

"Ooooh," said Grant. "I get it. You dog." He laughed.

"With your permission," Alastair said to Bill and Betty.

Amber's parents looked at each other.

"I don't like it," Bill said.

"What other choice do we have?" asked Betty. "Amber, honey, would you consider it? Joining us?"

Amber frowned. "What?"

"Imelda's a traitor. She can't be trusted anymore. She's out. And so the six of us are cut down to five."

"Unless you join," said Alastair. "You wouldn't have to do anything right now. Grant and Kirsty have already stepped up to the plate."

Kirsty beamed, and patted her belly. "We're just thrilled."

"And seventeen years from now," Alastair continued, "it would have been my turn with Imelda. But with Imelda gone... I'm going to need a new mate."

"I'm really not comfortable with this," Bill muttered.

"Why not?" Alastair said. "She's strong, she's beautiful, she's formidable. In seventeen years, she'll be thirty-three – a good age to start a family."

"No," said Amber. Astonishingly, after everything that had happened, she was shocked. "Just no. No to joining you, no to being a part of this… this sick cycle of murder, and definitely no to mating with you."

Alastair held up his hands. "I'm not saying it won't be weird, but you'll get used to the idea if you just give it a try."

"Screw you. I'd rather you eat me."

"Sweetie," said Betty, "you're not thinking this through. It might be for the best. Wouldn't it be nice, to be a family again?"

"A family?" said Amber. "With you and Bill? After what you've done? After what you've tried to do? We're not a family anymore, Betty — we never were. You're my parents by some unfunny cosmic joke, but we are not family."

"She's made her decision," said Bill. "We kill her, we eat her, just like we'd planned."

"Bill, wait," said Betty. "Give her a chance to think about it."

"She's not going to change her mind," Bill said irritably. "Have you ever known her to change her mind when she's in a mood like this? She'd rather die than admit that she's wrong. She'd rather die just to spite us. You know how wilfully obstinate she is, Betty."

"Bill, come on," said Alastair.

"Don't come on me. In a lot of ways, all this is your fault. You couldn't keep Imelda happy and now—"

Alastair dived at Bill, and only Grant and Betty held him back.

"Each couple looks out for each other," said Bill. "You think I'd have let Betty stray so far? You think I wouldn't have noticed her attitude changing? You think she wouldn't have noticed a change in me? Has Grant let Kirsty totter out on the precipice?

Has Kirsty been so inattentive that Grant finds himself alone with his doubts? We back each other up, Alastair. That's the deal we made, *ourselves*, when all this started. We would be each other's rock. We stayed true to that idea. You didn't."

Alastair pushed himself free of the hands restraining him. "You're not going to blame this on me," he said. "You and Betty were married before we ever talked to the Shining Demon. Grant and Kirsty were in love. But me? I barely knew Imelda, and yet suddenly she was a part of our group and I was told, hey, this is the woman you have to spend the rest of your life with. This is your mate from now on. There will be no others. I never loved her."

"She never loved you, either," said Kirsty.

Alastair glared. "I don't care. You get that? I don't give a damn. I was forced into this with her by my side and the rest of you were too busy gazing into each other's eyes to notice that Imelda was the weak link in the chain. But now we have a chance to replace that link with someone stronger."

"From the look on her face, I don't think my daughter loves you," said Betty.

"She'll grow to."

"If Imelda didn't, why would Amber?"

"What's our alterative? Kill them both? We don't know what that would do to how the power is divided between us."

"You're not killing Imelda," said Amber, "and you can shut up about all that other stuff. Bill's right. I'm not going to change my mind. Let Imelda go, and you can take me."

"We could take you, anyway," said Kirsty. "You really think you can outrun us all?"

"No," said Amber, "but I'd fight you all the way. If you let

Imelda go, I won't resist, as long as you promise not to make it painful."

The demons looked at each other, and Bill glanced at Imelda.

"You heard her. Get going. You want my advice, you won't stop running."

They stood aside, opening up a way out. Imelda looked at it, then back to Amber. She had tears in her eyes.

"Go on," Amber said. "You've saved me enough. Now it's time for me to save you."

Imelda sobbed behind her gag, and reverted. Amber felt a sudden wave of affection for the woman, the only person who'd ever shown her real, genuine love, and her heart broke as Imelda turned away.

But, at the last moment, Imelda whirled, broke into a sprint, running not for the way out but for the pyramid of broken pipes and steel rods. She ran straight into it. Amber screamed her name as Imelda came to a sudden stop, her impaled body hanging limply, her head lolling forward.

The demons stared in shock.

Tears streaming down her face, Amber backed away.

Alastair reached out slowly, like he couldn't believe what Imelda had done. He pulled her body from the pipes and laid it gently in the dirt. Then he knelt, and the others did the same. For a moment, Amber thought they were genuinely saddened by what had happened.

Then Imelda moaned softly, and Amber's hand flew to her mouth as the demons began tearing at Imelda's clothes, rending and ripping her flesh with their claws, biting and tearing with their teeth, blood flowing as they feasted.

A wail escaped from between Amber's lips when Imelda

turned her head, her eyes still open, almost as if she could see Amber hidden in the darkness.

They were eating her alive, and she only died when Bill plucked out her heart.

55

She watched them from the darkness as they gorged themselves on Imelda's body.

Once they had finished, they tossed the remains into the dirt and staggered away. It took Amber a few moments to realise they were drunk. Bill and Betty lay on the hood of their car while Grant and Kirsty waltzed through the yellow light, giggling and singing as they tried not to step on each other's feet. Alastair stumbled around them, muttering to himself. He tried using one of the cars to prop himself up, but he lost his balance, fell slowly and awkwardly, and once he reached the ground he stayed there, curling up and going to sleep.

Drunken demons, their red skin splattered with red blood.

Another set of headlights approached. Round headlights, and close together, much closer than any modern car. Amber moved, crouched over, to get a better look as the car neared. She didn't know what it was called, but it was an old one – from the 1930s or 1940s, the kind with the long fronts and the running boards, the kind that gangsters used to stand on after robbing banks.

Her parents were on their feet, scrubbing dried blood from their mouths and straightening their clothes. Grant kicked Alastair and Alastair woke, saw the car and scrambled up.

The car stopped and the engine cut off. A bald old man got out.

He was small, and stoop-shouldered, and he wore a woollen cardigan over his shirt and tie. He reached back into the car, taking out a big black case, the kind doctors used to carry. Next, he pulled out a folding table, carrying both into the brightly lit circle, to where the demons were waiting. He gave the table to Bill, who set it up. When it was done, the old man placed the bag on top.

He took out a neat pile of bandages and then six small jars, one at a time, and laid them in a row on the table. Bill stood before the first jar. Betty stood beside him. Only the last jar didn't have anyone standing before it.

The old man handed them each a long-bladed scalpel. He was left with one over.

Bill removed his jacket and rolled up his shirtsleeve. He ran the blade along his red skin and held his forearm over the jar. The blood fell in a steady stream. The others did the same.

When the jars were full, they placed wooden stoppers in the necks and wrapped their wounds with the bandages.

The old man looked at the jars. He eyed the sixth one disapprovingly.

"We are dreadfully sorry," said Bill, "but Imelda, she... she turned on us."

"The deal was for six jars," said the old man.

"You can have more of my blood," said Bill, but such a look

of disgust rippled across the old man's face that Bill actually took a step backwards.

"Your blood is already losing its potency," the old man said. "The terms of the deal were quite specific."

Betty smiled her million-watt smile. "We'll fill the sixth, I assure you. We're going to find our daughter. She's here, she's close. We'll feed again, and we'll give you enough for *another* six jars."

Amazingly, her words still hurt. Amber would have laughed if she didn't feel so much like crying.

"I have no interest in another six," the old man said. "I only require enough to fill this empty jar, as per the deal."

"We know," Bill said quietly. "You have our unreserved apology for the inconvenience. If you would like to stay here, we'll find her. We'll find her right now."

The old man sighed, and they took this sigh for agreement.

Amber ducked down as they spread out to search for her. They were sobering up fast, but they passed her hiding spot without even glancing down.

She circled round, came up in the shadow of the old man's car. She peered out at him and his glass jars. She could sneak over there, offer him her blood, get close, and then smash every one of them. Then he'd go back to the Shining Demon empty-handed, and the Shining Demon would be so furious that he'd smite Amber's parents and take care of her problem for her.

It was a good goddamn plan. It was also her only goddamn plan.

The old man turned in her direction. Impossible. He couldn't see her. He couldn't possibly—

His eyes locked on hers. He didn't say anything.

She stayed where she was, crouched down. "My name is Amber," she said, keeping her voice low. "I… I'm the one they're looking for."

"I have nothing to say to you, child."

"But I'm here to… I mean, I'd like to give blood. You need that jar filled, don't you? No matter how fast I run, eventually my folks are going to find me, catch me and… and kill me."

"Your fate is none of my concern."

Amber straightened up. She figured she could reach that table in six, maybe seven strides. "I understand that," she said, "I do, but since my blood is going to be used, anyway, I thought I'd give it voluntarily. Maybe that way I can take Imelda's place in the group. Maybe they'll let me live."

The old man had unsettling eyes. She didn't like the way he looked at her. "Perhaps. But I am merely the Shining Demon's representative – I do not speak with his voice."

Amber nodded. "That's good enough for me."

She stepped forward, but the representative held up a withered hand.

"When you have fed, you may approach."

He was a frail old man. One shove would be all it'd take to send him stumbling. And yet there was something about him, something about those eyes, that stopped her from making a move. He turned, then, stood with his back to her, but this only made her hesitate further. He'd called her bluff and now he was dismissing her, and so her only choice was to tackle him right now or start running.

She turned, and started running. She passed a prefabricated office and was almost to the gate when something charged at her from the darkness. A hand slammed into her chest and sent her crashing through a door. She fell backwards over a desk, sent a chair spinning, heard a heavy old computer hit the floor.

Alastair walked in after her.

"It didn't have to be this way," he said. "You could have joined us."

She got up. The office had only one door, and Alastair was blocking it.

"If you had said yes," he continued, "I wouldn't have to kill you. If you'd taken part, your blood would have been bubbling and boiling with all this incredible power and the representative would have gone back to his master with six jars."

A part of Amber wanted to plead with him, reason with him, get down on her knees and beg him – but he still had Imelda's blood smeared across his face, matted in his beard. And that made her angry.

Oh, that made her so *angry*.

"And all I'd have to do is have sex with you in seventeen years' time?" she said. "I think I'd rather you kill me."

Alastair shook his head as he came forward. "It's not a good idea to taunt me, Amber."

"Why? Are you going to try to kill me *more*? Jesus, no wonder Imelda dumped you."

"Watch it…"

"You're not exactly much of a man, are you?"

Alastair gave a roar and swung a punch that Amber ducked under. She raked her claws into his side and he bellowed, tried to grab her, but she dodged away.

"You little bitch," he snarled.

"Imelda told me about you," she said, backing away. "You

know the way we women like to gossip. She gave me every last detail, and she was not complimentary. Not that she had a whole lot to be complimentary *about*."

"I'm going to rip your head off," Alastair said, stalking after her.

"Did you really think I'd say yes?" Amber asked. "I may not be anything to look at normally, but check me out now. I am beautiful. My own mother pales in comparison beside me, doesn't she? I wonder how that makes her feel. How does it make *you* feel, Alastair?"

"Keep on talking," he said. "Won't make a bit of difference."

"My point is, I'm way too good for you. Even if I had wanted to join your club, you really think I'd settle for you? Grant, though, now he's a good-looking man, and from what I've heard he wouldn't disappoint…"

Alastair stopped walking. He smiled coldly. "You think I was born yesterday? You think I don't know what you're doing?"

"Of course you know what I'm doing," she said. "I'm goading you."

"It's not going to work."

"You moron, it already *is* working. You know why? Because you and I both know that everything I'm saying is one hundred per cent true, you pathetic excuse for a man."

He came at her too fast to dodge. One hand grabbed her while another punched. Her scales did nothing to dampen the pain. She fell back against another desk and flipped over it, landing badly. She tried to get up and he helped her with a kick to the ribs.

Suddenly she couldn't breathe, and he grabbed her jacket and hauled her to her feet when all her body wanted to do was curl up. He hit her again, and again, and when she tried to hit him back he laughed, and slammed her face into the wall.

Two people walked by the window. She tried to shout, but all she managed was a desperate gasp, and neither Milo nor the demon that was Gregory Buxton heard her.

Alastair's hand closed round the back of her neck, and he pinned her in place while he peered out. "Who was that?" he whispered in her ear. "I recognised your friend, the car guy, but who was the guy with the wings?"

She had no breath with which to answer.

"It doesn't matter," said Alastair. "We'll kill them both. Do you know how strong we are right now? What am I saying? Of course you don't. Our kind is always strongest right after feeding. If your friends want a fight, we'll pull their damn wings off. Especially after we eat you."

He dragged her towards the door.

"Why share?" she moaned.

He stopped, twisted her head so that he could look at her. "What was that?"

She sucked in a sliver of air. "Why share? Why not just... eat me yourself?"

"Because that's not how we do things."

She could take shallow breaths, but it was enough.

"Wouldn't you get even stronger?" she asked. "Is that how it... works? The more you eat... the stronger you get?"

"Yeah, that's how it works."

"So don't you... want to be the strongest?"

"I'm sharing you because that's what we do."

He started dragging her again.

"Sure you're not scared?"

He pulled her closer, tightening his grip on the back of her neck. "What did you say?"

Her breathing back under control, she gazed up at him. "I was just wondering if you're scared of what the others would do if they found out you'd eaten me by yourself."

"This has nothing to do with being scared. This is all to do with *how we do things*, and we share the—"

"Just so long as you're not doing this because you're scared of my dad."

He slammed her face down on to a desk and pain exploded behind her eyes. She crumpled to the floor. "You're getting transparent, Amber. You're not as sneaky as you seem to think you are. And is this really the route you want to go down – to goad me into killing you up here, right now? I don't think you've thought this through."

"Maybe not," she mumbled.

He grabbed her horns and hauled her up. "Be a good girl, and shut your mouth, and maybe we'll kill you before we eat you."

He pushed her ahead of him and she stumbled a little. She hit a desk with her hip. Her knees almost gave way.

"If I have to knock you out and carry you, I will," said Alastair. "Keep going."

"I'm seeing double," she said. "You hit me too hard."

He laughed. "Maybe that's because this isn't a game we're playing. If you think I hit you too hard, are you going to think we killed you too much? Go on, quit your complaining."

She let herself drop to the ground.

He stared down at her. "What do you think you're doing? Get up."

"Make me."

He kicked her and she cried out, rolled across the floor.

"Getting up now?"

She sat up, rubbing her back, but went no further. "Screw you."

He took hold of her arm, but she let her jacket slip off. Sighing, he threw it to one side, then grabbed her horns, started dragging her to the door. Her fingers closed round the edge of a desk.

"Jesus Christ," Alastair muttered. "Have a little dignity, would you?"

"I don't want to die."

"I don't give a crap." He yanked back on her horns and crouched, jabbing his finger into her face. "I will beat you into a coma, you little brat, and then we'll eat you. You got that? You hear me?"

She whimpered.

He let go of her horns, but kept the finger there. "You give me one more ounce of trouble and I swear to you I will—"

She bit his finger off.

Alastair squealed and fell back, clutching his hand. Amber spat out the finger and he lunged, grabbed her, slammed her against the wall, his fangs bared. She brought her fist down on his injured hand and he recoiled, and then she sank her own teeth into the meat of his throat.

Hot blood gushed into her mouth. She swallowed it instinctively, even as Alastair was staggering backwards. Amber clung on. He tried desperately to detach her, but he was weakening with every moment. He fell to his knees and Amber's weight came forward and he fell on to his back, and Amber wrenched her head to the side, coming away with a chunk of flesh.

She swallowed that, too.

A small part of her recoiled, but she ignored it. The taste was too good. The taste was amazing. Intoxicating. She tore out another chunk, dimly aware of the gurgling sounds Alastair was making. She chewed and swallowed and went back for more. The taste was better than anything she'd ever experienced. The blood was charged with energy, with raw power. She ate the flesh and drank the blood and it filled her and it was glorious, and the more she ate and the more she drank, the less she could hear of that small part of her, that pesky human part, that cried out in fear and disgust and dismay.

Alastair was dead. Amber didn't care. She ripped his shirt open and kept eating.

That's what demons did.

56

IT DIDN'T SEEM ALL that bad anymore.

The whole demon thing was weird, sure, but hell — so what? And as for her parents trying to kill her… that was just funny. It *was*, though. It was, like, the most unfortunate thing that could possibly have happened to her. Probably. She didn't know. It was kind of hard to take anything seriously right now, if she was being honest.

Was she laughing? She may have been laughing. She was pretty sure her laughing caught the attention of Milo and the big grey guy with wings, because they walked in to find her on the floor, covered in blood.

"Oops," she said.

Milo had the strangest look on his face. Half horrified, half concerned. It was funny, and she giggled. Yup, definitely a giggle.

"What happened?" Milo asked.

She stopped giggling and frowned. "What do you think happened? What does it look like happened? I got the munchies."

"Who is that?" he asked, looking at the remains scattered around her.

"This is Alastair," she said. "*Was* Alastair. *Is* Alastair? It *was* Alastair, and it will be again, when I poop."

That was funny, and it made her laugh.

"You okay?" Milo asked.

Amber did her best to stifle her giggles. She was still in an extraordinary amount of danger, after all. "I'm great," she said in a loud, loud whisper. "Peachy keen, jelly bean. I thought you were dead. Or Edgar told me you were dead, anyway. Hey, did you know he's a dick? He tried to kill me."

Milo's eyes widened in alarm. "Edgar?"

"Yep. Wanted to make a blood sacrifice of me to Big Shiny. Hey, what happened to you? How come you're palling around with the scary grey wing-monster?"

"You can just call me Gregory," said Buxton.

Amber shook her head. "That's a silly name for a wing-monster. From now on, you shall be known as... Steve."

"I prefer Gregory."

"Phillip, and that's my final offer."

Milo stepped forward. "Are you drunk?"

She clambered to her feet. "High on life, my dark and mysterious friend. Also, eating demons apparently gets you hammered, so... Who knew? I may not be able to operate heavy machinery for a little while, just to warn you."

"We have to get you out of here."

"No, no, no, Milo," she said. The words tumbled delightfully from her mouth. "No, no, no. No. I have a plan, you see, and it is as ingenious as it is clever. Did you happen to see an old man outside?"

"We saw him," said Buxton. "The Shining Demon's representative."

479

Amber nodded. "Very *good*, Phil. Can I call you Phil?"

"My name's still Gregory."

"That old man is indeed Big Shiny's representative. He comes to collect their offerings of blood. He currently has five jars." She listened to herself. She liked her voice. She liked how it sounded. Her whole life she'd been stifling that voice, choking on her own intent, but this feeling, this incredible feeling of speaking and being *heard*, was like the real her, the *true* her, bursting forth.

It was like being born again.

She frowned, and looked back at Milo and Buxton. "Where was I? Sorry, lost track. There are the words I'm saying and the words I'm thinking, and they're not the same. Kind of hard to keep everything where it's supposed to be. What was I saying?"

Milo hesitated. "Jars of blood?"

She snapped her fingers. "Yes! Thank you! He has five jars. He needs one more. My plan, as clever as it is ingenious, is to offer to fill that last jar myself. Once I am close enough – BABOOM!"

Milo looked unsure. "You explode?"

"What? No. I break the other jars."

"Oh."

"I thought she exploded, too," said Buxton.

"How come you two are friends?" Amber asked. "How did that happen? Did you bond over how scary you can be?"

"I caught up to him," said Milo, "and we got talking. He's going to help us."

Amber frowned. "So he wasn't flying around, carrying you? Edgar said that's what was happening. Though now I understand why Edgar was the one who kept on seeing you and not me. Guess he needed some way to get me here. He is a sneaky little fella, isn't he?" She shrugged, then grinned. "So now you're buddies. Super duper."

Milo winced slightly. "You've got, uh, something in your teeth."

"How embarrassing," said Amber, using her claws to rake between her fangs. "Is it gone? Is it?"

"It's gone," said Buxton. "And we should be too."

"Not yet," Amber said. "I am smashing those jars. The Shining Demon's going to be so mad at my parents and their dumb friends that no one's gonna give two hoots about my fine red ass. So what do you say, Phil? You in?"

"If you call me by my actual name, then yes."

"Cool," said Amber. "What's your actual name again?"

"Gregory."

She frowned. "You sure it's not Steve, Phil?"

"I'm fairly certain."

"Okay then, it's your name, you should know. What's the plan?"

"First we get the Charger," said Milo. "We need a fast getaway, and Gregory isn't able to carry us both."

"The creepy car it is," Amber said, nodding. "We get the Charger, I smash the jars, we drive away. Nice plan. Good plan. Let's do it." She held out her hand. "Go, go, Demon Squad."

Buxton looked unsure.

"It's what we do, Gregory," she explained. "It's a thing. A tradition. Now that you're fighting by our side, you've got to say it, too. Go ahead."

"Uh," Buxton said, placing his huge grey hand on top of hers. "Go, go, Demon Squad."

Amber laughed, dropping her arm. "Only kidding, we don't say that. You have no idea how dumb you just sounded."

"She's usually a lot more sensible than this," Milo muttered.

He led the way out and Amber followed, with Buxton coming behind. He looked so odd with his wings folded up behind him. She wondered how he sat down, or leaned against stuff. She wondered if a gust of wind had ever snatched him away like a kite. She planned to ask him. These were things she needed to know.

They gave the representative a wide berth on their way to the Charger. Milo took them the long way round, and they passed behind stacks of pallets and crates and splashed through stagnant puddles that waited in the dark. Amber could have complained, but this was very serious business, and so she kept her opinion to herself. Feeling very proud of how responsible and adult she could be sometimes, she walked into Milo.

"Oops," she whispered, "excuse you."

He didn't answer, which was rude. She looked beyond him, to where her mother was standing in front of the Charger.

Kirsty was there as well, and Grant, and of course Bill, who had his arm round Edgar. Edgar stood rigid like the slightest movement would cause Bill to tear his head off – which was probably true, now that Amber thought about it. But, as Amber stepped into the light, Bill smiled, and let go, and Edgar scuttled away.

"Hello, sweetheart," Bill said. "You're grounded."

"Aren't you going to introduce us to your friends?" Betty asked. "Mr Buxton, please forgive my daughter's manners. I thought we'd raised her better than this, I truly did. I love your wings, by the way. I'm a big fan of wings. Kirsty, haven't I always said how much I love wings?"

"For as long as I can remember," said Kirsty.

"For as long as Kirsty can remember, I have always said I love a good pair of wings. And they are a fine pair, Mr Buxton."

"Wait, wait, wait," said Grant. "One of these kids is definitely doing their own thing, aren't they? Here we have our beautiful Amber, resplendent in red, and Mr Buxton here, gracious in grey... but Mr Sebastian, I am afraid, is distressingly dull."

"Come now, Milo," said Bill, "we're all friends here, aren't we? After all, you drove off with my daughter – I imagine that makes us practically family. And your good friend Edgar has told us all about you, so why don't you join us? Show us your true face."

"This won't end well for you," said Milo.

Bill lost his good humour. "Grant, do me a favour, would you? Shoot him in the head."

Grant smiled, went for the gun tucked into his waistband, but Milo's gun leaped into his hand and suddenly the night was filled with gunfire and Amber was stumbling sideways, Buxton's arm round her waist.

She fell to her knees and Buxton was gone, and she felt a tremendous gust of wind and heard the beating of his wings. More gunshots, and shouting, and, just as Amber was making sense of it all, Kirsty was standing in front of her.

"You little pest," she said, and rammed a knee into Amber's face.

Amber fell back, the world a crazy place of tilting horizons and bright spots exploding before her eyes.

"You insufferable little bitch." Kirsty lashed a kick into her side that sent Amber rolling. "I never could stand you, you know that? Out of all of them, you've been the most annoying.

Just so goddamn *glum* all the time. Always watching that ridiculous TV show with all the pretty people moping around."

Amber tried getting up, but Kirsty's fist came down like a rock.

"Why'd you have to be so glum? What do teenagers have to be glum about?" Kirsty picked her up by the throat. "Why couldn't you have just learned to have fun?"

Kirsty headbutted her and Amber staggered back until she toppled.

In a daze, she watched Buxton throwing Bill against a cargo container, and Betty charge into him from behind. He was bigger than them, and probably stronger, but there were two of them, and when they worked as a team they were a lethal partnership.

Kirsty grabbed Amber's hair and yanked, and Amber cried out as she scrambled to her feet. Kirsty twisted her head round, till Amber was watching Grant pummelling Milo.

"Want to know a secret?" Grant said when Milo dropped. "I hate you guys. You know who I mean, right? You car guys. Your whole act just seems so self-conscious. You drive a cool-looking car. That's your entire thing. Where's the sense in that?"

He kicked Milo across the ground.

"How close do you have to be to it to get the full benefit of your deal? Closer than this, am I right?" He looked up at Kirsty. "Hey, honey, how close do car guys have to get?"

"Fifty paces is the standard, last I heard," said Kirsty.

"Fifty paces," Grant repeated. "You're, what, sixty paces right now, yeah? Around that? So close. So very close."

Milo started dragging himself towards the Charger.

"That's the spirit! Never say die!" Grant stood on Milo's leg. "Well, never say die until you *do* die, and by then what's the point, am I right?"

Kirsty laughed, and Amber slammed her elbow into her nose and broke free of her grip.

While Kirsty bellowed her anger, Amber went stumbling. Whatever high she was experiencing was beginning to ebb, but it had already lost its appeal. She was truly terrified, and she had no idea what to do.

She should have run. They all should have run when they had the chance.

Kirsty rammed into her from behind and Amber hit the ground, but managed to roll, managed to get up before Kirsty could grab her. She ducked the grasping hands and now she did run, but Kirsty was right behind her and sounding very, very angry.

Kirsty's hand found her hair and yanked again, even harder this time. Amber's head snapped back and she fell to one knee, and Kirsty had a hold of her now and Amber hurtled into a stack of pallets and they tumbled down around her, the edge of one smacking into her skull. The world spun and darkened. Hands on her. Kirsty's voice. Kirsty's face, hazy and bloody and furious. Pain blossomed and Amber fell against something. The Charger. She felt a tinge of surprise somewhere in the corner of her mind when it rolled backwards a few inches.

Amber's vision cleared in time to see Kirsty closing in. She braced herself against the car, got a hand to the hood, and pushed herself off, experiencing the dizzying notion that such a push was all the Charger had been waiting for. It rolled backwards at an unnaturally steady pace.

Amber swung a punch that Kirsty dodged, and got a swipe of her talons in return. They cut through her clothes, cut through her skin before her scales had a chance to form, and Amber made a noise like a wounded cat and Kirsty laughed.

Amber backed away, watching the Charger as it rolled silently along the even ground. Kirsty frowned, turning to see what was commanding her attention. Her eyes widened.

"Grant!" she yelled. "The car!"

Grant looked over, and Milo straightened up and Amber saw him, saw Milo, for the first time.

He was glorious. He had grown no taller and no broader, but his skin had darkened to an impossible black, a black that drank in the light around it so that his outline merged with the shadows behind him. The horns on his forehead were curved and sharp, three or four inches long, and when he smiled the same red light spilled from his mouth as shone from his eyes.

Grant turned and Milo plunged his talons into his gut, lifting him off his feet even as Kirsty screamed her husband's name.

57

Amber moved through a small maze of crates, away from the fighting, got to the crane and ducked behind the control cabin. She lifted her blood-drenched T-shirt. The claw marks across her side were not that deep, but the pain still made her grimace. She took a deep breath and moved on, keeping low until she neared the representative. He watched her approach, seemingly unimpressed by the sounds of violence from the other side of the stacks.

"You've eaten," he said.

"Yes, I have," she responded.

He peered at her. "You haven't got long before your blood is useless to me. Make haste."

Amber walked to the table, to the five jars of blood and the single empty one. The representative handed her a scalpel.

"Looks sharp," she said.

He didn't answer.

"Do I have to cut my arm? I'm already bleeding. Could I use that blood?"

"You may."

She nodded, moved the jar to her side, then looked up.

"What does he do with it all? The Shining Demon, I mean? Does he drink it? Bathe in it?"

The representative didn't answer.

Amber smiled nervously. "Not going to discuss your boss's personal habits, are you? I can understand that, I guess."

"You are wasting time."

She nodded. "Where'd your boss come from, anyway? Is he from hell? Was I in hell when I spoke to him?"

"Questions are irrelevant."

"Oh. Right. Yeah, okay."

"Your blood."

"Yes. My blood."

She put down the empty jar, and picked up a full one.

The representative frowned. "Be careful with—"

"I'm sorry?" Amber said, and flung the jar against the same pyramid of pipes that Imelda had impaled herself on.

Blood burst from exploding glass and the representative gasped, too stunned to move. Amber turned her hands to claws and destroyed two more jars before he barged into her. He was surprisingly strong for someone so old, but she scooped up one of the remaining jars while he grabbed the last one. He held it close to his chest, his eyes narrow.

"Why?" he snarled.

She tossed her jar into the air, caught it one-handed. "My parents are monsters. Your master's a Demon. Why would I ever want to be part of that?"

"You have no idea what you've done," the old man said. "You have no idea what this means for you."

Amber shrugged. "I imagine a lot of people are going to be very angry with me. But I don't mind that, because your boss is going to be very angry with you, too. You let this happen, after all. You were stupid enough to let me get this close. Looking at it like that, all this is kind of your fault."

"Give me the jar."

She held it up. "What's the point? Big Shiny won't be happy with two jars. It'd be an insult, right? So come on – I'll smash this one, you smash that one. Let's see who can throw it further."

"My master requires six jars," said the representative. "When your parents and their friends eat you, four more jars will be filled."

"Huh," said Amber. "I hadn't thought of that."

She went to throw, but the representative lunged, snatching the jar from her hand a split second before his shoulder rammed into her chest. Knocked off her feet, Amber hit the ground and rolled to a stop. The representative carefully placed the two jars back on the table.

"You're pretty spry for an old guy," Amber muttered.

"You have caused much disruption," he said.

"Yeah." She stood, the harbour wind playing with her hair. "So what are you going to do about it, old man?"

The old man looked at her, and grew. His arms and legs lengthened, tearing his clothes, reducing them to rags. He loomed over her, ten feet tall and rake-thin. His skin turned grey and smooth, almost rubbery like a shark, and his eyes closed over and his nose sank in and his lips stretched, impossibly wide, turned black and parted, revealing a second mouth that was no more than a hole ringed with curved teeth.

It wasn't a man anymore, it was a thing, a creature, and it shrieked at Amber, but she was already stepping backwards as a thousand different nightmares flooded her memory. She tried to run, but her foot slipped on some of Imelda's remains and then the creature was upon her.

With her left arm jammed under its chin, she tried to keep it at bay. The teeth of its second mouth were moving, undulating in their eagerness to get at her. Protective scales formed on her skin. Its breath was cold and foul, and it was strong, stronger than her, and no matter how hard she pushed, it drew closer and closer, and with one final surge it clamped its mouth on her shoulder.

Amber screamed as the teeth sank in like her scales weren't even there. Beyond the pain, which was exquisite in its striking clarity, she could feel those teeth beginning to bore through her flesh. She grew talons on her free hand and tried to plunge them into the creature's ribcage, but couldn't pierce its rubbery hide. She toppled, fell, the creature on top. Blood ran down her arm, her back, her chest. She screamed and raked and clawed and battered, but it didn't notice. It just drank.

She brought her knees in, got her feet against its body and tried to straighten her legs. The creature was too strong. Its grip was too secure.

"Please," Amber cried, "stop!"

The pain reached new heights as the creature adjusted its position. She turned her head away, looking desperately for something to use, something to fight it off with. Imelda's shoe was right there, but it didn't even have a sharp heel. Beyond it, no more than ten paces away, was the table.

She grabbed the shoe, doing her best to ignore the agony, and took careful aim. She threw, but the shoe sailed high and wide, missing both of the remaining jars.

She saw Imelda's other shoe. Her last chance.

She reached for it with her foot, managed to nudge it back towards her, then got her heel behind it and bent her leg, dragging it across the ground to her waiting hand. This time she didn't even bother to aim. She just lobbed, and the shoe missed the jars but hit the table, and the jars fell off the edge and smashed.

Instant relief as the creature snapped its head up, shrieking its fury when it saw what Amber had done.

She immediately pushed herself away, scrambled up, leaping to avoid its attempts to reclaim her.

Clutching her shoulder, she plunged into the stacks of pallets and crates. Didn't look behind her. Didn't want to and didn't need to. She heard it coming. It skittered and clattered and scraped and shrieked. She imagined it reaching for her with those long arms, those grasping hands, and pulling her towards its terrible funnel mouth. It wouldn't release her again, she knew that. The next time it clamped that mouth on her, it would be the end.

She darted left, wincing against the pain as she squeezed through a gap between cargo containers too narrow for the creature to follow. It reached for her, almost snagged her, but she kept moving, her horns knocking against the metal, preventing her from turning her head.

She emerged the other side, went stumbling, wanted nothing more than to curl up in a ball and cry, wanting this pain to just go away, but she kept running, across an open space now, trying to find cover before the creature found her.

She ran right into a dead end, whirled to try another route, and froze.

The night was cold. The night was freezing. Amber could suddenly feel every particle of air pressing against her skin. She could feel every strand of hair that the breeze played with. She could feel every bruise and laceration. She could feel everything now, on this cold night in New York, as the creature closed in.

Amber backed off. The creature moved closer.

An engine started up and she glanced to her left, saw Milo at the crane controls. There was a heavy whine behind her, a cargo container lifting off the ground, and she spun and ran right for it. She jumped, caught the edge with her good hand, looked down to see the creature leaping for her. Its fingertips grazed her leg, but it lost its grip. It hit the ground, scrambled up, screeched its rage as she heaved herself on to the top of the container. The crane took her higher and she clutched her shoulder, blood still pouring through her fingers. Higher she went, and higher, the sea breeze brushing past her skin, and she looked down, saw Kirsty throwing Milo into a pillar.

She lay back, grimacing in pain, looking up at the light-polluted night sky. The container swayed the higher it went, the breeze becoming a wind that was getting stronger and colder, but at least she was safe up here.

The container eventually stopped rising. Turning her head to her left, Amber could see the Statue of Liberty. She could see Manhattan, and across the Hudson into Newark. She could see tugs on the river, bright lights bobbing on blackness. What a sight.

She rolled on to her stomach and inched towards the edge. She'd never had a problem with heights before, but this was different. She wasn't strapped into a rollercoaster at Disney World here. She wasn't strapped into anything.

She looked down, down, all the way down. Whoa, that was a long way. Amber suddenly felt very vulnerable and very light, as if one of these strong gusts could just nudge her over the edge. She watched the people below fighting, couldn't really tell who was who with the way they kept moving in and out of the light. She looked for the creature, and frowned when she couldn't see it. Then she caught movement out of the corner of her eye — there it was, climbing up the crane arm.

Coming for her.

She moved back from the edge, got to her hands and knees, and crawled for the nearest steel cable. Gripping it tightly, she stood, watched as the creature reached the top of the crane arm and started across.

"Milo!" she screamed. "Gregory!"

The wind whipped her words away. She stood there, hanging on to the cable, watching the creature get nearer. She couldn't run, couldn't hide, couldn't escape and couldn't fight. She couldn't fight *that*. The only thing she could do was die. She looked down. She could end it now. Step off and plummet. Terrifying but painless, and infinitely better than what was to come if she stayed where she was.

Sobbing, Amber lifted one foot, or tried to, at least. But it wouldn't budge. She tried to fling herself forward, but her body disobeyed. Her legs wouldn't move and her hands wouldn't let go.

"Please," she whispered to herself, but her body didn't listen. It refused her commands. It wasn't going to go to its death quietly, no matter how much she might want it to. It wanted to fight. It wanted to *survive*.

Her body buzzing with an energy like electricity, an energy that could send her sprinting or make her seize up like jammed machinery, she watched the creature get closer. It was practically overhead now. Soon it would drop down, and she had nowhere to run, and it would clamp that mouth on to her again, and it'd kill her. There'd be no surviving that. Without a doubt, it would kill her where her parents had failed, and the witch had failed, and the vampires had failed, and the serial killer had failed, and that guy had failed, back at the diner. What was his name? The name of the guy whose finger she'd bitten off? What was his goddamn name?

Brandon, that was it. *Brandon*.

The creature dropped to the container and while it struggled for balance Amber let go of the steel cable and ran at it. She jumped, both feet slamming into its chest, knocking it back off the edge. She twisted, reaching for a handhold, but the creature's flailing arms caught her leg and then she was falling too.

They both fell.

Plummeting.

Spinning in rushing air.

Then something slammed into her and suddenly there were strong arms around her and she heard the beating of great wings, and she watched the creature hit the ground, so far below, and come apart in a wretched explosion of blood and body parts, and she was swooping upwards.

Buxton let go and her momentum took her through the

air, her arms and legs pinwheeling. She touched down and crumpled and went rolling, coming to a wonderfully painful stop.

She lay there for a moment, a nice long moment, then raised her head, saw her parents coming for her.

58

AMBER RAN INTO THE warehouse, started up the stairs, but then remembered that up there she'd be trapped, so she jumped back down, ran across the warehouse floor. Nowhere to hide here, nowhere except behind the engine block.

She went to duck behind it, found Edgar cowering there. He looked up at her with tears in his eyes and she hit him and he crumpled. She crouched over him, and listened to her parents' footsteps.

"We're not mad," said Betty, "are we, Bill?"

"Not mad at all," said Bill.

"You've proven yourself," Amber's mom said. "We're impressed. We are. Come on out, sweetie. We've got a lot to talk about."

Amber's shoulder was still bleeding badly. She couldn't fight them, and she couldn't run. They were stronger and faster and better. She had one option. Right here, right now, she had one way to escape.

She dug a hand into her pocket.

"We're going to need to make plans," said Bill. "The Shining Demon isn't going to be pleased with any of us – least of all you. We're stronger if we stick together."

496

Amber tore a match from the matchbook she'd taken from Edgar's house, back in Miami. She dropped the match on the ring of powder, and stood.

Her parents smiled, and Bill opened his mouth to say something, but Betty saw the flames at the last moment and she grabbed him, yanked him into the circle with her just before the flames met and turned blue.

And then they were in the Shining Demon's castle, with its five arched doorways and its obscene tapestries and stained-glass windows.

Bill and Betty whirled, confused. In their day, a summoning would mean the Demon appeared to them. Amber didn't bother telling them that times had changed.

Her breath crystallised as she adjusted to her new surroundings. Now she could hear the distant screams, and she could see better in the gloom.

"Hello, Fool," she said.

Her parents stood together, watching as Fool emerged from darkness. Thin rivers of sweat streaked its ash-pale make-up, but its glass-shard smile was as fresh as ever. "I've been waiting for you," it said. "Do you have him? Is that him there?"

It tried to peer at Edgar as he stirred, but Amber blocked its view. "First you give me what I want," she said.

Fool shook its head. "The Master's instructions were clear. First you hand over Gregory Buxton and then I give you this." It took a small vial of yellow liquid from its patchwork robes.

Her eyes locked on to it. "And what about the countdown?"

"Drink this," said Fool, "and the scars will fade."

She took a moment. "No, Fool," she said sternly, like she was talking to a child, or a dog. "I don't trust you."

"Where are we?" Bill asked.

Fool looked at him, started to answer.

"Your master's business is with me," Amber snapped. "Forget about them. They mean nothing. It's me you need to address. I don't trust you, Fool, so I am not going to give you Gregory Buxton until *after* you give me the vial."

"But the Master—"

"The Shining Demon wants Buxton," Amber interrupted, "and the only way that's happening is if you do what I say."

Fool licked its red lips. "Same time," it said. "Yes, yes, same time."

She couldn't put it off any longer, so Amber grabbed Edgar by the collar and hauled him to his feet. He moaned, almost toppled. "Here he is," she said. "Here's Gregory Buxton."

Fool looked at Edgar.

And nodded eagerly.

He held out the vial with one hand. In the other, he clutched a metal collar attached to a chain.

Amber nudged Edgar out of the circle as she snatched the vial from Fool's hand, and Fool snapped the collar around Edgar's neck with practised ease.

Edgar straightened up at once. "What? What's going on?"

"What *is* going on?" said Bill. "Creature, what did you give our daughter? What is that?"

"Seasoning," said Fool, and giggled. "It'll turn her blood to poison."

Bill reached for the vial, but Amber backed away. Betty moved behind her.

"Give it to me," said Bill. "Give it to me right this instant, young lady."

Amber snarled. "Screw you, *Dad*."

He dived at her and she held him off with one hand while she thumbed the stopper from the vial. Her mother was grabbing her from behind, trying to tear the vial from her grip. They had her wrist pinned so she leaned down, took the vial between her teeth and threw her head back. The yellow liquid splashed down her throat and burned. It reached her stomach and sent out hot jabs of pain, and her parents stepped away as she fell to her knees. Her vision dimmed. She couldn't feel her fingers or toes. Her blood boiled in her veins. Through blurred eyes, she watched the scarred numbers fade from her wrist.

And then, just like that, it was gone, and she gasped and blinked and looked up in time to see Fool tugging angrily at Edgar's chain.

"You *are* Gregory Buxton!" it said. "I know you are him! You are just trying to confuse me!"

"Gregory Buxton is a sixty-five-year-old black man!" Edgar cried. "I'm a forty-six-year-old white guy!"

Fool frowned at him, then its eyes widened. "You all look the same to me," it mumbled.

From one of the corridors, a rapidly intensifying glow. Amber's parents turned away instantly, and Edgar clamped his hands over his face. Amber screwed her eyes shut as footsteps thundered on the stone floor, so heavy she felt the vibrations through the soles of her own feet.

"You dare cheat *me?*" the Shining Demon roared. His brightness was blinding, even with her eyes closed, and his voice came from above. He was towering over her, towering over them all. "You come to my castle and you dare try to cheat *me?*"

Amber's legs were shaking and she desperately wanted to curl up in a ball and cry, but she forced herself to stay standing.

For a long time, there was not one other sound to be heard. Even the distant screams quietened.

Then the Shining Demon softened his voice. "Look at me," he said.

Amber didn't move for a few seconds. She certainly didn't open her eyes.

But then the brightness began to retract, and when it stopped hurting Amber dared to look up. For a moment she thought she saw a being of terrifying proportions and impossible appendages, but her squinting eyes adjusted as the brightness was reined in, and now she saw that the figure was of normal height, and not the monstrous thing she had glimpsed. The Shining Demon blazed with a fierce light from within. Tattoos dotted his translucent skin like archipelagos, black islands in a sea of burning orange. His face was calm. He had black eyes.

"My Lord Astaroth," Edgar said, falling to one knee, "the Duke of Hell whom we mortals call the Shining Demon, I ask of you only that you remake me, sire. I have so far been unworthy of your attentions, but look, I have brought to you a curiosity, a girl of—"

The Shining Demon looked at him like Edgar was something he'd stepped in. "You? You have brought me nothing."

"But... but I have everything to offer," Edgar countered, bowing his head. "I offer you my soul, sire. All I have ever wanted in my entire pathetic life was the power you have bestowed upon mortals like me. I offer you my flesh to remake how you see fit. I offer you my soul to sculpt, and my mind to twist, and—"

"You offer me nothing I do not possess," said the Shining Demon. "You are outside the circle, little insect. You have nothing to bargain with. Your soul is mine already."

Fool tittered, and yanked on the chain. Edgar fell back.

"No!" he cried. "Wait, it's not meant to be like this! All I want is power! Please, just—"

Another tug and the last of Edgar's words were choked from him. Fool started walking for the nearest of the arched corridors, and Edgar was dragged after him, kicking and spluttering. He reached out to Amber, but she just stood there, on her side of the blue flames, and watched him go until he was lost to sight.

Amber turned back to the Shining Demon to find his eyes fixed on her parents, who were still averting their gaze.

"Look at me," he commanded, and this time they obeyed. "Two of your brethren are dead, along with my representative on Earth. And I have received no tribute."

"We... we can make it up to you," said Bill. "We can—"

"You have failed to fulfil your part of our deal," said the Shining Demon. "You had better start running."

Bill and Betty clutched each other's hands.

The Shining Demon turned his gaze upon Amber. "And finally you. You have cheated me, you foolish, foolish girl. You think, because Buxton has eluded me, you stand a chance? Buxton made himself an expert in the arcane arts. Can you say the same?"

Amber swallowed. "No," she said. "But I found him in less than three weeks, and you've been after him for fifteen years. So it occurs to me that maybe you're not so hot at finding *anyone*, you dumb shit."

The Shining Demon stared.

"I don't care what your excuse is," she continued while a

significant part of her brain screamed at her to shut the hell up. "I don't care if you regard time differently or if you've got endless patience or what. Fifteen years is fifteen years. You've had all that time to learn how to google and instead you kept trying to find him on Demon radar. I mean, seriously? You might be shiny, but you're not too bright, are you?"

"I will make you pay for every insolent word."

"You sure you can count that high, you moronic pile of crap? Screw you. I'm not scared of you. Come after me. Send another representative after me and I'll kill him just like I did your last one."

She thought that'd make him explode. Instead, he just smiled. Which was worse.

"Amber," he said, "you are a brave girl. You are even a clever girl, in your way. But you are also an ignorant girl. I could command your parents to force you from that circle and then you would be my plaything for all eternity. But there is a certain way to do things. Deals. Negotiations. Collecting debts. Wreaking vengeance. All these things I have been doing for centuries upon centuries. Technology means nothing to me. If I want you, I will get you. Your body may fade, but your soul will burn as bright.

"Yet you have cheated me and insulted me. I do not easily forgive insolence. Your parents will run as they must." The Shining Demon smiled. "But you must run faster, for the Hounds of Hell will be coming for you."

The blue flames spluttered and went out, and they were suddenly back in the warehouse.

59

AMBER TOOK A MOMENT to adjust to her new surroundings, took a moment to absorb what the Shining Demon had said, and then she turned and Bill lunged at her and Milo said, "Stop."

Bill froze, though his body practically hummed with restrained violence. Milo and Buxton stood over the unconscious forms of Grant and Kirsty. Milo was back to normal, and his gun was pointed straight down into Grant's face.

"We'll pay you ten times what Imelda was paying you," said Bill. "Just walk away, Mr Sebastian. We'll pay you, too, Mr Buxton. This is a family matter."

"Indeed it is," said Milo, and he didn't budge.

Amber watched as the space between the two men became charged, and then Betty was there, her hand on Bill's arm.

"We have to go," she said. "We have to go *now*."

"Don't forget your friends," said Buxton.

Moving slowly, her father approached Grant and her mother went over to Kirsty. Amber just stood there, waiting for them to look at her. Her dad hauled Grant off the ground by his shirt collar. She was being ignored. They were going to walk out and walk away and she was being ignored.

"Apologise!" she screamed.

Everyone looked at her.

"I beg your pardon?" Bill said.

"Apologise," Amber repeated, trying to get her voice under control. She would not cry. Not in front of them. Not ever again. "After everything you've done, the least you can do is—"

"You ruined everything," her mother said.

Her words robbed Amber of her voice.

"We gave you life," said her dad. "For sixteen years, you wanted for nothing. We provided for you, we kept you safe, we let you have friends, go to school… We didn't have to. We could have locked you in the attic. But we allowed you to live. And this… this is how you repay us."

Her throat was so tight. "You wanted to kill me," said Amber.

"That was always going to be how it ended," Betty replied. "We knew you only had sixteen years so we decided to let you spend it however you wanted. We allowed you happiness, Amber."

"You think… you think I was happy?"

"You didn't know any better. And we were good parents."

Bill nodded. "We were very good parents. Did we ever shout at you? Did we ever ground you? We let you live your life however you wanted to live it. Do you think it's our fault that you never made any real friends? Are you blaming us for that? Not that we're complaining. One good thing about you being socially inept – we've got no one probing too deeply into your disappearance. We've been wonderful parents, and all we've tried to do is give you a good life."

Amber frowned at how incredible this was. "You think you've done me a favour?"

"Every minute," said Betty, "every second of your sixteen years was possible only because we needed you to boost our power. That is your *purpose*, Amber. That has *always* been your purpose. You were meant for nothing else, just like your brother and your sister were meant for nothing else but to sustain us, to keep us going. This isn't about you. This isn't your story, Amber — it's ours. We're not going to hand over the reins to the younger generation — not when we're better, faster, smarter and stronger. We deserve our power and our life because we carved it out for ourselves. You? Your generation? You expect to have everything handed to you. You never had to work, to really work, for anything. So what do you deserve? Really, what do you deserve?"

"A chance," said Amber.

"You've squandered it," said Bill. He put Grant over his shoulder. "You've ruined everything for everyone. Imelda's dead because of you. You killed Alastair. Now we have to run, and you… You have no idea what's coming for you."

He walked out while Betty took Kirsty's hands.

"You should have just let us kill you," Betty said, and followed her husband, dragging Kirsty behind her.

60

THEY WERE SIX DAYS into their drive to Alaska, and they were staying in a bed and breakfast outside of Edmonton, Canada. Amber's bag was by the door. She slept in her jeans and socks. That evening, she'd eaten her first real meal in days, and for the first time in a week she'd been able to shower. These were things she was beginning to view as luxuries. She already considered a good night's sleep as an extravagance she couldn't afford, and as for a general feeling of safety…

At the slightest noise her eyes would spring open and her body would tense. The house creaked and groaned around her and she hovered like this, on the edge of sleep, as the hours slouched by. She wondered if Milo was finding it as difficult to sleep in the next room. He'd been even more taciturn than usual, ever since they'd fled New York. She would have liked to believe he was angry with her, maybe for the mess she'd dragged him into, but she knew he wasn't, and she knew the truth.

He was scared.

The Hounds were after them, and Milo was scared.

She heard a voice call her name and she nearly screamed.

She didn't move. She didn't sit up. She just went rigid,

and she listened. Maybe she'd gotten it wrong. It could have been the wind, or the pipes, or her imagination. Amber lay there, a statue made of nerve endings stretched like bowstrings. She stopped breathing. She waited.

But she couldn't close her eyes. She couldn't allow herself to believe it had been the wind. Not without checking.

She got out of bed, standing in the cold, cold room, her bare arms prickling with goosebumps. It took seven steps to get to the window. She wished it had taken more. She parted the curtains.

Her room was on the second floor. Glen was outside her window, standing on darkness and nothing else. He looked so pale. He looked so sad.

With trembling hands, Amber closed the curtains.

She stayed where she was for five minutes.

When she looked again, he was gone. The half-moon struggled out from behind some clouds, did its best to cast a silver light on the buildings and homes around her. The people in those homes slept, whole families warm in their beds. In the morning, they'd wake and the kids would go to school and the parents would work or do whatever it is they did, and they'd have their arguments and their fights and the parents wouldn't understand and the kids would storm to their rooms, and life would continue on as normal, or as normal as it ever got.

But, of course, normal was subjective. And so was life, now that Amber thought about it.

She reached for the cord to draw the curtains closed once more and she happened to glance to the east, to the long dark road they'd driven in on. In the distance – way, way in the distance – she saw tiny lights coming closer. Five of them. Motorcycles.

Amber grabbed her sneakers and her jacket and her bag. She hammered on Milo's door and he rushed out, fully clothed.

They got in the Charger and they drove.

DEREK LANDY

– DEMON ROAD –

DESOLATION

Reeling from their **bloody encounter**
in New York City, Amber and Milo flee north.
On their trail are the **Hounds of Hell** — five
demonic bikers who will stop at nothing to
drag their quarries back to their unholy master.

Amber and Milo's only hope lies within
Desolation Hill — a small town with a
big secret; a town with a darkness to it, where evil
seeps through the very floorboards. Until, on
one night every year, it spills over onto the streets
and **all hell breaks loose.**

And that night is coming...

31.03.16

KEEP YOUR EYES ON THE ROAD

by following Derek @
po.st/demonroad
🐦/dereklandy

THE BEATTY PAPERS

Selections from the Private and Official
Correspondence
of Admiral of the Fleet Earl Beatty

Volume I
1902–1918

edited by
B. McL. RANFT M.A. D.Phil. F.R.Hist.S.
Formerly Professor of History, Royal Naval College,
Greenwich
Visiting Professor and Senior Research Fellow
Department of War Studies, King's College, London

PUBLISHED BY SCOLAR PRESS
FOR THE NAVY RECORDS SOCIETY
1989

Published by
Scolar Press
Gower Publishing Company Limited
Gower House
Croft Road
Aldershot
Hants GU11 3HR

Gower Publishing Company
Old Post Road
Brookfield
Vermont 05036
USA

British Library Cataloguing in Publication Data
Beatty, David Beatty, *Earl, 1871–1936*
   The Beatty papers: selections from the private
   and official correspondence of Admiral of the
   Fleet Earl Beatty.——(Publications of the
   Navy Records Society; v. 128).
   Vol. 1 : 1902–1918
   1. Great Britain. Royal Navy. Beatty, David
   Beatty, Earl, 1871–1936
   I. Title   II. Ranft, Bryan   III. Navy
   Records Society   IV. Series
   359.3'31'0924

Library of Congress Cataloging-in-Publication Data
Beatty, David Beatty, Earl, 1871–1936.
      [Correspondence Selections]
      The Beatty papers : selections from the private and official
   correspondence of Admiral of the Fleet Earl Beatty / edited by B.
   McL. Ranft.
         p.   cm. — (Publications of the Navy Records Society : vol. 128)
      Includes index.
      Contents: v. 1. 1902–1918.
      1. Beatty, David Beatty, Earl, 1871–1936—Correspondence.
   2. Admirals—Great Britain—Correspondence.   3. Great Britain—
   History, Naval—20th century.   4. Great Britian.   Royal Navy—
   Biography.   I. Ranft, Bryan.   II. Title.   III. Series:
   Publications of the Navy Records Society : v. 128.
   DA70. A1 vol. 128
   [DA89.1.B4]
   359'.00941 s—dc19
   [941.082'0092'4]   88–24–24517 CIP

ISBN 0 85967 807 5

Printed and bound in Great Britain by
Anchor Press Ltd, Tiptree, Essex

THE COUNCIL
OF THE
NAVY RECORDS SOCIETY
1988

PATRON
H.R.H. THE PRINCE PHILIP, DUKE OF EDINBURGH, K.G., O.M., F.R.S.

PRESIDENT
THE RT HON. THE LORD CARRINGTON, K.G., C.H., G.C.M.G., M.C., P.C.

VICE-PRESIDENTS
A. W. H. PEARSALL, I.S.O., M.A.
H. U. A. LAMBERT, M.A.
A. P. McGOWAN, M.A., Ph.D.
Admiral of the Fleet the Lord LEWIN, K.G., G.C.B., M.V.O., D.S.C., F.R.S.A., Hon.D.Sc.

COUNCILLORS
N. R. BOMFORD, M.A.
John GOOCH, B.A., Ph.D., F.R.Hist.S.
R. J. B. KNIGHT, M.A., Ph.D.
R. F. MACKAY, M.A., D.Litt.
A. J. MARSH, M.A.
Lieutenant-Commander Lawrence PHILLIPS, R.D., R.N.R.
P. M.H. BELL, B.A., B.Litt., F.R.Hist.S.
Lieutenant-Commander J. V. P. GOLDRICK, B.A., M.Litt., R.A.N.
Captain A. B. SAINSBURY, V.R.D., J.P., M.A., R.N.R.
Professor D. M. SCHURMAN, M.A., Ph.D.
Geoffrey TILL, M.A., Ph.D.
C. S. WHITE, M.A.
Jonathan COAD, M.A., F.S.A.
Miss P. K. CRIMMIN, B.A., M.Phil., F.R.Hist.S.
E. R. Ll. DAVIES, B.A., B.Sc.
J. D. DAVIES, M.A., D.Phil
Professor B. McL. RANFT, M.A., D.Phil., F.R.Hist.S.
K. C. BREEN, B.A., M.Phil.
R. P. CROWHURST, B.A., Ph.D.

CONTENTS

MAPS AND ILLUSTRATIONS

Frontispiece: Beatty reading out the terms of surrender of the German Fleet, 16 November 1918 (by courtesy of the Trustees of the Imperial War Museum).

Maps
(By courtesy of William Collins & Co.)

PREFACE

As always in works of this kind, the greatest editorial problem has been that of selection from the great number of documents available. The principle adopted has been to print as many as possible of those papers which have not appeared in previous collections or have not been thoroughly utilised in scholarly books. In consequence, the great majority of those selected have come from the collection of Lord Beatty's personal papers, now held in the National Maritime Museum at Greenwich, which has not previously been fully available. This source has been supplemented from other collections in the Museum, in the Imperial War Museum, London, and in the archives of Churchill College, Cambridge. In the latter the collections used have been the Drax and Godfrey-Faussett papers, and even from them comparatively few have been printed because they have been so thoroughly utilised in Stephen Roskill's *Admiral of the Fleet Earl Beatty, The Last Naval Hero: An Intimate Biography* (1981). For a similar reason the mass of Beatty's official papers in the Public Record Office and the British Library have not been included because they are so fully used in Arthur Marder's *From the Dreadnought to Scapa Flow* (London 1961–1978). These admittedly debatable decisions to concentrate on the Greenwich collection have been made on the grounds of the novelty of the material, the conviction that it provides a unique insight into Beatty's character and achievements, and the unity of theme that it gives the volume.

Some documents already printed in W. S. Chalmer's *The Life and Letters of David Beatty, Admiral of the Fleet* (London 1951) have been included because of their centrality and because Chalmers often printed severely pruned versions and is not always reliable in his interpretation of Beatty's handwriting and in his dating of letters. Some papers are included which also appear in the two volumes of the Navy Records Society's *The Jellicoe*

Papers, edited by A. Temple-Patterson (London, 1966, 1968) because of their importance, and a note in Section Introductions indicates other relevant documents from this publication.

The Beatty Papers, acquired by the National Maritime Museum in 1981 from the Trustees of the 2nd Earl Beatty, are excellently described by Dr Roger Knight in *The Mariner's Mirror* November (1981). Among them are 1026 letters from the Admiral to his wife, to whom he wrote daily whenever they were separated. She replied less regularly, sometimes by telegram, and there are only 415 from her, but apparently she preserved virtually everything he sent her. The Drax and Godfrey-Faussett papers at Churchill College are also considerable. Reginald Plunkett (the future Admiral Sir Reginald Plunkett-Ernle-Erle-Drax) as Beatty's Flag-Commander, was often responsible for drafting Beatty's orders and tactical papers. The copies of these at Churchill College sometimes incorporate Drax's manuscript observations on their precise provenance. Captain Sir Bryan Godfrey-Faussett was naval equerry to King George V from 1901 to 1936 and the relevant portion of his family papers is the correspondence between Beatty and Sir Bryan's wife, Eugénie. They deal with professional matters as well as with their intimate relationship but, as they were intensively used in Roskill's biography, only a few have been included here. It should be noted that Beatty's correspondence with his own wife continued in its fullness and regularity in parallel with his letters to Eugénie.

Although the bulk of the volume is concerned with Beatty's part in the Great War, the first section, dealing with his career as a Captain, is included to illustrate the beginnings of his mature professional thought against the background of changing naval policy as the war approached. His adventurous earlier career is fully covered and documented by his two biographers.

The treatment of the battle of Jutland is relatively short to avoid duplication of the vast amount of documentary and analytical material already available, and concentrates on the immediate evaluation made by Beatty and his associates of what had gone wrong and on their recommendations of remedies. Volume II will include a fuller consideration of the battle in the context of the post-war controversy about the conduct of the battle. It will also cover the peace negotiations as they affected the Navy and Beatty's term as First Sea Lord. In the present volume the longest section deals with his command of the Grand Fleet from November 1916 to November 1918. This contains a great deal of unpublished and underused material, especially the correspondence with Sir Rosslyn Wemyss, which provides a significant revision of the common image of Beatty as merely a gallant and dashing leader in battle.

The guiding editorial principle has been to reproduce the documents as accurately as possible. The only alterations have been to Beatty's extraordinary punctuation and over-use of capitals. When omissions of insignificant material have been made, longer passages are indicated by *** and those of a few words by. . . . Where handwriting has made interpretation difficult, doubtful words are marked [?] and completely illegible ones [—] according to the number of missing words. Dates are printed as Beatty and his correspondents wrote them, and shown in parentheses when approximated by the interpretation of postmarks on envelopes or internal evidence. His wife's addresses have been included whenever ascertainable as illustrative of her activities and way of life. Salutations have been included only when they illuminate the personal relationship between correspondents. All editorial material is in brackets and the numerals in the Section Introductions are designed to draw attention to the more significant of the succeeding documents.

ACKNOWLEDGEMENTS

My gratitude is due in the first instance to the Leverhulme Trust whose award of an Emeritus Fellowship has enabled me to edit the Beatty Papers, and to the Trustees of the National Maritime Museum and the Imperial War Museum, and to the Master and Fellows of Churchill College, Cambridge, for allowing me to print documents from their respective collections.

My particular thanks are due to Dr Roger Morriss and Mrs Jacqueline Hayton, whose scholarly arrangement and cataloguing of the Beatty Papers and constant advice greatly eased my labours in the Maritime Museum. The Reading Room staff of the Museum were always unfailingly helpful, as were Miss Marion Stewart, the archivist of Churchill College, and her associates during my visits there. I am also grateful to Mr Roderick Suddaby, Keeper of the Department of Documents at the Imperial War Museum, for finding and copying relevant papers. For specialised information on technological matters I am heavily indebted to Mr David Lyon of the Maritime Museum, Professor J. T. Sumida, and to my former pupils, Mr Eric Grove and Dr Andrew Lambert. The latter has given further help in the selection of illustrations and maps.

I have been sagely advised and encouraged by the Society's General Editor, Mr A. N. Ryan. Mrs Sylvia Smither has not only typed the greater part of the content but has also firmly corrected my (but not Lord Beatty's) syntax. Finally, my wife's patience with the flood of paper which engulfed our home in the later stages of the work went far beyond the call of duty.

GLOSSARY OF ABBREVIATIONS

AC	Aim Correction System
ACNS	Assistant Chief of Naval Staff
AP	Armour Piercing (Shell)
ASW	Anti-Submarine Warfare
BCF	Battle-Cruiser Fleet
BCO	Battle-Cruiser Orders
BCS	Battle-Cruiser Squadron
BEF	British Expeditionary Force
BIR	Board of Invention and Research
BL	Breech Loading
CinC	Commander-in-Chief
CID	Committee of Imperial Defence
CIGS	Chief of Imperial General Staff
CNS	Chief of Naval Staff
COS	Chief of Staff
COWS	Chief of War Staff
CPC	Copper Pointed Common (Shell)
(D)	Destroyers
DCDS	Deputy Controller of Dockyards and Shipbuilding
DCNS	Deputy Chief of Naval Staff
DID	Director of Intelligence Division
DMO	Director of Military Operations (War Office)
DMT	Director of Military Training (War Office)
DNAT	Director of Naval Artillery and Torpedoes
DNC	Director of Naval Construction
DNI	Director of Naval Intelligence
DNO	Director of Naval Ordnance
DNOT	Director of Naval Ordnance and Torpedoes
DOD	Director of Operations Division
DR	Dead Reckoning
DTSD	Director of Training and Staff Duties

xiv

(G)	Gunnery Specialist
GCT	Gunnery Control Tower
GF	Grand Fleet
GFBI	Grand Fleet Battle Instructions
GFBO	Grand Fleet Battle Orders
GFGO	Grand Fleet Gunnery Orders
GFMO	Grand Fleet Manoeuvring Orders
GFTO	Grand Fleet Torpedo Orders
HF	Home Fleet(s)
LC	Lyddite Common (Shell)
LC	Light Cruiser
LCS	Light Cruiser Squadron
MV	Muzzle Velocity
(N)	Navigation Specialist
NID	Naval Intelligence Division
NMM	National Maritime Museum
NRS	Navy Records Society
OOQ	Officer of Quarters
PV	Paravane
PZ	Flag signal for Tactical Exercises, and applied to the Exercises themselves
QMG	Quarter-Master General
R.Ad.	Rear-Admiral
RFR	Royal Fleet Reserve
RMLI	Royal Marine Light Infantry
RNC	Royal Naval College
RNR	Royal Naval Reserve
RNVR	Royal Naval Volunteer Reserve
(S)	Submarine or Supply
SFO	Secret Fleet Order
TB	Torpedo Boat
TBD	Torpedo Boat Destroyer
V.Ad.	Vice-Admiral
V.Ad.BCF	Vice-Admiral Battle-Cruiser Fleet
WL	Water Line
WT	Wireless Telegraphy
W/T	Water-Tight

THE NAVAL CAREER OF ADMIRAL OF THE FLEET EARL BEATTY, 1884–1927

The following is extracted from the Official Record of his Services and Appendix II of W. S. Chalmers, *The Life and Letters of David Beatty, Admiral of the Fleet* (London, 1951)

Ship	Rank	[Period of service] From	To
Britannia	Cadet	15 Jan. 1884	14 Jan. 1886
Alexandra	Cadet	15 Jan. 1886	14 May 1886
Alexandra	Midshipman	15 May 1886	20 July 1888
Cruiser	Midshipman	21 July 1888	20 Oct. 1888
Alexandra	Midshipman	21 Oct. 1888	19 Mar. 1889
Duke of Wellington	Midshipman	20 Mar. 1889	14 Sep. 1889
Ruby	Midshipman	15 Sep. 1889	13 May 1890
Ruby	Sub-Lieutenant	14 May 1890	15 May 1890
Duke of Wellington	Sub-Lieutenant	16 May 1890	10 June 1890
Ruby	Sub-Lieutenant	11 June 1890	31 Aug. 1890
Duke of Wellington	Sub-Lieutenant	1 Sep. 1890	1 Sep. 1890
Excellent	Sub-Lieutenant	2 Sep. 1890	13 Jan. 1892
Victory II	Sub-Lieutenant	14 Jan. 1892	4 Feb. 1892
Nile	Sub-Lieutenant	5 Feb. 1892	6 July 1892
Victoria and Albert	Sub-Lieutenant	7 July 1892	30 Aug. 1892

Ruby	Lieutenant (Seny. 25 Aug 1892)	31 Aug. 1892	30 Sep. 1893
Camperdown	Lieutenant	1 Oct. 1893	2 Oct. 1895
Trafalgar	Lieutenant	3 Oct. 1895	18 May 1896
Victory I	Lieutenant	19 May 1896	2 June 1896
Egyptian government	Lieutenant	3 June 1896	19 Nov. 1896
Ranger (in command)	Lieutenant	9 Jan. 1897	30 June 1897
Egyptian government	Lieutenant	1 July 1897	24 Oct. 1898
	Commander	15 Nov. 1898	
Barfleur	Commander	20 Apr. 1899	12 Sep. 1900
Duke of Wellington	Commander	13 Sep. 1900	30 Sep. 1900
	Captain	9 Nov. 1900	
Juno	Captain	2 June 1902	17 Dec. 1902
Arrogant	Captain	3 Nov. 1903	29 Sep. 1904
Diana	Captain	30 Sep. 1904	11 Oct. 1904
Mars	Captain	12 Oct. 1904	24 Oct. 1904
Suffolk	Captain	25 Oct. 1904	19 Sept. 1905
Victory I	Captain	20 Sep. 1905	14 Oct. 1905
Naval Adviser, Army Council	Captain	21 Dec. 1906	14 Dec. 1908
Queen	Captain	15 Dec. 1908	3 Jan. 1910
	Rear-Admiral	1 Jan. 1910	
Naval Secretary to First Lord	Rear-Admiral	8 Jan. 1912	1 July 1912
Aboukir	Rear-Admiral	2 July 1912	27 July 1912
Naval Secretary to First Lord	Rear-Admiral	28 July 1912	8 Jan. 1913
Lion	Rear-Admiral	1 Mar. 1913	2 Aug. 1914
Lion	Act Vice-Admiral	2 Aug. 1914	28 Jan. 1915
Princess Royal	Act Vice-Admiral	29 Jan. 1915	8 Apr. 1915
Lion	Act Vice-Admiral	9 Apr. 1915	8 Aug. 1915

Lion	Vice-Admiral	9 Aug. 1915	27 Nov. 1916
	Act Admiral	27 Nov. 1916	
Iron Duke	Act Admiral	28 Nov. 1916	15 Feb. 1917
Queen Elizabeth	Act Admiral	16 Feb. 1917	31 Dec. 1918
Queen Elizabeth	Admiral	1 Jan. 1919	2 Apr. 1919
Queen Elizabeth	Admiral of the Fleet	3 Apr. 1919	7 Apr. 1919
President	Admiral of the Fleet	8 Apr. 1919	31 Oct. 1919
First Sea Lord	Admiral of the Fleet	1 Nov. 1919	29 July 1927

GENERAL INTRODUCTION

I

Beatty has been fortunate in his biographers. Although Rear-Admiral W. S. Chalmers had served on his staff and was a great admirer, his *The Life and Letters of David, Earl Beatty* (London, 1951) is a work of considerable merit, balanced in judgement and clearly written. It should still be studied alongside Stephen Roskill's *Admiral of the Fleet Earl Beatty, The Last Naval Hero: An Intimate Biography* (London, 1981) which is likely to be the definitive biography. Roskill had the advantage of Arthur J. Marder's magisterial five-volume work, *From the Dreadnought to Scapa Flow* (London, 1961–1978) and freedom to use a mass of private papers not previously fully exploited — the most significant of these being Beatty's private papers, the Godfrey-Faussett papers and those of Sir Shane Leslie, intended as a basis for an account of Beatty's private life, which was never published. Roskill's biography, with its full list of sources, should be consulted on these points.

II

The Sectional Introductions in this present volume contain relevant biographical information, but Beatty's family background and early naval career should be kept in mind. David Beatty was born on 17 January 1871, the second son of David Longfield Beatty and his wife Katherine, née Sadleir. The family background was Irish and military, with a great devotion to the hunting field which David shared. His three brothers followed their father into the Army, but he, encouraged by his mother, chose the Navy.

He entered the training ship *Britannia* on 15 January 1884 at the age of 13 and passed out two years later. His first appointment was to the *Alexandra*, flagship of the Commander-in-Chief Mediterranean, the Duke of Edinburgh, Queen Victoria's second son. The *Alexandra* was representative of the transitional capital ship of the time. She was fully rigged and equipped with muzzle loading guns, but also steam-driven, heavily armoured and carried White-head torpedoes. Among Beatty's fellow midshipmen were Walter Cowan, Richard Phillimore and Reginald Tyrwhitt, all of whom were to serve under him during the Great War. This appointment to a fleet flagship with a royal admiral was a most promising start to his career. The next stage was aboard the corvette *Ruby* for nearly a year's intensive sea training during which he was promoted Sub-Lieutenant. He returned to England for Sub-Lieutenants' courses at Greenwich and Portsmouth in the autumn of 1890. In these his performance was mediocre, his only first-class pass being in torpedoes, and several of his contemporaries achieved greater seniority for promotion. Beatty was made Lieutenant in August 1892 and served a further year on *Ruby*, mainly in the West Indies and South Atlantic. It was not until October 1893 with his appointment to the modern, sailless battle-ship *Camperdown* in the Mediterranean that he became involved in the fleet steam tactics which were to dominate his wartime career. But the experience which led him to rapid promotion was of a radically different nature from the North Sea battles in which he was to make his name. His service on gunboats on the Nile in Kitchener's campaign to reconquer the Sudan showed that he possessed great qualities of leadership, determination and ingenuity and earned him both a DSO and special promotion to Commander. This, at the age of 27, with only six instead of the normal 12 years' service as Lieutenant, made him a marked man not only in the service but to a wider public, including the young Winston Churchill who had served as a cavalry officer in the campaign. Beatty's first appointment as Commander, in April 1899, to the battleship *Barfleur* on the China station, gave him further opportunity for active service. In May 1900 the anti-fore-igner Boxer movement was threatening the British and other communities in Peking. The British Commander-in-Chief, Admiral Sir Edward Seymour, led an international relief expedition, but this was repulsed and had to fight its way back to the river port of Tientsin, which itself came under attack. Beatty, with 150 men, was landed from *Barfleur* as part of a force to defend the town and assist the withdrawal of Seymour's expeditionary force, among whom incidentally was Captain John Jellicoe, the Commander-in-Chief's Flag Captain. Beatty played a gallant and effective part in the fighting but suffered serious wounds to his left arm. He was warmly recommended for his conduct and on 9 November 1900 was one of the four Commanders specially promoted to Captain. At 29 — the normal age for promotion being 42 — this gave Beatty a long start on the ascent to flag rank, for which he would become eligible when he came to the head of the Captain's list. He had previously returned to England where he was faced with a difficult operation and prolonged treatment to restore his left arm to full use. It was during this time that he pressed his courtship to Ethel Tree, whom he had met before going to China, and they were married on 22 May 1901. In the following year he was fit enough to take up his first Captain's appointment and a new stage in his career began.

It may well be said that none of Beatty's experience so far was an appropriate preparation for the final responsibilities which were to fall on him. The cramping education on *Britannia*, the long training under sail and the fighting on the Nile and in China were remote from the Heligoland Bight, the Dogger Bank and Jutland and the frustrations of his years in command of the Grand Fleet. But there had been advantages — experience in keeping the seas in all weathers, acceptance of responsibility and, a factor rarely recognised by historians, the ability to think and act under fire.

III

The only authoritative analysis of British naval policy in the later part of the nineteenth century is Arthur J. Marder's *The Anatomy of British Sea Power 1880–1905* (London, 1964). The story is taken up in the same author's already mentioned *From the Dreadnought to Scapa Flow*. The revised edition of Volume 3 (1978), dealing with Jutland, has significant additions to the original version of 1966. The concluding Volume 5 is particularly valuable for its overview of the whole war and its comprehensive bibliography. The official five-volume *History of the Great War: Naval Operations*, by Julian Corbett and Henry Newbolt (London, 1920–1931) is valuable for its highly detailed accounts of operations and its contents were an element in the post-war Jutland controversy. Sir Llewellyn Woodward's *Great Britain and the Great War* (London, 1967) is a reliable guide to the interaction of the sea and land operations. The Navy Records Society's *The Jellicoe Papers*, ed. A. Temple-Patterson, in two volumes (London, 1966, 1968) is an essential companion to this present publication. The most detailed and comprehensive source of information on the naval ships of the time is *All the World's Fighting Ships, Vol I, 1860–1905*, ed. Roger Chesnau; and *Vol II*,

1906–1921, ed. Randall Gray (London, 1979, 1985).

Among the scholarly work published or in train since Marder wrote, two significant topics have emerged which he did not treat in any depth. Both arise from welcome initiatives by historians to enter new territory by studying in detail the scientific and technological problems which affected the course of the war. This has begun with a re-examination of the quality of British gunnery fire-control systems and its impact on the major naval battles, and has centred on the proposition that far better results would have been gained if the Admiralty had accepted the system invented by a civilian, Arthur Hungerford Pollen, rather than relying on the designs of its own gunnery specialists. This has been treated, from a partisan point of view, by Pollen's son, Anthony Pollen, in his *The Great Gunnery Scandal* (London, 1980). The relevant technical documents are printed in J. T. Sumida (ed.), *The Pollen Papers* (London, 1984). Dr Sumida's further work is eagerly anticipated.[1] Obviously the difficulties involved in countering the German U-boats were of decisive importance. Willem Hackmann, *Seek and Strike: Sonar, anti-Submarine Warfare and the Royal Navy* (London, 1984), treats the problems of detection and location in terms of the scientific and technological problems to be overcome. The subject is taken further by Lt Commander M. B. Wignall in his London University Ph.D. thesis, 'Scientists and the Admiralty: Conflict and Collaboration in Anti-Submarine Warfare 1914–1921' (1987), which breaks new ground in its analysis of the problems involved in organising effective co-operation between the naval authorities and the eminent civilian scientists involved.

[1]His *Finance, Technology and British Naval Policy, 1889–1914*

IV

When Beatty joined the Royal Navy in 1884 the implications of the revolutionary technological changes of the nineteenth century were becoming clear but had not yet been completely embodied in ship design and equipment, or in tactics and strategy. Metal construction, heavy defensive armour, longer-range guns and more destructive projectiles, and more efficient boilers and engines were accepted as the essential elements of warship construction. What remained to be clearly established was the appropriate combination of these for the different types of vessels needed. An unknown factor for policy-makers and sea officers was the effect of the torpedo as it developed in range and accuracy. This involved not only the design of vessels to deliver the weapons and of those to counter them, but aroused more fundamental questions. Would the torpedo end the dominance of the battleship, or could the fleet still gain and exercise command of the sea by underwater protection, quick-firing guns and escorts designed to destroy enemy torpedo boats before they could launch their weapons? Would the advent of the torpedo, and its static counterpart, the mine, make the imposition of close blockade, the traditional pivot of British maritime strategy, no longer possible? In this connection the appearance of effective submarines was soon to raise further questions, although it took the experience of the Great War to show the extent of their significance, both on the strategic and tactical freedom of the fleet and on the vulnerability of merchant shipping.

The size of the British fleet had, since the Naval Defence Act 1889, been formally based on the absolute necessity of having a force superior to the combined strength of the next two naval powers, which were then identified as France and Russia. The Act, with its building programme of eight battleships and 42 cruisers, which was continuously added to in succeeding years, marked the beginning of the naval race so often identified with Anglo-German naval rivalry. Britain was not prepared to consider abandoning a superiority which she considered vital to the security of her metropolitan territory, imperial possessions and maritime trade. European rivals perceived this sea dominance as giving her excessive global influence which they were not prepared to leave unchallenged.

In 1902, when Beatty assumed his first Captain's command, a complete transformation of Britain's diplomatic and naval policies had just begun. The new German Empire, whose defeat of France in 1870 had made it the dominant European land power, had begun to think increasingly of overseas territorial and commercial expansion and was resentful of Britain's global position, of which naval supremacy was both a symbol and a cause. The Naval Act of 1898 set Germany on a path increasingly seen in Britain as a challenge which had to be met. Because of Germany's vast industrial resources, European allies and military strength, this demanded a diplomatic as well as a naval revolution. In 1902 the Anglo-Japanese alliance provided for the safeguarding of Britain's eastern empire in the event of her being involved in a European war. Two years later the Entente with France ended an old rivalry and underwrote Britain's interests in the Mediterranean. Finally, the 1907 agreement with Russia ended the land threat to India which had so long dominated British military thinking to the neglect of full consideration of a European continental commitment.

The naval repercussions of these changes in the country's overall strategic posture coincided with the adoption of the naval reforms of Sir John Fisher, appointed First Sea Lord in 1904. These consisted of changes in officer entry and training, the construction of the *Dreadnought* battleships and battle-cruisers, designed to make all existing capital ships obsolete, and the concentration of the fleet against Germany in the North Sea, facilitated by heavy reductions in the Mediterranean and the Far East. From 1904 there could have been no doubt in the minds of Beatty and his senior, Jellicoe, that the colonial-type wars, in which they had each achieved distinction, were to be replaced by a very different struggle in Northern waters, using ships and equipment as yet untested in war. What they were not mentally prepared for were the length, frustrations and disappointments of that struggle before the Navy completed its part in the defeat of the new enemy.

PART I

PRELUDE TO HIGH COMMAND, 1902–1912

INTRODUCTION

Beatty was promoted Captain on 9 November 1900 but protracted treatment of the wounds to his left arm sustained at Tientsin delayed appointment to his first command, the cruiser *Juno*, until 2 June 1902. His early adventurous career had been marked by bravery and dash which had earned him this early promotion.[1] He had now to prove himself in the less dangerous but equally demanding tasks of ship command in peacetime. Failure to achieve high standards would bar the path to the Flag List. Not only did Beatty soon demonstrate his aptitude for the work in hand but he also began to formulate ideas on naval policy and strategy and to show insight into the darkening international situation.

For the historian and biographer 1902 marks the beginning of the correspondence which provides a uniquely deep insight into Beatty's career and character. On 22 May 1901 he had married the American heiress Ethel Tree[2] and the separation entailed by his appointment to *Juno* saw the beginning of the virtually daily writing to her which was to persist throughout his career whenever they were parted. In addition to the light they cast on Beatty's professional development, his letters and her replies, even at this early stage, reveal the strains and jealousies which were to cause them both such pain.

When *Juno* ended her commission Beatty transferred to *Arrogant* in November 1903, and to the new armoured cruiser *Suffolk* in September 1904. The Mediterranean Fleet in which he served, the pivot of Britain's naval dispositions against France and Russia, had made great strides in efficiency and in readiness for war under Sir John Fisher, Commander-in-Chief, 1899–1903.[3] He had based

[1]See General Introduction, pages xix–xxiv.

[2]Ethel Tree, only daughter of millionaire Chicago chain-store founder, Marshall Field; divorced in the United States from Arthur Tree on grounds of her desertion, 12 May 1901.

[3]Later Admiral of the Fleet Lord Fisher of Kilverstone (1841–1920): entered RN 1854; DNOT 1886–90; Rear-Admiral 1890; 3rd Sea Lord & Controller 1892; Vice-Admiral 1896; CinC North America & West Indies 1897; CinC Mediterranean 1899; Admiral 1901; 2nd Sea Lord 1902; CinC Portsmouth 1903; 1st Sea Lord 1904–10; Admiral of the Fleet 1905; Chairman of Oil Committee 1912; 1st Sea Lord 1914–15; Chairman of Board of Invention & Research 1915–18.

3

his training on accurate long-range gunnery and high-speed manoeuvering as the only way to decisive victory. When *Juno* arrived in the Mediterranean, Fisher had been succeeded by Admiral Sir Compton Domvile,[1] who was followed in June 1905 by Lord Charles Beresford[2] during Beatty's last months on *Suffolk*.

It was, however, in manoeuvres under the eagle eye of Admiral Sir Arthur Wilson[3] that Beatty gained his first experience in command. Wilson, Commander-in-Chief of the recently formed Home Fleet, was accepted as the Navy's greatest expert in the handling of large fleets and renowned for the heavy demands he made on his subordinates. Once arrived in the Mediterranean Beatty was plunged into the annual manoeuvres, the climax of the training year. Since 1901 they had involved a combination of the Channel and Mediterranean Fleets so as to give Flag Officers experience in commanding large forces. A favourite exercise was to test the practicability of blockading an enemy force in the face of mine and torpedo attack. Beatty showed an early awareness of the particular threat from submarines in this context. For ships' captains the emphasis was on highly competitive evolutions centred on ship handling, gunnery and coaling. Beatty, determined to excel, was impatient of *Juno*'s shortcomings and confessed to losing his temper with his officers. On the other hand, in addition to following the normal practice of providing hospitality, he tried to involve them in discussions on the lessons of the manoeuvres, a much rarer procedure which he was particularly critical of his superiors' failure to follow at squadron and fleet level [1–6].

Concurrent with Beatty's determined efforts to make his mark in command came the first signs of strain in his marriage. Ethel, like any young naval wife, resented the separation which service life demanded, and at times hoped that her husband would change his career. But she was no ordinary naval wife. Her wealth had opened the doors of Edwardian high society, although her divorce

---

[1]Sir Compton Domvile (1842–1924) : DNOT & Rear-Admiral 1891; Mediterranean Fleet 1894–6; Vice-Admiral 1897; Superintendent of Reserves 1897; service in Admiralty 1900–2; Admiral 1902; CinC Mediterranean 1902–5; retired 1911.

[2]Lord Charles Beresford (1846–1919): entered RN 1859; Rear-Admiral & 2nd in Command Mediterranean 1897; commanding Channel Fleet 1903; CinC Mediterranean 1905; CinC Channel 1907–9; ordered to haul down flag after prolonged dispute with Fisher; MP for Portsmouth 1910–16; elevated to the peerage 1911.

[3]Later Admiral of the Fleet Sir Arthur Wilson (1841–1921) : entered RN 1855; commanded Channel & Home Fleets 1901–7; 1st Sea Lord 1910–12, forced to retire by 1st Lord, Churchill; served in Admiralty as adviser to 1st Sea Lord, October 1914 to June 1915; refused peerage.

prevented her formal presentation at Court until 1911. In her restlessness she junketed around British aristocratic houses and French and German resorts, a practice not long interrupted by the birth of a son, David, in Malta in February 1905. At times Beatty doubted her faithfulness and discretion and often reminded her how her conduct in influential circles could help or hinder his career. She had no illusions about the importance of money and was determined that her father Marshall Field's remarriage should not reduce her expectations. The size of the settlement he finally made enabled the couple to maintain a lifestyle far beyond the grasp of Beatty's fellow officers [7–9].

After two years as naval adviser to the Army Council, Beatty was given command of the battleship *Queen* in November 1908. She was part of the Atlantic Fleet commanded by Prince Louis of Battenberg[1] whom Beatty had encountered in the Mediterranean and respected, which was far from his attitude to Winston Churchill at the time [4].[2]

The naval background to this phase of Beatty's career was the completion of Fisher's plan to concentrate the Navy's main strength in home waters, and under a single Commander-in-Chief, to counter Germany's growing strength. This and other elements in Fisher's policies had caused a bitter feud with Lord Charles Beresford which split the Navy. Beatty avoided being identified with either camp. He liked Beresford personally but accepted Fisher's main policies, although, like many officers, he objected to his manner of forcing them through. Beatty's first information on the new fleet command structure proved inaccurate. When it was fully implemented in March 1909, the Atlantic Fleet remained

---

[1]Later Admiral of the Fleet, Marquess of Milfordhaven (1854–1921): father of Earl Mountbatten of Burma; entered RN 1868; DNI 1902–5; Rear-Admiral 1904; commanding 2nd Cruiser Squadron 1905–7; 2nd-in-Command Mediterranean 1908; CinC Atlantic Fleet 1910; 2nd Sea Lord 1911; 1st Sea Lord 1912; in July 1914 made crucial decision not to disperse the fleet after manoeuvres; resigned in October 1914 because of anti-German mania and criticism of the Admiralty's handling of war; renounced German title and took family name of Mountbatten, 1917.

[2]Later Sir Winston Churchill (1874–1965): commissioned into army 1895; took part in cavalry charge at battle of Omdurman 1898; Conservative MP 1900; joined Liberals 1904; Parliamentary Under-Secretary for Colonies 1905; President of Board of Trade 1908; with Lloyd George, prominent in Radical element of Liberal Party and advocate of reduced defence expenditure; Home Secretary 1910; 1st Lord of Admiralty 1911; resigned after Gallipoli failure and break with Fisher; commanded a battalion in France 1915–16; Minister of Munitions 1917–18; Secretary for War and Air 1918–21; for Colonies 1921–22; rejoined Conservatives and MP for Woodford 1924–64; 1st Lord of Admiralty 1939; Prime Minister and Minister of Defence 1940–5; Prime Minister 1951–4.

independent, with its own Commander-in-Chief, although assigned to work with the Home Fleet when required [10–12].[1]

Beatty's major concern was the efficiency of his ship, although his occasional thoughts on international affairs were strikingly prophetic of the events of 1914 [11]. He was becoming more critical of his superiors and when, in April 1909, the Channel and Atlantic Fleets combined for manoeuvres under Sir William May[2] his condemnations were severe. Night attacks by torpedo craft were still very much in his mind and he was particularly interested in *Queen*'s participation in gunnery trials using shrapnel as a counter measure [13–16].

Towards the end of 1909 Beatty's attention turned to the general election of January 1910 and the expectation of another Liberal victory. Although he was opposed to radical policies such as Irish Home Rule and reform of the House of Lords, what most alarmed him was the prospect of Churchill's becoming First Lord of the Admiralty. Like most naval officers, he was contemptuous of politicians and utterly opposed to the meddling in service matters which Churchill would certainly attempt. By now he was looking forward to promotion to Rear-Admiral but his pleasure was marred by fears that he was losing Ethel's love and support when he needed them most [17–19].

Promotion came on 1 January 1910, but for two years Beatty was unemployed, except for attendance at the War College in the spring of 1911. In the following July he was offered the post of second-in-command Atlantic Fleet but rejected it as not offering sufficient scope for his talents [20–23]. Such arrogance was strongly resented by his superiors and he might have remained unemployed for a longer period had not the event which he had so dreaded, Churchill's becoming First Lord, ironically set him on the upward path. He was among those interviewed by Churchill for the post of Naval Secretary. The new First Lord was impressed by the strength of his views and his clarity of expression, and he was appointed in January 1912.[3]

[1]Arthur J. Marder, *From the Dreadnought to Scapa Flow* (London, 1961), Vol. 1, pp. 26–7, 40–3, 71–104, 186–207.

[2]Later Admiral of the Fleet Sir William May (1849–1930) : entered RN 1863; Rear-Admiral, 3rd Sea Lord & Controller 1901; Vice-Admiral and CinC Atlantic Fleet 1905; 2nd Sea Lord 1907; Admiral 1908; CinC Home Fleet 1909–11; noted for conducting large-scale tactical exercises taking into account gunnery and torpedo developments; CinC Plymouth 1911–13.

[3]Randolph Churchill, *Winston Churchill*, London, 1966, Vol. 1, pp. 550–1, describes Churchill's reasons for selecting Beatty.

This was a decisive move which was to lead him to the command of the Battle-Cruiser Squadron. In the interval he accompanied Churchill at inspections and conferences which took him to the heart of the discussions which determined the Navy's posture in 1914. Although continually critical of Churchill's impetuosity and practice of interfering in matters beyond his competence, Beatty soon accepted his genuine concern for the service and hoped that his energy would enable him to overcome Cabinet indecision about increased naval strength, although he was never totally confident of this [24–25, 27–29, 32]. He saw his own role as ensuring that Churchill was given correct naval advice, in both conversations and written submissions. A paper by Beatty in April 1912 was particularly perceptive in foreseeing Germany's likely courses of action in the event of war [26].

Churchill gave Beatty's career a further boost by giving him command of an armoured cruiser squadron in the 1912 manoeuvres. His Flag Captain in *Aboukir* was A. E. Chatfield, who was to remain with him throughout the war.[1] As usual, Beatty was critical of the unreality of the manoeuvres and the performance of his seniors. His own success in bringing his reserve fleet ships up to fighting efficiency must have reinforced his reputation for leadership. There is no evidence of whether he appreciated the underlying lesson of the manoeuvres — the difficulty of locating the enemy and bringing him to action in the North Sea, even in summer [30–31].

---

[1]Later Admiral of the Fleet Lord Chatfield (1873–1967) : Rear-Admiral 1919 and joined Beatty at the Admiralty as 4th Sea Lord; between the wars occupied major staff and command positions; 1st Sea Lord 1933–8; Minister for Co-ordination of Defence 1939–40; author of *The Navy and Defence* (London, 1952) and *It Might Happen Again* (London, 1957); the most interesting link between the Navies of the two world wars.

1. *To his wife* [Wemyss Castle]

[BTY/17/8/20–1]   *Juno*
[at sea on passage to Gibraltar]
[22–27 August 1902]

My Darling Tata[1]

*   *   *

Saturday: Again we have been hustled about a good deal by
Wilson at Steam Tactics and have had a busy[?] morning and the
afternoon has turned out filthy cold and wet with a nasty sea and
weather and I was quite seasick. There is a good long Atlantic
swell which reaches to the bottom of one's interior and makes me
feel very uncomfortable and I do not feel inclined to do much
writing. So you must forgive this short scrap today as I am off to
be sick again.

Sunday: I really could not have written any more yesterday, it
was too melancholy and depressing altogether and this morning
there seemed to be no improvement, wet and muggy, and we had
to have Church down below on the mess deck and it tried me
very highly.

I have been thinking a good deal about what you said about
not going to Wemyss and Dunrobin[2] but going to your Father
instead. I hope and trust that you will do nothing of the kind. Of
course I do not wish you to do anything you do not want to do,
but I cannot think it would be of use to join your Father who
always has the most depressing effect on you. Whereas at the
other two places they would tend to cheer you up. And again I
had hoped that by going to Dunrobin you would have made
friends with the old Duke and that therefore in the future should
I ever require any outside assistance he would be more likely to
take an interest in someone he knew than someone he knew little
about, and therefore might be of the utmost assistance to me.
One has to think of these things when one lives a public life and
if one wants to get on, and not throw a chance away, and no one
in this world can afford when they want particular appointments
to let slip opportunities of making friends with those who can
assist you to get them. But of course if it is absolutely distasteful

---

[1]Beatty's pet name for his wife; he sometimes signed himself 'Jack'. Wemyss
Castle, the seat of the Wemyss family, then occupied by the 10th Earl who had
succeeded in 1863 (died 1914).
[2]Dunrobin, the seat of the Sutherland family; the 4th Duke had succeeded in
1892 (died 1913).

to you to go there you must not go, but I am sure that when there you would enjoy yourself, and the air would do you a world of good. So I really hope and trust and hope that you will go and have a pleasant stay. We are going to do more firing tomorrow and so I hope it is a flat calm and warm, otherwise it will be a failure . . .

Monday: It is a lovely morning with a strong breeze behind us. Wilson is again going to stir us up with more target practice which gladdens the heart of Tommy[1] who likes letting his guns off.

We have had a very busy day and it appeared to me that I had made myself excessively disagreeable to everyone and have not been in the best of tempers. The old Commander is a dear old thing but very trying at times.[2] He is so abominably slow and things have not gone well. I suppose it will all come out alright in the wash and it is no use disturbing oneself overmuch about anything. But I think my ill temper has probably been assisted by a touch of liver, as the change of diet, etc, have had a bad effect which I don't seem able to get over, and for the first time in my life I suffer from the frailties of the interior. The sun and sea air combined have as usual turned me black and very sore. Tomorrow we do some prize firing and I hope the beggars will shoot straight. It will not be for want of practice as we had them at it all day today, with poor results . . .

Tuesday Night: We have had a very busy and troublesome sort of day and I don't think I have had half an hour to myself since I was called at 6 a.m. My face is like a beefsteak and my temper almost as florid. We did Prize Firing with the small guns and the results were disastrous. Tommy and his blessed Captains of Guns could not hit the target nohow and it was a stormy day and I had to stop all prizes and abuse Tommy, who is for him, down on his luck. But it really was disgraceful and to help things into a better frame of mind, one of the cutters capsized and deposited everybody into the ocean. Thank God nobody was drowned but it was a near thing and very stupid.

*   *   *

Good-bye my own darling, with all the love of my heart,
With all my heart

David

---

[1]Lieutenant (G) Thomas Wardle.
[2]Commander Alfred Lafone.

2. *To his wife* [Dunrobin]

[BTY/17/8/43–51]   *Juno*
[at sea]
[29 August – 2 September 1902]

*   *   *

I walked over the Gibraltar Dockyard which is truly a remarkable achievement — or will be when complete. They have moved
away hills mostly of solid rock, by hundreds of square yards and
pushed the sea back ½ a mile in which to cut and make the
Dockyard and what was originally a bare coast line they have
turned into a mighty harbour. It certainly makes one stop and
think, when one realises that the greater part has been
accomplished in 6 years, that there is no end to the might of
science and brains nowadays. But as Mr Tommy Bowles[1] says in
the House that all these millions and years of labour are practically
at the mercy of a few good guns of the [—] and unenterprising
Spaniards at Algeciras, such is the frailty of common sense in big
undertakings . . .

Sunday: I got the old Warrant Officers into dine last night, that
means the Gunner, Boatswain, Carpenter and Torpedo Boatswain, and got the old Commander, Hulton and Mr Waterer,[2] the
fat Lieutenant in to help and they all got very hot and merry and
quite enlivened the evening . . .

I have had some of the Midshipmen in to lunch and they are
still full of spirits and ready to commit any crime or devilment.
Otherwise being a Sunday it has been a very quiet day with
nothing but morning Church to break the monotony.

Monday: We had this morning a great day of drill and we
flogged the Fleet and the men are getting quite pleased with
themselves . . . In the evening we play cricket and it is a fine
game to get the superfluous flesh off and provides a vast amount
of exercise and amusement. And then, all hands to bathe, the

[1]Thomas Gibson Bowles MP (1842–1922) had joined the Liberals from the
Conservatives in 1906; he was mainly interested in financial matters.
[2]Lieutenant Montague Hulton, 1st Lieutenant of *Juno*; Lieutenant Philip
Waterer.

ship stopping for the purpose and they do enjoy it. I wish I could bathe, but it makes me livery.

*   *   *

3. *To his wife* [Hotel Bristol, Paris]

[BTY/17/9/78–83]   *Juno*
                                                      [at sea on exercise]
                                                     [18 September 1902]

*   *   *

Yes, I think the Royal Yacht in a few years time will be quite a nice appointment in which to spend two or three years, and at any rate one would never go or be away for a length of time. And at the same time I must remark that you have done a great deal of grumbling in your letters of late and really Sweet[?] we have very little to complain of when one compares my good fortune with that of others out here and in many other parts of the world, who seem to consider themselves fortunate if they see their wives for a fortnight during the year. It makes me quite ashamed to utter a word against it. Only of course you have been brought up differently and like all American wives do not understand why their husbands should be anywhere else but with them. But, as I know you really understand, in a life that is to be made anything of, that is rarely possible . . .

4. *To his wife* [Paris]

[BTY/17/9/88–93]   *Juno*
                                                         [at Nauplion]
                                          Saturday [20 September 1902]

*   *   *

Our Admiral has gone sick and so we have been placed under the command of Prince Louis of Battenberg who is one of the Captains out here, in fact the senior one and supposed to be the most capable man. He is very nice but frightfully pompous and heavy in hand, but I think otherwise he is alright. You are quite right, Winston Churchill is not nice, in fact he is what is generally

described as a fraud, and to use a naval expression, all Gas and
Gaiters.

*   *   *

5.   To his wife [Paris]

[BTY/17/9/95–8]   *Juno*
[at sea]
Sunday 21st [September 1902]
*   *   *
We had a great gathering last night. First, all the cruiser
Captains dined with the cruiser Admiral and then went on to the
Bulwark where all the officers of the fleet had been invited to
attend, and there was a great gathering, there being over 900
officers on board of all sorts. And naturally one met a vast number
of fellows that one had not seen for years. It was rather a trial
for the memory and most amusing . . .

We get to Argostoli tomorrow afternoon when I hope to get a
wire from you and shall also send you a wire from there to let
you know we have got there. Then we shall fill up with coal, a
process we always seem to be at, scrape the ship's bottom to make
ourselves go faster & wait for future events. We are like a lost
child among strange children we are the only ship from the
Channel or Cruiser Squadron that are among this fleet; all of
whom Mediterraneans, and so we shall have to hustle up and
make a point of beating them every time. We began well by
beating them early this morning at unmooring the ship, if you
know what that is, and so accept[?] that as a good omen.

The idea is that we are one Fleet bottled up in Argostoli and
two others of equal value to each other, slightly inferior to us,
but together vastly superior, are sitting down outside blockading
us and we want to get out and go away, either to the right or left
without being brought to action by the enemy's combined fleet,
or the two fleets in detail. As a matter of fact it is a practical
impossibility, and the real value in the operation lies in the fact
that we are testing the circumstances under which a blockade
would be maintained in the present day without the presence of
submarines, which in that form of warfare must always be a very
powerful factor. The Authorities have made one or two rules
which have to be observed which, I fear, will stultify any real

beneficial knowledge being gained. Still we, the inside squadron, must do our best and keep them fairly busy. Blockades can always be worried and in time doubtless worn out, but our time will be too short for that. So we must make up for that by being an extra nuisance to them.

We finished the first part of the Exercises by having two tactical battles and they won't tell us the results, which is a poor way of keeping alive the interest among the officers. So they would not have any general discussion and so reap the real advantages of the work done. We had our own private discussion onboard and all the officers came in and we thrashed it out. But as far as I remember it appeared to me that most of the discussion came from me and the answers too. Still they all took an interest in it, which is the great thing and it produced a certain amount of argument, which is what is wanted as it makes them think. And we must repeat the experiment on other occasions.

*   *   *

6.   *To his wife* [11 South Audley Street, London]

[BTY/17/10/11–15]   *Juno*
                                                                  Argostoli
                                                            3rd Oct [1902]

*   *   *

We are all supposed to be coaling again this evening, but for some reason or other they have just stopped us in the middle. This is very annoying and they treat us very badly, not at all like the honoured guest which you would think they would, seeing we are the stranger to the party and belong to another Fleet. But they make us do all the dirty work and give us always the worst and most tedious and tiresome jobs. It is unreasonable[?] to do it every time and very trying to the temper. By the time I am an admiral, if ever I ever get as far, my temper will be of a devilish kind. But, thank heavens, we get away from them after tomorrow's venture, which, unless the other side are criminally slack, there is no possible chance of our getting through uncaptured. And, in my humble opinion, the expense of sending all these ships so far and at such an infernal time of the year, has not been justified by the results, from which they will gain nothing new and nothing we did not know some fifteen years ago. These are my private opinions & must go no further. Everything we do is of the most childish description and not in any single feature can it resemble the real thing. They had far better spent the money in trying to improve the shooting of the men by giving them some more ammunition and opportunity if no better plans of strategy in peacetime can be devised[?] than what we are now doing for which we have sacrificed all our gun practice and torpedo runs. Still I suppose it will all be the same a hundred years hence and so there is no use wearing myself out about it. One advantage we have had is that the mimic[?] war has produced about the most peaceful period we have had in the ship since I have been in it. The men land and play football and the officers hockey. I've toiled many miles through the vines[?] and climbed impossible places searching for quail & partridge, but although there are a fair number in the market, there are none to be seen alive. . . .

Saturday 4th: That wretched collier did not get alongside until 11 p.m. After tying her up and getting things ready we started at 11.30 and finished at 1 a.m. The men worked like Trojans and got the 166 tons in at the rate of 110 tons an hour, when they had never done more than 64 tons an hour before in the three years they have been in commission. Even the Commander was smiling, although at first he was much annoyed because I had torn up his arrangements and had made him carry out mine. But the end justified the means and the old dear doesn't bear any malice. We all sat down to a sardine and onion supper afterwards like so many Christy minstrels and consequently did not get to bed until 2.30 — which was bad training for tonight when we shall have to be up all night trying to break the blockade.

*   *   *

7. *From his wife*

[BTY/18/2/30–7]   Palazza Capua
                                                            Silene
                                                            Malta
                                      Sunday 16 [April 1905]

*   *   *

I got your letter this morning from Port Mahon — the first one — and it was so nice coming on Sunday as it is always such a difficult day for me to get through without you. I have read your letter over again & again. I think I quite understand what you mean, although you seem to be afraid I should not. I agree with *every* word you say. I have thought for a long time that your abilities where you are are wasted. I think, as you do, it would be the greatest pity for you to entirely break away from the Navy, as you might find that you wished to, but I am sure that you would succeed in [—] another trade[?] & would I am sure satisfy your ambition quite as much, if not more, & our life would certainly be very much happier, & after all, that is everything & sometimes I feel as if I really could not stand the strain of these terrible partings very much more. When you come back we must have a long talk about it all & really decide what is best. I look forward to this summer with a sort of terror & wake up in the night with a cold creeping feeling down my back at the very idea of it. It is too terrible. The Fleet came in early yesterday morning. It was most heartbreaking to see them & no *Suffolk*.

*   *   *

8. *From his wife*

[BTY/18/4/33–40]   Badenweiler
                                                                 27 July [1905]

Well, the interview is over & went off much easier than I had expected. Papa was really *very* kind & nice about it all. And I began by saying that on account of the small boy I felt that I must have his future assured, especially as Papa would soon be married and his new interests might of course affect us. He assured me it would do nothing of the sort & told me that Mrs Caton[1] had before they left America signed a paper that in no way her marriage to Papa would change our future, that is, the Will he has made in favour of us is not to be changed. He told me not to tell anyone, but of course I tell you. He then asked me how much I would like & I said $15,000 a year, but he said no, but he would give us $12,000 & we pay the London house [*sic*]. On the first of January he will send us the papers & we are to put them in the bank & before he leaves in September he will give me a cheque

---

[1]Marshall Field (1834–1906) married as his second wife Mrs Delia Caton.

for $2,000, and the first of January the $1,000 a month will begin regularly. It is a great relief off my mind. Now we know where we stand & can arrange our lives. Getting a lump sum in September will enable us to pay for our horses etc & we can now enjoy ourselves without the fear of running into debt & now I know if anything happens to me that you and Baby are all right. I asked Papa if anything happened to him between now & January what guarantee would I have not to be left penniless & he said you need not bother about that, you will have a great deal more than $1,200. So I think we are alright & we need not worry our heads any more about our money affairs.

*   *   *

9. *From his wife*

[BTY/18/17/61–7]   Biarritz
Friday night [13 March 1908]

Your letter written on Tuesday has made me very sad to think I should have caused you so much sorrow & heartache. As this whole trouble seems to come our way without helping it in any way [*sic*] & in this case, dear heart, I really think a great deal of it — most of it — has originated from your imagination. It was of course very stupid of me not to have talked everything over with you long ago. But I saw you did not like my friendship with Lion¹ & I thought it was stupid of you to care, and being very reserved [?] it was difficult for me to explain & so I went on like a fool without saying anything. As you know Lion & I were a great deal together & I became very fond of him, not the way I care for you dear but as you know I am a strange sort of person & really like so few & having no relations in the world & no one I care for but you and little David,² in all the big world, it was rather luck to find someone I really liked — and he also is rather a strange creature, we got on very well. And I don't think he had ever been much with a woman before in his life. And I really think he liked me & in my own mind I always felt it was a comfort to have him to go to when you are away as the miserable lonely feeling of being alone in England when you were at sea is always

¹Nickname of Brigadier L. W. Sadleir Jackson.
²David, their first son, the future 2nd Earl, born 22 February 1905, died 1972.

before me, & never shall I forget it. All this is stupid I know, and you could say there is Charlie,[1] but somehow Lion is different & in a way, rather like you, as he is strong and manly [?] with a good head on his shoulders & someone I really could depend on. And so it has all ended in unhappiness for us all. I am so sorry dear heart if you felt I no longer cared for you, as I have never cared for anybody else in the same way [– – –]. You have been everything in the world to me and have given me the only happy years I have ever known. . . . I honestly say I like the companion-ship of other men but that is I think because most women bore me & although I never get tired of being with you, it is always well to see others & that in itself always makes me appreciate you the more, as you stand alone in character etc, etc, & I appreciate your love for me the more than ever I shall be able to tell you. . . .

As far as Mr Fitzgerald goes, he is not worth talking about. I know quite well the class of man he is. I like him because it is always agreeable to have people about who make themselves pleasant. I think that quite settles him. I don't know how I can explain any better to you. As you know women are strange things & I fear I am a very difficult person and also *very* selfish to live with. I wish [?] I was not quite so strange but I will try to be different if I can. And now Sweetheart Mine, I thank you a thousand times for your dear kind letter. It has indeed upset me, you said so many sweet things in it.

10.   *To his wife* [15 Upper Grosvenor Street London]

[BTY/17/12/64–9]   *Queen*
[Bantry]
Feb 16 1909

Your two letters of Saturday and Sunday received today, so your domestics probably failed to post your Saturday letter in time. So, shake them up in the future. My non-receipt of an expected letter has far reaching results, as I make myself abomin-ably unpleasant to everybody all round. I am so relieved to know that you both are progressing so well and that your temperature

---

[1]Charles Beatty, the Admiral's elder brother (1870–1917) died of wounds suffered in France.

at night is normal, although I don't like to hear of the continued coughing of little David.

* * *

I just glanced through the *Times* and noted the constitution of the new fleets at home. The *Daily Mail*, I am told, goes further and I am told, had added the information that the Atlantic Fleet is to be a division of the newly constituted Fleet, the latter a new title. In which case Prince Louis is no longer a commander-in-chief but reduced to a mere admiral-in-command, a very different thing with a consequential reduction in his pay which I hardly think he will approve of. So I take it the Main Fleet is to be composed of 4 Divisions: North Sea Divn under Admiral May who will be commander-in-chief; Channel Division under Milne;[1] Atlantic under P. L.; [—] or Home Divn under Neville.[2] We are to have our Refitting Base at Gibraltar and two Home Bases or Bases in home waters, one at Dover and one here & our cruising ground will be the Irish coast. The former base to be used 3 or 4 times a year, a month at a time, when preparing for manoeuvres or marking time. The former base to be used for carrying out General Gunnery Exercises. This I think you will find a fairly accurate prognostication. Dover is a certainty, as I write they have brought me the official instruction to that effect: *i.e.* Dover is to be used by the Atlantic Fleet in conjunction with Berehaven as its principal harbour. Why the d — d old fools at the Admiralty should have made such a mystery about it, it beats me altogether. I suppose they think that unless they keep or wrap such changes in mystery they will not be thought to be doing their job well. Dover anyway is better than Berehaven all the year round. I shall be able to see you sometimes I presume, now that Prince Louis will very shortly formulate a programme of our movements, so that we can look ahead and see where we are.

Don't think, Sweetheart, that I am bored to death with nothing to do here. I have plenty to do and am glad of it and in fact make more work every day. To be here with nothing to do would be purgatory, but as it is, with the glorious weather we have at

---

[1]Admiral Sir Archibald Berkley Milne (1855–1938): entered RN 1869; Rear-Admiral 1904; 2nd-in-Command Atlantic Fleet 1905; 2nd-in-Command Channel Fleet 1908; commanded 2nd division Home Fleet 1909–10; CinC Mediterranean 1912–14; given no further appointment after the escape of the *Goeben* and *Breslau*, although cleared of all blame.

[2]Neville, Vice-Admiral Sir George; Rear-Admiral 1904; commanded 1st Cruiser Squadron 1905–7; Vice-Admiral 1908; commanded 3rd and 4th Divisions Home Fleet 1909–11; Admiral 1912; retired 1913.

present, which I am afraid is too good to last — and plenty of work which I hope to see bear fruit in the near future, and my books, I get through the days very fairly well. It is very different life [sic] to the last two years and a half, or is it 3 years, and on the whole a better & more wholesome, though very strenuous existence, and I shall feel in the end all the better for it, though exile it is from all that I care for and have to live for. Do you remember you complained once that I wanted to be tied to your apron strings? The comic side of the remark struck me at the time, that it could ever be applied to a naval officer. However you have your strings free now, so make the most of it, for I shall be back again tied up before very long. I should like to have a peep every now and then of my two treasures just to help me on the way. As I said before, tell me all you do. Every moment of your two lives are [sic] of the utmost interest to me. . . .

11. *To his wife* [Stratton Hall, Northampton]

[BTY/17/12/85–9]   *Queen*
[Berehaven]
Feb 20th [1909]

*   *   *

We wasted no end of time yesterday doing nothing but steaming through a very heavy swell which rolled us about a good deal. We were supposed to be carrying out experiments but the Flag Captain arranged matters so badly that we did nothing of any value except for one short half hour. I do hate wasting time when it could so easily be expended to much good purpose.

We had a very good morning's drill on Thursday and I really think we are coming on. The men are excellent, but some of the officers, although very nice, are infernally stupid and had very little knowledge. We had our first competition with the Fleet yesterday, in mooring the ship, and we beat them all to blazes, which was satisfactory. Last night I dined with the officers and played bridge. My dinner for the Commanders of the Fleet was a great success. They are more interesting than the Captains and have more go and zeal in them. The band is doing very well, although not brilliant. But we want sadly a good cello player and 1st violin. The former is on the way but the latter I must see about.

* * *

Yes, I believe it to be correct, that old J. F. has not a bed of roses in front of him, and C. B.[1] intends to stir him up properly before he has finished with him. And I think, in consequence J. F. will very likely go before it gets too hot.

* * *

I am thrilled with Carlyle's *French Revolution* which I read slowly and at intervals. A little goes a long way as you must read every word and no skipping or else you lose the context.

* * *

I have just glanced through the papers and what I have seen confirmed my opinion that Austria and Servia are as near blows as makes no matter, and I can't see how it can be avoided unless Austria entirely alters her attitude. Furthermore it if does come Russia cannot sit idle and see Austria absorb Servia, so in she comes. Then arises the question of the Triple Alliance and of how far Germany is involved to support Austria. It is a nice point & I cannot see Germany doing nothing. Then where is our friend France and the Russo-Franco Alliance, backed up by the spirit which they like to make out pervades the whole of France, but in reality does not, namely the one desire of a war of revenge for '70? Alors, where are we? The whole of Europe will blaze if it once starts and the outlook at present is of the worst. Another box of chickens came from Rumpelmeyer, more asparagus, and peas, sea-kale etc and the roll of felt stuff. How you do spoil me, you dear darling. . . .

12. *To his wife* [Hotel Meurice, Paris]

[BTY/17/13/35–40]

Queen
[off Deal]
April 6th [1909]

* * *

So we got underweigh & came to the target buoys at the mouth of the Medway and have been hard at it, banging away all day, with, I must say, most disappointing results, in fact the shooting was d–d bad. Consequently my temper has been at boiling point & I could chop a good many people into little pieces. . . . However

---

[1]A reference to Lord Charles Beresford's continuing attacks on Fisher's policies.

we shall go on again tomorrow with, I hope, better results. My poor Gunnery Lieutenant[1] is in the depths. It is not his fault, he has worked hard enough, but there are one or two that want straightening out, and they'll get it before we are done.

The world in general as represented by the monthly magazines, a large proportion of the Press, including the stolid & correct *Times*, appear [sic] to be waking to the conclusion that they in general, and the Navy in particular, have had about enough of John Fisher, and there have been many little articles of late against him and his methods. One long and vituperative article in the *National Review* going the length of saying that as long as he remains where he is nothing can be improved in the Navy. This is bad enough but I hear there is worse to come. Never before in the history of the Navy has any Admiral or officer been singled out for so much adverse opinion, except it be poor old Admiral Byng,[2] who committed one act of misjudgement and was promptly shot. Where are we going to and what is to be the outcome is the question on the lips of every sailorman. I of course have seen no paper today, but do not anticipate any change of feeling, unless it is an increase against him. It is quite extraordinary that a man who has jumped and bounced himself into such a position should have derived so much notoriety of an objectionable character [sic].

*   *   *

Wednesday 6 p.m. . . .

We were not very successful, and it was disappointing. One thing about it, we know the worst and we have I hope time to correct our mistakes before we carry out the exercise in earnest. We shall certainly not suffer from overconfidence or being too conceited. So there is hope.

---

[1]Lieutenant George Lewin.
[2]Admiral John Byng (1704–1757): court-martialled and shot for neglect of duty leading to loss of Minorca to France.

13. *To his wife* [Menton]

[BTY/17/13/68–71] *Queen*
[Cromarty]
13th [April 1909]

Arrived safely at 9.45 and are now in the midst of a naval whirl, battleships, cruisers galore with many minor craft: 21 battleships, a heap of big cruisers and torpedo craft, a truly fine sight. Many admirals, and not one that inspires a great deal of confidence, this is private, unless it be Prince Louis, and his national or birth qualifications are against him.

I went on board to see May, he Admiralissimo, who was very nice and pleasant, but not a man that impresses one as being possessed of the qualities of a great commander. I saw Prince Louis also and had some good news which I must impart to you. We are not going to Galway or to Ireland at all, but are going to do our gunlayers' practice off the mouth of the Medway, that is to say off Margate, which will convey to you something of the geography. . . . We shall be doing our firing after the 27th of this month and shall probably be in Dover about the 2nd or 3rd May. This ship has been told off by the Admiralty to carry out a series of experiments with shrapnel shell for night defence and we shall have to do a good deal of this, going out during the next month, or rather during the months [?] we shall be at Dover. But I have had visions of being left at Galway the whole of May. It is a relief off my mind that it is not as bad as that. We have to be at Dover on the 10th May to receive the King,[1] who wishes to inspect the Atlantic Fleet. Also we have to be at Spithead on June 10th for a review and then we go for a month's manoeuvring, so I imagine we shall start the latter about the 17th June and finish on or about the 28th July. After which we do our battle practice early in August when we give 10 days leave. And then the ship will set about finishing the experiments. And after a fortnight or three weeks, that is end of September, go to Gibraltar for our refit. . . .

---

[1]King Edward VII, eldest son of Queen Victoria, reigned 1901–10.

14. *To his wife* [Menton]

[BTY/17/13/75–82]   *Queen*
[at sea]
16th [April 1909]

*   *   *

We have been manoeuvring all day and go on again shortly, but we arrive at Scapa Flow at 5 tomorrow morning and shall be anchoring about 6.30, when I shall have a little more time to myself, but not much, as there are all the reports of these experiments we are to carry out [*sic*] to write and committees to form and preside over. But Sunday no doubt will be fairly peaceful. The two days have been most productive, principally in demonstrating how unpractised our admirals are in the manner and methods of handling large fleets. It is not their fault. We don't do enough of it, either sufficiently frequent or for sufficiently long periods to enable them to correct mistakes and put into full use the experience that is gained even by two days of continual manoeuvring. But then, I think we lack a strong man sufficiently energetic and hard who would drive home the object lesson of every mistake so that it should not be committed again. We have a very fine fleet and the best material. May the Lord help the Germans if they were to come along now. But we have *8* admirals, and there is not one among them, unless it be Prince Louis, (who is lazy & has other disadvantages) who impresses one that he is capable of great effort; and 34 captains, among whom there is really fine material, which seems wasted for want of a guide or leader. We have just arrived and anchored simultaneously and had a great contest in mooring the fleet, in which we defeated the whole fleet, doing a very good evolution.

*   *   *

I am a little vague at present as to what our plans are after leaving here on Wednesday. We are not going to Ireland, so expect shall go back to Dover or vicinity for practices to work up for the gunlayers' test which we shall do on the 27th and should complete by the 1st [?] May, when the rest of the ships will return to Dover. But we shall have to commence those experiments, for which purpose shall have to remain, either at sea or at some anchorage such as Deal or Margate, where we can fire our guns at night.

*   *   *

15. *To his wife* [15 Upper Grosvenor Street, London]

[BTY/17/15/8–19]   *Queen*
                                                   [At sea]
                                              [2–4 July 1909]
                                                     Friday

*   *   *

We waited yesterday evening from 6 p.m. until midnight with steam up and the ships without lights in preparation to go to sea. Not that the want of light bothered us much up to 10 o'clock as it was quite daylight until then. But at 11 it was quite dark and at midnight we set forth on our travels; cruisers in front & then a line of battleships. We steamed straight out expecting to be attacked by torpedo-boats and destroyers, but nothing happened and we got out without being discovered. As it was light again by 3 a.m. the night was not long and at 4 we could all go to lie down for a bit. I do not think we were discovered at all until quite late and then was cruisers only & not the battleships, the former having chased away & driven in the enemy's lookouts etc. And it was not until 8 a.m. that they got news of our battleships & then through a small cruiser which had been put out of action by an armoured cruiser quite early in the hunt [?] and without her information, although we used no subterfuge, I do not believe they would ever have received reliable information of our movements. So, it reduced matters to a farce. However we steamed away, presumably pursued by the whole of the enemy fleet, and such is the situation now. As 12 of their ships can go 1½ knots faster than our 11 they are bound to cross [?] with us before we meet with friends cruising through the English Channel.

*   *   *

Saturday 3rd. We truly had a poisonous night, very thick and drizzling rain. You could not see a ship's length ahead and we were booming along without lights, expecting to be attacked by torpedo craft every minute. But it was too bad for them to find us I expect, anyway we got through scatheless. I was very glad when daylight, such as it was, came at 4 a.m. and turned in, very cold and wet. But it was a miserable morning and only a little better than the night. However we could see a little distance which was all we wanted. We have now got in touch with our friends in the White Fleet and, unless a miracle happens we shall make good our junction, which is our principal and most important objective. We ought to meet at about 8.30 to-night. What happened to Sir

W. May and his 24 battleships and 22 armoured cruisers, not to speak of his 6 protected cruisers, 8 scouts and 100 destroyers, I can't think. I fear he committed the mistake of splitting them all up, battleships and cruisers, as we have only seen isolated battleships & cruisers and only two groups of destroyers, one of which we destroyed or put out of action, on the face of it. It would appear as if he has made some colossal errors and his reputation, if he ever had one, has gone. What the actual finding will be I don't know but nothing can prevent us making our junction now. When made, two courses are open to us: 1. to raid the enemy's territory, establish ourselves in one of his ports and, if we can, remain there 24 hours, land an armed force. Or 2, turn in our tracks, return North and endeavour to bring one of his divisions to action in the hope that they are still split up. But I cannot conceive that May, when he has realised that we have made our junction, would do anything but collect his battleships at a central rendezvous and, with his immense [?] screen of cruisers, endeavour to locate us and bring us to action. Our manoeuvres area is so small that he can hardly fail to find us, knowing as he must do, where we are within a 50 mile radius. Through our enemy's mistakes and through no subterfuge or guile on our part, the manoeuvres are much more interesting than I ever thought they would be & now I cannot understand what in the world they have been up to.

It is a fair beast of a day, enveloped in mist and drizzling rain, with a few short fair intervals, and I am afraid tonight will be equally as poisonous as last.

Sunday 4th. We found our allies at 9 o'clock last night and made good our junction and as there was a thick mist and rain it was not possible for the enemy's cruisers to have witnessed it. And, as it remained thick for some time, it was a grand opportunity to exercise a little deceit and, by altering course judiciously & using the armoured cruisers to demonstrate in another direction, we could have led them a dance for several more days. But our C-in-C was apparently content with what he had done and did not wish to trouble any more, so, after an hour, we altered course right round and steamed back in our tracks; to, of course, meet the enemy's cruisers. We continued during the night, expecting to be attacked by torpedo-destroyers every minute, but nothing happened; most un-enterprising they were. It wasn't altogether a pleasant night, but a great improvement on the other two. At daylight we could see their battleships in the mist every now & then and cruisers in every direction, and at 6.30 we formed order of battle and proceeded to manoeuvre our fleet of 18 battleships. We had lost one, old Packs,[1] who had been put out of action yesterday, and 8 armoured cruisers, against their 22 battleships, they having lost 2, and 18 armoured cruisers, with lots of smaller cruisers. The sea was fairly alive with ships whistling about. We banged away for an hour and a half and then stopped, and the manoeuvres were over. Results will be worked out after, but I don't think it will be found that they will redound very much to the credit of anyone, and very much the reverse in some cases. This is between you & I and not for publication.

We then shaped course for Oban again when we received fresh orders and the Mediterranean Fleet went off to their home ports while we in Atlantic Fleet came into Dingle Bay and anchored. It is an open bay on West Coast [sic] of Ireland with heavy swell rolling up it. . . .

Tomorrow we go to Foyne, up the Shannon, 25 [?] miles West of Limerick and the C-in-C says he is going to stop there until the 14th! — 9 whole days. What in heaven's name he is going to do in such a place I don't know. It is right up the river, so can do no firing or useful work of any sort. I think he must be mad, as he does nothing but get into a place & stick. It matters nothing what the place is or like.

*　　*　　*

16. *To his wife* [15 Upper Grosvenor Street, London]

[BTY/17/15/62–8] *Queen*
[Bantry]
13–14 July 1909

*　　*　　*

And now, what am I to write to you about that would interest you? Nothing I fear. Or how I spent last night. I said it was a poisonous night. Well, so it was and it wasn't. The sea fog rolled

[1]Later Admiral Sir William Pakenham (1861–1933): entered RN 1874; present as observer at the battle of Tsushima 1904; appointed 4th Sea Lord by Churchill 1911; Rear-Admiral commanding 3rd Cruiser Squadron Home Fleet 1913; commanding 2nd Battle-Cruiser Squadron 1915; succeeded Beatty in command of Battle-Cruiser Fleet & Vice-Admiral 1917; Admiral President RNC Greenwich 1919; CinC North America and West Indies 1920; Admiral 1922; retired at own request 1926.

up and enveloped us as we left the Shannon which increased the dangers of navigation, & at the same time added an excitement to the hour which prevented it from becoming humdrum & gave one something to overcome or compete against, after all, which is half the joy of life. And there is something uncanny about booming along in a wet fog, when you cannot see more than 100 yards in front on either side. As we passed Kerry Head we could hear the shore birds piping their wild music, saddest & most delightful of all, two curlews calling to each other like the wail of two lost souls. I am sure, with the Greeks, that distressed souls take up their abode in wild sea birds. And then we steamed into the fog, which got thicker towards midnight, and really I think, I enjoyed it; could see nothing, hear nothing except the wash of the water on the bow, and I sat on the rail of the bridge & opened my lungs and swallowed huge draughts of damp, soft, pure, warm air which had crossed the Atlantic from south west to north east and so was unpolluted for 10,000 miles, so felt it was doing me good. Yes, I really did enjoy it and Brandon[1] thought I was mad because I said what a nice night it was. And I pitied you in stuffy London, surrounded by a polluted atmosphere and the crowds of hunters after excitement which is principally composed of doing something which others don't do, and consequently the enjoyment lies in making one's friends envious, isn't it the way of life? By the aid of compass and sounding machine we found our way into Bantry in the dark and when at 7 this morning we found ourselves where we expected to be we were pleased & felt we had accomplished something, nothing in reality but it tickled our vanity, that's all.

*   *   *

What a grumbler I've been of late, how I have bored you with my nasty peevish letters. And all the world has been under my nose, with new joys to hand if I would only see, in the rain or sunshine or if I would only use my eyes. Nature is always with us & always ready to teach. Is it because I shall see my sweet one so soon that there is a golden haze over everything? . . .

[1] Commander (N) Claude Brandon RN.

17. *To his wife* [15 Upper Grosvenor Street, London]

[BTY/17/18/27–30]   *Queen*
                                                [Gibraltar]
                                    Monday 6th [December 1909]

*   *   *

I see in the papers that if the Radicals come in after the Election that Winston Churchill will become 1st Lord of the Admiralty. No greater blow could possibly be delivered to the British Navy. And, if the Unionists come in, Walter Long[1] will go there. He of course is imbued with Charles Beresford's ideas. So the result will be interesting to follow, but I grieve for the poor Service, tossed like a shuttlecock between two rival lines of ideas & of policies. When shall we settle down to continuity? Much will depend on Arthur Wilson & I trust he will be able to deal efficiently with a parlous state of affairs and he will have to be very strong and firm — and ought to have a strong lot to serve with him.

Again Tariff Reform if Unionists are returned is bound to come in & what the result outside our country will be, no man can tell, but I cannot but think that the Germans will not take it sitting down and they might well seize the opportunity of making use of it to put their recent strenuous efforts to increase their Navy to the test. For it will undoubtedly hit them hard, far harder than any other nation, and they will never be in a more favourable position than they will be at the end of 1910. After that their chance will grow smaller. So I feel that 1910 is to be the most difficult year to tide over & will take us all our time.

*   *   *

[1]Later 1st Viscount Long (1854–1924): Conservative MP. The election resulted in a minority Liberal government. Reginald McKenna (see note 1 on p. 33) remained 1st Lord. Long headed the Admiralty during 1918–21 when Beatty was 1st Sea Lord.

18. *To his wife* [15 Upper Grosvenor Street, London]

[BTY/17/18/46–53]   *Queen*
                                                                 [Gibraltar]
                                                               10. Dec. 1909

*   *   *

The political campaign appears to have fairly started and the Liberal party are not letting the grass grow under their feet — Winston Churchill being particularly busy. And from all accounts, Trafalgar Square, Albert Hall, & many other meetings, [*sic*] the Unionist party will be defeated before they begin if they do not set to work soon. I am afraid that 'Down with the House of Lords' will prove a very popular cry among the masses and it is very skilfully being made use of by the radicals.

You never mention such things in your letters, but do you never hear an expression of an opinion worth quoting among those that you meet, or is this subject tabooed as being too ordinary & uninteresting among the intellectuals? We in the Navy are naturally much interested, as the result will have very important and far-reaching results upon the Service generally also on our foreign relations with our great rivals, which must of necessity cause anxiety to all those in the Navy who look ahead or think about the future at all. But the idle public are as blind in England as they were in Russia before the Russo-Japanese war. Please God we will not have such a rude awakening or unhappy issue as they had. But in view of what we *know* one cannot but have serious misgivings & I should describe the outlook as gloomy in the extreme whichever party wins. I fear we are not governed or regulated in any particular or by any office by that single purposedness [*sic*] which alone can command success & which we know is & can see being put to such good effect by the Germans. I don't suppose you have seen considered or heard mentioned the German Naval Estimates which most assuredly will be passed in the Reichstag without comment or a dissenting voice. Such purposedness [*sic*] is illustrated by the toast drunk every night in every German man of war, 'To the Great Day'. While we waste our time listening to the quarrelling of politicians and admirals which provide the necessary copy for the newspapers & topics for discussion in the Fleet. Truly it is sickening in the extreme. What we truly need is a man, a big man who knows what is required and will get it. But fear [?] the national characteristic is against any such man making himself heard and felt until the moment

arrives, and in the preceding phases everything is left to the clap-
trap of the small politician. It was ever thus. When the blow falls
we shall be unprepared and suffer many losses & lose many lives
and valuable assets in the way of ships and possessions. And the
disasters will themselves breed the man and the strong points of
the national character and out of the debris we shall dig our way
to a successful issue. A long homily, but I have plenty of time to
read and think & am firmly of the opinion that it is tending that
way, but it sounds like 'A voice crying in the wilderness' just now,
doesn't it? But the time is not far when it will be proved and I
comfort myself by the thought that in the Navy at least the idea,
the same idea, is prevalent amongst all those who think deeply on
the subject, but who never voice their opinion for the uselessness
thereof & for the universal objection to being considered a scare-
monger and unduly pessimistic.

*   *   *

19. *To his wife*

[BTY/17/18/88–93]   *Queen*
                                                                   [Dover]
                                         Wednesday [29 December 1909]

I got down alright and found everything quiet and peaceful.
The men had had a very quiet but enjoyable Xmas, that is to say
they nearly all stopped onboard and the ship was beautifully
decorated and they enjoyed their dinners and *turkeys* and said
they had never had such a happy Xmas onboard a ship before.
The little Commander I find not at all well, but much better, so
I am bundling him off on leave to London for a few days, which
I think will do him all the good in the world. A ship is a miserable
place when not feeling well, especially this time of the year when
cold and damp, although this morning is delightful, quite calm,
and bright sunshine which I hope it will last [*sic*].
    I do hope, dear one, you are *happy*. It struck me very forcibly
on my return that you did not seem so and the afternoon we went
down to Brooksby, I felt as if I was an ogre dragging you to some
fearful place that you dreaded. You see, dear, your happiness is
the one thing I have to live for and if only you are happy and
contented, so am I. But I fear I am making a hash of it somehow,

and at times it appears that the point of a rift in the lute is inclined to show and I can't think why but have a sort of intuition it is there. For instance Dennis[1] told me yesterday that Muriel did not go to Sandown with you. It was à propos of her neuralgia that she hadn't left Leicestershire, except to go to London, since her trip abroad. Well, you told me she was going with you & led me to believe she was with you and did not enlighten me when I referred to her being with you. The fact of her not being with you is not a matter of much consequence in itself, although as I think I said before, I don't like you going to such places by yourself. But what does matter and what hurts more than I can say, is that you should have allowed me to be under the wrong impression. Of course I knew you were not by yourself because you referred to *we* doing this and *we* doing that. Moreover I know that you could no more spend a Saturday to Tuesday by yourself in a place like that than fly over the moon. I do not want to force your confidence if you do not wish to give it. But it is that very want of confidence in me which hurts and makes me think that something has crept in to destroy it which I do not wot of. If you have come to the decision that you want to go to [sic] your own way without interference from me, as apparently is the fashion nowadays, would it not be fairer to say so. God knows, I do not want to force myself at all times down your throat, but give me your confidence in *all things*. By plain speaking half the misery in the world could be done away with. I know you dear heart think the same as I do, so why should there be any subterfuge between us? I am not the sort of person who would wish to dictate to you your mode of life, or who your friends are to be or not to be, but I should like to participate with and in them. The end of this year is on us and a new year about to begin. I shall arrive at the same time at a higher status in life with greater responsibilities and possibly greater opportunities of which I shall want to make the most, and the first essential must be that I have you on my side, your advice, your assistance, and your confidence in all things, and moreover [?] that I can feel assured of your happiness and contentment of mind. I have many faults and no one can see them or be more aware of them than you. Won't you out of kindness

[1]Lieutenant-Commander (retd) Dennis Larking: a family friend of the Beattys who helped to manage their financial and property affairs both before and after the war. He was re-employed from 1914 in the 2nd Sea Lord's department and then as Naval Attaché, Rome, and promoted Acting Captain. Neither Chalmers nor Roskill recognises his importance in the Beattys' private lives. His papers are in the NMM.

point out where I fail and in what way I upset you, as it would appear that I do at times. You have the instinct and could put your finger on the sore spot if you would only speak frankly and tell me wherein I fail. For I truly feel that I do fail and I do so want to succeed in making you happy and not rub you up the wrong way. Will you try to understand me and this rigmarole? . . .

20. *From Captain E. C. Troubridge*[1] [Private Secretary to 1st Lord]

[BTY/2/2/1]   Admiralty
5.7.11.

Have I answered your letter? I cannot remember. I have been writing letters without ceasing these past few weeks but I imagine I told you the position. The First Lord cannot promise either of the posts you mention, i.e. 1st Division H. F. & King Hall's[2] post when he leaves here. Your not wanting the IIIrd Division or Atlantic has rather narrowed the choice, it must be admitted and the business of the other post is so far in the future that I am somewhat at a loss to give you any reply.

However I have made notes as follows:
  You want:
    1st Division H. F. vice Peirse[3] Jan 11
        or
    2nd Division H. F. vice Patey[4] Oct 11
        or
    Director of Mobilisation — when vacant.

[1]Later Admiral Sir Ernest Troubridge (1862–1926): entered RN 1875; Rear-Admiral 1911; Head of new Admiralty War Staff 1912; commanding Mediterranean Cruiser Squadron 1914 and held responsible for the escape of *Goeben & Breslau*; although acquitted by court martial, not given further active employment; adviser to Serbian government 1914–19. (See C. E. J. Fryer, 'The British Naval Mission to Serbia', unpublished Ph.D, thesis, London University, 1985.)
[2]Rear-Admiral Herbert King-Hall: Rear-Admiral 1909; Director of Naval Mobilisation 1909; commanding 2nd Battle Squadron Home Fleet October 1911.
[3]Vice-Admiral Sir Richard Peirse: CinC East Indies 1912; member of Central Committee Board of Inventions and Research 1916–18, involved in ASW research. Supported A. H. Pollen in his disputes with the Admiralty over the trials of his gunnery control system.
[4]Later Admiral Sir George Patey: Rear-Admiral 1909; commanding 2nd Division Home Fleet 1910; commanding Australian Navy 1913–15.

That is about how it stands is it not?

21. *To Reginald McKenna*[1]

[BTY/2/2/4]   Hanover Lodge
[Draft]   Regent's Park
                                                        London
                                      Tuesday [25 July 1911]

I am in receipt of your letter of the 21st only today and I regret
the delay in answering. I have been up North. The letter followed
me and caught me this afternoon.

I thank you for the time to think it over which you kindly gave
and regret extremely that I am unable to accept the offer of the
2nd in Command of the Atlantic Fleet. As I informed your Private
Secretary in the course of several conversations I was ready for
service anywhere at the Admiralty or at sea where there was
work to do and experience to be gained. But preferably a sea
appointment — and being invited by him where, I as early as the
beginning of March, asked that my name might be listed [?] for
the Home Fleet, where the greatest experience afloat is to be
gained, where the work is continuous . . . *one could fit oneself
better for High Command* [deleted]. I was given to understand
that this was quite likely to be favourably considered and I stood
as good a chance as any and that my seniority would be about
right. I have always stated that the one appointment I did not
wish to be considered for was that of 2nd in Command Atlantic
Fleet. There the work to be done & experience to be gained is
of the miniumum quality & a Rear-Admiral with a nominal
squadron of 6 ships frequently reduced to 5 and even 4 ships, has
absolutely nothing to do and occupy himself with — except a
study of naval history.

I appreciate your endeavours to find me another appointment &
the difficulties of satisfying the personal claims of other officers
and I trust that my assurance of my desire to fill useful appointments and my desire to become as efficient and capable as possible
may tend to lead me to hope that you will employ me in such

[1]Reginald McKenna (1863–1943): Liberal politician. 1st Lord of Admiralty
1908–11, when replaced by Churchill; Home Secretary 1911–15; Chancellor of
Exchequer 1915–16.

appointments as you may see fit for the good of the Service & in which I can do good work & gain much [?] experience.

22. *From Captain Troubridge*

[BTY/2/2/2]   Admiralty
                                                              26.7.11

I have your letter today and am truly sorry you have decided to refuse, for one can never tell from day to day whether an appointment afloat will turn out strenuous or otherwise. The fact is that the Admiralty view is that officers should serve where they, i.e. the Admiralty, wish and *not* where they themselves wish. This is the cold and brutal explanation of your being offered the appointment although I had informed the Powers That Be that you did not wish to be offered it.

*   *   *

23. *To Troubridge*

[BTY/2/2/6]   Hanover Lodge
                                                              26.7.11

I am glad to have your letter with explanations of methods employed at the Admiralty. If I had lived to be a thousand I should never have guessed them. There is something peculiarly subtle in inviting the poor devil yearning for employment to state his desires and hopes and then offering him the one thing he doesn't want, it savours of the guile and intrigue of the ancient Egyptians. It's a mercy that all the big offices are not administered in the same fashion or it is to be feared that there are few who would wish to serve under such conditions, and it is only the poor Naval officers who would put up with such as you well describe, brutal treatment. I presume that the gentlemen at the Admiralty have different views and a different code in so far as it effects themselves and they take care not to mix one code with the other. I have often heard that such was the case but never believed that it could have been possible. . . .

*　　*　　*

24. *To his wife* [Hanover Lodge, Regent's Park]

[BTY/17/20/9]   Admiralty Yacht
[Portsmouth]
Sunday [4 February 1912]

*　　*　　*
I have and am not enjoying myself. A ship in this weather is to
be avoided, but I've been able to do a good deal of work. Three
times I have pounded the snow round the Yard with the First
Lord, and have had some useful conversations with him & others
towards settling many knotty points. And, as I am the only Naval
representative on board, under no circumstances except the most
urgent, could I have conscientiously got out of it. But I do hate
these trips in the *Enchantress*,[1] but I am such a selfish brute. . . .

25. *To his wife* [Hanover Lodge]

[BTY/17/20/11–12]   Admiralty Yacht
[Portland]
Sunday [24 March 1912]

*　　*　　*
This morning the weather is better but none too good and looks
like rain at any moment. I hope it will improve before morning
or our firing will be much upset. The 1st Lord, Winnie, waits for
a telegram in the morning to decide whether we return tomorrow
night or not. It all depends on the state of the Cabinet & whether
they feel strong enough to get on without him. But I doubt our
staying here after Tuesday. I shall try to play golf with George
Warrender this afternoon.

*　　*　　*
I am very glad I came down. I had 2 hours solid conversation
with W. C. and in consequence matters are better & my mind is
not so perturbed about the questions of great importance I told
you of, & we see things from the same point of view & con-

[1]The Admiralty yacht.

sequently there will have to be some very considerable alterations made in the many schemes that have been without his proper consideration. I think he had rather a shock at first but in the end saw things with my eyes. But whatever happens, it will be done without causing any breach in the relations between I [sic] and the 1st and 2nd Sea Lords. So if nothing else happens my journey here will have been a fruitful one from many points of view.

*   *   *

26. *Beatty's paper for Winston Churchill on naval dispositions in a war against Germany*

[BTY/2/3/6]
[Copy]   [7 April 1912]

In any consideration of the distribution and disposition of our fleets with regard to the possibility of war with Germany, either singlehanded or with or against allies; due regard must be taken of the geographical condition of the seas in which the struggle will take place.

The principles affecting the struggle between the two dominating sea powers must remain the same whether one or the other enjoys the advantage of having allies or not.

Therefore by surveying the geographical situation of the waters between England and Germany, we arrive at a more proper appreciation of the problems that are before us.

The conclusions are that with a proper distribution of her fleets, Great Britain is capable of confining all or nearly all warlike operations within the North Sea.

The conditions of such waters are not repeated in any measure anywhere else in the world. The exits from the German sea ports and Naval bases to the great seas are in the North Sea, and by controlling the exits from the North Sea both North and South Great Britain confines and controls the sea power of the German nation.

The British Isles form a great breakwater across German waters thereby limiting the passage of vessels to the outer seas to two exits, the one on the South, narrow, easily blocked and contained, and the other on the North of such a width (155 miles) that with the forces at our disposal it could easily be commanded so as to preclude the possibility of the passing of any hostile force without our knowledge and without being brought to action by a superior force.

The possible and probable objects of the German Naval Forces at war with this country are —

(1) To interrupt and destroy the oversea trade especially food supplies, upon the safe carrying of which the existence of the nation depends.

(2) To endeavour by constant attacks by destroyer, submarine, and mine-layers so to reduce our fleets that they might reasonably hope for a successful issue when they give battle with their entire available force.

(3) By such attacks to drive our fleets etc such a distance out of the North Sea and contain them for sufficient time to enable a large expeditionary force to be launched — i.e. to hold the North Sea for a sufficient time to enable an invasion of the British Isles to take place.

There are two possible subsidiary objectives on the part of Germany —

(1) The seizure of a port or anchorage on the Norwegian coast or in the Shetlands or Orkneys from which their torpedo craft could operate and so make more feasible objective No. 2 and possibly No. 3.

(2) The occupation of the Texel. This latter would entirely depend on their relations with the Dutch as to whether this occupation would be of a peaceful nature or otherwise.

It is conceivable that war would break out — first — after a prolonged period of strained relations. Secondly — as a bolt from the blue with a bare 24 hours notice, if as much.

In either case the principle governing the disposition must remain the same and must be carried out to its logical conclusion, notwithstanding the many difficulties that would arise in the event of war breaking out as in No. 2.

The policy of Their Lordships provides for the immediate disposal of a force in home waters consisting of (at present) 22 battleships with 6 attendant small cruisers, one swift and 13 armoured cruisers. This force is only available if no portion of them are undergoing refit which is exceedingly improbable. In addition 4 flotillas of destroyers and 8 sections of submarines make up the complete force that can be reckoned on as available in the first 24 hours.

There are the 6 battleships of the Fourth Squadron which might be in home waters and available for immediate service without offending the susceptibility of our prospective foe or hampering the diplomatic discussions which might possibly lead to peace, but this force cannot be relied upon at all times.

It therefore remains to dispose immediately of the available force to meet the possible and probable objectives, taking advantage of the favourable geographical conditions.

To this end the Battle Fleet will proceed, if time permits, by the Western route to the North; if time does not permit then by the shortest route — remaining at sea North of Lat. 55° 30' and West of the Meridian of Greenwich, making use of the anchorage of Scapa Flow for the purpose of coaling only.

The 1st and 3rd Cruiser Squadrons will also proceed to the Northward visiting the Orkneys and Shetlands at the earliest opportunity and ascertaining that no hostile force has forestalled them and is already making use of anchorages in the above named Islands.

The 1st Flotilla will proceed to Scapa Flow — its primary duty will be to act as the Battle Fleet Flotilla and it is at the same time available for the purpose of watching and guarding the Shetlands and Orkneys and the waters between them.

The 2nd Cruiser Squadron will move to Dover. The 2nd Flotilla to Rosyth, the 3rd Flotilla to Yarmouth, the 4th Flotilla to Dover. The 4th section of Submarines to Harwich and the 6th Section to Yarmouth, the 7th Section to Dundee and the 8th Section to Dover.

On the precautionary telegram being received the Flotillas will patrol their beats in so far as they are able. The 4th Flotilla patrolling to the Northward supported by the 2nd Cruiser Squadron as far as the Latitude 52° and thereby watching the estuaries of the Thames and guarding against the approach of minelayers which might be anticipated as endeavouring to mine these waters at the earliest opportunity.

It is anticipated that on precautionary telegram being issued all flotillas will be brought up to full strength.

On the outbreak of war the fleets, squadrons, flotillas, submarine sections, minelayers, sweepers and air craft will be disposed as follows:- The 1st Battle Fleet stationed at the North will be brought at the earliest opportunity to its full strength of 28 ships.

It might be anticipated, that owing to circumstances, it would be desirable to complete it to full strength by the inclusion of the 5th Battle Squadron instead of having to wait for the possibly delayed arrival of the 4th Battle Squadron from foreign waters.

This Battle Fleet will be based for coaling purposes at Scapa Flow or possibly Cromarty, but it is to be understood that in the absence of efficiently defended and protected ports in those waters their greatest safety lies in keeping the sea.

The Battle Squadrons of the 2nd Fleet will assemble at Spithead. The Battle Squadrons of the 3rd Fleet at Portland. The 5th Cruiser Squadron to Dover in support of the 2nd Cruiser Squadron.

These squadrons will move up and form a patrol off the Texel when the waters South of the line of Smith Knowles Light Ship and the Haaks has been cleared of torpedo craft.

Details of patrol will be arrived at later.

The 6th Cruiser Squadron will proceed to Rosyth. The Training Squadron will proceed to Falmouth and complete with coal, the time that they might expect to be available would depend on the amount of warning of hostilities that we might receive and their movements would be governed by similar circumstances to those that govern the 4th Battle Squadron.

Yarmouth is placed at a point on the coast which would be much nearer the objective of the Force using it than Harwich and it should be used in preference provided the weather conditions permit.

The 4th Flotilla will proceed to Yarmouth on being relieved by the 6th Flotilla at Dover. The 5th Flotilla will also proceed to Yarmouth. The 7th and 8th Flotillas will proceed as detailed in special orders to form the East coast patrols. The 2nd Flotilla on being relieved by the 8th will proceed and place themselves under the orders of Officer Commanding, 1st Cruiser Squadron. The Nore Defence Flotilla will take over the patrol of the Thames Estuaries. The 8th section of submarines will be moved up to Lowestoft. The Minelayers will assemble at Sheerness.

By the stationing of the foregoing craft we have disposed of the total force that is available and which cannot be added to for at least six days. They are so disposed to meet the probable objectives of the German forces at the earliest opportunities, having due regard to the geographical conditions as before stated —

1st. In the South we have a force of two armoured cruiser squadrons, 3 Destroyer Flotillas and 3 sections of Submarines with which to hold the line between Smith Knowles Lightship and the Haak Lightship, thereby clearing the waters South of this line for the free entrance of our merchant shipping to the mouth of the Thames.

And for the launching forth of any expeditionary force that we might desire to throw across at the earliest opportunity and at the narrowest part of the Channel.

At the same time this force is in a position to prevent any occupation of the Dutch Islands by hostile torpedo craft.

The operations of this strong force of torpedo craft, consisting as it does of flotillas and submarines with a strong supporting force of armoured cruisers should not confine its operations to that of purely defensive holding of the line as indicated, but might well be considered as available for offensive operations which need not be continuous, and at the same time perform the duty of look out patrol and be capable of picking up knowledge of the departure of any large force from German waters in the Bight of the Elbe.

Such offensive operations should meet with some measure of success by the skillful handling and disposing of forces at command, such as — the destruction of the enemy's destroyer flotillas on their departure or return to their bases at Borkum, Norderney, etc., also skilful combined operations with flotilla and submarine against hostile cruisers which might endeavour to drive off flotillas.

Further, opportunities should occur of successfully mining the waters in the Bight under cover of the cruiser squadrons — All such operations must of necessity depend on the weather conditions at the time, but it can be assumed that should the conditions be such as to preclude the possibility of making use of destroyer flotillas for the purposes as detailed, it would certainly deter the enemy's torpedo craft from also making effective attacks, and in such case the armoured cruisers could patrol with greater safety nearer hand.

They should be capable of patrolling the waters so as to make it impossible for any large hostile force to break out South of the Line joining May Island and Terschelling Light.

A small expeditionary force should be prepared at Harwich for the occupation of Ameland anchorage and should the diplomatic relations between Great Britain and Holland be such that such an occupation would not jeopardize the successful issue of the war in its larger aspects, the anchorage should not be seized and made use of as an advanced base for our torpedo and submarine craft.

The advantages of such an anchorage are too obvious to need stating.

Turning to the North we have two armoured cruiser squadrons, 2 destroyer flotillas, whose duty it will be to search the waters between the Shetlands and Norwegian coast and endeavour to defeat that possible objective on the part of Germany to seize a port in Norway — then to establish a base either at Stavanger or at Fedde and form a patrol S. W. from Lister Point, but one destroyer flotilla is to remain within the vicinity of the Battle Fleet.

It is understood that the Germans keep a considerable force of destroyers at all times in the N. E. Danish waters, so it may be conceived more than likely that they contemplate operating in time of war in the Skagarak [sic] and as aforesaid from Norwegian ports.

It should be possible for this patrol to make certain that no large force of the enemy should pass to the N. W. of the line joining Lister Point and a point in Lat. 3.53.E.

The 6th Cruiser Squadron based at Rosyth will have two functions to perform — one to act as an observation squadron in the gap between the two patrols (N. and S.) which gap being large and their numbers small could not be a concentrated force but observation force only.

They will patrol between the Firth of Forth and the Meridian of 2° E., on a course due E. (true), spread by day at 1½ visibility distance, reaching the outermost point (i.e. 2° E.) at sunset, the most Northern look out not to be North of Lat.56.° 30'. At night closing in 5 miles apart or good signalling distance and returning towards their base. Their secondary duty which is subsidiary would be to act as supports for the coastal patrols.

The Fleet sweepers will proceed to Rosyth and Cromarty and place themselves under the orders of the Commander-in-Chief, Home Fleets.

It is as well to emphasise the opinion that during the preliminary stages of the war the safety of the battle fleets from submarine, destroyer attacks, and minelayers, is more perfectly assured by keeping the sea with constant change of positions, protected as they are by the six attendant cruisers, the swift and if necessary the first destroyer flotilla, rather than at rest in an anchorage, the approach to which lend themselves to being mined by hostile minelayers, wide enough for submarines to operate in and in thick weather to the successful issue to a determined attack by destroyer craft — such as Rosyth or to undefended ports, such as Cromarty and Scapa Flow.

Doubtless as the war progresses and the whole of the British Force is put into being, a firmer grip and control of events in the North Sea will be established, it *may* then be possible or advisable to make more use of the bases in the North.

The movements of the 1st Battle Fleet will depend and conform to the movements of the northern patrol, which as it clears and makes good the waters in which it operates will ensure a larger safe area for the Battle Squadron, and furthermore will permit of the Battle Squadron occupying a more southern area and so enable it to be in a more favourable position to bring to action in the shortest possible time a hostile force – should the enemy make an attempt to land on the shores of Great Britain supported by their full strength.

A second phase constituted by the fact of the addition to the available forces of the 5th Cruiser Squadron and the Battle Squadrons of the 3rd Fleet — which force amounts to the total strength of Great Britain in Home Waters.

Of these squadrons, one (the 11th) will be based on Lough Swilly and will co-operate with the Training Squadron already stationed at Falmouth in protecting the trade on its near approach to the British Isles — the forces being divided so as to provide for 2 armoured cruisers of the Training Squadron being moved to Berehaven, which Port and that of Lough Swilly, being defended ports, will be used as ports of refuge — all vessels of the North Atlantic trade being instructed to proceed to Lough Swilly, the South Atlantic trade to Berehaven.

This duty of trade protection will be supplemented by vessels of the *Hyacinth, June*, class, now attached to the Battle Squadrons of the 2nd Fleet, by forming a cordon due South from Portland — the remaining four squadrons will proceed to support the patrols in the North Sea as follows:-

The 10th Cruiser Squadron proceeding to Scapa Flow and will patrol between the Norwegian coast and the Shetlands in Lat. 60° 31'.

The 7th and 8th to Rosyth to support the 6th Cruiser Squadron.

The 9th Cruiser Squadron proceed to join the First Cruiser Squadron, whose position it will replace in the Northern Patrol, thereby freeing this Squadron to act as a supporting Squadron in a position half way between the Northern Patrol and the Battle Fleet.

It is to be remembered that in thus disposing of cruisers, both armoured and protected, the principals of effective use as patrols and look outs is governed by their value as fighting craft and therefore armoured cruisers, which have considerable fighting value, should be disposed in a concentrated form. On the other hand, protected cruisers, whose fighting value is small but whose principal duties are that of look outs, need not be so concentrated, more especially as they have a force of armoured cruisers acting as supports.

The forces at our disposal having been distributed as aforesaid, all of which dispositions should have taken place in the first week of the war — they might be described as an offensive defensive distribution.

But before proceeding to discuss further movements it would be as well to consider the effect of the failure of one or more of our endeavours.

1st The failure to establish a control of the waters on the Norwegian coast or the possibility of a strong German force of destroyers and submarines, backed by armoured cruisers forestalling us and establishing themselves in a strong position on the Norwegian coast. It would be then necessary to dislodge and destroy such a force at the earliest opportunity before established too strongly and to this end a particular force would be detailed.

The forces at the disposal of the enemy are limited and therefore a proportion of our forces are doing good work in holding, containing and eventually destroying any force of the enemy that should be detached for definite purposes.

2nd The possibility of a German Force of T.B.D.s and Submarines establishing themselves in Dutch waters. At all costs that force must be destroyed or turned out. But nothing, speaking generally, must be allowed to interfere with the dispositions of our fleets and squadrons as indicated above. They might be retarded and held up for a *short* time but they must eventually without the loss of too much time be brought into effect. And the advance of the British Naval Forces must resemble that of the steam roller crushing all obstacles and overwhelming all opposition, gradually confining the waters to which the enemy would have access to that only surrounding their own coast line and that only at the risk of capture or destruction. For instance with the

Ameland anchorage in our hands and being made use of by us as a base for destroyers and submarines it would appear a comparatively simple matter for us to maintain an efficient blockade of German waters. Still more so if it were possible for us to make use of an anchorage on the Danish coast in the vicinity of Blavaand Point, even if it were only a fine weather anchorage.

It is to be considered to what possible offensive effect the force in the South composed as it is of 2 armoured cruiser squadrons, 3 flotillas of destroyers numbering 54 T. B. D.s 3 flotillas of submarines numbering 12 C.s. and 8 D.s. supplemented by minelayers could be put to.

It is obvious that any offensive could only consist of a general sweep from the waters South of the Line Smith Knoll Lightship and the Haak Lightship round Terschilling Bank into the waters of the Bight of Heligoland, sweeping in front all but the heaviest combination etc. Such a movement must terminate either by return to their bases owing to the impossibility of keeping the sea for long periods of the destroyers and submarines or by establishing themselves somewhere in the vicinity.

A third alternative of keeping a portion of their force always in the vicinity of the waters of the Bight can be dismissed as involving too great a risk of the reduced force being crushed by an overwhelming force and by the difficulties that distance from their base would create to prevent it being effectively carried out. Therefore the sweep up clearing the waters from the narrow seas up to the German ports is in itself an operation of considerable effectiveness and importance and must terminate in one of two things —

(a) The return of all torpedo craft, destroyers and submarines. or

(b) The seizure of an anchorage when an advanced base can be established for torpedo craft, destroyers and submarines.

For (a) there is nothing to be said. For (b) much, both for and against. The only possible anchorage which could be utilised for this purpose is that between Ameland and Terschilling Islands in Dutch territory. If as I have said previously this could be done without jeopardising the successful issue of the war in its larger aspects it should be done immediately on the outbreak of war — the advantages of such a base are too numerous to need any elaboration. That it is a feasible proposition to seize is without question, that it is a practical proposition to hold and maintain when seized should be considered in all its branches but it does not appear to present any insuperable difficulties.

It would therefore be of the utmost value to prepare a scheme for organising a force of 2000 men fully equipped with guns, searchlights, and wireless to proceed immediately on the outbreak of war in a suitable vessel of small draft, similar to the *Bakana* that carried out the marine detachment to Scapa Flow.

Having decided that such operation is both feasible and practicable. The detail must be worked with the greatest care and minuteness.

The armoured cruisers and destroyers would clear the waters in advance of the submarines, minelayers and transport.

The 6th Flotilla of 21 boats from Dover would advance their patrol position from the Straits of Dover to the Smiths Knoll — Haaks Light Ship Line in rear of the submarines and destroyers watching the waters from the Texel for any hostile movement in their flank or Rear.

Owing to the obstruction to the entrance to the anchorage by shallow sandbanks and the shallowness of the waters in the Channel (17¾ feet at low water) it would be necessary for the transport to arrive at ½ flood tide as early as possible. Destroyer could be told off to investigate and locate the channel before her arrival owing to the constant change that the Channel-s are liable to and to make sure that the buoys marking the West Channel have not been tampered with.

27. *To his wife* [Hanover Lodge]

[BTY/17/20/38–9]   [Admiralty Yacht]
                                                          Naples
                                            24 [May 1912]

                        *   *   *

That old rascal Fisher arrived on board directly we got here, looking very well and young, never stopped talking and has been closeted with Winston ever since. Wasn't that something to come to Naples for? Do not mention in conversation to *anyone* that F is in close confidence with Winston. It would be most injurious to the Service if it ever got out, & the Navy would hate it. I took the opportunity to bolt to the shore and send you a wire, but found them together still on my return, & they are spending this afternoon together. Prince Louis hates it and keeps out of the way also as much as possible. I understand that we stay here until Sunday when we go on to Messina stopping at Sorrento on our way, possibly Palermo and then on to Malta. I find this wretched party on board getting duller and duller. There is not a high spot among the whole lot & don't think I can bear it. *If I break away* I shall be home by the 6th and will come with you to the Ball, but won't dance the Quadrille, but you must be ready to get me a costume to wear or I shouldn't be able to go.

*   *   *

28.   *To his wife* [Hanover Lodge]

[BTY/17/20/44–5]   Admiralty Yacht
                                                        [at sea]
                                                   27 May 1912

*   *   *

Oh dear! I am so tired and bored with the whole thing. Even the weather isn't kind; cloudy and cold with heavy rain storms. The Sunny South doesn't exist, we can do better than this in London. And the party on board bores me to tears. Winston talks about nothing but the sea and the Navy and the wonderful things he is going to do. Mrs Winston is a perfect fool, I never met a truer or better specimen of the amiable fool. Old Asquith[1] is a regular common old tourist; spends his time immersed in a Baedecker Guide and reading extracts to an admiring audience. On shore it makes one ashamed to have to introduce him as the Prime Minister of Great Britain. Prince Louis is of course charming, but not terribly exciting.

*   *   *

I can bear it no longer and shall be back by Thursday 6th. . . . Don't say a word to anyone about my coming back it would never do, but I really cannot stand any more of it. Of all the lot on board I like Winston the best. He is sincere, he does enthuse, he is keen and he is appreciative of the Navy so should not like to hurt his feelings and it will have to be managed skilfully.

*   *   *

[1]H. H. Asquith, later 1st Earl Asquith (1852–1928): Liberal politician; Home Secretary 1892–5 and 1905–8; Prime Minister 1908–16, replaced by Lloyd George.

29.   *To his wife* [Hanover Lodge]

[BTY/17/21/1–2]   Admiralty Yacht
                                                              [Malta]
                                                             1.6.1912

Just a line to let you know that I shall be with you on Thursday as I wired and shall probably be with you almost as soon as you get this. I have to stop in Rome and shall go to the Hotel Grande, so send me a wire there. The Prime Minister is in an awful fuss as his colleagues want him to come home and he jibs and keeps sending wires for more details. If he was to go, he will go to Marseilles on the *Sufflok* from Bizerta and would get home Wed. I thought of going with him, but there is a chance he won't go, in which case I should be stranded and then should be beat. The old silly won't make up his mind & I can't risk it. The C-in-C is going to let me have the *Hussar* to go to Sicily in, which, though not saving time will be more comfortable than the dirty *Carola*.

We've had a very busy day from 8 o'clock this morning and now are going to have a Conference Dinner Party of Prime Minister, Lord Kitchener,[1] Winston, Prince Louis and self, so it will be interesting and am moving in the highest intellectual circles, so must keep my wits about me. I've rarely had a busier 3 days, in fact 4.

*   *   *

30.   *To his wife* [High Chimneys, Sunningdale]

[BTY/17/21/6–7]   *Aboukir*
                                                             [at sea]
                                             Wednesday [10 July 1912]

*   *   *

We all filed out and pursued our way to our different ports before commencing the great war. It was a fine and wonderful sight, the sea was fairly black with ships, like a plague of flies, going to every point of the compass. We have steamed quite well for a lot of craft [?] that have been laid up for a long time and

[1]Later Field Marshal and 1st Earl Kitchener (1850–1916): commissioned in Royal Engineers 1871; British representative and virtual ruler of Egypt 1911–14; Secretary of State for War 1914–16; drowned in HMS *Hampshire* June 1916.

all but one will do well I hope. The one is slow and can't steam, but we will ginger them up a bit when we get in. It is a fine day, or at least has turned into a fine day, which is a blessing, the early morning was poisonous. I hope it will continue but fear that is asking too much, the glass is falling. We arrive at Rosyth tomorrow morning at 7 o'clock and commence to coal immediately & I hope the whole squadron will have finished by daylight Friday, as we start out, or are expecting to, at 8 am. I shall be back if nothing happens by the evening of the 17th, but I trust that before that a good deal will happen and should not be surprised if the 1st part of the Manoeuvres were over by then, and we had separated again for another phase. I hope so, indeed, as I do not think these very instructive, except in the way of how not to do things, and hope for better things from the next lot.

*   *   *

31. *To his wife* [High Chimneys, Sunningdale]

[BTY/17/21/12–15]   *Aboukir*
[At sea, North Sea]
14th [July 1912]

We departed from Firth of Forth on Friday at 9.30 and after steaming vigourously all day deposited ourselves on our war stations, which we have maintained intact up to the present. Now, alas, coal is running short so three of my cruisers have to return to fill up, so I am left with reduced numbers, only 7. We had a poisonous night Friday: the most terrific thunder storm which lasted 7 hours. I've never seen such rain so continuous, with the most vivid and voluminous lightening. We were apparently in the centre of it as it went round and round us. One ship was struck and all the compasses put out of action but otherwise no damage was done. We sighted 3 destroyers in the middle of it, running like rabbits. We pursued but lost them in the storm which was as well, as they must have been our own which got out of position. War was not actually declared until 5 am yesterday, so only has been in progress about 36 hours and up to the present we have seen nothing. I think the enemy must have gone North and left our end severely alone, but I hope to have some definite news during the day. We understand that two submarines have put out of action two of George Warrender's[1] destroyers and two of our destroyers have torpedoed an enemy cruiser. Otherwise nothing has happened. I wish they would get a move on & let us do something. They had a great opportunity the 1st night but they missed it and now every hour adds to our advantage. My destroyers had a great contest this morning, and, as far as I can gather, accounted for 8 of the enemies' which they claim to have sunk. No doubt there will be a lot of hard swearing when it comes to be argued out.

Three of my cruisers have to go in to coal and I hear they are stuck in a fog, which is a bore if they don't hurry up. I shall run out of coal as Wednesday morning is my limit and two ships or [–] have to be coaled before it comes to me. . . . I shall in all probability turn over to another ship and remain out in the line. I shall only lose the *Aboukir* for 36 hours but that might be sufficient to lose the threads altogether. . . .

They keep on reporting to me the near approach of the Battle Fleet (enemy's). I wish they would and we could have a Tourney of our own.

16th. We have had nothing but fog in patches which lays [?] us up, and I expect you are having perfect weather all the time. It is too disgusting, we cannot get on. We have been very lucky as it has always kept clear for us but everywhere else it seems to be very thick. The enemy with 1 Division and armoured cruisers broke through our line last night, George Warrender's end, & they've disappeared to the North. I have not seen an enemy ship yet, though some of my cruisers have, and sunk one & have lost one of our own in doing it. They seem to be taking their time about doing things and have not made any serious attempt upon us as yet, but should imagine they are trying to but are bottled up by the fog and can't get on; which in time of war they would not care a cuss about. I expect *Aboukir* will start off tomorrow and get to Firth of Forth tomorrow night & you should get this on Thursday. . . .

[1]Later Admiral Sir George Warrender (1860–1917): entered RN 1873; Rear-Admiral 1908; Vice-Admiral 1913; in December 1914, commanding 2nd Battle Squadron, was in overall command of operations which failed to intercept enemy raid on Scarborough; CinC Plymouth; retired on health grounds 1916.

32. *To his wife* [Hanover Lodge]

[BTY/17/21/18–19]   *Aboukir*
[Margate]
Tuesday [23 July 1912]

*   *   *

I have not yet seen in the paper what Winston said yesterday
in the House,[1] but whatever it was I know it will raise a storm. I
cannot think what has come over him. When I left him last everything was satisfactorily arranged, both for ship construction and
increasing the personnel, and I suppose his confrères in the
Cabinet have got at him and overcome his arguments. I fear he
is not a strong man when it concerns [?] a really big thing, only
about the little things which don't really count is he strong. It is
most disappointing and I fear he'll drag the Board into the
ignominy of it all with him. Truly the time has come for them to
kick out and wash their hands of it all or they too will be tarred
with the same brush. It is unfortunate that it should have come
at the [–] time when Prince Louis was away & what little influence
I have could not be brought to bear. Was it all done on purpose,
do you suppose? I don't understand the arguments that are being
used, principally because I haven't heard them, however I shall
know a little more [?] before long.

---

[1] In House of Commons debate on 22 July 1912 the Opposition criticised the
relative capital ship strength with Germany in the North Sea.

PART II

THE BATTLE-CRUISER SQUADRON TO THE EVE OF WAR
1913–1914

THE NORTH SEA THEATRE

Scale of Miles

0   100   200   300   400

ATLANTIC

OCEAN

NORWAY

Faeroe
Islands

Shetland
Islands

Oslo

Skudesnes

Ekersund

The Naze

Orkney
Islands

Pentland Firth

Loch Eriboll

Cromarty Firth   Moray Firth

Peterhead

SCOTLAND

Aberdeen

Long Forties

NORTH

Jutland

DENMARK

Loch Swilly

Bayth   May Is.

Glasgow   Edinburgh   Forth of Forth

Farne Is.

Newcastle
R. Tyne
Sunderland
Hartlepool

Scarborough

SEA

Dogger
Bank

Horns Reef   Esbjerg

Sylt

Hoyer
Tondern

Amrum Bank

SCHLESWIG-HOLSTEIN

Heligoland

Kiel

Kiel
Canal

Cuxhaven   R. Elbe
Hamburg

Belfast

IRELAND

Dublin

IRISH
SEA

Liverpool

R. Humber

The Wash

Bara
Deep

Terschelling

Texel

Wilhelmshaven   R. Jade

WALES

ENGLAND

King's Lynn

Broad
Fourteens

NETHERLANDS

R. Ems

Emden

Queenstown

Bantry
Bay

Cape Clear

St. George's Channel

Milford Haven

Bristol Channel

Yarmouth
Lowestoft

Harwich
The
Nore

London
R. Thames   Sheerness

Dover

Hook of Holland

Walcheren
The
Downs

Ostend   Antwerp

Zeebrugge

R. Rhine

GERMANY

Devonport

Portland Bill

Portsmouth

Scilly Is.

Start Point

Calais
Boulogne

Dunkirk
Brussels

BELGIUM

ENGLISH CHANNEL

Straits of Dover

Dieppe

Le Havre

Ushant   Brest

FRANCE

Paris

INTRODUCTION

When Beatty hoisted his flag on *Lion* on 1 March 1913 he had no doubt that the primary role of his force was offensive. In this he echoed Fisher's conviction that the heavy hitting power and high speed of the battle-cruiser made it the climax of the revolution in capital ship design necessitated by the development of long-range gunnery and effective torpedoes. Defensive armour had to be sacrificed in favour of hitting power and the speed which would enable it to evade destruction by the stronger but slower battleship. Beatty, of course, realised that battle-cruisers could not act alone. They needed the co-operation of light cruisers in reconnaissance and the protection of destroyers when executing offensive missions, as well as the support of battleships in fleet actions. What he did not realise, and had to learn by the experience of war, were the difficulties in achieving rapid and accurate gunfire with the fire-control systems available and the hazards of North Sea weather. Even less did he anticipate the vulnerability of his ships to the quality of the enemy's gunnery skill and equipment.[1]

In the meantime his aims were to impress upon his captains the spirit in which his orders should be interpreted and to inspire their ships' companies with his own aggressive spirit and determination to achieve the highest possible standards. His admirers, led by the journalist Filson Young,[2] were soon telling the public of Beatty's outstanding ability to accomplish this [34, 40]. An early draft Instruction, the basis of future formal Battle-Cruiser Orders, emphasised the priority he gave to his subordinates being always prepared to exercise initiative without detailed orders, in order to bring the enemy to decisive action [36].

On matters of detail he gave careful thought to the defence of

---

[1]J. T. Sumida's 'British Capital Ship Design and Fire Control in the Dreadnought Era', *Journal of Modern History*, June 1979, is a concise analysis of the problems.

[2]Filson Young, journalist and author, cultivated by Fisher in his search for publicity for the Navy; a great supporter and propagandist for Beatty, whose attitude to his efforts was ambiguous; for a short time, at Fisher's instigation, served on Beatty's staff as intelligence officer; his *With the Battle-Cruisers* (London, 1921) is strongly pro-Beatty.

his force against submarine and torpedo attack, the proper use of wireless telegraphy, and, claiming uniqueness in this, defence against Germany's formidable air force. His daily life settled into a demanding routine of correspondence, supervision of gunnery and other exercises and inspections designed to impress his personality on the sailors. He was conscious of the need to keep personally fit through the only means available — golf and long walks whenever he could get ashore [37–41].

Both Beatty and his Commander-in-Chief, Sir George Callaghan,[1] became increasingly concerned with the torpedo, both as an offensive weapon in fleet actions and as a threat to their own capital ships. They saw concentrated destroyer attacks at the beginning of fleet actions as being potentially decisive by throwing the enemy into disorder, and studied the deployment patterns needed to counter this threat. In their minds, at least, there was not the total dependence on the gun as the dominant weapon which has often been seen as a weakness in British naval thought at the time. By July 1913 Beatty was ready to issue Battle Orders which, in contrast to his earlier draft [36], considered the problems involved in an action with the whole High Seas Fleet and not just its battle-cruiser force. He also showed greater appreciation of the gunnery difficulties, especially in his insistence that helm changes should be kept to a minimum once firing had begun. Captains were again instructed to use their initiative, especially in deciding on concentration of fire and the tactics to be used against torpedo boat and submarine attack [42,43].

The 1913 manoeuvres were most significant for the success of the commander of the 'enemy' fleet, Jellicoe,[2] in landing an invasion force on the east coast without being brought to action by Callaghan's main force. This not only enhanced Jellicoe's reputation but revived fears of invasion. In their reports, Callaghan

[1]Later Admiral of the Fleet Sir George Callaghan (1852–1920): entered RN 1866; Rear-Admiral in Channel Fleet 1905; commanding 5th Cruiser Squadron 1907; 2nd-in-Command Mediterranean 1908; Vice-Admiral commanding 2nd Division Home Fleet 1910; Admiral commanding Home Fleet; replaced by Jellicoe on grounds of age on outbreak of war; CinC Nore 1915–18; Admiral of the Fleet 1917. An underestimated man — the quality of his strategic thought is demonstrated in 48 below.

[2]Later Admiral of the Fleet Earl Jellicoe (1859–1935): entered RN 1872; as a Captain, DNO and member of Fisher's Committee on Designs 1905; Rear-Admiral 1907; Controller & 3rd Sea Lord 1908; Vice-Admiral commanding Atlantic Fleet 1910; 2nd Sea Lord 1912; Acting Admiral and CinC Home Fleets August 1914; (the designation Grand Fleet not adopted until September); 1st Sea Lord 1916; dismissed by 1st Lord December 1917; Empire Mission on Naval defence and Admiral of the Fleet 1919; Governor-General New Zealand 1920–4; earldom 1925.

and the chief umpire, Sir William May, expressed alarm about the lack of port and coast defences. The subject was taken up by the Committee of Imperial Defence whose report in May 1914 was to recommend the creation of a territorial defence force.[1] During the manoeuvres Beatty enjoyed himself lecturing Churchill and his entourage on the unreality of the exercises and their own ignorance of naval realities. Although he made some private criticisms of Callaghan's slow reactions, he praised his calmness and good common sense, obviously considering him an acceptable Commander-in-Chief. A portent for the future emerged in Beatty's dislike of the Firth of Forth as a base because of its vulnerability to submarine attack [44–46].

Beatty's respect for Callaghan is supported by the quality of the Commander-in-Chief's review of the War Plans in the light of the manoeuvres. He too stressed the necessity of improving the Forth's defences, seeing it as the best strategically situated fleet base. He continued his anticipation of massed torpedo attacks on the fleet and saw concentration of his own destroyers close to the battle squadrons as the best defence against both torpedo boats and submarines. Above all, he insisted that a combined gun and torpedo onslaught on the enemy was infinitely better than a single arm attack [48].

Beatty's own preoccupations were with coaling provision, knowing that the high speed of his squadron would produce unprecedented demands, and gunnery problems. A submission from Chatfield, an eminent gunnery specialist, is remarkable for its admission of the battle-cruisers' vulnerability to shell and torpedo hits which could reduce their speed at the beginning of an action, thus depriving them of their one basic advantage. From this he deduced that they should never operate too far away from supporting battle squadrons in case they should be overwhelmed by a superior enemy force. Beatty was reluctant to accept this and insisted that risks must be taken. He was more in agreement with Chatfield's argument that he should aim to manoeuvre his squadron into a favourable tactical position before opening fire so as to avoid the inaccurate gunnery inevitably caused by major changes of course once the engagement had begun [49,50].

Convinced though he was that war was inevitable, and determined as he was to maintain the strength of his squadron in readiness for it, Beatty did not expect hostilities to begin in the

[1]For the 1913 manoeuvres see Marder, *From the Dreadnought* Vol. 1, pp. 353–8.

summer of 1914. He did not even foresee the ceremonial visit to Russia on which his wife was to join him.[1] Reality came with the decisions to keep the fleet mobilised after the Spithead review, and to send it North at the end of July. As he shouldered the burdens of war, Beatty was apprehensive of how Ethel would react and was relieved by her determination and energy in converting their yacht *Sheelah* into a hospital ship. She of course was delighted that this would enable her to follow the fleet to its war stations [51–59].

---

[1]For the Russian visit see W. S. Chalmers, *The Life and Letters of David, Earl Beatty* (London, 1951), pp. 126–31.

33. *From Admiralty*

[BTY/2/4/1]   Admiralty, S.W.
1st February 1913

I am commanded by My Lords Commissioners of the Admiralty to acquaint you that they have selected you to succeed Rear Admiral Lewis Bayly, CVO, CB[1] as Rear Admiral Commanding the First Battle Cruiser Squadron.

Orders have been given for your Flag to be hoisted at Devonport in such ship as the Commander-in-Chief may select on the 1st March and to be transferred to H.M.S. *Lion* on the following day.

Rear Admiral Bayly's Flag will be struck in H. M. S. *Lion* at sunset on the 1st March.

34. *Filson Young, 'The Things that Matter', Pall Mall Gazette*

[BTY/2/4/2]   3 March 1913

On Saturday at Devonport the flag of Rear-Admiral David Beatty was hoisted on H.M.S. *Lion*.

It was apparently an unimportant matter — merely a square of white crossed with the cross of St. George, floating up over the dirt and litter of the dockyard. The public knows little of the individual lives that are spent at sea in its service; half-a-dozen names at most become familiar, and David Beatty is too young to be even a name to the man in the street. But those who do know him look to him for more than name — for the highest fame, if time and the hour are favourable. He is not only the youngest Naval officer of his rank in the world, but by becoming an Admiral at thirty-nine he outstripped even Nelson in rapidity of promotion and established a record in the Naval service of the world. Distinguished war services in Egypt and China did that for

[1]Later Admiral Sir Lewis Bayly (1857–1938): entered RN 1872; Rear-Admiral 1908; President RN War College Portsmouth 1908–11; Commanding 1st Battle-Cruiser Squadron 1912; 3rd Battle Squadron 1913; 1st Battle Squadron 1914; Vice-Admiral commanding Channel Fleet 1914; Admiral President RNC Greenwich 1915; commanding Western Approaches in charge of ASW 1915; Admiral 1917; retired 1919.

him; and now, after two years as Naval Adviser to the First Lord
of the Admiralty, he goes to sea in command of the First Battle
Cruiser Squadron to put the crown — or the extinguisher — on
his naval career.

For there comes a time in the life of every such man when the
beams of a fortunate star, the promise and brilliant performance
of youth, must be answered for and justified if he is to make good
his title to greatness. No one who knows Beatty has any doubts
or fears for him. He will 'make good'. It will be done after the
manner of his profession, in the lonely places of the sea, out of
sight and knowledge of the public. All we can do is to give his
flag a cheer as it disappears below the horizon, and watch for its
coming again with honour and perhaps — who knows? — with
glory.

Perhaps there will be nothing for some years but brief sentences
in the small type devoted to Naval intelligence. But to such as can
discern his movements in that, I say 'Keep your eye on Beatty'.

35. *To his wife* [Monaco]

[BTY/17/22/15]   *Lion*
                                                     [Glengariff]
                                            Tuesday [1 April 1913]

*   *   *

We spent the day doing practice at anchor, so I trotted my
round little Flag Lieutenant for a good long walk ashore. He is a
very nice little man and I like him very much, more so than I did
my first one, and in fact I like all my staff. They are all intelligent
and charming, which is not a very common combination.[1]

*   *   *

The Germans are fairly setting about creating a formidable
Aerial Force & it behoves us to move rapidly to provide a means
of defeating them. I am busy preparing a scheme for the defence
of our ships, which at present are absolutely at their mercy, a
little matter which has been overlooked in the past, with a possible
case for disaster if we are not prepared soon.

*   *   *

[1]For an assessment of Beatty's staff see Roskill, *Admiral of the Fleet Earl Beatty,
The Last Naval Hero: An Intimate Biography* (London, 1981) pp. 59–60; the
Flag Lieutenant Ralph Seymour (1886–1922) was not a signals specialist and his
performance at the Dogger Bank and Jutland has been criticised.

36. Beatty's 'Functions of a Battle-Cruiser Squadron'[1]

[BTY/2/4/3]   *Lion*
[Holograph]   [5 April 1913]
[Draft]

A   Supporting a rapid reconnaissance by very fast light cruisers
    (27 or 25 knotters) on the enemy coast, at a high speed
    and sweeping a large area of hostile craft which sweep or
    reconnaissance could only be interrupted by a strong force of
    enemy battleships.
B   Supporting a blockading force of a patrol of armoured
    cruisers.
C   Forming the supports between an armoured cruiser force and
    the battle fleet when cruising.
D   Forming the supports to a cruiser force watching an enemy's
    battle fleet at sea.
E   *and Final Function:* Forming the first division of a battle fleet
    in a general action.

The squadron is composed of vessels possessed of the offensive
power of a battleship with a speed far greater than a cruiser but
with a considerably reduced defensive. The power of the ship is
to be gauged by her offensive rather than her defensive, and the
best defensive is an overpowering offensive. Therefore it cannot
be too much emphasised that when concentrated as a squadron
the fighting effectiveness of each unit of the squadron is increased
by the overwhelming offensive power it is able to develop as a
whole.

From a study of the great naval wars, it is impressed upon one
that cruiser Captains — which of necessity must include battle-
cruiser Captains — to be successful must possess in a marked
degree: initiative, resource, determination, and no fear of
accepting responsibility. To enable them to make the best use of
these sterling qualities, they should be given the clearest indication
of the functions and duties of the unit to which they belong, as
comprehended by the Commander of that unit. They should be
completely comprehensive of his mind and intentions.

Cruiser Captains cannot be too often reminded that: In war
more things occur to distract a man from the road he has entered

[1]For the provenance of this document and its connection with later Battle Orders
see Roskill, p. 381, n. 34. See also 43 below for draft orders of 17 July 1913.

upon, to make him doubt himself and others, than in any other human activity. Here therefore nothing else will help but an imperative maxim of von Clausewitz, which is 'In all doubtful cases adhere to the first opinion and not give it up until a clear conviction forces us to do so.' Von Clausewitz has impressed upon us that 'A great part of information in war is contradictory, a greater part false, and the greatest part doubtful.' Therefore a certain power of discrimination is necessary for the officer and the law of probability must be his guide.

War is a perpetual conflict with the unexpected. The far greater part of those things upon which action in war must be calculated are hidden in great uncertainty. Therefore it is imperative that Captains should be supplied with all the information available, to enable the Admiral to rely upon them to grasp the situation and pursue it with resolution, using their own discretion how to act under conditions which could not have been anticipated by him. Instructions issued should be such as not to interfere with the exercise of the judgement of the Captains and should — 'except in very exceptional cases' — be of a very general character.

In considering the functions of the battle-cruiser squadron as enumerated above, it becomes apparent that with the exception of the ones labelled A & E, the predominant factor is that of acting as a *support* and all cases can be considered as one. So, if we consider B in detail, C & D may be accepted as similar, supporting a force driven in by a superior force which would consist of a strong force of armoured cruisers, or battle-cruisers. In either case it would be safe to assume that the enemy force would be a concentrated force to meet which effectively our supporting force should be a concentrated force. In the event of the enemy force being a battle-cruiser force we must be prepared to meet it with a force superior to the known total battle-cruiser force at the disposal of the enemy. Our prospective enemy is known to at present have three BCs, very shortly to be increased to four. Furthermore it must be assumed that any offensive operation undertaken would be at his selected moment in a concentrated form.

In view of the fact that Function B would if undertaken be more than likely to continue for a very considerable period of time, which would necessitate a careful scheme of reliefs for coaling, it it obvious that out of a squadron of 5 BCs only 4 would be available or out of 4 only 3 to form the supports with which to meet this attack & prevent our armoured cruisers from being swallowed up in detail. Therefore it would appear to be imperative that in circumstances in which our prospective enemy can produce three BCs we should have at *least* four & when four at least five in the supporting force.In disposing of the supporting force in the performance of Function B, the factors which have to be considered are

(a)   The best relative positions of the support to the cruisers.
(b)   The distance of the support from each other.
(c)   The quickest and surest method of asking for support at the same time indicating position, course & speed in view of the almost certain W. T. interference.

In considering (a) and (b) we have to take into account the difficulties to be surmounted as represented by 1st; *Weather Conditions* which can be faithfully assumed to be as disadvantageous to our force as inversely they are favourable to the enemy force and vice versa, which can be considered as several points in favour of the enemy who has the advantage of selecting his moment. To meet this difficulty little can be done beyond closing in the lines of cruisers and supports and making more certain of a portion of the line. This is a doubtful advantage but local circumstances might point to its being advantageous.

2nd; *Destroyer attacks by night and submarine attacks by day*. Destroyer attack by night can be minimised by allotting a period of time before dark to each cruiser to steam at a high speed in the direction from which such an attack may be expected and breaking up any destroyer organisation that may be preparing an attack during the dark hours, returning to the fixed or arranged point at the allotted hour and retiring during the night at a reduced speed, thus causing any attack that would be made to in all probability come from an after bearing. At all times a cruiser can minimise the danger of a destroyer attack by turning to bring it on an after bearing.

The same remarks apply to the supports who are much less likely to be attacked owing to the screen of cruisers between it and the enemy. The cruisers, if not breaking up any attack, would give the supports ample warning.

Submarine attack can only be frustrated by a sharp look-out, speed and continual alteration of course.

Therefore we can assume that insofar as the difficulties brought about by bad weather conditions and destroyers & submarine attack, the relative position of the supports and the cruisers is not much affected provided the distance between them is not great, say under ¾ hours combined speed.

(a) To determine the best relative position of the supports to the cruisers, the factors to be considered are

1st   The strength of the cruiser force.
2nd   The length of line (Cruisers).
3rd   Visibility.
4th   The distance from the enemy base.
5th   The possible geographical advantages and disadvantages that might exist.

1st. & 2nd. can be taken together and in cases where the length of line is short and cruiser strength considerable they can turn to each other for mutual support in certain cases but such cases are likely to be rare, as stated before, attack on the cruiser line wd almost assuredly be of a concentrated nature. Therefore it might be accepted, as wd always be the case if the line was long with long intervals between cruisers, that it is to the supports that they would turn for assistance which wd also insure that the line wd not be broken except at the point of contact. This would also leave the remaining cruisers of the line free to investigate what was behind the advanced enemy cruiser force, & if enemy battle fleet, locate it & keep touch. Therefore it can be generally stated that in nearly all cases cruisers wd turn to supports for assistance rather than to their next in line. To preserve the utility of the cruiser line it should not be permitted to be broken for any length of time. Therefore the supports should not be too far.

3rd. Assuming a general visibility of 5 miles cruisers should be closely supported, say 20 miles or ½ hour combined steaming, or they are in serious danger of being overtaken and destroyed by enemy battle-cruisers. But with a visibility of 10, supports could be further away, say at 30 miles, but never more. Both distances should enable supports to receive ample warning of the approach of torpedo craft, the likelihood of attack from which is governed in a measure by Factor 4.5th Factor. Geographical conditions must invariably be taken into account as circumstances admit. Therefore we assume at this fact [sic] that supports should be between 20 & 30 miles in rear of the cruiser line.

We now come to;

(b) The distance of supports from each other. As has been

previously stated supports to be effective and to avoid themselves being overwhelmed must be concentrated, or so disposed as to be able to concentrate with ease. But they should always be in pairs, each pair should never be more than ½ hours combined steaming apart, i.e. 25 miles or 30 miles at the extreme.

Thus if [a] cruiser line 100 miles long had two pairs of supports 30 miles in its rear 30 miles apart, the wing cruisers would be 45 miles from supports or practically 1 hour's steaming at combined speed, & if supports were 20 miles in rear of crs. line, 38 miles from supports or ¾ hour combined steaming. Outside these distances it wd not appear to be practicable to go, but exercises of the nature of those to be carried out 15th to 19th April should throw much light on the subject.

We now deal with;

(c) The quickest and surest method of communicating with supports and supports with each other in view of the almost certain W. T. interference.

This requires minute investigation as it is a possible source of considerable embarrassment and on the successful overcoming of which the efficient supporting of each other depends.[1] [CCC/Drax/4/1]

To meet this the following points require attention:-

All ships should be carefully tuned with loose couplings, and receiving ships should have opportunity to get accurate adjustments for all ships that may send to them.

Signals *must* be brief. To contain the necessary information in its most concise form it is essential that the Officer drafting a signal should have a good knowledge of the Wireless Code book.

Ships in visual touch should exchange visually all information that they collect by W. T.

Cruisers in sight of the enemy must continue sending off information though interference may prevent them hearing any replies to their signals.

If interference is on a low note it may be possible to get through by changing quickly to a high note.

It is useful to fit a wavemeter in the receiving circuit as an additional rejector.

A thoroughly efficient code staff is essential; without it cruiser operations become almost impossible.

Wireless Officers should realise that the efficiency of material

---

[1]The holograph finishes here. A typed copy in the Drax papers (4/1) includes the missing section.

is only a small portion of the preparation necessary to success.
The training of personnel and a careful study of the organisation
of communications in all its details are factors requiring constant
attention.

It is important for cruisers while engaged to be able to send
wireless from behind armour, and to shift to or from that position
without delaying communications.

37. *To his wife* [Monaco]

[BTY/17/23/15–16]   *Lion*
                                                        [Bantry]
                                                       5.4.1913

*   *   *

We have had several additions to our squadron and consequently I am commanding quite a respectable force here; two
battleships, eight first class cruisers & battle-cruisers, 6 mine-layers
and two fast new light cruisers, so we are somewhat congested. I
spend most of the day, when not at sea, writing and inspecting.
The former takes most of my time, and my mornings are very
full, seeing officers who arrive and trying to keep pace with the
paper work. I play golf in the afternoon and return about five,
when I find time to read, and after dinner I spend again writing
and am kept at it until midnight most nights. In fact it is midnight
now and I haven't wasted many minutes during the day which
gives me a sense of satisfaction, whether one has accomplished
anything or not, and so the days go by. Tomorrow, Sunday, I
have a busy day inspecting one of the ships and seeing the men.
I stop on board to church and make everybody's acquaintance
and get to know them, and they get to know me, which is a good
thing for us all. Monday we are out firing all day. In fact I am
taking the squadron out and go on board each ship as she fires,
which means a busy day as we shall be out all day. And so the
world, our little world, goes on, no better & no worse than
anybody else. But if we achieve some modicum of success in the
end it will pay, but nobody else will ever know it. . . .

38.   *To his wife* [Monaco]

[BTY/17/23/22–3]   *Lion*
                                                            At sea
                                                          9.4.1913

We left Berehaven last night and have been exercising at sea
most of the day with varying results, but I hope much instruction,
certainly to myself. I learnt a great deal of the greatest value, and
others should have benefitted in a like degree. The great difficulty
is to drive the lessons home and see that none are forgotten.
Therefore one has to look at everything from the schoolmaster's
point of view so that nothing is lost that comes from experience.
No doubt I shall be better with practice. We have had a beautiful
day as far as weather is concerned but as we approached the
English coast it gradually became worse, colder and damper with
a strong N.W. wind, which is not so pleasant as that we have had,
but produces conditions from our point of view more realistic,
which has its advantages. We arrive at daylight tomorrow and
spend the next two days in coaling and conferring, both of which
very necessary adjuncts of the Naval Service.

*   *   *

39.   *To his wife* [Paris]

[BTY/17/23/25–6]   [Turf Club, London]
                                         Friday [11th] April [1913]

When we got in I found most people away so I made the
necessary arrangements and came up this afternoon and am now
trying to find somebody to dine with. We are all coaling today
and tomorrow, so shall go back tomorrow after noon for a conference of admirals on Saturday evening.

Winston has written to ask if I can take him out with me for
the manoeuvres or rather the tactical exercises, which commence
on Monday. So of course I shall and I hope to be able to squeeze
some sense into him, and something useful out of him for the
good of the squadron in particular and the Service in general. It
will add to the excitement any way as he will want to know so
much, but I hope it is not his intention to make a general practice

of it, or else it would be inclined to pall after a bit, fond as I am of our Winnie.

*   *   *

40. *To his wife* [Paris]

[BTY/17/23/28]   Hanover Lodge
Friday 11 April 1913

I hear there is a long article on the subject of my humble self in last Sat's *Saturday Review*, signed by Signifex, which is fulsome in its laudatory tone. This is Filson Young, I feel sure. I wish to heaven he wouldn't. I personally hate it and it does me no good. Everybody naturally asks me how much did I pay for it and classes me as an advertiser, which, whatever my faults, I am not. I suppose he thinks he is making me, as he said the journalist Stevens made Kitchener !!!? I don't like it. I don't want it and I won't have it. But how am I to stop it? Thank the Lord he hasn't very much left to say from all accounts & it will die a natural death. But it does me harm in the Navy who can't abide the advertisement of a newspaper, and those who don't know me, of which there are thousands, will wrongly construe it.

*   *   *

41. *To his wife*

[BTY/17/24/17–19]   *Lion*
[Portree, Skye]
[8 May 1913]

You must not bother Prince Louis or Winston by asking them where we are going to and to send them (the 1st Battle-Cruiser Squadron) here or there because you want to spend Whitsuntide with me. It won't do. It's good enough for the War Office but not the Admiralty, and they have a good deal to do without having to consider which port they send ships to will suit the wives best.

It was stupid of me wiring you to ask Eddy Marsh,[1] as when once one is started asking questions there is no end, and I thought he could answer himself. I wrote to Prince Louis myself urging him to send us back to the east coast if all dangers of complications were past, so that we could get on with our practices which we cannot do here, and he will think that it is collusion between us, which is the last thing I should like him to think of, and I wish I had never written him and if it hadn't gone when I got yours I would have torn it up.

Everything seems to have settled down and there is much more peace in the air than for some time. But that is always a dangerous period after a strained time and I don't honestly think we are out of the wood yet. The Albanian principality is like to raise questions of a complexity, to which that of Scutari was a mere nothing and we might still expect to see drastic action on the part of Austria which will set everybody by the ears again, and it looks to me as if it was leaning that way. Twice a year we have regular shocks of the same nature and they are getting too frequent now to be healthy and they will come oftener before long, when flesh & blood will stand no more & there will be a breakdown in the diplomacy which will upset everything.

*   *   *

It is still blowing like fury here but we are able to get on with our coaling and have just done a very good one, 300 tons an hour, a long way the best they have ever done and so they are all very pleased and elated. I've spent 5 hours writing and my fingers are getting stiff, so shall go ashore for a walk and get some fresh air which will do me good and easy [sic] my brain box a little. I can put in a lot of work in these places, which is something, but not getting very much real exercise shall soon get fat and bald, but no doubt I'll soon get it off again.

*   *   *

I went and had a good tramp by myself. It was blowing too hard to be pleasant & I hated it, but it no doubt did me good. It is not all beer & skittles here, nothing to do but to write.My recreation is my work and my labour is walking ashore to prevent getting livery and bad tempered, and the Lord knows I don't succeed very well. But all things considered, it is for the best & I feel that I am doing something and not idling. Everybody has

[1]Sir Edward Marsh (1872–1953): civil servant; Private Secretary to Churchill when Under Secretary for Colonies 1905; served him when in office for the next 23 years, including his time as 1st Lord 1911–15.

to sacrifice something in his life and if we only lived for pleasure &
the joys of life, they would soon pall and we would have nothing
to fall back upon.

42.   *To CinC Home Fleets*

[CCC/DRAX/4/1]   *Lion*
[COPY]   Queensferry
                                                              4 June 1913

   In accordance with Home Fleet Memorandum No. 0184 of 4th
May 1913, I have the honour to forward the following remarks
on the enclosure thereto.
   2. I am generally in agreement with the deductions stated in
the Memorandum, which presents a valuable and exhaustive
enquiry into the use of torpedo craft in battle. All things
considered, it appears fairly certain that the position for T.B.D.
operations will usually be on the flanks of the line of battle, where
it is possible that their influence might be so great as to decide
the action. It is on the flanks of the line however that light cruisers
and also the battle-cruisers will be required to act. I therefore
submit that the destroyer problem is one which particularly
concerns the 1st Battle-Cruiser Squadron, as representing the
most powerful force, and probably the Senior Officer, in that
area.
   3.   To consider the Memorandum in detail —
        EMPLOYMENT OF DESTROYERS IN COMPANY
        WITH A BATTLE FLEET.
        A.   *In a Fleet Action*
             There are two main considerations:-
             1st.   Attack on enemy ships.
             2nd.   Attack or counter attack on enemy torpedo
                    craft.
             1st. (a)   In clear weather.
                   (b)   In thick or misty weather.
                   (c)   The best position from which to deliver the
                         attack.
   (a) In this the long range torpedo, enabling the T.B D. to keep
out of range of the anti T.B.D. gun, is the deciding factor.
   (b) Misty weather increases opportunities for attack in the early

stages. Endeavour should be made to bring off a successful attack as early as possible. It cannot be emphasised too strongly that the Fleet which develops its T.B.D. attack first will gain an advantage the usefulness of which it would be difficult to measure. The effectivenes of the torpedo fire would not be the only ruling factor, as the moral effect produced would almost certainly cause a considerable alteration of course on the part of the enemy, thereby upsetting them at the commencement of an action and producing a tactical advantage for the development of our gunfire which at this stage would be of inestimable value.

(c) Attack from before the beam. The time taken to bring off the attack being of much shorter duration minimises the chance of its being interrupted.

Attack from abaft the beam — would not in any degree offer the same chances of success as that before the beam — certainly not at the commencement of a Fleet action. A destroyer attack from before the beam, if successful in securing a good position to fire torpedoes, would assuredly cause the enemy line to make some considerable alteration of course which they had previously no intention of making, thus presenting some tactical advantage to our line, whereas an attack from abaft the beam would not necessitate so large an alteration of course on the part of the enemy, and thus no great tactical advantage would be gained by our line. It must not be lost sight of, however, that during a Fleet action, what is abaft the beam in one phase might easily be before the beam in a secondary phase, by the Fleet being caused to make a 16 point turn to avoid a T.B.D. attack on the part of the enemy, as outlined above. Therefore the ideal would be to have strong flotillas at each end of the line.

4. To station destroyers *to attack disabled ships* would necesitate having a very large number at our disposal, which is unlikely and they would be better employed in endeavouring to make successful attacks on enemy ships still in the line, leaving these disabled to be dealt with afterwards.

5. The 'THROUGH THE LINE ATTACK' has so many disadvantages on the face of it that unles it is thoroughly practised, and all the advantages and shortcomings brought to light, it would be difficult to advance an opinion of any value on its possibilities.

6. *A* (2nd).   Attack or counter attack on enemy torpedo craft. The best possible defence against an enemy attack by torpedo craft would be by the proper disposal of light cruisers. Under no circumstances is it conceivable that our own Destroyer Force could

frustrate the enemy T.B.D.s attack on our Battle Fleet, once the latter had launched their attack, *unless* our destroyers were in a position ahead much nearer the enemy fleet than our own fleet, where they would be liable to be cut up by enemy light cruisers or, by a sudden alteration of course cut off from support and prevented from coming into action at all.

If they occupied a position as shown in Diagram I of Commander-in-Chief's Memorandum, and the enemy torpedo craft from a somewhat similar position with regard to their Fleet, launched their attack against our Battle Fleet (assuming that the enemy craft and torpedoes were as efficient as our own), they would be in a position to fire their torpedoes before any counter attack could be delivered to prevent them, as they would have to go only 2000 yards against the 3000 yards which the counter attacking force would have to cover before getting within effective gun range.

7. It would therefore appear that the only effective counter attack on the part of our T.B.D.s would be a similar attack upon the enemy Battle Fleet, with this disadvantage, that the enemy torpedo craft having discharged their torpedoes at our Battle Fleet are in a good position to turn their entire attention on engaging frustrating the attack of our T.B.D.s.

This again emphasises the absolute necessity of getting in our T.B.D. attack *first*.

8. As stated in H. F. 0184, light cruisers are the *only* proper means of defence against torpedo craft in a Fleet action, and destroyers could not, except under very exceptional circumstances, take their place. Ships of the line must depend upon their own gun-fire and alteration of course to frustrate the attack if allowed to develop.

The statement that light cruisers are the proper reply to enemy T.B.D.s applies only in cases where the attack is on a flank and not 'through the line', when the battle line can expect no extraneous support to ward off attack.

Light cruisers placed 4 points on the bow to prevent torpedo craft attack would also perform the duty of destroying any craft detached to drop mines as suggested in paragraph 20.

9. Light cruisers much be supported to avoid destruction by enemy armoured cruisers. This opens up a larger and more important question which affects the 1st Battle-Cruiser Squadron very considerably in the performance of its function as a fast division of the line.

If the 1st Battle-Cruiser Squadron occupied a position ahead of the Battle Fleet, light cruisers placed to prevent attack from enemy T.B.D.s would be immune from attack by enemy cruisers — the 1st B.C.S. providing sufficient support. But at the same time it must be considered that the 1st B.C.S. would themselves become the object of attack by enemy T.B.D.s, and in any endeavour to place themselves in a good tactical position ahead of the enemy battle line, they would undoubtedly have to be prepared to meet a strong T.B.D. attack.

For this purpose they *must* be able to fight *all* their anti torpedo craft guns, instead of only half as at present, while they are heavily engaged with their main armament.

It is thus seen that the duties of the 1st Battle-Cruiser Squadron, light cruisers and destroyers on a flank co-mingle and should be co-ordinated one with the other.

10. From the above the following principles are deduced:-

(a) Enemy's destroyer attacks from ahead, or the bow, must be repelled by all vessels at the head of the line: light cruisers for preference, battle-cruisers almost unavoidably, and T.B.D.s if necessary.

(b) For this duty, and in self defence, battle cruisers *must* be able to fight their anti T.B. guns while heavily engaged with their main armament.

(c) The primary duty of destroyers in battle, when possible, is to proceed ahead and pour in a long range torpedo fire at the enemy's leading battleships. If, say, 16 or 32 torpedoes were fired at the commencement of an action, 20 per cent of hits might well produce irreparable confusion.

Having delivered this attack, they should then assist in engaging the enemy's destroyers.

(d) The T.B.D.s in company should be as numerous as possible and should be divided in 3 equal groups, taking station as follows when the fleet deploys. One group on each flank, one in the centre of the line to proceed at full speed for the van as soon as it is seen which way the fleets turn on engaging. Thus ^{2}/$_3$rds of the available destroyer force will automatically be at the head of the line.

(e) As soon as the role of these vessels in action is definitely decided it is most necessary that every step of their possible movements should be fully practised in peace exercises. Also their training should be amended if necessary, particularly as regards firing salvoes of torpedoes from flotillas or half flotillas. Decisive results cannot be expected unless torpedoes are fired in large numbers.

(f) It may of course occur that our destroyers are required to attack the enemy's destroyers if no more suitable vessels are available. But destroyers are not ideally suited for this duty, and in performing it they would certainly be assisted by all other vessels in the vicinity. Assuming the head of the line to be the chief point of danger from enemy T.B.D.s, it seems more probable that we should have light cruisers and battle-cruisers in a position to repel them than we should have flotillas, which admittedly may be absent. The light cruiser is the ideal vessel for the purpose, but the battle-cruiser, in the performance of its primary duty (gun and torpedo attack on the flank of the enemy's battle line) will be so placed that not only it can aid in repelling a T.B.D. attack, but in self defence will be compelled to do so.

11.   *B. at other times* (not during battle).
         Destroyers with a squadron by day may be used —
         As look-outs.
         As a screen against submarines and hostile T.B. craft.

As look-outs, the remarks contained in paragraph 25 of H.F. 0184 are concurred in, and in consequence of the amount of fuel that would have to be used by them with all boilers alight it is not considered that they could maintain their position as distant look-out for any length of time in the performance of a duty which at best they could only carry out inefficiently.

12. As a screen against submarines; undoubtedly in this capacity T.B.D.s can perform a duty of real value; in fact it might be said that they would form the only useful protection against submarines. Their efficiency in this depends mainly on sufficiency of numbers.

13. Employed as a *defence* against hostile torpedo craft; in this capacity we have them employed in their proper sphere as pointed out in paragraph 2 of H.F. 0184. To perform this duty effectively they should be in close order not spread as a screen, if possible in two divisions one on each bow of the Flagship at fairly close signalling distance ready to be hurled at an enemy force directly it is sighted. It should be possible to combine the two duties of acting as a screen against submarines and at the same time protect the Fleet against attack by enemy torpedo craft by day, and the necessary essentials of being spread for the one and being concentrated for the other should be capable of combination by practice and due consideration.

43.   *Confidential Battle Orders for 1st BCS*

[CCC/DRAX/1/2]   *Lion*
[Draft]   Scapa Flow
                                      17 July 1913

No 015 MEMORANDUM

These orders are sub-divided for dealing with 3 cases:

A.   When engaged with battle or armoured cruisers.
B.   When engaging the rear ships of a retreating fleet, with a view to causing delay so that our own fleet may come up and engage.
C.   When forming the fast division of the Battle Fleet in general action.

2.   *Case A* might occur when acting as supports or in various other circumstances, and it is very probable that the squadron would be spread. In this event the principles laid down in paragraphs 3 and 4 of my 0142 of 11 June 1913 are to be taken as a guide. . . . The following further instructions apply generally to Case A: The order of battle, unless chasing, will be in single line ahead.

3.   After opening fire every effort must be made to keep the 'A arc' bearing steadily. Alterations of course should be small — not exceeding 2 points if possible — and made with small helm, usually 10 to 15 degrees.

4.   If ordered to form a line of bearing, or reform, while engaged, the smallest possible amount of helm should be used consistent with rapid execution.

5.   If, as may happen, the Admiral is not leading the line, the leader is to hoist 4 Pendant without signal.

6.   Re signals in action: guiding principle in single line, 'Each ship is responsible for her next astern'. If, as is quite likely, the Rear Admiral does not wait for all ships to repeat close up, the last ship that has repeated the signal is to keep it flying after Flagship hauls down, until next astern has seen it: ships in rear to act similarly until the last ship has got it.

7.   *Case B*. When fighting a retarding action with rear ships of an enemy's fleet, it is possible that some of them may be already damaged and reduced in speed. Fire will be concen-

trated on these, and the squadron will be manoeuvred in line abreast or quarter line, according to the bearing of the enemy, and opened out to considerable intervals when within range of the enemy's torpedoes.

8. *Case C. General Action.* It may be expeced that the Commander-in-Chief would use the fast division for attacking the enemy's flank and the squadron must therefore be prepared to attack either van or rear. To attain quickly a good tactical position full speed will be needed, not only during the approach but perhaps also while engaged.

9. Much will depend on whether the enemy's van or rear is attacked. If the van, one of our chief objects will be to pour in a steady fire with long range torpedoes.

10. Very probably we shall have to meet a determined attack by the enemy's torpedo craft, directed at either the battle-cruisers or our own battle line; in either case the anti-torpedo guns must be ready to open fire instantly for repelling this attack. Similarly the squadron must be prepared to deal effectively with the enemy's armoured cruiser force, whether acting as supports or attempting to attack the flank of our battle line with gun and torpedo. In so doing we should also afford necessary protection to our own flotillas near by, and thus assist and support them in advancing to make their attack.

11. If the enemy's rear is to be attacked, it will be necesary to open out to 4 or 5 cables apart when within range of enemy torpedoes, or to steer a course which will reduce their chance of hitting. A sharp look-out should also be kept for submarines, which may be found near the rear of the enemy's line.

12. Whether at the van or rear, our final aim must be to concentrate on the flank battleships of the enemy and to press in, provided they are engaged by our own battlefleet, to such [short] range that our fire may have decisive results.

13. Much must be left to the initiative and judgement of Captains. They are relied upon to act promptly in battle on their own initiative for dealing with all cases such as the following:-

(a) 2 or more ships requiring to concentrate fire on one of the enemy.

(b) Altering course to avoid torpedoes, or extending the gaps in the line as a precautionary measure.

(c) Making small alterations of course to fire torpedoes. N. B. Care should be taken to right the helm and resume station as soon after as possible.

(d) Hauling out of the wake of next ahead to avoid smoke or backwash. N. B. It is desirable that ships should not haul out more than 1 point, lest they hamper the squadron when turning in succession. If 1 point is insufficient, ships should avoid smoke interference by opening out.

(e) Altering line of bearing from Flag in order to get a clearer arc of fire.

(f) Or any other case in which Captains consider that prompt action is needed, and their movements are such as the Rear Admiral would certainly approve if they could be made known to him beforehand. The chief limitation in these cases is that no movement must mask the fire of other ships, or in any way inconvenience them from a manoeuvring point of view.

14. Concentration of fire to be arranged as laid down in Home Fleet General Order No 15.

15. The above describes briefly the main outline of our duties in a Fleet Action. . . .

The Commanding Officers,
   1st Battle Cruiser Squadron.

44. *To his wife* [Hanover Lodge]

[BTY/17/25/20–2]   *Lion*
[At Sea]
23.7.13

. . .

I found at Queensferry the 1st Lord in *Enchantress* with a large party of naval experts, all except one amateurs; Colonel Seely,[1]

---

[1] J. E. B. Seely, later Lord Mottistone (1868–1947) : Conservative MP 1900; followed Churchill to Liberals 1906; Parliamentary Under Secretary for Colonies 1908; Secretary for War 1912; resigned over Curragh incident March 1914.

Sir John French,[1] Ashley St Leger, a young soldier, name unknown, Jack Churchill the secretary of the Defence Committee who is a marine,[2] a Major Oliphant who apparently advises now on all naval strategy questions and old Custance[3] who never gives a direct opinion on any subject. They were just off to Scapa Flow when I pointed out that they would arrive there just in time to turn round & come back again, a distance of 430 miles, which the great strategists had evidently overlooked. So they elected to remain where they were and go out this morning. I played a game of golf with Chatfield which did me good and dined onboard *Enchantress* where I heard much as to how things might be done and I burst a bomb by pointing out that if Jellicoe did a certain thing, which he probably would, nothing that the Blue C-in-C could do would stop him. This apprently developed a flaw in the general orders which was never intended and wires were sent off in every direction for explanations.

We started at 8 this morning, found it blowing very fresh with a lump of a sea. This will upset the amateur strategists onboard *Enchantress* who have probably all taken to their beds, they looked very yellow last night.We were unfortunate in getting a very heavy sea onboard which damaged seriously Lieutenant Johnson[4] and 5 men. Lucky none were washed overboard. Poor Johnson dislocated his hip, which is serious and the others, broken bones and some severe gashes.

24th

Old Brock[5] in the *Princess Royal* got lost and I had a job to find him; lucky he wasn't required as a fighting unit before 9

[1]Later Field Marshal Sir John French and Earl Ypres (1852–1925): RN cadet 1866; transferred to Army 1870; distinguished service in Egypt and South Africa; CIGS 1912; CinC British Expeditionary Force August 1914–15.

[2]John (Jack) Churchill, Winston's brother (1880–1947): served in South African War and Gallipoli; a stockbroker in civilian life. 'The marine' was presumably Maurice Hankey, secretary to the CID. (See n. 2 on p. 156.)

[3]Admiral Sir Reginald Custance (1847–1935): DNI 1899–1902; Rear-Admiral 1902; Vice-Admiral 1906; 2nd-in-Command Channel Fleet 1907–8; Admiral 1908; not further employed and retired list 1912; a constant critic of Admiralty policies on both officers' education and ship construction; in favour of a study of war and strongly opposed to *Dreadnought* policy. His major work, *Naval Policy: A Plea for the Study of War* by 'Barfleur' was published in 1907.

[4]Lieutenant Hugh Johnson.

[5]Later Admiral of the Fleet Sir Osmond de Brock (1869–1947): entered RN 1882; Captain of the newly commissioned *Princess Royal* July 1913; Rear-Admiral commanding 1st Battle-Cruiser Squadron 1915; Chief of Staff to Beatty as CinC Grand Fleet November 1916; Vice-Admiral and DCNS when Beatty was appointed 1st Sea Lord 1919; CinC Mediterranean 1922–5; Admiral 1924; CinC Portsmouth 1926; Admiral of the Fleet 1929; retired list 1934.

o'clock this morning as he did not turn up till then, but now we are united. We hear wireless reports of all sorts of alarums going on in the southern area and I expect Jellicoe is doing exactly what I said he would do. We can get nothing very definite but gather that four battleships & 4 cruisers have escorted the transports to some landing place between Yarmouth and Flamborough Head and are endeavouring to land & there is certainly no force down there capable of stopping them, so they will in all probability succeed. In the meantime our C-in-C is dashing down there and has collected the squadrons (cruisers) in western areas to go there also, but they will arrive too late, I fear. We, with two cruiser squadrons, and our battle-cruiser squadron in support, are moving on our way unruffled and undisturbed except by the noise of the German guns away on the Norwegian coast at exercises, and have a great deal of interference from their wireless, which always chips in when we commence signalling, with such regularity that it has all the appearance of being done on purpose.

*   *   *

25th

We have just heard that the Red have landed 36,000 men at Grimsby and have decamped with the loss of one battleship, some destroyers and submarines and done what exactly I said they would do. Now we must wait for the next move. In the meanwhile we are ambling up & down doing nothing but burn coal, so much so that the *Princess Royal* will have to go in this afternoon to coal. . . .

45.   *To his wife* [Hanover Lodge]

[BTY/17/25/26–8]   *Lion*
                                                              [At sea]
                                                       Sunday, 27.7.13

. . .

The Admiralty on Friday, too late after the event, re-issued the Regulations & Instructions they imposed on the Blue, to give them at least a fair opportunity of dealing with raids. But the C-in-C for some reason made no alterations in his scheme of defence, with the result that Red started off another raiding party and, as far as I can hear, was as nearly as successful as the first one. We heard of them at midnight and all the cruisers were ordered down and we went in support at top speed. On the way we sighted the Red Battle Fleet, 2nd Division, their fast ships, at 5 am. This was the plum of their basket so got on to C-in-C and told him and then proceeded to dog them. They were much worried with our attentions and did all they could to shake us off, even cheating, as Jellicoe would, but it was no go.I thought we had him fairly as the C-in-C was in a splendid position to cut him off and he could never shake us off. But, there is always a but for some reason or other to be explained later, the C-in-C never came (he is a very slow starter), got involved in an engagement with the slow and unimportant division of the enemy, which he could well have left to his own slower ships, and wasted too long over them before getting started. We chased them right down, to nearly off Ostend!! before we had to give up as he could not get up in time. We gave them a real shake up and they went into the Nore to fill up with coal. They steamed wonderfully well, the six battleships and could do, apparently comfortably, 21½ knots which was very good. Of course for us it was nothing, but for battleships, very good. In the meantime Osmond de Brock in the *Princess Royal* coming out of the Firth of Forth got himself in the way of a submarine and was torpedoed and his speed reduced to 14 knots. So I've lost him for the rest of the Manoeuvres, which is a great nuisance. I haven't heard exactly what happened but apparently the C-in-C destroyed *Albemarle*, *Agamemnon* and *Vengeance*. The *Commonwealth* has been sunk and the *King Edward VII* & *Bellerephon* damaged, apparently all by submarines. We are on our way into Firth of Forth, so no doubt they will make a determined attack on us which we shall have difficulty in avoiding, and once more prove that the Firth of Forth is no use as a war anchorage. We have swallowed tons of coal and have a big coaling before us, but should finish at midnight and come out again in the dark when they won't see us. We had a very strenuous 24 hours during which I spent all but 2 on the bridge and slept like a log last night in consequence while we were returning to Firth of Forth.

Just as I expected, we were attacked by submarines outside the Firth and were only saved by making turns. It was the *Indefatigable* that was attacked. . . .

46. *To his wife* [Hanover Lodge]

[BTY/17/25/29–30]   *Lion*
[Firth of Forth]
28.7.13

We never departed at midnight after all as in the middle of the
night we received a signal to the effect [*sic*] that operations were
at an end. Consequently we put all the fires out, turned over and
went to sleep. . . .

I shall have in fact wired you Dover our movements, which are
to leave here tomorrow night or Wednesday morning, go to sea
for the tactical exercises or 2nd part of the manoeuvres, and which
will probably continue until Friday or Saturday, but where they
will finish up I cannot say. I should think in all probability somewhere in the region of this place, Firth of Forth or Cromarty. I
will wire you directly I know. It seems a great waste of coal for
you to go all the way to Plymouth, if you are going to come back
up the North Sea again. It is 480 miles there and back and actually
involves an expenditure of £40 on coal alone,to say nothing about
the stores necessary to run the yacht. . . .

I haven't seen a newspaper since Tuesday, except Saturday, so
do not know what has happened between. I thought when they
stopped the manoeuvres just as it was reaching a very interesting
stage, that it was on account of the Balkan situation again, which
certainly looks far from being settled or in a happy condition.

The manoeuvres as far as I can gather have turned out exactly
as I prognosticated. Nothing could stop Red landing if he made
up his mind at once, but there have been many interesting
features. Old Kit Craddock[1] was captured with his cruisers the
very first night. Since then he has not been heard of. They simply
can't find him.

Bayly was torpedoed three times in one day and is much upset.
In fact very few ships escaped altogether. The C-in-C however
bears up with the utmost calm and sang froid and nothing disturbs
him which is just what one wants in a C-in-C, except the old man
has got a very bad cold and ought to be in bed. He says he is
getting too old to be out of bed for more than three nights running.
He can just do 3 and no more. He is much more admirable when

[1]Craddock, Rear-Admiral Sir Christopher (1862–1914): entered RN 1875; Rear-
Admiral 1910; commanding North America and West Indies Station 1913; went
down with his ship at battle of Coronel November 1914.

things go wrong than when they go right, as he doesn't fuss and
takes things quite calmly, which is half the battle.

* * *

47. *To CinC Home Fleets*

[CCC/DRAX/4/1] *Lion*
Devonport
8th September 1913

In view of an Admiralty Letter S. 15000/13/17944 of 1st
September 1913, communicating Their Lordships' approval of an
estimate forwarded by the Admiral Superintendent, Malta for
fitting side-screens to *Indefatigable*, I have the honour to submit
that I may be informed whether it is intended to transfer that ship
to the Mediterranean Station.

2. Should this be the intention, the British and German Battle-
Cruiser Squadrons in the North Sea will be composed as follows:-

British	*German*
1. *Lion*	1. *Moltke*
2. *Princess Royal*	2. *Von der Tann*
3. *Queen Mary*	3. *Seydlitz*
4. *New Zealand*	4. *Goeben* (temporarily detached to Mediterranean)

3. I respectfully and earnestly submit that such a surrender of
numerical superiority in the North Sea would be a very great
error. The recent manoeuvres served to emphasise our need for
more battle-cruisers and it is considered that even if the *Indefatigable* were retained in this Squadron, the margin — 5 to 4 — is
insufficient.

4. It has been accepted that one of the principal functions of
the Battle-Cruiser Squadron is to provide supports for the cruiser
squadrons. Primarily of course, they need to be supported against
enemy battle cruisers, which are the greatest danger to our
cruisers, and therefore we must have in support a concentrated
force at least equal to that which could be sent out by the enemy.
Anything less than this would be courting disaster. With only four,
of which one would always be away coaling, we are reduced to a

bare equality leaving no margin for eventualities which, in a prolonged and active war, would be almost certain to reduce the strength of the squadron still further. Moreover this equality only exists until the *Derfflinger* is completed next summer, and provided that the *Goeben* is not brought home to the Squadron to which she belongs.

5. The main point to consider is the war stations and relative strength of the forces concerned. Taking first the German side, it is obvious that the *Goeben*'s war station is the North Sea. Alone in the Mediterranean she can achieve nothing, and her destruction is certain. But she can return at any time in a few days, she is due home shortly to refit, and it is therefore quite certain that her stay abroad will not be prolonged. This makes a force of 4 battle-cruisers in the North Sea on any date in the near future prior to strained relations.

6. It may be argued that if the *Goeben* returns home the *Inde-fatigable* could do likewise, but is is neither dignified nor politic that a German warship should have to be shadowed by a British one, particularly as this might happen at a time of strained relations. Obviously the situation turns on the *Goeben*, and one can look at it either way with the same result. If her war station is the North Sea, there is no adequate reason for sending the *Indefatigable* to the Mediterranean. But if her war station is to be the Mediterranean it will be for one reason only: because her detachment from the main theatre has been so successful in containing a larger (in fact vastly larger) British force, that the German Battle-Cruiser Squadron can hope for victory at the decisive point — i.e. in the North Sea.

7. I omit any discussion of the strategical situation in the Mediterranean, for I am sure it is already clear that our requirements there are not much better met by 4 battle-cruisers than they are by 3.

8. I doubt however if the gravity of the situation in the North Sea is sufficiently realised. The Germans can further increase their force by adding on the *Blücher*, only half a knot slower than the *Von der Tann*, while next year they add on the *Derfflinger* several months before the *Tiger* can possibly be ready.

9. Our Battle-Cruiser Squadron occupies a position of unique importance in war since it is, with its high speed and high offensive power, the one force to which the cruiser squadrons can look for support when employed in an advanced position: it should in fact by the keystone of the cruiser dispositions and as such should be

maintained at such strength that it would be capable of meeting under any circumstances that can be reasonably foreseen the German Battle-Cruiser Squadron consisting as it will in 12 months time of the *Derfflinger, Moltke, Von der Tann, Seydlitz* and *Goeben*, with the possible inclusion of the *Blücher*.

10. I submit that this situation calls urgently for the retention of the *Indefatigable* in Home waters.

48. *Admiral Sir George Callaghan's Review of the War Plans after Manoeuvres, 1913*

[BTY/2/4/5]   SECRET   2–3 October 1913

The Commander-in-Chief is held responsible for: —

(a) Frustrating invasion or serious military raids.
(b) Preventing the lines of the distant blockade (Northern Patrolling Force) being broken up.
(c) Effectually covering the transport of a British Expeditionary Force if such a course is decided upon.
(d) Bringing the enemy to battle on a good occasion.

According to paragraph 1 of part V (War Plans) the preliminary bases of the Grand Battle Fleet are on the west coast of Scotland, at such a distance from the theatre of operations in the North Sea that, in the event of Germany declaring war by attempting (a), it would be impossible for the Battle Fleet to arrive in time to prevent a landing if the attempt was covered by the German Battle Fleet.

It seems essential that the preliminary stations of the battle fleet should be on the east coast.

2. The natural and strategic bases on the east coast are, taking them in order from north to south:-

Scapa Flow
Cromarty
Firth of Forth
Humber
Thames

Of these, *Scapa Flow* is the best natural harbour, but it is unforti-fied, and its position is not strategically suited for our battlefleet under present conditions, owing to its distance from the probable area of operations.

The *Firth of Forth*, above Inchcolm and Oxcars, will hold any number of ships, and is protected by the heavy guns of the outer defences. The strategic position of the Firth of Forth is a very good one. The anchorage below the bridge is, however, not safe from attack by torpedo craft, while the berthing space at Rosyth is limited in extent, and will even now barely hold the First and Second Battle Squadrons; it will not do so when the newer and larger ships join the First Battle Squadron in lieu of the *Beller-ophon*s and *St Vincent*s.

The accommodation in *Cromarty* harbour for heavy ships is approximately similar to that at Rosyth, 27 big ship berths, 10 of which can take *Dreadnought*s. Guns are now being mounted for its defence; but its position is not strategically so good as the Forth.

The *Humber* is very well placed strategically and possesses a harbour which might be made suitable if large sums of money were spent on its development, but, besides being unfortified, it is within the easiest reach of the German bases, and is therefore the most liable to attack.

3. To whatever extent these harbours may be developed in the future, it is necessary to consider them as they are at present, and there seems no doubt that the Firth of Forth and Cromarty meet naval requirements better than the others.

The need, however, for increasing the available safe anchorage in the Forth is already very great, and will before long become imperative, and it is therefore strongly urged that steps should be taken to render the anchorage below the bridge safe for use by the Fleet.

This can be done by adopting the Inchcolm-Oxcars-Mickory line as the line of inner defence, as I have already recommended. I am prepared to report in more detail if required.

4. Briefly, my proposals are that, if matters become so acute between Great Britain and Germany as to require the concen-tration of our Fleet, the battle squadrons should be assembled at Rosyth and Cromarty.

In both places the sea-going flotillas, stiffened by light cruisers, would be required to patrol and guard the approaches. This is in addition to the torpedo boats and submarines of the patrol flotillas already earmarked for this work, and which might, or might not, be available.

Cruisers

5. With the withdrawal of the Fifth Cruiser Squadron and the appropriation of the Seventh Cruiser Squadron to the Southern portion of the North Sea, the cruiser squadrons remaining for duty with the Grand Fleet in the North Sea are:-

Ships

Second Cruiser Squadron	4 ⎫
Third Cruiser Squadron	4 ⎬ 12
Sixth Cruiser Squadron	4 ⎭

to which may be added the two light cruiser squadrons, making a maximum of 22 ships.

Cruisers must be withdrawn occasionally (by squadrons) to coal, and this, as far as experience goes, will reduce the number by one-third, leaving not more than 15 available at any moment for service.

If the Battle Fleet is in the North Sea, it must be covered by cruisers, to act as look-outs or as a screen; this is of far greater importance than the watching of areas, since it is essential that the battlefleet should be well supplied with intelligence of the enemy's movements, and that it should be guarded against surprise.

This being so, it is manifest that no provision can be made for any fixed observation system which has for its object the prevention of German ships breaking through to the North in order to deal with our 'Northern Patrolling Force', or to operate against our trade in the North Atlantic.

Destroyers

6. With regard to the offensive operations which can reasonably be expected of destroyers, the idea of using them for sweeping areas more or less remote from their bases, or out of immediate supporting distance of heavy ships, appears to be unsound, as such a policy militates against the principle of all available forces

being concentrated at the decisive moment. The subject generally is treated in a separate paper.

General

7. As long as the role of the British naval forces in the North Sea is to prevent this or that, and generally because we are debarred by geographical reasons from executing any strong offensive against an enemy unless they seek battle in the open sea, it is essential that our forces be concentrated.

The bare fact of having to act on the defensive means that we must continually be ready in some strategical position at sea; it means that our preponderance of power is reduced by almost a third owing to ships being absent fuelling or going to and from their stations; it means that we can never know when or where our enemy is going to strike, which greatly increases our difficulties.

To prevent raids, to defend the northern blockade, to cover the transport of the expeditionary force, to 'consider' the use of Norwegian fiords by the enemy, are all strings which pull the forces of the fleet in divergent directions, unless some strategically central position is made use of, which is a compromise to govern generally all directions of action without specially catering for one.

Northern Patrolling Force

8. With regard to the 'Northern Patrolling Force', for which the 10th and 11th Cruiser Squadrons (numbering at the outside twelve ships) are appropriated, it is observed that this force has to guard:-

(a) The Pentland Firth
(b) The Channel between Orkneys and Shetlands
(c) The space between North of Shetlands and coast of Norway (62° N)

To maintain the blockade for any length of time will necessitate at least one-fourth of the total force being off their stations, either coaling or going to and fro.

This reduces the number of ships available to nine, out of which:-

(a)   One must watch the Pentland Firth,
(b)   Two are required between the Orkneys and Shetlands,
(c)   Two are to be sent to the latitude of Tromsoe,

leaving but four (or five if (b) is reduced to one ship) to patrol a line 180 miles long. Such a blockade is not likely to be effective even supposing a condition of perpetual daylight, not to mention the periods of inaction which occur when dealing with the shipping.

It is considered that the remedy lies in providing Armed Merchant Ships of good steaming capabilities to reinforce this patrol.

Employment of Destroyers in War

The functions of our destroyers are two-fold:

(i)   *Defensive*, i.e. destroying the enemy's torpedo boats by gunfire;
(ii)   *Offensive*, i.e. torpedoing the enemy's capital ships.

The order in which these very distinct roles have been placed above should not be taken as indicating their relative importance. The Destroyer role being the most difficult is placed first, and, for that reason, it is proposed to give it preference of discussion.

2. It is necessary in the first place to consider in what manner the Germans would be likely to use their torpedo boats against us: if we can arrive at a reasonable answer to such a question we are the better able to judge how to employ our more numerous and more powerfully gunned destroyers.

It is supposed by some, that, in the early stages of a war, the Germans will utilise their torpedo boats to seek out our battlefleet and endeavour to reduce it in strength by torpedo attacks until their own battlefleet possesses a chance of bringing ours to action on equal or superior terms.

The North Sea comprises many hundreds of square miles, and so it does not seem wise to imagine that they will send flotillas hunting about the North Sea promiscuously in the hope that they will stumble across our squadrons. It would appear still more unreasonable if we adopted a counter plan on similar lines, and were to send our flotillas to scour the North Sea on the off chance of meeting theirs.

There is every reason to believe that the Germans intend to use their destroyers as torpedo boats, and there are strong indications to lead us to suppose that the intention is to use them in company with their battlefleet.

In any case their objective is the same. If they are to be used offensively it follows that they must first of all ascertain the whereabouts of the ships they are to attack. How they will do this is beside the immediate question and need not be discussed here.

3. One of the methods open to us to counter the offensive tactics of German torpedo craft is for *our destroyers to blockade the German exits*, either with a view to preventing their torpedo boats coming out, or, if they do, bringing them to action immediately, or, by cutting off their retreat and joining issue with them on their return.

It is understood that this policy of close blockade was seriously considered a few years ago and abandoned as being impracticable. As it appears to be still more impracticable now, it is useless to re-consider it.

4. To endeavour to encounter them mid-way between their objective (our battlefleet) and their harbours — by sweeping intermediate areas half way between the above — seems to be a compromise which is unsound in principle and dangerous in practice. Unsound because it would only be an off chance that they would meet, and dangerous because they might encounter a superior force too far from effective support. Since the German torpedo boats cannot be offensive until they get into striking distance of our battlefleet, the best disposition for our destroyers is in close touch with our battlefleet.

This position, it is contended, is the only one where they can immediately and directly defend our battlefleet.

5. The gist of the foregoing reasoning may be briefly expressed thus:—

'If our destroyers are intended to be employed in their defensive role of beating the German torpedo boats by superior gunfire (thus preventing their antagonists using their torpedoes), it seems a far better war policy to keep them in contact with our main force than to send them afield.'

This aspect of the problem is being laboured because it is supposed that the opinion is held that our destroyers should be used more as destroyers and less as torpedo boats, in fact that better effect is to be expected from their gun armament than from their torpedo armament.

Since the days when we built torpedo boat destroyers to counter the numerous torpedo boats then possessed by our latent antagonist, France, the situation has vastly changed. Our enemy *in posse* [*sic*] does not possess small torpedo boats, but has produced vessels approaching our destroyers in size, superior in torpedo armament and speed, but inferior with regard to gun power. It is apparent, therefore, that they are intended to be used as torpedo boats.

With the introduction of the long range torpedo, opinion, however decided it may have been previously, is now more favourably disposed towards using our destroyers offensively against the enemy's capital ships.

6. It is generally agreed that above water torpedo craft are not by themselves able to act against heavy ships in *daylight* with sufficient prospect of success to justify the attempt; at night or in thick weather, their chances of success, although much greater, are wholly dependent on the torpedo craft being able to locate the ships they are in search of; however likely this may be in limited areas, in open waters it is beyond dispute that the chances are remote.

It is also observed that, provided squadrons cruise in a flexible order and are able to alter course at once if torpedo craft are sighted, the difficulty of hitting with torpedoes is very considerable. It is considered therefore that, *so long as a fleet keeps in open waters and is properly screened by its attendant cruisers and flotillas*, the danger of torpedo attack from surface torpedo craft will not be serious.

It may be argued in answer to this that such precautions will not always be possible; this no doubt is true, but the occupation of what may be called 'the enemy's torpedo area' would be justified only when some great strategical object was involved.

7. The whole question may be summarised as follows:-

(i) The main function of seagoing torpedo craft is the destruction of the enemy's capital ships, and they will usually most efficiently contribute to that end by close co-operation with their Battle Fleet. Isolated and divergent efforts entail an inferiority of torpedo craft at the decisive battle and are therefore to be strongly deprecated.

NOTE: This statement must not be accepted as a stereotyped rule: exceptional conditions require exceptional treatment.

Such would exist if a fleet were in occupation of the enemy's torpedo waters — for following up the results of a day action — for covering the retreat of an inferior force or defeated fleet; for the attack of ships in harbour, or at sea if their position is known, immediately prior to the outbreak of war, or at any time if there is reason to believe such attack would succeed; perhaps for mining the mouth of a habour known to be occupied by the enemy's fleet; and under such circumstances it is to be expected that the employment of torpedo craft would be governed accordingly, unfettered by plans based upon different conditions.

As a case in point, the position of the Russian Fleet off Port Arthur during a period of strained relations was exceptional and invited attack. We know now also, that if the guns of the battle-fleet had followed up the torpedo attack, early next morning, the Russian Fleet would have been destroyed, because they were utterly demoralised and the forts were unprepared.

(ii) The destruction of an enemy's torpedo craft is no less a function of our destroyers than is that of the enemy's capital ships, but, as an objective, it is too indefinite to be pursued *in open waters* except when the chance arises. The strategy which successfully leads to (i) is considered most likely to lead equally to (ii). The two functions are therefore, in a sense, intermingled, and it is to be expected that sometimes one and sometimes the other will be the more important.

In *narrow waters*, or limited areas, the question is quite a different one; there is no reason why torpedo craft should not be employed to keep such areas clear of enemy vessels of similar class.

(iii) The number of seagoing torpedo craft required in support of the Battle Fleet on the day of battle is governed not by the strength of the enemy's flotillas, or even by what we consider sufficient for decisive victory, but *only* by the number which, by the most successful strategy, can be brought to the scene of action in time to take part. It is evident that gun attack by itself cannot have the same effect as combined gun and torpedo attack, and it is undoubtedly true that, in combination with the gunfire of a fleet, torpedo attack by large numbers of destroyers is a danger which a Battle Fleet, already heavily engaged, would find almost impossible to resist.

(iv) The idea that destroyers can be effectively used for search or observation duties far in advance of the main fleet is unsound under modern conditions, and no analogy from experience of 18th century warfare or the Dutch wars can properly be taken as proof to the contrary.

The advent of submarines and the introduction of ships which combine high speed and great gunpower have introduced factors which necessitate the concentration of cruisers and flotillas in the same area as the Battle Fleet.

If our torpedo craft are widely separated from the heavy ships, not only will they be absent when required, but they are liable to be destroyed in detail. It is not the enemy's torpedo craft that they may expect to meet but his cruisers and even battle-cruisers which can steam as fast as they can in ordinary weather, and may be frequently within gun range on sighting.

NOTE: There are, of course, exceptions: for example, the coastal cruisers and flotillas and cruisers exercising the control of trade routes. Also, in operating against a passive enemy, such as the Russians showed themselves to be in the war with Japan, the ordinary principles may be wisely neglected.

49. *From Chatfield* [with comments by Beatty marked with *]

[BTY/2/4/6]   [*Lion*]
                                                        [October 1913]

Fast Division Work from a Gunnery Standpoint

Rear Admiral.
                              Submitted.
To study the correct handling of a fast division from a gunnery standpoint requires very careful consideration and necessitates a slight investigation of the various aspects of fast division work.

The fast division forming, as it does, part of the Battle Fleet, is subject to some risk when it is detached from the main body.

The chief risks are:-

(A) It may have its speed reduced by gunfire or torpedoes.
(B) By incorrect handling, it may be inaccurately timed to come into action simultaneously with the main body.

With regard to (A), the fast division is especially liable to torpedo attack by the enemy's destroyers and submarines, which may cause loss of speed. Speed is much easier lost than any other part of the fighting power. A few well directed salvoes may be amply sufficient to wreck the funnels and casings, while a shell in the unprotected ends might also necessitate a large reduction of speed.

Battle cruisers acting as a fast division are especially vulnerable and if they lose their speed, they are immediately in a position of great inferiority to a battleship. They may then be cut off and destroyed, or left out of the action, as the *Princess Royal* and the *Indefatigable* were on 10th October 1913, and the three *Collingwood* class on 9th October 1913.

With regard to (B), there are two ways in which a fast division can be employed.

I.   It is detached early and, keeping out of range of the enemy, it gets to a position of tactical advantage <u>before fighting</u>*
II. It is detached after fighting has commenced, and endeavours, by its speed, to get an advantageous gunnery position while under gun fire.

The first method is necessarily risky. It assumes that the enemy's effective gun range is known, which is not the case. If the enemy's effective gun range is under-estimated, the fast division may suddenly find itself under heavy gun fire without the support of the main body. If, on the contrary, the fast division keeps a long way out of range, the difficulty of the task of closing to effective gun range *simultaneously* with the main body is very greatly increased. [*Yes but even so *not* difficult if in the van of enemy & with a proper understanding with the C-in-C beforehand.]

In all cases the present unknown factor, 'Effect of gun fire on the enemy', is the most important consideration. How long will it take to win a modern action at sea, or even to get a decisive effect with gun fire in the first phase of an action? It is undoubtedly a matter of minutes; but whether it is 5, 10 or 30 minutes is a matter of the utmost importance. On this depends the degree of accuracy to which an Admiral must work in effecting a combination with the other part of the fleet. If this factor is miscalculated, one portion may be overwhelmed before support arrives. Past land warfare, as well as naval, fully illustrates this.

The second method (B. II) is much less risky [*Yes, but less likely to achieve any result of real value and something must be risked to secure any advantage of value.]and therefore more certain to be effective. It consists usually in the fast division being stationed a short distance ahead of the main body when in line of battle, and gradually increasing this distance by high speed, but not to a greater distance than about two miles. This will usually be sufficient to give a definite advantage from a gun fire standpoint, and the courses being steady and not unduly acute to those of the enemy, the control should not be handicapped.

The Admiral commanding a fast division must always have uppermost in his mind the effect that any order he gives will have on the gun fire of his division. It is not sufficient to alter course and speed by eye, as such calculations are not accurate enough and will probably lead to a further alteration shortly, thus unnecessarily handicapping the gun fire. Before launching out on a new course, therefore, the relative positions at the moment must be accurately plotted on a mooring board, or better still by specially constructed speed scales, in order that the most advantageous course for gun fire may be correctly selected and the probable relative positions in 5 or 10 minutes time may be forecasted as far as the enemy's movements allow. [*Real tactical advantages are not to be gained once general action takes place, it must be secured beforehand.]

This is very seldom done in practice, and, in my experience, the attempt to obtain a tactical, or rather a gunnery advantage, usually results in a high and frequently changing rate due to constant change of course. This *must* affect the gun fire, possibly (especially in newly commissioned ships) to such an extent as to entirely neutralise the value of the position gained. [*This should be done before the action commences; once committed to serious action this should be reduced to a minimum.]

Visibility also affects these fast division tactics and especially makes B. I very risky when the visibility is short, as a detached division is then more liable to surprise and to lose touch completely with the main body.

The above arguments are not intended to imply that a fast [*YES] division should not be used in action in the present method but that there are strict limitations to its movements. These must be clearly understood and *agreed upon*. As guns get more efficient and long-ranged, the risks of detaching part of a fleet get correspondingly greater. While combined, full gun power can always be developed; once separated widely, exceedingly accurate manoeuvring by the Admirals commanding units is essential, and, a bad miscalculation or loss of speed may lose the day.

To summarise, therefore, I submit the following: —

*YES
1. The effective gun range of the enemy must be found out as accurately as possible, before war.

*YES
*IMPERATIVE
2. The detached division must be handled so as to open fire simultaneously with the main body.

*YES
3. The Commander-in-chief must decide and communicate to the Admiral commanding the fast division his intended range for opening fire, and must communicate to the latter also shortly before this will occur.

*YES AFTER GENERAL OR CLOSE ACTION COMMENCES
4. All alteration in course and speed must be considered primarily with regard to their effect on the gunfire and not only from what looks best to the eye.

YES, SHALL BE GLAD TO HAVE THIS AT ONCE
5. Arising out of 4, it is quite easy, with superior speed, to calculate suitable courses which will keep the range constant and the rate nil, a ready method of doing this to be prepared.

*YES
6. The 'T' must never be crossed at too broad an angle as this is unnecessary and causes a big and difficult rate.

*YES
7. It is especially necessary for the Admiral commanding a detached division to know fully the Commander-in-Chief's intentions in all emergencies, specially the following:-

(a) Under what circumstances will the Commander-in-Chief alter course 16 points, i.e., for torpedo attack, or if the enemy has already done so.

*NOT NECESSARY
(b) What is to be done if a ship is disabled.

*YES
(c) How many of the enemy's van (or rear) is the fast division to fire at, so as to ensure not confusing the fire of the main body.

Examples of perfect gunnery courses, speed of fast division 5 knots greater than enemy's:

1. *Squadron 2 points before beam of enemy* (10,000 yds)* An alteration of 1½ points (1 and 's' deleted*] will keep range constant, i.e., no rate, and the squadron will gradually draw ahead of the enemy (*& at end of 10 mins gained 1 pt in bearing.)

2. *Squadron 5 points before the enemy's beam.* An alteration of 5 points [*19 degrees substituted for 5 points deleted] inwards will keep range constant, i.e., no rate, and the squadron will gradually draw ahead of the enemy and eventually cross his 'T' (if he does not alter course) in 20 minutes.

50. *To CinC Home Fleets*

[CCC/DRAX/4/2]   SECRET   Lion
[Copy]   Devonport
                                        31 December 1913

In accordance with your Memorandum No. 066 of 20 September 1913, para. 2, I have the honour to report as follows:-

2. I concur in the provision of coal for the First Battle-Cruiser Squadron in peace, but I consider that the arrangements for meeting first requirements and maintaining an efficient supply for the Fleet in war do not appear satisfactory or sufficiently certain.

3. At the present moment there is, at the Northern bases, no coal available for heavy ships. The supplies mentioned in Form (2) page 2 are of use only for flotillas or light cruisers, and the two hulks now fitting out will not be suitable for taking heavy ships alongside in all weathers. In any case, when all arrangements stated in remarks column of Form (2) have been carried out, the total supply at Northern ports will be less than one day's estimated requirements for First Fleet.

4. The Fleet therefore is entirely dependent on a vast supply of coal which is to be embarked in South Wales when mobilisation commences, or on receipt of warning telegram. Experience shows that there is a tendency for the telegram, and mobilisation, to be delayed till the last minute, when relations are strained almost to breaking point. Time therefore may be very short.

5. Table 5 gives the following data:–

	Tons
Coal to be embarked in South Wales on receipt of warning telegram	289700
Coal to be embarked on mobilisation	348700
Total to be embarked at once	638400
Coal to be sent off by rail	150000
Total to be sent off at once	788400

When we consider the confusion due to mobilisation, the vast amount of coal to be handled, the need for more than 200 colliers, and the fact that they must take three days to reach Cromarty or Rosyth, it seems impossible to admit that the situation is satisfactory. Further it is not understood how it is intended to transport the 150,000 tons of coal sent by rail to Rosyth and Humber from the sidings to the large ships lying in the anchorage.

6. In the Manoeuvres of the last two years the coal for the Fleet has always arrived late at the place it was most wanted. Two and a half years ago, when foreign relations were severely strained, the Fleet lying in Northern ports was short of coal and quite unable to replenish. The situation today seems no better.

7. I submit that the whole question of fuel supply for operations in the North Sea requires careful examination and revision. The chief needs appear to be as follows:-

(a) There should be a peace reserve at the Northern bases similar to those of the Home ports i.e. sufficient to supply the first requirements of the Fleet in time of emergency.

(b) If stored on shore, there must be adequate means for placing it rapidly on board ships, and supplying several ships simultaneously, as at Portland.

(c) Where supplies by rail are relied on for immediate requirements, condition (b) must equally be complied with, and also it must be quite certain that no delay can occur from strikes, movement of troops, or other exceptional causes.

51. *To his wife* [on board *Sheelah*,[1] Gibraltar]

[BTY/17/27/17–18]   *Lion*
                                                    [Portland]
                                              2 February [1914]

*   *   *

I've had a seance this morning with the Captains and everything is reported well. Our probable programme for the spring and early summer is as follows:

March 24th and 25th, Fleet exercises.

March 26th, go to home ports for Easter.

April 15th, leave home ports for Cromarty.

Remain at Cromarty until the middle of May.

Return to Portland about 18th May until 10th June, when we have to go to Spithead for the biggest review that has ever been seen; intended principally for the glorification of Winston and incidentally to give some information to the taxpayer as to the way his money is being spent. This will be a great opportunity for you to instil proper ideas of the Navy into the minds of your very charming but perhaps not very clear thinking friends.

After 10th June and review I don't know what we shall do, some form of exercises if not manoeuvres I suppose. This year I hope to get most of our gunnery programme finished in the spring, so as to leave the autumn free for a cruise in Norwegian waters in August and September, which would be very pleasant; and you will like that also, won't you? I hope you had good weather on your way South, I watch the weather chart with great anxiety, and the *Sheelah* behaves herself and proves a good sea boat [*sic*]. . . .

52.   *To C in C Home Fleets*

[CCC DRAX/1/2]   SECRET   *Lion*
[Copy]   Villagarcia
                                          10 March 1914

No 01S

Sir,

I have the honour to submit herewith for your information a copy of my Memorandum 015 of 3rd March 1914 addressed to

---

[1]*Sheelah*, the Beattys' private steam yacht, 680 gross tons, built 1902; her captain was W. Grint (Lieutenant RNR).

the Commanding Officers of the ships of my squadron. In it I have endeavoured to summarise briefly the work carried out in 1913, and to draw attention to points which require further investigation in the present year.

2. It is now accepted that there are two principal duties for the battle cruisers to perform, viz:-

(a) Supporting cruisers.

(b) Acting as fast division of a battle fleet.

For the successful performance of both these functions, the numerical strength of the squadron is all important.

Insufficient strength for (a) might cause delay in carrying out the duties which are dependent upon the maintenance of the advanced line ships, whose failure might cause immense disadvantages to the Commander-in-Chief.

Insufficient strength for (b) might cause failure to perform adequately those duties that the Commander-in-Chief expects of the Battle-Cruiser Squadron in battle.

Our strength however is far short of that which you stated to be necessary in your letter to the Admiralty No H.F.75 of 18th September 1913.

3. In my letter No 79 of 9th September 1913 I submitted my views on this matter, and since then the gravity of the situation has increased. In June or July next the *Derfflinger* will join the German Battle-Cruiser Squadron in the North Sea. This will bring their squadron up to four ships, exclusive of the *Goeben*. The English and German battle-cruiser squadrons in Home Waters will then be nominally of the same strength. But, in time of war our squadron would generally be reduced to three, one ship being away coaling, since we must assume that while it will be necessary for us to maintain our strategical positions at sea, it is by no means probable that the enemy will adopt a similar policy. We are then faced with a preponderance of 4 to 3 in favour of the enemy, when he takes the offensive at his selected moment.

4. Even the above situation would be more favourable than we could rely on with certainty, as there is every probability that the *Blücher* of 25 knots would accompany the battle-cruisers when putting to sea for an offensive move.

5. I much regret having to reiterate my former arguments on these subjects, but my reason for doing so is that the situation is now more serious than it was before.

It must not be thought that I am mainly concerned because our inferiority might lead to the inefficient performance of the work dependent upon the Battle-Cruiser Squadron: indeed with *Lion, Princess Royal* and *Queen Mary* I feel that against any four enemy battle cruisers we could successfully accomplish all that was asked of us. At the same time, I consider it my duty to point out that the inferiority does exist, in a vitally important area, where failure to support the advanced line efficiently might cause it to crumple like a pack of cards without any sufficient compensating advantage for the losses incurred.

It seems that such a risk should not be permitted to exist when it can be avoided.

6. It may be argued that the Mediterranean battle-cruisers would come home on the outbreak of war, but in view of the possible serious effect of such a move in India and Egypt, it seems highly probable that the government of the day might not concur in such a complete evacuation of the Mediterranean.

7. Further, the battle-cruisers suddenly recalled from the Mediterranean would lack the advantage of homogeneous training and would be unused to North Sea conditions. It is difficult enough for ships which are always employed there to carry out the duties that fall to them.

8. If in certain circumstances this is the policy that Their Lordships would propose to adopt, and these ships may have to work in conjunction with me in time of war, I respectfully submit that I may be informed of the fact, in order that the principles which are to govern our strategy may be mutually determined and understood.

53.   *To his wife* [Brooksby Hall, Leicestershire]

[BTY/17/28/4–6]   *Lion*
                                                                 30.7.14

I was very distressed at leaving you all alone yesterday morning, but you had little David who is a host in himself to take care of you. I expect you found London in a turmoil when you got there. I hope you were able to glean some news, but expect not. However I do not suppose you waited there too long and got away down to Brooksby where I trust you found little Peter alright[1] . . .

We steamed slowly away and turned East in the Channel when out of sight, but of course ran into cross-Channel steamers who would have reported us certainly. However we were alarmed during the day by telegrams from the Admiralty and last night we made certain that this morning would see us at war. But it has not come and I feel in my bones that it won't. Everybody in any country who thinks seems to be of the opinion that it has got to come sooner or later but I fear we are too well prepared this time for it to happen. With the exception that we are short of cruisers we could not be in better circumstances, time of year, etc. And I feel that luck would be too great to permit of me going to war in this ship and in command of this fine squadron. No one could be better placed. I do not want to go war [sic] but if it has got to come I should like it to come now quickly while I am where I am.

We have been busy all yesterday and today making preparations. Last night we bolted through the Straits of Dover with lights out. All the fortresses round the coast are mobilised and we watched with interest the big searchlights at Dover. You must not mention to a *soul* where we are or where we went. You can say that we are at sea and the newspapers will provide you with the rest. We shall in all probability remain at sea until it is necessary to coal, when ships will go in one by one to fill up. I shall not go in with *Lion* but remain out and change over to another ship — But I will send you a wire and letters by the ships going in which will be in 4 days or so.

The situation is so acute that it cannot last in such a condition for any length of time. It is bound to get better or worse. Mercifully the weather is very fine and our visibility extraordinary. We passed the French ships which escorted Poincaré to Russia.[2] They were scuttling off home as fast as they could go in a terrible fuss. Everybody is very well and cheerful. Green[3] has a letter from Madame Dubois[4] written Friday last before sailing telling him she scented stirring time but he was not to fuss as he was in great [?]

---

[1] Beatty's younger son Peter, born 2 April 1910.

[2] The French President, Raymond Poincaré, paid a state visit to Russia 20–23 July 1914.

[3] Green, Engineer Commander, DP of *Lion*.

[4] Edyth du Bois: fortune teller. Beatty and his wife also consulted her and at least two others of her kind, see Roskill, *Admiral of the Fleet* pp. 34, 136, 253.

good luck. I wonder if you went to see her and if she told you anything fresh.

We get the Poldhu[1] telegrams but that tells us very little. Prime Minister is making the most of the situation to keep people from thinking too much of the Irish situation.

I shall get this away to you today Friday 31st but I am not allowed to say where we are but if you look in the *Daily Mail* or *Telegraph* they will probably be able to tell you.

It is the usual way we do things in England, terribly secretive in one sphere but in all others we leave them alone. We were much amused to read a telegram from the German high power wireless station to say that, 'The local press, Berlin, had reported that the German armies were mobolising but the authorities had announced in the official press that it was not true.' They must think we are simple idiots . . .

When there appears to be a chance of seeing anything of you I'll let you know and you can send *Sheelah* up, but not unless we know something definite and I should not send her yet & not further North than Firth of Forth — to travel by day and fly the Blue Ensign not the White — Present state cannot last long.

54. *To his wife* [Brooksby Hall]

[BTY/17/28/8–9]   *Lion*
                                                       1.8.14

Your letter of the 30th reached me this morning, which was pretty good I think. I am glad to hear of you all at Brooksby and to know that you are all well. I think you are better off there than in London where I hear the excitement is intense. I gather that both England and Germany are doing all they can to preserve the peace; the one trying to prevail on Russia and the other on Austria. But it looks as if it were too late. Russia is the turning point & all must depend upon her. Whatever happens Germany and Austria are in a very awkward position, hence the anxiety for Germany to preserve the peace, which she will only be able to do at the cost of her own humiliation. Italy I doubt taking any too active part in the war & is as likely as not to leave the Triple

[1]Poldhu, Cornwall, Marconi WT station, the first to transmit across the Atlantic in 1901. See Arthur Hezlett, *The Electron and Sea-Power* (London, 1975).

Alliance when the bell rings. One cannot see them engaged in a war of extermination hand in hand with Austria.

I think Madame Dubois is right & it won't come, I told the Engineer Commander, Green, who was packing up his belongings to stow below, when he ceased immediately and spread them all out again. What a far-reaching influence the Lady has . . .

Jellicoe has been appointed 2nd-in-Command of the Home Fleet, which I think is a good thing as he is the C-in-C designate after Callaghan. And a man called Grant[1] who has not been to sea for 4 years, knows nothing of cruiser work, has been appointed to command the 6th Cruiser Squadron. As he happens to be one place senior to me in the list, he is the senior cruiser Admiral afloat. It was done out of pure good nature to give him a job and the situation is complex; all Bertie Hood's[2] fault. It is maddening. The C-in-C is upset because I know his ideas, views and plans and intentions, and now chaos will reign supreme: a new man who knows none of the captains and the general working of cruisers & who actually hasn't been to sea for 3 years, & has never seen a battle-cruiser!!!!. . . .

55. *From his wife*

[BTY/18/17/13–18]   Brooksby Hall
                                              Saturday 1 August 1914

It certainly looks as if we were getting nearer & nearer, and [?] hang [?] on the precipice & I expect you have got into that state of mind that you wish something to happen & quickly, as it must be very tiresome being in the North Sea day after day, & only getting bits of news. I wonder if you are getting any mail. Bertie Hood won't tell me anything, except that it will be very difficult to hear anything from the Fleet. I heard from him this morning & he says if we do go to war, we are in a much stronger position than they ever considered possible, & it is just England's strength that may save the situation. Germany is indeed in a bad way. She

[1]Rear-Admiral W. L. Grant : senior Rear-Admiral on active list, 26 October 1909, compared with Beatty's seniority, 1 January 1910; Beatty's being made Acting Vice-Admiral on 3 August 1914 solved the problem.
[2]Rear-Admiral Sir Horace Hood (1870–1916) : appointed Churchill's Naval Secretary June 1914; commanding 3rd Battle-Cruiser Squadron 1915; lost in *Invincible* at Jutland.

seems surrounded on every side. I heard Jellicoe has gone to sea & he has been pitchforked into a new ship. Thank goodness you have been in your *Lion* for 18 months and so on every [—] & know all your officers and men, and they adore you, so I feel happier in that way alone. If you do have to fight, don't, for our sake, take any unnecessary risks. I know how brave you are & that makes me fear for you.

*   *   *

I am going to begin to take First Aid lessons in Leicester, & if we go to war will at once turn *Sheelah* into a hospital ship. I would ask Winston if it would be possible.

56.   *To his wife* [Brooksby Hall]

[BTY/17/28/11–14]   *Lion*
2.8.14

We are enveloped in fog and with our nets out, ready for most things. We spent all yesterday getting rid of superfluities and still preparing. The men are doing well, the spirit is excellent, light hearted, cheerful and high hearted. So that is good. Opportunities of sitting down quietly and writing letters are rare, so I am writing you at 4 am when everything is at rest. It is quite daylight and has been for an hour but still a beastly fog. It should not last long though at this time of the year.

We received telegram at 2 am that they had mobilised the Reserves, which means as far as the Navy is concerned we can do no more in preparation. I cannot think that such a step would have been taken unless war is inevitable. All I can say is, we are ready and will win through but it will mercifully be quick, at the rate of doing things nowadays. Once we start, I can't think it will last too long. Keep a strong heart dear one, you have much trouble, trial and tribulation before you. We've lived for 40 years in peace and comfort and now we are to be put to the test. It is good for us, will strengthen us and we shall be better men and women for it in the end, now we have come down to bed rock and look things fairly in the face. No weakness, no weeping, grousing, help others. There will be many that will need it. Thank God my babies are too young . . .

The *Sheelah* I should hold up for the present. It would not be safe for her to go up the North Sea when the trouble starts, as there will be mines all over the place, which we know of but she wouldn't. This quite private of course. Later she might by day journeyings get as far as Rosyth. She could anchor well up the Firth, clear of all danger, but would be many miles [*sic*]. If I can get there any time you could always get to Lady Eva at Wemyss, not far away, but you have to consider the desirability of leaving the children. Again, it is very doubtful whether I could ever get in at all. The ships will come but I shall in all probability remain out. Again, you might consider the desirability of offering the *Sheelah* to the Admiralty for purposes of sick etc. The *Maine*[1] has been wrecked, and, although small, she could do much if equipped properly with nurses, doctors and appliances. You might see Hood about it. It will give you much to do and think about, which will be good for you.

I spend my time visiting my ships and watching over their preparations which are complete now. My Captains are splendid and are not easily rattled. Whatever comes the battle-cruisers will give a good account of themselves. Please God I shall be able to put them in the right place and do as well by them as the circumstances will permit. We are at 4 hours notice and consequently ready to move. I have plenty to eat up to now and we are all well and going strong. Have no fear on our behalf, we are well off.

I suppose all my beautiful horses will be taken for the military. We must give everything without a murmur. One thing, the country is safe from invasion. Germany will have her hands full with Russia on one side and France on the other to find men to embark and waste on a futile attempt on our shores. So the only danger at home is that of riots caused by the absence of bread, but I think that would not be too serious . . .

---

[1]*Maine*, hospital ship, 4540 tons, stranded and sold July 1914.

57.   *From his wife*

[BTY/18/17/27–30]

Berkeley Hotel
London
Monday 3 August 1914

I came up to London this morning to try & fix things up about the yacht. Of course Fripp and Shields[1] are out of London but I hope by this evening shall be able to get hold of them. I am going off to the Admiralty after lunch to see the D.M.G.[2] [sic] to see about medical stores etc. We are also trying to find out how long it would take wireless on the yacht [sic]. The Admiralty says she can follow up after their hospital ships, one leaving tomorrow & one in a weeks time.

If it is true that Germany has captured some of our ships in the Kiel Canal, surely England can't hold out another moment. Dennis & I have [sic] a bit of food here. They have given him a job at the Admiralty under Philpotts[3] but he wants to go to sea & is frightfully keen for you to wire the Admiralty for him to come to the *Lion*, if you are short of officers. Poor thing, he is keen to be off . . . I am so glad they have made you admiral of the cruisers — splendid.You know my heart & soul is with you through all this & even now one feels perhaps the Germans are preparing to attack you [– – – – – –] before war is declared.

To see the crowds wandering round London you would not think anything is happening. They are in an awful state here as the government will not decide what they are going to do. It seems extraordinary that they should hesitate at this 11th hour. However Asquith is to make a statement this afternoon. What will it be? . . .

I have seen the D.M.G. & they will give me every assistance and will let me join the yacht probably at Cromarty. So I may be near you before many days are over dear heart. Bertie has been kindness itself.

---

[1]The eminent surgeons Sir Alfred Fripp & D. (later Sir Douglas) Shields were appointed Honorary Consulting Surgeons by the Admiralty.

[2]The Director-General Medical Department, Sir Arthur W. May, with the relative rank of Vice-Admiral.

[3]Dennis Larking, see n. 1 on p. 31. Captain E. M. Philpotts was Naval Assistant to 2nd Sea Lord.

PART III

HELIGOLAND BIGHT AND THE SCARBOROUGH RAID
1914–1915

INTRODUCTION[1]

The first five months of the war saw Beatty in a position exactly fitted to his capacities and ambitions. He, and general opinion, saw the Battle-Cruiser Squadron as the embodiment of the aggressive naval warfare which was to destroy the pretensions of the German navy. He had confidence in his ships, his staff, and, at first, the Admiralty. Although he deplored the supersession of Callaghan as Commander-in-Chief, he recognised Jellicoe's abilities and was sure that they would work well together. Above all, he was confident of his own ability to motivate his ships' companies to withstand the strains of modern war.

It would be wrong to say that he became disillusioned, but he was soon more realistically aware of the frustrations and disappointments that lay ahead than when he had welcomed the end of uncertainty on 4 August 1914. He was no longer confident that the war would be short, or a decisive action at sea easily attainable. He recognised, as he had not in peacetime, the limitations imposed on the fleet's movements by underwater weapons, and was increasingly dismayed by the failure to produce effective anti-submarine techniques. Experience had shown the ability of the climatic condition of the North Sea to deny him contact with enemy battle-cruisers on the rare occasions they were at sea. He now accepted that he had to face a future of fruitless searches for the enemy, followed by the feverish labour of coaling and the strain of maintaining constant readiness for sea [58–64].

The spirited action in the Heligoland Bight on 28 August was to reassure Beatty of the fighting spirit of his force and of his own ability to command in battle, but it also reduced his confidence in the Admiralty's ability to co-ordinate complex operations. His doubts on this were intensified by the revelations of the errors behind the escape of the *Goeben* in the Mediterranean at the beginning of the war, and turned to bitter criticism with the sinking of *Aboukir* and her two consorts by the submarine U–9 in

[1]The Jellicoe-Beatty correspondence relevant to this section is in A. Temple-Patterson (ed.), *The Jellicoe Papers* (London, 1966), Vol. 1, pp. 82, 92, 96–100, 103–6, 108, 110–15, 120–1, 126–7, 130–6.

September and the much greater disaster at Coronel in November. His own failure to bring the German battle-cruisers to action during their attack on the east coast in December was a more personal blow, especially as weaknesses in reconnaissance and reporting, and the performance of his own staff, were partially responsible for the failure.

The action which gave the battle-cruisers their first combat experience originated in a plan submitted to the Admiralty by the Commodore of Submarines, Roger Keyes.[1] This involved a sweep into the Heligoland Bight by surface forces to attack German patrols in combination with submarines stationed to intercept any heavy German units which might be tempted out. The Admiralty took over the organisation and added Sir Archibald Moore's[2] two battle-cruisers from the Humber, *Invincible* and *New Zealand*, to the light forces from Harwich under Commodore Tyrwhitt,[3] originally proposed by Keyes. Jellicoe's proposal that the Grand Fleet should move out in support was rejected by the Admiralty, but he was given discretion to send the battle-cruisers. This he wisely did, also giving Beatty the support of the 1st Light Cruiser Squadron under Commodore Goodenough.[4] The Admiralty's failure to inform these different elements of each other's involve-

[1]Later Admiral of the Fleet Lord Keyes (1872–1945): entered RN 1885; Commodore Submarine Service 1912; Chief of Staff to Admiral Sir Sackville Carden, and his successor Sir John de Robeck in the Dardanelles operations 1915; commanding *Centurion* in Grand Fleet 1916–17; Rear-Admiral 1917 commanding 4th Battle Squadron; Director of Plans, Admiralty, October 1917; Vice-Admiral Dover Patrol 1918; Attack on Ostend and Zeebrugge April 1918; DCNS 1921; CinC Mediterranean 1925–8; Admiral 1926; CinC Portsmouth 1929–31; Admiral of the Fleet 1930; retired list 1935; Conservative MP for Portsmouth 1934; Director of Combined Operations 1940–1; elevated to the peerage 1943. Three volumes of *The Keyes* Papers are published by the NRS, ed. Paul G. Halpern (London, 1972, 1979, 1981).

[2]Later Admiral Sir Archibald Moore (1862–1934): 3rd Sea Lord 1912; commanding 2nd Battle-Cruiser Squadron 1914; Vice-Admiral 1916; criticised by Beatty and Jellicoe for his conduct in the Dogger Bank action, he was moved to command a cruiser squadron in the Canary Islands area and relieved by Pakenham (see note 1 on page 154).

[3]Later Admiral of the Fleet Sir Reginald Tyrwhitt (1870–1951): entered RN 1883; long service in destroyers; served with Harwich force throughout war; Rear-Admiral 1918; commanding 3rd Light Cruiser Squadron in Mediterranean 1921; Flag Officer Scotland 1923–5; CinC China 1927–9; Admiral 1929; CinC Nore 1930–3; Admiral of the Fleet 1934.

[4]Later Admiral Sir William Goodenough (1867–1945): entered RN 1880; Commodore 1st Light Cruiser Squadron 1913, redesignated 2nd Light Cruiser Squadron in May 1915, and fought at Jutland; Rear-Admiral and commanding 2nd Battle Squadron 1916; Admiral Superintendent Chatham 1919; Vice-Admiral and CinC South African Station 1920; CinC Nore 1924–7; Admiral 1925; retired list 1930; joined Home Guard 1940.

ment, combined with Goodenough's failures in reconnaissance, produced confusion and near disaster. This was avoided by Beatty's bold decision to intervene despite risks from mines and torpedoes and the possible intervention of German heavy units. Equally meritorious was his decision to withdraw before the odds became too great. Chatfield's analysis of the gunnery experience of the action, especially problems of range-finding and fire control, was an important pointer to future difficulties. Beatty's mounting dissatisfaction with the Admiralty was intensified by the delay of any formal recognition of his achievement until the end of October [65–71].

The months following Heligoland were marked by increasing criticism of the Admiralty and frustration at his own impotence to do something to balance the mounting casualties in France. His discontent was accentuated by the failure of Jellicoe's plan to repeat the Heligoland operation on 7 September without its errors of co-ordination, and taking out the entire Grand Fleet in support. But the Germans could not be tempted out, and Beatty began to fear that he would never come to grips with his opposite number, Hipper[1] [72–74]. His letters to his wife are full of criticism of the Admiralty's failure to make the correct dispositions needed to ensure an encounter. As always, he told her to keep his views to herself but, knowing her as he did, it is probable that he expected her to pass them on to the influential people she met. At the same time he approached Churchill direct with an appeal for immediate action to make the east coast bases immune against submarines, which he saw as the root of the problem. He did not yet seem to have grasped the complex scientific and technological difficulties involved in locating and destroying submarines, and thought that getting the right man to organise offensive hunts was all that was needed [75–78].

Churchill's recall of Fisher to be First Sea Lord in October 1914 gave Beatty some hope, but he rightly foresaw that there would be friction between them. In his continuing efforts to influence policy he was to conduct a private correspondence with them both. It is noteworthy that with all his responsibilities and forebodings he continued, with Ethel's assistance, to give detailed attention to his men's welfare [79–88].

On 3 November the German battle-cruisers made their first raid

[1]Vice-Admiral Franz Ritter von Hipper (1863–1932): commanding High Seas Fleet Scouting Forces 1913–18; CinC High Seas Fleet August-November 1918. See Tobias R. Philbin, *Admiral von Hipper* (Amsterdam, 1982).

in support of mine-laying operations and bombarded Yarmouth. This increased Beatty's apprehension that he might have to encounter a future raid with inadequate force, a fear no doubt reinforced by the news of Rear-Admiral Craddock's defeat at Coronel, the result, as Beatty was convinced, of the Admiralty's failure to provide him with adequate force [83–90]. Sturdee's[1] victory at the Falklands would have done more for Beatty's morale had it not been for his conviction that the former Chief of the War Staff had been repsonsible for all the previous disasters, including Coronel itself. He continued to press his views on the Admiralty, claiming that Jellicoe was in substantial agreement, but his major anxieties continued [91–101].

In December Germany launched another mine-laying operation and raid, and this time brought out the High Seas Fleet in support of Hipper's battle-cruisers. 'Room 40', the Admiralty's intelligence centre, gave Jellicoe good warning of the raid but failed to detect the Battle Fleet's participation. Beatty's four battle-cruisers, with the support of Sir George Warrender's Second Battle Squadron, two cruiser squadrons and destroyer support, successfully concentrated in a good position for interception. But, after that, the encounter was marked by errors on both sides. The Germans succeeded in laying their mines, bombarding Scarborough and Hartlepool and regaining their base without loss, but von Ingenohl,[2] commanding the High Seas Fleet, missed a greater success. Thinking that the whole Grand Fleet was at sea, he avoided action when, in reality, he was in a position to achieve Germany's major strategic objective — the overwhelming of a weaker portion of Jellicoe's command.

On the British side, confused encounters with enemy cruisers and destroyers, accompanied by repeated errors in reconnaissance and reporting and combined with appalling weather, prevented the interception of the enemy battle-cruisers. In addition, an ambiguous signal by Beatty, causing Commodore Goodenough's light cruisers to lose contact with the enemy, was a major factor

[1]Later Admiral of the Fleet Sir Frederick Sturdee (1859–1925): entered RN 1871; COS to Lord Charles Beresford, CinC Mediterranean, 1905; followed him to Channel Fleet 1907; Rear-Admiral 1908; commanding 1st Battle Squadron 1910; Vice-Admiral 1913; Chief of Admiralty War Staff July 1914; appointed to command in South Atlantic after Coronel; defeated von Spee at Falklands 8 December 1914; commanding 4th Battle Squadron 1915–18; during this time he bombarded Beatty with papers on tactics (see NMM Beatty Papers BTY/7); Admiral 1917; CinC Nore 1918–21; Admiral of the Fleet 1921.

[2]Admiral Friedrich von Ingenohl (1857–1933): CinC High Seas Fleet 1913–15, relieved of command after the Dogger Bank action.

in the Germans' escape. Beatty and Jellicoe were both highly critical of Goodenough's conduct, but Jellicoe rejected Beatty's demand for his removal, recognising that there were more widespread faults to be remedied [102–111].

For both navies, the operations of 16 December demonstrated that technological change had not removed the influence of weather and chance on sea warfare. Only experience properly evaluated, training intensified to drive home the lessons learned, and improved intelligence of the enemy's movements, could ensure fleet contact. The future was to show that even if this were achieved and action joined, making it decisive involved other difficulties.

58. *Telegram Copies*

[BTY/3/2/5]   [*Lion*]
                                              [4 August 1914]

To: Winston Churchill
     Admiralty
     London

Private: contemplated change rumoured would cause unprecedented disaster. I beg of you to reconsider. Moral effect upon
Fleet at such a moment would be worse than a defeat at sea. It
creates impossible position for successor whose difficulties would
be incalculable. At present confidence of Fleet is high morale
magnificent which would be destroyed by this step.

                                              David Beatty

[BTY/3/2/6]   [*Lion*]
                                              [4 August 1914]

To: Admiral Prince Louis Battenberg
     Admiralty
     London

Private: following sent to First Lord begins: [as above with
additional concluding sentence] When you receive this I am sure
you will realise national gravity of the question which alone makes
me wire, other Flag Officers would be overwhelmed if they knew.

                                              David Beatty

59. *To his wife* [Hanover Lodge]

[BTY/17/28/18–20]   *Lion*
                                              5.8.14

We are at war as you will know. The long talked of and much
dreaded has happened and now we are to be put to the test after
all. I can hardly realise that it is so and it seems as if it were only
in a dream that I ever heard of such a thing. It is a cruel war

because there never has been any reason for it. We have been forced in entirely through the rapacity and thirst for power and a large portion of the world by Germany. Never in the history of the world has there been so little reason or so little cause. But there it is. Thank heavens it's summer months and before the dark nights of winter are on us it ought to be all over. There is not sufficient money in the world to permit such a gigantic struggle to be continued for any great length of time.

We left Scapa in a hurry Monday night to support cruisers who were investigating report that Germans were landing in Shetlands. Before doing so I went on board the ships and harangued them. The enthusiasm was immense. I never seen[sic] such a magnificent and cheerful spirit. War was a certainty at the time and we all knew it. We dashed out and spent the night, which mercifully are very short [sic], at the guns, as we shall for the next months. Nothing learnt, so we proceeded about the location, all apparently well with Shetlands. Yesterday we were told war would be declared at midnight. Had a scare last evening. Q.M.[1] of course started it & reported 2 enemy cruisers in sight. Away I went with our top speed to find old Packs[2] pottering off to coal. Afterwards a quiet night in which you will be surprised to hear I slept like a baby for the short spell off I took and am as fit as a fiddle this morning.

We received a royal message from the King and also the terrible news that the C-in-C has been relieved by Jellicoe. I fear he must have been taken ill. It is a terrible handicap to start a war by losing our C-in-C and it will break his heart. Jellicoe is undoubtedly the better man and in the end it will be for the best, but he hasn't the Fleet at his finger tips at present and I do not think is very well either.

I would give a great deal to have a newspaper, *Daily Mail* would be most sensational. We miss all the excitement, being on the ocean, but we have enough of our own. I am not anxious and feel able to deal with situations as they arise. If only I could only have a word with Jellicoe and learn his views. I knew poor old Callaghan's but this is different, and one of the curses of changing horses in the middle of the stream. Weather yesterday bad, blowing hard, which I like, but thick which I don't like. Today clear, see for miles and warmer. Everybody well on board,

[1]The battle-cruiser *Queen Mary*.
[2]Nickname of Rear-Admiral Pakenham.

Woodley,[1] Frank regular old campaigners already. The Secretary[2] rejoices that he has already earned a medal. All the Staff doing well & the spirit high and cheerful. My cabin is being dismantled to remove woodwork, otherwise we are much the same as ordinary manoeuvres . . .

It is a great relief to me and a weight off my mind that you are all well and at Brooksby[3] peacefully and quietly. I know well, dear heart what a sore trial it is though for you and know how much you would rather would [sic] be doing something. There will be plenty for you to do later, so reserve your energies and keep well and strong is your principal duty now. I send you the addresses of 4 young women who are engaged to be married to men, names attached, on board, whose banns have been published onboard. Will you write to them and tell them to be of good cheer, they are all well, I think they would like it and show them there is somebody in the world who takes an interest in them . . .

*　　*　　*

We are making history now, so courage Sweetheart, and it shall be a page that will not be behind those of the glorious past. All will be well in the end. I have great faith . . .

60.　*To his wife* [Hanover Lodge]

[BTY/17/28/22–24]　　　　　　　　　　　　　　　　　　　　　*Lion*
7.8.14

I got two letters from you yesterday and was glad indeed to hear you were busy about *Sheelah*. It will keep you from thinking too much and occupy your mind. It's people with nothing to do who suffer on these occasions. . . . We of course are very busy, night time of course is our worst period, and we generally have most to do then, so sleep has to be taken when we can get it. Mercifully it is a good time of the year, the days are long and at present we have a beautiful moon and the weather is fine, so we have nothing to complain of and we shall gradually get into

[1]Woodley, Beatty's steward.

[2]Fleet Paymaster, later Captain (S) Sir Frank Spickernell (1885–1956) remained as Beatty's Secretary throughout the Admiral's career. See Roskill, *Admiral of the Fleet*, p. 60.

[3]Brooksby Hall, Leicestershire, the Beattys' favourite country home, well situated for fox-hunting.

training for the winter months, or at least the autumn months with their short days and long dark nights. The men are splendid and I don't think that any conditions will damp their ardour.

The Germans are strewing mines broadcast. I am glad to say the 3rd Flotilla bagged one and sank her, which is all we can claim at present. You won't on any account come up with the *Sheelah* will you? And she must not come up until the Admiralty tell her when, and by what route, it would not be safe for her. Old Packs and I had a tremendous hunt today but unfortunately drew blank, which was a great pity. Don't encourage Dennis to go to sea. He has plenty to do at home and it's all good work and has to be done to bring success to the main body. I had a bleat from Filson Young, so thank him for it if you see him. Between you and I, I don't think he would like it if he was here. Woodley is doing nobly. Notwithstanding the whole thing I believe I am getting fatter, so it shows I am contented. In fact I would not change with anybody in the world just now . . .

Belgium has done well & nobly & appears to be having the brunt of the fighting. We ought to send the Expeditionary Force over at once to help her if it is to go at all. And move the Ulster Volunteers[1] over *en bloc* to the east coast of England, to defend it. But I don't think Germany could spare a man to launch at England. She'll want them all on the Continent, so the invasion scare must fall flat. We get Poldhu telegrams every now and then and I was delighted to hear this morning that Kitchener was to be Secretary for War. Just the right man, he'll do it splendidly & has the confidence of the country behind him.

The Admiralty has done awfully well up to now and have left nothing undone. I hope they will keep it up. Just heard of the disaster to *Amphion*. I trust the Captain, Fox got clear. He is a gallant fellow and would be a sore loss[2] . . . I see Winston answered [?] in the House of Commons about the strewing of mines. It's no use crying out when we are hurt. I always told him it would be so. This is not going to be a manoeuvre picnic . . . Our principal dangers are mines and submarines, and I think in time we shall be able to manage both satisfactorily. So don't fuss, dear heart. The *Lion* is stout and strong and it will take a big

[1] A volunteer force raised to resist the Liberal government's policy of Home Rule for a United Ireland.

[2] On 5 August 1914 Captain C. H. Fox in *Amphion* sank the minelayer *Königin Louise*. *Amphion* herself was sunk by a mine on following day with loss of 51 men and most of the prisoners from the minelayer; Fox himself survived.

thing to demolish her, which is not going to be yet. I am indeed fortunate to be in such a ship and have a fine lot of fellow officers and men with me . . .

61.   *To his wife* [Rosyth]

[BTY/17/28/30–32]   *Lion*
                                                                   16.8.14

I got your wire sent by the Senior Naval Officer Scotland this afternoon and was much relieved to hear that *Sheelah* had arrived safely Rosyth. I wonder how you managed to get him to send it off, as the wireless is very full just now and it's hard to get a message of importance through. I assume that you are up there in her and am wondering what you are doing with yourself as there is nobody to nurse or look after, and I don't think there will be for some considerable time yet.

We have some long and weary weeks to get through before we can do anything very definite, during which we can never relax, always be at tension for all eventualities. This is the wearing part of it without the relief of excitement, and constant anxiety as to what the day will bring forth, and night too for that matter. Mericfully we at present enjoy the most wonderful weather on the whole. Sometimes strong wind and sometimes fine & smooth, but always with a clear atmosphere and long visibility, which is everything to us. The days are shortening up and the nights, though still short, are getting longer. It is when the days are short and the nights are long, with fog and mist, that the real troubles will begin. But we are getting very good training for it and by the time it comes shall be ready to meet the new conditions.

My principal difficulty is want of exercise. I can manage a want of sleep and want of food, which doesn't apply now, but it is the want of exercise that finds me out. I walk up and down the deck for hours and only succeed in making my feet sore and tired. But everybody is very well and the spirit of everybody excellent, which is the great thing.

I cannot believe it will last very long. The economic pressure will be too great to permit that, and I think much will depend upon the result of the first big battle with the French. Let us hope that they will be forced to send their fleet to sea, which I am afraid will be very unlikely until they have caused us considerable losses from the mine and submarine, which has not been very successful up to the present, and I think the danger will lessen instead of increase as the war goes on, as long as we can exercise the same vigilance as at present . . .

It is very difficult to realise even now that we are at war and all that it means & it is very difficult to impress it on the minds of everybody. And, if one tries to forecast the future, it becomes worse. The Navy I hope & believe, will have served its purpose and then it will not be necessary to have always such a large force strung up to concert pitch as we have been for the last five years & there will be a general relaxation without loss of efficiency. We are undoubtedly becoming even more efficient every day the war progresses. I suppose the expeditionary force will be off soon and cause many gaps in the social life of England, with its attendant depression. We have had no news for over a week so know nothing, but I fancy every unit of life will be sorely affected by this time. Still, we are a sound race & will come through alright in the end. As a rule we are bad starters and it's our staying power which saves the situation. but on this occasion we have surprised the world and ourselves by starting uncommonly well.

We get news through Poldhu Telegram which is something and have heard of the *Goeben* having retired up the Dardanelles, presumably to become a Turk. In any case she ought never to be in a position to bother us and I hope now they will let the *Indefatigable* come home and join us. The Germans do not seem to have made any headway anywhere and to have been checked all down the line. They have moreover suffered losses all over the world from China, East and West Africa and in the Atlantic, so the strings against them are gradually being tightened and their outlook is not particularly rosy.

Woodley has done wonderfully well and feeds us like fighting cocks, in fact too well, and we are all getting fat on it notwithstanding the strains etc . . .

I sincerely trust it be all over by October and before winter sets in, but I doubt that very much. I don't think a great nation can be defeated in so short a time. It means the end of the German monarchy if it is so . . .

62.   *To his wife* [Rosyth]

[BTY/17/28/34–6]   *Lion*
                                                                         19.8.14

*   *   *

Yes, apparently the War Office is greatly alarmed at the idea
of a possible invasion but I do not think that anything of a serious
nature can take place. Our patrol flotillas ought to be able to
locate them in good time and a small force ought to be well looked
after by the Territorials. 40,000 men are not going to conquer
England and they are badly needed in other places, such as
reserves. I don't think it would be a bad thing for a certain
number to land, it would make the people of England realise more
properly their responsibilities and the necessity of being able to
defend their own country, which they never will unless they have
ocular demonstration . . . Last night I had a splendid sleep. It
was the first real night I have had in bed since I saw you last,
which seems years & years ago, and I enjoyed every minute of
it . . .

Kitchener is doing wonders, but then of course he would, the
right man in the right place. I wish we had one like him in
the Navy. Winston, I hear does practically everything, and more
besides . . . I see Kitchener has stated that the war will be over
in 6 months or it will last 2 years. This I cannot think possible for
a moment. The money in the world will run short before then or
they will have to construct some new form of barter & exchange.

All officers and men are very well, very cheerful and in great
spirits that something will come our way before long by which we
can prove our metal & efficiency. If we could have a blow up
every now and then to keep our spirits up & our hand in, it would
be something . . .

63.   *To his wife* [Rosyth]

[BTY/17/28/ 38–40]   *Lion*
                                                                         20.8.14

*   *   *

We are well up to date now with our news and have had papers
quite recently. Everything seems to be going well for the allied
forces and the great military big bear of Germany which has kept

everybody on tenterhooks for the past twenty years seems to be fizzling out and unable to do anything special. In fact their calculations have been so accurate and numerous that they have forgotton the most important of all, namely the personal element, and it certainly appears as if the heart of the personnel is not in it and they will consequently fail in all the big things they undertake . . .

I've used up the money for the horses to look after the wives and those dependent on sailors belonging to the squadron who are in a bad way. You will see that there will be heaps of money coming in for spectacular funds like Millie's[1] & the Princess of Wales fund, but nothing to help the wife and children of the poor badly paid sailor, stoker etc. Those whose homes are at Devonport, Portsmouth or any of the big centres will be alright as there are organisations to look after them & plenty of willing people. But for those whose homes are in remote & out of the way places in small villages etc in Ireland and all over England where the price of bread, sugar, tea and all necessities go [sic] up although they say they don't, there is nobody to look after them and the sailor's remittance monthly fails to arrive on time, & very meagre at that, there is nothing but starvation for many. So, I am starting funds onboard all the ships to go into the case of every man and see that his dependents are cared for, and am applying the money to that end, which is sorely needed. I get something out of it too because the sailor who knows that his dear ones are being looked after will be happier in his mind and will work better & more cheerfully, for that knowledge . . .

You won't hear from me for some days after this, so don't fuss. All is well, well fed, well housed, plenty to think about and now well stored [?] with sleep. The waiting is the part that tries one, never relaxing a second because never certain when the blow will fall. But be sure we shall be ready when it does, the sooner the better. The *Invincible* I hope will join us before long, so we shall be well off then for ships.

The news from London seems to point to everything being fairly quiet and resuming its normal condition. They will gradually lull themselves to sleep and even forget that there is such a thing as war, until some German soldiers land on the east coast, not that they can do much harm even if they do.

[1]Millie, Duchess of Sutherland.

64. *To his wife* [Rosyth]

[BTY/17/28/42–5]   *Lion*
                                                          24.8.14

We are still wandering about the face of the ocean and apparently get no nearer to the end. In fact we have not begun yet.
This waiting is the deuce and, as far as we can see, has no limit.
We are entirely in the hands of our friends the Germans as to
when he [sic] will come out and be whacked. We have established
economic pressure of a very thorough character and have trailed
our coats for him to come and tread on them, but he refuses to
come and we can do no more. It is tantalising but is to be expected
and I can see no reason why it should not continue for many
months. We have the anxiety and strain of being continually at
sea, expecting anything at any moment, and it is not pleasant, but
has to be, there is no other way out at present. Our news is
confined to telegrams from a German source called Norddeutsch
which continally reports magnificent victories won by the Germans
all along the front, Ostend down to Basle, which are immediately
contradicted by the telegrams we get from Poldhu, which were
amusing but have now become boring, and we wonder what is
the truth. We have our own scares daily about every three or
four hours, which always fizzle out to nothing. It's three weeks
tomorrow since we went to war and have seen and done nothing. I
won't say done nothing because we have steamed miles, consumed
thousands of tons of coal and, I think, are more efficient than we
were. Notwithstanding it all, our spirits are high and the weather
on the whole has treated us well . . . The days are getting shorter
and the nights longer which is gradually increasing the strain on
the personnel, but has its advantages as it lessens the number of
hours that we are likely to be subjected to submarine attack,
which is something gained. I believe there is a great battle going
on along the Belgian frontier and I suppose our troops are in
position by this time and taking their part, which will be no mean
part either. I fear it will be very heavy in casualties . . . I am sure
our soldiers will give a fine account of themselves. They are small
in numbers but they are undoubtedly efficient and will wager [sic]
they will hold up the Germans at their end. Lucky for them, it's
the fine weather season: will be very hot, but that is better than
the wet. I wish I was with them. For 30 years I have been waiting
for this day and have as fine a command as one would wish for,

and can do nothing. 3 weeks of war and haven't seen the enemy. We shall have to become more offensive. It's four weeks since we parted, dear heart, and it seems like four centuries . . .

[P.S.]   Send me a box of chocolates if you can. They would be very acceptable.

65.   *To his wife* [Rosyth]

[BTY/17/28/47–8]   *Lion*
29.8.14

Just a line to say all is well. I sent *Liverpool* in to Rosyth today with some prisoners and wounded. We got at them yesterday and got three of their cruisers under the nose of Heligoland, which will give them a bit of a shock. The ones in the *Liverpool*[1] were all that were saved out of one ship and, alas, none were saved from the others that sank. The 3rd disappeared in fog in a sinking condition and I doubt if she ever got back. I could not pursue her further, we were too close already and the sea was full of mines and submarines, and a large force might have popped out on us at any moment. Poor devils, they fought their ships like men and went down with colours flying like seamen, against overwhelming odds. We take no credit for such, but it was good work to be able to do it within 20 miles of their main base, Heligoland, and with the whole of the High Sea Fleet listening to the boom of our guns. We could not afford half measures and had to go in and out as quickly as possible. Three of our light cruiser flotilla cruisers got badly knocked about, and one or two destroyers, but the supporting force light cruiser squadron, which did very well and sank one ship, and my battle-cruisers, had no material damage, only a few hits, and only one casualty, very slight. The Flag Lieutenant trembles because he thinks he will have to be bled. Don't say anything about this until you read in the Press. I am not sure I am justified in telling you so much. Everybody onboard is well and the letting off of guns and doing execution did them all good. But it was sad seeing a gallant ship disappear. That is a side of the picture I cannot permit myself to think about and only

[1]The light cruiser *Liverpool* played a prominent part in rescuing German survivors from the *Mainz* in the Heligoland Bight action.

remember that if we had not been there in time one of ours would have the same fate.

*   *   *

66.   *To the Secretary of the Admiralty*

[BTY/3/1/5]   *Lion*
                                                              30 August 1914

In accordance with Admiralty telegram No 81 I have the honour to report that on Thursday 27 August at 5 a.m. I left Scapa Flow with 1st B.C.S. and 1st L.C.S. in company, proceeding South Eastwards to rendezvous with R.A. *Invincible*.[1]

2. At 4 a.m. 28th the movements of Flotillas commenced as previously arranged, B.C.S. and L.C.S. supporting as described in my signal 1653 of 27th.

3. The subsequent narrative of events is as follows:-

5 a.m.   Passed through pre-arranged rendezvous having been joined by R.A. *Invincible, New Zealand* and 4 T.B.D.'s. Asked R.A. what his instructions were: received reply- 'My instructions are to be in Lat 54° 30′ N, Long 6° 20′ E at 8.30 a.m. and from there to steer N 80 W, no speed given but by inference 12 knots.' Asked for positions of our submarines and formation of T.B.D. flotillas: replies as follows — 'R.A. to V.A. — submarines are as follows: 3 in Heligoland Bight, 3 in Longitude 6° 48′ E, Latitude unknown but as arranged by Commodore (S),[2] 2 off the Western Ems.' Commodore (S) is in *Lurcher* with *Firedrake*, searching for submarines South to South East of my 0500 position.
'Admiralty signal last evening says Commodore (S) reports enemy's submarines and warns battle-cruisers of the area in which they were seen. At noon a signal may be expected from *Euryalus* to say that operations are to cease and all vessels to return to their bases. I have no further information.'
8 a.m.   Passed through pre-arranged R.V., course W ¼ S, speed 16 knots, altering course 4 points every ¼ hour to evade submarines.

[1]Rear-Admiral Moore, see note 2 on page 108.
[2]Commodore Keyes, see note 1 on page 108.

8.10 a.m. Received signal from Commodore (T)[1] timed 7.50, 'Destroyers are in action with destroyers'. This was presumably in vicinity of their pre-arranged 8 a.m. position.

8.40 a.m. Informed S.O. L.C.S. I was marking time in vicinity of Lat 54° 32' N, Long 6° 35' E.

9.10 a.m. Received report from *Lurcher*, 2 enemy cruisers N.W., *Lurcher's* position 55° 10' N, 6° 48' E: course and speed not stated.

Intercepted signal from S.O. 1st L.C.S. that he was proceeding S 88 W, 20 knots. Also intercepted various signals to him to support Commodore (S).

9.30 a.m. In view of above and no news from Commodore (T) of his position since 8.15 a.m., I assumed that the whole sweep was moving West so proceeded West ¼ South at 20 knots with B.C.S. spread. Communicated my position to S.O. L.C.S., Commodore (T) and Commodore (S).

9.41 a.m. Received signal *Lurcher* to *Invincible* – 'Am being chased by 4 light cruisers and am leading them in your direction.'; no position, course or speed. On enquiring from *Invincible* as to where this position was likely to be, received reply: Lat 54°N, Long 4° 50' E.

9.45 a.m. Reduced to 15 knots. Felt that there was something wrong owing to having had no definite report from Commodore (T) since he was first engaged at 7.50 a.m. Commenced turning by 8 points turns every ¼ hour to mark time until 11 a.m.

10.10 a.m. Received signal from S.O. 1 L.C.S. – 'Commodores (S) and (T) had no knowledge of 1 L.C.S. taking part. I consider we should withdraw at once. Submarines are closing to us.'

10.50 a.m. Sighted L.C.S. to the southward, altered course to close them.

11.0 a.m. B.C.S. in 54° 20' N, 6° 13' E, steering S.W. at 16 knots was attacked by submarines: 3 were sighted. Ordered 4 attendant T.B.D.s to attack submarines: B.C.S. altered course to avoid them.

11.15 a.m. Ordered S.O. 1 L.C.S. to support the torpedo flotillas. Various conflicting signals had been received indicating that Commodore (T) or Commodore (S), or both, were being chased by light cruisers. Commodore (S) in *Lurcher* was aided first and was now in sight. It transpired that he had been running

[1]Commodore Tyrwhitt, see note 3 on page 108.

from our L.C.S. whose presence in the theatre of operations he had not been informed of.

11.25 a.m. Received signal from Commodore (T), 'Am attacked by *large* cruiser 54° 0' N, 7° 13' E.': no course received.

11.28 a.m. Received signal from Commodore (T), 'Respectfully request that I may be supported. Am hard pressed.'

11.30 a.m. Received from Captain (D) 1st Flotilla, 'Assistance urgently required 54° 0' N, 7° 0' E.'

At 11.30 the B.C.S. in 54° 9' E turned to E.S.E. and worked up to full speed.

These signals, received 11.25, 11.28, and 11.30 were practically the first news we had got since 7.55 a.m. as to movements of the flotillas or the result of an action which apparently had been in progress for 3½ hours. The situation appeared to me to be extremely critical. The flotillas had advanced on their sweep only 10 miles since 6 a.m. and thus were only 26 miles from an enemy base in their rear, with another base 25 miles on their flank to the westward of them. *Arethusa* was already reduced to 10 knots and there was the possibility of a grave disaster.

At 11.30 I therefore decided that the only course possible was to take the B.C.S. at full speed to the eastward. To be of any value the support must be overwhelming and carried out at the highest speed possible as there were indications of the presence of 3 or 4 enemy ships (one of which was reported a large cruiser). I did not deem the L.C.S., two of whose ships were detached, *vide* Commodore's report, to be strong enough to deal with the situation sufficiently.

I had not lost sight of the danger to my squadron from the following:-

(1) Enemy submarines. (2) Our own submarines. (3) The possible sortie of a large enemy force from their base, especially in view of state of the weather, which to the South East was misty.

(1) I discounted by the fact that our high speed made their attack difficult, and the smooth state of the sea made their detection easy, when keeping a sharp look out.

(2) I discounted, partly for the same reason, and partly because I had been able to communicate with Commodore (S), who was now in sight, and informed me at 11.55 a.m. that our submarines were 20 miles ahead, i.e. to the Eastward. This gave me room to manoeuvre, and his presence with me was some measure of protection.

(3) I discounted because our force was so powerful that we could

only have been stopped by a battle squadron, which was unlikely to be out in time if we were sufficiently rapid in our support.

12.15 p.m.   Weather misty, visibility 7,000 to 8,000 yards: sighted *Fearless* and 1st Flotilla retiring West. Then sighted L.C.S. engaging enemy ship ahead, they appeared to have her beat. B.C.S. steered N.E. for sounds of firing ahead.

12.30 p.m.   Sighted *Arethusa* and 3rd Flotilla retiring to Westward, engaging a vessel of the *Kolberg* class on our port bow.

12.37 p.m.   Opened fire.

12.42 p.m.   Enemy turned to N.E. Chased at 27 knots.

12.56 p.m.   Sighted and engaged 2-funnel cruiser ahead, which turned to Eastward. She seemed to be of the *Hansa* class and disappeared in the mist, burning fiercely, with heavy list and in a sinking condition (German Press telegram reports this vessel to have been the *Ariadne* and that she subsequently sank). This was not the vessel sighted by *Southampton*, reported of *Rostock* class. Floating mines having been reported by our destroyers to the Eastward I did not deem it advisable to detach a vessel to pursue; also it was very desirable to remain concentrated to meet eventualities.

1.10 p.m.   Made the general signal, 'Retire'. Turned North and circled to port to complete the destruction of vessel first engaged, which had disappeared in the mist.

1.25 p.m.   Sighted her again steaming S.E., colours still flying. *Lion* opened fire with 2 turrets and at 1.35 p.m. she sank after receiving 2 salvoes in latitude 54° 10' longitude 7° 8' E. 4 attached destroyers were sent at once to pick up survivors, but deeply regret that none were saved. The German ships fought against overwhelming odds with the greatest gallantry and sank with colours flying.

1.40 p.m.   Turned to Northward. All forces had retired by 1.50. Battle-cruisers covering the retirement of flotillas until nightfall.

2.0 p.m.   *Queen Mary* was attacked by submarine which she avoided by putting her helm over.

3.25 p.m.   *Lowestoft* reported a submarine approaching to attack. Avoided it easily by altering course.

4.45 p.m.   Turned to the Westward to remain within supporting distance of *Euryalus* and detached *Invincible* and *New Zealand* to form immediate support.

6.0 p.m.   It was apparent from intercepted signals that retirement had been well executed and all T.B.D.s accounted for.

Altered course to North, spread light cruisers and swept Northwards to the Eastward of meridian 4 E in accordance with orders received from the Commander-in-Chief.

7.45 p.m. Detached *Liverpool* with German prisoners to Rosyth (7 officers and 79 men).

No further incidents occurred worthy of report.

7.0 p.m. 29th   Arrived Scapa Flow

4. Report from Commodore 1st Light Cruiser Squadron is attached [67].

67.   *From Commodore Goodenough*

[BTY/3/1/2]   *Southampton*
29th August 1914

Sir,

I have the honour to report that I left Scapa Flow at 5 a.m. on Thursday 27th August with *Nottingham, Birmingham, Lowestoft, Falmouth* and *Liverpool* in company and proceeded in accordance with your orders.

2. At 4 a.m. on 28th August in latitude 55° 20′ North, longitude 6° 43′ East I met the Commodore (T) with destroyers and received the following signal from him, 'Are you taking part in the operations?'

At 8 a.m. I received a signal by W/T, 'Destroyers were engaged with enemy destroyers': proceeded at full speed until at 8.15 a.m. when I received a signal from *Lurcher* giving her position and reporting that she was in touch with two cruisers: I then went to her assistance.

Nottingham and *Lowestoft* had previously been detached to render assistance on my port side (to the East); these ships did not rejoin till late in the afternoon.

3. I fell in with *Lurcher* in latitude 54° 06′ North, longitude 6° 56′ East and received the following signal from the Commodore (S):-

'I was not informed you were coming into this area, your run great risk from our submarines. Position of Commodore (T) at 9.45 should read 45 miles West. Please give me your present position. Your unexpected appearance has upset all our plans. There are submarines off EMS.' [*sic*]

Shortly before this I sighted and attempted to sink a submarine; subsequent events tend to indicate that this was a British submarine. Fortunately I missed her.

4. At 10.08 a.m. I received signals from the Commodore (T) and *Euryalus* to support Commodore (S) who was then in sight of me in *Lurcher*.

The weather was thick closer inshore.

5. At 11.15 a.m. in latitude 54° 18′ North, longitude 6° 29′ East I received your signal to support Commodore (T) and at noon *Southampton* with *Birmingham, Falmouth* and *Liverpool* engaged and sank the German light cruiser *Mainz* in latitude 54° North, longitude 6° 45′ East.

Liverpool picked up 7 officers and 79 men from the *Mainz*.

I then rejoined your flag which was passing at the moment.

6. The four-funnelled cruiser reported by *Lurcher* was undoubtedly our own and had the Commodore (S) been fully aware of the situation and scheme of operations I should in all probability have been able to support Commodore (T) earlier.

7. At 1.10 p.m. a German cruiser of *Rostock* class was engaged by *Southampton* and *Birmingham* on the starboard beam at a comparatively long range. She disappeard to the Southward, apparently having received some slight damage.

8. The sea in the vicinity of the enemy appeared to be sown with floating mines.

9. There were no casualties in nor damage to any of the ships of 1st Light Cruiser Squadron during the operations.

68.   *From Captain Chatfield* [forwarded to Jellicoe]

[BTY/3/1/7]   *Lion*
                                                    31 August 1914

Remarks on Cruiser Action of 28th August

The action was fought with a bad light and a visibility of 5,000 to 7,000 yards. The enemy first appeared to view at about 7,500 yards through binoculars and about two or three minutes were taken to decide if he was a friendly or hostile ship, ships being on closing courses. The guns and Argo[1] were kept trained on enemy by bearing but it was impossible to take ranges and when the 'Commence' was sounded no range had been taken, nor was it possible to take any afterwards.

Even greater difficulty in seeing the enemy was experienced in the turrets, the periscopes getting damp also from spray added to the lack of illumination and gunlayers could not lay accurately. After firing each round, great difficulty was experienced in finding the target again. The Argo training gear having broken down with the first salvo, its Evershed[2] could not be used to direct the guns, otherwise it would have been invaluable. The control of Eversheds was shifted to 'B' turret, but owing to the difficulty experienced by this turret in finding the target after firing, the Eversheds bearing receivers were of little or no assistance to the turret trainers. Under similar conditions the use of a turret for controlling the bearing receivers is therefore not recommended.

The range on the sights on opening fire was 6,000 but this was rapidly spotted down to 5,200 and first straddle was obtained at a range of about 5,000. The spread was larger than it ought to have been at this range, undoubtedly due to difficult laying. This difficulty was not immediately realised and being ourselves under fire, the gunlayers were probably unduly hurried, consequently a small percentage of hits were obtained to rounds expended.

The smoke from enemy, and also the burst of our shell, made it still more difficult later to aim at anything but the flashes of the enemy's guns.

I think it should be realised that under short visibility conditions, unless you close enemy to a range 2,000 less than visibility, slow and deliberate firing with turret guns will be as effective as rapid, and great waste of ammunition will be avoided. The inclination, on the contrary, when at short ranges, is to fire very rapidly.

The *Köln*[3] opened simultaneously with *Lion* and fired good salvoes (possibly by director) but the spread was considerable,

[1]The Argo company was founded by the inventor A. H. Pollen to manufacture his fire-control system. The Admiralty did not adopt his entire system but did install some components. The central feature was the Argo Clock, a form of computer designed to keep guns correctly aimed despite changing ranges. See General Introduction, p. xxii, and note 1 on page 241.

[2]The Evershed bearing-indicator instrument was designed to keep guns on the same bearing as that ordered by the Chief Fire Control Officer; capital ships had this equipment situated in the main armament control position transmitting to receivers in the turrets.

[3]The light cruiser *Köln*, the German flagship, was sunk in the action.

with the 4″ projectiles at 6,000 yards; she must have fired some 200 rounds or more and made 5 hits. Her fire was not very rapid. The shell always burst on striking the water, those that struck *Lion* had of course no effect, with the following exceptions:- 1 projectile struck base of 'B' turret. Effect outside, nil. Effect inside was as follows: Electric light wiring torn away locally. Similar damage was caused by a shell which struck after deck. The circuits being in both cases switched off this was of no consequence and the damage was quickly repaired after the action, but is instructive.

It appears very necessary for bad visibility firing that turret officers should have some form of open sight to get their gunlayers on to the enemy quickly. This is being done in *Lion*.

Bearing plates in the Conning Tower are also essential even where Eversheds are fitted, as the latter are disappointing in thick weather.

69. *To Admiralty*

[BTY/3/1/4]   *Lion*
                                                        1st September 1914

I have the honour to report that on Thursday 27 August at 5 a.m. I left Scapa Flow with the 1st Battle Squadron and 1st Light Cruiser Squadron in company, proceeding south eastward to rendezvous with Rear-Admiral, *Invincible*.

2. At 4 a.m. the movements of the Flotillas commenced as previously arranged, the Battle-Cruiser Squadron and Light Cruiser Squadron supporting as described in my signal 1635 of 27th. The Rear-Admiral, *Invincible* with *New Zealand* and 4 destroyers having joined my flag, the squadron passed through the rendezvous respectively arranged for 5 a.m. and 8 a.m.

3. At 8.10 a.m. I received a signal from Commodore (T) 'destroyers are engaged with destroyers'. This was presumably in the vicinity of their pre-arranged 8 a.m. rendezvous. From this time until 11 a.m. I remained about this vicinity ready to support as necessary, intercepting various signals which contained no information on which I could act.

4. At 11 a.m. the squadron was attacked by three submarines.[1] The attack was frustrated by rapid manoeuvring and the four destroyers were ordered to attack them. At 11.15 various signals having been received indicating that Commodore (T) and Commodore (S) were both in need of assistance, I ordered the Light Cruiser Squadron to support the torpedo flotillas.

5. At 11.25 a.m. received signal from Commodore (T) stating that he was being attacked by a large cruiser and at 11.28 a further signal, 'Respectfully request that I may be supported. Am hard pressed.' At 11.30 the Captain (D), 1st Flotilla signalled 'Assistance urgently required.'

6. From the foregoing the situation appeared to me extremely critical. The flotillas had advanced on their sweep only 10 miles since 8 a.m. and were only about 25 miles from two enemy bases on their flank and rear respectively. Commodore Goodenough had detached two of his light cruisers to assist some destroyers earlier in the day and these had not yet rejoined. He therefore had only 4 ships with him, and as the reports indicated the presence of many enemy ships – one a large cruiser – I considered that his force might not be strong enough to deal with the situation sufficiently rapidly, so at 11.30 a.m. the battle cruisers turned to E.S.E. and worked up to full speed. It was evident that to be of any value the support must be overwhelming and carried out at the highest speed possible.

7. I had not lost sight of the risk of submarines and possible sortie in force from the enemy's base, especially in view of the mist to the south east. Our high speed however made submarine attack difficult and the smoothness of the sea made their destruction comparatively easy. I considered that we were powerful enough to deal with any sortie except by a battle squadron, which was unlikely to come out in time, provided our stroke was sufficiently rapid.

8. At 12.15 p.m. *Fearless* and 1st Flotilla were sighted retiring West – at the same time the Light Cruiser Squadron was observed to be engaging an enemy ship ahead. They appeared to have her beat.

I then steered N.E. to sounds of firing ahead and at 12.30 p.m. sighted *Arethusa* and 3rd Flotilla retiring to the Westward engaging a cruiser of the *Kolberg* class on our port bow. I steered to cut her off from Heligoland and at 12.37 p.m. opened fire. At

[1] A false alarm; see Julian Corbett and Henry Newbolt, *History of the Great War: Naval Operations* (London, 1920) Vol. I, p. 113.

12.42 the enemy turned to N.E. and we chased at 27 knots (& shortly after disabled her & she drifted down the line & was fired at by some other ships).

9. At 12.56 p.m. sighted and engaged a two-funnelled cruiser ahead. *Lion* fired two (a few) salvoes at her which took effect and she disappeared into the mist burning furiously and in a sinking condition. In view of the mist and that she was steering at high speed at right angles to *Lion* (& altering course 4 points every minute) who was herself steaming at 28 knots, the *Lion*'s firing was very creditable.

10. Our destroyers had reported the presence of floating mines to the Eastward, and as several of them were now being sighted, I considered it inadvisable to pursue her. It was also essential that the squadrons should remain concentrated and I accordingly made the general signal, 'Retire' at 1.10 p.m. — and the battle-cruisers turned North and circled to port to complete the destruction of the vessel first engaged. She was sighted again at 1.25 p.m. steaming S.E. with colours still flying. *Lion* opened fire with two turrets and at 1.35 p.m. after receiving two salvoes, she sank.

11. The four attached destroyers were sent to pick up survivors but I deeply regret that they subsequently reported that they searched the area but found none. The German ships fought against overwhelming odds with the greatest gallantry and sank with colours flying.

12. At 1.40 p.m. the battle-cruisers turned to the Northward to retire and *Queen Mary* was again attacked by a submarine. The attack was avoided by the use of helm — *Lowestoft* was also unsuccessfully attacked[1] — the battle cruisers covered the retirement until night fall. By 6 p.m. the retirement having been well executed and all destroyers accounted for, I altered course, spread the light cruisers and swept northwards in accordance with the Commander-in-Chief's orders. At 7.45 p.m. I detached *Liverpool* to Rosyth with German prisoners, 7 officers and 79 men, survivors from the *Mainz*. No further incident occurred.

[1]No confirmation of these attacks has been found.

70. *To his wife*

[BTY/17/29/2–4]   *Lion*
                                                    2.9.14

I got your message from the *Liverpool*, and the officer who
went on board *Sheelah* will have told you all we did on the
Friday. I had thought I should have received an expression of their
appreciation from Their Lordships, but have been disappointed,
or rather not so much disappointed as disgusted, and my real
opinion has been confirmed that they would have hung me if
there had been a disaster, as there very nearly was, owing to the
extraordinary neglect of the most ordinary precautions on their
part. However, all's well that end's well, and they haven't had
the opportunity of hanging me yet and they won't get it. Don't
breathe a word of this to a soul, but it's on record. Anyhow I
received a most charming telegram from the Prime Minister of
Canada, whoever he is,[1] to myself, officers and men. A bit of an
Imperialist whoever he is. They did not leave us at rest long, just
time to coal and get some more ammunition and we are now
scouring the sea again. The ships' companies are full of beans and
that little shooting and getting into touch with the enemy did them
no end of good and they feel warriors now. Of course, these
entertainments are the easiest part of our job and not to be
compared with the weary hours of looking out without much
release to the strain, which is far and away the worst side of our
picture. I had a long letter from Filson Young, who has gone off
as the honorary secretary of the Australian hospital, very down
on his luck, and wants to go to sea as the official chronicler of
naval events. He would hate it if he were here now . . .

I can only trust that our friends the Russians are the victorious
ones. Little von Essen[2] has done nothing up to now except some
of his ships have blown themselves up, apparently on their own
mines. The German cruiser *Magdeburg*[3] ran ashore, which, with
the three we sank, *Köln*, *Mainz* and *Ariadne*, will make a big
hole in their cruiser force. They seem to be terribly busy laying
mines, which is alright as long as we can locate them, which fact

[1]Sir Robert Borden (1854–1937): Prime Minister of Canada from 1911; member
of War Cabinet, 1917–18.
[2]Vice-Admiral Nikolai von Essen, Russian naval commander in Baltic.
[3]*Magdeburg*, German light cruiser sunk by the Russians in the Gulf of Finland
26 August 1914; her naval cypher books were recovered and handed to the
Admiralty in late October.

has saved us from a disaster up to now. They borrowed the *New Zealand* from me the other day to operate down south, and sent me the *Inflexible*, but I have managed to change it and get my *New Zealand* back again, which is a good thing, and I shall get the *Tiger* in about 3 or 4 weeks, so shall have my 4 pussy cats then. We have been engaged in another operation of sorts but nothing has come of it up to now.

We had a terrible scare last night, sighted a lot of vessels without lights, so turned round after them and followed for some time, trying to get the right side of the moon, so they should not see us and we could get a good view of them. This required great restraint on our part, as it is everything to get in the first blow. After an hour we got to a good position, when I thought they looked uncommonly familiar, and so challenged them, when they turned out to be our own destroyers. They were never so near being blown out of the water before. There is something wrong somewhere which would permit them being in a position in which we both run such unnecessary risks. War is bad enough without adding to it by making stupid mistakes of that nature . . .

71. *Secretary of the Admiralty to Jellicoe*

[BTY/3/1/3] *Admiralty*
22nd October 1914

Sir,

I am commanded by My Lords Commissioners of the Admiralty to acquaint you that they have had before them a letter dated 1st September, 437/023, from Vice Admiral (Acting) Sir David Beatty, KCB, MVO, DSO, reporting his proceedings on the occasion of the action off Heligoland on August 28th.

Their Lordships have read this report with much satisfaction, and I am to request that you will convey to Sir David Beatty their appreciation of the resolution and promptitude shown by him in bringing his Squadron into action with decisive effect notwithstanding the risks he had to face from submarines and floating mines.

I am,   Sir,

   Your obedient servant,

   O. MURRAY

The Commander in Chief
H.M. Ships and Vessels
Home Fleets

II

Vice Admiral, First Battle-Cruiser Squadron
   I have much pleasure in forwarding this expression of their
Lordships' appreciation with which I fully concur.

                                          J. JELLICOE
                                          29 October 1914

72.   *To his wife* [Aberdour House Rosyth][1]

[BTY/17/29/11–13]   *Lion*
                                                  12 Sept. 1914

                         *   *   *

We went out on Monday very slowly until we got to Inchkeith
when it was nearly dark, and then we went very fast so as to run
no risk of the submarines. Rosyth left me with the impression that
they were only playing at war and had not considered the matter
very seriously. No doubt the disaster to the poor old *Pathfinder*[2]
will help to enforce it upon their minds, but there is a lot to be
learnt there yet.
   We wandered into the North Sea and patrolled for Tuesday
and Wednesday; and, Thursday, had another look into the Bight,
but they knew we were coming and not a soul was in sight. I had
made certain they would be ready for us and give us a warm
welcome, but I fear we gave them much more of a shaking than
we thought of the first time and they haven't recovered from that
yet. I fear the rascals will never come out, but will only send out
minelayers & submarines. They seem to have a blight on them

   [1]Aberdour House, about six miles from the Rosyth base, rented by the Beattys;
Ethel spent most of the war there, interspersed with short trips to London.
   [2]*Pathfinder*, destroyer flotilla leader, Captain Martin Leake; torpedoed and sunk
off St Abbs Head by U–21, 5 September 1915.

and wanting initiative and dash with their battle-cruisers. They could have done so much by this time if they had set their minds to it. It really is very disappointing and looks as if we shall [?] go through the war without ever coming to grips with them. Such a thought is more than I can bear . . .

73. *To his wife* [Aberdour House]

[BTY/17/29/28–31]   *Lion*
                                                19–23.9.14

                   *   *   *

   I hope the generals are not making the mistake of trying to turn the Germans out of their position by a frontal attack. If so, they will lose very heavily and will not succeed. But apparently the Germans themselves have resorted to counter attack, particularly against the English troops and have failed, but I fear our losses in the Brigade of Guards have been very heavy. Oh dear, oh dear, if we could only do something at this end, but we can't. They never send one of their ships out now, only merchantmen or trawlers, which are hard to detect, full of mines, never one of their men of war. So we are just eating our hearts out in impotency, hearing of the great struggle, but can take no part in it. It truly is maddening and I can see no end. If we could strike one heavy blow it would do more to end the war than anything else, with the Russians advancing from the East in myriads, and if we could only smash their navy, they would be ready to make peace, with the French and English just containing them on the West side.
   This roaming about the North Sea day after day with no prospect of meeting an enemy vessel, I think is the heaviest trial that could be laid on any man. Added to which, the anxiety of the mine or submarine always present, provides a situation which requires the highest form of philosophy to compete with, to prevent it from clouding one's judgement. I have here the finest striking force in the world; 6 battle-cruisers and 6 light cruisers, and for all we can do they might be Thames barges. Under any circumstances we can never do anything because we are never in the right place. Who at the Admiralty is responsible for our movements, I do not know, but it is not the C-in-C, who concurs with me. Not a word of this to a soul. I must not criticise, it is

most improper, but my digestion under continual disappointments is giving way and my temper is becoming damnable . . .

Troubridge is being brought home to have the question of the escape of the *Goeben* and *Breslau* enquired into!!!! I suppose it will be hard swearing between him and old Arky Barky.[1] I am indeed sorry, but failures must be explained and it is correct and sound on the part of the Admiralty to insist on adequate explanations.

23rd. In the middle of the night we heard of the terrible disaster to the *Aboukir*, my old ship that I first hoisted my Flag onboard, and so had considerable affection for; the *Cressy* and the *Hogue*, all of my old squadron. We heard the *Aboukir* crying out yesterday morning, and then thought there was something wrong, although she was over 400 miles away, but never contemplated it was a disaster of this magnitude; that is three fine ships and the greater part of two thousand two hundred men that can be ill spared. It was bound to happen, they (our cruisers) had no conceivable right to be where they were. It is not being wise after the event, but I had frequently discussed with others that sooner or later they would surely be caught by submarines or battle-cruisers if they continued to occupy that position. It was inevitable, and faulty strategy on the part of the Admiralty. The trouble is not only shall we have sacrificed such [?] valuable lives and ships but the Admiralty will be panicked and we shall sacrifice positions which will enable further minelaying expeditions to be freely embarked upon by the enemy, and they won't realise that the disaster was to be expected in view of the dispositions made by them. We don't know the full tale or how many lives were lost. It will be terrible reading but can make no difference to the result. I am so sorry for all the poor mothers who had sons, little naval cadets onboard, just from Dartmouth, many of whom no doubt will be among the lost. Don't speak of this or my views. I'll take care they are heard in the right place *and only write this to you.*

[1]Nickname of Admiral Sir Archibald Berkeley Milne (see note 1 on page 18).

74.   *To his wife* [Aberdour House]

[BTY/17/29/37–40]   *Lion*
                                                                    29.9.14

Since my last letter we have been having a most poisonous time; blowing very hard with a bad [?] sea. Sunday night and Monday morning it was a full gale and it was not pleasant, and I haven't a dry spot in my cabin. The decks leak like a sieve and it's like living under a perpetual shower bath. It reminded me often of *Typhoon* by Conrad. It still continues but not so strong, but very unpleasant. We lost a top-gallant mast with the wireless and a gun went overboard. So, it has been no joy and this is the fourth day, one of which we spent practically hove to. It has been bad for some of the destroyers and two of our submarines, I don't know what has happened to them and hope they will turn up alright. However we continue our roaming about the sea, incessant patrol, it is one way we can make ourselves felt and we are always ready to seize the smallest opportunity, should they give us one, of getting at them.

Last time we had news it was so terrible, long lists every day of casualties, that one didn't want to go into harbour. So many we know have been taken, and the proportion of officers to men seems too high, as if they were foolish and exposed themselves too much, which is a foolish way of losing your life, unless it is absolutely necessary.

*   *   *

I've read a little of the book you sent me by Professor Cramp which is indeed interesting and no doubt is very correct as to the attitude adopted towards us by Germans of every class who think in those channels. I fear for them and their reasoning power after the war is over. It will be a rude awakening to find that we are not the decadent race they expected to find, simply because we haven't talked war and have talked about peace. They are evidently one of the lost tribes and are going to remain lost for all time. Ever since the Roman Empire they have striven in the same sort of way to achieve Empire & it has always ended in the same sort of way. Frederick the Great, the greatest warrior Germany ever produced, declined the job when the aspiring ones invited him to consider the time opportune to create a German Empire by saying it would not be worth the trouble. No, they are not cut out for it, talk they ever so loudly. One has only to travel

all over the world to see that & to see what a hash they make
of their efforts at colonising other countries. Literature, Music,
Philosophy they are pre-eminent in, as rulers & conquerors, No!
The poor effete worn out old England, who has constantly produced universal peace for the last twenty years, produces still the
predominant race and are not beaten [?] off our perch yet.

I am glad that Sept. is over, it has been a bad month for the
Navy. You would hardly believe it but we have already lost 120
officers and 2,000 men. We don't have missing & very few
wounded. This is very nearly as many as have been killed in
France up to the battle of the Marne if not more, but I fear the
battle that has been raging for the last fortnight on the river Aisne
will bring up their casualty list terribly high . . .

75.   *To his wife* [Aberdour House]

[BTY/17/30/14–16]   *Lion*
                                                          11.10.14

                    *   *   *

I am overwhelmed, and indeed the Navy is overwhelmed, with
the terrible blow that has fallen upon us in the shape of the
necessity of trying by Court Martial Troubridge for the escape of
the *Goeben* in the Mediterranean. What the charge is I do not
know, but it cannot be one which will be anything but a slur and
stain on the good name of the Navy. They had a Court of Inquiry,
Hedworth Lambton[1]and George Callaghan, and their finding was
such as necessitated a Court Martial, that speaks for itself. It is
very improper and unjust to judge before everything is made
clear, but I shudder to think that the honour of the Navy should
be tarnished by the suggestion as to the necessity of so extreme
a step. To think that amidst the wonderful sacrifices that are being
made, that have been made, the wonderful deeds of heroism that
are done daily by every class of English man & woman all over
the world, the simply tumbling over each other of the individual
to serve his country, to give his life for his country, to die if need
be heroically for his country. To think that the Navy should

---

[1]Later Admiral of the Fleet Sir Hedworth Meux, CinC Portsmouth 1912–16; in
1911 he changed his name from Lambton to Meux as a condition of inheriting a
fortune from the widow of the brewer, Sir Henry Meux.

provide and first and only instance of failure, God, it makes me sick. I fear the worst. I fear a stain that cannot be wiped out, even if in a lesser degree we don't talk about it, but we wait in fear and trembling. So, don't you [–] it's too ghastly to think of . . .

76. *To Churchill*

[CCC/SLGF/3/3]   *Lion*
                                                                17.10.14

I take the opportunity of an officer[1] going to London in charge of signal books, to write you of what goes on. I have written you before, or rather to Hood for you. I think it is right that you should know how things generally affect the Fleet. I trust that you will take this as it is written, in fact I know you will, as being written with only one idea of service to the country. I write as I do because I know that the plain truth at times such as these is the only thing worth hearing, and because you are the one and only man who can save the situation. Even at such times, official documents, requisitions and demands are of little value; they are met at once, I admit, but without understanding the time value of all that lies behind them.

At present we feel that we are working up for a catastrophe of a very large character. The feeling is gradually possessing the fleet that all is not right somewhere. The menace of mines and submarines is proving larger every day, and that adequate means to meet or combat them are not forthcoming, and we are gradually being pushed out of the North Sea, and off our own particular perch. How does this arise? By the very apparent fact that we

[1]Beatty's Flag Commander Reginald Plunkett, later Admiral Sir Reginald Ernle-Erle-Drax (1880–1967); changed his name in 1916 on inheriting an estate from his mother; entered RN 1896; torpedo specialist; had attended both Army and Navy Staff Colleges; joined Beatty as War Staff Officer in 1913; Captain cruiser *Blanche* 1916–18; first Director RNSC Greenwich 1919; a continuing advocate of staff training; Rear-Admiral 1928; commanding 1st Battle Squadron in Mediterranean 1929; Director of Manning 1930–2; CinC America and West Indies 1932–4; Vice-Admiral 1932; CinC Plymouth 1935–8; head of British section of Anglo-French delegation to Russia aiming at a Russian alliance against Germany; CinC Nore 1939–41; retired, volunteered in 1943 as a convoy commodore. In addition to his valuable papers at Churchill College, Cambridge, there are documents on his tactical concepts in the Beatty Papers in the NMM (BTY/7/2).

have no Base where we can with *any* degree of safety lie for coaling, replenishing, and refitting and repairing, after two and a half months of war. This spells trouble. It is a perfectly simple and easy matter to equip Scapa Flow, Cromarty, and Rosyth, so that vessels can lie there undisturbed to do all they want, and for as long as they want, provided material and men are forthcoming. The one place that has put up any kind of defence against the submarine is Cromarty, and that is because at Cromarty there happens to be a *man* who grapples with things as they are, i.e. Commander Munro,[1]and because they have trained artillerymen to man their guns. That was one of the best day's work you ever did when you insisted on taking the defences there in hand. At Rosyth it appeared to me in Sept. when there that to deny access to submarines and destroyers was a fairly simple task; it was an awkward place to get into, but when once in, it ought to be, and could be, very easily made a safe asylum for vessels in need of rest, repair, fuel etc. At Scapa something has been done towards blocking the many entrances, but that is all. I am sure that all the brain and intellect at the Admiralty could devise a scheme or method of defence which would make the anchorage practically safe, and which could be done in a fortnight. No *seaman* can dispute that these three bases could have been made *absolutely* safe from submarine attack during the 2½ months that the war has been in progress. As it is, we have been lulled into a sense of false security, because we have not been attacked before, but I can assure you that it has literally been recognised by all that it was only a question of time when we should have this sense rudely shattered. That time has come, and it is only a Divine Providence that has saved us from an appalling disaster. I maintain stoutly that each one of our three bases could have been made capable of resisting attack by submarines and destroyers, by means of obstruction gates, etc., and by strengthened patrol (local). At Portsmouth, Devonport, Clyde, Pembroke, and Queenstown, we have local defence flotillas; if others are not forthcoming these should be robbed to supply the same at Cromarty, Rosyth, and Scapa, where they are more urgently needed. These, with the aid of submarine nets, torpedo nets, piles or concrete blocks, sunken ships, wire hawsers, booms, and mines as passive defences, supported by well-placed guns manned by *trained* artillerymen, *not territorials*, who cannot be expected to handle efficiently the

[1]Acting Captain (retired list) Donald J. Munro: King's Harbour Master, Cromarty.

modern quick-firing gun against a fast moving target in an uncertain light, to do which requires years of training. These harbours defended thus would free the coastal patrol forces to be out in positions where they can cut off minelayers and locate submarines at a distance from, instead of being tied to, to protect a base which should be quite capable of protecting itself.

Having protected these bases, the point at issue is the question of getting there, as far as cruisers and battle-cruisers are concerned, by utilising the dark hours to arrive and depart, and proceeding at speed, Scapa has no terrors, neither should it have any for the battleships if it is thought necessary to have some stationed or based on it. Cromarty also during hours of darkness is fairly or comparatively safe, but requires more care taken than Scapa. Rosyth is difficult and practically impossible with any degree of safety *except for* a very small number of ships moving very fast; these latter should not in dark hours run great risk. Given freedom from danger of mines in the approach I can assure you I would have no fear of taking the B.C.S.into any one of the three Ports.

The situation as it is, we have no place to lay our heads. We are at Loch na Keal, Isle of Mull. My picket boats are at the entrance, the nets are out and the men are at the guns waiting for coal which has run low, but ready to move at a moment's notice. Other squadrons are in the same plight. We have been running now hard since the 28th July; small defects are creeping up which we haven't time to take in hand. 48 hours is our spell in harbour with steam ready to move at 4 hours notice, coaling on an average 1400 tons a time, night defence stations. The men can stand it, but the machines can't, and we must have a place where we can stop for from four or five days every now and then to give the engineers a chance. Such a place does not exist, so the question arises, how long can we go on, for I fear very much not for long, as the need for small repairs is becoming insistent.

The remedy is to fix upon a base and make it impervious to submarine attack; as I have pointed out I am firmly convinced this can be done.

Can I sum up the situation as it appears to me? We are driven out of the North Sea because of the menace of enemy submarines and mines. Presumably the North Sea is denied the enemy ships by our submarines; but is it? All the control we require to exercise over the mercantile traffic in the North Sea can be produced just as well outside the North Sea as in it; if we revert to the methods

142   THE BEATTY PAPERS

of the Napoleonic wars, and see that it is carried out by patrols off the coast of Ireland, Cape Wrath and Shetlands, and the Faroe Is. if necessary, but aren't we giving up too much by evacuating the North Sea and permitting their fast craft to lay mines and cut up our patrols ad lib, and if they think desirable, cause a panic by rushing 100,000 men across, which under these circumstances would be quite possible, they would command it, not us, which surely would be detrimental. Therefore, or rather anyhow, it is as well to examine the menace as it really is, and I think it can be summed up by saying that —

The menace is one of submarines and mines only. *Region of menace*, our coast lines and entrances to naval and commercial bases and arsenals extending to 60 miles from the coast, and in the case of mines possibly even up to 100 miles from the coast.

To meet this menace, we have a very large force and we are on the right tack. But up to the present this force has accomplished very little, if anything. It presumably consists of the patrol flotillas with a large number of submarines working with them. The 1st and 3rd flotillas are also enlisted practically in this work, and it is supplemented by a vast number of trawlers, etc. On the proper handling of this large force very much depends. What is essential is that whoever runs them should be somebody of great determination who can instil them with a great zeal and imbue them with the spirit of men knowing when they are [– –] and skilful enterprise; a man whom they will trust absolutely and follow anywhere. Such a man you had in John de Robeck.[1] He might not have been a genius, but with guidance from you at the Admiralty he is a born leader of men, of great energy and determination; in fact with those qualitites which come to the front only in war. I am sure that if he had been there he would have curtailed the depredations of the minelayer and the submarine.

Judging from what I have seen and heard of the force of trawlers in northern latitudes in Orkneys and Shetlands, they are practically valueless because they are undisciplined and uncontrollable. They receive high wage and are always drunk. To be of value

[1]Later Admiral of the Fleet Sir John de Robeck (1862–1928): entered RN 1875; Rear-Admiral 1911; Admiral of Patrols 1912; commanding 9th Cruiser Squadron 1914; 2nd in command & eventual successor to Vice-Admiral Carden in the Dardanelles and Vice-Admiral 1915; commanding 2nd Battle Squadron Grand Fleet 1916–19; CinC Mediterranean 1919–22; Atlantic 1922–4; Admiral 1920; Admiral of the Fleet 1925.

they must be manned by men who understand discipline, who will do exactly what they are told, and who can be depended upon. Such a force manned efficiently, and half at least equipped with a short wireless (which should not be impossible) would be invaluable as an adjunct to the coastal patrols. I would suggest their being manned by R.F.R., R.N.R. or R.N.V.R.,[1] equipped with wireless and a gun (hidden). Let them increase their activity by keeping more at sea, rushing numbers to the spot when a submarine has been sighted or reported, gradually pushing out further from the coast as their skill and efficiency increases, until they can hold a line 50 or 60 miles from it. Enemy minelayers laden with high explosives will not risk an encounter with any vessel armed with a gun. Submarines appear to work always with a trawler in the vicinity. In each case of *Pathfinder*, *Aboukir* and *Hawke*[2] a trawler was there, being or about to be examined. With all our resources and all our reserves of trained and disciplined men, we ought to ensure that minelayers and submarines are not permitted to act with impunity undetected along our coasts. The *centre* of the North Sea can be swept by vessels at high speed from time to time without running any great risk from submarines. Permanent patrol areas must be avoided. The submarine cannot act except from a floating base or in the vicinity of the coastline; navigational difficulties prevent it. Destroy his floating base and you control his action in the centre of the sea. Strong coastal patrol should be able to limit his activities near the coast.

In the case of creating extempore defences against submarine attack or destroyers, it is not sufficient to supply a quantity of material as asked for without also supplying a sufficient number of men to place and work them and to keep them constantly efficient and with experience gained to steadily improve. This again calls for disciplined men to be permanently stationed at each base for this purpose alone, which would entail a large amount of heavy work, particularly in winter months.

You might be told that this idea of making the entrances secure is chimerical. This is not so; and I will guarantee that if the fleet was instructed to defend the entrances to the ports named, and was provided with the material, they could and would devise not one but several methods which would satisfy most requirements, and which would keep out submarines. If the fleet cannot spare

[1]Royal Fleet Reserve, Royal Naval Reserve, or Royal Naval Volunteer Reserve.
[2]The cruiser *Hawke* of the 10th Cruiser Squadron (the Northern Blockading Force) was torpedoed off Peterhead with the loss of nearly 500 lives.

the time and labour, turn it over to Commander Munro and give him a free hand and what labour he requires, and he will do it in a fortnight.

I trust, First Lord, you will forgive this long bleat. I think you know me well enough to know that I do not shout without cause. The fleet's tail is still well over the back. We hate running away from our base and the effect is appreciable. We are not enjoying ourselves. But the morale is high and confidence higher. I would not write thus if I did not know that you with your quick grasp of detail and imagination would make something out of it.

Commander Plunkett takes this with him and is perfectly aware of all that I have in my head, so if there is anything in it that requires explanation, he can supply it. He is sound and clear-headed, and you can trust him to give you all information.

[P.S.]   If we ever use Scapa anchorage again, I trust that some steps be taken to deal with the spies that exist there, which are a very serious danger. Martial Law of a fortress is the best and only real method.

77.   *To his wife* [Aberdour House]

[BTY/17/30/33–5]   *Lion*
                                                              20.10.14

Your letters are turning up in driblets, the last I had was the 10th and now I have just received those of 17th and 18th so I have a good many to come. You appear to have been instrumental in putting the Authorities on to the track of spies. I hope they will catch them. God knows we are surrounded with them and do not take adequate steps to deal with them. The Offices or Government Departments take so much trouble in patting themselves on the back that they give everything away sufficiently for the Germans to take steps to counteract what measures have been taken; *vide* Admiralty publications and Home Office *not* the War Office which happens to be run by a man and not a politician. If we only had a Kitchener at the Admiralty we could have done so much and the present state of chaos in naval affairs would never have existed. It is inconceivable the mistakes and blunders we have made and are making — the papers you sent me are alright and I have sent them on.

I am glad now that Hall[1] is at the Admiralty, he might be of some use to me there as he is not afraid of speaking his mind and between you and I think Bertie[2] was. I used to write him screeds of useful information and opinion (not mine only) which were never acted upon and so either they are very mulish and obstinate or very self satisfied and complacent or they never went on. I incline to think the latter. Now I shall push them in to Hall and hope something will be done but he knows my views already.

I've seen George Warrender several times lately, he is very well and cheerful and we are in perfect agreement in all respects, and I know will support me in any way he can. I can get no news of Troubridge beyond they are going to try him by Court Martial. This I think is not a wise thing to do unless they prepared and have already made up their minds that they are prepared to exact the Extreme Penalty *if* it is necessary, 'Pour encourager les autres' not that that is necessary thank God nowadays.

Well there is no honour and glory attached to our work but it is very necessary work all the same and there is plenty of excitement every now and then caused by the enemy submarines, which have been very active of late, but I hope we have been able to bag one or two with proper care and precaution. I do not think they are a very great danger but if one is careless anything becomes dangerous in the game we are playing at. The Captain and Staff are all very well. Plunkett I have sent to London with confidential matter. He was delighted to go and no doubt will have much to tell us when he comes back. He is a good man to send because his opinion carries a good deal of weight among the younger men at the War Staff so I think my letter supported will have some effect. It is rather an extreme step to take but I hope it will have some effect and it will be better than none at all. Tomorrow is Trafalgar Day, the powers that be have forgotten it. Ye shades of Nelson that we should be in the hands of such is

[1]Later Admiral Sir William Reginald Hall (1870–1943): entered RN 1884; Captain of new battle-cruiser *Queen Mary* 1913; in 1914 moved to Admiralty as Director Intelligence Department, where he organised radio stations to intercept enemy radio traffic and 'Room 40' to interpret it; also covered German diplomatic messages, including the Zimmerman telegram which helped to bring the United States into the war in 1917. In addition he was active in counterespionage and virtually ran the whole of Britain's wartime intelligence. See Patrick Beesly, *Room 40: British Naval Intelligence 1914–18* (London, 1982), an excellent account of his career.

[2]Rear-Admiral Sir Horace Hood, see note 2 on page 101.

past enduring but one is powerless to do anything but wait wait day after day. 4 of our destroyers armed with 16 x 4" guns and cruiser of the most modern up to date type with 2 x 6" guns and 6 x 4" guns engaged 4 German torpedo boats armed with nothing and sank them and received paeans of selfsatisfied advertisement from the Admiralty — this is neither naval nor British and the Navy is disgusted.[1] Gosh I should like to tell them what I think. It is truly disgusting and more than I can bear — one can do nothing but grin and bear it and thank God that Navy afloat is not the same as Navy at the Admiralty. I hope to get more letters from you in the course of tomorrow. I cannot think what has happened to them all but they will turn up alright . . .

78. *To his wife* [Aberdour House]

[BTY/17/30/37–9]   *Lion*
                                                         23.10.14

*   *   *

Our news is of course very limited and in fact we have nothing to tell. We go the same weary periods at sea expecting and hoping from day to day for something to turn up and permit us to have the opportunity of striking a blow but it never comes. If anyone would have said that we should have been at war for three months without striking one blow or seeing the enemy for certainly 90 per cent of our ships it would not have been believed. We must not grumble I suppose but it is hard desperately hard not to. We in the battle-cruisers are buoyed up every now and then by the hope of something turning up and even that is denied to the battleships who really have a terrible time. We've been enjoying another gale from the Eastward, this time it did not blow nearly so hard as before but we got very wet and shipped tons of water principally because we have to steam through it.My cabins were again flooded out, it drips everywhere, it's just like living in a large wet cave with water dripping from the roof.

I've written Lady Henry Grosvenor I am sorry for her parting with both her sons to go to the front but as she says she is proud to let them go and as Milly says it's not the time to think of the individual, it's the country one has to think of, there will be time

[1]On 17 October 1914 the light cruiser *Undaunted* and her consorts sank the German torpedo boats, S. 115, 117, 118, 119.

enough to think of them and mourn for them if need be afterwards. No one must possess any other thought but what is best for the country. We are up against it hard and any softening on the part of anyone of us will let the country down. If they only understood the peril we are in as a nation that would indeed alter the outlook and aspect of this and that very considerably. The greatest offenders are the authorities in *all* the offices in London, except the War Office. The Home Office to acquire merit announce how clever they've been in dealing with espionage and by their very announcement nullify all the good they have done by making it public. The Post Office coupled with the Home Office are most culpable. Would you believe it but it is a fact that all over Scotland anywhere where there is a possibility of there being a Naval Base the Post Mistress (not Master) is a German!!! I know three two of which have been appointed since the war!!!! in little out of the way places that in all probability the Postmaster General or the Secretary at the Home Office does not even know exist — We have Sir Edgar Speyer, Waechters, Neumanns, Cassels, Oppenheimers and all the other Hoggenheimers free to do what they like, all German Jews. It is inconceivable.[1]

The Admiralty make announcements from time to time but always with the idea of patting themselves on the back, never anybody else, which gives something away which our enemies are not slow to make use of. For instance, they announced this morning that the three gunboats had assisted the military forces by bombarding the enemy's right flank presumably in the neighbourhood of Ostend, and had thus *justified their purchase* by the clever Admiralty. The Germans get it at once and probably before had not known they were there — next time [?] they'll have some submarines down there to look after them. Every instance of an

---

[1]Anti-Semitism was widespread in Edwardian high society and as many of the most successful Jews were of German origin, intensified during the war. It was involved also in the spy mania to which Beatty was addicted. Of his named victims the two most prominent were Sir Samuel Speyer (1862–1932) and Sir Ernest Cassel (1852–1921). The former, a financier and philanthropist active in Liberal politics, was a friend of Asquith's, who had obtained a baronetcy and a Privy Councillorship for him. In 1914 he was accused of signalling to German submarines from his Norfolk home and resigned his honours and appointments and moved the headquarters of his family's banking firm to New York. In 1921 his naturalisation and that of his family were formally revoked. Cassel, also a financier and philanthropist, had come to England from Cologne in 1869; he was subsequently awarded the GCB, GCMG and GCVO and made Privy Councillor. He was a close personal friend of King Edward VII. In the 1914 hysteria an attempt to deprive him of his Privy Councillorship failed and he gave valuable financial advice to the government throughout the war.

Admiralty announcement has been with the view of absorbing credit for themselves never giving credit. Even the dreadful Antwerp fiasco,[1] the destroyer action against torpedo boats and the Heligoland Bight which would have been a fiasco if it had not been for Jellicoe. Why haven't we got a Kitchener to help us? The Board of Trade another department which is continually undoing work done by the Navy —. our ships capture neutrals carrying contraband unquestionably for the enemy and the Law Officers of the Prize Court appointed by the Board of Trade let them go with food and supplies of all kinds which are admitted to be for the enemy. I suppose at the instance of the Foreign Office who are afraid of hurting the susceptibilities of a neutral state. Is it possible that they don't realise we are fighting for our very existence and the Germans are laughing at us for our pains. The *NZ*[2] captured a ship with iron ore which they admitted was for Krupp to make more guns and ammunition (shells) with. The Admiralty have ordered her to be released. I have strongly protested but what's the use? It is all so inconceivable and incomprehensible that any one should be so wickedly foolish when at war. Might is right as long as no injustice is done to a non belligerent. We argue about it in a Law Court.

Goodnight precious one, I must go on deck, it makes me cross thinking and writing about such foolishness at times like these. Love to you all and all my heart to you. Must send this at once.

79. *To his wife* [Aberdour House]

[BTY/17/30/56–7]   *Lion*
30th [Oct 1914]

The casualties go on climbing up and many good fellows are taken . . . It always seems as if the nice ones were taken. They have had a tremendous lot of casualties in the cavalry of late, but they do seem to be getting on and making progress. Oh dear, oh dear, I'd give anything to be there and would give up my battle-

[1]When Kitchener refused to send army reinforcements to defend Antwerp, Churchill sent a hastily improvised naval brigade. It could do little and Antwerp fell on 10 October 1914. The event reinforced Churchill's reputation for impulsive irresponsibility. See A. J. P. Taylor, *English History 1914–1945* (Oxford, 1969), pp. 11, 32.
[2]The battle-cruiser *New Zealand*.

cruisers if I could command one regiment of cavalry. Our lot is terribly irksome. Here I have 5,500 men and four magnificent machines, pining for something to do, and we can do nothing. All our time is taken up avoiding submarines but it [sic] striking a blow for the country, it is not possible. We stop ships on the High Sea at times, always at considerable risk from the submarines, I think, send some of them in and the Law Officers of the Crown let them go. I do not understand why but I suppose they have very good reason for doing so.

We hear in the Poldhu that Prince Louis has resigned owing to his close relationship to Germany. I thought they would get him out but that is not the reason why, which is because he did not keep a proper check on Winston and run the show himself, instead of allowing him (W) to do it. Now they have resurrected old Fisher.[1] I am afraid he is *too old* (74 years) and of course the Service don't trust him. But if he is what he was, he has energy, ideas and low cunning, which is what we want. It does not matter who goes there as long as it is somebody that can get something done, and I feel, provided he is not gaga, he'll perhaps be alright. But where are the young men? We want young virile active men with brains, imagination and courage, and we don't seem to possess one. It is lamentable. I cannot see Winston & Jacky Fisher working very long together in harmony. They will quarrel before long. The poor Navy, it's terribly sad, but nothing matters if we can get some proper policy initiated. Well we must hope for the best but the outlook is very black though on the whole I am inclined to think it is better than it was, which is something.

If the Germans are thoroughly defeated in their attempt to push through on the North East corner [?] and the Russians are able to turn what is not a considerable advantage into a reverse of the first magnitude, then the Germans in desperation might endeavour by a blow at England, of say 200,000 men, try to save the situation, and then our chance would come. We must be patient and keep fit and the spirit of the men up, but it is hard, though they really are wonderful in the optimism which pervades all ranks.

The weather is bad again and we are having a roughish blow from the N. E. which produces always a very steep and uncomfortable sea, which makes us very wet, and my cabins are not watertight yet . . .

---

[1]Prince Louis resigned on 28 October. Fisher returned as 1st Sea Lord at Churchill's invitation the following day.

80. *Beatty to Fisher*

[BTY/3/2/1]   *Lion*
[Holograph]   [Undated but probably
                                            early November 1914]
[Draft]

Dear Lord Fisher,

Thank you for your letter and for the repair ship. With it we should never require to go into dockyard hands except for docking.

Your plan of a 2nd divn of B.C.s is sound and will be very useful; 2nd divn, as opposed to a 2nd squadron, must be right, as they would be controlled by the same orders and instructions as 1st divn, that is all B.C.s would be imbued with the same ideas & principles which have governed our training in the past.

I am not quite clear why both divns should not use the same base, as: —

(1) They all would meet, exchange views and ideas, which I have found very valuable in the past; details of operations could be explained beforehand.

(2) Shall they all be required for combined operations they are already concentrated.

(3) Operating from 2 bases some distance apart there is always a possibility, owing to the reduced visibility in the North Sea, especially winter months, that they would never actually meet, with a consequent loss of valuable time. As to the best base to use, no doubt Rosyth strategically is preferable, but it has geographical disadvantages, such as a long narrow dangerous water [?] suitable for enemy submarines & which could be easily mined. These are not insurmountable and with a proper scheme and sufficient craft under an energetic & capable officer, they should disappear. As I have to use the place now I am going into the matter, and with Captain Fox,[1] who is in charge at Granton, am arranging a suitable scheme for the Admiral here's approval. It is unorthodox for me to have anything to do with it, but God helps the man who helps himself, so am taking an intelligent interest in the arrangements.

[1]Captain C. H. Fox, see note 2 on page 115 and 81. The CinC Scotland until 1916 was Admiral Sir Robert Lowry.

(4)   If any proportion of them in a divn were required by the C in C to perform any specific duty, they could be detached as well from one base as from another.

(5)   It conforms to your well proved [?] policy of being strong in one spot as opposed to being weak in several spots.

81.   *To his wife* [Aberdour House]

[BTY/17/31/2–5]   *Lion*
                                                              2.11.14

. . .

Well, Prince Louis has gone. The 3rd Sea Lord (1st) that has left that office in 3 years since Winston became 1st Lord.[1] He doesn't seem to have any luck.

You were quite right, they have resurrected old Fisher. Well, I think he is the best they could have done but I wish he was 10 years younger. He still has fine zeal, energy, determination, coupled with low cunning, which is eminently desirable just now. He also has courage and will take any responsibility. He will recognise that his position is absolutely secure and will rule the Admiralty and Winston with a heavy hand. He has patriotism and is a firm believer in the good qualities of the Navy; that it can do anything and will go anywhere, and please God, we shall change our present methods for a strong offensive and defensive policy. He is the head of the Navy now and as such must, in this great and terrifying crisis be supported by every officer and man in the Fleet and out of it. And I think under circumstances such as they are, if he is not too old, he will be able to do more than any other man that I know of. At least the situation cannot be worse than it was before. I trust old Charles Beresford will have the decency to sink his differences with him and not stump about the country endeavouring to calumniate him, as he has done in the past.

I, of course, have no news whatever. I hear from Filson Young, another letter. I don't know what to say to him but I certainly have no room for him here, but if he works his cards right, as he is a friend of Fisher he might get a job somewhere. Why doesn't

[1]The two other 1st Sea Lords removed by Churchill were Sir Arthur Wilson in 1911 and Sir Francis Bridgeman in 1912.

he become a Royal Naval Volunteer Reserve man, apparently anyone can become that, and he can join Winston's Naval Brigade!!!

We are having more wind and wet. The weather has been unpleasant but not very cold, so I suppose we must be thankful for such mercies.

I see Fox, Captain [*sic*] has been appointed to something in the Firth of Forth. I hear the poor fellow's nerves gave way *after* his destruction of the 4 German destroyers, as a result of his experience in the *Amphion*. You may remember she was sunk on a mine at the beginning of the war. He then got the *Undaunted*, which he was in the other day, and then his nerve went very suddenly. Very odd, so they have given him this appointment which is comparatively peaceful. Look after him as I expect he will be upset about it all, poor chap.

We are now at war with Turkey. What a poor benighted foolish country. It means the end of them as a power. I suppose they are alarmed as to what she may do in Egypt, possibly endeavour to invade it, and much will depend on the attitude of the Egyptian government. If the *Goeben* had been sunk by Troubridge, this could never have taken place — well they will perhaps have another chance of sinking her yet, who knows . . .

P.S.   I am afraid my letters are very inarticulate. But I hope, and don't think, the Admiralty find my communications the same.

82.   *To his wife* [Aberdour House]

[BTY/17/31/7–10]   *Lion*
                                                          3–4.11.14

. . .

I am sorry Filson Young thinks I am so inarticulate. I hope the Admiralty doesn't think so, or perhaps that is why I cannot always get done the dozens of things I am always asking for. He has been bothering me again. I told him I had no room but Brock had and he better get his friend Fisher to fix him up somewhere. Dear Heart, I did not tell you I was going to Cromarty because I did not know until just before we went there, and if I had known I should not have told you for reasons which I have already given and which you should understand. . . . Your idea of the Christmas Box is a beautiful one, *but* I think savours too much of self-advertisement, whacking out photographs of myself all round. I was thinking what I could do. I gave the *Lion* a turkey for each mess last year, which they liked awfully. But if I gave each mess in each ship a turkey, I don't think we could find enough. It would mean about 200 odd and would cost about £100, which is a lot. I might give them all a goose which would be cheaper, but I don't like thinking of the money side of the question in times such as these. What do you think? . . .

I am storing a lot of things like woollen scarves, gloves etc, and whacking them out as they are wanted and not wholesale, which is better as they will wear out. All the destroyers are very well off, in fact everyone is at present and I can feed other small ships with things as they want them, when we meet.

Prince Louis departed not for the reason given but to save the politicians. They thought that after Antwerp somebody ought to go, so he was sacrificed. I think however Fisher will do just as well, probably very much better. I think he will do something, which is everything, to meet the submarine and mine menace, and Winston will find him a very difficult person to deal with officially and will have to conform to Fisher's views . . .

We had a gallop yesterday and thought we should at last get at the Germans but they bolted home again and we got no further. It blew pretty hard with a nasty short sea which upset some of my small ships, and today, so if we had catched them we couldn't have seen them.[1]

*   *   *

You remember you asked me further addresses of sailors' wives who would want clothes for themselves and children, well really I don't think they are in any want now at all, in fact they are better off than they have ever been, as their husbands are spending no money & are saving and sending home all they collect. And they get a very good separation allowance from the Admiralty of from 8 shillings to 10 shillings a week, so they really are alright and have any amount of people to look after them. I expect there will be much more misery requiring attention among the unemployed at home and in the slums. Unemployment must

[1]On 3 November Beatty had sailed from Cromarty on reports of a German sortie. A force of three battle-cruisers and four cruisers had sailed from Heligoland Bight the previous evening but had retreated after sighting British light forces.

increase this winter and surely the price of some of the necessities of life will go up. And I fear for the widows & children of all the poor fellows that have been killed. I've no doubt in Leicester you would find ample room for rendering aid, but sailors' families are all right.

[P.S.] I expect with the advent of Jacky Fisher we will have many changes and among the first to go will be, I am sure, Sturdee whom he cannot abide.

83. *To his wife* [Aberdour House]

[BTY/17/31/12–13] *Lion*
5.11.14

* * *

I dare say we shall come to the Firth of Forth when they have fixed up the booms properly, but not until. . . . I have masses of work to do and spend hours writing and gingering them up about Cromarty defences patrols etc, which are sadly in need of reorganisation and additions.

We've had a tremendous upheaval. Sturdee, Chief of War Staff has departed, as I thought he would. Having failed in one appointment they give him another and he is going off in the *Invincible*. Moore has been [–] out and much to poor Halsey's disgust transferred into the *New Zealand*.¹ I suppose he is now looked upon as 2nd in Command of the Battle-Cruiser Squadron. If so, I'll have him put into the *Queen Mary* but I don't want him and he will have nothing to do. But I dare say he will find his way back to the Admiralty, which is the best place for him as he has got brains.

The poor Navy, it is almost inconceivable. The first three months of war and we have changed the Commander-in-Chief, the First Sea Lord, and the Chief of the War Staff, the three most

¹Moore had been displaced from command of 2nd Battle-Cruiser Squadron by Sturdee's taking *Invincible* and *Inflexible* to the South Atlantic (see note 2 on page 108 and note 1 on page 110). The future Admiral Sir Lionel Halsey (1872–1949) commanded *New Zealand* until June 1915 when he became Jellicoe's Captain of the Fleet; 4th Sea Lord 1916; Rear-Admiral 1917; 3rd Sea Lord 1917 and remained on board until 1918; commanding 2nd Battle-Cruiser Squadron 1918; COS to Prince of Wales on visits to Canada and USA 1919; and to Australia and New Zealand 1920; on Prince's personal staff until 1936; Vice-Admiral 1921; retired list 1922; Admiral on retired list 1926.

important men. It really is incredible. Percy Scott has been hoisted out. What will they make of him I don't know, but if they can keep him sober,[1] I've no doubt his natural low cunning will be made use of by Jacky Fisher. Who goes as Chief of War Staff I don't know,[2] unless Jackson[3] returns, but the chaos which reigns at present must be bad. But we shall win through, the Navy afloat, if they are not interfered with, will pull out alright.

News just received of an action in the Pacific. Poor old Craddock has been badly knocked and lost the *Monmouth* and very nearly the *Good Hope*, but I expect he has damaged severely some of the enemy ships. I don't understand it. The Germans had a concentrated force of two big cruisers and three small ones against his force: *Good Hope* which is not the equal of the German two, the *Monmouth* considerably inferior, and the *Glasgow* a small one. So I fear he saw red and did not wait for his proper reinforcement, the *Canopus*. He is a gallant fellow and I am sure put up a gallant fight, but nowadays no amount of dash and gallantry will counterbalance great superiority, unless they are commanded by fools or very incapable men. He has paid the penalty, but doubtless it was better to have fought and lost than not to have fought at all under certain circumstances. Commander Darley,[4] my 1st Lt in *Queen* was in the *Good Hope*. I hope he and old Kit are alright. . . .

[1] Admiral Sir Percy Scott (1853–1924): entered RN 1866; a great instigator of gunnery improvements; Captain of *Excellent*, the gunnery school 1903–5; Rear-Admiral and Inspector of Target Practice 1905; commanding 2nd Cruiser Squadron of the Channel Fleet, began dispute with Lord Charles Beresford, the CinC, 1907; Vice-Admiral 1908; hauled down flag 1909; continued campaign for adoption of director gun control system which he had developed; recalled to Admiralty for special service 1914–18; from 1915 organised anti-aircraft defence of London; after war public advocate of the abandonment of battleships in view of submarine and aircraft improvements. See his biography by Peter Padfield, *Aim Straight* (London, 1966).

[2] Sturdee was succeeded by Churchill's Naval Secretary, Vice-Admiral Sir Henry Oliver.

[3] Later Admiral of the Fleet Sir Henry Jackson (1855–1929): entered RN 1886; throughout his career an enthusiastic and effective proponent of the use of WT in fleet communications; his scientific knowledge was recognised by election as a Fellow of the Royal Society in 1901; 3rd Sea Lord 1905; Rear-Admiral 1906; commanding 3rd Cruiser Squadron in the Mediterranean 1908; Director of War College, Portsmouth; Vice-Admiral 1911; Chief of Admiralty War Staff 1913; in 1914 was destined to be CinC Mediterranean and made Admiral but retained at Admiralty for special services until May 1915 when appointed 1st Sea Lord to succeed Fisher; replaced by Jellicoe December 1916; Admiral President RNC Greenwich 1916–19; Admiral of the Fleet 1919; retired 1924.

[4] Commander T. Darley did not survive.

84.   *To his wife* [Aberdour House]

[BTY/17/31/15–16]   *Lion*
                                                                          6.11.14

No further news from the South Pacific, beyond that everything we have heard comes from a German source & is therefore to be treated with suspicion. But I fear that they have had a terrible disaster and the *Monmouth* has gone and the *Good Hope* very nearly so.

I cannot quite understand how it is that they were unable to inflict damage on the enemy ships, but fear they must have been caught napping. Poor old Kit Craddock, I am sorry for him. It cannot be altogether his fault, it's the policy that is wrong. The Admiralty are responsible and should have collected a stronger force there to meet them with. Nowadays no amount of gallantry will make up for inferiority of guns & matériel and the superior force must always win. I understand Craddock represented to the Admiralty that he was not strong enough. Moore with *Invincible* and *Inflexible* ought to have gone out there two months ago and then we should have had a very different story. But we are as much obsessed with the North Sea as the French are with Alsace-Lorraine.

I am glad you enjoyed your visit to the Balfours.[1] I was sure you would. So, Hankey[2] is responsible for the Naval Brigade, is he? Well, I shouldn't talk about it if I were him or he'll be the best hated man by the British Navy, which is subjected daily to attacks by submarines which could have been rounded up if they had used these men to man proper craft, which are available, and many ships have been starved of men and are undermanned in consequence. Would that I had him here.

The news, other than the Pacific, seems good and the enemy

---

[1]Arthur Balfour, later 1st Earl (1848–1930): Conservative MP from 1874; Chief Secretary for Ireland 1887; 1st Lord of the Treasury and Leader of the House of Commons in his uncle Lord Salisbury's administration and again in 1895; Prime Minister 1902–5; in war, at Asquith's request, active in CID; 1st Lord of Admiralty 1915–16; Foreign Secretary 1916–19; Lord President of Council 1919–22; led British delegation at the Washington Naval Conference 1921; earldom 1922.

[2]Maurice Hankey, later 1st Baron Hankey (1877–1963): entered Royal Marines 1895; served in NID 1902–7; Assistant Secretary CID 1908; Secretary 1912–38; Secretary War Cabinet 1916–18; Cabinet Secretary 1919–38; member of War Cabinet 1939–40.

have lost a valuable cruiser, the *Yorck*,[1] which apparently blew herself up on one of their own mines, or possibly it was one of our submarines, and is a good set off to the *Monmouth*. As a fact we could well spare the *Good Hope* and the *Monmouth*, but it is the loss of prestige which is bad, and we cannot afford the valuable lives . . .

85. *To his wife* [Aberdour House]

[BTY/17/31/18–20]   *Lion*
                                                                      7.11.14

We are again enveloped in fog, or rather a heavy wet mist, which encumbers our movements terribly. We can see about a mile and no more and I find it very difficult to find my ships, and never when I want them. It is poisonous, however it has its compensations because in it the enemy submarines cannot see us, so our dangers in that direction are greatly reduced. What is tantalising is that I am sure on shore the weather is perfect, in fact from all accounts you have had the most perfect autumn imaginable. Well, it has been a good thing for the poor soldiers and they deserve all the good fortune they can get, as they have done such wonders. My heart thrills with pride when I read the stories, official & unofficial, and would give much, very much, to be with them.

The anxieties of this sea life with valuable machines and the valuable thousands of lives depending on you is very very great and makes a very heavy burden & responsibility to carry. But I would not mind them, I can but do my best and make ready to meet every eventuality that experience has taught me, and having done all I can, the result must be in the lap of the gods, if every now and then we had some compensating event and achieved some real tangible success, which never comes, indeed the opportunity never comes. We get back to coal with a feeling of, thank God I've got in again. And yet when we go out again, the same day or the next, we are filled with hope that perhaps this time the opportunity will come and think of nothing else, and it never comes. Surely this is the hardest and the most cruelly trying kind

[1]German armoured cruiser *Yorck* blew up in the Jade minefield 4 November 1914.

of warfare. And one has to be cheerful and encouraging to the others and bring them up to live in hope every time, that this is *the* time, and surely we will have our reward, knowing that there is but small chance of finding somebody to fire a gun at and trying to wipe out the long list of scores we are totting up against them. Now I am beginning to grumble, our day will come, but one day is not enough, we want more. They are playing their game well in trying to *wear* us down, to upset our nerves and make us do foolish things, but they won't succeed and whenever I begin to think in the strain I have written, I pull up and say, that is what they want. If we consider the question from that point of view, it is one gain to them. So I shut down and only write it to you, but it is not true. The spirit of the officer and man is wonderful. The morale is very high and I am sure the whole Navy is imbued with the same spirit, and only get impatient every now & then. Opportunity is all we want.

I hear Sir Arthur Wilson[1] is at the Admiralty. What a wonderful combination: Fisher, Scott and Wilson, all three old, with no experience of modern naval conditions, and will probably fight like the deuce. Well, we must wait and see, but it is this waiting which I cannot do & is the hardest task of all. . . .

My new Captain of the *Queen Mary*[2] is a nice cheerful person and hasn't rammed me yet. I hope to get the *Tiger* this week which will be a great addition to my strength and I shall be glad to see her.

I cannot understand what the Admiralty are going to do with Moore. They have taken his ships away simply to find a job for Sturdee and they have hoisted him on to me. He, poor man I am quite sorry for, they have treated him abominably and should have sent him with his ships. I really don't know what to do with him but no doubt something will turn up . . .

[P.S.] Please send me a comb, the teeth of mine are gone.

---

[1]Admiral Sir Arthur Wilson acted from October 1914 as unpaid adviser in the Admiralty (see note 4 on page 4).
[2]Captain Cecil Prowse, in succession to Reginald Hall.

86. *To his wife* [Aberdour House]

[BTY/17/31/22–4]   *Lion*
10.11.14

. . .

Yes, I believe Mrs Prickett[1] was up at Invergordon. You see
the *New Zealand* has been in dock there and under no circumstances could go to sea under 24 hours, so there was no reason
why she or any other wife should not have come up and stayed
at Invergordon. But that is very different to the other ships which
are ready for sea at a moment's notice and all officers have to be
onboard at 6 p.m. When we have a long time like that, i.e. a
week, it will be different. . . .

Alright my dear, we will give each mess in each ship a turkey
for his [*sic*] Christmas dinner. It will mean something like 250
turkeys, so will you tell Mr James and Dennis. . . .

We are busy coaling and storing and shall be off again I suppose
at once. We don't stop long, but our stays at sea are shorter than
they were . . .

I am inundated with letters from fellows wanting to join the
battle-cruisers and F.Y. writes once a day, persistence will win if
determined enough.

Poor old Kit Craddock has gone, poor old chap. He has had a
glorious death but if it had only been in victory instead of defeat.
But I fancy he must have sunk one if not two of the German ships
(small). His death and the loss of the ships and the gallant lives
in them can be laid to door [*sic*] of the incompetency of the
Admiralty. They have as much idea of strategy as the Board
School boy and have broken over and over again the first principles. It is inconceivable that their intelligence does not make
them see it.

I see Troubridge is now being court martialled. If he had been
where Kit was and Kit had been in the Mediterranean, how
different the result would have been.

I am glad again that you enjoyed your visit to the Balfours. I
wonder what he thinks about the situation. I feel very gloomy at
times about the naval side. No one trusts the Admiralty. They
have made so many mistakes that should never have been made,
that it is causing distrust, and loss of confidence not only in the

---

[1]Wife of Lt Commander Prickett, gunnery officer of *New Zealand*.

country but in the Navy, which really in time will have a bad effect. But of course the sailorman doesn't think much. He is very trusting and he trusts completely those over him, such is his nice simple nature, which to those who do think makes it all the harder, knowing that things are not as they should be.

I have sent the cutting you sent me on to Hall. There are many instances in these parts and the authorities are not capable of dealing with it. Why, I can't think, but I am afraid it is that ruffian McKenna[1] who is at the head of the Home Office and I fancy that he is obstructing every suggestion put forward. He and old Haldane[2] should be locked up and removed from any responsible position.

I hear they have caught and destroyed the *Emden* at last and the *Chatham*, little Drury Lowe has got the *Köningsberg* [*sic*] cornered up a river on East coast Germany [*sic*].[3] That is indeed good news, at last the Navy is doing something. If only the Admiralty had had the sense to send the *Invincible* & *Inflexible* out to the Pacific instead of the *Good Hope*, what a difference.

87.   *To his wife* [Aberdour House]

[BTY/17/31/29–30]   *Lion*
                                                                    12.11.14

. . .

I am only waiting for the *Tiger* and am anxious to hear from her as to how she has been getting on with her practice. When she becomes efficient she will be a great addition to my fighting strength. I dont think you know the captain of her, Pelly by name, a very charming person and, what is more important just now, a very efficient officer. If I had only been able to keep Bentinck I

---

[1]McKenna: see 20–23 and note 1 on page 33 for Beatty's earlier dealings with him.

[2]Richard, Viscount Haldane (1856–1928): Liberal MP from 1885; Secretary of State for War 1905–12; Viscount 1911; initiated important army reforms including organisation of BEF, the Territorial Army and the functioning of the Imperial General Staff. He had been educated in Germany and consequent prejudice, presumably shared by Beatty, forced Asquith to omit him from his coalition cabinet of 1915.

[3]*Emden*, one of most successful German surface raiders, was sunk on 9 November 1914 by HMAS *Sydney*. *Köningsberg* was blockaded up the Rufiji River in East Africa.

should have had a real fine lot of captains, but Prowse I think will be alright. He has nerve which is everything and I dont think is easily rattled.[1]

I am curious to see Winston's statement as to the disaster in the Pacific, which the Prime Minister said he would make. I fear he will try and throw blame on to poor Kit Craddock, which would be absolutely unjustifiable. If ever there was an occasion which displayed bad judgement on the part of the Admiralty, you have it there. What happened was, they did not know where the *Scharnhorst* & *Gneisenau* were and hadn't the courage to say so. It was a surprise to them their turning up where they did.

The Germans are so much better at that game. They have made a business of it for years and are now reaping where they have sown. Whereas we have never, and even now, take no trouble about such things and they count a great deal in the end. You will see in the Parliamentary Report many incidents are being quoted, and there are many more much more flagrant and worse cases. And the steps we take to deal with them are childish in the extreme, and too simple for anything. I am going to take a hand in the game myself and see if I cannot bring some of them to earth, and I'll wager I succeed. We are absolutely surrounded with them in every port we go into and it is becoming a perfect scandal. I've just heard from the Commander-in-Chief that he concurs in a long expression of my views with their remedy [*sic*] which gives me confidence and I hope to be able to get something done in consequence that will improve matters from the point of view of my squadron. He is splendid, Jellicoe, he always understands and gives attention and consideration to one's views. I wish indeed he had as free a hand as the C-in-C ought to have. . . .

[P.S.]   Everybody says it will be all over much earlier than expected. I see in the papers Smith Dorrien[2] has come home. Why?

---

[1]Captain H. B. Pelly of *Tiger*; Beatty had wanted Captain Rudolph Bentinck to succeed Hall on *Queen Mary*; instead he went to the battleship *Superb* in the 1st Battle Squadron. In February 1915 Beatty was able to have Bentinck made his COS.

[2]General Sir Horace Smith-Dorrien (1858–1931): commanding II Corps BEF from 1914; criticised by CinC Sir John French for his conduct at Le Cateau 26 August; their relations deteriorated and he was removed from his command 1 May 1915.

88. *To his wife* [Aberdour House]

[BTY/17/31/32–3] *Lion*
13/14.11.14

. . .

You must not talk about old men of 45. I shall be 45 in another two months and I don't feel old. In fact I feel very young just now. . . .

I don't want another comb. The one of your own you sent me is a beautiful one and will do all I ask for it. In fact I shall have very little hair left if we go on much longer.
14th

We are being pushed about from pillar to post. There is nothing definite, nothing certain, no policy: ordered out one minute, ordered back the next. I honestly think at the Admiralty they are stark staring mad, but what can you expect when they produce two old men of over 70 years of age, who have no personal knowledge of the requirements and capabilities of a modern fleet, working with an ill-balanced individual like Winston. Perhaps they will settle down, let us hope they will. I do not understand the situation. It is a one man business and Jacky Fisher by himself might accomplish something, but working in combination with old Wilson and W.C. only the bad in him will come out, until they have a quarrel, which, please God, will happen soon. I am not happy with the situation at all and think from the naval point of view the outlook gloomy. Thank God, the Navy afloat is alright and, thank God, I am afloat and not at the Admiralty, which I hear is in chaos.

*   *   *

89. *To Jellicoe*

[BTY/13/21/3]   SECRET   *Lion*
[Duplicate]

13 November 1914

I have the honour to point out that, by the present disposition of my squadron I am confronted with the possibility of situations of great difficulty which I had never anticipated. Being in command of the *only* force which can deal effectively and rapidly with the enemy's 'cruiser squadron' I have always assumed that our duty would be to sail and engage it if it put to sea.

2. Having assumed hitherto that for offensive purposes the enemy's cruiser squadron would consist of 4 battle-cruisers, the *Blücher* and 6 light cruisers, my intention was to engage them when and where they could be found, and considered that the superior quality of our ships would have counter balanced the possible inferiority in numbers.

3. Now that the inferiority of our numbers has greatly increased (owing to detachment of *Princess Royal*, and *Tiger*[1] being as yet unfit to take her place) and a situation has arisen which has never been previously contemplated or considered possible, I am obliged to ask for a ruling as to what is considered the proper course for me to pursue.

4. It was accepted as a principle by the late C-in-C and concurred in by you that my squadron should always consider the enemy's Battle-Cruiser Squadron as their objective and it was never considered possible that our Battle-Cruiser Squadron would be *greatly* inferior to that of the enemy.

5. From the experience gained during the few operations of the war, it has been emphasised most markedly on each occasion that superiority will always annihilate inferiority, without the inferior force being able to inflict compensating damage on the superior force.

6. Again, it would be highly detrimental to the prestige of the Navy and cause considerable loss of morale, which at this juncture is of the highest importance, if an enemy force bombarded our coasts and arsenals and we did not engage them at once: or if the enemy cruiser squadron swept the North Sea and we could not bring them to action except with an inferior force, *viz, Lion, Queen Mary* and *New Zealand*.

7. I raise this question only because I feel that in a situation so extremely grave I ought to obtain guidance from higher authority who are conversant with all the circumstances and the exact disposition of the enemy forces.

8. It may be assumed that the enemy will take advantage of the detachment of the *Princess Royal* to undertake an offensive movement.

---

[1]*Princess Royal* had been detached by the Admiralty to strengthen trade-protection forces in North American waters after Coronel. *Tiger*, only completed in October, was not fully effective.

90.   *To Jellicoe* (telegram copies)

[BTY/13/21/3]   14 Nov. 1914

From: Ad. Cdg. 1st B. C. S.
To: Commander in Chief Home Fleets
Date: 14 Nov 1914

With reference to my letter of 13 November. In absence of other instructions I conceive it my duty as previously arranged to bring the enemy's battle cruisers to action to the best of our ability and regardless of their superiority. 11.00

Reply:
Your 11.00 of yesterday. Yes. This should not of course prevent you from attempting to separate his fastest and slowest ships by suitable manoeuvres. *Tiger* will be with you when next at sea. 12.14 17 November 1914

91.   *To his wife* [Aberdour House]

[BTY/17/31/35–7]   *Lion*
                                                    16.11.14

*   *   *

My dear, you were absolutely right. Sturdee has been one of the curses of the Navy since he went to the Admiralty as Chief of the War Staff. He was principally responsible for all our disasters afloat and Fisher showed his acumen by turning him out. All I regret is that he gave him employment at all.

*   *   *

Filson Young is full of beans and has settled down in the intelligence office under Plunkett. He was full of Fisher and Beresford and the sniffs from the latter when F. was sent to the Admiralty. I am having a bad time with the swinehounds at the Admiralty and a terrific war going on on paper. They do the most outrageous things which jeopardise not only my squadron but in fact the fate of the nation. I have pointed it out in no unmeasured terms. I have Jellicoe on my side and his support, but I am afraid I cannot move them. I wrote to Fisher a personal letter which I hope will have some effect, if he is not too old. But apparently they have no knowledge of the strategic side. One would think they never heard or thought of war before. They certainly have never read anything. It is very trying and difficult and I know of no remedy with the present lot. I think Wilson must be at the bottom of some of the stupid things they do. Perhaps my letter will bear fruit. Please God it will, or there will be the makings of a catastrophe (not with me so don't fuss). . . . Burn this page.

92. *To his wife* [Aberdour House]

[BTY/17/31/42–3]   *Lion*
                                                  21.11.14

I had an opportunity of meeting the C-in-C yesterday and had a long and interesting conversation on many matters, and though I am not permitted to acquaint you of their purport, yet I can say that we are in perfect agreement, and it left me feeling very much happier than I was before. The great thing is that we see eye to eye on every point which essentially affects me and my command, and, I might say, on all the principal features of the naval part of the war. What it has done is to leave me in greater wonderment than ever at the attitude adopted in not paying entire and complete attention to the views of the man who has to use the instrument of the fleet to carry out the work allotted to them [*sic*]. . . .

My dear you must understand the reason why my letters apparently take so long is because I write them on one day and perhaps am not able to post them for two or sometimes three days after. Further, all letters from the ships do not go direct to their destination but always go straight to the General Post Office London, where they are sorted and distributed. It is a precautionary measure of infinite value and certainly would be highly improper if was myself attempt [*sic*] or permit anybody else to post letters through the local Post Office. . . .

We have our scares almost daily from enemy submarines, but we are getting very used to them now. The *Tiger* has joined me, a fine looking ship and in every respect *looks* workmanlike, but I fear they have finished her in too much of a hurry & it will take a long time to get her right. Her guns are alright and she can steam, which is something. The only fly in the ointment is Moore, and it is an awful nuisance having him planted in my midst as he

is of no use to me and is only a stumbling block. Poor Halsey is
the worst off as he has to house him and this is a sore trial. But
it is only a temporary measure and he will move away shortly to
another squadron, and I hope to be shot of him altogether. And
if I can only get my 5 Bully Boys and the 6 light cruisers, I can
go anywhere and do anything. . . .

93. *From Churchill*

[BTY/3/2/2]   Admiralty
[Holograph]   22 Nov 1914

Mr dear Beatty,
    No one has done better than you. Keep your spirits up. We are
sure that your squadron will give the enemy's battle cruisers *plus*
Blücher, a most satisfactory trouncing if the chance comes. And
you are the man!
    The Navy is far ahead of the German Navy ships for ships, as
the Army has proved itself man for man. Steer midway between
Troubridge & Craddock & all will be well, Craddock preferred.
    I wish we could have a talk about it all.
    All my soldier friends are killed.
    And this time last year we had persuaded ourselves that it was
never coming!

                                                       Yours sincerely,

                                              WINSTON CHURCHILL

94. *To Churchill*

[BTY/3/2/3]   [*Lion*]
[Typed draft, written
amendments by
Beatty in square
brackets]   [November 1914]

My Dear 1st Lord,
    I thank you very much for your letter. It was nice of you to

think of writing to me and I am proud to think that I retain the confidence of the Admiralty. Your enjoinder to keep my spirits up, was, I feel, caused by my letter to the C-in-C which he forwarded, after the withdrawal of the *Princess Royal*.

I think you know me well enough that my confidence [as to the tactical side of the question] is not involved [?] and nobody realises more than I do that ship for ship and man for man we are fully capable of wiping the floor with them.

I confess however that when I think of the strategic side [my spirits are inclined to fall] I feel that my dream of annihilating the enemy may not be fulfilled. Nothing less than complete annihilation can or must be allowed to satisfy us. To ensure this it is necessary to have a superiority in each unit and not only in one. The German main fighting force on the surface consists of battle-ships and battle-cruisers. No amount of superiority in the former will compensate for inferiority in the latter, owing to the difference in speed.

[The *Tiger* is not yet an efficient unit. I took her firing last week & after 1st salvo her guns refused to go off, all electrical communications had broken down, troubles incidental to a new ship commissioned in a hurry, and in no circumstances can she be considered to have attained the same efficiency as the other 3 Cats for at least 6 months.]

What disturbs me therefore is not doubt whether my unit could defeat its German 'opposite number' but whether we can be reasonably certain of annihilating it, without which I should feel we had failed.

It is almost a platitude to say that the quintessence of strategy is to have the right force in the right place at the right time, but to be a 'right' force it must be a 'superior' force, and a battle-cruiser is the only ship that can reach the 'right' place at the same time as other battle-cruisers. So, a superiority in battle-ships won't help the battle-cruisers, even though that superiority is so vast as to verge on unwieldiness.

Nothing will convince me that it is sound strategy to gamble on individual superiority [with possible mischance from mine and submarine] when we have at our disposal a numerical superiority which would ensure the desired result, if only we had it in the decisive area.

95. *To his wife* [Aberdour House]

[BTY/17/31/47–9] *Lion*
26.11.14

. . .

I have no stirring deeds to relate, nothing new, only a repetition of the daily anxieties and risks, with never a saving clause. We hear hourly almost of the presence in the neighbourhood of the enemy submarines, accounts which are vivid and circumstantial, masses of them, but never get hold of one. But at last the bagging one [*sic*] the other day brought a vestige of hope that they are vulnerable and can be catched [*sic*], if we go the right way about it.

We had an interesting period at sea the last time, which was an extraordinary mixture of war and make believe or exercise in the practising of naval war movements, which struck me as being a very good example of the peculiarities [?] of the naval officer. I with the cruisers exercised against Jellicoe with the battleships, and I think we gave him something to think about, which I sincerely trust he will take to heart in time. . . .

The matter of the *P. R.* was supposed to be a profound secret and has been a question of a very great difference of opinion between me and the Admiralty. I've bombarded them with letters and been supported by the C-in-C, and by dint of hammering hope to achieve her return, but truly it is hard work to have to keep on representing [?] the muddle the Admiralty make. I have shaken them, which is something and have had private letters both from Fisher and Winston and hope to get her back in time. In the meantime anything might happen, and we have not the *P. R.*. The new captain of the *Q.M.*[1] is not quite the type of man required for a battle-cruiser, too slow in the brain, ponderous, and I fear the ship will deteriorate in consequence. . . .

They appear to have the fear of invasion very strong all over the country. I hear that Ireland is to be the *point d'appui*, that Ireland is full of traitors who are ready to rise on the first occasion and deliver Ireland into their hands. I wish it were true and should like to see 100,000 (Germans) actually landed in Ireland. They would do Ireland a lot of good and will solve the Home Rule question for ever. And when we had fixed the Germans on the continent we could pay a little attention to those in Ireland. . . .

[1]Captain Cecil Prowse.

The poor old *Bulwark*[1] was blown up, I feel sure, by dropping a shell into the magazine while they were embarking ammunition, a careless accident. It was no mine or submarine but sounds ghastly.

96. *From Churchill*

[BTY/14/4/1]   Admiralty
[Holograph]   30.11.14
Private

My dear Beatty,

I hope it will be possible to strengthen your squadron in the near future by the return of the straying cat and the addition of a still more formidable feline animal, to wit: the *Queen Elizabeth*.[2] But for the present you must just put a bold face on it. The *Derfflinger*[3] is new as well as the *Tiger* & of the two I have little doubt the *Tiger* would win. We are trying also to find you some kittens from our not unlimited litter.

You must all get the 60% standard out of your minds. No one has any ground for complaint at fighting on equal terms. But we shall do our best to reinforce you.

Everything in this war has shown that we are their match man for man & gun for gun. And no one is more capable of proving that than yourself.

With all good wishes

Believe me

Yours sincerely,

WINSTON CHURCHILL

---

[1]The battleship *Bulwark* had blown up in the Medway on the day of Beatty's writing; this, and a similar disaster to *Vanguard* in July 1917 were most probably due to spontaneous explosion of deteriorating cordite.

[2]*Queen Elizabeth*, the first 'super Dreadnought' with 15-inch guns; did not join Beatty but went to the Dardanelles in February 1915.

[3]German battle-cruiser *Derfflinger* completed in November 1914.

97.   *To his wife* [Aberdour House]

[BTY/17/32 5–7]   *Lion*
                                                          2.12.14

Of all the poisonous weather we have experienced the last few
months what we enjoy now is about the worst. *Four months!* It
seems extraordinary that it should be only four months since we
first started and we have accomplished very little in that time it
seems, and thousands of lives have been hurled into eternity and
we are not much, if any, the better for it.

The news from the East is somewhat disappointing. We were
led to expect great things, a veritable débacle [*sic*], and it would
appear that the Germans have wriggled out of what was a tight
place with great skill. Still they must have received a severe knock
and have certainly had a gruelling and will require very large
reinforcements to hold back the Russian advance and the latter
can still prosecute their advance on the Southern end of their line
and roll up the Austrians.

In the meanwhile on the Western side they appear to be
marking time. I assume that Joffre[1] has no wish to push him back
to the Rhine until the Russians get into Germany, as he contains
more of the enemy by holding them along the present line than
he would if he forced them to take up the position on the Rhine.

The naval situation remains the same. We can do but little
except wait — hold up all the traffic and prevent the escape of
enemy ships into the Atlantic and be ready to pounce if they make
any attempt to raid our coasts or force a landing. Our difficulties
are to avoid their submarines, which remain very active. It is
nearly time we took measures to curtail their activity. I have a
new Commander arrived yesterday and Parker is to leave.[2] I am
glad that he is going as he has been here too long and cannot
produce new ideas and he cows the spirits of the wardroom officers
to an alarming degree, which under war conditions is distinctly
bad. Chatfield gets more melancholic daily and very taciturn. He
is an outstandingly obstinate human being and inclined to be
narrow minded and tries me very highly and is really of very little
assistance. He always sees the bad side of things and never the
good, but I must have a go at him tactfully, but it does add to his
worries as I can unfortunately see the bad side of things myself

---

[1]Joffre, the French CinC, replaced by Nivelle in December 1916.
[2]Henry Parker, commander of *Lion*, was replaced by Charles Fountaine.

quite clearly, & like to put them out of sight when I have once considered them. I think he must have some secret sorrow, and that is a luxury nobody is entitled to in times such as these. The Secretary is my principal stand-by. I get more aassistance out of him than anybody else.

I was not surprised to hear that there is talk of Winston leaving the Admiralty as I cannot see him working in harmony with Jacky Fisher for very long and they certainly could not turn out the latter after all the flourish of trumpets with which he returned to the yoke. I had another letter from Winston in reply to mine taking exception at 'Keep your spirits up' — and evidently my representations are bearing fruit and I shall get the *Princess Royal* back again before long and, he tells me, the *Queen Elizabeth*. I shall be surrounded with Queens, Princesses & cats, but it is good news and *Private*, as the *Q.E.* is the *finest* fighting unit in the world.

*   *   *

We are not at Cromarty. It is quite impossible to say from day to day where we shall be next. . . .

98. *To his wife* [Aberdour house]

[BTY/17/32/9–11]   *Lion*
                                                                                     3.12.14

The weather remains perfectly impossible and makes it extremely difficult to get anything properly done. However we are pegging away and endeavouring to maintain our efficiency as best we can.

Halsey is of course delighted to get rid of Moore but the Admiralty have treated him abominably, as they always will anybody who does not have the courage to turn and insist. If you lie down they will wipe their feet on you and kick you always. Moore has been so long at the Admiralty that it is astounding he should be so afraid of them. Your letter of today amused me much. You must not be so plain spoken to old admirals, especially if you cannot alter them. It only makes them more obstinate. And old Packs will be very upset at your giving him such a bad character. But why won't he let them go ashore? Whenever I get the chance our men are landed and taken for a march to a field where they kick a football about, which gives them much pleasure, and then they are marched back again and they love it. We have as many as 300 from a ship at the same time.

You never sent me back Winston's letter which I asked you to do. I like keeping those letters as I never take risks of any kind with that type and it is evidence of a kind.

. . . Funnily enough I heard from old Jacky Fisher. . . . He wrote me a long letter (the 2nd, in a week) in answer to mine and I am glad to say he is in perfect agreement and promises to do all I ask. And if he had known as much as he does now he would not have sent the *Princess Royal* away, and, I assume, will get her back. He is on my side and that is something — this is quite private. . . .

French's dispatch was a most amazing story of intense interest, and really very easy to follow if you attack it slowly and use a map. . . . I have never read anything that thrilled me so much. Our soldiers are wonderful. There is not decadence there. Never in the history of the world has any army written such a glorious story on the pages of history. I think old French made a mistake in trying to do too much with them and was saved a disaster by the magnificent fighting qualities of the soldier. Officer & man alike, they have surpassed themselves. Would that we could have opportunity of showing that we belong to the same stock.[1]

Yes, a truly wonderful garment arrived. It is an astonishing thing to look at and I am sure would float anybody, but can only be put on at the critical moment and one could get nothing on over it. I don"t think I want to float in the water for 24 hours in this weather, it is much too cold, but might manage for ½ a dozen & will try it for that . . .

Well, my dear one, I hope, no one more fervently, that the Germans will come out, and I think they will, but fear not for a long time yet, and this waiting is trying and irksome to a degree. Still, we live in hopes. My days are very full. I am never idle and spend hours writing and scheming and going round my ships. The *Tiger* is a beautiful ship but in a very bad condition and will take a lot of pulling together, but it will be done.

---

[1]By November 1914 when the German offensive finally halted, the BEF, the old British Regular Army, had virtually ceased to exist. More than half of its original members were casualties — one in ten killed.

99. *To his wife* [Aberdour House]

[BTY/17/32/13–14] *Lion*
4.12.14

Another miserable day, snowing and blowing and very cold, but we are not idle and are carrying out our programme daily. Firing all day and completing with coal and ammunition, stores etc. The men I think are happy and feel that if there is anything to be done, we shall do it somehow. Every man in the squadron feels that everything depends on the battle-cruisers and they act accordingly, are proud of being where they are, and I am certain of them that when our hour comes they will not fail. And yet, the monotony of it all you would think, coupled with the discomfort and the long night hours, would be sufficient to crush them into apathy. Not a bit of it! . . .

I am glad my letters to Winston and Fisher moved them as they evidently have. I have received two letters from each of them in a week, which in itself is a remarkable fact, and both of them of a serious apologetic character and containing promises of a change in the direction in which I have urged. The situation is curious; two very strong and clever men, one old, wily and of vast experience, one young, self assertive with a great self satisfaction, but unstable. They cannot work together, they cannot both run the show. The old man can and will, the young man thinks he can and won't. Hence one must go and that will be Winston. I should not be surprised to see him removed at any time.

Fisher has sent me very sound letters. He agrees with all the arguments I have put before him, and they have been opposed to his own views & consequently criticised his action, but he has taken no offence; says he agrees and if he had known what he knows now, would have done differently, and I think will do as I want in time, but old men must never be hustled. He told me if I ever wanted anything to wire him direct, and I should have it. No man could say more and all we have to do is to wait and see him do it. . . .

100.   *To his wife* [Aberdour House]

[BTY/17/32/23–6]   *Lion*
                                                          10.12.14

. . .

We had glorious news last night which I sent on to you by telegram this morning. Poor old Kit Craddock has been truly avenged and the *Scharnhorst, Gneisenau* and *Leipzig* have been sunk by Sturdee's squadron. Truly the ways of providence are strange, as Sturdee is the one man who was really responsible for the disaster to poor old Kit, in that he sent out a weak squadron on a hopeless quest. The victory ought to have been Kit's if they had only done what they ought and sent the *Invincible & Inflexible* out to him long ago. Now the victory belongs to old Fisher, & nobody else, who sent them out directly he arrived at the Admiralty, and all credit is due to him. We do not know what force Sturdee had with him, but I expect he was pretty powerful. Well, there is not much left of the German Navy outside their own ports; two small cruisers, the *Bremen* and *Karlsruhe*,[1] and possibly one big one, but that is doubtful.

I fear it will act as a deterrent to prevent them from coming out, which would be maddening. It has done us all a tremendous amount of good getting the news and I hope will put a stop to a lot of unpleasant remarks one can detect in a certain portion of the Press, that the Navy *has* been an expensive luxury and is not doing its job. . . .

I never heard such nonsense as forming a Women's Volunteer Reserve, really it is too ridiculous. There is plenty for a woman to do if she will but set about it. Work that a man cannot do, and, as you say, for married women, to look after the home and children should be enough. That sort of thing sickens me when women try to ape men in their [?] sphere of life, which is bad enough for them, and would be worse when women put their fingers into the pie. . . .

[1]Light cruiser *Karlsruhe* sank in Caribbean on 4 November 1914 following an internal explosion; this not known by Admiralty until March 1915. *Bremen* sunk by mine in Baltic, July 1915.

101.   *To his wife* [Aberdour House]

[BTY/17/32/28–9]   *Lion*
                                                  11.12.14

It was a great sweep-up they had in the South Atlantic and up
to the present they have got all except one, and should be able
to catch her also.[1] Sturdee retrieved his mistakes well and deserves
well for what he has done. We do not know yet what force he
had, but I think he was very well off in that respect. I do not wish
to be mean or narrow minded, especially when a man does well,
but somehow I grudge the victory to him. As Chief of the War
Staff he committed terrible blunders which have cost us many
valuable lives, the ships were nothing, and it is given to few people
in this world to be permitted to make mistakes wholesale, and
then given an opportunity of effacing them. If the right steps had
been taken and the strategical situation been properly appreciated, this victory would have been poor old Kit's on the 1st
November. As a matter of fact all credit is now due to Jacky
Fisher, who first initiated the battle-cruiser, which has justified
itself, and then saw the strategical necessity of having a strong
force at the right place and sent them out.

I am sorry for Moore who was taken out of his squadron to
find room for Sturdee who had to be got rid of — and they say
there is no such thing as luck. Truly Fate is ironical.

It really is splendid to think that the naval power of Germany
has ceased to exist outside the Kiel Canal and their own ports —
and, please God, even there it will be destroyed before long.

*   *   *

There is very little for me to write about. We go on hour by
hour and day by day, trying to make ourselves more efficient,
using what little knowledge our experience, and that of others,
during the war, has given us, to improve the position, and I
believe that we are, under the many [?] circumstances, as efficient
as we can be and good enough. But it is to the supreme test that
we must apply for any certainty, and when that will be, who
knows, if at all, which I fear now will never be. Well we mustn't
think too much about it but just go on. . . .

---

[1]*Dresden*, scuttled on 14 March 1915 in Chilean territorial waters after action
with *Glasgow*.

102. *From Goodenough*
Operations, 16th December 1914

[BTY/3/3/1]   *Southampton*
                                          18th December 1914
No 0037

Sir,

In compliance with your signal 1535 of to-day I have the honour to report that at about 11.25 a.m. on Wednesday, 16th December, with the 1st Light Cruiser Squadron spread N.N.E. and S.S.W, 4 miles apart and *Lion* bearing E. 5 miles from *Southampton*, one enemy light cruiser accompanied by a flotilla of 7 or 8 Destroyers steering South was sighted by *Southampton* approximately 3 miles distant ahead.

2. The weather at the time was misty, wind West (force 5–6); heavy spray and some sea was coming over the forecastle, the speed of ship being 24 knots.

The ship was turned to starboard to get to windward of enemy, as there was too much sea to fire to windward. The enemy continued South at high speed; *Southampton* was turned to follow them and engaged them and the destroyers.

Birmingham joined from her look-out station.

I signalled the light cruisers to close.

The enemy was followed and engaged until 11.50 a.m., accurate shooting being a matter of great difficulty owing to the motion of the ship and the spray which obscured the gunlayers' telescopes.

Three more light cruisers or cruisers were sighted to the South-Westward.

3. At 11.50 a.m. I received a signal by searchlight, made both by *Nottingham* and *Birmingham* — 'Light cruisers resume previous look-out stations'; I then relinquished the chase and returned to my station.

4. At 11.55 a.m. a cruiser, apparently of the *Prinz Adalbert* class, was sighted steering approximately S.E. Shots were exchanged with her and the fact of her presence reported to *Lion* by searchlight.

5. Owing to the mist and the spray breaking over the ship the situation was not at all clear, but I am of the opinion that there were five or six enemy cruisers or light cruisers and certainly one flotilla of destroyers in the immediate vicinity.

6. One torpedo was seen to come to the surface short and astern of *Southampton*. The ship was struck by a few splinters of shell.

7. I enclose a copy of the Signal and W/T logs of *Southampton* in accordance with your signal 1535.

The times in the Signal Log can only be regarded as approximate, for everything on deck was being washed down when steering West and South.

A signal to the light cruisers to close was made but not logged, also a signal to turn 16 points to follow the enemy. These signals were made approximately at 11.25 a.m. when the enemy was first sighted.

8. In addition, I beg to enclose on a separate sheet a copy of a signal made by me to *Nottingham* today, together with the reply.

Enclosure No 3 in Light Cruiser Squadron letter No 0037 of 18th December 1914, addressed to the Vice Admiral Commanding, First Battle Cruiser Squadron

COPY OF SIGNAL
From. . . . Commodore, 1st L. C. S.
To. . . . . *Nottingham*
Date. . . . 18th December 1914
Time. . . . 8.57 a.m.

To whom did you pass the signal to 'resume your previous look-out station' at about 11.45 a.m. the day before yesterday ? 0855

REPLY

Signal 'L Y' made by S. O. 1st B. C. S. to 1st L. C. S. on 16th passed to ships on both sides of *Nottingham* about 11.55 a.m. 0930

Enclosure No 1 to Goodenough's Report dated 18 December 1914

[BTY/3/3/18]

Extracts: Signal Log H.M.S. Southampton

11.55 a.m.   *Lion* to Commodore (by searchlight): What have you done with enemy light cruisers?

Reply: They disappeared steaming S. when I received your signal to resume station.

12.00 noon   *Lion* to *Southampton* (by searchlight): Engage the enemy.

12.13   Reply: There is no enemy in sight now.

12.20   Reply: When & where did you last sight enemy? When you sight enemy engage him. Signal to resume previous station was made to *Nottingham*.

12.50   *Lion* to *Southampton* (by searchlight): My signal to resume previous station was sent to *Nottingham*. I cannot understand why under any circumstances you did not pursue enemy.

103. *To Warrender*

[BTY/3/3/14]   SECRET   *Lion*
19 December 1914

No 01   Sir,

I have the honour to submit the following narrative of events after joining your Flag at 11 a.m. 15th December and receiving the instructions contained in your signal 1141. The 1st Battle-Cruiser Squadron took station as ordered for the night 5 miles ahead of the 2nd Battle Squadron with the 1st Light Cruiser Squadron 5 miles on the starboard beam and the 3rd Cruiser Squadron 5 miles on the port beam, Destroyers with Battle Squadron, and proceeded to Rendezvous 54.10 N 3.0 E, where it was hoped to meet Commodore T.

2. Between 5.40 and 7.30 a.m. on 16th Dec received and intercepted various signals indicating that Destroyers were engaged astern of the Battle Squadron and that enemy cruisers were present. Telefunken heard from 5.30 onwards.

A.M.   7.30   Battle Cruisers and Cruisers altered course N 17 W to conform with orders received and to close enemy reported. Squadrons disposed as follows — L. C. S. spread to Nd, 3rd C. S. to Sd 5 miles.

7.55   Dawn. Sighted Battle Squadron and received signal

'Are you going after *Roon*':[1] Reply 'Have heard nothing of *Roon*. What course are you steering'

8.00   Signal from *Shark* 'Position 54.22 N 3.20 E am keeping touch with large cruiser *Roon* and 5 Destroyers steering East 0705'. B.C.S, and L.C.S. altered course to the Ed to cut off *Roon*, and worked up to 24 knots. Ordered 3rd C.S. to preserve station on B.S.

8.35   From *Shark*[2] 'Am being chased to West by —— 54.34 N 3.48 E 0815'.

8.42   Intercepted *Patrol*[3] to *Jupiter* 'Heavily engaged with 2 Enemy B.C's.' (no position. German interference)

8.45   Intercepted 'Scarborough to Admiralty — Scarborough being shelled'.

8.54   Altered course to N to support *Shark*

8.56   From Admiralty. Urgent. 'At 8.20 a.m. Scarborough was being shelled. 0855.'

9.3   Altered course for Scarborough W.N.W. and informed V.A.C. 2 B.S.

9.12   L.C.S. reported 3 columns of smoke to the Nd and later that they were 4 of our Destroyers steaming at high speed.

9.25   From *Shark* 'Am being chased by Light Cruisers. 0918.'

9.30   I made to *Southampton* 'Light Cruisers are probably enemy if so engage them.' 0923

9.33   Intercepted Sheerness to *Aurora* 'Tynemouth intercepted. 3 battleships of *Dreadnought* class attacked *Waveney* off Hartlepool.[4] Hartlepool reports 3 three-funnelled cruisers S.E. Urgent'. (interference)

3. At this time the situation appeared to be that various forces of enemy battle-cruisers and cruisers were bombarding our coast towns leaving a screen of cruisers to indicate our approach. A

[1]*Roon*, German cruiser of the *Yorck* class.

[2]*Shark*, one of seven TBDs escorting the battle-cruisers. She was to be sunk at Jutland.

[3]*Patrol*, light cruiser, ship of SNO Hartlepool, had moved out to attack the German battle-cruisers. *Jupiter*, guardship in Tyne.

[4]*Aurora*, a light cruiser in Harwich Force. *Waveney*, TBD, one of four stationed at Hartlepool, came under fire from enemy battle-cruisers when attempting an attack.

portion of this screen, or probably an outpost, had been located by our destroyers who were being chased to the Westward by them, to the Northward of us. Large operations were taking place off our coast — how large was uncertain. It was imperative that we should not be deflected from getting into touch with the larger force by endeavouring to concentrate on the minor force to the Nd. It was also imperative that this outpost or cruiser screen should be driven off and engaged by our light cruisers before 1st B.C.S. was seen and reported by them. I therefore made the following signal —

9.40   To *Southampton* 'Your duty is to clear enemy L.C's from our front so that they will not obtain information as to our position. Do not close me any more. 0934'.

9.50   Made to V.A.C. 2 B.S. 'Shall have to haul to N 40 W to clear S.W. Dogger Bank patch. Enemy appears to be working up the Coast. 0950'.

4. My reasons for steering to the North of the Dogger Bank were (i) the gap in the minefield lay between 54.50 N and 54.20 N. Our chance of catching the enemy was to watch the gap between these two parallels. (ii) It was possible for him to escape to the Nd of the Dogger Bank or to the Sd, and if we were late in arriving at the gap by the Sd route he might get away to the Northward unobserved.

10.30   From V.A.C. 2 B.S. 'I think you might probably cut him off about 55.0 N, 1.20 E. 10.30.'

10.35   From V.A.C. 2 B.S. Urgent. 'Keep to South of Dogger Bank. Go through gap between 54.40 N and 54.20 N up to 20 minutes E. 1026.' This arrived too late to be acted upon.

10.35   Made to V.A.C. 2 B.S. 'Propose to steer W.N.W. at 11 a.m. with L.C's ahead of me to fill gap through minefield. 1035.'

10.50   Made to V.A.C. 2 B.S. 'Propose we should block gap between mine fields, L.C's to Nd, 3rd C.S. to Sd. 3rd B.S. guards by Farn Is. Commodore T off Flamborough Head.'

5. In the absence of any instructions from you I assumed that you concurred in my submission and at 11 a.m. the situation appeared to be as follows. My position was 54.37 N, 2.23 E, course W.N.W., 24 knots. L.C's 5 miles ahead spread 5 miles apart, which with a visibility of 5 miles covered a front of 25 miles. The 2nd B.S. was to Sd of Dogger Bank and 3rd C.S. pushing forward to continue the line of look outs to the Sd of L.C.S.

6. From various signals received (*vide* enclosure) it was evident that enemy B.C's were off Hartlepool at 9 a.m. which gave us time to get to the Westward of the Dogger Bank and reach the strategical points before him. I anticipated that we should receive information from our patrols as to the position of the enemy B.C's, but a signal intercepted from *St George* to A.O.P.[1] at 11.13 (have raised steam for full speed, Destroyers ready. 0921) showed that this was improbable.

11.12   B.S's eased to 18 knots to allow the L.C's to get sufficiently ahead, it being all important that the Battle Cruisers should not be sighted by enemy's cruisers. Wind and sea had increased considerably.

11.33   *Lion* observed light cruisers on her port bow firing at enemy.

11.38   I received signal from S.O. L.C.S. 'Engaging a cruiser and destroyers. 1130.'

11.47   I received from S.O. L.C.S. the signal 'Chasing an enemy light cruiser and destroyers steering South. 11.44.'

11.50   I signalled to *Nottingham* and *Falmouth*, who were proceeding to join Commodore, to resume their station ahead. I considered *Southampton* did not need their assistance, as only 1 cruiser was reported and I assumed that 3rd C.S. was to the Sd of them. Also it was important for *Nottingham* and *Falmouth* to look out ahead of me for other enemy ships.

11.54   I altered course to S.S.W. and at

12.5 p.m.   resumed course W.N.W.

12.10   I received signal from S.O. L.C.S. 'Enemy cruiser bearing S 60 W.'

12.13   Observed *Southampton* closing me steering to N. Wd and not engaged. I signalled 'Engage the enemy.' She replied 'No enemy in sight. They disappeared steering S when I received your signal to resume station.' The following signals passed —

12.25   *Lion* to *Southampton* 'When and where was enemy last seen. When you sight enemy engage him. Signal to resume previous station was made to *Nottingham*. 1220.'

12.25   *Southampton* to *Lion* 'At 11.55, bearing S 5 miles, steering about S.S.E. 1225.'

[1]*St George*, depot ship for TBDs in Humber; flagship of Rear-Admiral G. A. Ballard, Admiral of Patrols, who was responsible for east coast defence with flotillas based in Dover, Humber, Tyne and Forth.

12.50   *Lion* to *Southampton* 'My signal to resume previous station was made to *Nottingham*. I cannot understand why under any circumstances you did not pursue enemy. 1250.'

12.25   At 12.25 p.m. I was about to alter course for centre of gap between the minefields when I received your signal 'Enemy cruisers and destroyers in sight. My course N.E. by E. 1218.' I therefore turned 16 points to port to ensure being to the Eastward of enemy B.C's.

12.41   I received your signal 'Enemy's course East. No battle cruisers seen yet. 1238.' Then, at

12.56   received your signal '2 B.S. has resumed original station. 1250.'

7. The situation now had to be again reviewed. The various reports we had received of enemy battle-cruisers off Hartlepool at 9 a.m. made it practically certain that they must still be West of us. The enemy light cruiser sighted by you, which I assumed to be the same as that engaged by *Southampton*, made it probable that our battleships would be reported south of the Dogger Bank and the enemy battle-cruisers would then attempt to break away north of it. In any case, with visibility varying as it was from only 1 to 5 miles between 11.30 and 1.30, and with this new information at his disposal the possibility of catching him became remote. Therefore at 1.15 p.m. I turned to the North with L.C.S. still spread to the Westward and reported to you accordingly.

1.43   Received signal from Admiralty 'At 12.15 G.M.T. enemy battle cruisers were 54.33 N 1.7 E steaming E by S 23 knots. Urgent 1325.'

8. The course was obviously incorrect as he was not likely to steer from W to E over the whole length of the S.W. patch of Dogger Bank. Had he steered Nd of it our line of look-outs would certainly have already sighted him. Therefore he must have steered Sd of that course or else turned away again. As there was a doubt, and it was imperative he should not get to the Ed of us, I altered course E by S and reported to you (*vide* my 1355). I hoped to get further information and continued Ed assuming that having received no further instructions from you, you concurred in my movements.

9. It was not until 3.22 that I received Admiralty signal 709 'Enemy Battle Cruisers position at 12.45 was 54.26 N 1.25 E steering N by E 21 knots. Urgent 1450.' This reaching me 2½ hours late was of little value but I turned to the Nd still hoping

that if the enemy steered N by E and then turned again Ed we might be able to hit [*sic*] him off.

10. It is interesting to note that if I had received the Admiralty 1450 signal as soon after the event as in the case of Admiralty 1325 signal, we should have been in a fairly good position to intercept the enemy had his movements been as reported.

11. From the later signal received at 1.20 p.m. on 17th (see enclosure), it would seem that he probably turned West again and then through South so as to proceed East after dark.

Enclosure: [see Para. 6 above]

From	To	Time	Message
Sheerness	*Aurora*	9.33 16th	Tynemouth intercepted. 3 battle-ships *Dreadnought* class attacked enemy off Hartlepool. Hartlepool reports 3 three-funnelled cruisers S.E.
Aberdeen	C-in-C	10.10	Following message received from Tynemouth. 3 enemy battleships *Dreadnought* class reported 8.47 a.m. off Hartlepool. 0910
Aberdeen	C-in-C	10.50	Following message received from Newcastle. Off shore battleship *Dreadnought* class attacked *Waveney* off Hartlepool. Hartlepool report query S.E. firing N.E. 0945.
Aberdeen 14	C-in-C	11.15	Following message received from Newcastle. Whitby reports 2 hostile battleships of class unknown bombarded signal station 9.0 a.m. to 9.15 a.m. when vessels left proceeding E at high speed. 1047.
Aberdeen	C-in-C	11.24	Following from Newcastle. Off shore battleship *Dreadnought* class attacked *Waveney* off Hartlepool. Hartlepool reports 3 three-funnelled cruisers S.E. steering N.E. 0945.
Aberdeen 15	C-in-C	11.45	Following from Newcastle. Scarboro' bombarded from 8.7 to 8.30 a.m. Hartlepool 8.20 till

			8.50 am. enemy last seen proceeding N. 1108.
Admiral of Patrols	S.O. 1st B.C.S.	12.44	Am off Flamborough Head in *Skirmisher*. There is no sign of the enemy between Flamborough Head and Humber. 1210.
do	S.O. 2nd B.S.	1.18	All German vessels steered E from neighbourhood Whitby and Filey Bay, about 9.0 a.m. and have not since re-appeared. 1250.
Aberdeen	C-in-C	1.20 p.m.	Trawler reports 6 German men-of-war 57 miles E.N.E. Flamborough Head steering N 6 W at 1.7 p.m. yesterday. Admiralty has been informed.

104. *To Jellicoe*

[BTY/3/3/16–17]   SECRET   *Lion*
No 01   19 December 1914

Sir,

In accordance with your signal 1800 of today and 2307 of 17 December, I have the honour to forward herewith a copy of the report which I have addressed to the Vice-Admiral Commanding, 2nd Battle Squadron,[1] giving a detailed narrative of the operations of 16 December.

2. Since compiling this narrative I have received Commodore Goodenough's report of which a copy is attached [105].

3. From this report it appears that he sighted no less than 5 German cruisers and actually engaged 2.

4. The reports signalled to me at the time indicated the presence of only *one* cruiser and some destroyers, and nothing in the Commodore's subsequent signals led me to assume that he had sighted more.

5. The following are the reports referred to, and signals concerning them, extracted from the logs of *Lion* and *Southampton*:

[1]Sir George Warrender had been in overall command.

11.38	W/T	*S'ton* to *Lion*	Am engaging a Cruiser and destroyers. 1130.
11.48	W/T	*S'ton* to *Lion*	Am chasing Light Cruiser and destroyers steering south. 1144.
12.10	S.L.	*S'ton* to *Lion*	Enemy Cruiser bearing S by E (reported in *Lion* as S 60 W)
12.13	S.L.	*Lion* to *S'ton*	Engage the enemy.
12.14	S.L.	*S'ton* to *Lion*	No enemy in sight.
12.25	S.L.	*Lion* to *S'ton*	When and where was enemy last seen? When you sight enemy engage him. Signal to resume previous station was made to *Nottingham*. 1220.
12.30	S.L.	*S'ton* to *Lion*	At 11.55, bearing South 5 miles steering about S.S.E. 1225.

6. Commodore Goodenough's written report makes the whole situation perfectly clear. It shows that our light cruisers and battle-cruisers had attained the right strategical position, and in spite of the low visibility had actually succeeded in getting in touch with the advanced enemy cruisers.

7. Had *Southampton* and *Birmingham* reported fully all that was sighted, or pressed their attack or even maintained touch with the enemy whom they had sighted, it may be taken as almost certain that the whole German force would have been brought to action.

8. I do not understand how the Commodore could have thought that the signal made to *Nottingham* and *Falmouth* applied to him, observing that *Lion* was in visual touch with *Southampton* and in fact nearer to him than the *Nottingham*, the apparent source of his information. Even though the wrong call sign was used in addressing *Nottingham* I consider that the situation in which the Commodore was placed should have made him doubt the intention of my order. I say this more especially as I had in personal interviews previously impressed on him that he might always use the freeest discretion; and that if he, on the spot, considered any of my orders unsuitable to the existing situation, he should never hesitate to vary them and report to me. This indeed is an elementary duty of cruiser officers.

105.   *Goodenough to Jellicoe*
       Copy to Beatty

[BTY/3/3/3]   SECRET   *Southampton*
No 0037   20th December 1914

Operations, 16th December 1914

Sir,

In accordance with your message 1800 of 19th December, I have the honour to report as follows with regard to proceedings on 16th Instant:-

2. At 6 a.m. on 16th December *Southampton*, with *Birmingham, Nottingham* and *Falmouth* in company, was in position Lat 54° 15′ N, Long 2° 50′ E, stationed 5 miles on starboard beam of 1st Battle-Cruiser Squadron, with orders to close Battle-Cruiser Squadron at 7.30 a.m.

Subsequent proceedings were as follows:-

7.00 a.m.   Squadron was closed on Battle-Cruiser Squadron to 1½ miles, and was in that station by 7.15 a.m.

7.26 a.m.   Squadron was ordered to take station North (true) 5 miles from *Lion*, spread North (true). Squadron was spread accordingly 4 miles apart.

7.30 a.m.   *Birmingham* was put on 'D' tune.

8.05 a.m.   Course E.N.E., 22 knots, by order of Vice Admiral, *Lion*.

8.10 a.m.   Course E.½ N., 24 knots, by order of Vice Admiral, *Lion*.

8.15 a.m.   Course E.

8.50 a.m.   Course N.

9.00 a.m.   Course W.N.W.

9.10 a.m.   (about) Signal came through light cruisers from the Northward that our destroyers were approaching (see Signal Log).

9.55 a.m.   Three more light cruisers or cruisers were sighted to the South-Westward.

4. At 11.50 a.m. I received a signal by searchlight, made both by *Nottingham* and *Birmingham* — 'Light cruisers resume previous look-out stations'; I then relinquished the chase and returned to my station on *Lion*, in visual touch with her. I now understand that the signal was meant for *Nottingham* only. (See further letter)

5. At 11.55 a.m. a cruiser, apparently of the *Prinz Adalbert*

class, was sighted steering approximately South-East. Shots were exchanged with her and the fact of her presence reported to *Lion* by searchlight.

6. Owing to the mist and spray breaking over the ship the situation was not at all clear, but I am of the opinion that there were five or six enemy cruisers or light cruisers and certainly one flotilla of destroyers in the immediate vicinity.

7. One torpedo was seen to come to the surface short and astern of *Southampton*. The ship was struck by a few splinters of shell.

8. Subsequent proceedings of the Squadron were as follows:-
12.35 p.m. Course E.S.E. by order of Vice Admiral, *Lion*.

1.40 p.m. Course N.W. by order of Vice Admiral, *Lion*.

2.12 p.m. Course E.S.E., 24 knots, by order of Vice Admiral, *Lion*.

2.30 p.m. Course, S.E., 24 knots, by order of Vice Admiral, *Lion*.

3.40 p.m. Course North, 20 knots

9. As directed in your message 1800, extracts from the under-mentioned documents, covering the period 6 a.m. to 4 p.m. on 16th December, are enclosed [not included]:-

Signal Log,
W/T Log,
Intercepted W/T Log,
Cipher Log, and
Intercepted Cipher Log.

The times in the Signal Log from 11 a.m. can only be regarded as approximate, for everything on deck was being washed down when steering West and South.

A signal to the light cruisers to close was made but not logged, also a signal to turn 16 points to follow the enemy. These signals were made approximately at 11.25 a.m. when the enemy was first sighted.

106. *Goodenough to Jellicoe*

Operations, 16th December 1914
[BTY/3/3/3]   SECRET   *Southampton*
No 0037   20th December 1914

In obedience to your W/T message 1051 of today and in

continuation of my No 0037 of today which this accompanies, I have the honour to submit that my reasons for relinquishing the chase of the enemy at 11.50 a.m. on 16th December were as follows: —

2. The signal I received from *Nottingham* was clear, viz:-S——LY = 'Light cruisers resume previous look-out stations'.

I took the signal to be a positive order from *Lion*. The situation, as it appeared to me, was that the enemy I had in sight was heading straight for the position where I believed the 3rd Cruiser Squadron and 2nd Battle Squadron to be. I took it that the enemy's battle cruisers were the principal objective, and that the light cruisers were required to assist in locating them.

I therefore obeyed what I took to be the orders of the Vice Admiral, H.M.S. *Lion*.

3. I enclose a copy of a signal made by me on 18th December to *Nottingham*, together with the reply.

107. *[Signals Copies after the Scarborough Raid]*

[BTY/3/3/4–13]   17–20.12.14

[I]

Admiral Commanding 1 B.C.S. to Admiral Commanding 2 B.S. 17.12.14 Time 10 a.m.

> Submit with reference to your 1500 to C-in-C; after full consideration no enemy ships could have passed between us unseen as I was 10 miles to the North of you and light cruisers covered the front between us.
> The cruisers and destroyers sighted by you were those sighted & engaged by *Southampton* & *Birmingham*.
> Enemy battle cruisers must have been to the Westward of us at dark.

[II]

Senior Officer 2 B.S. to C-in-C 17.12.14 10.15 a.m.

> An intercepted signal reported battle-cruisers off Hartlepool at 9.20 a.m. Admiralty had previously informed me they were off Scarborough at 6.20 a.m. Beatty therefore went North of Dogger Bank.

I wirelessed him to come South, but evidently too late; mist and rain between 11.30 a.m. and 1 p.m. assisted enemy to escape as I never saw them.

[III]
S.O. 2 B.S. to A.C. 1 B.C.S. 17.12.14 3.10 p.m.

I calculate enemy passed you in the rain about 11.30; visibility with me was then less than 3 miles. By the time you got my signal that cruisers & destroyers were in sight, they were 30 [sic] from you. Please accept my best thanks for all you did. Do you understand why *Shark* did not rejoin as soon as she could?

[IV]
S.O. 1 L.C.S. to C-in-C 17.12.14 7.51[p.m.]

Your 1702: *Southampton* and *Birmingham* were in action from about eleven thirty-three to eleven fifty-five with a cruiser or light cruiser and flotilla, with others in sight. Later at long range with cruiser of *Prince Adalbert* class for a few minutes. Heavy spray owing to high speed and rough sea rendered shooting very difficult. First enemy disappeared into mist and rain on being chased.

[V]
S.O. 2 B.S. to S.O. 1 B.C.S. 17.12.14 10.1 p.m.

I am much inclined to agree with you that battle cruisers were in Admiralty position at 12.45 and cleared to the Northward.

[VI]
S.O. 1 L.C.S. to C-in-C 18.12.14 11 a.m.

Your 2307: 1st L.C.S. spread NNE 4 miles apart WNW from *Lion* until 11.35 a.m. when *Southampton* five miles W from *Lion* sighted an enemy cruiser with flotilla on port bow steering about South. Engaged and followed them with *Birmingham* until 11.50 [?]. Sighted three other enemy ships to SE. Weather thick with mist and rain. At 11.50 received signal by searchlight to resume station and did so. This signal was apparently meant for *Nottingham* only. Enemy disappeared in mist and rain to Southward. At 11.55 sighted one large cruiser for a few minutes steering about SE. Remainder of time in company with battle cruisers.

[VII]

S.O. 2 B.S. to C-in-C 18.12.14 5.37 p.m:
My destroyers engaged about 6.15 a.m. on 16th Dec and I did
not see them again. 1st L.C.S. drove off enemy. Arrived at the
rendez-vous 7 a.m. 17th and on receipt of intelligence
proceeded towards Scarborough. 11.30 1st L.C.S. engaged light
cruisers and 5 destroyers. 12.11 numerous vessels N by W.
12.15.54°: 23′ N, 2° 14′ E [?] made out cruisers and destroyers
about 5 miles.
No opportunity to open fire. Enemy not again seen and at 3.45
chase was abandoned. Battle-cruisers never saw enemy.

[VIII]

C-in-C to S.O. 1 L.C.S. 20.12.14 12.27 p.m.
My 1800 yesterday: your report should explain your reasons
for abandoning chase at 11.50 a.m. as reported in your telegram
0230 of 18th.

[IX]

C-in-C to S.O. 1 B.C.S. 20.12.14 12.43 p.m.
Your signal of 19 Dec No 01 to V.A.C. 2 B.S.: telegraph by
land your positions at (1) 5 a.m. (2) 7.30 a.m. (3) 9 a.m. (4)
10 a.m. (5) 11 a.m. (6) noon (7) 1 p.m. and (8) 2 p.m. on 16th
December.

[X]

A.C. 1 B.C.S. to C-in-C [no date or time given]

	Position	
	Lat N	Long E
(1) 5 a.m.	54.37	2.41
(2) 7.30 a.m.	54.6	2.12
(3) 9.00 a.m.	54.19	3.36
(4) 10 a.m.	54.23	2.58
(5) 11 a.m.	54.37	2.24
(6) noon	54.38	1.54
(7) 1 p.m.	54.35	1.53
(8) 2 p.m.	54.45	2.2

108.   *Jellicoe to Goodenough*

[Copy to Beatty]

[BTY/3/3/19]   23 Dec 1914

Operations in the N Sea 16th December

Having before me the reports of the operations of the 16th
instant of the force of which the Light Cruiser Squadron formed
a portion, I have to make the following remarks.

2. I am of the opinion that whilst the escape of the enemy's
battle-cruisers was largely due to the weather conditions prevailing
at the time, it is at least conceivable that they might have been
brought to action had the *Southampton* and *Birmingham* kept
touch with the three light cruisers sighted by you at 11.45 a.m.
The reason given by you for the light cruisers having rejoined the
battle cruisers at 11.50 a.m. is that a visual signal to this effect
was made by the Vice Admiral 1st Battle-Cruiser Squadron at
11.40 a.m. Immediately afterwards however you sighted the three
light cruisers, and knowing the Vice Admiral 1st Battle-Cruiser
Squadron was unaware of their presence when the recalling signal
was made (as it turned out later, in error) you should most
certainly have kept touch with these vessels and informed him of
their presence.

109.   *Beatty Memorandum To Commanding Officers and the Engineer Captain, 1st Battle-Cruiser Squadron*

[HTN/17]   *Lion*
                                              28 December 1914

. . .

I have had under consideration the question of how to utilise
to the fullest advantage the resources at our disposal for dealing
with the defects that arise in the ships of the squadron.

2. The practice hitherto has been to report through the
Engineer Captain on my staff only those defects which come under
the heading of engineering. In future this should be extended to
include all requisitions for work etc connected with hull, gunnery
and torpedo fittings and the like, in which his advice and opinion

can be of value. He is to be recognised as my expert adviser on *all* such questions of materiel.

3. To assist the Engineer Captain in carrying out these duties, Asst. Constructor Stephens now serving in *Lion*, is to be lent to *Tiger* for duty under the Engineer Captain, and is to be regarded as being on my General Staff for this purpose.[1]

4. Commanding Officers should bear in mind that valuable time may be saved and expert advice obtained by requesting the Engineer Captain personally to inspect defects or alterations of the nature described. He will delegate the Asst. Constructor to attend to structural questions as necessary.

5. Application has been made to the Admiralty for 7 additional Engine Room Artificers to be drafted to *Tiger* for squadron work under the Engineer Captain. If this proposal is approved, the fact will be notified later.

6. Every effort is to be made to reduce the calls made on yards and repair ships. The best results can only be achieved by the most intelligent co-operation of all departments and the use of all their resources for the common end.

110.   *Jellicoe to Flag Officers and Commodores*

[BTY/3/3/20]   *Iron Duke*
Secret And Personal   30 December 1914
H.F. 0022   *Memorandum*

Having had under consideration the reports of the various Flag and Senior Officers taking part in the Operations on 16th December, I have to make the following remarks for information and guidance, as a result of the experience gained.

2. Under all circumstances of sighting any enemy vessels in the vicinity of our own coast, it is very necessary that the coast patrols in the vicinity should be warned immediately. This warning saves valuable time in the departure of local flotillas of all sorts from their anchorages if not already at sea, permits of concentration of forces, and may facilitate the defence of ports.

3. The Admiralty and Commander-in-Chief should also be

[1]The Battle-Cruiser Squadron's Engineer Captain was Charles Taylor, accommodated on *Tiger*; the Assistant Constructor was A. K. Stephens, holding the equivalent rank of Engineer Lieutenant.

informed at once, as well as other senior officers in the vicinity. This saves time in ordering such vessels as are deemed necessary to proceed to sea.

4. Officers commanding squadrons or Captains of single vessels should be most careful to give full information to the nearest Flag or Senior Officer as to any enemy vessels sighted. Attention is once again directed to the absolute necessity for indicating the position of the reporting ship and of the enemy.

5. Should the officer commanding a squadron, or the captain of a single vessel, when in actual touch with the enemy, receive an order from a senior officer which it is evident may have been given in ignorance of the conditions of the moment, and which, if obeyed, would cause touch with the enemy to be lost, such officers must exercise great discretion as to representing the real facts before obeying the order. It must be realised that a signal made under such conditions is in the nature of an *instruction*.

6. It is very undesirable, when in proximity with the enemy, that anticipated positions should be given in advance. They are liable to be misunderstood, and moreover are very probably not realised. It is correct to give position, course, and speed at the moment.

7. The senior officer on the spot, when actual contact with the enemy has been gained, must assume general control of the operations of all naval forces in the vicinity, in order to ensure co-operation between the various units.

8. The experience of German mining methods is instructive, and needs study in order that the methods may not be successful in mining our vessels. On the 16th December, the enemy laid mines apparently close inshore north and south of the positions of the vessels engaged in the bombardment. These were obviously intended to catch our vessels coming to intercept the enemy. Further mines were laid in the proximity of the gap in the existing mine field in order to catch our vessels entering through this gap, and more mines were also laid across the line of retreat of the German squadron. These facts indicate the necessity for due caution being exercised when closing the enemy.

111. *To Admiralty*

[BTY/3/3/24]   *Princess Royal*
[Copy to Jellicoe]   26th February 1915
No 01

Sir,

With reference to Admiralty Letter M.04953/14 of 6 January 1915, I have the honour to point out that the conclusions drawn by Their Lordships make it clear that my orders and dispositions on 16 December were not such as they consider to have been best suited to the circumstances that arose, but I would respectfully submit that those conclusions appear to be based on data which on many points disagree with the records kept in *Lion*.[1]

2. With reference to para 5 of the above quoted letter, the spreading and working of the cruisers was *intended* to be left to me, but this became impossible when I proceeded to chase the *Roon*, as the 3rd Cruiser Squadron, on account of their limited speed, was incapable of keeping in touch with us. I therefore ordered them to rejoin the 2nd Battle Squadron and they never again rejoined me or came under my orders.

The front covered by the Light Cruiser Squadron was 25 miles. The number of ships available was 4. Though the extent was small it was, in view of the visibility at the time being only 5 miles, as much as was practicable with that number of cruisers.

3. At 10.40 a.m. the distance apart was reduced to 4 miles because the visibility became reduced and fluctuated between one and four miles.

I would point out that I altered course at 10 a.m. not 9.50 a.m. to N 40 W and when clear of the SW patch of the Dogger Bank turned again at 11 a.m. to WNW which brought the 2nd Battle Squadron 15 miles on Port beam *not astern*. The space between us was filled by the SW patch of Dogger Bank, over which it could safely be assumed that the enemy heavy ships would not pass, and the distance between the 2nd Battle Squadron and most Southern light cruiser was only 10 miles.

4. In para 7 it is inferred that I turned to SSE and remained on that course making no further attempt to investigate to the

---

[1]The Admiralty letter had criticised the 'spread' of Beatty's cruisers. Beatty and Jellicoe rejected this as contrary to the principle of concentration which their experience showed to be paramount (see Roskill, *Admiral of the Fleet*, p 104). For Beatty's original report see 103.

Westward. I would respectfully point out that as is clearly shown in my report, I altered course to SSW at 11.54 a.m. and resumed my original course WNW at 12.5 p.m. — an interval of 11 minutes only.

The object of the turn to SSW was to clear a fleet of trawlers, which might have been enemy minelayers; but on investigation by our TBDs they were proved to be British. This turn also helped me to close Commodore L.C.S., whereas if I had turned to the Northward I would have opened from him.

On resuming my WNW course I *did* push to the Westward in such a manner that any Force advancing behind the enemy cruisers and in sight of them would certainly have been sighted by us.

I held on this course until at 12.25 p.m. I received the signal from *King George V* saying 'Enemy's Cruisers and Destroyers in sight. My course NE by E 1218.'

I then considered it imperative to turn for the reasons stated in my report.

Speed was reduced to enable the light cruisers to keep ahead. I would remark that at this time it was blowing with considerable force and the sea was affecting the speed of the light cruisers, which were not able to make good their full 25 knots.

5. In para 9 it is inferred that my battle-cruisers and light cruisers should have been in a long line N & S. I would submit that to do so would have been against all the experience gained and principles evolved during the past 2 years, which have received the entire approval of two successive C-in-Cs.

The one main principle by which I have hitherto been guided is that battle-cruisers should be concentrated, more especially when the enemy force is equal if not superior to ours, and the visibility is low (as was the case on this occasion). To illustrate my point, if the line is advancing West and an enemy at high speed strikes the Northern flank and drives back and destroys the light cruisers composing it (visibility was at most only 6000 yards) our battle-cruisers at the other end get the news 15 minutes later (allowing for coding, transmitting and decoding) during which time they steer an opposite course to enemy. They then alter course and commence to chase, in misty weather, after the enemy has got a start of 10 to 12 miles besides being 20 miles to a flank and *out* of sight.

In these circumstances it appears that the enemy would break the look-out line and never be brought to action.

We had of course a Battle Squadron also in the vicinity, but in view of their being 5 knots slower than the enemy's ships they could only be considered an uncertain aid.

6. In further proof of the undesirability of spreading I would point out that though my squadron on 24 January was in close order, the rear ships never came into action except with a vessel whose speed had already been reduced by gun fire. Had the battle-cruisers been one mile apart, I can assure Their Lordships that they could never have come into action in time, without running grave risk of being destroyed in detail as they successively came in range of the enemy's concentrated squadron, and we should then have accomplished nothing at all.

7. In para 9 it is stated that the movements of the Battle-Cruiser Squadron had no relation to the probable course of the enemy, yet a perusal of my report will show that the probable course of the enemy was my *only* consideration. I respectfully submit that paragraphs 3, 4, 6, 7, 8 & 9 of that report make this obvious.

8. I might have been wrong in my decisions, but I am at a loss to understand how it can have been supposed that the movements I ordered had no relation to the probable course of the enemy.

Furthermore, the fact that our lookouts did actually succeed in sighting 5 or 6 enemy cruisers and light cruisers and a flotilla of destroyers indicates that the Light Cruiser Squadron and Battle-Cruiser Squadron attained the right strategical position in spite of the low visibility.

9. I attach a copy of the report which I have quoted in paragraphs 4 and 7.

PART IV

THE DOGGER BANK AND AFTER
1915–1916

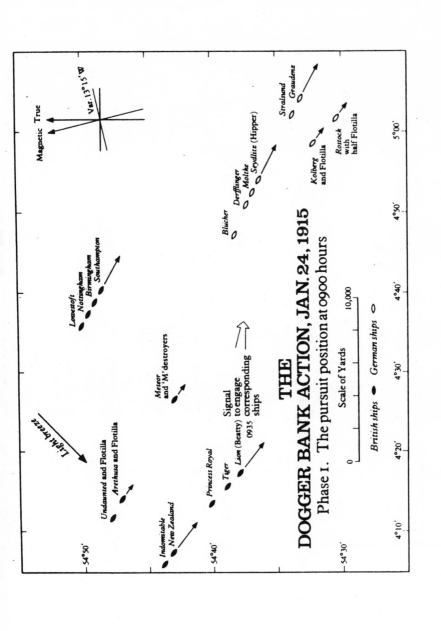

THE
DOGGER BANK ACTION, JAN. 24, 1915
Phase I. The pursuit position at 0900 hours

Scale of Yards

0   10,000

British ships ● German ships ○

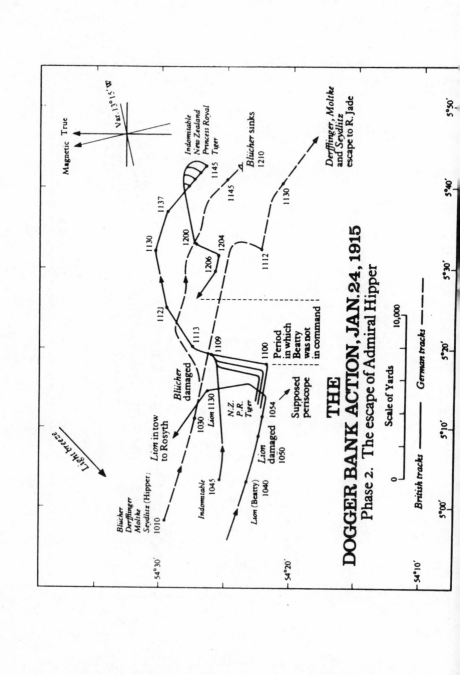

THE
DOGGER BANK ACTION, JAN.24, 1915
Phase 2. The escape of Admiral Hipper

Scale of Yards

British tracks ———   German tracks – – –

INTRODUCTION[1]

On 20th December 1914 Beatty was ordered to move his force to Rosyth, and the Admiralty produced a new command procedure. Jellicoe remained in overall command but, on receipt of intelligence of German activity, the Admiralty would directly order the battle-cruisers, Tyrwhitt's Harwich force and Keyes's submarines to an appropriate rendezvous. As soon as Jellicoe was at sea and in contact he would assume command of the whole force.[2] On Christmas Day 1914 the battle-cruisers were at sea in support of a seaplane raid against Cuxhaven, and again on 18–19 January 1915, this time supporting another sweep through the Bight by the Harwich Force. In neither case was there any contact with enemy battle-cruisers. However these moves encouraged von Ingenohl to attempt to intercept any future sortie, believing that he could overwhelm it before reinforcements arrived. His plan for 23–24 January was to be executed only by his battle-cruisers and their attendant cruisers and destroyers. The High Seas Fleet was not to participate. In London, the Admiralty, aware of German moves, produced a well-conceived counter-plan to deploy a superior force between Hipper and his base. Beatty, with five battle-cruisers and supporting forces, was to sail on the 23 January and rendezvous with Tyrwhitt the following morning some 30 miles north of the Dogger Bank. The Pre-*Dreadnought* Third Battle Squadron and an armoured cruiser squadron were to take position some 40 miles north-west to prevent any enemy breakaway. Finally, the Grand Fleet was to move south from Scapa Flow in case the High Seas Fleet should sail. Although, as von Ingenohl had estimated, Jellicoe was unable to reach the scene of action, the British had five battle-cruisers to the Germans' four in addition to the heavy gun power of the battle squadron.

The British dispositions were successful and cruiser contact made with the enemy at 8 a.m. on 24 January. When Hipper

[1]The Jellicoe-Beatty correspondence relevant to this section is in Temple-Patterson *Jellicoe Papers* Vol. I, pp. 142–50, 152–3, 155–7, 161–7, 170, 174, 177–9, 187–90, 198, 204, 207–10, 219, 221, 231–2, 235–7.
[2]Corbett and Newbolt, *Naval Operations*, Vol. I, pp. 50–1.

realised that he was confronted with battle-cruisers and not just Tyrwhitt's light forces, he turned for home. But that was 150 miles away and, having included the slower armoured cruiser *Blücher* in his line of battle, he had no hope of escaping the pursuing Beatty. The weather was good and *Lion, Tiger, Princess Royal, New Zealand* and *Indomitable* seemed certain of a decisive victory over *Seydlitz* (Hipper's flagship), *Moltke, Derfflinger* and *Blücher*.

It was not to be. Although *Blücher* was sunk and *Seydlitz* heavily damaged, just escaping destruction, Beatty failed in a unique opportunity to eliminate the enemy battle-cruiser force. The documents which follow point to the conclusion that the failure was due to weaknesses in combat, particularly in gunnery and communications, for which Beatty was directly or indirectly responsible. Any judgements on that responsiibility must be made remembering that the battle was fought at unprecedented ranges and speeds unpractised in peacetime exercises, and that the battle-cruisers came under heavy fire for the first time. In addition to all this was Beatty's legitimate fear of running into a submarine or mine trap.

By 9.20 a.m. all Beatty's battle-cruisers, with the exception of the slower *Indomitable*, were in action and *Blücher*, in the rear of the enemy line, badly damaged, but, some 30 minutes later, the first mistake occurred. Captain Pelly of *Tiger* misinterpreted Beatty's fire distribution instructions and, instead of engaging his opposite number, *Moltke*, joined *Lion* in her engagement with *Seydlitz*. Not only was *Tiger*'s gunnery highly inaccurate, but *Moltke*, left free from fire, joined the attack on *Lion*. From 10 a.m. Beatty's flagship was hit repeatedly, her speed seriously reduced and, at 10.50, she lost all electric power. This meant the loss of her radio and searchlight signalling capabilities, leaving two pairs of signal halyards as Beatty's only means of communication. *Tiger, Princess Royal* and *New Zealand* overhauled *Lion* in pursuit of the enemy battle-cruisers but were delayed by Beatty's ordering an abrupt change of course, claiming himself to have seen the wash of a submarine periscope. Later research has produced no evidence of submarine presence at this time.[1] This turnaway increased the fleeing enemy's lead and Beatty's signal urging his own ships to close the gap was so worded that Rear-Admiral Sir Archibald More, now in command in *New Zealand*, interpreted it

[1]Roskill, *Admiral of the Fleet*, p. 113; Marder, *From the Dreadnought*, Vol. 2, p 133.

as meaning he should concentrate on the already doomed *Blücher*. Further attempts by flag signals to correct this failed and when Beatty, transferred by destroyer to *Princess Royal*, resumed control it was too late to overtake the enemy. At 12.54 p.m. he turned for home and the battle was over.

During the following month the official correspondence between Beatty, Jellicoe and the Admiralty, as well as between Beatty and his subordinates, concentrated on establishing what had gone wrong and what lessons could be learned for the future. In addition to identifying the tactical errors already mentioned, there were detailed investigations into gunnery difficulties and the scale and type of damage inflicted by enemy shells. Chatfield in particular was keenly aware of the implications of these last two. It was during this process that Beatty chose to consolidate and circulate the development of his own thought on the role and deployment of battle-cruisers since his appointment in command in March 1913 [112–118].

Recent research has revealed the poor showing of the battle-cruisers' gunnery equipment and performance. Ignoring *Blücher*, they inflicted only an estimated six hits of their main armament on their enemy counterparts, compared with the 20 or so they received.[1] One of *Lion's* hits on *Seydlitz* would have sunk her but for the timely flooding of a threatened magazine. But the relative performance as a whole points strongly to the basic fire-control defects which were to re-emerge at Jutland. It would seem that the Germans benefited most from the post-mortem in at least one vital respect — precautions against explosions in turret ammunition handling procedures. Examination of *Lion's* damage, which put her out of action for two months, showed that her 5 inch and 6 inch armour was inadequate against German A P shells — a vulnerability again not remedied before Jutland. The realisation that smoke made by enemy destroyers had handicapped gunnery observation boosted the equipping of British capital ships with director control systems. Only *Tiger* had been so equipped at the Dogger Bank, and she had to resort to independent firing after failure of the equipment [120]. Changes were made in signal books, including the reintroduction of 'Engage the enemy more closely', to avoid one of the difficulties experienced by Beatty,

---

[1]Roskill, *Admiral of the Fleet*, pp. 118–19, citing N. J. M. Campbell, *Battle Cruisers, Warship Special No 1* (London, 1978); Marder, *From the Dreadnought*, Vol. 2, pp 170–2.

and Jellicoe rephrased the Grand Fleet Orders on distribution of fire, which Pelly had pleaded in justification of his failure to fulfil Beatty's intentions [125, 131].

The excitement of the Dogger Bank was followed by a long period of operational frustration arising from inability to bring the enemy to action. For Beatty this coincided with a resurgence of acute domestic strain 132–140, 142]. The stress of this, combined with the feeling that his correspondence with the Admiralty and politicians, including the Prime Minister himself, was having no effect, made this one of the most frustrating periods of his career. His relationship with Jellicoe can be described as that of a young and eager subordinate urging a Commander-in-Chief whom he respected to be more forthright and emphatic in demanding the battle-fleet superiority essential to victory. He felt that Jellicoe was not making clear enough the disadvantages under which he would have to fight in the face of German superiority in torpedo craft, submarines and Zeppelins [143, 145].

Against this background Beatty was greatly concerned about the strength of his own command. This was reorganised in February 1915 as the Battle-Cruiser Fleet, designed to be made up of three squadrons each of three ships, with *Lion* in addition as fleet flagship. They were to be supported by three light cruiser squadrons and a destroyer flotilla, totalling 13 light cruisers and 16 destroyers. The whole force was to be based at Rosyth. In February 1916 Beatty, supported by two of his squadron commanders, Brock and Pakenham, apprehensive that they might have to meet enemy battleships and not just Hipper's battle-cruisers, recommended that the fast ships of the 5th Battle Squadron should be included in his command. Jellicoe was opposed to this on the grounds that it would tempt Beatty to become involved in an independent action instead of fulfilling his proper role of leading the High Seas Fleet towards the Grand Fleet. Although he rebuked Beatty for corresponding directly with the Admiralty, the general tone of their correspondence was cordial and shows underlying agreement. For instance, Beatty strongly supported Jellicoe's resistance to Admiralty pressures for any risky operations, including further seaplane raids designed to tempt out the German fleet. Nor is there any evidence that he would have differed from Jellicoe's cautious summary of the relative advantages and disadvantages of the Forth as the main fleet anchorage. What Beatty did press for was closer 'community of thought' between Jellicoe and the Admiralty, the Commander-in-

Chief and his subordinates, and they with each other. That means to ensure this were needed, is exemplified by the meeting between Beatty and Jellicoe in February 1916 being the first for five months [146–154].

112.　From Rear-Admiral Moore

[BTY/4/6/7]　　　　　　　　　　　　　　　　　New Zealand
(No 2/17. Confidential)　　　　　　　　　　January 25, 1915

I have the honour to submit the following report on the action of the 24th instant. A report as to the lessons learned during the action is being forwarded separately.

2. On the morning of the 24th instant the First and Second Battle-Cruiser Squadrons were steaming in single line ahead in the following order: *Lion, Tiger, Princess Royal, New Zealand, Indomitable*, speed 18 knots, when at 7.25 a.m. gun-fire from our destroyers and accompanying light cruisers was observed ahead. The subsequent movements, course, and speed of *New Zealand* are shown on the accompanying track chart [not reproduced]. For clearness only the tracks of that ship and the *Blücher*, the rear ship of the enemy, are shown. The narrative will explain the relative positions of the remaining ships of the opposing battle-cruisers.

3. At 7.54 a.m. the enemy's battle-cruisers, four in number, were made out on the port bow, and, as far as could be ascertained, they were in the following order: *Derfflinger, Seydlitz, Moltke, Blücher*.[1] They were a long way out of range, but at 9 a.m. *Lion* opened fire at the rear ship, the enemy replying some five minutes later; as was natural, the firing was very deliberate at the great range, estimated to be about 21,000 yards, and the shot of both sides fell a long way short. The wind was on our port bow, and consequently very favourable to our squadron; the sea was calm, yet the spray thrown up by the high rate of steaming was a considerable inconvenience throughout the action.

4. The other ships with 13.5-inch guns came into action soon after *Lion*, and the fire of these ships was gradually shifted to the ships ahead of *Blücher*. *New Zealand* could not get enough elevation to open fire until 9.35 a.m., when she did so at *Blücher*. *Indomitable* dropped a long way astern, and, of course, could not get within range until much later.

5. Our destroyers and accompanying light cruisers were gradually dropping back to a position on our port quarter and to starboard of the enemy. The Light Cruiser Squadron was apparently

---

[1] The order of the German battle line was in fact *Seydlitz* (Flag), *Moltke, Derfflinger, Blücher; Derfflinger* was a ship of a new class not previously seen by the British.

well up astern on port quarter of the enemy, but the leading ship was soon driven off by heavy gun-fire. The enemy's destroyers were hull down ahead of our squadron. The action thus continued with the range, decreasing slowly, and the enemy's zig-zagging to confuse the rate until 10.30 a.m., when *Blücher* had a serious fire amidships and she made a complete circle, resuming, however, her original course, but with somewhat reduced speed. At this time she was firing at *New Zealand*, and her shots were falling short and with a very large spread, showing that she had lost the good control with which she started the action.

6. At 10.10 a.m. it was observed that the enemy made a large alteration to the northward for a considerable time before resuming original course; at this time our squadron had reached a position where there were some half-dozen trawlers or vessels resembling them; these vessels hoisted various neutral colours, chiefly, however, red ensigns. I cannot help thinking that we had been purposely led to these vessels, which were really marking where submarines were stationed, or the edge of a prepared mine-field. At the same time the enemy's destroyers left the position ahead of us and worked to port. They never afterwards came back to the original position; this may have been because our destroyers were now working ahead between the opposing squadrons to engage them, or because they had dropped mines and their purpose had been effected.

7. At 10.50 a.m. *Indomitable* received a W/T signal from the Vice-Admiral, *Lion*, to attack enemy breaking away to the north; this was *Blücher*, but she quickly resumed her original course, as stated. About this time *Lion* appeared to be struck by a mine or torpedo and she listed heavily to port, gradually dropping out of the line.

8. At 11.10 a.m. the Vice-Admiral made a signal turning the whole squadron 8 points to port, bringing them approximately N by E and almost at right angles to the enemy's course, the three leading ships of the enemy quickly increasing their range in consequence. At 11.20 a.m. the Vice-Admiral made a general signal: 'Attack the rear of enemy bearing NE'; this was apparently the *Blücher* (she bore approximately NE from *New Zealand* at the time). *Princess Royal* and *Tiger* apparently acting on this, altered course to circle around *Blücher*, passing ahead of *New Zealand* in doing so, *Indomitable* passing astern and turning up to port.

9. By the track chart it will be seen that the original course was gradually resumed by 11.40 a.m., but by this time the distance

lost through the turn of 8 points to port had allowed the three leading ships to get out of range. Visual touch was lost with the *Lion* at 11.30 a.m., and I then took charge of the squadron. The *Blücher* struck at about 11.50 a.m.,and as the other enemy battle-cruisers were then far out of range, distant about 12½ miles and steaming at least 25 knots, there was no prospect of regaining effective gun range for a couple of hours, by which time they would be close in to Heligoland, and, as I also had grave fears for the safety of *Lion* — W/T communication could not be obtained — I retired in her direction, leaving a light cruiser and some destroyers to rescue the crew of *Blücher* and complete sinking her. *Blücher* had, in addition to her other severe injuries, been torpedoed about 11.45 a.m. by a destroyer, so that she was not likely to remain long afloat.

10. A Zeppelin airship had been hovering near the scene of action for about an hour, and now approached the spot where *Blücher* sank and commenced dropping bombs at the rescuing ships, which were consequently ordered by *Southampton* to leave the spot at once.

113.   *From Goodenough*

[BTY/4/6/7]   *Southampton*
(No 0037. *Secret*)   January 25, 1915

I have the honour to submit the following report of operations carried out on the 24th instant.

2. The First Light Cruiser Squadron, consisting of H.M. ships *Southampton* (wearing my broad pennant), *Nottingham, Birmingham*, and *Lowestoft* arrived at the rendezvous ordered (55° 13′ N, 3° 12′ E) at 7 a.m.

3. At 7.15 a.m. gunfire was observed ahead; speed was increased to 25 knots and the squadron turned towards it.

4. At 7.30 a.m. *Aurora* reported enemy's cruisers ESE and battle cruisers SE.

At 7.35 a.m. enemy was sighted by *Southampton* (ship's position 55° 2′ N, 3° 16′ E), and in a few minutes was made out to consist of four battle-cruisers, with five or six light cruisers and destroyers.

The enemy light cruisers at once passed to the southward of

their battle-cruisers, and remained there, which rendered it impossible for the First Light Cruiser Squadron to get at them. They appeared to be steaming considerably faster than their battle cruisers.

5. Enemy's courses — When sighted, NW; immediately afterwards, between SE and S; at 8 a.m., NE; afterwards, between E and SE; and at 10 a.m., E. He appeared to zigzag during the earlier part of the action.

6. The First Light Cruiser Squadron, steaming at full speed, kept touch with the enemy's battle cruisers from a position on their port quarter, at ranges varying between 20,000 and 13,000 yards, until the enemy was lost sight of at 12.4 p.m. on the squadron being ordered to retire to the north-west.

7. At 9.45 a.m. one enemy battle-cruiser (not *Blücher*) was seen to be badly on fire a little abaft of amidships, and fires were noticed in this ship and another twice afterwards.

8. At 10 a.m. the squadron was under somewhat heavy fire from the enemy's rearmost battle-cruiser; no casualties nor damage resulted.

9. At about 10.30 a.m. *Blücher* dropped astern of remainder of enemy and afterwards sank.

10. At 10.58 a.m., at a range of 14,000 yards, fire was opened by the First Light Cruiser Squadron and was effective against *Blücher*, who had been heavily hit by our battle-cruisers. *Blücher* replied from two turrets.

11. At 10.50 a.m. a Zeppelin airship was sighted, and kept almost continuously in sight until about 12.30 p.m.

12. At about 11.15 a.m. the Zeppelin was fired at by *Southampton* (with 6-inch guns) and by other ships: this appeared to cause her to alter course away from the First Light Cruiser Squadron.

13. Shortly after the Zeppelin appeared the German flagship fired light balls, which burst into a number of brilliant stars. This was done two or three times, but details were not very clear.

14. At 12.20 p.m. I received a signal from *Aurora*, asking me to close and assist in rescuing survivors from *Blücher*. I turned to do so, but found on approach that the Zeppelin was taking advantage of the destroyers being stopped by attempting to drop bombs on them. I then ordered *Aurora* and destroyers to leave the spot at once and turned my squadron away.

15. Separate reports are forwarded herewith — (1) with regard

to gunnery matters, and (2) with regard to the use of the private signal in connection with the action yesterday.

114. *From Chatfield*

[BTY/4/6/7]   SECRET   *Lion*
                                             January 27, 1915

In accordance with your orders, I have the honour to make the following report of the action in which H.M. ship under my command was engaged on the 24th January, 1915: —

At 7.24 a.m. the course being S12 W, 18 knots, in a position latitude 54° 55′ N, longitude 3° 12′ E, flashes of guns were sighted SSE. Shortly after a report was received from *Aurora* that she was in action with the enemy, followed by a report that four enemy's battle-cruisers were bearing ESE from the *Southampton*. Course was at once altered towards the enemy, and speed increased to 22 knots. About 7.45 a.m. the enemy's battle-cruisers were sighted bearing SE by E, and speed was increased to full speed.

2. The wind was light in the NE, and course was shaped to keep on the lee quarter of the enemy, who was apparently steaming at full speed to Germany. At 8.15 a.m. the enemy's rear ship was observed to be 25,000 yards distant by range-finder (approximately). At 8.45 a.m. the rear ship of the enemy opened fire at a destroyer on her port quarter, causing the destroyer to withdraw. It was now obvious that we were overhauling the enemy. *Lion* was steaming at 288 revolutions, the engine-room having been called on for the utmost speed possible. At 8.52 a.m. the range of the enemy rear ship was taken as 20,000 yards, and a shot was fired from 'B' turret at that range, which fell short. A second shot fired 2 minutes afterwards at extreme range on the sights 20,200 fell over, and slow deliberate firing from 'A' and 'B' turrets were commenced.

3. It was impossible to distinguish hits at this distance. Owing to the speed the periscopes of 'A' and 'B' turrets were considerably affected by spray, but *New Zealand* reports *Lion* commenced hitting *Blücher* at 9.9 a.m.

4. *Lion* continued to gain on the enemy, who at 9.14 a.m. commenced to return her fire. About 9.22 a.m. *Tiger* (the next

astern) opened fire on the enemy's rear ship, and *Lion's* fire was shifted at 9.24 a.m. to the third ship in the enemy's line, probably the *Moltke*. Range, 18,000 yards. Course was slightly altered to starboard to bring the after turrets into action. Course SE. At 9.25 a.m. the control reported that they were hitting *Moltke*, and regular salvos were commenced.

5. At 9.35 a.m., as *Lion* was still drawing ahead, permission was obtained to shift the fire to the leading ship, assumed to be *Derfflinger*, the signal being then made by the Admiral, 'Fire on your opposite numbers'. Range of *Derfflinger* 17,500 yards. At 9.35 a.m. a heavy shell hit the water line abaft the stokers' bathrooms, penetrating into the bunkers. This was speedily shored up with hammocks and mess stools. The *Derfflinger* opened fire on *Lion* about 9.35 a.m., her shots falling short at first. At 9.50 a.m. she was on fire by the mainmast, and the two after turrets appeared to cease fire altogether, as only two-shot salvos were seen to fall for a long time.

6. The smoke of the enemy coming almost straight towards us, combined with the gloom, made spotting very difficult. Flashes of the enemy's guns were extraordinarily vivid, so that it could not be seen whether we were hitting or not. The splashes of the enemy's shorts came over the conning tower and Argo hood like green seas, drenching everything. About this time the right gun of 'Q' turret ceased fire from breech trouble, which was thought to be more serious than it was, and the gun remained out of action unnecessarily.

7. The range was still decreasing, and at 9.54 a.m. it was 15,300 yards. 'A' turret roof was now struck by a shell, the plate was driven down but not penetrated. Left and centre sighting hoods were blown off, damaging periscopes and the vertical armour plate above the gun port, and also the port shield was badly damaged, jambing the left gun and wounding the left gunlayer, and trainer. The right gun continued in action. At 10.1 a.m. an 11-inch shell from the *Seydlitz*, who was also concentrating on *Lion*, pierced the armour in the engineer's workshop, which was flooded, and efforts of the Chief Carpenter to seal it with leak stoppers failed. The after switchboard compartment also commenced flooding, short-circuiting Nos 2 and 3 dynamos. This compartment was finally abandoned at 10.10, the compartment being flooded and the watch-keeper wounded. This put the after-fire control and 4-inch gun circuits out of action.

8. Ship listed slightly to port. At 10.18 the effect of the enemy's

concentration began to be felt, though their shooting was very wild at times. Their salvos were rapid, and shots fell well together. *Lion's* course was ESE, 27 knots. At 10.18 a salvo of two 12-inch shells from the *Derfflinger* hit the ship. The shock was very great, and was thought at the time to be due to a torpedo. One shell pierced the armour near the water-line in the torpedo-body room, where it burst, causing damage which flooded the fore submerged flat, the torpedo-body room, and the port-cable locker, injuring several men and blowing open the hatches. These compartments flooded up to the main deck. The other shell hit the armour below the water-line, driving in several plates through the backing and flooding several of the port foremost bunkers.

9. Course was altered 1 point to starboard and subsequently 2 points to port, causing enemy to lose the range. At 10.35 a.m. two shells hit the Engine Room Artificers' bathroom, penetrating the armour and also the upper bunkers in the vicinity, which were flooded. Another shell burst in 'A' turret lobby, doing local damage, and causing a small fire, which was rapidly extinguished. At 10.41 a.m. 'A' turret magazine was reported on fire, and I gave the order to flood the magazine. After 2 feet of water had been admitted, the report was discovered to be erroneous. Between 10.49 and 10.51 a.m. several hits occurred with 11-inch or 12-inch shell. The only serious one drove in the armour plates below the water-line abreast 'F' boiler-room shaking the ship considerably. The port feed-tank was injured and some damage caused in the port engine-room. The rush of salt water through the overflow pipe necessitated the stopping of the port engine, and the ship heeled considerably to port.

10. No 1 dynamo, the only one remaining, was thrown off by a short circuit, so that all light and power failed.

11. The other shell that struck the ship at this time penetrated the funnels and upper deck, and in several cases did not burst, nor was any important damage done by them, with the exception of one which burst in the bakery, a splinter from which penetrated the armour gratings of the port after engine-room and injured the induction pipe.

12. The speed of the ship was now reduced to 15 knots, and with a list of about 10 degrees to port she lost her place in the line and was passed by the other ships, otherwise she was perfectly fit to continue the action with all turrets. At 10.52 course was altered to ENE, 10 knots, and subsequently to north. Ship ceased firing owing to being out of range about 11 a.m.

13. The range at which *Lion* fought was largely decided by the threatening attitude of the enemy's destroyers, which took up a position about 8 miles on the port bow. At 9.35 they closed to about 10,000 yards, and the port 4-inch guns were manned, and opened fire, driving them off, and it is thought that some of the torpedo-boats were hit by 4-inch shells.

115. *From Captain Pelly*

[BTY/4/6/7]   [with instruction to Flag Cdr   *Tiger*
                   & side markings by Beatty] 31st January 1915

(Flag Comdr Look up C-in-C's Instructions)

In accordance with your No 01 of 29th January 1915 I have the honour to report that the signal AP was received at 9–41 a.m. at which time I, in accordance with all orders for distribution of fire, was engaging the leading ship of the enemy's line, i.e. concentrating with *Lion*, as there were five ships in our own line but only four in theirs. This signal AP was followed after 10 minutes by a reduction in speed signal to 24 knots and 15 minutes later by an increase to 26 knots, this confirmed my previous decision that all our five ships were engaged and added to this the rear ship of the enemy had already been badly hit by *Lion* or *Tiger* or both.

2. I also had in mind the following instructions: —

(1) GFGO No 15 Pt 1, General Principles.

W (b) It is of the greatest importance to disable the leading ships of the enemy's line, with the object of throwing those astern into a state of confusion.

(2) GFGO No 15 Pt 1. Concentration Para 2.

X 'It is also to be remembered that if we are to establish superiority of fire by concentration on the leading enemy's *ships, they will probably be unable to concentrate on ours.*'

(3) GFBO Gunnery Addendum. Distribution of Gun Fire. 11 (b)

Y 'In a fleet action with fleets deployed on similar courses, the Commander of the leading division is to concentrate his four leading ships in pairs on the two ships of the enemy's van.'

(c) In concentrating on the leading ships of columns it is quite likely that the angle of an enemy's approach will permit of two

Z { ships at the head of a column being fired at and if so, this should be done as a matter of course, one pair of a division of four ships taking the leading ship and the other the second.

(4) GFBO Gunnery Addendum. Last para (11).

'The two chief objects to be kept in view are:- To disable the enemy's leading ships in order to throw his line into confusion.'

In conclusion I beg to submit that in acting as I did, I had hoped that by concentrating with such force on the leading ship, the chances were greater of reducing her speed and I had no doubt in my mind but that I was carrying out your wishes.

116. *To Jellicoe*

[BTY/4/6/7]   *Princess Royal*
                                                              February 2, 1915

*Report of Vice-Admiral Commanding First Battle-Cruiser
Squadron*

(No 01. *Confidential*)

I have the honour to report that at daybreak on the 24th January 1915, the following vessels were patrolling in company:-

The First Battle-Cruiser Squadron, consisting of *Lion*, flying my flag, *Tiger*, and *Princess Royal*, in the order named.

The Second Battle-Cruiser Squadron, consisting of *New Zealand*, flying the flag of Rear-Admiral Sir Archibald Moore, KCB, CVO, and *Indomitable*.

The First Light Cruiser Squadron, consisting of *Southampton*, flying the broad pendant of Commodore W. E. Goodenough, MVO, *Nottingham*, *Birmingham*, and *Lowestoft*, were disposed 5 miles on my port beam.

The whole force was steering S 12 W at 18 knots.

2. Shortly after 7 a.m. I ordered the First Light Cruiser Squadron to spread for look-out duties NE by N.

3. Commodore (T) R. Y. Tyrwhitt, CB, in *Arethusa*, with a half flotilla, was sighted ahead at 7.10 a.m. At 7.25 a.m. the flash of guns was observed SSE. Shortly afterwards a report reached me from *Aurora* that she was engaged with enemy's ships. I immediately altered course to SSE, increased to 22 knots, and

ordered Light Cruiser Squadron and flotillas to chase SSE to get in touch and report movements of enemy.

4. This order was acted upon with great promptitude; indeed, my wishes had already been forestalled by their respective Senior Officers, and reports almost immediately followed from *Southampton, Arethusa* and *Aurora* as to the position and composition of the enemy, which consisted of four battle-cruisers, six light cruisers, and a number of destroyers steering NW. The enemy had already altered course to SE. From now onwards the light cruisers maintained touch with the enemy and kept me fully informed as to their movements.

5. The battle-cruisers worked up to full speed, steering to obtain the leeward position, and if possible to get to the southward between the enemy and their base, with the object of forcing them to the northward away from it. The wind at the time was NE, light, with extreme visibility. At 7.50 a.m. the enemy battle-cruisers, four in number, were sighted on the port bow steaming fast, steering approximately SE, distant 14 miles.

6. Owing to the prompt reports received we had attained our position on the lee quarter of the enemy, and so altered course to the SE parallel to them, and settled down to a long stern chase, gradually increasing our speed until we reached 28.5 knots. Great credit is due to the engineer staffs of *New Zealand* and *Indomitable* — these ships greatly exceeded their normal speed and actually reached 27 and 26 knots respectively.

7. At 8.52 a.m. we had closed to within 20,000 yards of the rear ship, and the battle-cruisers manoeuvred to keep on a line of bearing so that guns would bear; *Lion* fired a single shot which fell short. The enemy at this time were in single line ahead, with light cruisers ahead and a large number of destroyers on their starboard beam.

8. Single shots were fired at intervals to test the range, and at 9.9 a.m. *Lion* made her first hit on the *Blücher*, No 4 in the line. The *Tiger* opening fire at 9.20 a.m. on the rear ship, the *Lion* shifted to No 3 in the line, at 18,000 yards, this ship being hit by several salvos. The enemy returned our fire at 9.14 a.m., scoring their first hit at 9.28 a.m. on *Lion*. *Princess Royal* on coming into range opened fire on *Blücher*.

9. Three of the enemy ships were now concentrating on *Lion*, the range of the leading ship being 17,500 yards, so at 9.35 a.m. I made the signal, 'Engage the corresponding ships in the enemy's line'. By this time *New Zealand* was within range of *Blücher*,

which had dropped somewhat astern, and opened fire on her. *Princess Royal* shifted to the third ship in the line, inflicting considerable damage on her.

10. Our flotilla cruisers and destroyers had gradually dropped from a position broad on our beam to our port quarter, so as not to foul our range with their smoke; but the enemy's destroyers threatening attack, I ordered Commodore (T) to take station ahead. This he was unable to do without passing between us and the enemy and masking our fire with his smoke. The *Meteor* and 'M' division succeeded later in passing ahead of us by virtue of their great speed, and I fully concur in the remarks of the Commodore (T) as to the able and gallant manner in which Commander Hon H. Meade handled this division.[1]

11. About 9.45 a.m. the situation was as follows: *Blücher*, the fourth in their line, already showed signs of having suffered severely from gun-fire; their leading ship and No 3 were also on fire. *Lion* was engaging No 1, *Princess Royal* No 3, *New Zealand* No 4, while the *Tiger*, who was second in our line, fired first at their No 1, and when interfered with by smoke at their No 4. This was unfortunate, as it left the second enemy ship unfired at, and she concentrated on *Lion*.

12. The enemy's destroyers emitted vast columns of smoke to screen their battle-cruisers, and under cover of this the latter now appeared to have altered course to the northward to increase their distance, and certainly the rear ships hauled out on the port quarter of their leader, thereby increasing their distance from our line. The battle-cruisers, therefore, were ordered to form on a line of bearing NNW and proceed at their utmost speed.

13. Their destroyers then showed evident signs of an attempt to attack, and I signalled to the squadron to that effect. *Lion* and *Tiger* opened fire with 4-inch and 6-inch guns respectively, and caused them to retire and resume their original course. The 6-inch guns of *Tiger* performed very useful service at long range, and certainly succeeded in placing two salvos among them at 12,000 yards.

14. Any attempt on our part to close the enemy by altering course to port was met by the enemy's torpedo craft steering more to starboard, and so putting us in a position of having to cross their track: this had to be avoided, owing to the danger of their

[1] 'M' division consisted of 7 new destroyers, completed in 1914, capable of 33 knots.

mine-laying. We had, therefore, to depend on maintaining our speed and establishing an overlap ahead before we could close sufficiently to force them to the northward or bring them to close action.

15. The First Light Cruiser Squadron maintained an excellent position on the port quarter of the enemy's line, enabling them to observe and keep touch, or attack any vessel that might fall out of the line. They were also in a good position to mark the effect of our fire and the fall of the shot. *Southampton* reported that one ship, probably *Tiger*, was firing consistently 'over'. This might have enabled her to correct her range.

16. From 10 a.m. onwards *Lion* suffered considerably from the concentrated fire of the enemy's two leading ships, and two alterations of 1 point inwards were made accordingly, ships turning together. *Lion* then zig-zagged to throw out the enemy's range. About 10.40 a.m. *Lion* received heavy punishment. By 10.51 a.m. her port engine was stopped, all lights were out, she was making water rapidly, listing heavily to port, and was unable to maintain her place in the line.

17. At 10.48 a.m. the *Blücher*, which had dropped considerably astern of enemy's line, hauled out to port steering north, with a heavy list, on fire, and apparently in a defeated condition. I consequently ordered *Indomitable*, which was astern, to attack enemy, breaking to the northward.

18. At 10.54 a.m. submarines were reported on the starboard bow, and I personally observed the wash of a periscope 2 points on our starboard bow. I immediately signalled 'Turn 8 points to port together'. This signal was hauled down at 11 a.m. As this turn would take us across the track of enemy destroyers, it was important that it should be sufficiently large to take us clear of it before we reached the position they were in at this moment, so as to avoid the mines which they would probably take the opportunity of dropping. *Indomitable* subsequently reported that a torpedo had been fired at her, crossing her bows 40 yards ahead after leaving the vicinity of the sinking *Blücher*, so it may be assumed that the enemy submarines had closed and attacked her.[1]

19. It was now clear that *Lion* could no longer remain 'guide' of the fleet, and as our zig-zagging might have caused doubt as to the actual course to be steered, I hoisted the signal 'Course NE'

[1]There is no evidence of the presence of submarines in battle area (Marder, *From the Dreadnought*, Vol. 1, p. 161).

at 11.2 a.m. This course would have cut the enemy battle cruisers off the *Blücher* should they turn to support her, as I anticipated they would. Should they leave her to her fate our ships could have again turned to a parallel course when clear of track of their torpedo craft.

20. At 11.5 a.m. I hoisted the signal 'Attack the enemy's rear', hauled down the course signal, and hoisted 'Keep nearer to the enemy'. At this time *Lion's* wireless apparatus was out of action and only two signal halliards remained, preventing me from informing Admiral Moore of the reason for my sudden 8 point turn or from exercising any further command. I kept the signals 'Attack the rear' and 'Keep closer' flying till the remainder of the squadron has passed out of sight.

21. At 11.3 a.m. the injury to the *Lion* being reported as incapable of immediate repair, I semaphored to Commodore (T) to close and to detail destroyers as a submarine screen and directed *Lion* to shape course NW. At 11.20 a.m. I called the *Attack* alongside, shifting my flag to her at about 11.35 a.m. I proceeded at utmost speed to rejoin the squadron, and met them at noon retiring NNW.

22. Having made a signal to turn 16 points to resume pursuit of the enemy, I boarded and hoisted my flag in *Princess Royal* at about 12.20 p.m. Captain Brock acquainted me of what had occurred since *Lion* fell out of the line, viz, that *Blücher* had been sunk and that the remaining enemy battle-cruisers had continued their course to the eastward in a considerably damaged condition. He also informed me that a Zeppelin and a seaplane had endeavoured to drop bombs on the vessels which went to the rescue of the survivors of *Blücher*. I re-formed the squadron and proceeded to pick up the *Lion*.

23. The good seamanship of Lieutenant-Commander Callaghan, in placing his vessel alongside the *Lion* and subsequently the *Princess Royal* while both ships were under way, enabled the transfer of flag to be made in the shortest possible time with the minimum risk of submarine attack.

24. At 2 p.m. I closed *Lion* and received a report that her starboard engine was giving trouble owing to priming, and that possibly she would not be able to steam for more than twelve hours. At 3.38 p.m. I ordered *Indomitable* to take her in tow, which was accomplished by 5 p.m.

25. I directed the destroyer flotillas to surround the two ships to form a submarine screen. Throughout the homeward journey

this duty was performed under the direction of the Commodore (T) in a most masterly and skilful manner, providing almost complete security from submarine attack.

26. The greatest credit is due to the Captains of *Indomitable* and *Lion* for the seamanlike manner in which the *Lion* was taken in tow under difficult circumstances and brought safely to port.

27. The Second Light Cruiser Squadron which had now joined me was stationed SE 10 miles and First Light Cruiser Squadron E 10 miles to act as screen from destroyer attack, the battle-cruisers taking station to be in a position where necessary.

28. Before concluding this report I desire to remark that during the critical moments of uncertainty as to the condition of the *Lion*, the officers and men of that ship exhibited a coolness and indifference to danger worthy of the best traditions of the service.

29. The excellent steaming of the ships engaged in the operation was a conspicuous feature. . . .

117.   *From Moore*

[BTY/4/2]   *New Zealand*
No 2 / 17   7th February 1915

With reference to your report of 6th instant on the action of 24th ultimo, a copy of which you have forwarded for my information, I find that certain signals were made by *Lion*, which were either wrongly received in *New Zealand* and other ships, or not received at all. As this resulted in your intentions being wrongly interpreted, I desire to point out exactly where differences occurred in signals, as made in *Lion* and as received in *New Zealand* and the bearing these had upon the course of the latter part of the action.

2. In paragraph 10, the time given for hauling down the signal to 'turn together 8 points to port' is 11 a.m. In my report, I stated it to be 11.10 a.m.; further comparison of notes taken during the action shew that our signal log times were 6 minutes fast, so that my corrected time should be 11.04 a.m.

3. Paragraphs 19 and 20, shew that the signal received in *New Zealand* as 'AF — Comp B', 'attack the enemy's rear, bearing NE'; was made in *Lion* as two separate signals, Comp B being hoisted at 11.02 a.m. and hauled down at 11.05 a.m., when AF

was hoisted. Inspection of the *Tiger*'s log by my Flag Lieutenant shows that the signal was received by that ship in exactly the same form as in *New Zealand*. *Princess Royal* does not appear to have received the Compass B signal, only the AF. *New Zealand* undoubtedly repeated the signal as seen flying in the *Tiger* and passed it on by searchlight to *Indomitable*.

4. Paragraph 19 explains the reason for making the signal 'Course NE', and had the two signals Comp B and AF been received as separate ones, never flying together, or, if together, with the Compass B superior, the intention would have been clearly understood and acted upon, in which case gun range with the enemy would have been maintained, by *Tiger* and *Princess Royal* at all events. As it was, the reason for the 8 point turn to port was unknown, *and as the course it brought the ships on to headed them to pass astern of Blücher*, the signal (as now known to have been erroneously received in *Tiger* and *New Zealand*) AF — Comp B appeared therefore to offer the explanation, viz:- to attack the *Blücher*, since, as I pointed out in paragraph 8 of my report, the *Blücher* bore approximately NE, she was nearly NE by E from *New Zealand*, the remaining enemy ships bearing approximately E by N. The signal 'Keep nearer to the enemy' made by *Lion* at 11.05 a.m. was never received by *New Zealand* and I believe not by *Princess Royal*; had this signal been received it probably would have assisted to a correct understanding of the Vice-Admiral's intentions. The fact that, after the 8 point turn, *Tiger* and *Princess Royal* shifted their fire to *Blücher* and bore down on *New Zealand* to such an extent that they actually crossed her bows, fire having to be checked on the occasion of each ship passing, confirmed the opinion that the Vice-Admiral's intentions were being rightly interpreted, and threw no doubt upon the correctness of the reading of the signal 'AF — Comp B'.

118.   *To Admiralty*

[BTY/4/6/7]   *Princess Royal*
                                                                      February 9, 1915

Remarks on Action, January 24, 1915

(No 97/01)

Submitted herewith are some notes which I have prepared after considering the events of the action of the 24th January.

I enclose also reports from HM ships under my command.

Enclosures

1. Signal notes [119].
2. Lessons learned [120].
3. Report from Rear-Admiral *New Zealand* [121].
4. Report from *Lion* [122].
5. Report from *Princess Royal* [not included].
6. Report from *Tiger* [123].
7. Report from *New Zealand* [not included].
8. Report from *Indomitable* [not included].
9. Report from Commodore, First Light Cruiser Squadron [not included].
10. Report from *Southampton* and First Light Cruiser Squadron [not included].

Enclosure 1

119. *Signal Notes*

[BTY/4/6/7]

Signals were made by flags, searchlight, main and auxiliary W/T whilst under fire and being hit.

2. At the commencement of the chase battle-cruisers were ordered to haul out on the weather quarter to receive signals, and the wind being 2 points on the engaged bow, conditions for flag signalling were ideal.

3. All flag signals were observed to be correctly and smartly repeated by *Tiger* and *Princess Royal* up to the time *Lion* was forced to quit the line, and fell to leeward. The signals to turn 1 point to port actually took 2 minutes to hoist, repeat, and haul down.

4. *New Zealand* reports a difficulty in distinguishing visual signals, which might have been disastrous, and did have unfortunate results. This was due to the fact that the signal staff were in the conning tower and signal tower, which were swept by spray and so interfered with their vision.

Princess Royal and *Tiger* reported that signals were clear and easily read.

5. The *Lion*'s bridge was abandoned by signalmen at 9.30, but there was no reason why ships astern should not have maintained

signalmen in a good visual position, at least until the enemy's fire made such a position untenable.

6. Protection should be rigged to enable men to remain on the bridge as long as possible to keep a look-out, work a searchlight, and assist the next astern.

New Zealand reports that men stationed in her after armoured tower were of great value.

Breakdowns

7. At 9.50 starboard halliards from action position and centre section of main aerial shot away, the latter falling across the feeders and earthing main and battle aerials.

10.34 auxiliary W/T office had to be abandoned owing to fumes, and shortly after all electrical supply failed, thus putting out of action searchlights and arc lamps.

W/T.

8. When main aerial was shot away signals were passed by auxiliary W/T to *New Zealand* for retransmission.

When electrical supply failed emergency sets were rigged, but working on half aerial in main office, with other half up, only a very small spark could be obtained, giving a range of two or three miles. Later, when both sections were connected up, *Aurora* received signals strength 6 at about 5 miles.

9. Auxiliary W/T office was remanned when fumes allowed and emergency set rigged which gave satisfactory results.

Internal Communications

10. Conning tower and manoeuvring platform are connected to both action signal stations by voice pipe and telephone. Voice pipe was used throughout and was satisfactory. Conning tower and both wireless offices are connected by three buzzers working in parallel and also by telephone. Coding and decoding are done in the main W/T office, except short enemy reports and signals from Fleet Signal Book, which are done in the conning tower.

Signals are passed between main and auxiliary offices by buzzer, between main office and conning tower by buzzer or telephone as convenient. All these arrangements were in order at the end of the action and worked perfectly throughout.

Conning tower operator wore telephone receivers attached to the buzzer and enabled him to receive messages at any time during the action, and prevented gun deafness.

General

11. *New Zealand* recommends more use be made of auxiliary, and this was fairly busy throughout the action, and it is desirable

to keep it clear when visual signals are available. Unfortunately when visual signals did fail when *Lion* dropped astern, main and auxiliary W/T were both out of action.

12. It is recommended that in all ships arrangements should be made to:-

   (a) Provide operator in conning tower with telephones attached to buzzer.

   (b) Have emergency set ready for auxiliary office.

   (c) Fit preventers from every section of main aerials to the mast and not the yard.

13. After action was over the power circuit on the starboard side of the ship was temporarily repaired and the W/T distributing box was fed by a wandering lead from the side, thus putting the buzzer and operating circuit in action. By means of the change over switch fitted in the alternator supply all gear was in action in thirty-six hours fed from the starboard section of the ring main.

Duplicate leads to the W/T office distributing box should be a permanent fitting, supply being drawn from either side of the ship as desired by means of a switch in the main office.

Enclosure 2

120. *Notes re Lessons Learned from Action on January 24, 1915*

[BTY/4/6/7]

Importance of avoiding delay

The number of lessons learnt is very numerous. Many of them apply to all ships in the Service and involve alterations to machinery.

As the Germans also will have learnt valuable lessons, we can only hope to gain advantage from the battle if we can apply our lessons in a practical manner without delay.

Machinery

2. Ships' reports show numerous small mechanical failures in turrets, and in *Lion* there are many questions re flooding and draining which require the attention of all ships.

Zigzags

3. As the enemy zigzag whenever they are being hit, it is most

important to practice this at spotting tables or when doing towed target practice. Rates and Dumaresqs[1] become almost useless under these conditions. Range-finders may help, but spotting must be the primary aid for keeping on the target.

4. There can be no doubt that we should make a turn, in or out, when enemy begins to hit; 2 points would be ample, or at high speed 1 point. Small helm should be used.

This has often been practised, and will in no way interfere with our gunnery.

Projectiles

5. Hits with AP shell are usually impossible to see at long range. Lyddite common would be better seen, and on account of its greater destruction to personnel it seems desirable to fire LC in at least equal proportion to the AP (usually LC first and then AP). For ranging, or whenever spotting is unusually difficult, it is probable that powder common is far the best shell to use. Its flash on bursting is more distinctive, and the immense column of smoke from it is visible under the most difficult conditions.[2]

Lee Position

6. This is usually much superior to the weather position, but there are many pros and cons to be carefully considered:—

(a) Against lee position: spray will come on board from enemy's shorts; but this will happen almost equally in weather position. Spray is bad when steaming fast and when firing before the beam, particularly so if wind is fresh.

(b) Against weather position: Smoke is the only hindrance, but this is very serious when steaming fast. The after guns will rarely get a clear view, and if smoke is blowing towards enemy the whole armament and the Control Officers may be masked.

Vide reports from *Invincible* and *Blücher*, smoke difficulty may be partially got over by opening out the ships and by using director, but the Germans did both these on the 24th January and their shooting was usually much worse than ours.

We have, therefore, to balance smoke *versus* spray, taking into consideration the special circumstances of each case. On most

[1]Lieutenant J. Dumaresq's invention of a device to measure rates of change in range and deflection.
[2]See also 130.

occasions, as we have proved so often at battle practice, the lee position is the best.

Spray

7. Every effort must be made to keep gun telescopes clear of spray. Hoses must not be running on the weather side of upper deck — in fact, nowhere near a gun.

Every gun telescope must be readily accessible for wiping over from inside. An absorbent swab (dry sponge?) is necessary when there is much wet. Chamois leather is no use in this case. . . .

Fighting Range

8. The Falkland Islands Fight and the 24th January have proved that hits can be made without difficulty at 19,000 or 20,000 yards, but this range is not decisive, and the percentage of hits is too small.

An hour's fighting may find guns disabled and ammunition running short with no decisive result obtained; therefore there is no harm in slow firing at long range, but we *must* try to get in closer without delay. Probably 12,000 to 14,000 yards would suit us well, this being outside the effective range of enemy's torpedoes and 6-inch guns.

We must try to combine early hits with *decisive hitting* soon afterwards.

Director

9. Will prove most valuable whenever target is difficult to see. Director 'Pattern' is a very important point. The spread for elevation is not likely to be too great, but it is distinctly possible for it to be too small.

This was most noticeable with enemy ships on the 24th January. Probably quite twenty salvos fell so close to *Lion* that, if they had had a bigger spread, one shot in each salvo would have hit her. The theoretical advantage — that perhaps the whole of a salvo may hit — did not occur. *Lion* was never hit by more than two shots simultaneously.

A very big spread is known to be bad. A very small spread, which approximates to a single shot, makes it most difficult to straddle, and spotting thereby loses half its efficiency. There must be some figure, between 10 feet and 10 cables, at which the spread of a salvo gives most efficient results. It would obviously have some relation to range, danger space, and number of shots in a salvo, but I submit that it is very important to work this out carefully — not forgetting that it *may* be necessary for director ships to be able to increase the spread of their salvos.

Secondary Lighting

10. Oil lamps are blown out at once by concussion and are practically useless. Electric power *may* fail totally at any moment, therefore it is essential to make elaborate arrangements for secondary lighting with candles, accumulator and dry batteries or torches.

Tactics

11. The tactics of pursuit are certainly difficult owing to the inevitable concentration on leading ship and the menace from mines and torpedoes. Some advantage can be obtained, however, by getting on enemy's lee quarter and thus causing him serious smoke interference.

The presence of enemy torpedo-craft on our engaged bow was most inconvenient. Our 4-inch guns could never prevent torpedo firing at long range, and manning the guns means exposing a large number of men.

Trim

12. It is perhaps desirable to remind Captains that fore and aft trim is vital to stability and should be the first thing corrected when ships have compartments flooded. It is said that change of trim was mainly responsible for capsizing of two at least of our ships that have been torpedoed.

Enemy's Shell

13. German shell, for incendiary effect and damage to personnel, are far inferior to ours. Their only good quality lies in armour penetration and damage to material.

On this account it is necessary to consider most carefully the effect of any possible damage and the best means to localise it.

Lion's puncture in capstan engine exhaust pipe, though occurring right forward, flooded the auxiliary condenser with salt water. This is a typical failure, like flooding of compartments through ventilation trunks, which should not be able to occur.

14. There are a great number of useful recommendations and notes in the *Lion*'s report. To avoid duplication these points are not commented on here, but they are entirely concurred in, and I think it most necessary that the extra stores asked for (e.g. collision mats, larger shot-hole stoppers, electric torches, &c) should be supplied to all ships without delay.

Enclosure 3

121. *From Moore*

[BTY/4/6/7]   *New Zealand*
(No 2/17. Confidential)   January 29, 1915

I have the honour to report, in remarking upon the lessons to be learned, that the first thing which impresses me is the limited amount of elevation it is possible to give to turret guns of many of our ships, as compared with what the Germans are capable of obtaining. The result is that, unless we are able to close the range very rapidly, we must expect to be under fire from German ships for a considerable period before we can reply; this is very trying for the gunlayers, and must tend to make them impatient and unsteady, besides which there is distinct evidence that, although the German fire control is excellent to start with, it very soon deteriorates when they are being fired at, especially if a hit can be obtained; an early hit being of such importance, we ought at all costs to pass through the zone lying between German and our own extreme ranges as quickly as possible. With the guns of *New Zealand* on the stops, the ship could not open fire for some time after getting within enemy's extreme range, as the nature of the chase prevented a quick approach. Having the gunlayers trained to take an alternative aim at top of funnels, control tops, &c, enables fire to be opened a little earlier.

2. With a light wind and practically calm sea the lee position was a positive advantage; we were never troubled with smoke except once or twice from our own destroyers passing between the lines. The enemy must certainly have been greatly inconvenienced by smoke, for the flashes from our opposite number's guns were nearly always dimmed, showing that a considerable smoke haze hung in a direct line between his guns and target (ourselves). The wind was light; had there been more wind or sea I fear we could not have claimed much advantage from the lee position; as it was, spray from our own speed was a great nuisance to 'A' turret. The periscope sights were nearly always affected by this, and constant wiping hardly got over the trouble. The conning tower also suffered, as the spray driving through the openings wetted all glasses which it was absolutely necessary to use, owing to the great distance. I am not sure that the wind on disengaged bow is not an advantage if wind is strong or sea high.

3. It is extremely difficult to spot 'overs' or 'hits' when once the enemy has got well engaged. It was said in report of *Sydney-Emden* action[1] that the flash from enemy's guns could be distinguished from shell explosions. This may be true of light guns, but it was certainly not my experience in this action, particularly as the smoke haze round enemy damped down both types of flash. Stop watches would be of great assistance in this matter, but even counting carefully one is often deceived, as the arrival of an enemy's shell at full range time frequently proves it was their flash that had been noted; the best test is of course to get a short at same time as a flash on enemy. Shorts are very valuable guides.

4. An assistant spotter in conning tower is very useful. Control top aloft frequently found it necessary to get confirmation from conning tower.

5. There were undoubted cordite fires at least three times in *Blücher*.

6. A wet upper deck is a positive disadvantage. Water on it, either from sea or running hoses, is sprayed up by blast from one's own guns, and of course interferes with the periscope sights and range-finders. If a hole is made in upper deck by a shell, then a steady stream finds its way below.

7. Independent firing is not advisable at long ranges, especially if more than one ship has the same target.

8. The *New Zealand* and *Indomitable* were not hit, so I can only express certain opinions from my inspection of *Lion* and *Tiger*. The first thing that strikes one is the very limited explosive power of German shells and the considerable number of blind shell. This is a matter of much comfort to us, and we ought on no account to let it be known how inferior their shell and fuzes are compared with ours; we ought rather to encourage the idea that we are much impressed with their efficiency. If they know how little damage they do they will very soon take steps to improve burster and fuze. The blast from any large shell exploding is so great that *all* armoured doors and shutters fitted as protection against shell-fire should be properly closed at all times. On the other hand, unimportant compartments above the main deck should not be closed up; a good vent to the gases of explosion is necessary, otherwise the structural damage will be very great.

9. There does not appear to be much danger of fire being caused by enemy's shell — why, I cannot imagine; but I understand their

[1]See note 3 on page 160.

shell-burster is a special high explosive, and is not either TNT or lyddite.

10. Turret roofs and conning-tower tops are not nearly thick enough against heavy shell fired at the long ranges at which we must expect actions to be fought. Immediate thickening should be carried out. I suggest one or two extra thicknesses of 1-inch high-tensile steel being bolted on; the total thickness should not be less than 5 inches in all.

11. Sights hoods on turret roofs are not secured nearly firmly enough. A shell striking a roof, even an 8-inch, breaks the rivets from jar and the hoods are violently displaced, probably damaging the sight.

12. Plunging shell will probably burst in compartments below the water line; these compartments must of necessity be closely shut up in action, consequently the blast from the burst of the shell will certainly blow up the deck above, making it leak over large areas, and athwartship bulkheads will be distorted, so conveying the effect of explosion to compartments whose surroundings are connected to these bulkheads and decks. Water-tight hatches will often be blown off from pressure underneath. These possibilities should be taken into consideration when preparing shores, &c, for stowage in the various compartments.

13. Visual flag signals are very difficult to distinguish with the interference from smoke from funnels, exploding shell, &c, and ought to be sparingly used, unless a repeating ship is available. There were two cases in the recent action that I specially mention. One, when a signal was made for a line of bearing NNW to be formed. This was read as 'Course NNW'. Had it been obeyed as such when hauled down we should have been thrown out of position to such an extent that we probably should never have got in range again. It was palpably an incorrect signal, or reading, and so ignored. Again, when the signal was made to 'Attack the enemy's rear' with a compass signal inferior (NE), this apparently was read by all ships to mean 'Attack the enemy's rear bearing NE', consequently all ships proceeded to attack *Blücher*, which ship was the nearest to a NE bearing, *Tiger* and *Princess Royal* shifting from *Derfflinger* and *Moltke*, with which they were engaged. This certainly appeared to be the intention of the signal as the squadron had been turned 8 points to port heading to pass astern of *Blücher*, and had been so steaming for quarter of an hour. I now understand the two hoists were intended to be 'Course NE, Attack the rear of the enemy', in which case one would have

expected the course signal to be hoisted superior. This may have been done, but it was not so taken in, and the leading enemy ships got far out of range in consequence. Short distance W/T is strongly recommended. *New Zealand* repeated some signals by searchlight when there was much smoke interference.

A signal position aft is a necessity with voice tube or other direct communication with the conning tower. This was attemtped in *New Zealand* by using the after control tower, and in several instances proved most useful.

14. It is understood that *Birmingham*, or one of the light cruisers, was so placed that she was in a position to observe the fall of shot from our ships, and did actually send wireless reports from time to time. If such an arrangement could generally be made it should yield valuable results.

15. The line of bearing on which the line was formed 7 points abaft the beam proved of great value in enabling flagship's movements to be observed in good time.

16. The enemy zigzagged very much at first, and frequently threw out the control with marked success; of course he lost ground in doing so, and thus in a measure he gave us back the equal of what he took away.

Zigzagging, if full speed is not essential, is certainly to be recommended at very long ranges, but at short ranges with a time of flight of 10 or 12 seconds, it does not appear to offer much advantage.

Enclosure 4

122.   *From Chatfield*

[BTY/4/6/7]   *Lion*
(No 21. *Secret*)   February 2, 1915

I have the honour to forward some further remarks on the action on the 24th January 1915, which may be of value to the Grand Fleet.

I also attach the personal reports of various officers which are of interest.

I. GUNNERY

1. *Lion* dropped out of action owing to her being unable to keep up with the enemy with one engine disabled. She was temporarily

overwhelmed by the combined fire of two battle-cruisers, who must have fired about 1,000 shell at her.

2. A mistake was made in firing too slowly during the earlier stages of the action, influenced by G.0800/14 of the 3rd September, 1914, and the general impression there has been since the 28th August that ammunition expenditure must not be excessive, subsequently — when *Lion* was being hit from 10.30 on — due to obstructed view of gunlayers by enemy's many shorts.

3. *Lion*'s control at the ranges fired at, viz, 20,000–15,300 yards, was very good, and at first far better than that of the enemy. Hits were obtained on each of the three ships fired at within five or ten minutes.

Blücher was fired at at 21,000 yards from 8.52 a.m. to 9.22 a.m., and hitting was commenced at 9.5 a.m. at about 19,000 yards.

Seydlitz was engaged from 9.24 a.m. to 9.35 a.m., and was quickly straddled at 17,000 yards range, and hit several times.

Derfflinger was engaged at 17,500 yards, 9.35 a.m. to 10.52 a.m. At 9.50 a.m. her two after turrets stopped firing, and she had two big fires aft, which did not, however, last long.

4. From this it appears that at any range under about 22,000 yards hitting *can* be attained within a few minutes. The mistake made was in not at once going into rapid independent and putting forth our whole volume of fire, regardless of ammunition expenditure. Enemy would then have been overwhelmed and never recovered.

5. *Lion*, however, certainly had the measure of the *Derfflinger* at the time, and it is thought that it was only the great support given to her by the *Moltke* which saved her and enabled them to combine eventually to injure *Lion* severely, otherwise *Lion* would have sunk *Derfflinger*.

Moltke being unfired at had a clear run at the *Lion* for one and a quarter hours.

6. The enemy's fire was slow at first but got faster, and at the end was a maximum. *Lion*'s fire was fairly quick at first, but got slower, due to the enemy's shorts interfering with gunlaying, spotting and control, until eventually it was almost impossible to return the fire for this reason alone, although all turrets were in action.

7. The general feeling when *Derfflinger* was on fire and only using two turrets was that we had her, not anticipating that we should be concentrated on. There seemed therefore plenty of

time, and that it was better to continue deliberate salvos and not to throw away ammunition at the long range. This proved an error.

8. *Recommendations for Control* — The chief lessons to be learnt are—

(a) That *rapidity of fire* is essential. The difficulties in controlling it are nothing compared to the disadvantages that ensue once the enemy's volume of shorts is greater than your own.

(b) That it is absolutely misleading to think hits will be seen, at any rate at long ranges. Shorts are the only guide, and the great value of them must be impressed on control officers. The main object when opening fire must not be the straddle, but to obtain a big *volume of fire* short, and then work it up by *small* 'ups' till hitting commences. If shots go over they are lost, and very large corrections must at once be resorted to.

Fairly reliable corrections for all ranges are: 'down, 1,000'; or 'up, 200'.

When being hit, the enemy will undoubtedly alter course towards or away, which will require the larger down correction in the former case in order to get short, hence the reason for 1,000 yard [*sic*], even after straddling.

(c) Spotting is so vital and so tiring that additional spotters in various positions are essential.

(d) Salvos when gunlaying are impracticable, as, owing to interference with aim, the rate of fire becomes a minimum.

(e) Directors must fire rapid double salvos as soon as range is found.

Derfflinger and *Moltke* at the end fired about two salvos a minute, i.e., from their seven turrets, fourteen shots a minute at *Lion*, whose rate of fire at that time was about two rounds a minute.

(f) That no emeny must be left unfired at must be further driven home.

(g) Sights of 13.5-inch guns and all corresponding instruments, time of flight watches, &c, to be graduated up to 25,000 yards.

9. If enemy commences hitting, course should be at once boldly altered about 2 points in or about for about three minutes, and then reversed. Care must be taken not to do this before enemy hits, as shots look much closer than they are, and *Lion* was

continually straddled, but only hit fifteen times. The small number of hits was probably caused by the very small spread of the *Derfflinger*'s salvos, which practically acted as one big projectile.

10. Accidents in turrets:-

'A'   Left gun put out of action from an 8-inch gun hitting 3-inch roof, blowing off the trainers' and left gunlayers' hoods, depressing roof a little, damaging periscopes, port shield, and vertical armour inside secured to roof badly shattered. Portions blown about turret fouling the gun, which was put out of action till noon.

'B'   Very slight delay due to choked vents at right gun. Left gun hinged tray bent on reloading after the last round (fortieth) fired. Spare one placed.

'Q'   Right gun of 'Q' ceased fire at 9.50 after firing fifteen rounds; the lock, actuated by spring link, failed to pass over tube. Lock and box slide, tube, &c, were shifted, and vent rimer used, then loading officer, incorrectly, commenced shifting link. In spite of the fact that rimer was used, the failure is attributed to fouling in vent chamber.

Left gun run in and out cylinder leather gave out after thirty rounds. Gun had to be depressed to run out quickly.

'X'   No accidents, delays, or failures.

All turrets report on extreme value of Evershed training indicators.

All turrets seriously handicapped by spray from ship's speed and enemy shorts. 'X' also from smoke, and the latter fired very few rounds.

Rounds fired —

'A' . . .	Right gun	27	42
	Left gun	15	
'B' . . .	Right gun	37	77
	Left gun	40	
'Q' . . .	Right gun	15	59
	Left gun	44	
'X' . . .	Right gun	28	57
	Left gun	29	
		Total	235

'A' and 'B' in action 8.52–10.50 a.m.

'Q' and 'X' in action 9.25–10.50 a.m.

Slight delay in all turrets caused by raising breach after each round from high angle of elevation, and guns ran out very slowly, but under circumstances these matters were not so important. At 10.25 a.m., after LP switchboard flooding, the bearing transmitters to 'X' and 'Q' failed, but Eversheds remained correct.

11. *Nature of projectile* — The nature of projectile to be used against armoured ships requires further consideration. ('Grand Fleet Battle Orders, Gunnery Addendum', p. 2)

A report on the damage sustained by *Derfflinger* and *Moltke* would, if available, decide whether fire should be opened with lyddite common or AP lyddite. Possibly *Lion* would have done better to change the nature of shell used to lyddite common.

12. *Rate of fire* — It is thought that an 'assurance' is needed to remove the great caution caused by Admiralty memorandum G.0800/14 of the 3rd September, 1914.

It is certain that battle cruisers, and probably battleships, may have to open fire at much greater ranges than 15,000 yards, and that rapid fire will be employed by the enemy at 18,000 yards, which must be answered by rapid fire.

13. *Point of aim* – Under certain conditions it is undoubtedly necessary to use the 'brown',[1] and it is essential that every gunlayer be schooled to the correct interpretation of this order.

14. *Periscopes* — Chamois leathers are unsuitable for wiping glasses with when being washed down. A swab capable of absorbing the water is much more serviceable.

II. GENERAL

1. There was only one small fire, and that was rapidly extinguished by the smart action of a seaman. The enemy's shell are not incendiary, and, unless improved, fires need not apparently be anticipated.

2. A number of shells penetrated armour near water-line, causing a rush of water and flooding of engineer's workshop, submerged flat, body room, after LP switchboard room, capstan room (partly), port feed-tank, port 'A' lower bunkers, 'D' upper bunker, 'F' lower bunkers.

[1]'Use the brown' meaning to shoot in the general direction of the enemy.

3. Several of those rents in side were at once plugged with hammocks and mess stools. Eventually damaged hatches were made watertight by mats and mess tables cut up and shored down with mess stools, these proving very suitable for the purpose.

4. The general angle of descent of shell was 18–20 degrees, and this was relatively increased by the heel of ship to port.

5. Oil lamps went out continually with shock of gun-fire and shell-fire. They were most unsatisfactory.

Candle lamps are better, and the allowance should be increased.

6. Smoke pads were invaluable in many places.

7. 'A' magazine was reported on fire at 10.35 a.m., and was flooded by order 2 feet, when it was found to be a false alarm.

8. Very few of the enemy's hits really affected the ship. Fifteen were made as follows in approximate order:-

(1) Mess deck near WL, and through deck into 'D' upper bunker aft.

(2) 'A' turret roof. Left gun of 'A' out of action.

(3) WL in engineer's workshop. Flooded two compartments.

(4) Below water forward. Flooded 'A' bunker's port.

(5) Torpedo body room. Extensive damage. Flooded several compartments.

(6) ERA's bathroom. Flooded 'D' upper bunkers forward.

(7) Ditto.

(8) Bakery.

(9) Armour amidships, did not penetrate.

(10) Through No 1 funnel, then burst in Captain's bathroom.

(11) Through No 2 funnel, then burst on upper deck.

(12) Through No 2 funnel, and then overboard.

(13) 'A' turret lobby, through upper deck, and burst below it.

(14) Port side aft below WL. Injured feed-tank and stopped port engine.

(15) Upper deck, and burst as it passed through ship's side.

Of these only (5) and (14) were really such as to affect the fighting efficiency. (1), (3), (4), (5), (6), and (14) flooded compartments, and gave ship a 10-degree heel.

(8) A splinter injured exhaust bend to port inner condenser.
The other six did no harm at all except locally.

RECOMMENDATIONS

(a) Collision mats of various sizes should be at once supplied for stopping holes and making hatches, &c W/T.

(b) Plenty of shores to be placed everywhere, as little danger of fires.

(c) A large increase in supply of candle lamps. *All* officers, where darkness may occur, to have electric torches.

(d) Plunging fire is a great danger to ammunition anywhere between decks.

(e) Lids of powder cases should not be removed faster than necessary to keep up with the rate of loading, and rapid opening of cases should be practised.

(f) Very thorough organisation of fire parties and repair parties necessary to avoid confusion and anxiety in the dark. There should be a leader and second leader of each party who should have a candle lantern.

(g) The electric pumps failed, as was expected, and this would have been serious if ship had subsequently been torpedoed. Although leaks had been stopped, water could not be pumped out for two days. More efficient pumps that will work under water are most necessary, as ship might have been lost from this cause.

III. DAMAGE TO ENGINES, &c

1. *Damage to feed-tank. Hit No 14* – The large board with the gauges on it was thrown on to the thrust block of the HP engine: the brass casting, forming the face of the engine-room telegraph, was hurled across the engine-room: the feed-tank being open to the sea, after the ship's side was forced in, it overflowed into the reserve feed-tank, and when this was full the water rushed into the engine room. The discharge pipe from the air pumps to the feed-tank was badly distorted, and if this had been carried away the engine room would have been flooded, but it luckily held.

   A stop valve should be fitted between this pipe and the feed-tank.

2. *Hit No 8* — A portion of the shell which wrecked the bakery passed through the armour gratings and struck the exhaust bend to the port inner condenser, made a hole in it, and landed on the frames for the testing doors; this saved the tubes in the condenser from being damaged. Breathing pipes

from condensers, air pumps and filters in the casings were completely destroyed.

3. *Hit No 5* — Shell explosion in the torpedo body room. The auxiliary exhaust pipe in the submerged torpedo room from the capstan engine was punctured by a splinter. As the only valves fitted to this system are spring-loaded valves, which can be kept open but cannot be screwed down in the closed position, the sea water came through the punctured pipe and was drawn into the auxiliary condenser.

As a result of the same explosion, a length of auxiliary steam pipe in the submerged torpedo room and one in the capstan engine room were dented, and, probably owing to the same explosion, a splinter went down the hatchway to the motor generator room and badly dented a length of steam pipe to capstan engine.

The spindle of the port cable holder was badly cut into and probably bent: the gland cast where it goes through the armoured deck is fractured.

4. *Hit No 4* — Owing to the concussion in the vicinity of No 94 bulkhead the circulating water outlet valve of the turbo-dynamo condenser was apparently driven in, and wheel and spindle for working it came in about 2 feet and carried away the air pump guides. Damage to outlet valve not yet known as the wing is still flooded.

5. *Bunkers* — Port 'A' boiler room lower bunker was flooded with a full pressure of water in it. Owing either to its being actually pierced itself, or more probably owing to damage done to the armour deck above it when the side armour was driven in (hit No 4).

'D' boiler room (hit No 6): the upper bunker was flooded on account of shell in ERA's bathroom carrying away the deck by the ship's side.

'F' boiler room (hit No 14): the forward lower bunker was flooded with a full pressure of water, the damage to the ship not yet known.

The after bunker is apparently intact, it was flooded owing to the damage at No 200 bulkhead.

IV. NAVIGATIONAL

1. In early stages of action conning was done from the bridge, the plot of courses and speeds being kept on a mooring board as usual, and the position placed on the chart every half hour. About

half an hour after opening fire chart was taken to the conning tower by Commander (N), and the Midshipman with plotting board went to the lower conning tower as arranged. He also had a duplicate chart. Subsequently both charts were kept going, one in the conning tower by the Navigator, and the other in the lower conning tower where the position could be referred to by the Commander who might have to take charge any moment.

2. No difficulty was experienced in the conning tower except at the end, when chart with everything else in the conning tower was completely flooded by short shots.

3. Steering was from upper conning tower throughout, but when electric light failed, ship had to be steadied from below, as the gyro had stopped and projector could not be seen.

4. Maximum deviation obtained on a north-westerly course was 4 degrees after the action.

5. The standard gyro receiver and pedestal had been stowed below before the action in case the standard compass had been shot away, but as current had failed this would not have been any use if wanted.

V. TORPEDO AND ELECTRICAL

1. No torpedoes could be fired owing to enemy being out of range on a forward bearing.

2. At 10.1 a.m. *Lion* was hit heavily aft and load on port dynamos gradually increased from 360 amps to 1,000 amps on each. At 10.20 a.m. both dynamos came off owing to short circuit. No 2 dynamo then isolated and remained on for about five minutes when it was again finally thrown off due to short circuit, *Lion* having been hit twice in the meantime.

No 3 dynamo isolated but again thrown off due to ring main being short circuited in after LP switchboard compartment which commenced flooding at 10.1.

10.10 a.m. — After LP switchboard compartment abandoned, flooded, and watch-keeper wounded. All after fire control and 4-inch gun circuits out of action.

10.15 a.m. (about) — Shell burst in torpedo body room (over submerged flat). One torpedo thrown on to the deck, others struck by splinters, and two of the crew wounded in submerged flat. Flat commenced to flood from body room and lighting failed.

10.18 a.m. — Heavy explosion close to submerged flat on port side. Flat flooded rapidly, and had to be abandoned. Ship listing slightly to port. The gunner (T), Mr Burton, opened one of the air reservoirs, which relieved the crew's breathing, and asked the conning tower's permission to abandon the flat.

10.50 a.m. — No 1 dynamo, the only remaining one, thrown off by short circuit, probably by water in the submerged flat reaching the ring main. All light and power failed. Until this the forward fire control system was in operation with the exception of Evershed's bearing transmitters, which stopped with No 2 dynamo, 10.20–10.30.

11 a.m. — Lights, power, &c, forward got on again for some minutes when, owing to the impossibility of keeping the dynamo on the ring main, temporary lighting direct from Nos 1 and 3 dynamos terminals had to be resorted to (No 2 dynamo steam pipe shot through).

Later — Sawed through ring main before No 1 dynamo, starboard ring main then available.

VI. MEDICAL, BY FLEET SURGEON MACLEAN

I was in the lower conning tower during the action, and I have nothing to note until after 10 a.m., when the first wounded man came down. He had walked below from 'A' turret, left gunlayer. I went up and saw him in fore distributing station, where Staff Surgeon Hingston attended him. Later I received reports by voice-pipe and telephone that there were injured men in 'A' turret, and aft on the mess deck, and I arranged for stretcher parties to collect them and take them to the after distributing station, which is the only one accessible to stretcher cases. I only had to go up to the 4-inch flat to communicate with the stretcher parties in the fore station (who went to 'A' turret and submerged flat), and I communicated with Staff Surgeon Cox by telephone, and he went over to the after station and sent out his stretchers from there to collect the wounded from aft.

About this time there was a heavy explosion, which seemed to lift us up from the deck, and the ship soon heeled over. Later a shell burst somewhere near, and the mess decks filled with smoke. All lights went out, and I heard men screaming on the mess deck. I went up with a smoke pad on and groped about, but was unable to find any wounded in the dark, and the crying ceased.

I should not have been able to remain any time in the smoke had it not been for the smoke pads, which were very useful. I then returned to my station and found that we had hauled out of line and ceased fire.

I then visited both stations and found all the wounded had

already been brought in. In the fore station had only walking
cases and one stretcher case. In after station all the bad cases had
been collected and were being attended to by Staff Surgeon Cox.

Owing to the water rising on the mess deck (port side) we had
to move the men to the issue room, and there hastily inspected
them by the light of an oil lamp and candles.

I then went round the ship and found no more wounded, and
also decided on using the sick bay for after treatment. The
wounded were removed there and taken in hand one at a time,
and when treated were put to bed and fed. We only had oil lamps
and candles to begin with, but afterwards got portable electric
lights and a wandering lead.

Water was nearly unobtainable, and had to be carried down in
mess kettles.

Chloroform was only necessary in three cases.

The stretcher parties were only just sufficient to deal with the
small number of wounded which we had.

The wounded behaved very well considering that they thought
the ship was sinking, especially Mechanician Cannon.

Staff Surgeon Cox did a lot of hard and painstaking work, and
Staff Surgeon Hingston did one of the operations most rapidly
and skilfully in a very poor light. All the staff worked well.

The majority of the injured were hurt by being thrown down
by concussion, not by direct hits. There were few burns, and, so
far, only one case who may have been affected by high explosive
fumes.

Enclosure 6

123. *From Pelly*

[BTY/4/6/7]   *Tiger*
                                                      January 25, 1915

*   *   *

Appendix V
Gunnery Notes

Fire was opened at 20,000 yards by director, and was continued
by director until about 10.35 a.m., when — owing to all the guns
which were ready missfiring — the order 'Individual firing' was
given.[1]

---

[1]*Tiger* was the only British battle-cruiser involved equipped for director firing.

2. During director firing no difficulty at all was experienced in shifting target or in shifting the point of aim. This latter advantage was made use of to increase the range at which firing could be carried on, and the salvo—which resulted in the *Blücher* leaving the line—was fired with 20,750 yards on the sights, and the point of aim her foretop.

3. Spotting was very difficult; the enemy's ships appeared to fire about the time our salvos [*sic*] were due to fall. As the enemy were to windward, their cordite and funnel smoke partially obscured them, and the funnel smoke from their destroyers on occasions nearly hid their leadng ship. On only one occasion did their short shots obscure the target from the top at the moment of our salvo falling. On one occasion heavy spray from their shell came over and into the top.

4. In 'Individual firing', 'A' and 'B' turrets had great trouble in picking up the target and laying on it, owing to spray covering the glasses of the sights. This also prevented these turrets obtaining ranges; in fact, very few ranges were obtained, and no attempt could be made either to obtain or keep a rate. In this connection it is pointed out that the scale on the Dreyer table only runs up to 17,000 yards, which range was not reached during the first phase of the action.[1]

5. All officers of turrets complained of blast through their look-out slips. The forward bow position was quite useless owing to spray.

6-inch Control

6. The spotting officer's station is in the top, and he passes all ranges, orders, &c, to the 6-inch gun control tower of the side in action.

7. During the action no difficulty was experienced with the port guns, as no damage had occurred while they were in action. The starboard side came into action after the damage to the gun control tower occurred. This included carrying away the voice-

---

[1]In 1912 Commander (later Admiral Sir Frederick) Dreyer had invented a mechanical plotting table to produce rates of change in a target's course and speed. See J. T. Sumida (ed.), *The Pollen Papers* (London, 1984), pp. 293–5. See also Admiral Sir Desmond Dreyer, 'Early Development of Naval Fire Control', *The Naval Review*, July 1986, which suggests a balanced assessment of the relative contributions of his father and Arthur Pollen to fire-control development. See also note 1 on page 128.

pipe from the top to the starboard gun control tower partially, and the voice-pipes from the starboard gun control tower to 6-inch TS and starboard OOQs hood completely.

8. No difficulty in spotting was experienced, except when firing at long range at their destroyers.

9. Owing to the damage to the voice-pipe between top and the starboard GCT, the opening range and deflection were missed, but the officer in the starboard GCT estimated the range by eye and put this on. Spotting corrections were heard correctly.

10. The GCT would have had great difficulty in spotting even at 6,000 yards, owing to the necessity for keeping the exonite screen up for protection from blast when the turrets are trained aft, and this screen, with spray on it, could not be seen through satisfactorily.

6-inch Ammunition Supply

11. During the twenty minutes the 6-inch guns were engaging the *Blücher* no difficulty was experienced with the supply. The guns started with twenty lyddite and full charges on the gun deck, and twenty more in the passages each, and this amount was not greatly reduced during the firing.

12. There was some difficulty in removing the charges from the 'T' and Clarkson[1] cases, as the bands had in many cases been removed. This had been done, as many of the bands are made of bleached calico, and it was considered that there was some risk from smouldering portions of this remaining in the gun, and also that a missfire might occur owing to the calico obstructing the flash of the tube to the primer.

13. The dredger hoists worked satisfactorily, except for a delay at one of the two of about ten minutes, owing to one of the screws securing one bucket becoming unscrewed and allowing the bucket to partially fall. Fortunately this happened where the bucket could be got at, and it was remedied by removing the bucket.

14. The motor hoists worked from the passages satisfactorily, but at one period they all stopped. This happened at the moment

[1]With the introduction of cordite as the standard propellant, the leather Clarkson cases for powder propellant were abandoned. It was the lighter bag which replaced them which was now being found unsatisfactory. After Jutland the overriding need for protection for the cordite charges against flash led to a readoption of the Clarkson cases, fire-proof canvas being soon substituted for leather.

when the shock of a shot striking the side was felt, and was probably caused by this.

Other Accidents and Delays

15. 13.5-inch — The left guns of all turrets were fitted with the spring-link device, and the right guns with the shearing-wire device. No trouble with the former can be traced; with the latter, a delay in loading occurred due to a tube jambing and carrying away both the shearing wire and the tube retainer. This was remedied by the armourer of the turret in less than ten minutes. Due to the slow rate of fire the turret did not miss a salvo owing to this cause, as the left gun was loaded in time.

16. Great trouble was experienced in removing the pins of the lyddite fuzes, although pliers were provided for each gun. At the 6-inch an additional man had to be employed on the gun-deck removing these.

Missfires

17. Several missfires occurred in the turrets, but the causes have not been ascertained definitely. At the 6-inch there were some missfires in electric and two in percussion firing; the latter were probably caused by the breech not being fully closed.

Hydraulic Pumps

18. All three pumps were in use the whole of the time. At the after-pump great trouble was experienced in keeping the water above the suction to the pump, and some salt water had to be used; fresh water was being pumped in continually. This pump and its tank are on the upper platform deck, and the forward two are on the lower platform deck. The exhaust water is found to fill the forward tanks and overflow through their breathing pipes on the main deck before it will flow into the after-tank. This possibility was pointed out to the contractors when the ship was being built. New lengths of piping are being made in *Akbar* to enable the breathing pipes to be extended to the next deck with a view to obviating the difficulty.

19. The mains, with the exceptions of those parts under the steam-pipe tunnels, have been examined since the action and found to be all correct.

Electrical Instruments

20. No trouble was experienced with these, even in those parts of the ship which were most seriously damaged. In the 13.5-inch GCT the repeat range and deflection receivers were in good order at the end of the action, although they are placed in the part of the tower where the worst of the explosion was felt.

21. In 'Q' turret the lighting and instruments were not damaged, except those quite close to the hole in the roof. The director receiver of the left gun is in step electrically, although its glass cover was completely destroyed.

Other Points

22. Large tubs of water were placed in rear of each 6-inch gun for wetting the rammer; these were found to be quite insufficient and required refilling. Some trouble was experienced in obtaining more fresh water for this purpose.

23. Better securing arrangements are required for the sight port covers and door of director tower, which were found to swing to and fro when the guns fired.

24. Some method of wiping windows of range-finders from inside the turret should be made.

*   *   *

124.   *Jellicoe to Admiralty*

[BTY/4/1/1]   *Iron Duke*
[Copy]   10 February 1915
No 290/HF 0022A

With reference to Vice-Admiral Sir David Beatty's despatch No 01 of the 2 February 1915, of which a duplicate was transmitted direct to the Admiralty, relative to the engagement of 24 January 1915, be pleased to lay the following remarks before the Lords Commissioners of the Admiralty.

2. The important features in this report which require elucidation are the following:

(a) The reasons which induced Rear-Admiral Sir Archibald G.H.W. Moore to discontinue the pursuit of the three enemy battle-cruisers, two of which were seriously damaged and on fire.

(b) The fact that the second ship in the enemy's line was not engaged by *Tiger* in spite of the Vice-Admiral's signal to engage opposite numbers.

3. As regards (a), the Rear-Admiral gives certain reasons in his report of the engagement, but he does not mention the receipt of the Vice-Admiral's signal 'Course NE', which was hoisted at 11.2 a.m. only two minutes after the signal to turn together 8 points to port together was hauled down, nor of the signal 'Keep nearer

to the enemy' hoisted at 11.5 a.m. Had these signals been acted upon the enemy would not have increased his distance to any appreciable extent. Further enquiry on this point is necessary to enable a true appreciation of the situation to be obtained. Copies of the Signal and Wireless Logs of all ships engaged for the period covered by the despatch are being obtained.

4. In regard to (b), a report has been called for from *Tiger* as to the reasons for not complying with the Vice-Admiral's signal to engage opposite numbers.

5. It is suggested that in any publication of these despatches, the mention of the fact that the squadron passed through a certain position at 7 a.m. on the 24th January (as stated in the first and second paragraphs of the Vice-Admiral's report) should be omitted, as tending to afford information to the enemy which it is highly desirable should not be known to him.

6. I fully endorse the Vice-Admiral's comments on the remarkable steaming performances of all ships of the squadron, which is in the highest degree creditable to the engine-room staffs.

7. I also entirely concur in the Vice-Admiral's mention of those officers and men who had the opportunity of specially distinguishing themselves during the engagement.

This letter was dictated by the Commander-in-Chief.

125. *To Pelly*

[BTY/4/5/1]   *Princess Royal*
No 01 *Memorandum*   11 February 1915

With reference to my memo 01 of 29 January 1915, the reasons stated in your reply of Jan 31st are not concurred in.

Both HFGO 15 and the GFBO deal specifically with 'Instructions for a Fleet Action by Day' which is very different to chasing a retreating cruiser force such as in the Falkland Islands fight or on Jan 24th.

In regard to the various extracts you quote, the first is qualified by a note as follows:- '(b) is of equal importance if numbers or tactical position admit of concentration . . .'. It is obvious that tactical position was *not* suitable for a concentration on van.

The second quotation is one which quite obviously did not apply to the existing circumstances. From the same paragraph one may quote 'Enemy ships within effective range must not be left unfired at; the fire of modern ships is too severe to permit of its being unanswered'.

The third quotation applies to circumstances totally different from those of 24th January.

The fourth quotation explains that the angle of enemy's *approach* may make concentration on his van practicable. It is equally clear that the angle of his *retreat* may render it impracticable (or at all events undesirable).

2. Apart from the above I cannot understand why *Tiger* on shifting her fire from leading ship at 9.50 should have selected the rear ship to fire at. This only served to inconvenience the fire of *New Zealand*, vide her report, and the rear ship was being adequately dealt with while number two was still un-fired at.

3. With reference to *Tiger*'s firing, I attach extracts from other ships' reports which throw further light on the subject. Your report contains the following items:-

'9.3.   Range 20000 yards at least.

9.10   Enemy opened fire. *Tiger* hit rear ship with two salvoes.

9.35.   Observed *Tiger*'s 13.5 strike leading ship.

10.22   Salvo from *Tiger* hit rear ship, causing fierce fire. Range 20000 yards. Point of aim *Blucher*'s top.

10.29.   Another salvo from *Tiger* hit rear ship.

10.40   Salvo from Tiger struck thid ship, causing fierce fire.'

4. For various reasons I think it possible that observers in *Tiger* may have been misled as to these hits, either by hits made from other ships or by the flash of enemy's guns being taken for bursting shell. The following reasons suggest that possibility:-

(a)   *Tiger* was at all times firing at a target which another of our ships had been ordered to engage.

(b)   Other ships report that hits with AP shell are very difficult if not impossible to see at long range.

(c)   *Tiger* did not appear to be obtaining that proportion of short shots which is usually considered essential for effective control.

(d)   The ranges reported by *Tiger* are very large.

(e)   Reports from four other ships remark on *Tiger*'s salvoes falling considerably a long way over.

5. The following extracts are typical:—

Birmingham.   'About this time (10.0 to 10.30 a.m.) *Tiger*'s salvoes were plainly distinguished as going very much over, I should say 800 to 1200 yards. The guns were shooting very well together but all consistently over.'

Nottingham.   'At the beginning of the action, *Tiger*'s fire was observed to be going considerably over.'

Southampton.   'For some time it appeared that the fall of shot from one ship was considerably over that from the remainder of our Battle Cruisers.

These "overs" fell very close together, with a very much smaller spread than that of the other ships, and during the period in question 3-gun salvoes appeared to be in use. it is thought that these came from HMS *Tiger*.'

6. I hope you will impress on Control Officers that a correct proportion of short shots is the best guarantee of accurate fire and that hits at long range are not easy to spot with certainty even when using an accurate time of flight watch and with no other ship firing at the same target.

It has been stated that time-of-flight arrangements were not used in *Tiger*, which would further account for bad results.

7. With reference to movements of *Tiger* after *Lion* hauled out of line, I wish to emphasise the extreme importance attaching to the post of second in the line.

He is provided, when the leader drops out, with a golden opportunity to display initiative and take steps for achieving successfully the main object in view—which is the complete destruction of the enemy. Standing orders make it clear, and the existing circumstances make it more so, that a disabled ship which has hauled out of line should not be attacked by four battle-cruisers. My signals and standing orders are intended for guidance, as I have often stated, and not for rigid obedience if they tend to hinder the destruuction of the enemy, but the signal 'Attack the rear of the enemy' should have sufficed to indicate my requirements.

My Battle Orders, para 13 f, should at least have prevented *Tiger* hauling across the bows of *Princess Royal*, which not only masked her fire but prevented her from pursuing the enemy.

8. This, in some measure, contributed towards the enemy's escape, but I consider that the heavy concentration of fire which disabled *Lion*, and afterwards somewhat damaged *Tiger*, was directly due to *Tiger*'s failure to 'Fire at her opposite number'.

Had this order been obeyed I can see no reason why we should not have annihilated the enemy's squadron.

9. In making these remarks I have no wish to express censure in any form. I realise that a newly-commissioned ship in her first action has many difficulties to contend with, and I am quite ready to make the fullest allowance for them. My chief aim is to ensure that our next action shall be a complete success.

126. *From Moore*

[BTY/4/2]   *Europa*
No 2 / 23   13th February 1915

With reference to your Memorandum No 014 of the 9th instant, I regret that my report No 2/17 of the 29th ultimo[1] on the lessons to be learned from the action of 24th idem unintentionally conveyed the impression that *New Zealand* was at times unable to distinguish signals due to smoke or bursting shell. My paragraph 13 was intended to refer generally to what must be anticipated in action, except under most favourable circumstances. I was careful to say 'Visual signals *are* very difficult, etc' not '*were* very difficult etc', but I admit the paragraph is badly worded and can easily convey a false impression. The two cases I gave were intended to be illustrative of the importance of, if possible, confirming visual Flag signals by Auxiliary W/T or Searchlight.

2. I understand *New Zealand* was able at all times to see correctly flag signals repeated by her next ahead, and frequently those flying in *Tiger*, which ship was at times more than 10 cables off.

3. Searchlight was used by *New Zealand* to pass two or three signals to *Indomitable*.

[1] See 112.

127.   *To Admiral Sir Frederick Hamilton*[1] (2nd Sea Lord)

[HTN/117]   *Princess Royal*
                                               17.2.1915

Thank you for your congratulations. I wish we could have
completed the job properly.

I am sorry if I put any scheme into the 1st Lord's head re
manning ships. I do not remember making any suggestions on the
subject at all, and most certainly never enlarged on any scheme
simply because I have not considered the question and have never
thought of a scheme of any sort.

I did say that *Tiger* had a very mixed ship's company with a
large number of recovered deserters, and that it was an uphill
task for the Captain to pull them together in war time, and the
same efficiency could not be expected from the *Tiger* as from the
other ships. No, you have not had any complaint from me or from
Pelly. It is not the time to complain, but to do the best we can
with the material available. I was assured [?] her ship's company
would have been better if it has been possible to make it so. If
they had had time to work up together and get to know each
other as your system provides for now, there would have been a
vast difference. The higher ratings are excellent and are gradually
making themselves felt, but it takes time.

I know the First Lord is obstinate when set on a thing, but
really it only requires firm treatment to make him realise when
he goes off the rails, but indeed it must be astonishingly firm. . . .

The Engineer Commander of *Indomitable*[2] is a hopeless fellow.
Kennedy tells me he tried before to get shot of him and they had
a Court of Inquiry which whitewashed him. He has by want of
care caused the brick work in every boiler to be in a hopeless
condition. Every other ship has kept hers going by repair work,
and in many cases have re-bricked whole boilers. The Senior
Engineer is first class and has kept the ship going under adverse
circumstances. If you think it necessary I will represent it officially,

[1]Admiral Sir Frederick Hamilton (1856–1917) had been 2nd Sea Lord since 30
July 1914; Commander-in-Chief Scotland 1 July 1916.
[2]Commander (E) James Mountfield was replaced by Thomas Jameson on 17
March 1915.

but I thought under the circumstances he might be removed or exchanged without going to this length.

128. *Revision of Battle-Cruiser Fleet Orders*[1]

[CCC/DRAX/1/3]   18th February 1915
                (B.C.F. No. 017 of 18th Feb. 1915.)

Part S, OPERATIONS, STRATEGY, TACTICS, &c.

1. General Principles (*Revision of B.C.S. 015 of 15–4–13.*)
1. From a study of the Great Naval Wars it is impressed upon one that Cruiser captains and battle-cruiser Captains, to be successful, must possess, in a marked degree, initiative, resource, determination, and fearlessness of responsibility.

To make the best use of these qualities they must be given a clear outline of the functions and duties of the force to which they belong, and of the principles by which the Admiral is guided in handling them.

War is a perpetual conflict with the unexpected, so that it is impossible to prescribe beforehand for all the circumstances that may arise.

The Admiral will therefore rely on Captains to use all the information at their disposal so as to grasp the situation quickly and anticipate his wishes, using their own discretion as to how to act in unforeseen circumstances and carrying through every operation with resolution and energy.

2. Cruiser Captains cannot be too often reminded that, in war, there is an immense increase in those things which occur to distract a man's judgment and overwhelm him with uncertainty. As Clausewitz has said, in war much information is contradictory, more is false, the greatest part is doubtful.

In all doubtful cases a carefully considered first opinion should not be abandoned until a clear conviction forces us to do so. That

---

[1]The copy of this document at Churchill College, Cambridge, has a manuscript note by Drax saying that, while he had initiated and drafted some passages, the wording of Sections I & II, General Principles & Battle Cruisers, was Beatty's own.

line of action which promises the greatest possible damage to the enemy is very seldom wrong.

3. As a rule, instructions will be of a very general character so as to avoid interfering with the judgement and initiative of Captains.

Orders should be complied with in spirit but it is not desirable to be tied by the letter of a standing order in circumstances where perhaps it was never intended to apply.

Orders issued by signal frequently indicate the Admiral's intentions or requirements; they may perhaps have to be obeyed literally by some ships and not by others. For example, a course signal when ships are widely spread would probably indicate that the Admiral and ships near him will steer the course indicated. More distant ships may find that a slightly different course will better suit their requirements.

4. Functions and duties of the battle-cruisers. These are concisely summarised in a later memo. *See* **2**.

5. The attainment of good results in fast vessels is enormously dependent on rapid and efficient signalling. All forms of signalling require careful attention, particularly wireless.

To meet this the following points require attention:—

All ships should be carefully tuned with loose couplings, and receiving ships should have opportunity to get accurate adjustments for all ships that may send to them.

Signals *must* be brief. To contain the necessary information in its most concise form it is essential that the Officer drafting a signal should have a good knowledge of the Wireless Code Book.

Cruisers in sight of the enemy must continue sending off information even though interference may prevent them hearing any replies to their signals.

If interference is on a low note it may be possible to get through by changing quickly to a high note.

It is useful to fit a wavemeter in the receiving circuit as an additional rejector.

A thoroughly efficient code staff is essential; without it cruiser operations become almost impossible.

Wireless Officers should realise that the efficiency of material is only a small portion of the preparation necessary to success. The training of personnel and a careful study of the organisation of communications in all its details are factors requiring constant attention.

It is important for cruisers while engaged to be able to send wireless from behind armour, and to shift to or from that position without delaying operations.

2. Battle-cruisers (*Revision of B.C.S. 015 of 3–3–14.*)

1. Having completed one year in command of the First Battle-Cruiser Squadron, and being now at the commencement of another year of work, the moment is opportune to summarise and review the results of the work of the past year. From this we can revise, if necessary, the General Principles upon which we have based our exercises hitherto, and at the same time determine the points requiring further attention.

2. I stated in my memorandum 015 of 15 April 1913, issued on taking command, that the functions of the Squadron included:—

Strategical. To provide a fast and powerful force for supporting the operations of advanced cruisers, or armoured cruisers, whether employed for patrolling, watching, searching, making a reconnaisance, or for other duties.

Tactical. To form the fast division of the line of battle for a general action.

These two functions, as shown by the lessons of last year, cover practically all the most important duties of the B.C.F.

The following remarks are compiled as an aid to further investigation in the coming year:-

3. *Strategical Principles.* From the experience gained from exercises carried out in April, June, July and October, also from the naval manoeuvres, I think it has been clearly demonstrated

(*a*) That there are many limitations and difficulties in carrying out efficiently the work of support.

(*b*) That supports should never be divided so that any portion of them could be overwhelmed in detail by a superior force of the enemy. Even when spread, the battle-cruisers should always be *in sight* of one another.

There can be no certainty of effecting a rapid junction with ships *out of sight* and dependent on wireless.

The support should be of such strength as to be at least equal to the greatest force of enemy battle-cruisers that can be brought against them.

(*c*) One unit of supports can only provide support to a very limited front of cruisers, the actual length of line from wing to wing being dependent upon the visibility, but not more than 50 miles, with supports 30 miles from the line, under the most favourable circumstances. In low visibility they should be very much closer, ten or fifteen miles in rear.

(*d*) The Batttle-Cruiser Squadron in performance of support duty must be prepared to man and fight every gun of its Anti-Torpedo Armament at the same time as its main armament, by day as well as by night.

(*e*) Strategically, and in many cases tactically, full use can be made of the Battle-Cruiser Squadron only when it is working in co-operation with other vessels. By itself it can accomplish something, but with small fast cruisers it could be made of infinitely greater value to the Commander-in-Chief, and would not be exposed to the same risks as at present.

(*f*) The destroyer menace compels retirement by night; the dangers of submarine attack by day, though undoubtedly large, have not yet been fully investigated.

(*g*) The safety and utility of all advanced or detached vessels will depend very considerably on the efficiency of the coding and wireless staffs. Thorough training in peace is essential and should be directed towards studying the principles of wireless communication, and means of saving time in signalling, decoding and delivering messages, rather than in studying the technical peculiarities of the instruments.

(*h*) It is essential that vessels which would co-operate with the Battle-Cruiser Squadron in war should be frequently exercised with it in peace.

4. *Tactical Principles*. The following lessons learnt during the past year deal with all phases of tactics including the earlier movements prior to engaging.

(*a*) My Battle Orders contain sufficient general instructions for the internal conduct of the Battle-Cruiser Fleet in action. *See* **3**.

(*b*) Further questions relating to the co-operation of all forces in a general action have been, after practical trial, discussed fully in correspondence between the Commander-in-Chief and myself from October to December last, the principal points are as follows:-

(*c*) It is most important that the B.C.F should join the C.-in-C. in time to take part in the Fleet action.

(*d*) From experience gained during the principal exercises last year, the battle-cruisers on approaching the Battle Fleet will probably be employed in advance of it to gain information of the enemy's movements, strength, formation, etc., until shortly before the line of battle is formed.

(*e*) Their future movements would depend upon one of two factors, viz., the presence of a squadron of battle-cruisers with enemy's fleet or not.

If hostile battle-cruisers are present they must form the objective of our battle-cruisers, so that they may be held by ships of equal power and speed to prevent them choosing their position.

We should engage with sufficient strength to annihilate them, while our surplus battle-cruisers, if any, would be sent to attack enemy's flank battleships. The choice of flank would depend on circumstances. If possible, it is useful to have battle-cruisers at each end of the line.

(*f*) If there are no battle-cruisers with the enemy fleet, our B.C.F. will act as a fast division of the Grand Fleet. Our B.C. Squadrons may be concentrated in an endeavour to crush the enemy's van, or may be separated so as to act on both flanks simultaneously.

In carrying out the objects mentioned in (*e*) and (*f*) it is essential that our movements should be governed by the following factors:-

(1.) The B.C.F. should run no risk of fouling or masking the front of the Battle Fleet when deployed.

(2.) It should not come into range of enemy Dreadnought *Battle* Fleet until our own Battle Fleet is engaged.

(3.) It must be in a position to open fire immediately after our Battle Fleet is engaged, and if possible should have reached a good tactical position beforehand.

(4.) The smoke of the B.C.F. must never be liable to interfere with the view of the Battle Fleet at a critical moment.

These four factors all make for the desirability of forming in good time on the selected flank.

Good work can be accomplished by the B.C.F. working on conjunction with light cruisers and flotillas.

5. In the light of past experience, and the principles learnt, it is now necessary to consider the training and exercises that we need during the current year. For training, we must of course practice all the strategical and tactical operations that we may have to perform in war. This can only be done efficiently when working in concert with the other forces which in war would actually co-operate with us.

Further, we must endeavour by practical trial to clear up all outstanding problems which are at present unsettled or in the controversial stage.

6. The following list gives a few of the exercises desirable for battle-cruisers and cruisers.

Strategical.

(1.) Exercise bringing in cruisers and destroyers from a distance to surround a fleet that has been located at sea.

(2.) Follow this with shadowing duty by day, making long range torpedo attacks if visibility is less than 11,000 yards.

(3.) Then shadowing exercise by night, making torpedo attacks with destroyers and long range attacks from cruisers.

(4.) Finally, by day, own Battle Fleet approaches and all vessels take stations for a general action.

Tactical. In tactics, even more than in strategy, what we specially need to practice is the concerted action of all arms in a simultaneous offensive. The following should be exercised:-

(*a*) Closing the Battle-Cruiser Fleet when spread, and forming order of battle for a cruiser action.

(*b*) Joining the Commander-in-Chief for a general action; first, when detached out of sight; second, when keeping touch with the enemy's fleet.

(*c*) Taking up preliminary station ahead of Commander-in-Chief and thence operating to drive back enemy cruisers and gain information of enemy's fleet.

(*d*) Proceeding to engage battle-cruisers when present with enemy's fleet.

(*e*) Falling back to form a fast division of the battle line. This entails first manoeuvring for a good tactical position, then closing to engage simultaneously with our main fleet but never before it.

(*f*) Practice concerted attacks on van or rear, battle-cruisers co-operating with light cruisers and flotillas. Also practice co-operation of the same forces for repelling attacks by the enemy's flotillas.

(*g*) Exercise as in (*f*) but firing salvoes of torpedoes sometimes from a Battle-Cruiser Squadron and sometimes from the light cruisers or flotillas.

(*h*) Exercises as above, but with submarines also taking part.

7. The exercises quoted above are retained in the present reprint because, although they cannot be practised as exercises, they describe operations which we may very possibly have to carry out.

3. Battle orders for Battle-Cruiser Fleet (*Reprint of B.C.S. 015 of 17–7–13.*)

The following orders are generally applicable for an action with battle or armoured cruisers, but they apply mainly to the requirements of a Fleet action.

1. It may be expected that the Commander-in-Chief would use the fast division for attacking the enemy's flank, and the battle-cruisers must therefore be prepared to attack either van or rear. To attain quickly a good tactical position full speed will be needed, not only during the approach but perhaps also while engaged.

2. Much will depend on whether the enemy's van or rear is attacked. If the van, one of our chief objects will be to pour in a steady fire with long range torpedoes.

3. Very probably we shall have to meet a determined attack by the enemy's torpedo craft, directed either at the battle-cruisers or our own battle line; in either case the anti-torpedo guns must be ready to open fire instantly for repelling this attack. Similarly the squadron must be prepared to deal effectively with the enemy's armoured cruiser force, whether acting as supports or attempting to attack the flank of our battle line with gun and torpedo. In so doing we should also afford necessary protection to our own flotillas near by, and thus assist and support them in advancing to make their attack.

4. If the enemy's rear is to be attacked, it will be necessary to open out to 4 or 5 cables apart when within range of enemy torpedoes; or to steer a course which reduces their chance of hitting. A sharp look-out should also be kept for submarines or small craft laying mines, which may be found near the rear of the enemy's line.

5. Whether at the van or rear, our final aim must be to concentrate on the flank battleships of the enemy and to press in, provided they are engaged by our own Battle Fleet, to such range that our fire may have decisive results.

6. Much must be left to the initiative and judgment of Captains. They are relied upon to act promptly in battle on their own initiative for dealing with all cases such as the following:—

(*a*) Two or more ships requiring to concentrate fire on one of the enemy.

(*b*) Altering course to avoid torpedoes, or extending gaps in the line as a precautionary measure.

(*c*) Making small alterations of course to fire torpedoes. N.B. —

Care should be taken to right the helm and resume station as soon after as possible.

(*d*) Hauling out of the wake of the next ahead to avoid smoke or backwash. N.B. — It is desirable that ships should not haul out more than one point, lest they hamper the squadron when turning in succession. If one point is insufficient, ships should avoid smoke interference by opening out.

(*e*) Altering line of bearing from Flag in order to get a clearer arc of fire, or to close nearer the enemy.

(*f*) Or in any other case in which Captains consider that prompt action is needed, and their movements are such as the Vice-Admiral would certainly approve if they could be made known to him beforehand. The chief limitation in these cases is that no movement must mask the fire of other ships or in any way inconvenience them from a manoeuvring point of view.

7. After opening fire every effort must be made to keep the 'A' arc bearing steadily. Alterations of course should be small — not exceeding two points if possible and made with small helm, usually 10 to 15 degrees.

8. Should any ship or squadron find itself being heavily hit, it is permissible to alter course 1 or 1½ points to upset the enemy's control. In doing this, however, it is most important not to drop astern nor to make the line so ragged as to interfere with manoeuvring.

9. If ordered to form on a line of bearing or reform while engaged, the smallest possible amount of helm should be used consistent with rapid execution.

10. If, as may happen, the Admiral is not leading the line, the leader is to hoist 4 Pendant without signal.

11. *Re* signals in action; guiding principle in single line, 'Each ship is responsible for her next astern.' If, as is quite likely, the Admiral does not wait for all ships to repeat close up, the last ship that has repeated the signal is to keep it flying after Flagship hauls down, until next astern has seen it; ships in rear to act similarly until the last ship has got it.

4. Instructions for concentrating battle-cruisers when spread and forming order of battle (*Reprint of B.C.S. 015 of 17–7–13.*)

1. When spread, ships must remember the importance of quick action and quick communication of intelligence on sighting the enemy. For this, and equally for concentrating, it is essential that ships should be within visibility distance. A sudden alteration of course by the ship sighting the enemy is seen by those on either

side of her far more rapidly than any signal could be sent, and being an almost certain indication of an enemy having been sighted it should be acted on immediately.

2. All ships that *may* be required to support must proceed to do so until they know definitely that they will not be required.

3. The immediate sequel to concentrating is forming order of battle and engaging the enemy. In future this will be done so far as possible without signal, and each Captain is to use his discretion in handling his ship as he considers that the Admiral would wish.

The following principles are to be accepted as a guide for concentrating and forming line of battle:-

4. Concentrating must be understood to mean placing each ship as rapidly as possible in a position to support her consorts by engaging the enemy with effective gunfire. This naturally does not require that all ships shall be in close order, but those near one another must form line of battle at the first opportunity after concentrating; leading ship automatically taking guide.

5. Ships that are able to close must form line ahead roughly at right angles to bearing of enemy, in the order in which they then are, leading ship taking guide, all without signal. Those ships furthest ahead of the enemy should not sacrifice their position in order to take station on others abeam of him, nor is it desirable to form in close order if heavy smoke on the engaged side is liable to mask the guns of ships astern. These exceptions must of course depend on existing circumstances.

6. When ships are widely separated and perhaps on opposite sides of the enemy, they are to hoist action signal 98 to indicate 'I am now nearly in range of the enemy and will close to engage as soon as sufficient support has come up.'

Each detached ship should, at her discretion, close and engage the enemy at the earliest moment she thinks justified, without waiting for further orders. The signal should be repeated by searchlight, and if necessary by wireless. Ships of Battle-Cruiser Fleet are to note the above signification in pencil against action signal 98 in the signal book.

7. If possible no signal other than this will be used. Ships must never suppose that the absence of a signal implies that any given action is not sanctioned by Flagship; on the contrary it usually denotes that the Admiral relies on each ship to take whatever action may be necessary without waiting to be told.

8. The above principles apply equally for separated divisions of 2 or 3 ships when concentrating to attack a superior enemy

squadron. The sole object of these instructions is to enable ships to understand beforehand the principles of rapid co-operation, so that the enemy may be brought to action at the earliest possible moment without any ship needing or wishing to wait for detailed orders from the Admiral.

5. Training (*Revision of B.C.S. 015 of 17–7–13.*)

It is desired that all exercises and training for battle shall be, so far as possible, carried out with a view to practising the conditions and operations described in my 'Orders for Battle.'

2. A few of the principal requirements are as follows:-

(*a*) That guns shall be able to shoot effectively when ships are steaming at full speed and perhaps making frequent alterations of course.

(*b*) That ships shall be able to carry out concentration of fire, either with ships of their own squadron, or with others firing from a different direction.

(*c*) That turrets in local control shall be able to make good shooting at both long and short ranges.

(*d*) That ships shall be able to steam full speed, and keep roughly in station, while closely engaged.

(*e*) That ships while engaged shall be able to fire torpedoes steadily and accurately until every torpedo is expended.

(*f*) That ships can man their light guns and repel torpedo attacks while simultaneously engaged with armoured vessels.

(*g*) That arrangements be made to keep a good lookout, throughout an action, for the enemy's submarines or torpedoes (the latter are not likely to be visible unless running shallow), also for minelayers or destroyers laying mines ahead.

3. The above requirements must be kept constantly in view, and every effort made to comply with the principle that 'Any exercise or training which does not reproduce as closely as possible the actual conditions of war is almost inevitably bad.'

4. It is desired to impress on all officers that the object of training is not merely to attain success in target practices and competitions, but to ensure that the fighting value of the squadron as a whole shall be as high as possible. To this end it should be remembered that good comradeship and cordial co-operation are among the first essentials for success in war.

(4 and 5 were previously issued as Appendices to Battle Orders.)

129.   *To Hamilton*
(2nd Sea Lord)

[HTN/117]   *Princess Royal*
                                                                   21.2.15

Re the Engineer Commander of *Indomitable*. I am sending you
an official request that he may be relieved, accompanied by a
report which should be strong enough. The brick work of his
boilers were [*sic*] in a disgraceful condition, necessitating 40!!
bricklayers being placed on board. Apparently they had sat down
and done nothing, although they were *3 weeks* in Gib. dockyard.
Every other battle cruiser has kept her brick work going during
the war, and in many cases entirely rebricked boilers in their ship.
They have rebricked 14 boilers completely. Again, the fire they
had in the engine room might have been caused by want of care &
supervision, and at least the Court of Inquiry revealed a condition
which reflects very gravely upon him. There are great objections
to Courts of Inquiry in war time and I think you will agree that
those who are responsible for, and have to run the machines
should be given latitude in such cases. There is no doubt there
is considerable friction between the Captain and the Engineer
Commander, so one of them must go, and I do not propose
to recommend the removal of Kennedy!!! The Senior Engineer,
Knothe, is a very good man and it is due to him alone that she
has done as well as she has.

This is how the ship's company of the *Tiger* are [*sic*] made up
at present; *i.e.* actually on board now. A number of men have
left the ship for misconduct.

A.B's: G & T ratings	18 recovered deserters
Old seamen	8 recovered deserters
Old seamen—short service	46 joined Service between May & July 1914
Boys	65
RNVR seamen	52
Stokers 1st Class	31 recovered deserters
Stokers 2nd Class	8 recovered deserters
Stokers 2nd Class	12 joined Service July 1914

Stokers RNR	50
Signalmen	4 recovered deserters
Marines	3 recovered deserters
Marines	50 newly joined recruits

You will observe 73 are recovered deserters and I think I am right in saying that at least 10 more are in prison. The 6″ gun crews had to be made up practically from old seamen and boys and over [?] 275 of her company are untrained material. In a ship of the complication of the *Tiger* this is difficult — with so many men capable of having a bad influence among them. They have had considerable trouble, but are gradually settling down and are tackling the job manfully. So no doubt they will come out alright. As she is never dry when at sea, it doesn't make it any easier for them.

P.S.   Will you please support my Secretary being confirmed as a Paymaster. It will make a considerable difference & he is a 1st class fellow.

130.   *From Chatfield*

[BTY/4/5/6]   *Lion*
                                                          2nd March 1915
No 55

Sir,
I have the honour to forward a report made by Lieutenant-Commander G. Longhurst[1] of this ship on the effect of certain shell hits on the ship. All pieces of shell were collected after the action and an examination of these has furnished certain instructive information.

   2. The damage under water is not touched on in this report, but it has already been described in the report sent in by Engineer Captain Whitingham of 2nd Battle Squadron in his letter of 7th February 1915.

   3. The further damage below water line since revealed will form

[1]Gunnery officer of *Lion*.

the subject of a separate letter shortly, when the drawings have been completed.

4. I have also to report that, generally speaking, the effect of the German shell was very slight and entirely local, except in three cases. In these cases, viz,

    1. Body Room,
    2. Below water, 94 station,
    3. Below water, 200 station,

detonation probably occurred.

The other shell merely exploded, and the effect is much that which one has been instructed to expect from Powder Common, and, as far as the fighting efficiency was concerned, they were entirely harmless.

This bears out the experience reported after the action on 28th August 1914, when Powder Common proved very ineffective.

5. In this connection I would point out that clause V of the recently issued Gunnery Addendum of the Grand Fleet Battle Orders, paragraph 2, recommends Powder Common for commencing a long range action. This is opposed to *Lion*'s experience on 24th January, where AP Lyddite hits were obtained early and at very long ranges which did vital injury to enemy, such as reducing *Blucher*'s speed, setting *Seydlitz* on fire, and silencing half *Derfflinger*'s main armament. This could not have been done with Powder Common.

Lyddite also have the advantage of being incendiary and giving off fumes which are poisonous to life.

It is recommended therefore that Lyddite AP and Lyddite Common alone should be used, and that every effort should be made to have all Powder shell removed at once and replaced by the more efficient projectiles. Nothing should be allowed to stand in the way of this. *The damage done early is of the utmost value* and far outweighs subsequent damage.

6. The disadvantage of Lyddite Common as regards AP Lyddite is that it has a quick acting fuze and therefore does not penetrate, and I doubt its stopping power compared to the AP projectile. Both however have their peculiar merits, and the natural solution is to fire both simultaneously, i.e., to load one or two turrets with Lyddite Common and the remainder with AP, but before this can be done, accurate calibration of these shell must be carried out at Shoeburyness and sights altered accordingly.

Until this can be done, the following rule is recommended–
    Long visibility, start with AP Lyddite and finish

with Lyddite Common.
Short visibility, start with Lyddite Common and
    finish with AP Lyddite.
7. With regard to Grand Fleet Order 66, I submit the following corrections:-

Page 18, line 1 should read 'Overs' were practically *always* impossible to distinguish and hits could never be seen, except when large structural damage was caused.

Lines 4 and 5 are not quite right. The flash of the German guns was plainly visible to the naked eye as if red searchlights were switched on, there was no mistaking them on this dull day.

Page 20, clause 12, for 18,000 read 10,000.

Page 20, clause 18, German shell fragments show that semi AP were largely fired as they had large cavities and comparatively thin sides.

131. *From Jellicoe*

[BTY/4/5/1]   SECRET   *Iron Duke*
HF 0022A/6   3 March 1915
MEMORANDUM

Having had under consideration the explanation furnished by Captain Pelly of the *Tiger* in reply to my Memorandum HF 0022A dated 10 February, 1915, I have to remark as follows:-

Under the conditions prevailing at 9.30 a.m. during the action of the 24 January when the Vice-Admiral's signal to engage corresponding ships of the enemy was hoisted, the *Indomitable* was some distance astern, and there were four ships in action on each side. The duty therefore of the *Tiger* was clearly to engage the second ship in the enemy's line.

Special emphasis is laid in Grand Fleet Orders on the fact that no ship of the enemy should be left unfired at, and a consideration of this rule should have led to the *Tiger* engaging No 2 in the line.

The concentration rules cannot be taken to apply to a chase of four ships by five when firing at extreme range.

132. *To his wife* [Claridge's Hotel, London]

[BTY/17/33/14–15]   *Princess Royal*
                                          Monday 15th [March 1915]

*   *   *

Great excitement, everybody very busy, even old Lowry is getting a move on: submarine has been knocking at the door all day and they have located him near Oxcars with microphone. I popped down to see what I could do, but of course nothing and cannot afford to be away from the ships, but I feel sure they'll make a mess of it and they ought to get him this time. Old Lowry plaintively bleats what a pity Ryan isn't here to work the microphone, which amuses me as he never fussed about it before, and says, I am afraid that he will be gone before Ryan gets back, which is like a child or an old woman. If they hunt him with sufficient determination they are bound to get him in the end. Oh dear, I wish I was not stuck to these big ships. I'm sure I could catch him. But I suppose one cannot do everything, but these spells of inactivity and masses of paper work and continued wrestling with the Admiralty, and the C-in-C now, are making a crabbed old man of me. It goes on for ever and is never ending. They have taken my beautiful repair ship away from me now, just as we were getting everything fixed up and making it into a such well-arranged self-contained going concern. Old Green is in the depths of despair. But she has to go out to the Mediterranean, so I suppose it is a case of dire necessity, so must not grumble.

I think we are all getting rather hipped [?] and I am sending the Secretary for a few days to have a night in a bed and a rest. 8 months in the same spot, the same faces, the same atmosphere, is trying to anybody and we are beginning to dislike each other. So, if ever you think I am cranky or queer, you must make allowances and remember I have a very great deal to think about and do, all of a type of work I am not at my best at. I spend hours writing which is certainly not my métier, is it? . . .

133.   *To his wife* [Aberdour House]

[BTY/17/33/17–18]   *Princess Royal*
                                                              19.3.15

Just a line as I shall not see you today and might have to go
out tonight. What for? I hope something worth doing. It at least
is better than being stuck in harbour, better all round for ships
and men, and certainly for me. The stress of paper work is trying,
and it makes an escape.

I am not cross patch. I think you often think I am bad tempered
when I am *really* not, and consequently you treat me with diffi-
dence, which is upsetting. Not, sweetheart, that I want you to go
to the trouble of smoothing me or stroking [?] me down. I suppose
circumstances make one sensitive, which I have no right to be,
and there is no reason at all why I should bother you with any
point of view but your own. You always say nice things to me but
I feel in your heart of hearts you think I am rather a fool who
has had tremendous luck who succeeds in spite of himself. I shall
not be accused of conceit if I say that I think you are wrong. I
have had luck, I admit freely, great luck, but there has been a
little something else besides. My dear, you must bear with me
and make a little allowance for my idiosyncrasies. My position is
fraught with difficulties which you can have no idea of. I am not
trying to make myself important in your eyes, merely trying to
explain, very indifferently, why I am at times supersensitive about
nothing at all.

I am making up a box of stuff which I am sending to Dennis
to be locked away in the Bank for future requirements, in case.
I shall take care my memory is not blackened anyhow if anybody
cares to make use of the material I leave behind.

I have forced several admissions out of the Admiralty which
will be useful.

You say I am better off than in the trenches. The parallel is
hardly just. If I was a soldier, I would not be in the trenches, I
would be putting others in them and watching the results outside.
I am grown out of the trench stage which is difficult to realise . . .

134. *To his wife* [Aberdour House]

[BTY/17/33/19–20]   *Princess Royal*
                                                       Saturday [20 March 1915]

Please bear with me and forgive me my irritableness, peevishness, what you will. One becomes at times supersensitive, I have no right to be, I know. No one in the 7 countries at war has a braver, truer and more gallant helpmate than you, and no one *truly* recognises it more than I do. Don't say 'You have a strange way of showing it'; don't think please that I haven't had time to think of you & the boys. If you will cast your mind back you will remember that no day passed that I did not find time to write you a line *every* day in the early days of the war, when our times were in many ways much harder than now, when we were constantly at sea in circumstances that were not easy. And I wrote because I loved doing so, because the fact of doing so brought me nearer to you and I felt I was communing with you quite near. And in those days I got to lean upon receiving your letters, and you were good to me and wrote to me each day, and the receipt of them meant a great deal. That is why I still when not with you, like to get a scrawl however small, and not getting them causes a disappointment which I have really, I know, no right to feel.

Latterly you have disagreed with me so frequently when I have tried to explain my point of view of certain happenings, that it has disheartened me. You must remember and truly believe that I have faith in your judgement on many matters, matters of plain common sense in which woman's intuition is often so valuable. And I have been really [?] disheartened when I have tried to explain my point of view, and you have replied rather (as it seemed to me) brusquely, 'I don't understand you, it's no use talking about it, I think you are very foolish.' I know you did not mean anything, but being fretful, having thrashed the whole thing out in my own mind, over and over again, it has quite unnecessarily, needlessly, indeed foolishly, irritated me. You see, I like to talk things over with somebody. There is nobody here that I can talk it *all* over with, there are so many wheels within wheels. Even if it is only to hear myself reiterate my own views and opinions out loud, it is something. So, when you begin by disagreeing and say you cannot understand, that shuts me up altogether, and I feel that I've been wrong and must go to work & thrash it all out again when I get back. It's not for what has been done, that, I have finished with, but just to see if I have made a mistake, so that it shall not happen again, by the simple process of re-elimination.

It seems very involved and I have no right to bother you. You have enough worries of your own, and I won't harass you again as it only upsets you. Forgive me, I have no grievance. You say there is always something. What, where, when? It's my cursed manner that's at fault. I am afraid I truly am a pig. Please don't bother your dear head about me at all. I was not annoyed at your going to London. I was glad for you to have the opportunity of a change and I hope you will go again whenever you feel like a change and don't think or fuss about me at all. I am not worth it. If you would ever let me tell you in my own way about the happenings of the 24th January and the subsequent happenings, I think you would realise more clearly the [–] I was batting up against.

Forgive me for bothering you. I don't want to add to the troubles you already have to contend with.

135. *From his wife*

[BTY/18/23/1–7] Aberdour House
May 1st [1915]

I am writing this hoping perhaps to clear away the cloud which has come between us & which one feels is very stupid and quite unnecessary between two people who have lived together as long as we have. Of course I see now how much of it in the past has been my fault as I have always run after you like a little dog, which, after all is a silly thing to do with any one like you who after all is not the ordinary person but one who had & has big things to do in the world. And I should have realised long ago you did not want a dog at your heels. And then you got in the habit of looking upon me as always being there, & that was not a good thing either. I began to realise all this when you were at Cromarty & I wrote begging you to let me come up to see you, if only for a few hours & you were quite firm (& quite right too). But one begins to see things in a different light & one seems suddenly to have grown older & sees things differently & realised what a big work you had to do in life & that I must in no way interfere with that. But then you on the other hand must know that I must also have a little life of my own & [– –] friends that are congenial to me. But this, as I see, annoys you & as I wrote & told you some time ago, it is a great pleasure to have a pleasant & intelligent man to talk to & one also feels that one has been able to be of some use to the sailor, who is only too grateful to have a cheerful house to come to instead of a dirty hotel at the end of a pier. [–] all this does not matter. You must realise that when I make friends, & pleasant ones, I do not like to feel that you are antagonistic & that I cannot live with only society butterflys [sic], but as one gets older, appreciate & prefer real people. I should be very happy here, as I also like Gladys Prickett very much, as her mind is far above the average woman's & her interests and mine are the same. So, if you would try & see things as they are I think we should all be very much happier. I do fully realise how much you have on your mind & the difficult problems you have to solve, & as you know, only too glad to share your burdens, were it possible. But it annoys you when I feel deeply any injustice has been done to you. I am sure I feel it far more than you do & I should like to kill every one, especially Winston, when they have put you in the wrong light. However [?] I suppose one must just take things as they are & make the best of them.

Please forgive this long letter, but I wanted to try & have you understand. And I would rather not talk about it so have just written what I feel about it all.

136. *To his wife* [Aberdour House]

[BTY/17/33/23–5]   *Lion*
                                                                  2.5.15

Your letter indeed was a bomb. This seems a curious moment in our lives, which are already full of problems, to be wanting to lead different lives, to have different friends. It seems to me that we *are* leading different lives, to have different friends. Circumstances only permit my seeing you on an average of about 14 hours per week. I have no friends except my Staff whose business it is to be friends with me & who put up with my vagaries, and my Captains.

You have your friends and are *quite quite* wrong when you

think I wish to interfere with them & am antagonistic. I am delighted you should have people with you who are congenial & interest you. As to Ryan, who I presume is the one referred to, you may remember that I wrote to you a long time ago that he was a nice person & you would like him & told you to look out for him. That you should have him to live in the house is your business; if it suits you, it is pleasant for him to live in the house, & I am sure he is grateful. I do not in any way wish to interfere between you and your friends — why they should not be mine also, I do not quite understand.

This cloud, where does it come from? It does exist, but dear heart, it is not of my making. In token of which I will ask you to read the letter I wrote some days ago and left with Captain Grant to give it you in case of certain eventualities. But, under the stress of this new circumstance I think you had better read it now.

I will tell you how this cloud appears to have grown up to me; by a complete change in your manner, a certain coldness that has crept in during the past two or three months, noticeable by the manner of your greeting or bidding farewell, which has been of the formal 'Helloa, Good Morning, Good Night' type, without any accompanying caresses. If you submit to any kiss from me I am presented with the tip of your ear. I remember on one occasion I kissed you with perhaps unnecessary warmth and there was an immediate shrinking. I am not a very demonstrative person, but I am sensitive & in times such as these perhaps hypersensitive, which is foolish. During the past two months I do not remember a single endearing adjective being applied, a loving or familiar phrase. Your letter which threw the brick was cold, almost conveying a veiled threat. On one of the last occasions when we returned after a very disappointing time, and indeed a very anxious one, when we had been at one time practically surrounded with submarines, & mind you, the responsibility lies on me only of the safe conduct of a great many ships, I was greeted very coldly on going on board the *Sheelah* by 'Halloa, what have you been up to?' as you presented me with your left ear. No doubt I exaggerated greatly the coldness, my mind was not in tune. I was fretful, disappointed, probably weary, no doubt bad tempered, and therefore made a mountain out of a mole hill. Still, the impression left was that there was a coldness. When we were at 12 hours the other day I had made arrangements to have my things ready to come over to Aberdour & was looking forward to a night out of the ship. After 9 months sitting down with the same people it is a real pleasure to get away. But alas, you were so extremely stand-offish [*sic*] on that day & made no such suggestion yourself when I told you I was at 12 hours notice, that I felt I should be very unwelcome and I cancelled everything & went back to the ship. No doubt I was again hypersensitive. I think perhaps in times such as these one is more highly strung, more ready to take offence, in fact, not quite normal. This, doubtless, living your quiet life, you will have difficulty in understanding. I know what a very honest minded person you are & that you cannot play a part, or pretend where you don't feel & I thank God for it. I also recognise that you have a great sense of doing your duty and that you feel it is your duty to do many things you wouldn't do otherwise. This, I appreciate greatly. I *simply hate* to think that you come to the *Sheelah* to lunch, come for a walk, come & play golf with me out of a sense of duty; that truly is worm & gallwood to me & I just cannot bear it. And so many times I feel that is exactly why you do these things. And in the same way, I should hate to think that you are trying to look pleased to see me, trying to be affectionate, trying to put warmth into our companionship from a sense of duty in trying to please. No, dear heart, it must be spontaneous or not at all. If you feel that the old comradeship that existed between us has departed you must say so. You have helped me much in the past and indeed, I am grateful. I have many difficult questions to deal with which occupy very fully my time. I am always at war with the Admiralty & frequently don't see eye to eye with the C-in-C, which causes me many hours of writing, very often fruitless but sometimes productive. I rarely go to bed before 12.30. I tell you this not to try and make myself more important in your eyes, but to show you that my brain is full of many things besides what appears on the surface.

Now, what I should like for the future is for you to do *exactly always* what you wish as to your day. Please do not think that it is ever necessary from a sense of duty for you to do this or that (that I cannot bear). If your feelings have changed towards me, please say so. As I said to the sailors, you have a great courage & a great heart. Do not let us be petty. I can stand anything but that in times such as these. I do not wish in any way whatsoever to dictate to you what you are to do as to your friends, or interfere with them & their relations with you. I trust you absolutely & entirely (I expect the same trust in return) to do always what is right. I sincerely hope that your friends will be my friends.

137. *From his wife*

[BTY/18/23/17–22]   Aberdour House
[3 May 1915]

I am afraid you did not quite understand my letter & believe me it is far from my wish for us to lead different lives & have different friends. I only wanted you to know that if I did like people I wanted you to like them too, just as I always like your friends & put myself out to be pleasant to them, not that it is any effort, but because I like doing so. But it always seemed to me the few times you met Commander Ryan here you were displeased. And I did not like to ask him to come on that account. And as he is a very hard working person & would have enjoyed [– – –] us, it always seemed a pity there had to be an uncomfortable feeling when he came. However, let us not be foolish any more on that subject but let us all be friends together.

As to the cloud, I think a great deal of it has come because, if you say that you are sensitive, I suppose I am *too* & when you first arrived here it seemed to me (I was probably wrong) how much you would have preferred to have remained at Cromarty and not have been bothered with me. Then, another thing, I felt deeply. You never wanted to sit & talk with me but always said you must take long walks. I quite understand that & you must keep fit, that is the most important thing, but I suppose all that hurt in a sort of way & so I got the habit of greeting you in a cold sort of way. At first I felt most keenly every time you went to sea & all the autumn I [–] feel miserable & [—] growing old over it. But one cannot go on like that for ever & it is very much the same sort of thing as the hospital nurse who gets hardened to terrible sights [?]. . . .

I love going & playing golf with you & lunching on the [-] but I have felt too often that I spoil your game because I cannot play more than a certain length of time, and I have annoyed you too often by saying it was cold or some such silly remark. When you have been angry & cross with me I have taken it frightfully to heart & felt I could sit down & cry my soul out. You may say hard things to your Staff, but they do not feel it as they do not care, but you see, I do. You see, other people feel things beside yourself. [Letter incomplete]

138.　*To his wife* [Aberdour House]

[BTY/17/33/28–29]

Lion
4.5.15

Truly I am a beast, thinking all you have [*sic*]. I wonder indeed you spoke to me at all. But, dear heart, I am glad you have voiced & written all you thought, because it gives me an opportunity to not repudiate them but exterminate [?] them.

1st.　I wouldn't let you come to Cromarty? But I ask would it have been just if I had, in view of the fact that I had given orders (strict) that no wives were to be allowed up there at all?

2nd.　I seemed to prefer to remain at Cromarty and not come here and be bothered with you? I did say several times that Cromarty was far preferable to the Firth of Forth as a base, but it never entered my head (and I don't believe yours at the time) that it could have been applied except in purely a naval service point of view. The advantages of one over the other are so obvious that it is no use bothering you by repeating them. Surely dear one, you couldn't dream of thinking that what I said had any connection other than that of a service one.

3rd.　When you come & play golf with me I am frequently angry & rude to you.

4th.　When you don't come but wished to go & skate or go out in a trawler, I dislike it and am disagreeable about it.

Surely I am a pig of pigs and terribly grieved to think that you have put these interpretations on anything I've said. Indeed they were not so meant and you have been truly an angel to bear with anything so abominably poisonous.

5th.　I made myself disagreeable to Commander Ryan and caused an uncomfortable feeling. Surely this last is the strangest and most unjust of all. Why in the wide world should I be rude to the poor man? It isn't my custom to be rude to people without reason. I was under the impression that I had been of some slight service to him and enabled him to get his devices adopted & secured for him his present appointment, which I understood was preferable to his previous one. And really, to think I have been rude to him & made him uncomfortable; no wonder you did not wish me to come to Aberdour for the night & so spoil the evening. And no wonder you don't want to have him there when I am there. But really and truly Tata, isn't it rather far fetched? Is there any justification for such an astounding statement, that he can't come to Aberdour because I am there & has to wait until I am gone and *vice versa*? I can't come there because I make an uncomfortable feeling, and apparently am such an atrocious bad tempered individual that I attack harmless & inoffensive people stopping in your house. Truly I had no idea that I was as bad as all this.

I know my temper is bad & uncertain, but not so bad as this. I apparently seem to be becoming a kind of savage.

139. *To his wife* [Hanover Lodge, Regent's Park]

[BTY/17/33/33–5]   *Lion*
                                                            21.5.15

It seems years since Monday & our visit to the dentist.

We went out for another abortive attempt to find the enemy, which went the way of all our former efforts and when the other ships returned I went North to bring off my long wanted visit to the Commander-in-Chief. I have had two very valuable days with him and much fog has been swept away and I think I have been able to put things to him from a very different point of view to that from which he was accustomed to look at them. Coming as it did at the time that matters reached a climax at the Admiralty, was most fortunate, and I do hope & think that much good will come out of it.

I warned Winston a long time back that if Fisher went to the Admiralty that one of them would have to leave that one would not be Fisher!!!

Thank God it has ended as it has. It would have been a national calamity if Fisher had gone. He is the only man capable of filling the position adequately, and the Navy breathes freer now it is rid of the *succubus* Winston. I know very litttle of what has happened, indeed nothing at all beyond the bare & important fact that a coalition government has been formed and that probably Balfour relieves Winston. I sincerley hope Balfour will remember the substance of our long conversation upon the *Sheelah*.

I saw several old friends at Scapa, gloomy most of them. The most cheerful man there is the Commander-in-Chief, who, thank God, is well, very well and as bright & far seeing as one could wish, but I do wish he were not *so simple* and charitable. It's nice to meet but it's dangerous in times such as these. I heard rumours of terrific casualties and am sick at heart at what the news might bring forth. I don't think dear heart you will ever realise the effect these terrible happenings have upon me. It seems to turn everything upside down in my mind and leave only the one desire, to do something, to destroy, to inflict punishment upon the German breed. And I feel we are so impotent, so incapable of doing anything for lack of opportunity; almost that we are not doing our share & bearing our portion of the burden laid upon the nation. I can hear you say how utterly foolish I am and that it's no use talking to me when I am like that. That does not make it any easier. It is foolish no doubt but can't you understand that this feeling of hopeless inactivity which comes over me from time to time, when we spend days doing nothing when so many are doing so much. At times life is nothing but the desire to accomplish something & the seeming impossibility of being able to do so is like a weight on the end of one's heart, which makes me feel sick at heart as if it had turned into lead.

My dearest Tata, I ask you to bear with me when I am in moods like this. Poisonous I am, I know, unreasonable & altogether impossible. I chafe at the inactivity & think only of all that we might do. I fret at the ineptitude & apparently the scandalous want of energy & zeal on the part of the Authorities, which is so bad that it makes me almost believe anything of them. We could do so much more than we do. Please God, the change of government control will bring about a change. It tickles us all to death that the resuscitated old man of 74 should have brought about the fall of the strongest ministry of all time.

I don't know where you are or what your plans are. Perhaps I shall hear from you when I get in and know where to send this, London, I suppose.

Bless you darling mine. Whatever you may think, whatever I may do, remember that all my heart and thoughts are with you always.

140.   *To his wife* [Aberdour House]

[BTY/17/34/10–11]   *Lion*
                                                                 29.6.15

This is not a [–], I know you hate being bombarded with my
letters, but an apology. Really truly, honestly, if I die tomorrow
I was not angry or annoyed or put out or upset in any possible
way when I came to Aberdour. I had not intended to come at all,
as I tried to explain, and I wish indeed I had not, as I upset you
so, though try to believe me it was not intentional.

Just after I had telephoned that we were at too short a notice
for me to come Aberdour [*sic*] I got orders putting us back. I did
not want to upset your arrangements by telephoning again and as
I was very gloomy I thought I would go for a good tramp, it's the
best thing for me when I get the Blues, which I fear I do rather
too often now. At times our inactivity frets me to such an extent
that I can hardly bear it. The greatest war of all time is proceeding,
the finest deeds of heroism are being performed daily, the dreams
of the past, of glory & achievement are being uprooted & proved
impossible of accomplishment. The country is in such need, the
spirit is so willing, and yet we are doomed to do nothing, achieve
nothing & sit day after day working out schemes that will never
be carried out, endeavouring by pen & paper to impress the
Admiralty with the possibility of our doing something. Even small
things are met with a stone wall. You are quite right, it is infernally
foolish for me to fuss. But you can imagine that it is painful,
humiliating almost [?] to see all the ideals & hopes of one's life
being rent in twain & reduced to nothing. At times I feel I can't
bear it, and I have to preserve a hopeful aspect, to keep on
smiling & saying our time will come, when I feel in my heart that
it never will. Tata dear, do not be too matter of fact, try to
understand me. I would gladly give my life to strike a real blow,
to achieve a real success, to destroy this cursed & poisonous
enemy. I think of nothing else and the futility of it all gives me
the Blues. And then you accuse me of being cross, bad tempered,
saying cutting things, which indeed indeed [*sic*] were far from my
thoughts or intention. I fear this has become an obsession which
[– – –] & caused you to acquire an antipathy to me.

I had got rid of this devil, or thought I had, perhaps he left a
mark behind & made me look bad tempered, cross, what you
will. Truly I am not fit for the society of anybody but those who

have got to be with me, or the antipathy will grow into an active and permanent dislike.

But, if you can believe me, I had not a disagreeable thought in my head when I came into your room this afternoon.

Do not trouble to answer this. I am sorry to bore you with it but I must try for my own sake to kill this perpetual idea that I am bad tempered (which I so often am) & love [?] making disagreeable & cutting remarks to hurt your feelings. It is not true really & truly it isn't. I express myself badly perhaps, but to hurt your feelings is the last thing in the world I wish to do.

Try & believe me.

P.S.   Thank you dear heart for the flowers. My cabin looks quite different.

141.   *To Hamilton*

[HTN/117]   *Lion*
                                                                      21.7.15

Do you think you could secure an expression of Their Lordships' appreciation etc for my Secretary with regard to the success achieved in bagging U–40?[1]

The scheme was entirely his, worked out to the smallest detail by him, every one of which was adopted and is in use now. I understand that you rewarded with DSOs and DCM the officers concerned in the carrying out of the operation and sent an expression of appreciation to others concerned with it, but nothing has come the way of the originator of the idea.

It would be of great value generally & of great assistance to me in keeping up the interest & enthusiasm in my little lot if Their Lordships could see their way to recognise the value of everybody giving his whole thought to the furtherance of the destruction of the enemy, by saying they were pleased in this case. At present it is assumed because an officer is of the Accountant Branch or other non-Executive branch that it doesn't matter.

But in the B.C.F. *everybody* digs out & thinks. Doctors, Chap-

---

[1] U–40 had been sunk on 23 June 1915 by a trawler and submarine working together.

lains and Paymasters as much as the others, and generally speaking they would appreciate that their efforts are recognised if, when they did something to deserve it, they received some mark of Their Lordships' satisfaction. This, I know you will readily recognise and the value contained in it.

Spickernell is a very bright and able officer, who, you may remember, I asked to have confirmed in his acting rank, but which was not concurred in. So, I hope you will be able to do this for me. . . .

142. *To his wife* [Brooksby Hall]

[BTY/17/34/13–15]   *Lion*
                                                                    30.7.15

. . .

No news from Packs. I had been hoping to have a bleat from him and kept everybody ready to move at short notice, but the bleat never came and he'll be back in the morning and another effort will be wasted and another opportunity, which are becoming so deadly rare, will fade away into nothing. There are times when I feel I can't bear it, and I cannot show it. The monotony of this deadly waiting is truly refined torture.

Now I am beginning to grumble and you'll see no real reason for it. . . .

I hope dear heart that I have not in the past month or so given you any further cause for unhappiness and am playing my part better. You must give me a little more time to get accustomed to the new conditions and your changed feelings.

You see, in the past you have spoilt me horribly & have given me so much love and sympathy that it is difficult to realise that I must do without it. It is unfortunate (for me) that it should come at a time when one can do with so much more. No doubt when the war is over and if we are still alive, I shall be able to secure as much as anybody could want, but this pressing need for it will have passed. However, let me impress upon you that I am really [–] to the altered conditions, that I in no way wish to monopolise your entire life, that I have no wish to be the orbit against your will around which everything will revolve, to be the centre of your

278 THE BEATTY PAPERS

efforts to live, as you put it, and makes me a horribly selfish egotistical person.

I truly am not that really. I know you did not mean to imply that I was, but that is what it came to. That is altered for ever. I realise you like to be more independent & indeed am thankful for it, and all I ask & wish is that you should do exactly what you wish at all times. All I truly care for is that you should be happy & contented. . . .

I have read the Archbishop's letter to the Fleet. I do not agree with you that he has laid the butter on too thick. It is not butter, he doesn't turn them into heroes or make them into superior beings. He simply states the plain facts and they are simple enough, but when represented in simple language it comes rather as a surprise to the inarticulate ones.

I fear you get your views from your invisible friend Ryan, and they are not quite just. It is true that for 12 months the Fleet has been enduring the strain of *immediate readiness* for battle. For the 1st 5 months we were constantly at sea. We had no harbours secure from danger. We were constantly in foul weather, moving at high speed without a light to show where our next door neighbour was. Anyone who had any idea of what Fleet work was would readily recognise that the strain & the risk of moving these monsters about was considerable. As the A.B. put it, we had all the strain and responsibilities of war without the thrill of battle, & one might well add, with the quite possible prospect of being sent into the next world by the agency of the mine or torpedo from the submarine. All that was welcomed, & I think can truly say was far preferable to the subsequent six months during which the inactivity has added a burden far harder to bear than the over-activity of the 1st period. You judge everything in the Fleet by me. I am having a perfectly easy & comfortable time. Not so the men. They haven't their wives & families here. They can't go ashore. They are, as a fact, allowed ashore for a march for 2½ hours in one day out of 8. They are almost in sight of their homes, but they can't go. And yet their spirit of cheerfulness is wonderful. They have played the game and they might so easily have not done so. And, if I ask them to do a big thing, I know that I can depend on them. They have not performed heroic deeds as their brothers have in Flanders or Gallipoli, but they can and will when the time comes. If you think of what the fact of being immediately ready for battle means in mind & spirit, as well as in organis-ation & detail, you will easily recognise that it is not a frame of mind or condition of life that one wants to dwell in for longer than can be helped, and one would be glad to relax. No, my dear, I don't think the Archbishop over-stated the case for the sailor. If applied to me and the Captains perhaps, yes, but not to the men of whom he was talking.

Now I have written enough. It is a horrid east wind, cold & damp, probably the forerunner of a fog but damnation unpleasant. Hug my two boys for me. I hope they are happy and glad to be back.

Take care of yourself & don't do too much to tire yourself. Have a good time and come back soon.

143.   *To Jellicoe*

[BTY/13/21/22]   *Lion*
[Copy]   12/8/15

My dear Commander-in-Chief,

Thank you very much for yours, and the remarks on the War Game, and on my paper — Lessons learnt from the War Game. Might I say at once that I know, and indeed the whole fleet knows, that of all people, you are more fully alive to the increasing menace of the new weapons that are likely to be mustered on the field of battle by the enemy than anybody else. I thank God for it. My remarks were intended to impress it upon others. I am *not* a pessimist, and the difficulty is to strike the happy mean between being unduly optimistic, and the natural tendency to appear pessimistic, when pointing out the difficulties we shall have to contend with.

But is the Admiralty fully alive to the disadvantages under which you will have to give battle? I fear greatly they are not.

What does it amount to?

We have the gun, with a possible superiority which we are entitled to keep up our sleeve.

They have the gun, *plus* the Zeppelin by which they obtain earlier and more definite information as to our whereabouts, strength, movements, etc, — *plus* a superiority in the number of torpedo craft and torpedoes, — *plus* minelayers to which the Zeppelin information will be invaluable – *plus* a considerable number of submarines which the War Games have indicated can be made to attain without difficulty really good tactical positions from which to attack.

Against the Zeppelin, I fear from what you say our position is not likely to improve for some little time. But no doubt even in this matter you will be able to achieve something.

The superiority in torpedo craft will I trust gradually disappear; and before long we will produce an equality in numbers to the enemy, as most certainly ours possess a superiority in quality. I am a very firm believer in getting our T.B.D. attack with the *torpedo* in first, which would place them admirably for frustrating a counter attack of enemy craft. On the other hand, I believe that if the enemy torpedo craft attack first, ours would never get into a position in sufficient time to enable them to frustrate it. The moral effect of the first attack with these vessels, I think, will be very great, and reflect very considerably upon the subsequent phases of the battle.

Minelayers, it is truly a misfortune that we do not possess an efficient and reliable type of mine in sufficient quantities.

The submarine appears to me the most important question of all.

Your request for some to be stationed at the Tyne would meet the case. The Admiralty simply *must* provide them. What do they do now, they have accomplished nothing. They would be just as available for the work they are employed upon from the Tyne or Humber as they are at Harwich.

The idea that they will be used by the Admiralty to intercept the German Fleet on its return, i.e. *after* a grand action, is inconceivable. Surely all vessels should be at the disposal of the Commander-in-Chief, who has got to fight the great action, rather than the Admiralty *after* we have suffered for the want of them. Surely the value of the submarine will be far greater at the commencement and during an action than it will be after it is over. To be decisive all weapons must be used at the right moment at the same time.

It seems positively foolish that we are deliberately arranging for one of our most important classes of vessel, whose destructive power should be enormous, to come into action only <u>after</u> the battle has been fought.

Does the Admiralty anticipate that they will turn a German victory into a defeat?

I know that on all the large questions we are of the same opinion.

I feel so strongly on them that I think it is imperative that the Admiralty should be induced to see them from the same point of view.

Writing seems so futile, and apparently only causes annoyance. Will they not discuss these questions personally with you?

Could I not be there to support you?

Decisive victory is the only thing to aim at. To achieve which has fallen to few men in the World's history of naval warfare.

Nothing but decisive victory can be considered, therefore what is the use of the Admiralty considering the employment of submarines *after* we have failed to achieve it.

We must utilize every weapon we possess, concentrated at the right spot, at the right time, in the greatest possible strength to achieve decisive victory. Unless we do this we shall be boiled — and deserve to be.

In view of your 1437 of 13th, I wired asking for opportunity of doing subcalibre and full calibre practice with one Battle-Cruiser Squadron at a time North of 62°N, and West of 3°W. We must keep our Gunnery up; our opportunities here are nil. As it is at present, it is our only asset.

I propose that the *Invincible* shall proceed to Newcastle to dock at the Tyne after the *Canada* in the floating dock, some time first week in September, if you would approve. Power, Captain Superintendent, tells me this will be convenient. She would be in dock 6 days.

You did not state definitely that battle-cruisers on being docked should *not* give leave to their ships' companies.

I understand, of course, that it is invidious that one class should get more leave than another, and in the case of the *Invincible* they had a good whack as recently as May. But in some cases they have had only 48 hours and have *not* visited their Home Ports and so enjoyed the chances of night leave.

The mining in the Moray Firth was an audacious and successful enterprise.[1] I only wonder they have not done it before and outside here. If we only had more torpedo craft!!!

Please don't over do yourself. You are our only hope and must take care of yourself.

---

[1] Probably laid by *Meteor*; she had been scuttled on her way home after interception by Tyrwhitt's forces on 9 August.

I am writing in a hurry to catch the messenger, so please excuse the scrawl.

Yours for ever,
David Beatty

144. *To Hamilton*

[HTN/117]

Lion
25.8.15

Thank you for yours which I found here on my return, and for what you have tried to do for my Secretary. I have adopted your suggestion and sent in a Service letter. No doubt there are many claimants.

But *it is* a *fact* that we had been at war for a matter of 10 months before anything was done in this matter, and then on the actual scheme evolved by Spickernell, although Captain Haggard had had nothing else to think about, as a matter of fact he was opposed to the idea, being like most N.O.s a conservative person & opposed to innovations. That is why I came into the hunt and personally took it to Lowry, who took it up. The details worked out by Haggard did not exist. There weren't any. It was just a question of common sense to take the S.M. in tow, and depended upon the submarine officer. It was when I was informed that Haggard had been commended for his initiative etc that I thought, that if anybody should receive credit, it was the originator of the idea, and not the man who sat there through ten months of war and evolved [?] nothing, and was quite prepared to sit through another 10 months. Why some of these fellows don't burst with the desire to do something, beats me. . . .

145. *To Asquith*

[BTY/5/2/2]

Lion
3rd February 1916

I have just left the Commander-in-Chief, whom I have not seen for five months, and left him so perturbed and despondent about the delays in new construction that I feel impelled to write to you, privately on matters which I feel to be of the greatest importance.

The Admiralty I understand are powerless to prevent the depletion of the ship building yards of labour which goes away daily to supplement the making of munitions, with the result that the programme of completing destroyers and light cruisers and battle-cruisers has been thrown back four to eight months. No doubt you are aware of this, and have been duly informed by the Admiralty. But what you cannot be aware of is the very serious view of the situation taken by the Commander-in-Chief, which I feel is of national importance and so take the liberty of calling your attention to it.

A year ago the Commander-in-Chief was oppressed with the knowledge that should we be fortunate enough to meet the German Fleet it would be with a considerable numerical inferiority in destroyers, but he was buoyed up with the idea that by Christmas 1915 with the great additions that had been projected this inferiority would disappear.

In the meantime, we have no knowledge of what the enemy have done in the matter of increasing their destroyer force. But we do know that they are quick to learn and apply the lessons of the war; therefore we can be assured that they have made great additions to their destroyer force and that most certainly, from their experience gained in the various actions they have fought during the War, they will have built and turned out destroyers the equal of ours in speed and gun power. Whereas we are practically six months behind our programme.

In light cruisers also, delays are great. Amongst other duties, they are to the Grand Fleet what Zeppelins are to the High Sea Fleet, and it is imperative that nothing should be allowed to prevent our Fleet being provided with a full supply of them. The light cruiser is our antidote to the Zeppelin and by using a sufficiency of them we can curtail the discovery of the position, composition and disposition of our Fleet. We thereby limit the successful use of enemy minelayers and prevent the enemy submarines acquiring information which would be invaluable to enable them to reach a most favourable position for attacking our Grand Fleet. Later, the light cruiser causes them to submerge and thereby reduces their radius of action and dislocates their pre-arranged plans. Again, our light cruisers operating against those of the enemy will drive them in and prevent them from obtaining the necessary and valuable information desired by the enemy Fleet to enable him to obtain the best tactical position. Finally, in view of our inferiority in numbers of destroyers, the light cruiser is the principle protection to our Fleet against enemy T B D attack. Consequently, considering the various functions and duties, all essential, that have to be performed by our light cruisers it is obvious that delay in completion and delivery is a matter to cause grave concern to those who have to be dependent upon them.

In battle-cruisers the situation is also urgent and pressing. It is not necessary for me to go into the proved enormous value of this type of vessel. It is sufficient to state that since August 1914 we have added one battle-cruiser to our strength, i.e. the *Tiger*, whereas the enemy has added three, i.e. *Derfflinger, Lützow* and *Hindenburg*. Again — this year, and possibly at an early date, the enemy will complete two more, i.e. *Ersatz Victoria Luise* and *Ersatz Freya*, and surely it must be wise to calculate on the possibilities as well as probabilities when our information is practically nil. Against this further addition of two, we have two under construction which owing to the shortage of labour are becoming delayed indefinitely and therefore must not be expected before the end of the year. So if this depletion of labour continues the situation before the end of the year may very well stand as follows:

German		British
Ersatz Freya		*Tiger*
Ersatz Victoria Luise	} 15-inch	*Lion*
Hindenburg		*Queen Mary*
Lützow		*Princess Royal*
Derfflinger		*Australia*
Seydlitz		*Indefatigable*
Moltke		*New Zealand*
Von Der Tann		*Indomitable*
		Invincible
		Inflexible

On paper it will no doubt appear that ten British battle-cruisers should be able to deal with eight German. This would be so, even though the Germans are of later date and more heavily armed, but the crux of any tactical encounter lies in the fact that a slow ship cannot catch a fast one.

By comparison, the 3 *Invincible* class are no better to us than battleships — they can never get into action if the enemy decides not to permit them to. If the enemy avoid the tactical error they made on 24th January 1915, and decide to leave the *Von der Tann* in harbour, it then becomes impossible for the 3 *Australia*[1] class to get into action. This leaves the Germans with 7 fast battle-cruisers, four of them armed with eight 15-inch or possibly 17-inch guns, to our 4 battle-cruisers armed with 13.5-inch. Owing to the necessity for docking and sending men on leave, one battle-cruiser refitting may well leave us with only 3 of adequate speed.

Therefore again it is demonstrated that it is absolutely necessary that delays caused by shortage of labour should not be permitted to interfere with the completion of our two new battle-cruisers, so as to ensure their delivery before the enemy acquire their additional two and be so placed in a position of considerable superiority.

I make no mention of the freak ships which with no defensive power and greatly reduced offensive (only 4 guns) could not be expected to engage successfully a heavily armoured ship with double their offensive power, though under fortunate circumstances they might be of considerable value. But I would point out that if *Lion*, on 24th January 1915, had not had protection from 7″ and 9″ of armour, which burst the projectiles, it is probable that she would have been destroyed.

No remedy can avert the risks we are now accumulating unless immediate action is taken to prevent delays in construction. Also, I am not presenting to you new or controversial opinions, but merely supporting the views of all Sea Officers, and most certainly those of the Commander-in-Chief. No doubt the heads of the Admiralty will have made similar representations to you, but I feel that I must bring to your notice from personal knowledge how gravely this responsibility is weighing on the Commander-in-Chief and how deeply he feels about it.

Further, I am very directly involved in the problem. We have still no destroyers that can keep pace with the battle-cruisers in a sea way, and on asking the Commander-in-Chief for the flotilla promised me in December he replied that I might get it in April. On having my command reduced by two light cruisers, he sent me one temporarily to replace them, and pointed out that delays in ship building made it impossible to do more. On the subject of fast battle-cruisers, as on other points, he fully agrees that we urgently need more.

I feel sure that the Admiralty will agree also and that I am only

---

[1] *Australia, Indefatigable* and *New Zealand*; because of lack of speed.

expressing what they also would say. But the final responsibility for fighting and winning battles must rest with the Sea Officers alone. They desire, as the whole nation desires, that when we fight the result should be decisive and overwhelming. This can be done if the ship yards give us punctually the new construction promised, and it is for this reason that I have felt it my duty to write to you. My letter is of course quite unofficial but I know that, as the leader of the nation, you would wish to have matters which must be vital brought to your notice no matter from what source it may come. More especially as I recognise that the subject is one on which my Commander-in-Chief feels so strongly, I shall send him a copy of what I have written to you as I think that is only right. I offer no apology for the length of this screed.

146. *From Rear-Admiral Brock*

[BTY/5/2/3]   SECRET   *Princess Royal*
                                            18 February 1916

The following remarks are based on the existing distribution of the Grand Fleet:-
     Battle Fleet at Scapa
     Battle-Cruiser Fleet of Rosyth
On receipt of information that the German Fleet has left its base, there are two courses of action open to the Commander-in-Chief–
     I.   Order B C F to get into touch with the enemy as soon as posible.
     II.   Concentrate with the whole fleet — including B C F — at some position in North Sea.
The first course appears to be most likely, taking into consideration that the earliest information of enemy movements will refer to their Scouting Groups, and the B C F would in consequence be ordered to sea at once. The B C F will be longer at sea, steam at higher speed and for a greater distance than the Battle Fleet. It is therefore essential that the accompanying light cruisers and destroyers should be of the type most suitable for these objects. This is not the case at present, especially as regards destroyers, and the substitution of a flotilla of the latest 'M' type for the present 1st Flotilla is clearly indicated.
The German battle-cruisers now number six, of which all

excepting perhaps the *Von der Tann* are faster than the *New Zealand* and *Invincible* classes. (This is, I think, quite certain notwithstanding the speeds given in Part II, Quarterly Return of War Vessels; moreover it must not be overlooked that the German vessels come out with clean bottoms and with their coal storage reduced to the minimum required for the intended operation.)

They have the advantage of the strategical offensive and can be in full force with submarines and minelayers in known positions.

It follows that we cannot bring them to action except on their own terms, unless we meet them in a particularly fortunate situation, such as between them and their Battle Fleet; even then the superior German speed would soon reverse our initial tactical advantage.

The Germans will probably adopt similar tactics to those of 24th January, i.e., a retreating action, and it is unlikely that they will commit the mistake a second time of sending the battle-cruisers beyond supporting distance of the Battle Fleet.

The B C F will therefore have to be extremely careful not to be drawn on top of the enemy's Battle Fleet, and must be prepared to withdraw at any moment unless our Battle Fleet is near – an unlikely condition in view of the considerations in paragraph 1.

In the action indicated above, the 4 *Lions*[1] are the only ships likely to be engaged, and in view of the superiority of the enemy no result can be expected; if anything the damage is likely to be on our side, and one or more ships may be reduced in speed. Under these circumstances i.e., the proximity of the German Battle Fleet, we may have to fight a retreating action under considerable disabilities, and the question arises whether the existing composition of the B C F is the best suited to meet all emergencies.

In my opinion the substitution of three, or even two, *Queen Elizabeths* for the three *Invincibles* would be a great improvement; the *Queen Elizabeths* are better protected, more heavily armed, and the difference in speed is not great. With two *Queen Elizabeths*, it would be possible to fight a withdrawing action with every prospect of success, and the probability of having to abandon ships with reduced speed would be much lessened.

The *Invincibles* can perform the duty of attacking the head of

---

[1] *Lion, Princess Royal, Queen Mary* and *Tiger.*

the enemy's battle line as satisfactorily as the *Queen Elizabeth*s, and if only two *Queen Elizabeth*s were attached to the B C F, it would leave a fast squadron for each end of the line, viz, three *Invincible*s and three *Queen Elizabeth*s.

The question to some extent resolves itself into a decision between the relative importance of the Battle Fleet and the Battle-Cruiser Fleet. Undoubtedly the ultimate command of the sea will rest with the result of the action between the Battle Fleets, but if the Germans established a superiority in battle-cruisers by defeating ours, they would continue their present policy of avoiding an action between the main fleets and use their fast ships to menace our trade, raid coast ports etc, and we should be unable to reply.

The conclusion is that, until the new battle-cruisers are ready, redistribution of our forces is necessary on the following lines:-

1. Substitute three *Queen Elizabeth*s for three *Invincible*s in the Battle-Cruiser Fleet.
2. Light cruisers with the Battle-Cruiser Fleet to be the best available.
3. A flotilla of the latest type of destroyers to be attached to the Battle-Cruiser Fleet.

147. *From Rear-Admiral Pakenham*

[BTY/5/2/3]   *Australia*
H.1.   19 February 1916

Reinforcement of Battle-Cruiser Fleet

Sir,

Circulation of the programme of British naval construction having rendered it possible to compare the relative powers of the opposed fleets, I have the honour to submit certain conclusions, which I hope may not be considered incompatible with the efficient performance of the prime duty of the Grand Fleet.

I. That the British Battle-Cruiser Fleet is in grave need of reinforcement by fast and powerful units.

Or, alternatively, that fleet strategy should be changed.

II. That the Battle-Cruiser Fleet requires the attendance of light cruisers faster than the *Town* class,[1] and of destroyers of the greatest speed and endurance.

I

Heavy ships

1. With reduction of her Battle-Cruiser Fleet to definite inferiority, Great Britain would have lost a most important factor in command of the sea. Indeed, it is probable that Germany would then have gained a position whence she could dictate terms of peace to this Empire.

2. British preponderance in heavy vessels of speeds around 20 knots has hitherto confined the German main fleet to the southern part of the North Sea; but owing to the distances which now separate British from German naval bases, no preponderance in slow vessels can enable the British to deny the Germans freedom to move at will their whole fleet in any direction within about 200 miles of Heligoland.

3. Within this considerable area, the Germans can execute any rapid fleet operation without much prospect of serious interruption by enemy surface vessels. It is true that on 24th January 1915 the Germans threw out an inadequate and unsupported force, but it should be accepted that they will not again commit this hazardous strategical blunder; and hence also it should be presumed that future operations will be conducted in consonance with military prudence, and that the fullest support will always be at hand.

4. The probability that this is the German attitude indicates the strategical utilisation of our fleet. It has been customary to employ the fast division at great distances ahead of the main fleet; but unless control of the southern area is practically to be abandoned to the Germans, either the method of employing our fast division must be continued, or the distance between the opposed bases must be reduced. Of these courses the former is preferred, provided that the precautions here advocated are considered feasible.

5. The only conditions in which the present method can be continued in safety are that our fast fleet shall have an indisputable

---

[1] *Southampton, Birmingham, Lowestoft* and *Nottingham* of Goodenough's squadron.

superiority of fighting power. It is desirable that this shall be so decisive that the Germans will never be willing to encounter it; but it is vital that it shall be sufficiently great to guarantee that in all possible circumstances our fast division will be able to break off engagement and withdraw without being exposed to great loss. Power to attack is desirable; but power to withdraw is essential. The former requires only superiority in speed; the latter can be satisfied by vessels which, though not the fastest, are yet faster than the bulk of their opponents, and of greater fighting power than all which can overtake a squadron hampered by the duty of safeguarding the retreat of wounded comrades.

6. Let us now examine the condition, present and in the near future, of the rival fleets, in so far as it is either known or surmised. The tables on the last pages of this paper shew the British slow fleet has a great and growing preponderance of numbers and weapons. They also shew that the situation of the fast fleet is by no means so reassuring. Its superiority is doubtful in the present; while in the future, diminution of relative fighting power seems inevitable unless remedy is found and applied.

7. The battleship tables require no comment. Turning to those of the battle-cruisers it will be remarked that the German list is headed by three very fast powerful vessels, which may be armed with 15″ guns. It is true that the British are superior in number, but if defensive armour is taken into account, it will be found that six of the British ships have little armour protection, and that even the best protected have armour of less thickness than the *Moltke*, possibly even than the *Von der Tann*. It must also be remembered that one of the British vessels, perhaps one of the best, may be undergoing refit, a deduction to which the German force is not liable.

8. The list of battle-cruisers building also shews formidable vessels will be added to the German force at no distant date, and rumour gives these additions guns of calibre larger than 15″. On the British side only two vessels are promised, neither of them to be available for some time, and, unless wrongly stated, neither carrying an effective area or thickness of defensive armour.

9. It has already been pointed out that power to break off an engagement ranks next in importance to power to defeat an enemy. But the possession by Germany of so many vessels superior to our best both in speed and power warns us that we shall be able to do neither the one nor the other, unless some change is made in the present relation of battle-cruiser forces.

The question then is — How can the Battle-Cruiser Fleet best be reinforced? The tables appear to furnish a ready reply. A fast and powerful squadron is there shewn as attached to the main fleet. It would be yet better for our purpose if its speed were greater; but its fighting power is all that can be desired. As the prime need of the Battle-Cruiser Fleet is an addition of fighting strength, it is deemed that at least three of the *Queen Elizabeth*s should be at once transferred from the main fleet to the Battle-Cruiser Fleet, and that the others should follow when the *Royal Sovereign*s have come into service.

10. Again I say that although attack may be optional, where the force attacked will almost certainly be very strongly supported, possibly be vessels of great power and with speeds not greatly less than those of our fast division, the scientific justification for initiating and pressing home an attack must be based on possession of force strong enough to assure that withdrawal shall not be disastrous. The Battle-Cruiser Fleet therefore cannot be made too strong.

11. Although during an operation fast vessels attached to the main fleet can seldom reinforce the fast advanced fleet, it will almost always be possible for the latter to fall back upon the former. Thus, while the measure advocated would guarantee the safety and greatly enhance the power of the advanced fleet, it is possible that the proposed redistribution would not be detrimental to the battle efficiency of the main body.

12. Though it is thought they had better remain where they are, the *Invincible*s might be transferred to the Battle Fleet, if their speed would render them useful.

13. It is possible that even while agreeing that our fast fleet has not the requisite strength, it may be decided that neither can it be adequately reinforced, nor can the base of the Grand Fleet be advanced to the Forth. As the fast division could not then operate in reasonable safety on the lines hitherto customary, its movements at sea would be restricted to the neighbourhood of the Grand Fleet, or of considerable detachment from it.

II

Light cruisers and destroyers

14. My final submission is so closely related to the first that separate argument could only result in repetition. Moreover it is believed that this part of the case has already been conceded.

15. As speed makes no difference in the principles on which sea battles should be conducted, these principles should be applied whenever circumstances permit. When battle fleets enter action, squadrons of light cruisers and flotillas of destroyers are required for certain duties, one essential to the performance of which demands from these vessels the possession of speed greater than that of the main body. If battle-cruisers were faster than existing light vessels, it is evident that such attendance would often be unnecessary, and must frequently be impossible. But, in ordinary weather, the highest speeds belong to light vessels already existing in considerable numbers. Unfortunately the fastest light vessels are already absorbed by other duties, while of those attached to the battle-cruisers many are both too slow to maintain their proper relative stations, and of endurance unequal to their task. Here again, redistribution is considered to be urgently necessary.

SLOW FLEET

*BRITISH   GERMAN
BUILT

Class	Broadside	Class	Broadside
†5 Queen Elizabeth	8 — 15"	2 Worth	8 — 15"
1 Canada	10 — 14"	4 Markgraf	10 — 12"
1 Erin		5 Kaiser	10 — 12"
4 Benbow	10 — 13.5"	4 Heligoland	8 — 12"
3 King George V	10 — 13.5	4 Nassau	8 — 11"
4 Orion	10 — 13.5		
1 Agincourt	14 — 12"		
2 Colossus	8 — 12"		
1 Neptune	8 — 12"		
3 St Vincent	8 — 12"		
3 Bellerophon	8 — 12"		
1 Dreadnought	8 — 12"		

TOTAL

BRITISH		GERMAN
29	—Ships	— 19
	Guns:	
40	—15"	— 16
10	—14"	——
160	—13.5"	——

94	—12″	—122
–	– 11″	– 32

29	– Ships	– 19
304	– Heavy Guns	– 170

*One ship would be absent refitting
†Temporarily classed as battleships

TO BE COMPLETED SOON

BRITISH	GERMAN
3 *Royal Sovereign* 8–15″	1 *Worth* 8–15″ or larger

FAST FLEET

	*British			German		

BUILT

Class	Broadside	Armour	Class	Broadside	Armour
2 *Queen Mary*	8—13.5″	9/4	1 *Hindenberg*	6—15″	13/4
2 *Lion*	8—13.5″	9/4	1 *Lützow*	or	13/4
3 *Indefatigable*	8—12″	6/4	1 *Derfflinger*	8—12″	13/4
3 *Invincible*	6—12″	6/4	1 *Seydlitz*	10—11″	11/4
			1 *Moltke*	10—11″	11/4
			1 *Von der Tann*	8–11″	10/7

*One ship would be absent refitting

TO BE COMPLETED SOON

British					
1 *Repulse*	6—15″	5″	2 *Hindenberg*	6—15″ or 8—12″	13/4

148. *To Jellicoe*

[BTY/5/2/3]   *Lion*
[Copy]   21st February 1916

Reinforcement of the Battle-Cruiser Fleet

I

Submitted. As regards (I), I entirely concur in the opinions and deductions of Rear Admiral Pakenham.

Having regard to the relative strengths of the British and German Battle-Cruiser Forces, and the fact that, profiting by their experience of 24th January 1915, they will probably be closely supported by a portion of the High Sea Fleet in any future ventures, I am very much impressed by the desirability of revising the dispositions of our faster units.

2. To this end I respectfully suggest that the Fifth Battle Squadron should be based on Rosyth instead of the Third Battle Squadron. They would then be in a position to afford support to my Fleet in secondary operations, giving us a definite superiority over anything less than the High Sea Fleet.

For operations preliminary to a general action they could perform similar functions and should yet be available to assume the position assigned to them in your Battle Orders when the Main Fleets gain contact.

3. By this disposition, I submit, the maximum use would be made of their superior speed under all circumstances. They would be available to carry out all the duties now required of them, with others of the greatest value in addition.

4. As regards (II), I think that the superior armament of the later *Town* class compensates for their lack of the highest speed, making them suitable units of the Battle-Cruiser Fleet. This, however, is not the case with the *Bristol*[1] class, whose deficiency in speed is not redeemed by superior armament. These ships should, I submit, be relieved in Home Waters by vessels of the *Chatham* class.[2]

I have previously urged that the number of light cruisers in this Fleet should be increased to thirteen, in order that the front may not be unduly restricted by the absence of one refitting. The

---

[1] *Bristol, Glasgow, Gloucester, Liverpool* and *Newcastle*.
[2] *Chatham, Dublin, Sydney, Melbourne* and *Brisbane*.

advent of the special light cruisers now building will improve the situation.

5. You are already acquainted with my views on the matter of destroyers. The operation which took place on 11th February emphasised very clearly the lack of speed and the small radius of action of the First Flotilla. It was necessary to send them in to fuel after 24 hours. They are the oldest and slowest flotilla now working with the Grand Fleet.

149.   *From Jellicoe*

[BTY/5/2/3]   [*Iron Duke*]
                                                   24th February 1916

I have received your minute BCF 016 of the 21st February, 1916, forwarding a letter from the Rear Admiral Commanding, Second Battle-Cruiser Squadron, No H1 of the 19th February, 1916, and am forwarding the correspondence to the Admiralty, together with a copy of my remarks on it.

2. In regard to the strength of the battle-cruisers, I think the proposal in paragraph 2 of your minute is based on a misapprehension of the speed of the Fifth Battle Squadron. The ships composing this squadron have not carried out any measured mile trials, but, so far as it is possible to arrive at a conclusion without measured mile trials, I have formed the opinion that their maximum speed, with the fuel on board which they would probably have on leaving port, does not greatly exceed 23½ knots. It is certainly less than 24 knots.

3. Under these conditions, I am very doubtful whether the Fifth Battle Squadron would, as suggested by you, afford any material support to the battle-cruisers in an offensive operation.

4. The danger with which we shall be faced when the *Lützow* and *Hindenberg* join the First Scouting Group is that our Battle-Cruiser Fleet will be unable to bring them to action, owing to the high speed of the German vessels. For this purpose, the Fifth Battle Squadron would be of no assistance.

5. If the First Scouting Group is supported by the German Third Battle Squadron, and it would certainly not be supported by anything less than this squadron if supported at all, the Fifth Battle Squadron as at present constituted, would not be a match

for this support, whereas, in the event of the Battle-Cruiser Fleet meeting this support, they would in any case be forced to retire.

6. It is unquestionably true that the First Scouting Group possesses a very marked superiority in regard to protection over our battle-cruisers. There is, in fact, no comparison in this respect. On the other hand, it must not be forgotten that, allowing the *Hindenberg* and *Lützow* to have eight 15-inch guns on a broadside, and allowing for one of our battle-cruisers being absent, we still possess a broadside of 66 to 68 guns to the German 52, and, as a whole, our guns are heavier than the German.

7. I have had the question considered of the effect on the *Lützow* of substituting 15-inch guns for 12-inch. The additional weight involved would certainly total 1,500 tons. This might be in some degree met by a reduction in the amount of fuel carried. If it were not so met, the increase in draft would be approximately 15 inches, with the corresponding reduction in speed, and the decrease in metacentric height would be probably about one foot, but owing to the great beam of the ships there would still be ample stability. There is, therefore, apparently no insuperable objection to the substitution of the heavier guns, and it is a question which we must face.

8. Undoubtedly, with the advent of these two vessels, the German First Scouting Group will be able to carry out raids against our coast with a very good chance of our being powerless to prevent such raids, mainly because of the high speed possessed by the German vessels, more especially if the *Von der Tann* is left behind, but I fear that the addition of the 5th Battle Squadron to the Battle-Cruiser Fleet would in no way assist to prevent such an operation. It is an unfortunate result of our policy of abandoning the construction of battle-cruisers, and substituting for battle-cruisers vessels of the *Queen Elizabeth* class.

9. In regard to the question of light cruisers, raised in paragraph 4 of your minute, the Admiralty inform me that the *Dublin* will relieve the *Lowestoft*, and the *Chatham* will relieve the *Falmouth*, but no relief has been detailed for the *Gloucester*, owing, as I understand it, to the impossibility of bringing home from abroad any more light cruisers.

10. In regard to paragraph 5, you are aware of the intention to form the 13th Flotilla based on Rosyth as soon as the 12th Flotilla is complete. I am, as you know, most fully in agreement with you as to the dangers which we run from the inadequate numbers of our destroyer flotillas.

II

BCF 016
Rear Admiral W. C. Pakenham, CB, MVO,
HMAS *Australia*
I should be glad to see you on this subject at your convenience.

DAVID BEATTY
Vice Admiral

Lion
28th February, 1916

150. *To Jellicoe*

[BTY/5/2/3]   SECRET   *Lion*
BCF 016   3 March 1916

In reply to your communication HF 0010/113 of 24th February, while recognising the existence of the limitations that you specify, I venture to submit the following remarks.

2. Paragraphs 2 and 3 of your communication question the value of the 5th Battle Squadron as support to the battle-cruisers on account of their lack of speed. I submit that even if they are unable, when leaving port, to do more than 23½ knots, their value would be enormous. It is however assumed that with a considerable reduction of their fuel on board, say by 1000 tons, it would so reduce their draught as to enable them to acquire the speed for which they were designed, i.e. 25 knots — equal to the 3rd Battle-Cruiser Squadron.

3. It might be said that this would reduce their radius of action to a dangerous extent. Against this I would submit that, being based at Rosyth, 100 miles nearer the probable scene of operations, this point is not of vital importance in an area restricted to the North Sea, and that in any case it would provide them with sufficient fuel to enable them to last at 20 knots for approximately the same time as the ships of the Battle-Cruiser Fleet.

4. Past experience shows that they would in all cases be able to keep with us until the moment when we sight the enemy. If we are then East of the enemy, the 5th Battle Squadron would be invaluable. Taking the worst case, we may be West of them and may have a long chase at full speed. After chasing for three hours,

i.e. a distance of at least 75 miles, the 5th Battle Squadron with their 23½ knots would then be at most 4½ miles astern of the 3rd Battle-Cruiser Squadron. I can imagine no better or more valuable support.

5. If the enemy battle-cruisers were supported by the High Sea Fleet, it would be necessary to retire, but even in this case the presence of the 5th Battle Squadron, with their speed greater than enemy forces, except battle-cruisers, would enable us to fight a rear guard action with great chances of causing considerable damage to the enemy and in any case the speed of our force would enable us to extricate ourselves from a position in which a slower force might be seriously involved.

6. If on the other hand the enemy were supported as suggested in your paragraph 5, by their 3rd Battle Squadron, it is possible that our retirement might be prudent, depending upon considerations at the time, i.e. time of day, geographical position, distance of the Grand Fleet, visibility, etc. But here again support would make an immense difference.

7. We may finish a successful action before the German support arrives and have two or three of our ships reduced in speed. The presence of the 5th Battle Squadron at this juncture would be invaluable and if necessary enable us, with our 14 or 15 heavy ships, to take on with a light heart the 14 enemy ships. At all events the chance of our battle-cruisers fighting a successful action and then being destroyed by enemy supports would be reduced to a minimum. It is a contingency such as this that I feel to be at present unprovided for.

8. The support organisation I suggest is similar to that ordered on the 16th December 1914, when, as now, the German *fast* battle-cruisers were superior to ours. This was an affair such as outlined in your paragraph 8 and on that occasion we were within an ace of being successful. Instead however, of using a slow support squadron which the enemy might overtake with battleships, I suggest the use of a battle squadron which in point of speed is no less immune than the battle-cruiser itself, from interference by enemy battleships.

9. In view of these points, which I venture to think are urgent, I trust you will favourably consider the strategic rearrangement I have submitted to you.

P.S.　As you have already forwarded former correspondence to

Admiralty, I have ventured to send them a duplicate of this direct.

151. *From Jellicoe*

[BTY/5/2/3]   SECRET   [*Iron Duke*]
                                                6th March 1916

With reference to your letter of 3rd March, BCF 016, relative to the 5th Battle Squadron, a duplicate of which you have forwarded to the Admiralty, I should prefer that any future discussion of proposals regarding the strategical distribution of vessels of the Grand Fleet, other than those under your immediate orders, should be addressed only to the Commander-in-Chief, unless the matter is one of such urgency as to render direct communication with the Admiralty a necessity. This is clearly not the case in the present instance.

152. *Jellicoe to Admiralty*

[BTY/5/2/3]   SECRET   *Iron Duke*
[Copy]   10 March 1916
No 588/HF 0010

With reference to my letter of 24th February, 1916, No 429/HF 0010, relative to a suggestion by the Vice-Admiral Commanding, Battle-Cruiser Fleet, as to the employment of the Fifth Battle Squadron, the Vice-Admiral Commanding, Battle-Cruiser Fleet, informs me that he has sent to the Lords Commissioners of the Admiralty a copy of a further communciation, dated 3rd March, 1916, BCF 016, on this subject.

2. Be pleased to lay before their Lordships my remarks on the question.

3. The Vice-Admiral's arguments in favour of adding the Fifth Battle Squadron to the Battle-Cruisers Fleet have weight only under two conditions:-

(a)   That the Battle-Cruiser Fleet is weaker than the First
      Scouting Group;

(b) That the First Scouting Group is supported by one Battle Squadron only.

4. The condition at (a) has not yet been reached and need not therefore be discussed at the moment. It may, however, require discussion later.

The condition at (b) may arise, but it is more probable that the First Scouting Group would be supported by the High Sea Fleet as a whole or by the First and Second Squadrons, seeing that there is no particular object gained by half-hearted support, and it is opposed to prevailing German tactical methods.

5. If the High Sea Fleet is in support, it would be wrong for our Battle-Cruiser Fleet to become seriously engaged either with or without the support of the Fifth Battle Squadron. The Vice-Admiral must keep touch, but fall back, on the main Battlefleet. If the Second or Third Squadron only is supporting, it is the case that the presence of the Fifth Battle Squadron might be of value in either permitting withdrawal, or enabling the Vice-Admiral to continue action with prospect of success, but I do not consider that this contingency should be provided for in view of the objections that exist to dividing the fleet.

6. To be quite clear on the point it is necessary to consider the conditions under which the Battle-Cruiser Fleet and First Scouting Group may meet again.

These conditions appear to be those of a raid on our patrols, a bombardment of our coast towns, or a trap designed to draw the Battle-Cruiser Fleet into a position in which it could be intercepted by the German Battlefleet.

For the two first the Fifth Battle Squadron would arrive too late to take part in the engagement, whilst under the last condition the Fifth Battle Squadron would not save the Battle-Cruiser Fleet, but would hamper the Battle-Cruiser Fleet by its lack of speed.

7. The whole truth of the matter seems to me to be that the Fifth Battle Squadron has not the speed necessary to work with the Battle-Cruiser Fleet, and the omission of 1,000 tons of oil would, I imagine, certainly not raise the speed by even half a knot.

8. I fully realise the disadvantage under which we labour in having the Battlefleet based so far north, but nothing short of a move of the whole Fleet to Rosyth, which would (even if the anchorage below the Bridge were used) necessitate basing the Battle-Cruiser Fleet on the Humber, will cure the evil without departing from the principle of concentration.

9. The weather conditions in the North Sea are so frequently such as to make it quite possible that the Battle-Cruiser Fleet and the Battlefleet might not meet, at a given rendezvous, that I hold a strong opinion that concentration of the Battlefleet is very necessary.

10. Should the addition of further battle-cruisers to the First Scouting Group place our Battle-Cruiser Fleet in a position of inferiority or even equality of strength, it may be necessary to reconsider the question, but the proper remedy, which I recognise is impracticable, is, of course, the addition of battle-cruisers of equal strength and superior speed to those of the enemy.

153. *From Jellicoe*

[BTY/5/2/3]   SECRET   *Iron Duke*
HF 0010/118   13th March, 1916

I beg to thank you for your letter of 10 March, 1916, No 016, and quite appreciate the fact that your action was taken with the desire to further the interests of the Service, but as it was necessary for my remarks on your proposals to be forwarded to the Admiralty the necessity of sending a duplicate direct did not appear evident, and it moreover might possibly lead to cross correspondence. It was for this reason that I addressed you on the subject.

154. *From Jellicoe*

[BTY/13/22/8]   *Iron Duke*
(Holograph)   11.4.16

It was unfortunate that I left Scapa an hour after *Falmouth*'s arrival & before your letter reached me. I am glad to say that firing is taking place in the Firth today, so 3rd Lt C.S. should finish . . .

There is a feeling at the Admiralty which I think may lead them to persuade me into what is called a 'more active policy'. I notice signs of it and it shows itself in the air raids heavily supported [*sic*]. I am being pressed to plan another, the idea being that it will bring the German fleet out. But the difficulty is this. The raid *must* take place at daylight, otherwise the force would be reported approaching and 5 sea planes would certainly not succeed in achieving anything, with a mass of Zeppelins & aeroplanes against them. If carried out at daylight & the German heavy ships do move, they won't be clear of the minefields & in a position where we could engage them before about 4 p.m.

This is no time to start a fight in these waters. It also involves our hanging about for a whole day in a bad locality, expending fuel, especially from T B Ds. You can't wait for the following day as by then the T B Ds are out of fuel & the light cruisers very short.

If we could stir them up at dusk and catch them coming out next morning the matter would be different, but I can't see how to do that.

The real truth to my mind is that our policy should be to engage them *not* in a position close to their minefields and therefore close to their SM, TBD and aircraft bases, but to accept the position that we must wait until they give us a chance in a favourable position. Patience is the virtue we must exercise. I am still trying to devise a means of drawing them out, but I am bound to say I don't think air raids will do it.

What do you think?

At the same time an air raid is a minor operation, especially if combined with some minelaying is all to the good. I am asking Tyrwhitt whether he could start the sea planes from a position north of Horn Reef. The distance is very little greater and leaves the field clear for SMs to the south of it. One SM says he saw Tyrwhitt & I gather he did not fire at him as he knew he was going to be there. If a torpedo was fired it looks as though an enemy SM were too!! . . .

I am going into the question of a sweep of L & M channels. I fear it is rather too far to send the sloops from Scapa as I should have nothing left to sweep up north.

Personally I think the Zeppelin raids are pure revenge & also reconnaissance of the southern part of the North Sea.

Those who opposed building Zeppelins in this country 3 years ago have a heavy responsibility now. . . .

155. *To Jellicoe*

[BTY/13/22/10]   *Lion*
                                                    14th April 1916

My dear Commander-in-Chief,

Thank you for your letter. You ask me what I think? Well, I think the German Fleet will come out *only* on its own initiative when the right time arrives.

Air Raids on our part will *not* bring them out. They may, and possibly will, bring out a portion which could be snapped at by the Supporting Force we choose to utilise to support the Air Raiding Force. If the force they push out is large, i.e. battle-cruisers supported by Battle Squadrons (one or two), it would go no farther than is necessary to reconnoitre and expose the full strength of the force that we had in support. And as soon as they had made clear what constituted our force they would act accordingly. If we were greatly inferior they might be tempted to prosecute their investigations and attack further afield, otherwise they will withdraw. It is on such occasions we might be able to inflict some damage, risking something to do it. But I am firmly convinced that under no circumstances could we ever by taking the initiative induce them to commit themselves to an action which in any way could be considered decisive.

I am not arguing against air raids. Anything that we can do to harass and annoy has great advantages. And there is always the possibility that they may be tempted to overstep themselves, go too far with an inferior force etc, which could be punished severely before it got back; and such operations fairly frequently may produce something which will be worth the risks. They would also have the advantage of denying him (the enemy) the initiative, and so prevent him from bringing off any of his set pieces. But it is certain that he will not come out in grand force when we set the tune, i.e. to fight the great battle we are all waiting for.

Your arguments re the fuel question are unanswerable and measure the situation absolutely. We cannot amble about the North Sea for two or three days and at the end be in a condition in which we can produce our whole force to fight to the finish the most decisive battle of the war: to think it is possible is simply too foolish and tends towards losing the battle before we begin.

As I said, my contention is that when the Great Day comes it will be when the enemy takes the initiative; and I think our principal business now is to investigate the North Sea with mine-sweepers so that we can have a clear and fairly accurate knowledge of what waters in it are safe, and what are not; so that when he does take the initiative we can judge fairly accurately in what waters we can engage him. I think we can be quite sure that it will not be North of lat 56°.

What I am disturbed at, is your remark that 'there is a feeling at the Admiralty etc, to persuade me into a more active policy — and being pressed to plan another —'. This is truly deplorable.

I have often been tempted to write to you in the past on the subject of community of thought between the administrators and those who have to use the instruments which they command. Many a time have I felt that we have suffered considerably for the lack of it. I have always held back from doing so because of the circumstances of myself and command, and felt it would be out of place. But this is not the time to blink the question, and when we have reached to crisis in the life of the Nation it is meet and proper to say what we think; and that is, that there should be a proper and personal exchange of views between the Admiralty, i.e. the First Sea Lord, and the Commander-in-Chief, which should be constant and frequent, and that Officers Commanding Units which are used independently, such as the Battle-Cruiser Fleet and the Harwich Force, should also know exactly by personal interview what is in the minds of the First Sea Lord and Commander-in-Chief and of each other. I have had many operations with the Commodore (T) and have seen him once, for five minutes! Surely this is not wise or practical. One hour's conversation is worth a volume of correspondence. In every other phase of the war, military, political, diplomatic, economic, the value of conversation has been realised. Generals, politicians, diplomatic and other representatives have travelled from the ends of the earth to attend conferences and exchange views. The Commander-in-Chief of the Expeditionary Force in France has had periodical meetings with the Minister for War.

Surely it is not beyond the bounds of practical possibility that meetings of those who run the great force upon which the safety and future of the Empire depends can take place. That they are necessary is practically proven by many things, and much good might come out of exchange of ideas.

I have asked Commodore (T) to ask the Admiralty for permission to come and see me. He replies that there was a strong opposition at the Admiralty to his doing so!!

I enclose you a copy of a report by Commander Ryan on Directional plates he has fitted to a B 3 Submarine.[1] I have been on board B 3, conversed with her Captain, a sharp and intelligent fellow, and feel that they will provide a most valuable adjunct against enemy submarines. They hunted C 25 all over the Firth of Forth and could not miss him. It will, if generally adopted, revolutionise submarine warfare, and I think is the answer to meet the submarine menace. Like most things of great value it is so simple. Could you send Bellairs or somebody whose opinion you can rely upon to look at it. Then the work of fitting every submarine with it requires expediting. The circular plates require about a week to prepare. Actual time required to fit when everything is ready, six hours. The Lieut. in charge told me that it is the best thing they had ever had, and if every submarine had had them at the beginning of the war they would have been able to keep the enemy submarines out of the North Sea. The 1st Sea Lord, I understand, is quite keen on it, but no Admiralty official has seen it or tested its possibilities which to me seem immense — especially if used in conjunction with sound signalling apparatus to avoid contretemps with friendly submarines.

B 3 has had the Evershed and Vignoles Sound Signalling apparatus[2] in since October, but things move slowly and it has not been pushed. It is excellent for sending and can be heard 9 miles. The Directional Plates with Hydrophone receivers make perfect receivers. If we could only short circuit delays and obstructions we should soon be in a position to curtail the activities of the enemy submarines. If you can send somebody to look into the matter I am sure it would help.

We cannot go on as in the past, viz our Kite Balloons (11½ knot steamer attached to BCF) and our Zeppelin construction about which the Chief of the War Staff wrote me 3½ months ago that they were building but they would be no use *this war*!! How long do they take to build and how long does the War Staff think the war is going to last, presumably about another three months!!

Re *Constance* I never heard until last night that she had a piece out of one propeller. This is quite sufficient to account for the leakage caused by the vibration, and although they can make

---

[1]For Ryan's experiments in giving hydrophones directional capability see Willem Hackmann, *Seek and Strike: Sonar and Anti-Submarine Warfare and the Royal Navy, 1914–1954* (London 1984), pp. 48–50.

[2]Sound signalling apparatus originally developed as a navigational aid, produced by the firm of Evershed & Vignolle.

good leaks now, the cause remains and more leakage will be experienced as soon as she does any steaming at high speed; hence my wire to you re changing propeller before she leaves here and the sooner the better. They have not dealt with it very intelligently. Conflicting reports as to extent of leaky rivets, a frame bracket, ship's side, etc — lucky I have Sheen and a good Asst Constructor.

May the Second LCS come up to Scapa after the First LCS for practices; it would be a great boon for them. *Southampton* can be received 25th at Newcastle, but if this delayed her a day I think they would be glad at Newcastle on account of the holidays.

First BCS and *Lion* are in need of an opportunity for sub-calibre and torpedo practices and would be glad of an early opportunity but I assume it must depend upon movements of First Scouting Group.

Third BCS *Inflexible* and *Indomitable* will have completed director tower fitting and circuits early in May; the former changed six guns; last firing did not show any vital necessity for calibration. But both ships would require preliminary adjustments of the director before firing. *Invincible* will complete her docking about 15th May, so if the squadron could get to Scapa as soon as possible after about 16th May and have an opportunity—*Inflexible, calibrate if* you think necessary, *Indomitable* and *Inflexible, test the Director*, and all three ships *fire sub-calibre 4" and full calibre and Whitehead* — it would be very beneficial but of course requires some little time to do all.

I am afraid I have given you a terrifically long letter to consider but I do not write you to bother you with unnecessary detail and the points I have dwelt upon appear to me to be of very great importance. More especially that of improving the conditions of community of thought and the desirability of my being acquainted with all your views and those of the First Sea Lord on the subjects which are of paramount importance. So I do not apologise. I hope you are fit and well. Thank God the winter is drawing to a close.

Your's ever
DAVID BEATTY

156. *To Jellicoe*

[BTY/13/22/12]   *Lion*
                                                              7th May 1916

My Dear Commander-in-Chief,

The Seaplanes as usual were disappointing.[1] The sea appeared to me to be entirely satisfactory, but apparently there was a lump which upset them and moreover I gather the bombs were slung in a position (and the only position possible as at present arranged) which put the seaplanes down by the head which caused the propellers to strike the water as all the propellers were damaged. They evidently have not paid that attention to trim which is part of a Naval Officer's training and thought that what went well in a landlocked harbour with smooth water would meet all cases.

However Lt. Rutland of *Engadine*, an excellent Officer, told me the sea conditions were the worst he had experienced in making attacks on enemy positions and I understand he has taken part in most of them.

I have never laid much stress or importance on the value of these air raids except as a means of telling the enemy we are about and asking him to come out, much the same as the Irishman trailing his coat. Evidently the one seaplane did not attract much attention. And it was the fortunate circumstance of meeting the Zep and its destruction that really produced the desired effect of stirring them up. But it was not until after 9 a.m. that he sighted the light cruisers and then the air was flooded with wireless. I do not think he sighted the BCs until after this, and it was when attempting to get closer to get material for a fuller and further report that he came under the gunfire of the *Galatea* and *Phaeton* and they evidently effectually prevented any further report being made as we never heard him call again.

I cleared out to the North to join you before being sighted by anything more and everything promised well towards fulfilling our final objective at daylight the next day.

I had husbanded my destroyers' fuel and they were well able to have had a good period of full speed the next day and get home at 15 knots if required.

You can understand my disappointment when we were ordered

---

[1] On 3–4 May a combined mine-laying operation in German swept channels and a sea plane attack against Zeppelin sheds at Tondern had failed to produce a reaction from the High Seas Fleet.

to return to base. Why cannot the Admiralty leave the situation to those on the spot? As you have pointed out, under any circumstances they could not get to Horn Reef until late in the day, and in the special circumstances obtaining they had evidently started late and would not get up until later still; therefore at daylight the *next* day there were infinite possibilities of striking him a very severe blow.

The subsequent signals received and the report of the SM E.31 substantiated this, and if we had been in the vicinity of the Horn Reef at dawn we should have had a glorious time.

To miss opportunities which are so few and far between is maddening.

I am sending you the results of the recent firings. The *Tiger*'s was as usual unsatisfactory, so much so that I addressed a letter to the RA 1st BCS,[1] copy of which and his reply I send to you without comment [not included].

I heard from Bartolomé who said that 'Pelly might perhaps go as Commodore R N Barracks'. Eustace leaves shortly.[2]

This I think would provide the necessary solution without causing heartburnings, discussion etc.

He suggested Keyes to relieve him; this I do *not* want. Keyes is a good fellow but has had no experience of big ship command, has not too many brains and I do not want any more experiments therefore would wish Bentinck to have *Tiger*. I know and you know that he is the right man. She is such an important unit that we cannot afford to take any more risks. I shall hate losing Bentinck but it is for the good of the Service so I hope you will support me.

I should like Brand to relieve Bentinck. Will you support me in this also? I shall do nothing until I hear from you.[3]

Invincible, date fixed 22nd May. This will be kept, after which I should like 3rd BCS to go to Scapa for exercises. Will you send the 5th BS to take their place as *Australia* will not be back until 10th June.

2nd LCS will leave here tomorrow night Tuesday. I will write you again by then and will let you know result of preliminary conference re berthing GF here. I am not at all sure in my mind

[1]Rear-Admiral de Brock.

[2]Later Admiral Sir Charles de Bartolmé (1871–1941): Naval Secretary to 1st Lord; 3rd Sea Lord & Controller June 1918. Rear-Admiral John Eustace, commanding RN Barracks Portsmouth.

[3]Captain Rudolph Bentinck, Beatty's COS, was succeeded by Captain Hubert Brand on 29 June 1916.

that it is a sound proposition and feel that the politician and not the strategic requirements are trying to rule the situation whereby history is once more repeating itself.

I am becoming sick at heart of continual disappointments and feel you are too.

157.   *To his wife* [Hanover Lodge]

[BTY/17/35/11]   *Lion*
                                                                7.5.16

We have returned disappointed beyond measure. These constant and continual disappointments are wearing to a degree. There were great possibilities, *but*, there is always a but, they were not made use of, and the opportunity passed away never to return again. It really is heart-breaking. For the life of me I do not know what to do to bring about the desired result. But something must be done, we simply cannot go on missing chances like this. You will have seen in the papers that we succeeded in baggng one Zeppelin. It was a good bit of work, well done by Sinclair, and eminently satisfactory that it should have been the 1st LCS that did it, as they are all good and the only squadron that had not been blooded. . . .

I am very tired as well as disappointed, so am going to bed.

158.   *Jellicoe to Admiralty*

[BTY/5/2/4]   SECRET   *Iron Duke*
[Copy]   11th May, 1916

Putting aside all but the most important considerations, the question of transferring the main fleet base from Scapa to Rosyth is dependent upon whether the advantages gained by —
  (a) Shortening the distance for intercepting the enemy's fleet,
  (b) There being a far greater certainty of the flotillas being able to screen the battlefleet south, and remain in company with it whilst waiting,
  (c) The concentration of minesweepers, destroyers, trawlers,

and other small craft, in one port, and searching one set of approaches,

are greater than the disadvantages of —

- (a) Greater facility for mining the fleet in,
- (b) More foggy weather,
- (c) The presence of neutral traffic.

2. There are two spheres in which the Grand Fleet is likely to operate. One is in, say, Lat 56.0 N, Long 6. 15 E, for offensive operations on the Schleswig coast; the other is in, say, Lat 54. 0 N, Long 4. 10 E, for operations designed to intercept and bring to action the High Sea Fleet, or to prevent a raid on the southeast coast or Channel.

3. In the first case, the difference of distance to the points named from Scapa and Rosyth is only 30 miles, 360, as compared with 330. In the second place, the difference in distance, if the forces went by 'M' channel, is 130 miles, i.e. 450 from Scapa and 320 from Rosyth, or, if a direct route is followed from either Scapa or Rosyth, neglecting Mine Area I, the difference is 100 miles, namely, 400 from Scapa and 300 from Rosyth. The difference in distance for the point off the Schleswig coast is not material, because any operation of that nature would be deliberate on our part, and we know exactly before starting how long we mean to be out. The difference in distance for the second point named is very material, because if the fleet is proceeding there it is probably on account of news having been received that the German fleet is out, and every minute that can be saved is of importance.

4. There is no doubt whatever that strategically Rosyth has the greater advantages. I have constantly recognised this point in communications to the Admiralty.

5. The question of minelaying is that of the greatest importance. I think it may be accepted that with the fleet based on Rosyth the concentration of small craft would be so great that it should be very difficult for any surface minelayer to act effectively. Indeed, the result of moving the fleet south should be to gain a positive advantage in this respect. With the comparatively small forces now based at Rosyth surface minelaying at some little distance to the eastward of May Island should be comparatively a simple matter, and a minefield could be placed so that it is not only a menace to the Rosyth force, but to the Scapa force also.

6. There remains the question of submarine minelayers. There is no safeguard against this, except constant sweeping, and the

knowledge that our patrols are very strong, and that such defensive measures as deep minefields, explosive indicator nets, etc, are fully used.

7. The larger the fleet based on Rosyth, the greater, presumably, will be the efforts in this direction.

8. With regard to fog, there is no doubt that Rosyth is at a disadvantage; there is this to be said, that the difficulties of leaving the two bases in foggy weather are very considerably less at Rosyth than at Scapa, and the difficulty of returning to the base in a fog will be largely minimised at Rosyth if the obstruction from Elie Ness to Fidra is laid.

9. So far as regards the time required to leave the bases, I am inclined to think that the advantage should lay with Rosyth, at any rate at night. It might be necessary to keep the Battle-Cruiser Fleet at shorter notice than the battlefleet, in order to ensure rapidity of departure.

10. The above arguments do not deal with the question of a division of the battlefleet, which is involved by the movement to Rosyth. It has to be recognised that the Fourth Battle Squadron must be based on the Humber. There is as a consequence a risk that the Fourth Battle Squadron might not be concentrated with the remainder of the battlefleet, but I do not think that the risk is a heavy one, because the concentration point would be within 60 miles of the Humber, and consequently an enemy force endeavouring to engage the Fourth Battle Squadron whilst on its way to concentrate would run exceedingly heavy risk of meeting the remainder of the Grand Fleet whilst so engaged.

11. The Humber is, of course, a most objectionable base for a squadron, and any means that can be devised to avoid placing a squadron there would be most beneficial. It is possible that should the Elie Ness — Fidra obstruction prove to be a really efficient obstacle, it might be safe to base the Fourth Battle Squadron inside Inchkeith, at any rate for a good portion of the time.

12. There is one other point which requires to be considered in connnection with the change of base, namely, the safeguarding of the North Sea exit and the support of the Tenth Cruiser Squadron. With the battlefleet removed from Scapa, the Tenth Cruiser Squadron is very open to attack should the enemy care to risk battle-cruisers for this purpose. I think myself that the risk is not so heavy as to weigh in the scale when considering the re-disposition of the fleet. The removal of the battlefleet to southern ports would leave Scapa free as a secondary base of the Tenth

Cruiser Squadron in place of Swarbacks Minn, and I would propose that the Tenth Cruiser Squadron move to Scapa.

SECRET
NEW DISPOSITION OF FLEET

THAMES	— 3rd Battle Squadron
	12 destroyers (1st Flotilla)
HARWICH	— 5th Light Cruiser Squadron
	9th and 10th Flotillas
HUMBER	— 4th Battle Squadron
	1st Cruiser Squadron
	4th Flotilla (Local work)
	15th Flotilla (with squadron) 18 boats
BLYTH	— *Titania*
	Talisman
	Trident
	12 Submarines ('J' and 'G' classes)
FORTH	— Battle Cruiser Fleet and 5th Battle Squadron
	13th Flotilla (28 boats)
	1st Battle Squadron
	2nd Battle Squadron
	2nd Cruiser Squadron
	4th Light Cruiser Squadron
	11th, 12th and 14th Flotillas (54 boats)
	Active and 12 'K' class Submarines
CROMARTY	— Ships repairing
SCAPA	— 3rd Cruiser Squadron (5 ships to include *Hampshire* and *Donegal*)
	10th Cruiser Squadron (Base)
	8 destroyers of 1st Flotilla

N.B.   The destroyers must be at Scapa for escort duty as well as for screening 3rd Cruiser Squadron.

It will probably be necessary to increase their number to 12, in which case 4 should come from 4th Flotilla.

PART V

JUTLAND—EARLY REACTIONS
1916

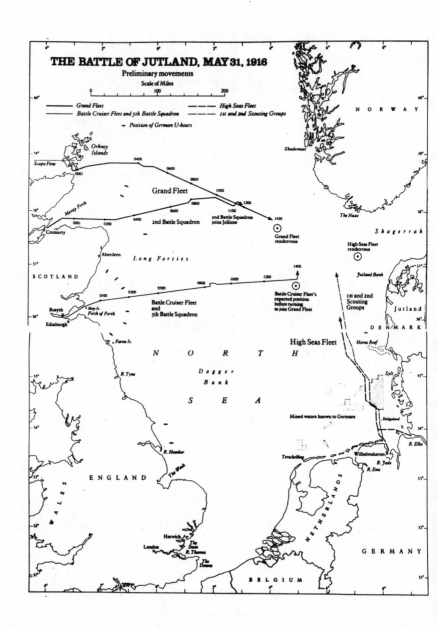

THE BATTLE OF JUTLAND, MAY 31, 1916
Preliminary movements
Scale of Miles
0   100   200

———— Grand Fleet   – – – – High Seas Fleet
———— Battle Cruiser Fleet and 5th Battle Squadron   –·–·– 1st and 2nd Scouting Groups
– Position of German U-boats

NORWAY

Orkney Islands

Scapa Flow

0001

0400

0600

0800

1000

Grand Fleet

Shudesnaes

Moray Firth

0001   0200   0400   0600   0800   1000   1100   1200

Cromarty

2nd Battle Squadron

2nd Battle Squadron joins Jellicoe

1430

⊙ Grand Fleet rendezvous

The Nase

Skagerrak

High Seas Fleet rendezvous ⊙

Aberdeen

Long Forties

1400

SCOTLAND

0100   0300   0500   0800   1000   1200

⊙ Battle Cruiser Fleet's expected position before turning to join Grand Fleet

Jutland Bank

1st and 2nd Scouting Groups

Jutland

Rosyth

May Is.
Firth of Forth

Battle Cruiser Fleet and 5th Battle Squadron

DENMARK

Edinburgh

High Seas Fleet

Horns Reef

Farne Is.

N   O   R   T   H

Sylt

R. Tyne

Dogger Bank

Helgoland

S   E   A

Mined waters known to Germans

R. Elbe

R. Humber

Terschelling

Wilhelmshaven

R. Jade

ENGLAND

The Wash

R. Ems

WALES

NETHERLANDS

GERMANY

Harwich

London   The Swin
R. Thames

The Downs

BELGIUM

INTRODUCTION[1]

For Beatty and the Battle-Cruiser Fleet, in addition to sharing in the whole Grand Fleet's disappointment at the failure to gain a decisive victory, the most painful episode of Jutland was the sinking of *Indefatigable, Queen Mary* and *Invincible*. The destruction of the first two in the early stages of the battle during which Beatty fulfilled his task of leading the High Seas Fleet into the jaws of Jellicoe's numerically superior force, was the occasion of Beatty's well-authenticated understatement to Chatfield, 'There seems to be something wrong with our bloody ships today.'[2] The loss of the three battle-cruisers, caused by no more than five hits each from their German counterparts, was a clear demonstration of the vulnerability of their construction to the accuracy of German gunnery and the destructiveness of their projectiles. The later realisation that none of the enemy battle-cruisers, although badly damaged, had actually sunk and that casualties were only 398 killed and 169 wounded compared with British losses from the battle-cruisers of 3,454 killed and 185 wounded, served to drive the lessons home.[3] That there is no evidence to show that these losses and the overall disappointment of the battle produced any loss of morale or readiness to fight again, is a tribute to Beatty's leadership and the quality of his ships' companies.

Both Beatty and Jellicoe rapidly set up a range of enquiries into the deficiencies in gunnery performance and ship construction which had led to the losses, and later, to analyse the tactical lessons to be learned. The wider questions on the strategic handling of the battle, which led to the bitter post-war controversies between Beatty and Jellicoe and their supporters, will be dealt with in the second volume of this work, but their seeds can be detected here as the two men began to examine their command decisions and the performance of their forces. In this they were no doubt spurred on by a desire to justify themselves in the light

---

[1]The Jellicoe-Beatty correspondence and other relevant material for this section is in Temple-Patterson *Jellicoe Papers*, Vol. I, pp 253–308.

[2]Roskill, *Admiral of the Fleet*, p. 160, establishes the authenticity of the wording.

[3]Ibid., pp. 164–5, citing N. J. M. Campbell.

of widespread criticism of the outcome of the battle and, certainly on Jellicoe's part, by anxious self-questioning.[1]

Beatty's first reaction was to alert the Admiralty to his conclusion that the loss of the three battle-cruisers was due to magazine explosions following hits on turrets, and the need for immediate remedies both in procedures and protection. The committee he appointed to identify the gunnery lessons learned reinforced this with detailed recommendations. The parallel committee on construction was much more radical, claiming that Jutland had demonstrated that all existing and planned capital ships were inadequately protected. Even the *Queen Elizabeth* needed greater speed, increased offensive and defensive power and diminished draught, to present a smaller underwater target. A first-hand account of the effect of shell fire on *Lion*'s 'Q' turret adds a personal dimension to the committee's analysis [159, 162, 169, 170, 172, 173].

The gunnery committee, having been sent reports from the battle-cruisers and the 5th Battle Squadron which had been under Beatty's command in the battle, came to the general conclusion that in the early stages it was poor visibility which had hampered British gunnery and assisted the enemy. They then made detailed recommendations to improve capability for early and rapid hitting, but admitted that existing range finders were inadequate when the enemy was constantly changing course. They emphasised that, although enemy gunnery had been very accurate at the beginning, it had deteriorated as the action developed. A first-hand narrative of one of *Lion*'s director layers confirms the importance of varying visibility and clearly shows the confusion and uncertainties of combat compared with later judgements made in calm retrospect.

Beatty's first formal expression of the lessons learned came in his additions to the Battle-Cruiser Orders issued on 31 August [168, 169, 171,173, 176].

There is no trace of recrimination in Jellicoe's early letters to Beatty, although the hidden seeds of future disputes were there. What concerned him most was the validity of his own crucial decision on the deployment of the Grand Fleet so as to cut off the Germans from their base. His chief difficulty had been in establishing the location and course of the enemy, partly due to the weather but also to the lack of early and accurate information from those ships already in contact. These had of course been

[1]For the post war Jutland controversy, see Roskill, chapter 15 and Temple-Patterson, *The Jellicoe Papers* (London 1968), Vol. II, Part IV and Appendix.

under Beatty's command. This weakness had been compounded by significant differences in reckoning of position between *Iron Duke* and *Lion*. In the light of all these difficulties Jellicoe believed that he had decided rightly. [160, 165].

Beatty's first detailed official report to Jellicoe was equally free from open recrimination and was full of praise for the commander of the 5th Battle Squadron, Rear-Admiral Evan-Thomas,[1] but was wildly out of touch with reality in its optimistic estimates of enemy capital ships sinkings. [164] But by 26 June, at an Admiralty meeting with Jackson, the First Sea Lord, Commodore Everett, the First Lord's Naval Secretary, and Jellicoe, Beatty's resentments began to emerge. In reply to criticisms by Jackson he had retorted sharply that if the 5th Battle Squadron had been allocated earlier to his command it would have become more used to his methods and thus avoided the delay in coming to the battle-cruisers' support, which he now seemed to be seeing as the cause of his heavy losses. This was a direct criticism of Jellicoe, who had opposed the transfer. It was only by chance that the battle squadron had been with Beatty at Jutland as a temporary replacement of a battle-cruiser squadron withdrawn for gunnery practice which was not feasible at Rosyth. More unpleasantly ominous for the future was Lady Beatty's virulent criticism of Jellicoe which she was unlikely to have kept from the social circles in which she moved [174–175].

Beatty's anger had already been aroused by the ineptness of the Admiralty's release of information about Jutland, which had led to alarmist public dissatisfaction with the Navy's performance. He was apprehensive that his Jutland dispatches would only be published in garbled form, as he alleged to Arthur Balfour his reports on the Heligoland Bight and Dogger Bank actions had been [161, 163, 164, 167].

The coming months were not to make his relationship with Jellicoe and the Admiralty any easier.

---

[1]Later Admiral Sir Hugh Evan-Thomas (1862–1928): entered RN 1876; Rear-Admiral 1912 & 2nd-in-Command 1st Battle Squadron; commanding 5th Battle Squadron 1915–18; Vice-Admiral 1917; Admiral & CinC Nore 1920; retired 1924.

159. *To Admiralty*

[HTN/122/B]   SECRET   3rd June 1916
[COPY]

SUBJECT: MAGAZINE DOORS IN TURRETS

Submitted in confirmation of my telegram No 447 (code time 1115) of today.

This matter is one of the most urgent and vital importance. Commander Dannreuther confirms the conclusions of Captain of *Lion*. Undoubtedly loss of *Invincible* was due to magazine doors being left open. All evidence of witnesses in other ships points to the destruction of *Queen Mary* and *Indefatigable* being due to exploding of magazines, following shell striking of turrets or beneath turrets.[1]

2. Witnesses from *Queen Mary*, a Midshipman and Gunlayer of 'Q' turret, report that 'Q' turret was hit, an explosion following which wrecked the turret. Turret was evacuated, upper deck being below water. Another explosion occurred, sinking the ship.

3. Pending Admiralty action as to fitting supply scuttles to all magazine doors, with watertight provision, I have given orders to battle-cruisers that magazine doors are to be kept closed on one clip, and only opened to replenish handing room from time to time. This will necessitate four or five full charges being kept in handing room, but will minimise danger of magazine explosions.

4. A copy of this submission is being sent to the Commander-in-Chief, Grand Fleet.

---

[1]Commander Hubert Dannreuther, gunnery officer of *Invincible*, who survived her sinking. The most recent research more precisely describes the cause of the battle-cruiser sinkings as flashes reaching the magazines and igniting the cordite in gunhouse working chambers (see John Campbell, *Jutland: An Analysis of the Fighting* (London, 1986), p 60).

160. *From Jellicoe*

[BTY/13/22/13]   *Iron Duke*
[Holograph]   4.6.16

I am, as you will guess, very busy but cannot miss the opportunity of sending a line of deep sympathy to you.

I gather from Evan Thomas that the conditions of light were most adverse to you. He says that on his disengaged side he could see 12 miles at least, whilst towards the enemy he could see only flashes of guns firing when engaged with the enemy ships. I do not wonder at your ships being heavily hit under these conditions.

My great difficulty, apart from low visibility, was between the difference in reckoning between *Lion* (12 miles), 2nd L.C.S. (20 miles) and *Iron Duke*.

This caused me to find the enemy and you in a totally unexpected direction & made deployment very difficult, and as the first thing I saw was firing from right ahead to abaft the beam it was impossible to guess the position of enemy battle fleet [*sic*]. In fact I did not know it until some time after deployment.

I knew in the early morning next day that the enemy had returned to harbour. Had it not been for the fact that our 11th Flotilla mistook enemy battle-cruisers at 9.30 p.m. for you, we should have added [–] to the bag. As it was they refrained from attacking and *Castor* got rather punished, also 4th Flotilla.[1]

During the battle fleet action the enemy flotillas & battleships fired a large number of torpedoes at the centre & rear of battle fleet [*sic*] spent a lot of time in dodging them. The only hit was on *Marlborough*.[2]

I found signals difficult to get through in the mist, although W.T. interference was very small, to my surprise. But it took an appalling time to get course alterations through the fleet for closing.

[1]4th & 11th Destroyer Flotillas of the Grand Fleet; light cruiser *Castor* was leader of the 11th (Commodore J. R. P. Hawsley).
[2]*Marlborough*, 1st Battle Squadron, flagship of Vice-Admiral Sir Cecil Burney, 2nd-in-Command Grand Fleet; her speed seriously reduced by a torpedo hit, she fell behind on the night pursuit. This was the only torpedo hit on a British capital ship in the action.

161. *To Dennis Larking*

[LAR/1/24]   *Lion*
                                                              5.6.16

. . .

Don't believe the b – y papers, they are all wrong.

We gave them a d – d good hammering and might have done more, but it was not the fault of yours ever.

162. *Admiralty to Commanders-in-Chief and other Flag Officers*

[HTN/122/B]   5th June 1916
[Copy]
Confidential

I am commanded by My Lords Commissioners of the Admiralty to acquaint you that the provision of some form of handing scuttles in the magazine doors is under consideration with a view to preventing the flash from a shell detonating in the turret gun house or working chamber reaching the magazine, and further instructions will be issued as soon as possible.

In the meantime the following general recommendations are forwarded for your information and guidance, so far as they apply to the different classes of ships —

(1)   To keep all openings in the gun house, working chamber and trunk closed whenever possible during action.

(2)   All inspection doors must be kept closed.

(3)   Pending new fittings, magazine doors to be kept closed excepting when actually passing charges out of the magazines.

(4)   Chain of cordite must be broken at working chamber, i.e. *normal state*: —

    (a)   Gun loaded

    (b)   Gun loading cage loaded in working chamber

    (c)   Main cage at bottom of trunk loaded with shell only, and charge in handing room hopper

    (d)   No accumulation of charges in the handing room.

163.   *From Hamilton's Journal*

[HTN/106]   7 June 1916
[Holograph]

On Saturday I visited Rosyth to see houses and took the opportunity to see Beatty, Phillpotts,[1] Pelly & Goodenough and went on board *Warspite, Tiger* and *Southampton*. I found Beatty very well and cheerful but very angry with the Admiralty for their very stupid communiqué sent out on Friday evening, which was really an apology for missing [?] a victory. I subsequently on my return found that Masterton-Smith was the author of it, Jackson & Oliver having been too busy to attend to it properly, and having told them to say anything they liked, as long as it was true.[2] They may be partly excused as they could hardly expect that knowing what we did of the German losses through the Japanese telegram, the Germans would lie in the barefaced manner they did. On the other hand we could make no use of our knowledge acquired through the Japanese, as it would have risked giving our sources of information away. In this respect Japanese [*sic*] are very bad for Their Lordships as they are rapidly converting us into habitual liars. However their value is worth the morals of any Board.

Beatty showed traces of indignation that he had not been supported earlier by Jellicoe but I hope when the facts are sifted out it will be shown that Jellicoe acted rightly. When I condoled with Beatty for the loss of *Hood*,[3] his face lighted up and he said 'You should have seen him bring his squadron into action, it would have done your heart good, no one could have died a more glorious death.'

*   *   *

[1]Captain E. M. Phillpots of *Warspite*.
[2]Later Sir James Edward Masterton-Smith (1878–1938): private secretary to 1st Lord (Balfour); Sir Henry Jackson, 1st Sea Lord; Sir Henry Oliver, Chief of War Staff. Marder *From the Dreadnought* Vol. 3, pp. 240–1, suggests that Balfour himself was responsible.
[3]Rear-Admiral H. Hood, commanding 3rd Battle-Cruiser Squadron; lost in *Invincible*.

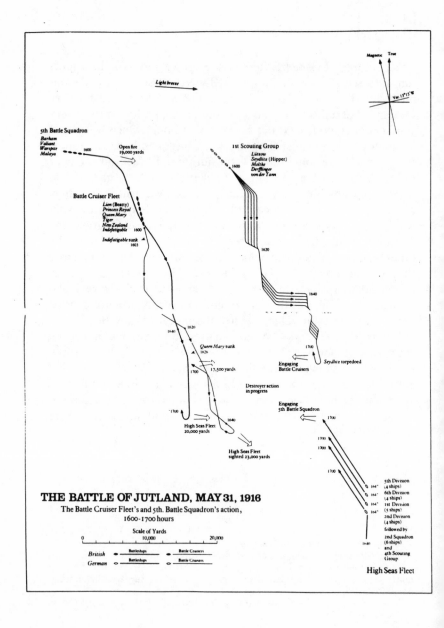

Light breeze

Magnetic True

Var. 13°15'W

5th Battle Squadron
Barham
Valiant
Warspite   1600
Malaya

Open fire
19,000 yards

1st Scouting Group
Lützow
Seydlitz (Hipper)
Moltke   1600
Derfflinger
von der Tann

Battle Cruiser Fleet
Lion (Beatty)
Princess Royal
Queen Mary
Tiger
New Zealand   1600
Indefatigable

Indefatigable sunk
1603

1620

1640

1620

1640

Queen Mary sunk
1626

1700

17,500 yards

1700

Engaging
Battle Cruisers

Seydlitz torpedoed

Destroyer action
in progress

Engaging
5th Battle Squadron

1700

1700

1700

1700

High Seas Fleet
20,000 yards

1640

High Seas Fleet
sighted 23,000 yards

5th Division
(4 ships)
6th Division
(4 ships)
1st Division
(5 ships)
2nd Division
(4 ships)
followed by
2nd Squadron
(6 ships)
and
4th Scouting
Group

164°
164°
164°
164°

1640

High Seas Fleet

THE BATTLE OF JUTLAND, MAY 31, 1916
The Battle Cruiser Fleet's and 5th. Battle Squadron's action,
1600-1700 hours

Scale of Yards
0   10,000   20,000

British	Battleships	Battle Cruisers
German	Battleships	Battle Cruisers

164. *Beatty to Jellicoe*[1] (Beatty's original Jutland dispatch).

[BTY/6/1/3]   SECRET   *Lion*
[Copy]   12 June 1916
BCF01

Sir,

I have the honour to report that at 2.37 p.m. on 31st May, 1916, being in Lat. 56.47 N., Long. 4.59 E., I altered course to the Northward to join the Commander-in-Chief, in accordance with previous orders.

2. The force under my command was as follows:-

Lion (Captain A. E. M. Chatfield, C.V.O.) flying my Flag, *Princess Royal* (Captain W. H. Cowan, M.V.O., D.S.O.) flying the Flag of Rear Admiral O. de B. Brock, C.B., *Tiger* (Captain H. B. Pelly, M.V.O.), *Queen Mary* (Captain C. I. Prowse), *New Zealand* (Captain J. F. E. Green), flying the Flag of Rear Admiral W. C. Pakenham, C.B., M.V.O., *Indefatigable* (Captain C. F. Sowerby), *Southampton*, flying the Broad Pennant of Commodore W. E. Goodenough, M.V.O., *Nottingham* (Captain C. B. Miller), *Birmingham* (Captain A. A. M. Duff), *Dublin* (Captain A. C. Scott), *Galatea*, flying the Broad Pennant of Commodore E. S. Alexander Sinclair, M.V.O., *Inconstant* (Captain B. S. Thesiger, C.M.G.), *Phaeton* (Captain J. E. Cameron, M.V.O.), *Cordelia* (Captain T. P. H. Beamish), *Falmouth* (Captain J. D. Edwards), flying the Flag of Rear Admiral T. D. W. Napier, M.V.O., *Birkenhead* (Captain E. Reeves), *Gloucester* (Captain W. F. Blunt, D.S.O.), *Yarmouth* (Captain T. D. Pratt), *Champion* (Captain J. U. Farie, Captain D, 13th Destroyer Flotilla), with Destroyers *Nestor* (Commander Hon. E. B. S. Bingham), *Nomad* (Lieut. Commander P. Whitfield), *Narborough* (Lieut. Commander G. Corlett), *Obdurate* (Lieut. Commander C. H. Sams), *Petard* (Lieut. Commander E. D. O. Thomson), *Pelican* (Lieut. Commander K. A. Beattie), *Nerissa* (Lieut. Commander M. C. B. Legge), *Onslow* (Lieut. Commander J. C. Tovey), *Moresby* (Lieut. Commander R. V. Alison), *Nicator* (Lieut. in Command J. E. A. Mocatta), *Fearless* (Captain C. D. Roper, Captain D, 1st Destroyer Flotilla), with Destroyers *Acheron* (Commander C. G. Ramsey), *Ariel* (Lieut. Commander A. G. Tippet), *Attack*

---

[1]Jellicoe's despatches and relevant documents are in Temple-Patterson, *Jellicoe Papers*, Vol. I, pp 285–308.

(Lieut. Commander C. H. N. James), *Hydra* (Lieut. F. G. Glossop), *Badger* (Commander C. A. Fremantle), *Goshawk* (Commander D. H. Moir), *Defender* (Lieut. Commander L. R. Palmer), *Lizard* (Lieut. Commander E. Brooke), *Lapwing* (Lieut. Commander A. H. Gye), Destroyers from the Harwich force temporarily attached to my command, *Lydiard* (Commander M. L. Goldsmith), *Liberty* (Lieut. Commander P. W. S. King), *Landrail* (Lieut. Commander F. E. H. G. Hobart), *Laurel* (Lieut. H. D. Stanistreet), *Moorsom* (Commander J. C. Hodgson), *Morris* (Lieut. commander E. S. Graham), *Turbulent* (Lieut. Commander D. Stuart), *Termagant* (Lieut. Commander C. P. Blake), and Seaplane Carrier *Engadine* (Lieut. Commander C. G. Robinson).

The Battle-Cruiser Fleet was accompanied by four ships of the 5th Battle Squadron under the command of Rear Admiral H. Evan-Thomas, M.V.O., flying his Flag in *Barham* (Captain A. W. Craig). The other three ships were *Warspite* (Captain E. M. Phillpotts), *Valiant* (Captain M. Woollcombe), and *Malaya* (Captain Hon. A. D. E. H. Boyle, C.B.)

3. The force was disposed as follows: 5th Battle Squadron N.N.W. 5 miles from *Lion*, screened by *Fearless* and 9 destroyers of 1st Flotilla. The 2nd Battle-Cruiser Squadron was stationed E.N.E. 3 miles from *Lion*, screened by 6 destroyers of the Harwich Force. *Lion* and 1st Battle-Cruiser Squadron were screened by *Champion*, 10 destroyers of 13th Flotilla, *Turbulent* and *Termagant*. Squadrons were in single line ahead, steering N.b E. Light cruisers were in L.S. 6, centre of screen bearing S.S.E., line of direction of screen E.N.E. and W.S.W. *Engadine* was stationed between B and C.

4. At 2.20 p.m. reports were received from *Galatea* indicating the presence of enemy vessels to the E.S.E., steering to the Northward. The direction of advance was immediately altered to S.S.E., the course for Horn Reef, so as to place my force between the enemy and his base. *Galatea* reported at 2.35 p.m. that she had sighted a large amount of smoke as from a fleet, bearing E.N.E. This made it clear that the enemy was to the Northward and Eastward, and that it would be impossible for him to round the Horn Reef without being brought to action. Course was accordingly altered to the Eastward and North Eastward, the enemy being sighted at 3.31 p.m. They appeared to be the 1st scouting group of five battle-cruisers.

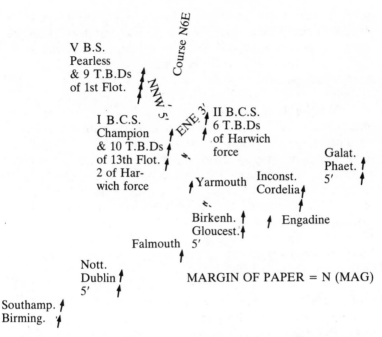

5. After the first report of the enemy the 1st and 3rd Light Cruiser Squadrons changed their direction and without waiting for orders spread to the East, thereby forming a screen in advance of the Battle-Cruiser Squadrons and 5th Battle Squadron by the time we had hauled up to the course of approach. They engaged enemy light cruisers at long range. In the meantime the 2nd Light Cruiser Squadron had come in at high speed and was able to take station ahead of the battle cruisers by the time we turned to E.S.E., the course on which we first engaged the enemy. In this respect the work of the Light Cruiser Squadrons was excellent and of great value.

6. From a report from *Galatea* at 2.25 p.m. it was evident that the enemy force was considerable and not merely an isolated unit of light cruisers, so at 2.45 p.m. I ordered *Engadine* to send up a seaplane and scout to N.N.E. This order was carried out very quickly, and by 3.8 p.m. a seaplane with Flight Lieutenant F. J. Rutland, R.N. as pilot, and Asst. Paymaster G. S. Trewin, R.N. as observer, was well under way; her first reports of the enemy were received in *Engadine* about 3.30 p.m. Owing to clouds it was necessary to fly very low, and in order to identify 4 enemy light cruisers the seaplane had to fly at a height of 900 ft. within

3,000 yards of them, the light cruisers opening fire on her with every gun that would bear. This in no way interfered with the clarity of their reports, and both Flight Lieutenant Rutland and Asst. Paymaster Trewin are to be congratulated on their achievement, which indicates that seaplanes under such circumstances are of distinct value.

7. At 3.30 p.m. I increased speed to 25 knots and formed line of battle, the 2nd Battle-Cruiser Squadron forming astern of the 1st Battle-Cruiser Squadron, with destroyers of the 13th and 9th Flotillas taking station ahead. I turned to E.S.E., slightly converging on the enemy, who were now at a range of 23,000 yards, and formed the ships on a line of bearing to clear the smoke. The 5th Battle Squadron, who had conformed to our movements, were now bearing N.N.W., 10,000 yards. The visibility at this time was good, the sun behind us and the wind S.E. Being between the enemy and his base, our situation was both tactically and strategically good.

8. At 3.48 p.m. the action commenced at a range of 18,500 yards, both forces opening fire practically simultaneously. Both appeared to straddle the target early, and at 3.51 p.m. *Lion* received her first hit. Course was altered to the Southward, and subsequently at intervals, to confuse the enemy's fire control; the mean direction was S.S.E., the enemy steering a parallel course distant about 18,000 to 14,500 yards. For the next ten minutes the firing of the enemy was very rapid and effective. *Lion* was hit repeatedly, the roof of Q turret being blown off at 4 p.m. Immediately afterwards *Indefatigable* was hit by three shots falling together. The shots appeared to hit the outer edge of the upper deck in line with the after turret. An explosion followed, and she fell out of the line sinking by the stern. Hit again by another salvo near A turret she turned over and disappeared.

9. At 4.8 p.m. the 5th Battle Squadron came into action and opened fire at a range of 20,000 yards. The enemy's fire now seemed to slacken. It would appear that at this time we passed through a screen of enemy submarines. In evidence of this a torpedo was sighted passing astern of *Lion* from starboard to port. The destroyer *Landrail* of 9th Flotilla, who was on our port beam trying to take station ahead, sighted the periscope of a submarine on her port quarter, and at the same time the track of a torpedo which passed under her and crossed the line of the battle-cruisers between *Tiger* and *New Zealand*. Though causing considerable inconvenience from smoke, the presence of *Lydiard* and *Landrail*

undoubtedly preserved the battle-cruisers from closer submarine attack. *Nottingham* also reported a submarine on the Starboard beam.

10. Eight destroyers of the 13th Flotilla, *Nestor, Nomad, Nicator, Narborough, Pelican, Petard, Obdurate, Nerissa*, with *Moorsom* and *Morris* of 10th Flotilla, *Turbulent and Termagant* of the 9th Flotilla, having been ordered to attack the enemy with torpedoes when opportunity offered, moved out at 4.15 p.m. simultaneously with a similar movement on the part of the enemy. The attack was carried out in the most gallant manner and with great determination. Before arriving at a favourable position to fire torpedoes, they intercepted an enemy force consisting of a light cruiser and 15 destroyers. A fierce engagement ensued at close quarters, with the result that the enemy were forced to retire on their battle-cruisers, having lost two destroyers sunk, and having their torpedo attack frustrated. Our destroyers sustained no loss in this engagement, but their attack on the enemy battle-cruisers was rendered less effective owing to some of the destroyers having dropped astern during the fight. Their position was therefore unfavourable for torpedo attack.

11. *Nestor, Nomad* and *Nicator*, gallantly led by Commander Hon. E. B. S. Bingham of *Nestor*, pressed home their attack on the battle-cruisers and fired two torpedoes at them at a range of 6,000 and 5,000 yards, being subjected to a heavy fire from the enemy's secondary armament. *Nomad* was badly hit and apparently remained stopped between the lines. Subsequently *Nestor* and *Nicator* altered course to the S.E. and in a short time, the opposing battle-cruisers having turned 16 points, found themselves within close range of a number of enemy battleships. Nothing daunted, though under a terrific fire, they stood on, and their position being favourable for torpedo attack, fired a torpedo at the 2nd ship of the enemy line at a range of 3,000 yards. Before they could fire their fourth torpedo, *Nestor* was badly hit and swung to starboard, *Nicator* altering course inside her to avoid collision and thereby being prevented from firing the last torpedo. *Nicator* made good her escape and subsequently rejoined the Captain D, 13th Flotilla. *Nestor* remained stopped, but was afloat when last seen. *Moorsom* also carried out an attack on the enemy's Battle Fleet.

12. *Petard, Nerissa, Turbulent* and *Termagant* also, pressed home their attack on the enemy battle-cruisers, firing torpedoes at a range of 7,000 yards after the engagement with enemy

destroyers. *Petard* reports that all her torpedoes must have crossed the enemy's line, while *Nerissa* states that one torpedo appeared to strike the rear ship. These destroyer attacks were indicative of the spirit pervading His Majesty's Navy, and were worthy of its highest traditions. I propose to bring to your notice a recommendation of Commander Bingham for the Victoria Cross, and other officers for some recognition of their conspicuous gallantry.

13. From 4.15 to 4.43 p.m. the conflict between the opposing battle cruisers was of a very fierce and resolute character. The 5th Battle Squadron was engaging the enemy's rear ships, unfortunately at very long range. Our fire began to tell, the accuracy and rapidity of that of the enemy depreciating considerably. At 4.18 p.m. the 3rd enemy ship was seen to be on fire. The visibility to the North Eastward had become considerably reduced and the outline of the ships very indistinct. This, no doubt, was largely due to the constant use of smoke balls or charges by the enemy, under cover of which they were continually altering course or zigzagging.

14. At 4.26 p.m. there was a violent explosion in *Queen Mary*; she was enveloped in clouds of grey smoke and disappeared. From the evidence of Captain Pelly of *Tiger*, who was in station astern, corroborated by Rear Admiral Brock in *Princess Royal* ahead, a salvo pitched abreast of Q turret, and almost instantaneously there was a terrific upheaval and a dense cloud of smoke through which *Tiger* passed barely 30 seconds afterwards. No sign could be seen of *Queen Mary*. Eighteen of her officers and men were subsequently picked up by *Laurel*.

15. At 4.38 p.m. *Southampton* reported the enemy's Battle Fleet ahead. The destroyers were recalled, and at 4.42 p.m. the enemy's Battle Fleet was sighted S.E.. Course was altered 16 points in succession to starboard, and I proceeded on a Northerly course to lead them towards the Grand Fleet. The enemy battle-cruisers altered course shortly afterwards, and the action continued. *Southampton* with the 2nd Light Cruiser Squadron held on to the Southward to observe. They closed to within 13,000 yards of the enemy Battle Fleet and came under a very heavy but ineffective fire. *Southampton*'s reports were most valuable. The 5th Battle Squadron were now closing on an opposite course and engaging the enemy battle-cruisers with all guns. The position of the enemy Battle Fleet was communicated to them, and I ordered them to alter course 16 points. Led by Rear Admiral Hugh Evan-

Thomas, M.V.O. in *Barham*, this Squadron supported us brilliantly and effectively.

16. At 4.57 p.m. the 5th Battle Squadron turned up astern of me and came under the fire of the leading ships of the enemy Battle Fleet. *Fearless* with the destroyers of 1st Flotilla joined the battle-cruisers and, when speed admitted, took station ahead. *Champion* with 13th Flotilla took station on the 5th Battle Squadron. At 5 p.m. the 1st and 3rd Light Cruiser Squadrons, which had been following me on the Southerly course, took station on my starboard bow; the 2nd Light Cruiser Squadron took station on my port quarter.

17. The weather conditions now became unfavourable, our ships being silhouetted against a clear horizon to the Westward, while the enemy were for the most part obscured by mist, only showing up clearly at intervals. These conditions prevailed until we had turned their van at about 6 p.m. Between 5 and 6 p.m. the action continued on a Northerly course, the range being about 14,000 yards. During this time the enemy received very severe punishment and undoubtedly one of their battle-cruisers quitted the line in a considerably damaged condition. This came under my personal observation and was corroborated by *Princess Royal* and *Tiger*. Other enemy ships also showed signs of increasing injury. At 5.5 p.m. *Onslow* and *Moresby* who had been detached to assist *Engadine* with the seaplane, rejoined the Battle-Cruiser Squadrons and took station on the starboard (engaged) bow of *Lion*. At 5.10 p.m. *Moresby*, being 2 points before the beam of the leading enemy ship at a range of 6,000 to 8,000 yards, fired a long range torpedo at the 3rd in their line. Eight minutes later she observed a hit with a torpedo on what was judged to be the 6th ship in the line. Later analysis of the director setting indicated a probability of this result. *Moresby* then passed between the lines to clear the range of smoke, and rejoined *Champion*. In corroboration of this, *Fearless* reports having seen an enemy heavy ship heavily on fire at about 5.10 p.m., and shortly afterwards a huge cloud of smoke and steam similar to that which accompanied the blowing up of *Queen Mary* and *Indefatigable*.

18. At 5.35 p.m. our course was N.N.E. and the estimated position of the Grand Fleet was N.16 W., so we gradually hauled to the North Eastward, keeping the range of the enemy at 14,000 yards. He was gradually hauling to the Eastward, receiving severe punishment at the head of his line, and probably acting on information received from his light cruisers which had sighted and were

engaged with the 3rd Battle-Cruiser Squadron (vide *Indomitable*'s report). Possibly Zeppelins were present also. At 5.50 p.m. British cruisers were sighted on the port bow, and at 5.56 p.m. the leading battleships of the Grand Fleet bearing North 5 miles. I thereupon altered course to East and proceeded at utmost speed. This brought the range of the enemy down to 12,000 yards. I made a visual report to the Commander-in-Chief that the enemy battle-cruisers bore South East. At this time only 3 of the enemy battle-cruisers were visible, closely followed by battleships of the *Konig* [sic] class.

19. At about 6.5 p.m. *Onslow*, being on the engaged bow of *Lion*, sighted an enemy light cruiser at a distance of 6,000 yards from us, apparently endeavouring to attack with torpedoes. *Onslow* at once closed and engaged her, firing 58 rounds at a range of from 4,000 to 2,000 yards, scoring a number of hits. *Onslow* then closed to within 8,000 yards of the enemy battle-cruisers and orders were given for all torpedoes to be fired. At this moment she was struck amidships by a heavy shell, with the result that only one torpedo was fired. Thinking that all his torpedoes had gone, the Commanding Officer proceeded to retire at slow speed. Being informed that he still had three torpedoes, he closed the light cruiser previously engaged and torpedoed her. The enemy's Battle Fleet was then sighted at a distance of 8,000 yards, and the remaining torpedoes were fired at them; having started correctly, they must have crossed the enemy's track. Damage in her feed tank then caused *Onslow* to stop.

20. At 7.15 p.m. *Defender*, whose speed had been reduced to 10 knots, while on the disengaged side of the battle-cruisers, by a 12" shell which damaged her foremost boiler but failed to explode, closed *Onslow* and took her in tow. Shells were falling all round them during this operation, which, however, was successfully accomplished. During the heavy weather of the ensuing night the tow parted twice but was re-secured. The two struggled on together until 1 p.m., 1st June, when *Onslow* was transferred to tugs. I consider the performances of these two destroyers to be gallant in the extreme, and I am recommending Lieut. Commander J. C. Tovey of *Onslow* and Lieut. Commander Palmer of *Defender* for special recognition. *Onslow* was possibly the destroyer referred to by the Rear Admiral Commanding the 3rd Light Cruiser Squadron as follows:— 'Here I should like to bring to your notice the action of a destroyer (name unknown, thought to be marked with the number "59" (? *Acasta* ?) which

we passed close in a disabled condition soon after 6 p.m. She apparently was able to struggle ahead again and made straight for the *Derfflinger* to attack her. The incident appeared so courageous that it seems desirable to investigate it further, as I am unable to be certain of the vessel's identity.'

21. At 6.15 p.m. *Defence* and *Warrior* crossed our bows from port to starboard, necessitating our hauling to port to clear. They were closely engaging an enemy light cruiser, but immediately after clearing us they came under the fire of enemy heavy ships, and passed down between us and the enemy on opposite courses.

22. At 6.20 p.m. the 3rd Battle-Cruiser Squadron, consisting of *Invincible* (Captain A. L. Cay) flying the Flag of Rear Admiral Hon. H. L. A. Hood, C.B., M.V.O., D.S.O., *Indomitable* (Captain F. W. Kennedy) and *Inflexible* (Captain E. H. F. Heaton-Ellis, M.V.O.) appeared ahead, steaming South towards the enemy's van. I ordered them to take station ahead, which was carried out magnificently, Rear Admiral Hood bringing his Squadron into action ahead in a most inspiring manner, worthy of his great naval ancestors. At 6.25 p.m. I altered course to the E.S.E. in support of the 3rd Battle-Cruiser Squadron, who were at this time only 8,000 yards from the enemy's leading ship. They were pouring a hot fire into her and caused her to turn to the Westward of South. At the same time I made a visual report to the Commander-in-Chief of the bearing and distance of the enemy Battle Fleet. At 6.33 p.m. *Invincible* was struck by a complete salvo about Q turret and immediately blew up.

23. After the loss of *Invincible*, the Squadron was led by *Inflexible* until 6.50 p.m. By this time the battle-cruisers were clear of our leading Battle Squadron then bearing about N.N.W. 3 miles, and I ordered the 3rd Battle-Cruiser Squadron to prolong the line astern and reduced to 18 knots. The visibility at this time was very indifferent, not more than 4 miles, and the enemy ships were temporarily lost sight of. It is interesting to note that after 6 p.m., although the visibility became reduced, it was undoubtedly more favourable to us than to the enemy. At intervals their ships showed up clearly, enabling us to punish them very severely and establish a definite superiority over them. The damage recieved by our ships during this period, excepting the destruction of *Invincible* was slight. From the reports of other ships and my own observations it was clear that the enemy suffered severely, battle-cruisers and battleships alike. The head of their line was crumpled up, leaving battleships as targets for the majority of our battle

cruisers. Before leaving us the 5th Battle Squadron were also engaging battleships. The report of Rear Admiral Evan-Thomas shows that excellent results were obtained, and it can be safely said that his magnificent squadron wrought great execution.

24. From the report of Rear Admiral T. D. W. Napier, M.V.O., the 3rd Light Cruiser Squadron, which had maintained its station on our starboard bow well ahead of the enemy, at 6.25 p.m. attacked with the torpedo at a range of 6,000 yards. *Falmouth* and *Yarmouth* both fired torpedoes at the leading enemy battle-cruiser, and it is believed that one torpedo hit, as a heavy under-water explosion was observed. The 3rd Light Cruiser Squadron then gallantly attacked the heavy ships with gunfire, with impunity to themselves, thereby demonstrating that the fighting efficiency of the enemy had been seriously impaired. Rear Admiral Napier deserves great credit for his determined and effective attack. *Indomitable* reports that about this time one of the *Derfflinger* class fell out of the enemy's line.

25. At 7.6 p.m. I received a signal from the Commander-in-Chief that the course of the Fleet was South. Subsequently signals were received up to 8.46 p.m. shewing that the course of the Grand Fleet was to the South Westward. Between 7 and 7.12 p.m. we hauled round gradually to S.W. by S. to regain touch with the enemy, and at 7.14 p.m. again sighted them at a range of about 15,000 yards. The ships sighted at this time were two battle-cruisers and two battleships, apparently of the *Konig* [sic] class. No doubt more continued the line to the Northward, but that was all that could be seen. The visibility having improved considerably as the sun descended below the clouds, we re-engaged at 7.17 p.m. and increased speed to 22 knots. At 7.32 p.m. my course was S.W., speed 18 knots, the leading enemy battleship bearing N.W. by W. Again after a very short time the enemy showed signs of punishment, one ship being on fire while another appeared to drop right astern. The destroyers at the head of the enemy's line emitted volumes of grey smoke, covering their capital ships as with a pall, under cover of which they undoubtedly turned away, and at 7.45 p.m. we lost sight of them.

26. At 7.58 p.m. I ordered the 1st and 3rd Light Cruiser Squadrons to sweep to the Westward and locate the head of the enemy's line, and at 8.20 p.m. we altered course to West in support. We soon located two battle-cruisers and Battleships, and were heavily engaged at a short range of about 10,000 yards. The leading ship was hit repeatedly by *Lion* and turned away 8 points, emitting

very high flames and with a heavy list to port. *Princess Royal* set fire to a 3-funneled battleship; *New Zealand* and *Indomitable* report that the 3rd ship, which they both engaged, hauled out of the line heeling over and on fire. The mist which now came down enveloped them, and *Falmouth* reported they were last seen at 8.38 p.m. steaming to the Westward.

27. At 8.40 p.m. all our battle-cruisers felt a heavy shock as if struck by a mine or torpedo, or possibly sunken wreckage. As, however, examination of the bottoms reveals no sign of such an occurrence, it is assumed that it indicated the blowing up of a great vessel. This seems a very probable explanation in view of the condition in which the enemy was last seen.

28. I continued on a South Westerly course with my light cruisers spread until 9.24 p.m. Nothing further being sighted, I assumed that the enemy were to the North Westward and that we had established ourselves well between him and his base. *Minotaur* was at this time bearing North 5 miles, and I asked her the position of the leading Battle Squadron of the Grand Fleet. Her reply was that it was not in sight but was last seen bearing N.N.E. 5 miles at 8.10 p.m. My position, course and speed had been made to the Commander-in-Chief at 7.30, 8.40 and 9 p.m., the latter signal giving the bearing of the enemy as N. by W., steering S.W. by S. which as near as could be judged was correct. At 9.16 p.m. I received a signal from the Commander-in-Chief that the course of the Fleet was South.

29. In view of the gathering darkness and for other reasons, viz. (a) Our distance from the Battle Fleet, (b) The damaged condition of the battle-cruisers, (c) The enemy being concentrated, (d) The enemy being accompanied by numerous destroyers, (e) Our strategical position being such as to make it appear certain that we should locate the enemy at daylight under most favourable circumstances, I did not consider it desirable or proper to close the enemy Battle Fleet during the dark hours. I therefore concluded that I should be carrying out the Commander-in-Chief's wishes by turning to the course of the Fleet, reporting to the Commander-in-Chief that I had done so.

30. My duty in this situation was to ensure that the enemy Fleet could not regain its base by passing round the Southern flank of our forces. I therefore turned to South at 9.24 p.m. at 17 knots, and continued this course until 2.30 a.m., with the 1st and 3rd Light Cruiser Squadrons spread to the Southward and Westward. My intention was to ask permission to sweep S.W. at daylight,

but on receiving a signal that the Commander-in-Chief was turning to North, and ordering me to conform and close, I proceeded accordingly and rejoined the Commander-in-Chief at 5.20 a.m.

31. The movements of the Light Cruiser Squadrons and Flotillas are described in detail in their own reports. *Champion* and most of the 13th Flotilla were in visual touch after the destroyer attack on the enemy line at 4.40 p.m. on 31st May, but they became detached later and stationed themselves at the rear of the Battle Fleet for the night. At 0.30 a.m. on 1st June a large vessel crossed the rear of the Flotilla at high speed. She passed close to *Petard* and *Turbulent*, switched on searchlights and opened a heavy fire which severely damaged *Petard* and disabled *Turbulent*. At 3.30 a.m. *Champion* was engaged for a few minutes with 4 enemy destroyers. *Moresby* reports 4 ships of *Deutschland* class sighted at 2.35 a.m., at whom she fired one torpedo. Two minutes later an explosion was felt by *Moresby* and *Obdurate*. On investigation I find the *Moresby* was in station with *Obdurate* astern of *Champion*. Some of the strange vessels were sighted by *Champion* and *Obdurate*, who took them to be some of our own light cruisers. This was impossible, and it is very much to be regretted that *Champion* did not take steps to identify them. If, as was probable, they were the enemy, an excellent opportunity was missed for an attack in the early morning light. More important still, a portion of the enemy might have been definitely located.

32. *Fearless* and the 1st Flotilla were very usefully employed as a submarine screen during the earlier part of the 31st May, but their limited speed made it almost impossible for them to regain their proper stations when the battle-cruisers altered course. At 6.10 p.m. when joining the Battle Fleet, *Fearless* was unable to follow the battle-cruisers without fouling the battleships, so turned 32 points and took station at the rear of the line. She sighted during the night a battleship of the *Kaiser* class steaming fast and entirely alone. She was not able to engage her, but believes she was attacked by destroyers further astern. A heavy explosion was observed astern not long after. The incident could be identified by the fact that this ship fired a star shell. By midday on 1st June all the 1st Flotilla were getting short of fuel and had to be detached in pairs to make their base at 15 knots.

33. The 1st and 3rd Light Cruiser Squadrons were almost continuously in touch with the battle-cruisers, one or both squadrons being usually ahead. They were most valuable as a submarine screen when no destroyers were present; they very effectively

protected the head of our line from torpedo attack by light cruisers or destroyers, and were prompt in helping to regain touch when the enemy's line was temporarily lost sight of. The 2nd Light Cruiser Squadron was at the rear of our battle line during the night, and at 9 p.m. assisted to repel a destroyer attack on the 5th Battle Squadron. They were also heavily engaged at 10.20 p.m. with 5 enemy cruisers or light cruisers, *Southampton* and *Dublin* suffering severe casualties during an action lasting about 15 minutes. *Birmingham*, at 11.30 p.m., sighted 2 or more heavy ships steering South. A report of this was received by me at 11.40 p.m. as steering W.S.W. They were thought at the time to be battle-cruisers, but it is since considered that they were probably battleships.

34. The work of *Engadine* appears to have been most praiseworthy throughout, and of great value. Lieut. Commander C. G. Robinson deserves great credit for the skilful and seamanlike manner in which he handled his ship. He actually towed *Warrior* for 75 miles between 8.40 p.m., 31st May, and 7.15 a.m., 1st June, and was instrumental in saving the lives of her ship's company.

35. I have not referred to *Chester* as she did not come under my personal command or observation. Her report shows that she fought gallantly and successfully against superior forces and sufferfed considerably in casualties and damage.

36. It is impossible to give a definite statement of the losses inflicted on the enemy. The visibility was for the most part low and fluctuating, and caution forbade me to close the range too much with my inferior force.

A review of all the reports which I have received, however, leads me to form the following estimate of the enemy's losses during the course of the operations described in this report:-

> 3 battle-cruisers,
> 2 Battleships,
> (*Konig* [sic] or *Kaiser* class)   } sunk
> 1 *Pommern* class,
> 2 light cruisers,
> 3 destroyers

> 2 battle-cruisers,
> Several light cruisers   } severely
> and destroyers.   } damaged

This is eloquent testimony to the very high standard of Gunnery and Torpedo efficiency of His Majesty's ships. The control and drill remain undisturbed throughout, in many cases despite heavy damage to material and personnel. Our superiority over the enemy in this respect was very marked, their efficiency becoming rapidly reduced under punishment, while ours was maintained throughout.

37. As was to be expected, the behaviour of the ships' companies under the terrible conditions of a modern sea battle was magnificent without exception. The strain on their morale was a severe test of discipline and training. Officers and men were imbued with one thought, the desire to defeat the enemy. The fortitude of the wounded was admirable. A report from the Commanding Officer of *Chester* gives a splendid instance of devotion to duty. Boy 1st Class John Travers Cornwell of *Chester* was mortally wounded early in the action. He nevertheless remained standing alone at a most exposed post, quietly awaiting orders till the end of the action, with the gun's crew dead and wounded all round him. His age was under 16½ years. I regret that he has since died, but I recommend his case for special recognition in justice to his memory, and as an acknowledgment of the high example set by him.

Our casualties were very heavy, and I wish to express my deepest regret at the loss of so many gallant comrades, Officers and Men. They died gloriously.

38. Exceptional skill was displayed by the Medical Officers of the Fleet. They performed operations and tended the wounded under conditions of extreme difficulty. In some cases their staff was seriously depleted by casualties, and the inevitable lack of such essentials as adequate light, hot water, etc., in ships battered by shell fire, tried their skill, resource and physical endurance to the utmost.

39. As usual, the Engine Room Departments of all ships displayed the highest qualities of technical skill, discipline and endurance. High speed is a primary factor in the tactics of the squadrons under my command, and the Engine Room Departments never fail.

40. I have already made mention of the brilliant support afforded me by Rear Admiral H. Evan-Thomas, M.V.O. and the 5th Battle Squadron, and of the magnificent manner in which Rear Admiral Hon. H. L. A. Hood, C.B., M.V.O., D.S.O. brought his squadron into action: I desire to record my great regret at his

loss, which is a national misfortune. I would now bring to your notice the able support rendered to me by Rear Admiral W. C. Pakenham, C.B. and Rear Admiral O. de B. Brock, C.B. In the course of my report I have expressed my appreciation of the good work performed by the Light Cruiser Squadrons under the command respectively of Rear Admiral T. D. W. Napier, M.V.O., Commodore W. E. Goodenough, M.V.O., and Commodore E. S. Alexander-Sinclair, M.V.O. On every occasion these Officers anticipated my wishes and used their forces to the best possible effect.

41. I desire also to bring to your notice the skill with which their respective ships were handled by Captains F. W. Kennedy (*Indomitable*), who commanded the 3rd Battle Cruiser Squadron after the loss of Rear Admiral Hood, C. F. Sowerby (*Indefatigable*), H. B. Pelly, M.V.O. (*Tiger*), J. F. E. Green (*New Zealand*), W. H. Cowan, M.V.O., D.S.O. (*Princess Royal*), C. I. Prowse (*Queen Mary*), A. L. Cay (*Invincible*), E. H. F. Heaton-Ellis, M.V.O. (*Inflexible*), C. B. Miller (*Nottingham*), A. E. M. Chatfield, C.V.O. (*Lion*), on whom lay special responsibility as commanding my Flagship, J. D. Edwards (*Falmouth*), A. A. M. Duff (*Birmingham*), E. Reeves (*Birkenhead*), W. F. Blunt (*Gloucester*), T. D. Pratt (*Yarmouth*), A. C. Scott (*Dublin*), B. S. Thesiger (*Inconstant*), R. N. Lawson (*Chester*), J. U. Farie (*Champion*) Captain D, 13th Flotilla, J. E. Cameron, M.V.O. (*Phaeton*), T. P. H. Beamish (*Cordelia*) and C. D. Roper (*Fearless*, Captain D, 1st Flotilla). With such Flag Officers, Commodores and Captains to support me, my task was made easier. The destroyers of the 1st and 13th Flotillas were handled by their respective Commanding Officers with skill, dash and courage. I desire to record my very great regret at the loss of Captains C. F. Sowerby (*Indefatigable*), C. I. Prowse (*Queen Mary*) and A. L. Cay (*Invincible*), all officers of the highest attainments who can be ill-spared at this time of stress.

42. I wish to endorse the report of the Rear Admiral Commanding the 5th Battle Squadron as to the ability displayed by Captains E. M. Philpotts (*Warspite*), M. Woollcombe (*Valiant*), Hon. A. D. E. H. Boyle (*Malaya*), and A. W. Craig (*Barham*).

43. In conclusion I desire to record and bring to your notice the great assistance that I received on a day of great anxiety and strain from my Chief of the Staff, Captain R. W. Bentinck, whose good judgment was of the greatest help. He was a tower of

strength. My Flag Commander, Hon. R. A. R. Plunkett, was most valuable in observing the effect of our fire, thereby enabling me to take advantage of the enemy's discomfiture, my Secretary, F. T. Spickernell, who made accurate notes of events as they occurred, which proved of the utmost value in keeping the situation clearly before me; my Flag Lieutenant Commander R. F. Seymour, who maintained efficient communications under the most difficult circumstances despite the fact that his signalling appliances were continually shot away. All these Officers carried out their duties with great coolness on the manoeuvring platform, where they were fully exposed to the enemy's fire.

44. In accordance with your wishes, I am forwarding in a separate letter a full list of Officers and Men whom I wish to recommend to your notice.

45. I enclose the reports rendered to me by Flag Officers, Commodores and Commanding Officers regarding their proceedings during the period under review. A sheet of diagrams is attached; a track chart has already been forwarded [not included].

I have the honour to be,
Sir,
Your obedient Servant,

VICE-ADMIRAL.

165.   *From Jellicoe*

[BTY/13/22/14]   *Iron Duke*
[Holograph]   13.6.16.

I know you have been as busy as myself and I hated to worry you about the dispatch but I was being pressed so to send in mine. It is impossible to find time for writing or I would have written to you more and earlier. Moreover I am disgusted at our luck in the weather line [?] and have been wondering whether I could not have got at them better. But I am arriving at the conclusion that I did the right thing with the knowledge at my disposal at the time. I never felt so 'out of it' as at the meeting. I could not make out the situation a bit. Whether the enemy B.F. was ahead, abeam or on the quarter. Of course *Marlborough* could see much better, but it took time to get signals from her & from you and precious moments were lost.

THE BATTLE OF JUTLAND, MAY 31, 1916
The deployment of the Grand Fleet, 1815-1826 hours

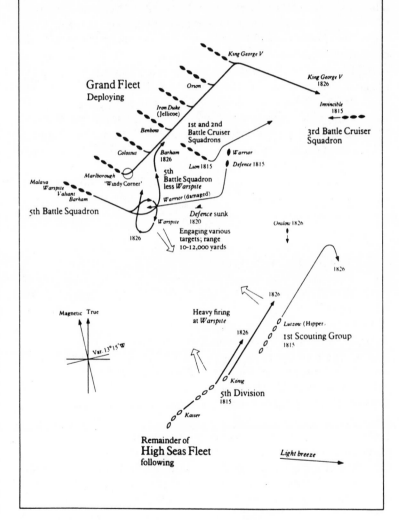

Scale of Yards

0	5000	10,000

British   Battleships   Battle Cruisers
German   Battleships   Battle Cruisers

King George V

Grand Fleet
Deploying

Orion

King George V
1826

Iron Duke
(Jellicoe)

Invincible
1815

Benbow

1st and 2nd
Battle Cruiser
Squadrons

3rd Battle Cruiser
Squadron

Colossus

Barham
1826

Warrior

Lion 1815

Defence 1815

5th
Battle Squadron
less Warspite

Marlborough

Malaya
Warspite
Valiant
Barham

'Windy Corner'

Warrior (damaged)

5th Battle Squadron

Warspite

Defence sunk
1820

Onslow 1826

1826

Engaging various
targets; range
10-12,000 yards

1826

Magnetic True

Heavy firing
at Warspite

1826

1826

Lutzow (Hipper)

1st Scouting Group
1815

Var. 13°15'W

1826

König

5th Division
1815

Remainder of
High Seas Fleet
following

Kaiser

Light breeze

That difference in reckoning between *Lion* & *Iron Duke* was most perplexing. Impossible to avoid of course, but nevertheless it put me out very much. Then all or one of your cruisers turned to port and I could not make out why.

Well, I don't want conditions like that again with a big fleet to handle and equal difficulties to contend with.

There is much to learn and much to arrange for the future. *Iron Duke* refits at the end of this week. I want to get it done whilst the Germans are repairing. I shall come to you by rail, have a talk and then probably go on to London & discuss future dispositions and operations. I also of course want to let the B.C.F. know how much I valued their work. I hope about the middle of next week will see me your way.

H.M.'s visit tomorrow does not reduce my labours, as you may imagine, but of course it is splendid for the fleet. I don't know whether he has been to you, but if not, I shall beg him to go to you on the way south, and he should in that case arrive Friday. I will send you a wire directly I have ascertained his intentions.

I am not very fit just at present, rheumatism & lack of exercise, but I hope it is only temporary.

I can't think of poor *Hood* & those good fellows who are gone. All right for them but terrible for those they have left.

166.   *To H. A. Gwynne* (editor of *Morning Post*)

[IWM/GWYNNE]   *Lion*
[Holograph]   18.6.16

Thank you for yours and your kind congratulations. I apologise for the length of time in replying but I have been inundated with work. The aftermath of the naval action is terrific.

I was very glad the *Morning Post* did not fall into the error that most of the Press did in proclaiming that we had received a severe reverse.

The Press generally seems very jumpy. The Admiralty pronouncement was downright bloody foolishness. But even so one did not expect the Press to put the interpretation on it that they did. It does not say much for their faith, so long and frequently vaunted, in the Navy. Naturally my men were furious. They had done gloriously, none could have done more, or approaching it. They had suffered heavily, many comrades and pals had gone. Their experience would have tried the morale and nerves of the superman. They had come out of hell undaunted, and were told they had been whacked. Their own feelings consequently were indescribable. No government official has even yet expressed sympathy with their losses, or gratitude for maintaining the highest traditions of our great Service. They had a memorial service at St. Paul's last Wednesday. In it there was no reference to the sea, sailors, Navy or victory, & consequently was a farce to the hundreds of poor women who went there for some small measure of comfort. You might well comment on that.

167.   *To A. J. Balfour* (1st Lord of Admiralty)

[BTY/6/3/15]   *Lion*
[Copy]   21st June 1916

Dear Mr Balfour,

I am moved to address you on the subject of despatches and their publication.

I have now had occasion to write three sets of despatches, the 1st on the Heligoland Bight operation, the 2nd on the Dogger Bank engagement, and the 3rd on the recent engagement off the Horn Reef. By 'despatches' I refer also to telegraphic reports.[1]

In the first two instances my reports were distorted and cut about, so that what eventually appeared in the Press bore a considerably different sense from what I wrote. May I explain.

As regards the 1st case, Heligoland Bight. All reference to the fact that, owing to faulty staff work at the Admiralty, one portion of the force employed was unaware of the presence and co-operation of another, was eliminated and not permitted to appear. The result of the fault was that the first support for Commodore T, a Light Cruiser Squadron, was drawn away in pursuit of our own destroyers, and so prevented from rendering the support urgently required by Commodore T. This made it necessary for me to use the battle-cruisers to support him in a position close to Heligoland, where they ran very considerable risk from mine and submarine. The end justified the means, but if I had lost a battle-

---

[1]See 103, 104, 111, 116, 124.

cruiser I should have been hanged, drawn and quartered. Yet it was necessary to run the risk to save two of our light cruisers and a large force of destroyers which otherwise would most certainly have been lost.

Again, on the 2nd occasion, the Dogger Bank fight. In the telegraphic report published, purporting to come from me but altered to meet Admiralty views, I was made to say that 'at — I broke off the engagement owing to the presence of submarines'. This was neither in accordance with the facts nor with my telegraphic report. Consequently I came in for a large amount of hostile criticism, perfectly fair and perfectly sound if the facts had been as published. I have a very vivid recollection of one perfectly sound and justifiable criticism finishing a very pungent article with the following, 'The British Admiral let the enemy escape because of the presence of submarines etc. What risks would he take? Admiral Beatty's report is given out officially by the Admiralty. It proves on his own showing that he deserves not glory, but a Court Martial — once more "pour encourager les autres" — with the ghost of Admiral Byng present as an interested spectator'!

My written despatch on this same occasion was so altered that I asked that an announcement should be made in the Gazette that it was an abridged copy, altered in the interests of the Service. I received a reply that the Admiralty recognised the undesirability of publishing a mutilated despatch; and they issued instructions that in future two despatches should be written, one for official record and one for publication.

I am not unduly sensitive to criticism, but in the best interests of the service it cannot be good for Admirals to be laid open to unfavourable criticism based on inaccurate data provided by the Admiralty.

In the present instance I would ask your consideration before it is too late, that is before the despatches are published. If it is necessary to publish them at all, it seems only right that they should be left as written by the officer who signs them.

As far as I can judge there is nothing in my expurgated despatch which would be of value to the enemy, except perhaps the latter part of paragraph 26, starting with the words 'My position, course and speed had been made to the Commander-in-Chief . . . (to the end of the paragraph), which might be left without detriment to the story.

168. *Lessons from Battle of 31 May 1916*
[Notes from Vice-Admiral Sturdee to Beatty]

[BTY/6/17/8]   21 June 1916

The following notes re lessons learnt are, I believe, corroborated by one or more other observers. In certain cases it seems very desirable to issue orders or take other necessary action as early as possible.

1. Speed of Battle Fleet was too slow. It is a vital necessity of successful tactics that the van division should steam at high speed so as to assist the battle-cruisers in enveloping the enemy's flank. This will also assist to open out the battle line, thereby reducing smoke interference and danger from torpedoes. Nothing could be more dangerous than ships getting jambed up at the rear of the line and having to reduce to slow speed, which actually occurred on 31st May. Greater speed in the whole battle line will also reduce danger from submarine attack and give greater manoeuvring power for dodging torpedoes.

2. Clearing the front of the Battle Fleet is a matter of great difficulty, particularly for slow cruisers. This does not seem to have been sufficiently realised by all concerned. If the same number of vessels are to cover the front of the Fleet in future, I think their safety cannot possibly be guaranteed in misty weather unless they retire between the columns of the main Fleet instead of going right round the flank.

3. Instructions in G.F.B.O. seem to go into too much detail and in some cases are rather too rigid. Initiative is certainly permitted, but is not specially encouraged.

4. We seem rather to have under-estimated our enemy, particularly in supposing that a Fleet which remains in harbour cannot prove efficient in battle.

5. The greatest problem of modern battle, perhaps even more so than in the past, is to decide what risks should be avoided and what risks should be cheerfully accepted as a part of the price of victory. The unavoidable risks are so great that it might seem essential to refuse every other that can possibly be avoided. On the other hand the total risks that *must* be run before a complete victory is achieved are so heavy that a few more or less would seem to be almost immaterial. A right decision in any given case is profoundly difficult, but one thing is certain: once it has been decided that the moment is opportune for a general action, there

can be no question of half measures from that moment onwards. If our forces are properly concentrated and properly handled, it should be possible to take all the necessary risks and still leave a margin (though perhaps a very small one) to give us a fair chance of achieving decisive victory.

6. There can be no doubt that our system of peace training has not been ideally suited to the requirements of modern war. The ready resourcefulness of the British seaman is a tradition dating from the Trafalgar epoch, but even in those days of constant war the display of initiative and bold leadership in battle was somewhat of an exception, practised only by Nelson and a few others of his type. It is almost inevitable now that we must reap what we have sown, but anything that can be done to foster and encourage those qualities will, even now, be of infinite value to us.

7. It seems to be of great importance that we should open fire before the enemy, and establish hitting before he does.

8. Provided that increased rate of fire gives a reasonable chance of increased rate of hitting, the rate of fire should be increased to the furthest possible limit. This particularly applies to the early stages of an action.

9. Once we have commenced hitting the enemy, his offensive power appears to be enormously reduced.

10. Zigzagging when hit is of undoubted value to us. It may be well to devise a uniform method of doing this and to enable any ship in the line to make a signal when she wishes to alter course on account of receiving punishment.

11. I am more than ever convinced that efficient concentration of fire is essential for decisive success in battle.

12. German night firing is very efficient. In conditions such as 31st May, it would have been very easy for them to force a general action during the night. Unless we do a great deal more night target practice, it seems probable that such action on a future occasion may be decidedly in the enemy's favour.

13. Owing to the large weights that have been put into ships since war began, and the greater weights now urgently needed (for magazine protection, etc.), it is recommended that nets be abolished and at once landed from all battle-cruisers.

14. Torpedo look-outs must be stationed aloft. In smooth water torpedoes can be seen approaching, but when the surface is ruffled by wind the torpedo will without doubt be a very serious menace. Look-outs must have direct communication to Captain, and must always report bearing on which torpedo is sighted.

15. Day attacks by destroyers on heavy ships may well prove very effective, but care should be taken not to go in any closer than is necessary. Destroyers should certainly not go inside 6,000 yards by day unless the enemy's ships are heavily engaged. The use of smoke screens for covering the flotilla's retirement is strongly recommended, so long as it does not hamper the view of our capital ships.

16. We had many very narrow escapes from enemy submarines and torpedoes. It would not have been surprising if we had lost six battle-cruisers instead of three. (Both *Princess Royal* and *Indomitable* state that two torpedoes went under their bottom). Anyway, the submarine on the field of battle is bound to have great value, and it is therefore suggested that the new 'J' class be attached to the Battle-Cruiser Fleet as soon as possible for tactical and other trials.

17. Directional wireless has proved itself of considerable value, and is recommended to be fitted in five or six other ships.

18. In Fleet action conditions, and also before and after, it is most important for all units to maintain visual touch. Any squadron likely to become detached by day should drop back a linking ship. Once a squadron or unit has gone out of visual touch, it is a matter of great difficulty to get them in again: Vide 1st B.S., *Champion*, and various other forces.

19. Recommended that enquiries be made and steps taken to prevent destroyers getting detached, either by day or night, in the way that they appear to at present. Also recommended that the Battle-Cruiser Fleet should, if possible, sight the Grand Fleet and check positions before proceeding to engage the enemy.

20. In view of the inferior defensive power of our battle-cruisers, it is now more necessary than ever that they should be adequately supported. The 5th Battle Squadron is an undoubted aid, but its value can only be very limited when the enemy battle-cruisers are supported by their whole Fleet.

21. The past indications that the German Fleet would come out and be brought to action (which were scoffed at by so many) tend now to suggest equally strongly that they will come out again. It would be a grave mistake for officers to settle down and assure themselves that the High Sea Fleet will never fight again.

22. It is quite possible that the enemy has been encouraged by his alleged victory, and we may therefore expect the demands from the Kaiser or the Army will impel his Fleet to come out for a further effort. In that event we should aim to make him fight

more or less at our own time and place, i.e., early in the day and
further from his base. It is easily in our power to do this, for we
have nothing to gain by operating near the enemy's base, while
he has nothing to gain unless he comes over to our coast or
attempts to attack our cruiser patrol lines which hold up and
strangle his trade.

23. It is worth noting that both Scheer and Hipper were
distinguished torpedo officers, and it is therefore quite certain that
the torpedo will play a large part in their battle tactics. Submarines
will certainly be present in as large numbers as possible, and the
torpedo menace will be a very serious one to us in future if the
weather chances to be more suitable than before to the German
requirements. (i.e. misty or windy).

24. The next naval battle will take place quite possibly in July
or August. Its result will largely depend on whether we or the
Germans take most pains to study the lessons provided by our
recent experience and to apply them with skill and unsparing
energy.

169. *Advance Report of Gunnery Committee*

[BTY/6/17/5]   *Lion*
                                               22nd June 1916

Sir,

We have the honour to forward an advance report of the
Gunnery Committee formed by your orders to consider the lessons
learnt on May 31st 1916.

Rear Admiral Brock and Commander Egerton have been
absent from the meetings on leave, but in view of the importance
of certain lessons being promulgated without delay, we have not
waited for their return before issuing the immediate report.

A further and more thorough report will be sent in later.

We have the honour to be,
Sir,
Your obedient Servants,
(Signed)   A. E. CHATFIELD
Captain, HMS *Lion*
(Signed)   E. R. RUSHTON
Acting Captain, HMS *Southampton*

(Signed)   S. R. BAILEY[1]
Commander (G)
The Vice Admiral Commanding
Battle Cruiser Fleet

Gunnery Lessons learnt from Action of 31st May

Having reviewed the reports of all ships of the B.C.F. and 5th B.S., the Committee consider that from a Gunnery stand point three main features stand out as requiring immediate consideration and action in view of a possible early meeting with the enemy. Should the recommendations meet with your approval either wholly or in part, they are such as can be immediately put into operation without delay, and it is with this idea in mind that they have been framed.

2. The Committee accordingly have dealt with these more urgent questions in this advanced report in order to meet the immediate necessities of the B.C.F. and 5th B.S. Their intention is to forward a further report on the many other points of value and interest which have arisen.

3. Under the weather and light conditions of the recent action the British system of fire control was put to the severest test imaginable, and on the whole it may be said to have stood the test successfully in that it proved our ability to inflict heavy damage on the enemy even under conditions most difficult for us and most favourable to him. At the same time these conditions have shown weak points with which we propose to deal.

4.   The three outstanding features are:-
(a) The necessity of rapid and early hitting.
(b) The use of defensive tactics to avoid being hit.
(c) The safety of magazines and ammunition.

5.   (a) *THE NECESSITY OF RAPID AND EARLY HITTING*

(i) *Rapid ranging*

At the commencement of the recent action it is known that the fourth salvo from an enemy ship was fired after 1½ minutes, while the fourth salvo from our ship was fired at 4 minutes. This shows that the enemy have a system of ranging by a succession of rapid salvos.

[1]On Goodenough's promotion to Rear-Admiral on 10 June 1916, Rushton was made Captain of *Southampton*; Bailey was on Beatty's staff; Wilfred Egerton, Flag Commander to Rear-Admiral Evan-Thomas.

There are undoubtedly great advantages in this method as compared with that of waiting for the fall of shot before firing the next salvo.

While, therefore, there is no great difference in accuracy in their opening range as compared with ours, they have, undoubtedly, greater chances of first hitting.

We therefore recommend that this form of attack should be countered by a 'ladder' system of salvoes – the general idea of which is as given below, and it is meanwhile being further investigated on the spotting table. We are strongly of opinion that though the ladder system appears, on first sight, to be extravagant of ammunition, this is not the case; on the contrary the present system has shown itself to be so when the enemy is zigzagging.

Firstly, because the rate of spotting is not sufficiently quick to give the necessary indication as to change of enemy's course.

Secondly, because the universal experience in the B.C.F. and 5th B.S. was that a correct rate was only achieved at considerable intervals for short periods.

(ii) *Ladder system of finding or re-finding the target*

On opening fire. Range, deflection, and rate to be calculated as at present, but 2 or 3 salvoes (according to the time of flight) to be fired in rapid succession without waiting to spot fall of shot. Sights to be adjusted as follows:-

1st salvo: A determined amount below the estimated range.

2nd salvo: Mean or estimated range.

3rd salvo: A determined amount above the estimated range.

Should these combined salvoes not cross the target, repeat the ladder until the target is crossed.

It is not for a moment intended that the Control Officers' hands should be tied, in any way, by a hard and fast rule; according to circumstances it may be best to fire a three salvo ladder before spotting, or to fire two ladders of two salvoes each – much must depend on how soon the target is crossed. In considering this system it must be borne in mind that on several occasions on 31st May the enemy re-appeared from the mist and fire was immediately re-opened before a single rangefinder reading had been obtained. These conditions have now been experienced so frequently that they cannot be considered other than usual, and they must be catered for.

The Control Officer, using this system, would decide on the number of salvoes in the ladder and the size of the steps by the information received from the rangefinders, if any, in precisely the same way that he now is guided as to the size of the bracket.

This ladder should be repeated until the target is crossed, (by which it will be known within what limits the range lies), then the ladder should be repeated with reduced steps until one salvo straddles the target.

As soon as the straddle is obtained deliberate or rapid salvoes should be continued, as at present, until the target is entirely lost, and then we consider that the ladder system is the quickest way of regaining touch.

(iii) *Rate finding and keeping*[1]

From the difficulties experienced by Control Officers, and from the observation of *Galatea* and *Yarmouth*, the fact is established that the enemy altered course frequently, but on what system there is no evidence.

Generally speaking, the rate was in error, due to this, but during occasional intervals it was correct, and hitting was established for a short time.

The action, taken through all its phases, appears to show that more value was obtained from rangefinders by some ships than by others, and that at such times as the enemy was on a steady course undoubted assistance was received from the plot.

It is again strongly emphasised that the enemy system of continuously altering course defeats any system of fire control based on rate-finding, for the reason that by the time the plot has established a rate it is no longer applicable.

It is considered that eventually a fully developed rangefinder system will give quicker information than any other, as to the movements of the enemy; i.e., an alteration of range will tend to be known in *advance* of firing rather than after the process of spotting has been resorted to.

A system by which the mean of the rangefinder readings is transmitted direct to the sights would cope with this, and every effort towards advance in such a direction is imperative. Whether this can be achieved with the existing service rangefinders is doubtful except under abnormally favourable conditions.

(iv) *Immediate action as regards rangefinders*

The Committee consider that immediate action should be taken as follows:-

[1]A detailed account of types of Rangefinder is in *Handbook on Naval Rangefinders and Mountings* (CB 269) and *Admiralty Technical History, Fire Control*, both in the Admiralty Library, Ministry of Defence.

(a) The Admiralty be asked to immediately provide means of lower magnification as an alternative to the present high power. It is understood that this could be applied to all existing range-finders by the provision of a special face-piece.

(b) The supply of one 15 ft rangefinder to each capital ship should be hastened.

(c) The provision of yellow tinted shades for use on rangefinders in misty weather should be proceeded with.

(d) All rangefinder mountings (not in turrets) should be fitted with bearing racers, particularly in light cruisers.

(e) In light cruisers every possible means must be taken to reduce vibration of the rangefinder platform.

(f) The training of operators must be intensive and on standard-ised lines. *Note*: This point will be dealt with separately as regards B.C.F.

(g) Further arrangements to reduce to a minimum the interval between the cut being obtained and its appearance on the plot.

(h) The capacity of a Sextant type of rangefinder to give rapid indication of change of enemy course should be investigated. The new type of Hurliman rangefinder might be used to start with on a ship zigzagging at the extreme range obtainable in Scapa Flow. It is probable that by working on the masthead height and apparent ship's length a very much quicker indication of change of course would be obtained than is the case with the present rangefinder.

(j) A high power glass fitted with a pair of vertical and also a pair of horizontal cross wires, one wire of each pair being adjust-able, was suggested some years ago in this connection, and might prove effective.

Trials on the above lines are recommended.

6. (b) THE USE OF DEFENSIVE TACTICS TO AVOID BEING HIT

(i) To have the best light is an enormous gunnery advantage. All Gunnery Officers emphasise the extreme difficulties when firing to the Eastward on 31st May when, on the contrary, (as observed by ships not then engaged), ships to the Westward made a splendid target. This *must* be taken into consideration in future tactics.

(ii) Alteration of own course did not hamper the control and director layers to any great extent, and it should be understood that in this respect Gunnery must meet the requirements of tactics.

Future practices for B.C.F., both rangefinding and firing, should allow for this. It is imperative for ships to slightly alter course for defensive purposes, when to do this must be left to the discretion of Captains of ships, and certain limitations to govern this matter should be laid down.

7. (c) *THE SAFETY OF MAGAZINES AND AMMUNITION*
   The Committee are of opinion that the following points with regard to magazines and ammunition are established:—

Turret Magazines

(i) With existing designs of turrets it is impossible to safeguard the Handing Room from the flash of a shell burst, or from cordite flash caused by shell burst, in the gun-house or working chamber.

(ii) Magazines must therefore be able to withstand flame under pressure, and in this connection it is pointed out that the bulkheads of Q Magazine in *Lion* were considerably buckled, although they were supported by the water which, by then, had probably completely flooded the magazine.

(iii) Doors opening inwards into the Magazine from the Handing Room are extremely dangerous and should be altered immediately.

(iv) One of the venting plates in *Lion* admitted a tongue of flame into the Magazine; this plate was of the old type, and had not been modified in accordance with A.W.O. 1331 (D.2945/15 – 13.8.15) and G.F.G.O. No 459 – 15.5.16. *All ships should have this alteration fitted forthwith.*

(v) The type of handing scuttle finally decided to be fitted must be designed to withstand the pressure mentioned in (ii), and it is highly undesirable that the handing scuttle or airlock should contain more than one-quarter charge at a time, owing to the consequent danger of bursting the airlock.

6″ and 4″ Magazines

(vi) It is the opinion of the Gunnery Officers of the B.C.F. and 5th B.S. that it is too dangerous to the safety of the ship to keep the magazine hatches of the secondary armament open in action, excepting when actually obligatory for replenishing the ready supply kept in cases at the guns. Wherever it is possible, handing rooms with airlocks must be fitted without delay to all 6″ and 4″

magazines. A letter with definite proposals for the 4″ Magazine of *Lion* class has, we understand, already been forwarded to you. This alteration is still more vital in the case of light cruisers, where the magazine must of necessity always be kept open when engaged.

Stowage of ready use cordite at guns and method of transport to guns

(vii) K.A. cases containing charges have been proved dangerous in action in more than one ship. For secondary armaments flame-proof stowage for 20 single charges must be provided at each gun, the ordinary ammunition cases being used to replenish this ready supply whenever required. Dredger hoists should never be used for cordite, but only to replenish shell when the ready supply is exhausted. At other times they must be kept closed down. A similar type of flame-proof case is also required in light cruisers, and in addition these must be used for transport from the magazines to the battery and for storage on deck in all weathers.

Igniters

(viii) The danger of a chain of cordite conveying fire from the gunhouse to the magazine is invited by the system of permanently attaching the igniters to the charges. The advisability of altering this should receive the immediate attention of the Admiralty as affecting the safety of our ships in the next action. It is known that trials were carried out some years ago in which the igniter was secured to a hook on the mushroom head. This method, however, is not now advocated owing to the high temperature which the mushroom head reaches after long firing; and it is preferred to place the igniter on the rear quarter charge (only) whilst on the gunloading cage tray, immediately before ramming home, — a wooden packing piece being fitted in rear of the cordite compartment of the gunloading cage so that on delivery of the cordite there is enough clearance between the rammer head and rear quarter charge to affix the igniter. This important question is also entirely applicable to handworked B.L. guns.

Drowning exposed charges

(ix) There is a strong expression of opinion that some extremely rapid method of flooding is required for all cordite positions in a turret or battery outside the magazine. With this the Committee entirely concur, and accordingly forward herewith a proposal placed before them by Engineer Commander W. C. Johnson, H.M.A.S. *Australia* [not included]. In the meantime they strongly recommend that, as a temporary measure, an immediate and ample supply of water should be stored at every position where exposed charges lodge during their transport to the gun. For this purpose a 25 gallon drum is recommended. Had it been possible to rapidly drown the charges in the handing room hoppers and main cages of Q turret in *Lion*, it is possible that the second and belated explosion might have been prevented, so saving many casualties and much damage to material.

Mantlets

(x) It was proved in *Southampton* that on the upper deck a rope mantlet saturated with water prevented the flame of a bad cordite fire reaching the other charges at the top of and in a neighbouring ammunition trunk, and in addition saved the supply party. The Committee therefore urge that the fullest use should be made of this method, and that so far as possible every gun with its ready supply of ammunition and every supply opening should be completely screened by saturated mantlets.

170.   *Private H. Willons RMLI*

[BTY/6/14/1]   *Lion*
[Copy]   31 May – 1 June 1916

Reminiscences of Q Turret, HMS Lion

At 3.35 p.m. the hands were all at their usual work or asleep as the case may be, whether they were watchkeepers or daymen. Five mintues later the bugle sounded (Action). In a few moments the crew were rushing from place to place to get as soon as possible to their different stations. Mine was the magazine of Q

Turret, my duty was to select the cordite from the magazine in accordance with the age and lot number, for if cordite is fired without knowing the exact quality it is impossible to get good shooting. However, our Chief Gunner had the different bins marked with cardboards, No 1 action and so on.

On arriving in the magazine I got rid of my superfluous clothing. When we had been down a few minutes we got the order to load with armour piercing lyddite and full charge of cordite. We started slinging out quarter charges until all No 1 action was used up in the starboard mag. About fifty-four rounds had been fired before we changed over to the port-mag. The change had been effected and about ten rounds fired when a heavier explosion than usual occurred and dense smoke came down the trunk, stopping progress until we had shipped our respirators. The time was 4.20 or thereabouts. Two men were then brought up from the Shell Room, both had been working in the Gun house, and were badly wounded, they were passed along the messdeck to the medical station. Standing by the magazine door I heard the Officer of Turret[1] give the order (CLOSE MAGAZINE DOORS—Q TURRET OUT OF ACTION). The Corporal and I closed the port magazine door and clipped it up, by the time we had finished, the handing room crew had gone up the iron ladder to the switchboard flat which is immediately above, and being rather a small place, was rather crowded; from this flat is another iron ladder which leads to the messdeck. About then the Chief Gunner[2] came along to see everything was in order, finding the turret was out of action he ordered several of us to put out fires on the messdeck. Just as he and I got clear the ignition of the cordite occurred and the blast pushed us along. The space of about ten minutes elapsed between the projectile exploding and the ignition of the cordite, which happened to be in the cages, hoppers and possibly a charge in the handing room (Broken ¼ charges that got damaged while handling).

Doubtless some burning clothing fell from one of the ramming numbers into the open cage and caught the cordite afire. Owing to the fact that the top of the turret was partially blown off, there was no explosion, but the flames travelled right through the turret and the adjacent compartments. After I had assisted the stokers under the Engineer Lt. to put out a fire on the messdeck, which

[1]Major Francis Harvey RMLI, awarded a posthumous Victoria Cross, also ordered the magazines to be flooded and thus saved *Lion* from total destruction.
[2]Alexander Grant.

was caused by a shell exploding in the funnel casing, I reported myself to the Captain R.M.[1] in the after battery. My job from then was to carry the wounded from the engaged side to the disengaged side of the ship as was requisite. We carried the severely wounded to the bathrooms, where they were put under anaesthetic. The news then came through that *Queen Mary* had been sunk, and that we were engaging the German Battle Fleet. The Commander came along giving us the cheerful information that Jellicoe was in sight and we were hauling out, and I am sure we all felt anxious after the loss of *Q. M.* During that period we were mostly engaged (that is those below decks) in listening for concussions and trying to locate the place that had been hit. A great amount of small calibre shell must have hit the armour belt and dropped off. One eleven inch went through the port side and destroyed the navigator's cabin, incidentally my kit also, it afterwards exploding in the funnel. The *Lion* even now has a kink in her midship funnel that appears rather odd. There was about four inches of water on all the messdecks from the fire hoses, and washing about in it were odds and ends of clothing, boots and burnt articles; the electric light gave out and we had to stumble through the water in the dark, striking matches or by the dim light of a candle. The Chief Gunner and I went down to the Shell Room at about six o'clock to find out if it was possible to salve any of the ammunition. The Handing Room, Switchboard, Flat and Shell Room were completely burned out, the crew were lying in all directions, some still hanging on the ladder in a last attempt to get out. On finding that it was impossible to salve any of the projectiles for use in the other turrets the shell room was flooded. The Captain of Marines sent for me then to go to the Gun house to find the Major and remove some of the casualties. I got into the Gun house through the manhole on top and assisted by another marine got out seven people from the right cabinet. The Chaplain was one of these.[2] The Major was in the range-finder position close by the voice pipe. There was a great deal of smoke coming from behind the ready use shell bin and we gave the alarm that four common shell were being roasted and were likely to cause another explosion. With the assistance of several more marines the fire was put out and the remainder of the casualties were removed. They were then taken aft, identified if possible and sewn into hammocks.

[1]Captain Francis R. Jones.
[2]The Revd Cecil Lydall killed in action.

This carried on most of the night 31st of May.

We were served out with a ration of corned beef as the bake-house and galley had suffered, and at sundown on the 1st of July, the men who had given all were buried in the sea.

The upper deck was a chaos, and the ship had been holed in many places. However, when we arrived into port we coaled and ammunitioned ship and were prepared for sea in two hours.

171. *Petty Officer Dan Sheppard* (director layer)

Notes on Jutland

[BTY/6/14/2]   *Lion*
[Copy]   [31 May – 1 June 1916]

When action was sounded the light was good, the first bearing Red 20, put us on the enemy, and onto the cruisers which appeared to me to be 3 of *Lutzow* [sic] class, with *Seydlitz* and *Moltke*; but I had no time to note peculiar or special points, as Red 32 Right Hand Battle-Cruiser was ordered — this was one of *Lutzow* [sic] class. Soon after this the enemy ship opened fire, using pairs of guns; fore turrets, after turrets. She had only 4 turrets. With alterations of course the ship was now yawing considerably. Straddle was reported and rapid salvoes ordered. There was not much increase of fire due to the following:

The light was now getting bad. Trainer was experiencing great difficulty to see and keep on the object. X turret wanted Auxiliary Director Circuit, so I had to give orders for training, the smoke from small craft between the target and director tower making it almost impossible to keep a good point of aim; we carried on after bearing and target was obscured by smoke — picked her up again about Red 140, the enemy appearing to turn.

Next trained to Green 90. From there trained left onto a battle-cruiser, left hand ship, which looked like *Moltke*, I forget how many gun flashes she showed, lost the target and found it again at Green 110 or thereabouts. We lost this target and was [sic] ordered to another bearing, I could barely see the object and reported — there was considerable smoke about and also mist, so we had a lull, trained fore and aft and had a check on director readings. All found correct. About 6.30 p.m. Stand by again Green bearing. Could not do much, fired couple of salvoes, lost the target in the mist, enemy in sight again further aft — this was also stopped by mist. There appeared a lull in enemy's fire; he burst out again in 2 gun salvoes, we were ordered to take the rear ship. Here I fancy we picked up a battleship as target, she had 5 turrets. Next we got a shift to battle-cruiser. Then was back to one of the latest battle-cruisers. Here I lose myself and do not know what training we were on, but it was here and there firing a few salvoes when we could see. It was battle-cruisers, but the conditions were about as bad as one could imagine. We were ordered to train on a light cruiser, but she was very hard to see, and appeared someone else's target — this would be somewhere about 9 o'clock.

We were doing plenty of Green bearings, getting in a couple of shots, and then the enemy was obscured by smoke. There were three battle-cruisers. They made behind smoke screen of destroyers. At last they drew out of the smoke screen and we opened fire at left hand battle-cruiser. She fired back in 8 gun salvoes. We got nicely into her. Two more ships appeared to be firing at her, but she soon turned away and was lost in the smoke. She was easily our best target. There was a cruiser with 3 funnels to be seen just after this dust-up, which ended at 9.30.

Director Notes

Elevation. Two speed elevating gear would assist the layer greatly especially where big rates, and change of bearing and ranges occur. A ship in action behaves differently to peace practice with continual small a/c. The ship gets a dragging roll on, and lies over for an appreciable time, especially when hit.

Training. Becomes very difficult with continual small a/c and the ship works up to a big yaw — the sight carrier rocking is very good at these times. *Telescopes*. Layer used 5 to 15 V. P. glass mostly at power 5, and it was seldom moved from 5 power. 2½ Power Trainers glass was useless, and 5 to 15 V. P. glass, spare in tower, was used, and the carrier rocking glass at Power 5.

Circuits. A simple device connecting the Main and Aux Pistols and Triggers is advisable, as the layer then has left hand for training.

172. *Interim report of Committee on Construction to Vice-Admiral Commanding Battle-Cruiser Fleet*

[BTY/6/17/4]   SECRET   *Australia*
                                                      23rd June 1916

The Committee ordered by B.C.F. 29 of 10th June have the honour to submit the following general conclusions and recommendations.

2. The Committee can observe no certain indication that in any near future the evolution of the submarine will be such as to deny the sea to the fast heavy vessel.

3. The Committee consider that British battle-cruisers whether in service or about to be commissioned, are unequal to the duties assigned to them, as their protection is insufficient to enable them to encounter the capital ships of the enemy without incurring undue risk of destruction.

4. For these duties the Committee are of opinion that vessels of very great protection, offensive power and speed are requisite; and that having regard to the existing naval situation and to the latest known foreign construction, the vessel required must be of fast battleship type, rather than on the lines of a battle cruiser. The *Queen Elizabeth* type appears more nearly to fulfil the conditions required than does any other; but higher speed, greater protection and greater offensive power should be attempted, in conjunction, perhaps, with draught diminished to reduce under water target.

5. After consultation with Director of Naval Construction, who stated the outlines of Admiralty proposals for constructing armoured vessels of great size and speed, the Committee are of opinion that in these vessels, as now designed, above water protection is quite inadequate; but as it is understood the designs are still capable of modification, the Committee recommend that it should be attempted to convert projected vessels into fast battle-ships by improving above water protection.

6. To this end, on evidence obtained from ships injured in action, and in view of the increasing power of artillery, the Committee think that for main belt armour that of *Queen Elizabeth*, thickened to 9" at upper edge, might be adopted.

7. As against plunging fire they consider the armoured decks of *Queen Elizabeth* are not strong enough, and that their disposition might be improved. Above the lowest armoured deck there should be another complete armoured deck, so that shell should

burst before reaching the former, which must be strong enough to resist perforation even by the largest fragments. Thus, before reaching the lowest armoured deck, shell would always have to pass either through side armour or through an upper armoured deck.

8. To limit the effects of shell bursting after passing through side armour, there should be continuous 2" vertical bulkheads placed about 20 feet behind it, between the armoured decks.

9. Embrasures are a source of weakness which should be avoided.

10. Tapering the thickness of redoubt armour is a matter requiring careful consideration.

W. C. PAKENHAM
Rear-Admiral

T. D. PRATT
Captain, H.M.S. *Yarmouth*
W. CRUMP-JOHNSON

GEORGE P. W. HOPE
Captain, H.M.S. *Queen Elizabeth*

Engineer Commander,
H. M A. S. *Australia*

EDW. HEATON-ELLIS
Captain, H.M.S. *Inflexible*

173. *Additional report of Gunnery Committee*

[BTY/6/17/7]

Lion

Confidential   24th June 1916.

Sir,

In furtherance of our advanced report, we have the honour to forward some additional remarks on various points of interest gathered from the ships of the Battle-Cruiser Fleet and 5th Battle Squadron.

1. *NOTES ON ENEMY'S GUNNERY*

The general impression is that at first fire was very rapid, and accurate for range, but frequently bad for line, the spread was as a rule very small. It appears to be uncertain whether the spread was not occasionally opened out intentionally either by pairs of guns or singly; certainly in some cases the enemy fired salvoes in pairs of turrets. In this connection it is interesting to note that no ship which survived the action appears to have been hit by a complete salvo, but on several occasions ships were undoubtedly hit by two shell in one salvo which struck within a few feet of each other.

Evidence shows that both instantaneous salvoes and some form of very rapid ripple were in use. It appears that one ship at least fired by individual when damaged. The light cruisers certainly fired by director.

Evidence is very inconclusive as to what extent the enemy's early hitting and rangekeeping were dependent on the accuracy of their rangefinders, but, undoubtedly, on some occasions the enemy's opening ranges were not accurate, and when our ships slightly altered course salvoes fell off and some time was taken in regaining the range.

Many officers noted the efficiency with which the enemy concentrated a rapid fire from more than two ships on a particular ship or on the turning point of our line.

The general impression is that the enemy's fire in the battle-cruiser action fell off gradually, but whether this was due to our fire, the conditions of light, or range, is quite uncertain. In the 2nd phase of the action the enemy's fire was undoubtedly slow and spasmodic, but the light conditions were then entirely reversed, and this is probably sufficient to account for this lack of response to our fire.

On the contrary it must be remembered that on 24th January the enemy, after being severely hit for a long time, suddenly increased his rate and accuracy of fire and never fell to pieces in any way.

Although heavy ships were infrequently hit by shell of small calibre, the enemy made no great use of their secondary armament, except against light cruisers and destroyers. There is no evidence as to whether their secondary armament was fired by director or not.

Rear Admiral 2nd Battle Cruiser Squadron, and the Captains of *Valiant* and *New Zealand* remark on the noticeably small splash made by the enemy's heavy shell.

2. *SMOKE INTERFERENCE BY OUR OWN DESTROYERS*

Some ships complain of interference from torpedo destroyers' smoke, and this raises the question as to whether the position of our submarine screen when cruising is a suitable one for action.

In the case of a High Speed Squadron, a position well ahead appears to meet requirements, for the higher the speed of the screened squadron the further ahead the screen *can* be placed to keep down submarines. Again, in such a position they are advantageously placed for delivering and countering torpedo craft attacks, and smoke interference will be reduced.

We recommend trials being made of the utility of our own destroyers making smoke on the disengaged side of the large ships to render them more difficult to range and spot on, especially in the event of the enemy having the advantage of the light. It should be possible to rapidly control this by signal.

3. We consider it desirable that in the Senior Officer's ship of every squadron, heavy or light, there should be an experienced officer whose sole duty it is to keep the Senior Officer informed, during an action, on gunnery matters other than those upon which his attention is at the moment rivetted. For example, the following are important points which can only be observed to the best purpose by some officer who has no other duty:-

    (a)   When at a suitable range for opening or re-opening fire.

    (b)   Whether the squadron is keeping at the desired fighting range from the enemy.

    (c)   The general effect of our own and enemy's fire from time to time, and any necessary signals as to concentration of fire.

    (d)   When it is desirable to make use of destroyers' smoke.

In the heat of an action so many other points have to be considered that these may be overlooked unless an organisation for such details has been prepared; and this is especially the case when the action opens and attention tends to be distracted by watching the result of one's own gunfire.

4. *DISTANCE APART IN LINE*

There appears to be a very general opinion that increased distance up to four cables between ships would be an advantage under many conditions, and would give more freedom for altering course to avoid torpedoes and gunfire, and also under bad conditions of smoke.

5. *POSITION OF CONTROL OFFICERS*

The opinion of Control Officers as to the best position from which to control is nearly equally divided. It is, however, pointed out that both in *Lion* on 24th January, 1915 and in *Warspite* on 31st May, 1916, a heavy concentrated fire absolutely prevented any view from the gun control tower, and control from this position was impossible. It is therefore recommended that all ships should develop the use of their foretops as, at least, an equally important position as the gun control tower, and that all ships should attach the greatest importance to the development of this position both as regards protection and communication, and that this point should be considered in future construction.

6. *AID TO SPOTTER DEVICE*

Whenever the target was difficult to distinguish, due to visibility, in ships controlled from aloft, an 'aid to spotter' device was proved essential. In ships controlled from the gun control tower, Evershed's Training Indicators, where fitted, met requirements — if not fitted between the control tower and director tower, immediate instalment should be provided for.

7. *EXCHANGE OF INFORMATION BETWEEN CONTROL OFFICERS*

Communication between control positions in action was not made use of; those ships which attempted to do so state they were unable to get answers to their signals. It appears from this that the want of the information was felt by some ships. It is therefore recommended that the intercommunication should be the responsible duty of the Assistant Control Officer, where there is one, and that he should continuously communicate by arc lamp the range and the rate (but not the deflection) to the ship to which it is likely to be of most value. The necessity of avoiding time lag is emphasised. The enemy ship fired at should continue to be indicated as at present. Attention should be drawn to G.F.G.O No 65.

8. *FATIGUE OF CONTROL OFFICERS, etc.*

Fatigue or eyestrain of either Control Officers, Director Layers or Rangetakes was not experienced to any inconvenient extent; but ships were seldom continuously engaged for more than three-quarters of an hour.

9. *STATE OF CONTROL INSTRUMENTS*

Reports show that control instruments generally were unaffected by the action — only one rangefinder being reported as getting seriously out of adjustment.

10. *DIRECTOR FIRING GEAR*

That director firing is absolutely essential in all light cruisers is the unanimous opinion as the result of the action. The reasons are:—

(a)   To prevent our light cruisers being outranged by German light cruisers as occurred frequently on 31st May.

(b)   Efficient direction of armament for training both day and night.

(c)   Use in rough weather.

11. *COMMUNICATIONS*

In some cases further extension of communications has been advocated, but as this does not apply to all ships it is considered that Admirals Commanding Squadrons should be instructed to take the necessary action.

12. *RANGE CORRECTORS*

The range corrector was not used by any ship. This is doubtless due to opinions formed in peace practices at comparatively short ranges and under easier conditions, when the corrections were consequently small. The Committee consider that at the very much greater ranges and more difficult conditions that we now have to contend with, these corrections being greatly increased, *must* not be neglected if early hitting is to be established. This should be pointed out to the Fleet, and the use of the range corrector insisted upon, all ships being supplied.

13. *ALLOWANCE FOR LOSS OF M.V.*[1]

The majority of ships made continuous allowance for loss of M.V. during the action. It is considered most important that this should be arranged for on the dip corrector scales in all ships.

14. *USE OF AIRCRAFT*

It is recommended that immediate use should be made of existing aircraft with the B.C.F. to practise passing information as to movements of enemy ships for the use of the Control Officer.

15. *LESSONS TO BE LEARNT FROM NIGHT ACTIONS BETWEEN LIGHT CRUISERS ONLY*

The situation experienced by the 2nd L.C.S. on the night of 31st May was approximately as follows. Two forces approached on converging courses, the enemy being to Westward could be seen but, there being doubt as to their identity, a short period elapsed trying without success to identify them, the challenge was then made but shortly after it was started enemy made compass sign by flashing lamp and switched on a combination of coloured lights at the masthead. *Southampton* then switched on searchlights and opened fire, upon which the whole of the enemy line (five ships) did the same. The other three ships of 2nd L.C.S. did not switch on searchlights but used the enemy light as a point of aim. The German lights, were high, widely separated and were on their object before switching on, and appeared to be controlled by Director and Master Switch.

Not more than two lights appeared to be used in any ship.

[1]Muzzle velocity.

Enemy appeared to fire at and between our searchlights, as practically all the hits in *Southampton* were made between them. It appears that all five enemy ships concentrated on the *Southampton* and the second ship *Dublin*, whereas the other two ships were not hit and were able to develop a very effective fire. As far as can be ascertained, fire was opened by both squadrons at the same moment. Three of the *Southampton's* guns probably opened at the wrong ship. The engagement lasted for about 3½ minutes, the enemy using 'rapid independent'.

On these facts the Committee make the following recommendations:—

(a) The enemy's recognition signals were instantaneous while ours required a long signal, which admits of no action being taken until a similarly long reply has been made, and failing such reply there is bound to be some slight indecisive pause before opening fire. This interval may be of the greatest value to the enemy to complete his preparations before attacking. The question of recognition signals therefore requires reconsideration.

(b) It is considered essential that all ships should extemporise arrangements for training their searchlights as well as their guns dead on to a suspicious vessel, ready for instant attack, before making the challenge.

(c) *Use of searchlights*

(1) Lights should never be switched on if it can be avoided, thus denying the enemy a defined point of aim, whilst firing at his lights if he uses them, remembering that his lights are high. (vide Jane, 1914) [*sic*]

(2) If searchlights must be used, then in one position only; the use of two searchlights widely separated gives away the position of the ship and her alterations of course.

(3) As searchlights form a focus for enemy fire, those on the Bridge should not be used if it can be avoided.

(4) It appears that the best position for our own single searchlight would be right aft. A portable mounting could be used in calm weather.

(5) Searchlights should be fitted high up with the operators beneath them and suitably protected against splinters.

(d) The method of firing recommended to be employed is training by director, with individual laying. Undoubtedly some form of indirect training is essential.

(e) Spare lengths of flexible voicepipes for repairs to communications should be supplied to light cruisers as to battleships.

(f) Open sights fitted on the side of gun shields were of the greatest value in getting and keeping guns on the target.These should be fitted in all light cruisers.

16. *EFFECT OF OWN SHELL*

Bearing out the experience of previous actions, hits with heavy shell were seldom seen, especially with Lyddite A. P., which constituted the chief proportion of shell fired from battle-cruisers. Lyddite Common, especially from light cruisers, shewed up well. Some ships ranged with C.P.C.[1] and this practice of changing the Committee do not consider promotes hitting.

17. *SYMPATHETIC DETONATION OF LYDDITE SHELL*

No case occurred of our own shell being detonated to enemy's fire, although in three ships shell burst within a few feet of them, and in some cases the projectiles were dented and driving bands cut.

18. *SAFETY PINS OF LYDDITE COMMON*

Most of the ships which fired Lyddite Common (both turret and light guns) experienced difficulty in extracting the safety pins; in a few cases shell were fired with the cap on, owing to the pins breaking, although pliers were used. Pliers in most cases met the difficulty.

19. *ENEMY'S SHELL*

There is no conclusive evidence that shrapnel shell were used. Star shell were undoubtedly used by some ships as night, generally before switching on searchlights. Enemy fired Very's lights during duty action continually, but for what purpose is not known.

20. *GUN TUBES*

Remarkably few missfires were caused by defective V.S. tubes.

21. *SUPPLY OF SPARE PARTS*

It is pointed out that no spare gear is supplied for the director. Spare parts as follows should be supplied to each gun, observing that serious delays occurred in one ship through lack of them:—
Box slide, electric lock, and vent. bit to each turret gun.

In one ship the supply of $3\frac{1}{8}''$ flexible voicepipe was found of the utmost value in effecting rapid repair of communications.

22. *CHOKED VENT*

A serious case of this occurred in one ship, a wad of shalloon and silk cloth choking vent so effectually that the mushroom head had to be shifted.

23. *FLASH DOORS, Etc.*

[1]Copper pointed common shell.

It is strongly recommended that the existing flash doors of the marking position in working chamber should be actuated by the transfer rammer heads instead of by the gunloading cage, and that this alteration should be hastened as much as possible in 13.5″ mountings and, where applicable, in 12″ mountings.

It is strongly recommended that the clearance between the trunk and the floor of the walking pipe space should be screened by strong flash plates, fitted so as to prevent the flash of a shell penetrating the turret armour going down from the turret, but so as to allow escape of gas pressures from the Handing Room.

As regards turret handing room hatches, it is a very debateable point whether these should be securely closed or not. In 'Q' turret of *Lion* it was open and relieved the pressure set up by the explosion of several full charges in the handing room: if this hatch had been closed it is probable the magazine bulkheads would have been blown in, observing that they are already distorted. We therefore recommend that handing room hatches should be closed, but not clipped, so as to prevent flame coming down and to relieve pressure going up.

24. *DIRECTOR*

Generally speaking, the existing director gear gave satisfaction. In one ship only is it reported as having occasionally 'got out of step', and larger fuses to stand more current are suggested.

The rocking trainers' sight proved valuable in one ship with a list.

One ship suggests that two-speed elevating gear to director sight would assist the layer considerably; with frequent alterations of course, ship gets a 'dragging' roll, and lies over for an appreciable time.

25. 12″ *BREECH MECHANISM*

Serious delays having been caused through fracture of tube retainers in a ship with 12″ Mk. X guns, it is strongly recommended that either spring link gear or hand operated locks should be supplied for these guns.

174. *Notes by Beatty* [Holograph]

[BTY/6/3/16] 26 June 1916

Notes in Remembrance of Conversations Held At Admiralty on
26th June, Monday, at 3.15 P.M.

Present: 1st Sea Lord, C-in-C, Commodore Everett[1] and V. A.
B. C. F.

The 1st Sea Lord commenced by saying that he understood I
(V.A. B.C.F.) had objections to the 5th B.S. being
sent to Scapa.

Reply: Yes most certainly, and if it was definitely settled to
do so, as I understood it was, I wished to enter a protest
in the strongest & most emphatic manner possible.

1st S. L. said that the C-in-C was of the opinion that the whole
Fleet should in future support the B.C.F. and that this
should be closer than hitherto.

I concurred and said that this was what I had
represented as being desirable and necessary over and
over again during the past 18 months, but as the G.F.
could not come to Rosyth until October, in the interim
it was most important that the 5th B.S. should support
the B.C.F. until they did. That I had argued and
written many letters on the subject for a considerable
time now and that in no way were the contentions that
I had put forward altered by the occurrence of the 31st
May.

The C-in-C said that the speed of the 5th B.S. was insufficient for
them to be utilised in such a way. They could not get
away from the enemy 3rd B.S.

I replied there was no evidence in support of this. The
occurrence of 31st May threw no light on the subject.
Further, I was confident that both the B. Cs and 5th
B.S. could have broken off the action any time they
wished.

The 1st Sea Lord stated that the next time I had them with me
he hoped that '*I would keep them in line with me*'.

I stated that I did not understand what he meant and explained
my cruising [*sic*].

[1]Later Admiral Sir Allan Everett (1868–1938): Naval Secretary to 1st Lord.

The 2nd B.C.S. was actually 3 [*sic*] apart — as we were so well off for T.B.Ds that 2 [*sic*] gave them insufficient room, formation which was in accordance with the C-in-C's wishes, except that I had been at 5 miles away instead of 8 as laid down in G.F.O.

That if I had had them with me constantly as I had asked and so enable them to be trained with me so that the R.A. and myself should have thoroughly understood each other they would have been at 2 miles. But as this was the first time we had ever been to sea together, it was considered advisable to give them more sea room. Squadrons of the heaviest ships moving at 25 knots require room unless they have been previously manoeuvred together.

(Furthermore during the manoeuvring before contact was made with the enemy, there was ample opportunity for the 5th B.S. to have closed the B.C.s as they were on the inside of the half circle described by the B.C.s — see plans. That they did not do so was due to the fact that I could not get a signal to them, and to the absence of training together, which if we had had the opportunity the R.A. would have done the right thing instinctively without orders as was done by every other squadron commander and ship.) — In brackets, not stated at the meeting as I had no wish to impute bad manoeuvring on the part of the R.A. 5th B.S. who had supported me so well. But I did point this out to C.O.W.S.[1] subsequently. Further I pointed out that their position was a very suitable one to meet all exigencies, not only the one that actually occurred. For instance, we might have sighted the whole H.S.F. in the same position as that of enemy B.Cs, in which case as they were, the 5th B.S. were less likely to be cut off from the G.F. This was an important consideration in view of the fact that their speed was at this time an unknown factor. The speed of the B.Cs on the other hand precluded the possibility of their being cut off.

The 1st S.L. then said it was a *pity* that on sighting the enemy B.Cs I did not turn away to join the 5th B.S., that I

[1]Sir Henry Oliver.

should probably have done better if I had done so as the enemy B.Cs might have followed me!!!

175. *Lady Beatty to Larking*

[LAR/2]   Aberdour House
                                                      [10 July 1916]

I do feel ashamed of myself never having written since the Great Battle. . . .

Now that it is all over there seems to be very little to say except to *curse* Jellicoe for not going at them as the B.C.s did & never stopped until we had annihilated them. I hear he was frightened to death in case he *might* lose a B. Ship. I think the real truth he was [*sic*] in a *deadly* funk & of course it makes one perfectly sick with the Admiralty trying to make out he is a great man & did all he could & that he is a great *leader*. He failed hopelessly & not only that but he does not tell the truth in his *dispatch*. He says he was in action for over two hours & all the others say it was quite [–] & that none of the B.S.s were in action more than 15 minutes. The map he has made is also untrue & the Admiralty know it. It makes one boil, as now one feels the B.C.s will have to fight again & one has less confidence than ever in the Commander-in-Chief, & they will not make any change & seem quite pleased with lies and mistakes.

Jack[1] went to the Admiralty when he went to London. He gave Jackson 'What For' & told him what he really thought, but I don't think it has done any good. It is a bit hard on the country & all those splendid men who did fight so splendidly.

It makes one so *furious*. I feel I can't bear it.

We had quite a good 'Jolly' in London & saw many friends, Jack being a great 'Hero' & I think he liked it & it was good for him. He of course felt terribly poor Bertie's death & all the others & to have three of his ships go within a few minutes was a bit of a shock. However he bore up splendidly & is very well. . . .

---

[1] 'Jack' was his wife's pet name for Beatty.

176. *Addition to Battle-Cruiser Orders*

[CCC/DRAX/1/3]   SECRET   31st August 1916
(*BCF.017 of 18th Feb. 1915*)[1]

38. Lessons learnt from action of 31 May 1916.

The following important lessons may be learnt from the action of 31st May. It is hoped that they will be fully applied when the next opportunity occurs.

2. It is of paramount importance that an enemy force once brought to action should not escape in fog, under a smoke screen, or in gathering darkness, and it must be the duty of destroyers as well as light cruisers to assist in making sure that no chance of escape is allowed to his heavy ships.

3. It has been proved again and again that nothing is more fatal than 'waiting for orders.' The Senior Officers may be closely engaged, their signal apparatus may be destroyed, or for many other reasons they may be unable to issue orders by signal. It therefore becomes the duty of subordinate leaders to anticipate the executive orders and act in the spirit of the Commander-in Chief's requirements. There are only two and they are very simple. So long as the enemy heavy ships remain afloat we must 'locate and report,' 'attack and destroy.' But to perform either duty without the other is to fall short of that co-ordination which ensures success, nor should it be thought that, to perform one duty efficiently, it is necessary to abstain from the other.

4. If a destroyer night attack sinks an enemy battleship it has done much, but if it also reports the enemy's position and course so that the whole force can be brought to action at daylight it has done more. On the night of 31st May our light cruisers and destroyers were almost continuously in contact with, or in sight of enemy heavy ships. Yet hardly one signal was received to state their position and course or what enemy vessels were located.

5. In future, at nightfall or at any time when the enemy appear to be getting out of sight, light cruisers or destroyers that are in a position to do so must move off without orders and get in touch.

It is preferable that reports of the enemy should not be duplicated but it is far better that they should be too many rather than too few. In any case, a report every ten minutes through the night would not be too many.

[1]See 128.

6. As regards day attack, it appears that destroyers between 6,000 and 4,000 yards from the enemy are liable to be damaged by the fire of 6" guns, but it should be quite possible to fire torpedoes that will cross the enemy's track after running 6,000 or 7,000 yards, without risking the loss of the destroyer that fires them.

7. Destroyers in company with battle-cruisers, if ordered to act as submarine screen, should remain ahead throughout the action. There is little need for them to seek shelter on the disengaged bow for they are probably safer ahead. They can of course haul out temporarily or push further ahead if subjected to an unpleasant fire. Every endeavour should be made to avoid their smoke interfering with the heavy ships engaged. Destroyers with the battle-cruisers before junction has been made with our own Battle Fleet should not move out without orders to attack the enemy heavy ships with the torpedo unless the opportunity is so obviously a good one that it would certainly be ordered by the Senior Officer if recognised.

8. It is imperative in the next action that no opportunity should be missed for firing torpedoes from battle-cruisers and light cruisers. Every effort should be made to seek positions where torpedoes can be fired effectively at the enemy's line. A good position to fire torpedoes is a good tactical and good gunnery position. Having found such a position it should be the aim of each Captain to fire every torpedo in his ship. Therein *B.C.O. 15* should be taken as a guide.

9. Light cruisers ahead of the battle-cruiser line should keep well ahead, so as to get a good torpedo position on the enemy's bow and also to be able to give early warning of movements ahead of either line such as minelaying operations or the arrival of reinforcements, and to report movements of the enemy.

10. Light cruisers and destroyers should be prepared to make smoke screens if required. In misty weather they might greatly aid the retreat of a light cruiser that has suddenly sighted heavy ships (e.g. it was probably the experience of 28th August 1914 that caused the adoption of 'smoke boxes' in the German Navy). A light coloured smoke, such as phosphorus, would be most useful as a background on the disengaged side of the battle-cruisers if there is an unfavourable light behind them (as on 31st. May). The question of smoke screens generally is now being considered.

11. At nightfall it is important for our destroyers to be informed, if possible, as to the position and movements of our own and the

enemy heavy ships. Flag and Senior Officers should give them visually any information they possess and the Captain's D or Flotilla Leaders should make enquiries, without using wireless, if they are not given the information they need. The ideal is that our own ships should haul off and leave the whole area occupied by enemy free for our destroyers to operate in. In practice this is doubtful of attainment and it is possible that our destroyers searching for the enemy may meet some of our light cruisers trying to keep touch with him. Hence the necessity for all information being given to Captain D as referred to above.

12. When destroyers sight a column of ships which, if enemy, would form a favourable target, it is imperative when in doubt that steps should be taken to identify them. If friends, there may be risk of being fired on, but at all costs we must avoid letting an enemy squadron escape through believing erroneously that they are friends.

13. A re-perusal of *B.C.O.s Nos 1 to 8* will show that the main principles governing most of the items above referred to have been clearly laid down two or more years ago.

PART VI

COMMANDER-IN-CHIEF GRAND FLEET
1916–1918

INTRODUCTION[1]

Beatty's appointment on 27 November 1916 as Commander-in-Chief in succession to Jellicoe, now First Sea Lord, inaugurated the most frustrating and stressful period of his career. Yet it can also be seen as a time of high achievement. The frustration originated in his inability to bring the High Seas Fleet to action and thus redeem what he increasingly felt to have been the humiliating failure of Jutland. Further frustration came from the long delay in finding an effective counter to Germany's submarine campaign against merchant shipping, which he rightly saw as a matter of national survival. The solution inevitably lay with theAdmiralty and he continually raged against their lack of urgency in tackling the problem, even after their reluctant acceptance of the convoy system in April 1917. His criticisms became increasingly directed against Jellicoe for what he and others saw as weaknesses and pessimism. These frustrations were made more bitter by the contrast Beatty so strongly felt between his fleet's lack of achievement and the army's costly struggles and final victory on land. [193–194, 196–197, 199–200, 204–207, 209, 214–222, 230, 232, 267, 271, 281].

These professional burdens were increased by continuing strains in his marriage and he felt particular resentment of his wife's failure to provide the sympathy and understanding which would have helped him to bear them. It is true that he found compensation in his growing relationship with Eugénie Godfrey-Faussett,[2] but his determination to keep this secret imposed further strains. Although Eugénie satisfied his emotional needs, it is noteworthy that he maintained regular and frequent correspondence with his wife, entrusting her with all his professional problems and seeking her help in getting information and circulating his own views in

---

[1]The Jellicoe-Beatty correspondence relevant to this section will be found in Temple-Patterson *Jellicoe Papers*, Vol. II, pp 1–109. The Jutland controversy is covered in Part IV and in the Appendix which contains the Harper Papers.

[2]Eugénie Godfrey-Faussett (née Dudley Ward), wife of Captain Sir Bryan Godfrey-Faussett (1863–1945): entered RN 1877; a friend and equerry to King George V.

influential circles [184–188, 196–197, 203, 206–8, 210–212, 216, 220, 224–227, 230, 238, 239, 242, 245, 249, 258, 260, 280, 289]

In contrast to this unpromising background lay Beatty's high achievement in leadership. He developed increasing understanding of what was needed to remedy the weaknesses shown at Jutland. In his training exercises and Battle Instructions he practised and promulgated offensive but not foolhardy procedures which, combined with his numerical superiority, were calculated to produce decisive victory in any future fleet action. Equally important was his success in keeping the confidence of his subordinate Flag Officers and in maintaining the morale and fighting spirit of his ships' companies in such difficult circumstances. He was denied the opportunity of a decisive battle but, without his success in maintaining and increasing the Grand Fleet's fighting capabilities, the success of the anti-submarine campaign and the blockade of Germany could never have been achieved. His reward came in a manner which accurately reflected the failures and successes of his command when the German fleet steamed into internment on 21 November 1918, not defeated in battle but reduced to ineffectiveness by a collapse of leadership and morale.

Beatty's appointment as Commander-in-Chief arose from the Prime Minister's lack of confidence in Sir Henry Jackson's ability to deal with the submarine threat and his consequent supersession by Jellicoe. The latter had hoped to be succeeded by his chief of staff, Sir Charles Madden[1] and referred slightingly to Beatty's 'many mistakes', but the First Lord Balfour strongly preferred the younger man. Beatty, at 45, was junior to other Flag Officers in the Grand Fleet, Burney,[2] Jerram[3] and Sturdee, and it says much for them and their estimation of Beatty that they all agreed to serve under him. Madden also agreed to stay as second in

[1]Later Admiral of the Fleet Sir Charles Madden (1862–1935): entered RN 1875; Rear-Admiral 1911; 1st Division Home Fleet 1912; 3rd & later 2nd Cruiser Squadron 1913; COS to Jellicoe August 1914-November 1916; Vice-Admiral 1915; 1st Battle Squadron & 2nd-in-Command Grand Fleet 1916–19; Admiral 1919; CinC Grand Fleet & later Atlantic Fleet 1919–22; Admiral of the Fleet 1924; succeeded Beatty as 1st Sea Lord 1927–30.

[2]Later Admiral of the Fleet Sir Cecil Burney (1858–1929): entered RN 1871; Rear-Admiral 1909; 5th Cruiser Squadron 1911; Vice-Admiral & CinC Atlantic Fleet 1911; 3rd Battle Squadron 1912; commanding 2nd & 3rd Reserve Fleets1913; 1st Battle Squadron & 2nd-in-Command Grand Fleet 1914; Admiral & 2nd Sea Lord 1916; CinC Scotland 1917; CinC Portsmouth 1919–20; Admiral of the Fleet.

[3]Later Admiral Sir Thomas Jerram (1858–1933): entered RN 1871; Rear-Admiral 1908; 2nd-in-Command Mediterranean Fleet 1910; Vice-Admiral & CinC China Station 1913; 2nd Battle Squadron Grand Fleet 1915; Admiralty for special service 1916; Admiral & retired list 1917.

command. Beatty, made Acting Admiral, took over on 27 November. Lloyd George's replacement of Asquith as Prime Minister on 7 December led to Balfour's going to the Foreign Office and the appointment of the Ulster leader, Sir Edward Carson,[1] to the Admiralty. In the following months, as the new appointments failed to bring success in the anti-submarine campaign, there was some agitation for the return of Fisher — now 76 — to the Admiralty. For a while Beatty appeared to favour this and even considered Churchill's return, although his distrust of the latter was increasing [177–83, 185–186, 211, 219, 222, 238–239, 254].

Beatty's dissatisfaction with the Admiralty became more extreme when Germany's adoption of unrestricted submarine warfare in February 1917 produced no adequate response. He was particularly critical of Jellicoe's failure to delegate and make full use of his staff. The only factor inhibiting his attacks was the fear that he might be made First Sea Lord and thus miss the fleet action he still hoped for. The further Admiralty changes in May 1917, including Jellicoe's being given the additional title of Chief of the Naval Staff, Sir Henry Oliver's being made DCNS and Alexander Duff ACNS[2], were dismissed by Beatty as of no practical significance [214, 221–223, 225, 227–8, 230, 232].

Pressure for more radical change came from Lloyd George, increasingly dissatisfied with what he saw as the Admiralty's inertia. In July Carson moved to the War Cabinet and was succeeded by Sir Eric Geddes[3] who, although a civilian, was already serving as Controller of the Navy, in charge of ship production. Geddes, a businessman, was determined to improve

[1]Sir Edward, later Lord, Carson (1854–1935): barrister & politician; prominent in campaign to preserve Anglo-Irish union; elected leader of Irish Unionists in House of Commons, led opposition to Home Rule Bill and asserted Ulster's determination to fight for continuing union with Britain; Attorney-General 1915; 1st Lord of Admiralty 1916; moved to War Cabinet 1917; resigned on Home Rule issue 1918.

[2]Later Admiral Sir Alexander Duff (1862–1933): entered RN 1875; Rear-Admiral 1913; 4th Battle Squadron Grand Fleet 1914; Admiralty War Staff 1916; Director of Anti-Submarine Divison; ACNS & Board Member 1917; Vice-Admiral 1918; CinC China Station 1919; Admiral 1921; retired 1925.

[3]Sir Eric Geddes (1875–1937): business man; made Controller of the Navy, a Board Member and Honorary Vice-Admiral by Lloyd George May 1917 and 1st Lord September 1917; in 1916 had been Director of Transportation in France; Inspector of Transportation in all theatres 1917; after war chiefly known as Chairman of Committee on National Expenditure which resulted in drastic cuts in naval personnel — 'The Geddes Axe'.

efficiency and in September 1917 appointed Sir Rosslyn Wemyss[1] to be Deputy First Sea Lord to relieve Jellicoe of routine responsibilities. By now, however, both Geddes and Lloyd George were convinced that Jellicoe was the chief obstacle to improvement. He was brusquely dismissed on Christmas Eve and succeeded by Wemyss.[2]

Although he deplored the manner of Jellicoe's dismissal, Beatty expected much closer co-operation from Wemyss and the new DCNS, Sir Sydney Fremantle.[3] Wemyss did everything in his power to provide this and to inject some cordiality into the relationship. Friction between the Admiralty and commanders-in-chief had always featured in the Navy and was probably inevitable. In addition to a significant sensitivity to what he considered an Admiralty attempt to monitor the fleet's gunnery standards, Beatty seemed capable only of seeing problems from his own point of view and not to understand the wider political and diplomatic pressures bearing on Wemyss. Typical of this were his arguments over the Northern mine barrage. Wemyss met Beatty's increasing assertiveness by continuous efforts to explain and mollify, without sacrificing his undoubted right to have the final word [253, 256–257, 259, 261–266, 268–269, 272–278, 282–284, 286].

Beatty's practical concerns centred on continuous efforts to increase the fleet's fighting efficiency in preparation for the anticipated encounter with the High Seas Fleet. Particularly interesting in this process was an exercise on 24th February 1917 in which torpedo attacks were met by turning towards, rather than away, and submarines stationed to challenge the fleet turn-away manoeuvre which had twice extricated the enemy at Jutland [184, 188, 190, 192, 196–197, 202–203, 211, 222, 224, 229, 232, 246–247, 255, 271, 282].

In addition to training for the day which was never to come, Beatty's preoccupations were with daily operations against submarines and surface raiders and the maintenance of the econ-

[1]For the background to these changes, see Marder, *From the Dreadnought*, Vol. 4, pp. 54–62, 192–209, 213–24; 323–49.

[2]Later Admiral of the Fleet Lord Wester Wemyss (1864–1933): entered RN 1877; 1st Captain of Osborne Cadet College 1900; Rear-Admiral 1911; 2nd Battle Squadron Home Fleet; 1st & 2nd Cruiser Squadrons 1914; Governor of Lemnos Base for Gallipoli campaign; participated in landings April 1915; Vice-Admiral 1915; CinC East Indies Station 1916; appointed CinC Mediterranean but selected by Geddes to be Deputy 1st Sea Lord 1917; 1st Sea Lord December 1917 & Admiral; resigned and Admiral of the Fleet 1919.

[3]Later Admiral Sir Sydney Fremantle (1867–1958): DCNS January 1918; a valuable link between Beatty & Wemyss; papers in NMM.

omic blockade of Germany [186, 189, 192–193, 195–196, 198–199, 205–210, 213–214, 217, 225, 231, 235, 237, 240, 243].

An interesting feature in his search for effective anti-submarine methods was Beatty's strong backing of Captain C. P. Ryan's efforts to produce efficient hydrophones and in his continuing clash with civilian scientists working under the Board of Inventions and Research, of which Fisher was chairman.[1] [190, 196, 198–199, 201, 208, 230, 233, 238–239, 260, 262–263, 272].

Beatty claimed to have been an early advocate of the convoy. The fact that he made his views known in influential places, and a particularly timely meeting with the Prime Minister, must have added substantially to the arguments which led to the Admiralty's change of heart in April 1917. In June he was so convinced of the absolute priority of defeating the submarine that he temporarily immobilised the Grand Fleet by denuding it of destroyers and aircraft to provide convoy escorts [209, 212, 237].

The spirit of Beatty's training of the Grand Fleet is most fully revealed in the Grand Fleet Battle Instructions which he added to Jellicoe's Battle Orders in March 1917. That they were Instructions and not Orders signified that they were guides to conduct rather than mandatory commands to be followed in detail. This characteristic was reinforced by their stress on the necessity for subordinate Flag Officers and individual Captains to take initiatives when circumstances unknown to the Commander-in-Chief had developed. Also stressed were offensive measures such as destroyer torpedo attacks, turning towards enemy torpedo attacks, sustained close pursuit of the enemy after dark and the offensive use of aircraft. The two pages of the first issue were gradually extended in more detail but never abandoned these basic principles based on the spirit of Beatty's Battle Cruiser Fleet Orders.[2] They did not reach their final form until 1918 [252].

Apart from ASW the most important operations were directed against German surface attacks on the lightly escorted Scandinavian convoys. These revealed that, despite Beatty's drive for efficiency and improvements in Admiralty organisation, things could still go badly wrong. On 17 October 1917 nine out of 12 merchantmen and two escorting destroyers were sunk by two enemy cruisers before supporting forces could get to the scene. A similar disaster on 12 December aroused doubts about the policy adopted to provide the fleet with intelligence and led to

[1]See note 1 on page 536.
[2]For Battle-Cruiser Fleet Orders see 128, 176.

the Admiralty's taking control of the organisation of convoys, although not their operational protection, with satisfactory results[1] [217, 250, 251, 254–7, 261, 272–3, 279].

Prior to this, on 17 November, a more alarming failure had occurred. A major sweep was made into the Heligoland Bight by a cruiser and battle-cruiser force with a battle squadron in support. The operation was marked by a lack of co-operation between the formations involved and by confusion over the location of minefields. In what engagements there were, the German gunnery was the more accurate. This action, which had offered an opportunity for Pakenham, who was in command, to overwhelm an initially inferior enemy force, bears so close a resemblance to the unsatisfactory actions of 1914 as to show that both Admiralty control and Grand Fleet performance were still far from perfection.

Beatty himself had no doubts that if the Admiralty's intelligence system, combined with his own correct disposition of his superior numbers, could place him in a strategically advantageous position, the greater weight of his gunnery and the fighting spirit of his men would give him the victory. Such a decisive encounter could only take place if the German fleet sought it. Its high command was prepared to do this, but not its men. By August 1918 signs of mutiny were beginning to emerge under the impact of unimaginative leadership, boredom and the increasing hardships imposed on their families by the Allied blockade. As the year progressed, the news of defeats on land and the growing evidence of the inability of the Imperial government to remedy the situation, brought matters to a head. On 30 October the fleet sortie planned by Hipper, which would have put Beatty's confidence to the test, had to be abandoned.[2] [286]. The High Seas Fleet had ceased to be a fighting force and Beatty had to be content with staging a formal surrender and the meticulous planning of its internment, so aptly described by Stephen Roskill as a 'Victory of a kind'[3] [287–289].

[1]For the problems of Scandinavian convoys see Marder, *From the Dreadnought*, Vol. 4, pp. 293–315.
[2]See Daniel Horn, *Mutiny on the High Seas* (London, 1973) & Holger Herwig, *The German Naval Officer Corps 1890–1918* (Oxford, 1973).
[3]Roskill, *Admiral of the Fleet*, title of Chapter 12.

177. *From Balfour*

*   *   *

[BTY/7/1/1]   Admiralty
[Telegram]   22. 11. 16

84: Secret and Personal from 1 Lord.

I beg to offer you the command of Grand Fleet in succession to
Jellicoe who becomes 1st Sea Lord. I hope change can be effected
without delay. Will you meet Jellicoe and myself at 10.0 am next
Saturday morning at the North British Hotel Edinburgh where I
shall arrive late Friday night.

178. *To Balfour*

[BTY/7/1/1]   *Lion*
[Telegram]   [22.11.16]

704: Secret & Personal from V.A.B.C.F.

I have the honour to accept the appt which you have offered me.
I will meet you as proposed on Saturday.

179. *To Admiralty*

[BTY/7/1/2]   27/11/16
[Signal Copy]

707 — Secret and Personal for First Lord

I most strongly represent that it is most desirable that officers who
fill the important commands under me should be those with whose
personal capabilities I am acquainted and in whom I have perfect
confidence. Admiral Pakenham may be lacking in seniority but in
experience for the appointment of V.A.C.B.C.F. he is second to
none. Admiral de Robeck also is an officer of tried ability with
whose capabilities I am well acquainted and I would submit for

your decision the appointments of Admiral de Robeck to 2nd
B.S., Admiral Pakenham to B.C.F. and Admiral Calthorpe to
3rd B.S.[1]

I am most anxious to have Admiral de Robeck in the Grand
Fleet.

180.   *From Balfour*

[BTY/7/1/2]

27/11/16

[Signal Copy]

94 — Secret & Personal from 1st Lord

I am quite prepared to fall in with your strongly expressed wish
to have Admiral Pakenham in command of Battle-Cruiser Force.
I should prefer however to keep De Robeck where he is for the
moment. The 2nd Sea Lord has claims both of merit position
and seniority, which cannot be ignored. He must therefore go to
2ndB.S. if he wishes to do so. I have the highest opinion of De
Robeck and his chance will surely come. I greatly hope you are
better. As you are one of the lucky people who are never ill please
remember that influenza never forgives the victim who meddles
with it.

181.   *From Admiralty*

[BTY/7/1/5]   27.11.16
[Signal Copy]

96 — For Sir David Beatty

You are appointed CinC G.F. with acting rank of Admiral as
from today Monday 27th Nov. Sir John Jellicoe has been ordered

---

[1]Later Admiral of the Fleet Sir Somerset Gough-Calthorpe (1864–1937): entered
RN 1878; Rear-Admiral 1911; 1st Battle Squadron 1912; commanding 2nd Cruiser
Squadron 1914; Vice-Admiral 1915; 2nd Sea Lord 1916–17; CinC Mediterranean
1917–19; Admiral 1919; CinC Portsmouth 1920–3; Admiral of the Fleet 1925.

to transfer command to you and haul down his Flag and proceed to London. Admiral Madden has been ordered to hoist his flag as Acting Admiral on the 28th November in *Iron Duke* and take command temporarily of Battle Fleet pending your arrival when he will transfer his flag to *Marlborough* as Admiral Commanding 1st B.S. and 2nd in command of the Grand Fleet. Admirals Burney and Jerram have been ordered to haul down their flags and come ashore. Admiral Pakenham with his flag in *Australia* will command the B.C. Force and the title of B.C. Fleet will be discontinued. Rear Admiral Brock is appointed your C.O.S. You should proceed at once to Scapa Flow. All Captains should remain in their ships until further orders. Addressed to Sir David Beatty, repeated to Sir John Jellicoe.

Acknowledge. (2145)

182.   *To Admiralty*

[BTY/7/1/6]   [28.11.16]
[Signal Copy]

I consider it most important that Officer commanding Battle Cruiser Force should be in *Lion*, which ship has necessary accommodation for the staff, speed, offensive and defensive qualities greatly superior to *Australia*, If it is decided that Officer Commanding Battle-Cruiser Force should also command a Battle-Cruiser Squadron, it should be the 1st B.C.S., but I consider present system preferable as [sic] relieving him of administrative work of a squadron. Further for tactical purposes it is desirable to have a junior Flag Officer or Commodore in *Repulse*.[1] I concurred in Admiral Phillimore relieving Admiral Brock for this purpose. If this is approved I will submit the name of an officer to command 2nd B.C.S.

(approved by No 28)

---

[1]*Repulse*, 15″ gun battle-cruiser and her sister ship, *Renown*, completed in August and September 1916, because of Fisher's priority for speed, were always regarded as underprotected. Jellicoe insisted on their being given additional armour in 1916–17.

183. *From King George V*

[BTY/15/4/2]   Buckingham Palace
[Holograph]   December 3rd 1916

My Dear Beatty,

On your taking over the command of the Grand Fleet from Sir
John Jellicoe, I wish to say what pleasure it gave me to approve
of this appointment.

I have known you for upwards of thirty years, ever since we
were shipmates together in the Mediterranean.[1] I have watched
your career with interest & admiration & I feel that the splendid
fleet which you now command could not be in better hands; that
you enjoy the full confidence of your officers and men as surely
as did your distinguished predecessor.

You have my hearty good wishes & those of the whole Empire,
may God bless you & my fleet and grant you victory.

> Believe me
> my dear Beatty
> very sincerely yours
> GEORGE R. I.

184. *To his wife* [Aberdour House]

[BTY/17/36/17–18]   *Iron Duke*
                                         Monday [4 December 1916]

We arrived here yesterday morning and have been very busy
since, interviewing, examining and considering, and, as I felt
rather a worm, it was rather a burden. But the weather has been
fine, very cold but bracing and a little sun, so I am getting better
by degrees. Poor Sturdee was very *piano* but is eating out of the
hand and ready to help all he can. Madden, Evan-Thomas are
the other two squadron commanders here and they are alright.
Generally speaking I have not much time to think but am wrestling
with the multitude of things to be done and think with a little
reorganisation I can put things on a better footing. There seems
at present to be such an enormous amount of time wasted on

[1] In 1888 both served on *Alexandra*, the future King as Lieutenant, Beatty as
Midshipman.

details which can be much better performed by others than by me, and so free me for the more important things. I fancy the late C-in-C. loved detail and messing about finicky things, and consequently the big questions got slurred [?] over and overlooked altogether. But I must go slow for the present and gradually get things put down on a broader basis, and in their proper places.

This blessed flu left me rather slack & weak and I seem to lack energy, but no doubt I shall soon get over that, but it is inclined to cramp my style. The Doctor has given me a good tonic which I think is already doing good.

There seems to have been an upheaval in the Cabinet, but from what I can gather from telegrams it only means a reshuffle and we shall have the same lot in different places, and I expect Winston Churchill will find a place somewhere!!

Of course there is no news here, the war hardly touches this place, certainly not the rank & file, only the Commander-in-Chief & his staff, & the number of telegrams that roll in is amazing.

The Sec. is alright again. Flags had a go and this flu is going through the ship, all picked up at Rosyth they say.

I hope my old battle-cruisers are alright. I will get them up here at the end of the month and have a good shake up all round.   . . .

185.   *From his wife*

[BTY/18/25/46–51]   Hanover Lodge
                                Wednesday [13 December 1916]

*   *   *

I did not have much of a talk with old Charlie this morning, but he thinks it is an excellent thing Carson going to the Admiralty, & I think I am going to meet him at their house at dinner tomorrow night [?]. He says he is quite sure he will work with you & has great pushing power. He says you must see him often & all will be well. I saw Captain Hall yesterday & he seems really hopeful about [?] the Admiralty & does not think they will interfere with you. He told me it was entirely Mr Balfour's doing making you C-in-C & that when he saw you some weeks ago on the *Lion*, he made up his mind then that you were not the rash devil J. & others made out, but that when you did meet the

Germans, it would be a fight to the finish. Regie Hall blinked a good deal, but seemed pleased & sent you many messages.

*   *   *

186. *To his wife* [Aberdour House]

[BTY/17/36/29–30]   *Iron Duke*
                                                                           15.12.16

*   *   *

Well, now that Carson is at the Admiralty we shall see the manner of man he is. But I fancy you will find Jellicoe will stop there much longer than you think. I certainly hope he will, as he knows the Grand Fleet conditions, and, if Carson supports him strongly, he will do. The trouble with him, i.e. J, is that if Carson doesn't support him, he, Jellicoe, is not strong enough in character to make him.

Lloyd George is a dirty dog, but I assume that he was determined to move [?] Asquith by fair means or foul, and that on the whole I think he was right. It seems to me that some of the late government knew of the possible peace manoeuvres on the part of Germany and were quite prepared to nibble at them, which would have been fatal.

*   *   *

Here I am very busy. We have had a very exceptional busy time which has tried us all highly; raiders and submarines, and I have kept our light cruisers fairly on the gallop. But alas, have not been able to achieve anything.

I shall come down to Rosyth the first week in January. I may go to Invergordon on the 24th. The late C-in-C had promised the *Iron Duke*s that she should be there then, and they have arranged to have all their wives up. So, poor dears, it would seem hard to disappoint them, and I have to go there to examine and inspect the place sometime, and I shall come to Rosyth from there about the 2nd or 3rd of January.

I hope you will meet Carson. It is absolutely essential that I should see him sometime *soon*, and Jellicoe or his chief of staff, whoever that is.

Our weather has been very good for this part of the world, a certain amount of rain, but no gales. I have had a walk of 1 hr and a quarter nearly every day, otherwise am glued to desk, but that will get better. There are so many big questions just now and the after effects of the flu are wearing off so my brain is more active and I am begining to be a thorn in the Admiralty's side. . . .

187. *From his wife*

[BTY/18/25/53–60]   Hanover Lodge
                                        Friday [15 December 1916]

*   *   *

I went to dinner with Lady Charlie[1] last night & Sir E. Carson & wife there [*sic*]. I think you will like him, he is very direct in what he says, he said at once — 'I don't know your husband, but hope to, very soon. I shall go up to see him every month.' So I said, 'That was good & what you had always wanted.' I did not talk about the Navy much. I only said, in course of conversation, that the Grand Fleet had been an obsesson [*sic*] (I don't know how you spell it) — but that other things had been lost sight of for the big thing, & that it was very difficult for you to [–] to it just at this moment, the seas full of submarines & mines. He is delighted because you are Irish too. I am sure you will get on. I meet them at lunch today [–] & shall ask them when they come North to come & stay at Aberdour. . . . I am lunching with young Lady Londonderry to meet them. The poor Carsons will be sick of my name soon, as I think they have been asked to meet me at every meal for the last few days. Carson has a boy in a submarine. I am really glad he is at the Admiralty. He told me Burney is ill & will probably not be able to take up his duties for a long time & a temporary Lord will have to be put in his place. I remarked that Burney had been ill for a long time. . . .

[1]Wife of Lord Charles Beresford.

388 THE BEATTY PAPERS

188. *To his wife* [Aberdour House]

[BTY/17/36/41–43]   The Grand Fleet
21.12.16

We arrived today after a cruise with the whole fleet which was,
as far as an exercise is concerned, a very instructive and interesting
one. All the admirals have just left me and said it was the best
that they had ever had, which was something. Even Madden
enthused over it. At any rate it was very valuable in many ways,
and being the first time the battle fleet had been to sea with me,
it was satisfactory. I think Packs will agree that it was good. He
did very well in the battle-cruisers. It was strange seeing the dear
things booming along from the outside and they looked fine and
I envied him being in command.

The weather was fickle, on the whole we were lucky, but it
was the cause of a terrible disaster. Two of the battle-cruisers'
destroyers, or a flotilla leader & a destroyer had been detached
by Packs because one had its steering gear gone wrong and he
sent the other with it to look after it. They collided in the middle
of the night, blowing a gale with a very bad sea, and both sank.
I am afraid the loss of life is considerable, but might have been
worse. I heard of it and luckily was not very far away, so sent
them 1 cruiser and 4 destroyers, and they saved all but 8 of one,
but only 1 officer and 33 men of the other. So it seems that about
6 officers and about 45 men were lost in the *Negro* and 8 men in
the *Hoste*. It all seems very inexplicable at present, but no doubt
we shall hear more in time.

*   *   *

I hope to get Sir E. Carson up to Edinburgh about the 4th.
Could you put him up about then? The difficulty would be his
secretarys [*sic*]. Those sort of fellows never travel about without
one or two, and they are a nuisance.

You must not mention anything about my movements, they are
supposed to be a deadly secret. The Admiralty make a particular
point of that, but I know of course that you are discretion itself.
I am having a little trouble on the *Queen Elizabeth* question, and
it may come to a struggle[1] So don't mention that, although no
doubt most people seem to know everything. . . .

[1]Beatty wanted to have the *Queen Elizabeth* as his flagship instead of the *Iron
Duke*; see 193.

189. *To Hamilton* (C in C Scotland)

[HTN/117]   The Grand Fleet
                                        26th [December 1916]

Thank you for yours. Our cruise was interesting, marred by the most *amazing* accident to *Hoste* and *Negro*, with consequent serious loss of life. The weather was damnable and finished them off.

The *Vanguard's* delay was very tiresome and I think with you that the Captain is a bad prophet, and is saying the best we can.

I am not acquainted with what the S.M.s in the Firth of Forth do now, but may I suggest that they should patrol at times outside the Firth, across the entrance about 30 or 20 miles, on a true North and South line. Enemy S.M.s have been there and I should say frequently, and ours fitted with the directional plates will stand a good chance of getting one.

From information collected, the enemy patrols are all fitted with trawler hydrophone sets and hunt our S.M.s properly and make their life a burden. We must do the same and equip all our patrol vessels with this device, which I gather is greatly superior to that used by the enemy. We are only slow in adopting it, and like everything else new, view it with the eye of suspicion. Having equipped the patrols, they must be taught how to use it and also be drilled or exercised in applying it the right way.

We know nothing here about the exchange of *Recovery* & *Dapper*,[1] and don't know where it started or why. I should certainly deprecate very strongly anything that would be likely to interfere with the completion of the boom. I hope to see you in a few days and we can talk many things over.

---

[1] *Recovery*, mooring vessel, and *Dapper*, lighter, working on the anti-submarine boom essential for protection of Rosyth anchorage.

190. *To his wife* [Aberdour House]

[BTY/17/36/56–7]   Grand Fleet
                                         Saturday [30 December 1916]

. . .

For the first time since I took over my new duties I begin to
see daylight and have got ahead of my work. I have started several
campaigns which has kept me busy but they are well under weigh
[sic], and I have been able to get the Cabinet to take an interest
in them and give them consideration. So I am beginning to feel
more hopeful. When I see Carson I hope to be able to enforce
some further attention. One hour's conversation is worth pages
of writing.

Tell Ryan I want 3 sets of directional gear, including electrical
arrangements besides the 3 the Admiralty say they have ready.
These are to complete the 2nd & 3rd S.M. Flotillas which are
under the orders of R.A. East Coast. They are not under my
orders but I am pressing for them to be fitted at once, and not
one is fitted at present. Then there will be 27 sets for the Harwich
Force, which again do not belong to me, but I am insisting on
them being equipped. I believe only 2 S.M.s of this force have
been fitted, but will wire as soon as I know definitely. Excuse this
disgression but it will get to him quicker this way. I have asked
for Dumas's head on a charger. [1] . . .

I will write to the King and tell him how things go but he is a
difficult person to write to and it is hard to differentiate as to how
much to tell him and how much to leave unsaid, and my time is
so very much limited. But, I am sure it is wise, as you say. . . .

---

[1]For hydrophone development see Hackmann, *Seek and Strike*, Chapter 3.
Dumas, later Admiral Sir Peter Dumas (1868–1948); Assistant Director of
Torpedoes.

191.   *To Hamilton*

[HTN/117]   Grand Fleet
                                                    20.1.17

Thank you very much for yours and information *re* the *Courageous*.[1] I should imagine that you are about right, but the Admiralty take a very optimistic view and state she will be alright in 4 weeks. This I doubt very much. However we shall see.

I am sorry to hear the B.C.s had trouble in getting out the other night. I cannot understand why, but no doubt shall hear. I have been out of there with a strong ebb and strong westerly wind and have never had trouble. In any case the question of showing a lot of lights would not have made it any easier. I am averse to showing lights unless it is absolutely necessary, because it discloses the fact that you are going out. Many times in the past two years we have gone out in the dark and it has not been known until next morning that we have gone. But of course the safety of the ships comes first. I shall probably hear from Pakenham on the subject.

Will you do something for me? Ask the P.O authorities to fix me up a private wire (telephone) from your exchange to Aberdour House. I will pay for it. Jellicoe had one put up between Invergordon and Tarbet House. I don't like communicating over the public telephone and it is desirable when I am there to be in telephonic communication with your office and the ship. I do not fancy there will be any trouble as the posts are there. I'll exercise the B.C.F. on 28th if the situation permits, but am awaiting your letter before I deal with it officially.

P.S. Brock has got the Flu, so am working double tides which accounts for the scratchiness of this.

---

[1]*Courageous* and her sister ship, *Glorious*, built as light battle-cruisers; rebuilt as aircraft carriers after the war.

192.   *To his wife* [Aberdour House]

[BTY/17/37/22–3]   Grand Fleet
25.1.17

*   *   *

I am very busy trying to stop raiders and have cruisers in every
direction and consequently am very anxious. The sea is full of
enemy submarines and I dread to hear of a disaster to one of my
ships, and am relieved when night falls [?] without bad news. Now
the wind is howling and the sea rising and so am anxious for my
destroyers which are also sweeping the seas hunting submarines.
So there is no rest from anxious moments. I was glad to hear the
hydrophones had located the S.M. west of May Island but why
didn't they act on the information and hunt him? I am asking for
information officially on the subject.

I shall have to move the battle-cruisers and another light cruiser
squadron up here, this is for you only. Old Packs is very good at
times, but they make a hopeless muddle of things sometimes. He
has got such an extraordinary bad staff. He would be splendid if
he had a good staff, but as it is, it is very tiresome. . . .

193.   *To Hamilton*

[HTN/117]   Grand Fleet
28.1.17

Thank you for your letter and for taking the trouble over my
telephone.

I am exercising the B.C.s tomorrow and exchanging 3rd for 2nd
L.C.S. I fancy from what I hear from a *very secret source* that we
may expect increased enemy mine laying off our bases & which
may possibly entail the use of surface craft vessels, so our own
light cruisers will have to be out in reliefs to frustrate this. It is
possible that the enemy may demonstrate with the H.S.F. with
the idea of getting us out and then lay mine fields against our
return. This must be dealt with by your local craft and it may be
necessary to put into force the 'Action to be taken etc in the event
of a fleet action' or any modification of it you may think necessary.
For instance, it would be obviously too late to do so if we waited
until the G.F. had reached a position some way from their bases.

Therefore it would appear necessary to have a modified edition of Secret Fleet Order No 14 so that such an enterprise on the part of the enemy would be frustrated. And it would thus require an organisation to put into force directly the fleet went to sea, which it would be possible to maintain for some time. The signal to do so would be 'Put into force Secret Fleet Order No 25' which is now being got out. Will you let me have a copy of your orders to meet such a situation as soon as possible. Of course if the fleet action took place, Secret Fleet Order No 14 would come in as before automatically.

I am glad to hear that the hydrophone system proved of value. It was fortunate that the enemy gave us time to have it installed.

I hope you will have the boom ready again by the 8th as I wanted to come down to turn over to the *Q.E.* about that time and was going to ask if we could put the *Q.E.* and the *Iron Duke* into the basin alongside each other to facilitate the turn over, which is a somewhat formidable operation with the printing presses and archives that have been collected on board here. . . .

194.   *To his wife* [Aberdour House]

BTY/17/37/28–30]   Grand Fleet
                                                             30.1.17

. . .

Yes Indeed, Russia is in a bad way and I greatly fear her internal legislative troubles will reflect greatly on her efforts in the coming Spring and we shall not be able to depend upon her to do much pushing. Even now the enemy are removing troops from the East to the West front in great numbers. So it looks as though they felt confident they can hold them. You say she has got a *Man*. Who is he? I have not been able to discern him.

France is becoming exhausted. Italy is becoming tired. Neither can keep their factories going owing to the shortages of coal, and we cannot keep up the supply because our steamers are all being sunk. The war is going to be won on the sea. Our armies might advance & slay the Hun by thousands, but the real race is whether we shall strangle them with our blockade before they defeat us by wiping out our Mercantile Marine. In the meantime the battle fleets are idle, except that we are making it possible for our blockade to be maintained. I have written pages on the subject and am rousing them to a sense of the desperateness of the situation by degrees. But it is uphill work, and they are very slow movers. I cannot see the end for a long way yet and we shall have to suffer much more than at present before it will even come in sight. And I am none too hopeful. Everything that we hear points to great privation & destitution in Germany and Austria, but they are so disciplined & well organised that they keep it within bounds.

If we made strenuous efforts in the right direction, all will yet be well, but if not we shall go to the wall, or be fighting Germany by ourselves in the end. I am not sure that in the end that would not be better. Our Allies make such terrifically heavy demands upon us, that to meet them & fight the enemy is almost more than we can do. However we must struggle on. This is for you alone, dear heart, don't quote me or mention my views, as it really is serious.

* * *

We are very busy here; have got a lot of ships out, which is a constant source of anxiety from submarines, but we keep a long line under watch now. I think we have prevented their raiders from getting out, but we cannot sight them.

The battle-cruisers will be here in the morning & I shall be glad to see them. I do wish Packs had a better staff. He gives me a lot of extra work. I must get at him when I see him.

195. *To Admiralty*

[BTY/7/9/1]   *Iron Duke*
[Copy]   31 January 1917

No 245 / H.F. 005

In reply to Admiralty letter M.0441 of 27 January 1917 be pleased to lay the following before The Lords Commissioners of the Admiralty.

2. My letter No 80/H.F. 005 of 10 January 1917 was intended to present a policy to deal with a menace the gravity of which is daily increasing. I am not aware of the Admiralty view on this matter. I asked for information in my letter No 132/H.F. 0022 of 18 January, but have not yet received a reply.

My proposals were obviously tentative, and as such were open to considerable criticism of a destructive character. I would submit, however, that at this extremely critical situation of the war, something more than destructuve criticisim is required. The difficulties are no doubt great, but are certainly not insuperable. It surely cannot be beyond our capabilities to overcome those commented on in the Admiralty letter under reply. I have not the staff required to evolve a detailed scheme, neither have I access to the technical experts at the Admiralty's disposal.

3. With reference to the particular points raised in the Admiralty letter, it is suggested that the barrage should be laid as near as possible to the ports of egress, thereby curtailing the distance to be mined to the smallest possible limit, which would appear to be the area bounded on its northern and western sides by a line drawn through:-

lat 55° 10′ N.,	long 8° 30′ E.,
55° 10′ N.,	7° 00′ E.,
54° 15′ N.,	5° 50′ E.,
53° 30′ N.,	5° 50′ E.

This area does not include the field recently laid by Princess Margaret[1] *when 38-day sinking plugs were used* [underlined]

4. The barrage would be watched by light cruiser and destroyer sweeps at varying intervals, with submarine patrols. I am aware of the difficulties connected with submarines maintaining a correct position at present, and therefore urge the necessity of providing them with the sounding apparatus for which, I understand, they asked some time ago.

5. With regard to the breaking away of mines, it should be practicable in the waters of the Heligoland Bight to ensure that the mines laid will remain in position for a considerable period. The depth of water is not excessive, and the tides are by no means strong. This is a matter which the enlarged experimental staff proposed in paragraph 3 of my letter No 80/H.F. 005 of 10 January 1917, should have no difficulty in overcoming. From the reports received, the enemy's mines laid in deep and difficult waters do not appear to break adrift in the same manner as British mines, and failing other ideas it is suggested that a complete copy of the enemy's devices in this respect should be resorted to.

---

[1]*Princess Margaret* a merchant ship converted for mine-laying. For Beatty's plan and defects of British mines see Marder, *From the Dreadnought*, Vol. 4, pp. 85–8.

6. Mines swept up by the enemy must be replaced by mines laid by shallow draught vessels such as the *Hunt* class minesweepers. Minesweeping is a daylight operation which would be interfered with by our watching craft or patrols. The operations of enemy minesweepers should be further interfered with by the laying of an obstruction barrage inside the mine barrage.

7. It is recommended that double mines should be laid in depths of 30 and 60 feet, 40 to 50 feet apart, and that two lines [?] should be arranged for. The mines should be laid in groups, six mines in a group, with the groups outside countermining distance of each other. The second line would cover the spaces between the groups of the first line. To complete the barrage vertically and prevent submarines diving under, a line of heavy ground mines could be laid behind or in front of the moored mines. There are several suggestions for these ground mines in existence, all of which promise success. The design of Captain Ryan's, with magneto-phone attachment, has demonstrated the possibilities of this device for anti-submarine work. To lay mines thirty feet apart in groups undoubtedly presents a difficulty, but, again, it should not be impossible of solution by the experimental staff already referred to.

8. The type of mines to be used is, again, entirely a technical question for the mining establishment, and demands the organis-ation of a design staff adequate to the work involved, and supply arrangments. But I am credibly informed the [?] mines can be produced.

9. To keep Dutch or Danish fishing vessels away from the barrage requires no further notification than at present, and such diffi-culties cannot be seriously considered as an argument against mining operations.

10. I note with concern the remarks on supply of mines. From the statement attached to the letter under reply, it would appear that at the date of the letter –

   a) We had only three hundred mines available (presumably now we possess more [?])
   b) 34,000 are likely to be available shortly.
   c) Orders are about to be placed for a large number.

In this matter I would again urge that the Ministry of Munitions may be impressed with the necessity of supply of mines taking precedence of other war material.

11. As regards paragraph 6, I would strongly represent the desir-ability (whatever minelaying is undertaken) of its being in the

form of a barrage, and that to enable it to be of the most efficient character it is imperative that mines should be laid on a scale hitherto unthought of. Isolated minefields laid at infrequent intervals and in small numbers are of doubtful value and tend to hamper further mining operations.

196.   *To his wife* [Aberdour House]

[BTY/17/38/2–3]   Grand Fleet
                                                                  1.2.17

*   *   *

The battle-cruisers arrived safely and I had a long talk with Packs, and I think he is alright. He has the right ideas in his head and I feel would do the right thing in the presence of the enemy, which, after all, is something. It is his administration work which is badly done and things are forgotten, which means bad staff work, and he hasn't the knowledge or imagination to keep them right, but that will come & he will learn, especially as I am continually pointing out his mistakes & never lose an opportunity, but it is tiresome. Still, he is such a gentleman that he (like many others would) never takes offence or tries to shirk the question. So I have hopes, but his staff are not good.

The enemy submarine activity is on the increase and we are not tackling them in the right way. But I hope to make them hear & see with my eyes before long, but in the meantime we are going downhill. I have got them to do a lot of things but not help enough yet. . . .

I have got in a lot of my ships this morning & feel better about them, but I must send out a lot more to keep fairly on the move. I shall be glad when the day comes that I shall never hear mention of mines or submarines, they are a veritable nightmare, but am bearing up. The Huns have pronounced a war to the knife policy with the S.M. & going [sic] to sink everything they see. I thought they had been doing that all the time. It sounds worse than it is, and is on a par with many things they do.

I was glad when Lord Milner[1] and his party got safely across. They were sent up in my care and so were an additional anxiety.

[1]Alfred, 1st Viscount Milner (1854–1925): High Commissioner to South Africa 1897–1905; member of War Cabinet 1916; took part in missions to Italy and Russia on munition supplies in 1917.

Lord Cromer[1]will be a great loss, he was a fine sound old man. It seems that all our best men are old and dying off like flies.

Did you ever hear from Lady Londonderry what Carson thought of his visit, or was she hurt at your not taking her in? The *Queen Elizabeth* is now on my mind as she is at Newcastle & I have got to get her to Rosyth and they are laying mines to catch her. I have sweepers in all directions and if all goes well, she ought to be alright. I shall know the worst by this time tomorrow.

[P.S.]   Thank Ryan for his letter; ask him if he is fitting any *C* class or *D* class with the directional *[sic]*.

197.   *To his wife* [Aberdour House]

[BTY/17/38/5–6]   Grand Fleet
                                                                        3.2.17

New phases are taking place in the contest. The newspapers in America, according to the telegrams, are shouting for war!! That has happened before and I am quite prepared to see that Mr Wilson considers the situation sufficiently serious to make it necessary for him to sit down and write another note. But indeed the interpretation of it all is exceedingly difficult.

Apparently the German move has raised a shout of anger from all the neutrals. She must have been aware that it would, therefore there are only two conceivable interpretations to the announcement. Either she feels that she is able to bring the war to a satisfactory conclusion by doing what she threatens,or does it knowing that she will cause the whole world to turn against her, and so enable her to save her face in making peace. The latter I cannot believe. It is too far fetched, and I think she believes that she is able to enforce *[sic]* on the world by means of her submarines. It is her last wriggle & it looks like the beginning of the end in reality. And I think we may expect some strenuous times ahead. Her fleet is still intact. She is suffering from the effects of our

[1]Evelyn Baring, 1st Earl Cromer (1841–1917): made his reputation as British representative in Egypt; appointed Chairman of Dardanelles Committee, he died on 29 January 1917 before its First Report was completed.

blockade & her rulers, Hindenburg & Co,[1] might well now say that the time has arrived when the fleet must do something and endeavour to raise the blockade by an attempt to defeat us on the sea – in exactly the same way that Napoleon did when he sent Villeneuve out to be defeated at Trafalgar, against the advice of all the naval authorities. In any case they would not be worse off and they would have much to gain with a success. In fact a success on the sea would win them the war. But the result would be the same, our losses would be great, but we shall annihiliate them with anything like a fair chance, because we are right, our cause is just, and we are prepared, or nearly so. We are not quite prepared yet. There are portions of our service [?] which are not instilled with the right spirit. It's not their fault, poor dears, they have had bad times and have been treated abominably, nobody to look after them, & their morale has sunk below our standard. I've only just found it out. Give me another month and they will be alright. The heart is there but it has crushed in the most extraordinary way & wants reviving. I must not say any more.

*   *   *

198.   *To his wife* [Aberdour House]

[BTY/17/38/7–8]   Grand Fleet
                                                Monday [5 February 1917]

. . .

Events seem to have moved quickly over the water in the last 48 hours, and the U. S. A. seems to be committed to war. But I still think that it won't go so far as that. Germany will climb down or Mr Wilson will put a new interpretation on the actions of the submarines. It certainly looks like the efforts of a despairing nation. How in the wide world they could expect to starve us out or seriously interfere with our prosecution of the war if the United States comes in too, is past my comprehension. They might have had a chance if she remains neutral, but to force her in also seems

---

[1]Field Marshal P. von Hindenburg & General E. Ludendorf, as his Quartermaster General, commanded the German armies in the West from 1916; they increasingly dominated German national policy and eventually pressed for an Armistice in 1918.

mad. I assume that it is one of their diplomatic mistakes, and they have made a great many.

In the meantime we sweep the seas more persistently and tighten up the blockade which is most effective, and indeed it is the only thing that is winning the war for us. Our armies cannot advance, but slowly & surely we are strangling them with my old 10th Cruiser Squadron. They are doing wonderful work, no gale is too much for them and they stop 95 per cent of the ships passing through, and the weather has been pretty bad.

*   *   *

Ask Ryan if he is fitting any of the *C* & *D* boats, or those at Harwich with the Directional *[sic]*. There are 37 wanted for the former and some 28 for the latter. If he would send me a wire and say how many sets he has on order and when he expects delivery, it would help.

*   *   *

199. *To his wife* [Aberdour House]

[BTY/17/38/10–13]   Grand Fleet
                                                                      6.2.17

. . .

I hear you had a further visitation of submarines in the Firth and the hydrophones detected them in good time and consequently the patrol was able to get to work and demolish him *[sic]*. I am not quite clear what they did or how they did it, but certainly having fixed him within a narrow compass he ought never to have been allowed to get away. Whether this is so, I do not know. It at least has proved the efficacy of the hydrophone up to the hilt and it makes me ill to think that we ought to have had them everywhere 18 months ago.

I am afraid the enemy submarines are inflicting upon us immense losses and all the Admiralty do is to make bombastic announcements, and yet fail to take the most elementary precautions. I have written and wired until I am sick of it. Unfortunately the sphere of this activity is outside my domain, and I am reduced to hurling insults at them. But the matter is very serious. I am glad to say they are adopting some of my suggestions, but the provision of certain essentials is so inadequate that it will take a long time before we can really expect a satisfactory return. Still, I suppose better late than never, if we don't lose all our Mercantile Marine in the meantime.

The situation of U. S. A. versus Germany is truly comical and I do not think Mr Wilson has any intention of going to war. He has severed diplomatic relations, which in any other country would mean war. Not so in this case, he will now wait until Germany commits a hostile act. In the meantime Germany will express surprise at Mr Wilson's interpretation of her note & say, of course, if it will in any way incommode or inconvenience the U. S. A., they are quite prepared to alter it, & will do nothing for the simple reason that U. S. A. has no mercantile marine, and so we shall go on. There is just the possibility that Mr Wilson's feigned righteous indignation will have stirred the hotheads over there, like Mr Roosevelt and others, that he won't be able to slip back into a *non compos [sic]* situation.

*   *   *

I have no news of any kind beyond war, submarines, mines, raiders, blockade, sweeps, patrols, gunnery and torpedo, and accidents innumerable, all of which I shall be glad of the day when I never hear of such things again; and a consequent argument with the Admiralty. It was ever thus. History may repeat itself.

*   *   *

We are all going strong here, everybody working hard and doing their bit, and I do think we have advanced things a good deal in more ways than one.

200.   *To his wife* [Aberdour House]

[BTY/17/38/19–21]   Grand Fleet
                                                              9.2.17

I am sending the battle-cruisers back this evening. I hope they won't get into trouble on the way down, and I hope to follow on the Monday. I have got to get Madden here on Sunday to turn over things to him, and there are a lot of things going on which I shall have to see finished before I leave. I fear I shall not be able to stop down for more than a week on account of the astonishing activity of the enemy submarines prevalent at this time, and it may forebode further activity on the part of their main Fleet. In any case I cannot be separated from my fleet, and the Firth of Forth is not ready yet to take us all, and I do not like dividing the fleet. I am sure that is unsound and I have always said so and I shall stick to it. When there is room for everybody then I will bring them all down, but not before.

* * *

There are hard times ahead. Much will depend upon whether our armies can make an advance in the spring. If they can really break through, then the enemy may break up, but I doubt the possibility very much. It has always been said that when the Germans begin to be defeated they will crumble up quickly; that I cannot see any possibility of happening. They are much too well organised to admit of that. We, on the other hand, are so slow to move, that when we do it is nearly always nearly too late. And one feels like a voice crying in the wilderness.

I hope to get hold of Sir Edward Carson next week. If he can't come up to me, I shall have to go down to him. But I think he will come. I do not want to go down because I feel that things are reaching a climax, and any moment something might happen which will alter the whole situation.

* * *

201. *From Rear-Admiral Halsey* (4th Sea Lord)

[BTY/13/16/3]   Admiralty
[Holograph]   14.2.17

* * *

As to Colliers and Oilers, you are doing us really well and I know you fully realise how vital the tonnage question is just now. All will be done at this end to ensure that the Fleet is not let down on account of your surrenders. We have had a bad time with Oilers this week and the question of oil stocks is somewhat worrying me. I wish you would put in a strong letter about the absolute necessity of running pipes into the dockyard at Rosyth in order to oil ships in basin *or* dock.

* * *

Hydrophones — We are going at this as hard as is possible and are now forming a flotilla of 12 destroyers for experimental work with 2 or 3 C-class submarines. There is *no* doubt that this work is the real answer to the S/M menace and it is beyond belief that so many obstacles should have been put in Ryan's path in spite of all you have done to back up.

*   *   *

202.   *Notes on tactical exercises carried out on 24 February 1917*

BTY/7/2/8

The object of the C-in-C in these exercises was to practice deployment under unfavourable conditions in which the enemy fleet was primarily in a position of advantage, and to endeavour from this postion to bring the whole fleet into action at the same time reducing the torpedo menace to the lowest possible limit.

Exercise 1.

In this exercise the Guides of columns of the British Fleet were placed on a 4 point bearing assuming that the enemy were going to be met the centre approaching from the starboard bow. Actually the enemy were right ahead. These conditions representing the case of our fleet meeting the enemy under low visibility, or should inaccurate reports have been transmitted from our Light Cruiser Screen.

On the enemy being sighted the rear was moved up to approximately a beam bearing from the *Queen Elizabeth*, the range at this time from the *Queen Elizabeth* being 20,000 yards. Meanwhile, the 1st and 2nd Divisions being on a 4 point bearing from ahead, were approaching into 15-inch gun range, and the Admiral leading the van led round in consequence to edge away from the enemy. The movement was followed shortly afterwards by *Queen Elizabeth* and by the rear. Deployment took place without any actual signal as laid down for low visibility. Meanwhile the enemy had deployed and were in position of great advantage. The British Van Squadron was within gun range of the whole enemy fleet, whilst the British centre and rear with the exception of *Queen Elizabeth* were outside. The position was one in which the Van would, undoubtedly have had to refuse action unless the 15-inch guns had been able to establish a superiority over the enemy and had succeeded in crumbling some of his ships throwing his line into slight confusion and prevent him carrying out completely accurate movements. Generally speaking, under these conditions the van would have to move away until the centre and rear can be brought up and 12-inch gun ships able to open fire at a range of approximately 18,000 yards. The guiding principle must be that so far as practicable the whole of the Battle Fleet must come into action at the same time; and in the majority of cases this means that the van will have to edge away whilst the 12-inch gun ships are brought up into position. The above does not apply when the British Fleet is able to obtain in the approach a position of advantage over the enemy: the van can then press in and obtain a superiority by concentration over the enemy van.

The situation developed with the enemy in an excellent torpedo position with the *Queen Elizabeth* leading the centre at a range of about 18,500 yards from the enemy centre; this is, just outside torpedo range of the 15,000 yard torpedoes. Under the conditions, with the enemy in this torpedo advantageous position, the speeds of both squadrons being approximately the same, it was impracticable to move on the arc of a circle keeping outside the 15,000 yard torpedo range. The turn was therefore made directly towards the enemy who was then steering directly towards the supposed position of Heligoland. The torpedo menace was accepted, but at the same time the tracks of torpedoes would have been comparatively easy to avoid, coming straight at the British Fleet the units of which presented a narrow torpedo target.

Exercise 2.

This was a normal exercise it being assumed the enemy was met approximately right ahead and steering towards Heligoland the British Fleet having obtained a position between the German Fleet and the Heligoland base. The movements of the C-in-C were guided with the object of keeping just outside torpedo range and moving on the tangent to the torpedo danger circle from the van and centre of the enemy fleet, the deployment being approximately a beam one. This movement was practicable, at the same time keeping the British Fleet in gun fire.

The 'K'[1] class submarines appeared from the *Queen Elizabeth*

---

[1] 'K' class steam turbine driven submarines with speed up to 24 knots surfaced, designed to work tactically with the fleet; 14 had been ordered in 1915, but were never in action. See Arthur Hezlet, *The Submarine and Sea Power* (London 1967), p. 75, and note 1 on page 511.

to develop a good attack, but it is not possible to say this definitely until the full information is available. In considering the turn away by the enemy, it is possible the 'K' class submarines, when all these have joined the fleet, will exercise a considerable influence on the enemy's tactics. It will be the C-in-C's object in the approach to manoeuvre the 'K' class into a favourable position to attack the enemy fleet, and it should be possible for each submarine to concentrate 4 torpedoes on one ship in the enemy line, if possible, the van. Assuming $1/3$ of the torpedoes fired get home the turn away movement of the enemy may be frustrated and the gun attack by the main British Fleet developed. The torpedo attack of our flotillas and squadrons of the van will be launched as early as possible also with this object in view.

Exercise 3.

In this exercise the British Fleet was again placed in an unfavourable position the C-in-C basing his tactics on an acceptance of the torpedo menace and not attempting to avoid it as in Exercise 2, and in the preliminary part of No. 1.

From the exercise it was apparent that if in the approach the enemy are allowed to obtain a favourable position, either the torpedo menace must be accepted or action avoided. The decision on this point must depend entirely on the stragetic situation: if the approach commences early on a long day, it may be possible for the Commander-in-Chief to refuse closing within decisive torpedo range for some hours during which time the enemy may be expected to have fired the majority of his torpedoes. On the other hand, if the action is later in the day, the need for decisive results quickly may entirely over-ride the torpedo menace. In considering the turn away tactics of the enemy it is important that the torpedo menace should not be exaggerated. If the tactics of the British Fleet are to be guided by this menace, it means that the movements of the British Fleet after the turn away of the enemy, are dictated for a period of about 20 minutes whilst the British Fleet are endeavouring to keep outside the danger zone. The difficulties of the enemy in firing torpedoes under these circumstances must be taken into account.

Actually, what he is probably doing is firing torpedoes on a turn away, when outside torpedo range, on the speculation that the British Fleet will turn towards and run into the torpedo danger zone. If he fires his torpedoes with the director setting on the original course of the British Fleet, the Fleet, by a turn towards will miss a great number of these.

If he fires, assuming a 4 point turn towards, at the centre of the British Fleet, provided the centre and rear turn 6 or 8 points for a short time, the greater part of the danger zone will be entirely avoided; the enemy's torpedoes will not have effected their object; whilst the enemy will be closed and brought under gun fire. Continous turning away on the part of the enemy, as is possible on the tactical board, presupposes practically no damage to the enemy fleet by our gun and torpedo fire. So soon as damage occurs and the speed of the enemy fleet is reduced, the situation will become easier for the British Fleet. The situation will also be greatly modified by the presence of the German 2nd Battle Squadron with its speed of 17 knots.

In these exercises the whole German Fleet were purposely allowed a speed of only 1 knot less than the British Fleet, thus making the conditions so much the harder.

It is intended to investigate these problems considerably further on the tactical boards, and to arrange further exercises for practically testing the points raised.

203. *To his wife* [Aberdour House]

[BTY/17/38/31–32]   Grand Fleet
Wednesday [28 February 1917]

*   *   *

So, old Fisher says I will let the Grand Fleet down in gunnery, does he? It might interest him to know that the general opinion of the *fleet* is that we have advanced more in our gunnery methods in the last 3 months then we have in the previous *2 years*. This is a fact. It *was* said by one distinguished officer after the 31st May that the reason we lost 3 battle cruisers that day was because the battle cruisers shot so badly. It has since transpired that on that occasion the enemy was hit by the *battle-cruisers* a great deal more than they were hit and the reason why they did not suffer immense damage was because our projectiles were not capable of penetrating the enemy's armour.[1] Similarly, if we had had decent projectiles on the 24th January we should certainly have destroyed *3* of the enemy's ships instead of only *one*. Lord Fisher was the 1st Ld [*sic*] of the Admiralty at the time that Jellicoe was the Director of Naval Ordnance, who was responsible for the production of the inefficient projectiles.

However I think at present we can afford not to take too much notice of the vapourising of these old gentlemen. But what is a matter of consideration is where does he get his information from, and his views, they certainly are not his own.

*   *   *

204.   *To his wife* [Aberdour House]

[BTY/17/39/2–4]   Grand Fleet
                                         Thursday, 1st March [1917]

. . .

4 years today since I joined the *Lion*. It seems to me as if it were not more than 2, and 3 months I have been in command of the Grand Fleet [*sic*] and we have not struck the enemy a severe blow yet. We have got some submarines, but that is not what is required to satisfy the longing to do something. I keep on saying to myself, 'patience, just have patience', but it is hard to act up to that. We have had our disappointments and our disasters too. This morning a destroyer went out on patrol at 5.30 and at 6.10 she ceased to exist, simply disappeared. There was an explosion, and not a vestige of her was left, except a little wreckage and a few dead bodies. It must have been a mine floated in to the coast from a minefield that was laid 18 months ago. 85 fine fellows in one pouf [*sic*], and nothing to show for it. Such is life and 'Death is but a bend in the road of life'. After all, nothing really matters, in a few short months [?] it is forgotten, or remembered as an incident. But it is hateful to be blown up in such a manner without striking a blow.

[1]Campbell, *Jutland: An Analysis of the Fighting*, pp. 354–5, argues that the German battle-cruisers received only 32 hits compared with the 52 suffered by the British. The same source, pp. 384ff, gives detailed comparisons of the relative effectiveness of the two sides' projectiles. See also Marder, *From the Dreadnought*, Vol. 3, pp 196–214.

Friday morning

. . .

The news from France is good, but it would appear that the enemy is retiring on his own accord and is not being pushed, which means he is not demoralised, & is going to stronger positions, still it is something that he should be going back.

A splendid box of asparagus has arrived & we shall fairly enjoy ourselves tonight. The chockies [*sic*] have not yet turned up. Thank you dear heart. You spoil me and in fact you spoil everybody. . . .

I am glad you told Masterton-Smith that I liked having Carson come up and see me. It is good for him to get the views of the Fleet and he can balance them against those of the Admiralty, which, as we do not always see eye to eye, is a good thing for him and for the prosecution of the war. . . .

We have a regular epidemic of Rubella or German Measles on board. A lot of officers have gone down with it, and the Secretary is very seedy. I hope he has not got it, but fear he has, which is an awful nuisance as he will be laid up for a fortnight, & he is an important person in my machinery.

We had the international conference party from Russia arrived today; British, French and Italian, a large party. I was glad to get them in safely as there are a lot of submarines & mines about; Lord Milner; Revelstoke; General Sir Henry Wilson,[1] the principal British members. I gathered that Russia was none too happy inside but was determined enough about the war, but that is of no use if everything is disorganised by internal trouble. I fear the Empress is playing Old Harry with things and causing the Czar to be very unpopular, he being entirely under her thumb. A revolution is not very far off. . . .

I think there is real need to cut things down, but not for you, you have already done so. We are cutting down in the Mess a good deal. Flags is my Food Dictator & is very arbitrary.

---

[1]Later Field Marshall Sir Henry Wilson (1864–1922): joined Army 1882; DMO, concerned with joint planning with the French 1910; staff of BEF 1914; Liaison Officer French HQ 1915; Command of IV Army Corps 1915; mission to Russia 1916; British representative on Allied Supreme War Council 1917; CIGS 1918–22; Conservative MP 1922; assassinated by IRA in London 1922.

205. *To his wife* [Aberdour House]

[BTY/17/39/16–18]   Grand Fleet
                                                                      12.3.17

. . .

The situation remains very much the same and we wrestle with the submarine menace. We are having some success which is encouraging and have fairly rattled a good many which curtails their sphere of activity and so saves some of our poor merchantmen. I hope we shall increase our successes by degrees, but it is very difficult and requires constant attention. In the meantime the country is getting short of supplies, they won't like that, and yet they must stick it out. Carson I think was very good at Aldwich [?] and his words should carry weight. But I fancy, as soon as the B.P.[1] begin to be pinched in their food supply they will begin to cry out. As it is, they have suffered hardly at all, not as much as Switzerland, Norway, Sweden & Denmark, which are *not at war*. Anyway they will have to suffer a great deal more before we have done, whether they like it or not. In the meantime the enemy appear to be in sore straits and the situation there is undoubtedly becoming acute. But the same applies to Russia and Italy. France seems to have been able to deal with the situation better than the others. It is odd [*sic*] situation, the old world appears to be starving and it is a question of which side can last longest against the pangs of hunger.

Baghdad has really fallen. This is the best bit of news for years and will shake Turkey to her foundations. It was a grand piece of work and our troops must have done extraordinarily well. The Dardanelles Commission Report,[2] which I have not read entirely, is an appalling revelation of incompetency and muddle. I should think from it that as far as Winston and Fisher are concerned, they are done. I certainly if I was Prime Minister would not allow any time for the evidence to be discussed, as asked for by old Asquith. Enough time has been wasted already, and we had better devote all our time to getting on with the war.

*   *   *

The Admiralty are slowly adopting my suggestions as quietly as possible, but after the loss of valuable time, and doing so as if it was on their own volition. I never hear from them about it. They

[1]The British Public.
[2]Two Reports: 12 February 1917 and 4 December 1917.

are not very generous. But it doesn't matter as long as it is done, which is the only thing that matters. They are welcome to all the credit they can get out of it. . . .

206.   *To his wife* [Aberdour House]

[BTY/17/39/20–22]   Grand Fleet
                                                              14.3.17

The very air is full of tragedies, at times they are inclined to depress me, but they are also having the effect of making me more determined than ever to prosecute the submarine hunt to the uttermost. We have had some losses and some fine fellows have just disappeared, no more, nothing to show where or how, but they just didn't come back. The silence of it is uncanny and has a baneful [?] effect, but I keep it to myself, and others take their places. I am wondering how long it can go on. We have been successful again and are to the good on the balance and I think will in the end be able to stand it longer than they can. If there was only a tangible result to hold up and show, but that is impossible. This gambling with men's lives is making an old woman of me and is worse than any general action. But it must go on and we must not turn back but prosecute our purpose up to the hilt. I am now hoping for some good result from a new disposition I have made, but luck is a tremendous factor and it has not been good lately, but we have had 3 undoubted successes. This is for you only. It is something to hearten one up. But it is a wearing-out game and leaves an indelible mark behind. . . .

I'll look up what I have got on the despatch and let you have it, but I have not much written in my own hand as I dictated most of it, but I have some, and of course I could give you a typewritten copy of the whole. The [–] despatches (copies) are already lodged at Lloyds bank in a despatch box.

                        *   *   *

The enemy are not beat & are a very long way from being so. I do not think their SM campaign has yielded the result they quite expected, but it has been terrific and it is indeed a big pill for us to swallow. I think we can say we know the worst and that as time passes we shall be able to minimise it some, but not very much unless we take the very strongest measures, which even now the authorities seem to be incapable of doing.

I expect to get Carson up to Rosyth beginning of the month, and Lloyd George, also I hope, get Sir Wm Robertson.[1] . . .

207.   *From his wife*

[BTY/18/28/68–71]   Aberdour
                                                      Saturday [17 March 1917]

I was so upset by your letter written on the 14th. You really must not take so to heart the submarine tragedies. I know how you must feel whenever our splendid men do not return, but if you take it so to heart you will become an old man, & it won't do anyone any good, & you are needed for so much & such big things. The loss of men & ships must *be* & you must just feel that about it, and in time we *must* get the better of these cursed Germans.

208.   *To his wife* [Aberdour House]

[BTY/17/39/26–27]   Grand Fleet
                                                                       18.3.17

I've just seen old Martin Leake, very elated in his dry way. He did very well & made a good job of it, no survivors. Somebody whispered into his ear 'submarine', so he remembered the old *Pathfinder* and took no risks, though he was somewhere near the North Pole.[2] It is not clear whether she was a new one going out or the old one going home. When he saw her first she was going towards home, but it might well have been the other way. In any

---

[1]Later Field Marshall Sir William Robertson (1860–1933): rose from the ranks; Major-General & Commandant Staff College 1910; DMT 1913; QMG in France 1914; COS in France 1915; CIGS 1915–18; Dismissed by Lloyd George; Eastern Command 1918; CinC Home Forces 1918 & Army of Rhine 1919–20.

[2]On March 16 Captain Martin Leake in *Achilles* of Northern Patrol sunk a surface raider trying to break out into Atlantic; his previous ship *Pathfinder* had been sunk by a U-boat, see note 2 on page 134.

case it was a splendid thing getting her and justifies a good deal that I have been trying to do.

I was very interested about your account of the enemy motor-boat directed by wireless. I wrote to the Admiralty a year ago about Ryan's invention and have subsequently urged them to take it up, but they would not and boomed it off. Now, as you say, when they find the enemy have taken it up they are stirring themselves. I wrote a long time ago referring to an American type of torpedo controlled by W/T and stated Ryan had the very thing.

We had a good week last week, one raider and 4 SMs, but very dear we have paid for it. The price is heavy but it is more than balanced. Still it is very wearing and I am rapidly ageing. If we could only get to grips properly I should be rejuvenated. Weather bad, wind and rain, but it is March so cannot expect anything better and must not grumble.

*   *   *

209.   *To his wife* [Aberdour House]

[BTY/17/39/38–39]   Grand Fleet
                                                                  28.3.17

Just a line to catch *Princess Royal* which is now returning to Rosyth. Something has gone wrong inside and she is *hors de combat*, which is indeed a very serious matter at this juncture of the war, because I feel that something might happen at any time now and her loss is a considerable reduction in our strength in battle-cruisers, & will take a month at least to put right, if not more. Poor little Cowan[1] is in a terrible state of anxiety, but it cannot be helped, and we have to face it.

*   *   *

The outlook on the sea does not improve. Raiders get out apparently when they like because the sea is large and we have an insufficient number of ships to patrol the vast spaces & the Admiralty will not introduce the system of convoy. The enemy

[1]Later Admiral Sir Walter Cowan (1871–1956): entered RN 1884 (with Beatty); Flag Captain to de Brock in *Princess Royal*; Commodore 1st Light Cruiser Squadron; Rear-Admiral 1918; commanding RN Forces in Baltic 1919; commanding Battle-Cruiser Squadron 1921; Vice-Admiral 1923; Commander-in-Chief Scotland 1925; CinC America and West Indies 1926–8; Admiral 1927; retired 1931.

SMs are sinking ships by the score, and I gather the Admiralty are at their wits end to know what to do, and they will not take advice, or if they do, will not adopt it in its entirety.

*   *   *

I hope to be down on the 4th or 5th if things are sufficiently quiet and I hope to get Sir E. C. and the Prime Minister up at that time and make an effort to startle them into doing something different to what we are doing now. . . .

210. *To his wife* [Aberdour House]

[BTY/17/39/41–43]   Grand Fleet
30.3.17

The weather is just awful, blowing a blizzard and bitterly cold, heavy snow & sleet. . . . Somehow down South on the West coast they do not seem to have had this weather, which does provide some means of security for the submarine, and consequently our losses have been great. Indeed I do not see how we can continue losing ships at the rate we are doing. I feel that we are living on a volcano and that we shall suddenly wake up and find that we cannot go on. I shall be glad to see Sir E. C. again. I have just had a wire from him saying that the Prime Minister cannot get up at Easter, but he will come on the 13th (This is a secret so don't mention to *anyone*), so I shall probably be delayed in arriving at Rosyth, as I cannot afford to be away from the Fleet for more than a week. I must see the P. M. and put my views before him, so I sincerely trust that nothing will interfere with that plan.

I shall get down on the 6th. It will be nice to see you and the boys again, and nothing but the advent of the enemy shall interfere with that.

The weather has been so bad the last three weeks that it has interfered very considerably with our operations against the S. M. Our light craft have suffered considerably and consequently, even if opportunities had occurred, they would in all probability not have been able to take advantage of them. However it can't last for ever. They seem to have had some terrific rumours down South this week, all caused by that silly old man, French, supported by our old friend Fisher, who have made up their minds that we

are about to be invaded, and consequently caused shocks all
round. . . .

I wish you would find out from the Bishop of Edinburgh the
name of his eye doctor. My eyes are the only things that trouble
me. They get so tired and worn out working with the electric
light, and all they really want is a tonic. . . .

You must not begin to consider who is going to win the war,
because it is a certainty that we are, in spite of all the handicaps
we make for ourselves by our muddling methods and crass
stupidity. We have the best human material in the world, who
simply cannot be defeated but the many mistakes drag it out so
long and increase the suffering so much that it makes one angry.
In the end, we shall win, because we are right, our cause is just,
and our hearts are in the right place, but the end is not in sight
yet.

The retreat of the enemy in the West is beginning to slacken
up, but the morale cannot improve with such tactics & in a little
time [?] they will have them out of France altogether. If it is done
with the intention of shortening their line they must go back a
long way yet before they can achieve that. They are massing
troops in so many places, according to rumour, that it is hard to
foretell where they will strike next. They must strike somewhere
after this [?] retreat. They simply must feed their nation on
victories, as they haven't got food. I shouldn't be at all surprised
if they settled on the Italians and went for them & they would
find them a comparatively easy prey I fear. . . .

211.   *To his wife* [Aberdour House]

[BTY/17/40/2–3]

Grand Fleet
1.4.17

*   *   *

Everything as far as the fleet is concerned is going hot cakes,
and all my admirals are in good humour and think the fleet has
improved in morale 50 per cent. This is an uncalled for remark
from our old friend Sturdee & was supported by Madden this
evening, so naturally perhaps I am feeling elated. I hope not
unduly so. But everybody is pulling together in the fleet, there is
no friction and no *jealousies* and they all tell me they think we

are more efficient. I must not buck about it or shall have a heavy fall, but cannot help being puffed [*sic*]. We are now getting ready for a new fine weather campaign against the submarines in these latitudes, but fear it is little we can do when we consider the whole areas we have to operate in, but live in hopes of some small successes. Really we are too far away from the root of the evil and cannot expect over much. They must be tackled nearer home.

*   *   *

We have a great gathering of ships here now, all the squadrons except the 2nd & 10th Cruiser Squadrons which are out and the 1st & 2nd Light Cruiser Squadrons at Rosyth. So the place is very full and plenty of work to be done.

212.   *To his wife* [Aberdour House]

[BTY/17/40/8]   Grand Fleet
Sunday [15 April 1917]

Packs will take this down to you. . . .

The Prime Minister wanted to see us both, so we arranged to meet at Invergordon where I arrived last night and am off again to Scapa tomorrow. The P.M. arrived at 4.30 this afternoon having travelled from Dundee!! today, and left again at 7 o'clock to go back to Inverness to pick up Winston Churchill!! and they go on to Aviemore for the night.

There is no doubt he is a wonderful man with a mass of energy and will allow nothing to stand in his way when he wants to find out something. Our conversation was interesting and varied and, I hope, will have far reaching results. You will of course say nothing about it, not even to Packs, who will certainly not mention it to you beyond a possible necessary reference, as it might make it awkward for him to answer questions. And there is nothing that I could put into writing. You will understand . . .

213.   *To his wife* [Aberdour House]

[BTY/17/40/10–11]   Grand Fleet
                                        Saturday [21 April 1917]

Just a line to let you know we arrived safely this morning. We had a good passage, but the first part was full of shocks, as just before we got to May Island we heard that mines had been discovered to the north of the channel we were to go out by, and 7 miles to the eastward of May Island they reported an explosion on the starboard bow and a ship on fire. We had just time to see an unfortunate steamer standing on its tail and disappear, about 2 miles off. It all happened in 2 minutes. The question was, was it a mine or a torpedo? If the former it was dangerous to turn round, as were on top of the minefield, and, if the latter, it was dangerous to go on. I considered the latter was the least dangerous and rammed the spurs into the Good Queen Bess, and we got through. The *Valiant* was ten miles astern, and so I stopped her and sent her back. I sent one of my destroyers to pick up what they could find of the crew of the unfortunate steamer, and they picked up 13 floating in the water, which I fancy was the whole crew, as she was a very small steamer. And I think now that it must have been a submarine that torpedoed her. It seems cruel that these poor little steamers should be sunk in this way. There never was a more cruel and heartless war than this one.

It was a good thing I came back, as they are all at sixes and sevens and apparently quarrelling among themselves, Madden, and Brock and the admiral of the base, and things in somewhat chaotic conditions owing to the attack on the merchant shipping. But we have fixed it all up, and I hope to straighten everything out.

*   *   *

We got 2 Zeppelins yesterday in the North Sea and up at this end we got 2 enemy submarines, *this last part is secret*, our distant patrols got them during this week. So we haven't done badly lately, perhaps our luck is going to turn. God knows, we want a bit of luck just now.

*   *   *

214.   *To his wife* [Aberdour House]

[BTY/17/40/16–17]   Grand Fleet
                                                              25.4.17

A box of daffodils and mignonette arrived last night as fresh as if they had just been picked and the latter scents the cabin. Your dear letter came with them and was a joy to receive.

The two ships in the Straits of Dover did well but I fear you will never prevail upon a naval officer or man (British) not to save life when he can do so. He simply could not do it, although I quite agree it would be more in keeping with the methods of modern warfare, as played by the Hun, if he did not do so. What we should do would be to confiscate all enemy property in this country for the benefit of those who are left behind, the widows and orphans, instead of preserving it, to hand back to them when the war is over. If they announced their intention to do this it would do more to stop their devilish tricks than anything else.

The Western news is good as far as it goes. We keep pushing on against increasingly stubborn opposition and slaying Huns & taking prisoners. The best bit of news is that which indicates that we are gradually gaining the upper hand in the air. Everything depends upon that and from the latest information it would appear that we are succeeding in this important feature of the fighting.

I hear the papers are beginning to make attacks on the Admiralty & caustic remarks as to the failure of the Sea Lords. That I fear is invevitable and not to be wondered at. It is a thousand pities Jellicoe is not strong in his dealings with the S. M. menace. God knows where it will lead us to and every day it is put off the more difficult it becomes. Everything at present is given up to the defensive attitude, and even that is not being well done.

I am terribly exercised over the question of getting the neutral traffic across the North Sea and down the coasts, and hope to establish a system by means of which our losses will not be great. It requires perfect co-operation of all concerned & that seems the most difficult thing to achieve, but we have done well up to the present.

I have not heard from Carson yet, but hope to the next 24 hours & to hear about this conference the P. M. intended to have.

215. *From King George V*

[BTY/15/4/5]   Windsor Castle
[Holograph]   April 26th 1917

*   *   *

I quite agree with you that our principal concern now is to
defeat the S/M menace which has become most serious. Last week
we had 55 ships of over 1,000 tons sunk & can't afford that for
any length of time. As it is, we shall soon be on short rations. I
hope you in the Grand Fleet will do all you can to economise in
bread & flour & prevent all waste. I am pleased to hear you are
going to try a system of convoy which I hope may ensure the
safety of our ships, without too great a strain on our destroyers.
I wonder if seaplanes might be used more now that the weather
has become fine, to locate the S/Ms & drop bombs on them. We
have no doubt sunk some but not enough.

Your having been able to meet the Prime Minister, the First
Lord, Jellicoe & Sir William Robertson, to discuss the various
questions connected with the Grand Fleet in this important
moment of the war, must have been of enormous help to you in
solving the many difficulties which confront us, & I trust that
these meetings may be repeated whenever an opportunity offers.

I must hope that America will be able to help us by sending
dedstroyers & other small craft over here. Adml. Sims has
arrived & I know wishes to do all he can.

I am delighted to hear the health of the men in the Grand Fleet
continues to be excellent & I have no doubt their morale is of the
highest, as always. I can't help thinking that the German fleet will
come out again some day, as when they know they are beaten
they will be forced to come out & do something by public opinion
in Germany.

*   *   *

216.   *To his wife* [Aberdour House]

[BTY/17/40/19–21]   Grand Fleet
                                                                      27.4.17

You spoil me with good things, a box of *new* potatoes arrived
the night before last and were perfectly excellent. Yesterday some
asparagus & cauliflowers, which we shall guzzle tonight.

The situation at sea seems to get worser and worser [*sic*] and it
is difficult to see the end, unless it will be the return of the
archdevil Jacky Fisher. If he were only 10 or 15 years younger,
but he isn't, so there it is. The Army are [?] doing all they can to
win the war and we are doing our best to lose it, which is heart-
breaking. The battle raging on the West [*sic*] Front does seem
like playing a very decisive part in the conduct of the war. The
enemy are fighting for time until they can prepare their next strong
line of defence, and are being heavily punished. If we can but
break them now it may cause a débacle. Both sides seem out for
a decision. So it would seem that a decision will be arrived at one
way or another.

Our grand fellows are doing wonderfully. There are no finer
fighting troops in the world than the British, that sounds insular,
but it has been proved over and over again. The heart-breaking
point is that the Navy, upon which so much depends, cannot show
that they also are the salt of the earth, and we are getting a bad
reputation by the muddling of those in authority. And I cannot
see the remedy with those in authority remaining where they are
and would welcome even Jacky Fisher if I thought it would do
any good. I pray not for tranquillity nor that my tribulations may
cease, but for opportunity and strength to overcome adversity
and make use of opportunity when it comes. They always say
opportunity makes the man but what is more to the point is that
man makes the opportunity, and that is where I am beat. I cannot
see any way to make the opportunity. Can you help, dear one,
with your clear-sighted view of things?

*   *   *

217. *To his wife* [Aberdour House]

[BTY/17/41/2]   Grand Fleet
                                                      1.5.17

May Day is anything but May-like, blowing a gale of wind with
torrential rain and my small ships are getting sadly knocked about.
But the weary work has to go on, hunting, hunting, all day and
night, and endeavouring to protect the merchant craft. We have
been successful up to now and have not lost one that was under
convoy. 'So be it said' touch wood; and we have brought over
and down the coast a great number. But the cursed weather plays
the devil with my escorting vessels. But I try not to grumble.

The Press and the House are making a dead set at poor Carson
and the stupid Admiralty. It was to be expected, but what will
the outcome be? I have suggested a remedy, reorganisation, we
shall see what will be done. I only hope and pray they won't leave
out Carson. That's the stupid thing they will do, and that won't
do any good to anybody. But indeed the situation is bad. . . .

218. *To his Wife* [Aberdour House]

[BTY/17/41/4–5]   Grand Fleet
                                                      2.5.17

. . .
I fear the Admiralty are in for a bad time with attacks in the
House and the Press. It is not surprising, indeed it was bound to
come. They must bear with it and do things better. I have endeavoured to help them by pointing out the way I should change. They
are good enough to accept my principles, but fail to provide
sufficient material or efficient staff to make them effective. I have
now pointed out it is not the principle which is wrong but the
execution of the method. I must wait and see what effect that will
have. I am not very hopeful, but you can be sure I will keep
pegging away at them.

*   *   *

219.   *To his wife* [Aberdour House]

[BTY/17/41/7–9]

Grand Fleet
3.5.17

I fear the agitation will result in removing Carson who gave me the impression that he was only too ready to go the last time I spoke to him. I think with you his heart is in the Irish question and he feels that he has not much scope at the Admiralty, it being a very technical service, and that he must support his naval advisers, and does not like acting on his own initiative. Well, we are all made of clay and the poor country suffers. We fly to opposites; first we have Winston with great ideas (generally impossible) and quiet determination, who over-rides a lamentably weak Board of naval officers, including the redoubtable Jacky Fisher; result—disaster. Then we have a philosopher[1] who, learning from his predecessor's mistakes & aided by a natural tendency to not interfere, allows an even more lamentably weak Board of sea officers to do worse than nothing; result – literally nothing done and everything allowed to fall into a deplorable condition of unreadiness to meet any menace. And then we have a lawyer,[2] who is still imprisoned by the memory of the disaster caused by the impetuous, interfering Winston, takes over, with a new Sea Board which came into office with all the flair of a sea officer straight from the sea and 2 years experience of war, and the authority of the late Commander-in-Chief, and he also feels with his want of knowledge, he cannot interfere. And the great sea officers are not great enough and fail miserably to appreciate the necessity of the strongest measures, with the result we sink deeper into the mire and are losing ground instead of gaining it. And the lawyer, with his knowledge of human nature and human affairs knows it, and yet feels powerless to put things right, so will take refuge in resigning and let somebody else wrestle with it. Is it possible, do you think, under such circumstances to do anything to pull the fat out of the fire, with an old vulture like J. F. sitting on the rail waiting for the corpse to give its last kick? The man who, if he gets there, has pledged himself to turn me out as I am a danger to the nation because I do fight the enemy when I meet him. Ye Gods, was there ever such an astoundingly

[1] A. J. Balfour.
[2] Sir Edward Carson.

humorous [?] situation? How they must laugh. And in the meantime our magnificent mercantile fleet is rapidly being destroyed.
And the task is gradually assuming proportions that the Archangel
Gabriel couldn't put right under six months. What is to be done?
I've had my say. I will wait and see what happens, and if no
attention is paid, I must reconsider. There is not a man that I
know of who could go to the Admiralty and put it right, not *one*,
unless it's Winston!!!

* * *

220. *From his wife*

[BTY/18/30/7–13]   Hanover Lodge
                                                  Monday [7 May 1917]

I lost no time on my arrival & telephoned to Mr Pollen[1] to
come & see me, which he did. He tells me he has declared open
warfare against Jellicoe & he is going to have him removed in a
month's time. He has his list of men [?] he says who are clever
fighting admirals. The whole Admiralty MUST go, with Jellicoe
as 1st Sea Lord it will always be hopeless. He would do well as
Admiralty Secretary in place of Greene, but that he has proved
himself hopeless as a fighting man at sea & on land, & that Carson
does not care enough & is too old and tired to take a stand &
that things will only go muddling on as they are. I do think he is
right. He is going to send you the article which was censored. He
just wants you to see his views & does not want to bring you [–]
the controversy. He says what they MUST have at the Admiralty
are men who understand war & want to fight, & I think he is
right. I wish you had heard him. He says Fisher will never get
back. If there was any chance of it, he would start meetings all
over London & speak in Trafalgar Square.

* * *

Pollen's article just arrived. I have not had time to read it, but
send it on to you. The epitaph for J. J. good, 'He never risked a
life or lost a ship.'

---

[1]Arthur Hungerford Pollen, in reaction to the Admiralty's rejection of his
gunnery control system, had by 1917 become one of its fiercest critics. See note
1 on page 128.

221.   To Admiralty

[BTY/22/5]   [*Queen Elizabeth*]
[Cypher Signal]   8 May 1917

If there is any question of reconstructing Admiralty War Staff
I strongly urge [?] that the new organisation should provide for
free and constant interchange of ideas and opinions between War
Staff and C-in-C, every possible opportunity being taken for meetings of 1st S. L. and C-in-C: personal touch being maintained by
staff officers in the meantime.

222.   *To his wife* [Hanover Lodge]

[BTY/17/41/14–15]   Grand Fleet
                                                              8.5.17

. . .

I see there is a large amount of criticism being levelled in the
Press about [?] the inactivity of the Grand Fleet. They will be
wanting my head on a charger soon. Custance and Winston have
joined in the fray. The former asking questions as usual, but
providing no useful suggestions, as usual, and the latter saying
what a fine fellow he is and how different it was when he was at
the Admiralty. Then they were so active and offensive that they
paralysed the enemy. As usual, talking about himself and not
about the Navy and the country & providing nothing useful in the
way of suggestions. I find, on looking up my old papers, that I
made suggestions on 8th December 1914, which, if they had been
accepted and put into force, would never have permitted the
submarine menace to reach the proportions it has now. But he
and *Fisher* would not accept them or make provisions for dealing
with the S. M. trouble in any other way. And now he has the
cheek to say that it was throttled by those heroes, when as a matter
of fact it hadn't begun in real earnest & they never recognised that
it would. They have enough material at the Admiralty to stop
those two rascals W. C. and J. F. talking for ever.

And now, where are we? The Admiralty again once more seems
to be the target at which all and sundry are letting fly. The fact
of the matter is that the Admiralty (the present one) inherited an

almost impossible task to make up lee way and tackle the question. And, being made up of a mediocre crowd, are not only failing, but failing with ignominy. As constituted, it simply was beyond their powers, and they have gone the wrong way to work and, instead of improving matters, have made them worse, and we are getting deeper and deeper into the mire. There are rumours of changes, but I pity any poor devils that have to go there and work under the present régime. It is simply impossible to make it a success. Nothing but a clean sweep would be of any value. They will tinker with the question and call the same people by different names and all will go on as before until another disturbance greater than the last will have an up-rooting effect.

I am not consulted & do not know what is going on. I have given Carson my opinion and I doubt if he is strong enough to take it. But we shall see. Of one thing I am certain. I have no idea or liking of leaving the Grand Fleet and clearing up the mess for them. I can do my duty best by keeping the fleet ready and prepared against the day, which cannot be far off, when we shall have to fight like the deuce. After which I am prepared to do anything.

223. *To his wife* [Hanover Lodge]

[BTY/17/41/17–19]   Grand Fleet
10.5.17

There does indeed seem to be a hub-bub in the Press over the Admiralty organisation. But as usual we are on the wrong tack. It is not the organisation that is wrong, although it can be improved, but those who form the organisation who are not equal to the job. I have pointed this out until I am tired, they are going to make some alterations, principally to consist of calling the same people by different titles, and expect that to alter things. Which it won't of course. However, I can do no more unless I leave the Grand Fleet and go there myself, which I will not do. Because I still consider that the Grand Fleet is the end of all things as far as the country is concerned. I mean by that, if the G. F. came to an untimely end we may as well put the shutters up and we are finished as a Great Power. Bad as it is, the submarine menace won't accomplish that.

I feel rather like Achilles who sat in his tent and sulked during the siege of Troy. Is that very conceited? But I haven't sulked. I have done my best by making representations and offered plans and suggestions, which have been taken up months too late, in a half hearted way which is worse than useless. They don't ask me to help. I force it upon them, and they don't like it, more especially as they haven't the energy or courage to accept it entirely and only do so half-heartedly. I give them a little more time and they will be run out. Carson is disappointing and will not take a strong line.

There is a lovely story of old Fisher's that he is coming to stop with me. What a welcome we would give him, but he hasn't been asked yet, and he certainly shall not come unless he is. I have half a mind to ask him anyhow. He is a man, unscrupulous, but still a man. Which is more than anybody at the Admiralty is.

I see old Custance has again returned to the Press, the nebulous old fool, always destructive criticism, never constructive. It is so cheap and nasty. He now says, 'The controlling mind is imbued with the one idea that the safety of our ships is more important than the destruction of the enemy.' *Perhaps* he refers to the Admiralty, but I, and not the Admiralty, am the controlling mind of the Grand Fleet, and I am not aware that my actions during the war have been such as to permit him to make such an appalling statement. In any case, it does not make it any easier for me, and should make his statements clearer as to what he does mean, instead of damning wholesale the senior officers of the service which has suffered him for so long. Anyway he has roused a considerable feeling of resentment in the fleet. His animosity against some has led him to damn the whole Navy in the eyes of the world. Why should the mistaken ideas of some be laid at the doors of the whole Navy or Grand Fleet? I should like to pull his nose.

Mr Pollen's article is very scathing & I do not wonder they would not publish it. . . .

224. *To Eugénie Godfrey-Faussett*

[CCC/SLGF/14/1/A]   The Grand Fleet
                                                                  10.5.17

Eugénie, you are a darling, and I love your delightful letters. Nobody can write letters like you do. They are human, and have the effect of causing a swelling of the head which I like. Indeed, my dear, they do me good, and when I think that somebody believes in me it increases my belief in myself and I feel that I can accomplish great things,in fact they *inspire*. Your idea of dealing with the Admiralty is a splendid one, and indeed I don't laugh at it because it is exactly what I have thought of doing myself many times. And in fact have actually done it, but unfortunately the other play actor in the Drama has failed to take his cue and make the impassioned speech of his life, so what am I to do about that, make it for him!! No, as a matter of fact, they are now doing what I have been pressing them to do for months, but alas in only a half-hearted way. J. J. was always a half-hearted man. However, I insult them once a week and goad them into more determined efforts and an upheaval has been the result but I fear the Mountain will only bring forth a Mouse. However, we shall see. I have not relaxed my efforts and do not intend to. But I am also faced with a quandary. If I go the whole length of denunciation of the Adlty, and their ways and I am successful, it means that *I* should have to go to the Admiralty, that means leaving the Grand Fleet, and for the life of me I do not know who to put into the Grand Fleet. It is a question of which is the most important appointment to the Nation, and will have the most important effect upon the War. To my mind, there is no question, and that is, the Grand Fleet, which if that was mismanaged a second time we meet the enemy we are done for good and all and we cannot for a second risk that. I believe in myself to the extent that if we can once get in touch with the enemy we shall never let him go and I believe in the Fleet that under those circumstances we shall destroy him utterly. Is that very conceited? It's your fault if it is!! — And I do not know of anyone that I could trust to do the job as I would do it myself — more conceit — your fault again. It is a very complex question and is a question of which is the greater or lesser of two evils. My place is the G.F., then who should go to the Admiralty if J. J. departs as he would if I started a war to the knife. Perhaps you will have another inspiration in that dear head of yours.

I honestly think J. J. would do very well there if he had the right sort of men behind him but he simply seems totally incapable of selecting good men to serve under him. He apparently dislikes men of independence and character and loves sycophants and toadies. What a diatribe and a bore I am becoming with my conundrums and appallingly egotistical (you'll have to look that up in the dictionary) it seems. But I write to you as I think, and you are so delightful you don't mind. You won't write me any more in the diffident way, will you? Do you think I could possibly hear often enough what you told me in the non-diffident letter. No, my dear, I am like the Bear and the Honey Pot. You remember that John Knox called Mary the Honey Pot and instead of providing one grain of happiness it supplies me with a stack full and I walk on air and feel capable of doing anything. You spoil me with your letters and I regret that I have so little time to write oftener in reply. But being of great understanding you will forgive and understand.

My dear, the weather is ghastly. Bitterly cold, heavy snow and a foul wind. Mid-winter weather, and I understand the sun shines with you. Well you deserve it and I suppose we don't. But it is hard to keep on hoping for the best under such conditions. Bless you, dearest Eugénie. Much love. I think of you more than is good for me.

Yours
David.

[P.S.]   I am wondering whether you will be able to read and understand this rigmarole.

225.   To his wife [Hanover Lodge]

[BTY/17/41/21–2]   Grand Fleet
                                                         11.5.17

*   *   *

I wonder what Charlie B. wanted, or if you got anything out of Carson?

I have come to the conclusion that I must move warily. If I

attack the Admiralty too vigorously and successfully! it will end
in my having to go there, and that means leaving the Grand Fleet,
which I should not like, and moreover I do not think would be a
good thing. As I am kicked [*sic*] if I know who to put in command.
I also am of the opinion (perhaps I am biassed) that of the two
appointments, i.e. the C-in-C or 1st Sea Lord, the most important
one from the national point of view is the Grand Fleet. If that
went wrong, or if it did not succeed in destroying the enemy, for
a second time, on meeting them, then we may as well put the
shutters up. We should be done.

Whereas the S.M. menace might reduce us to great straits, but
it would not defeat us, and from my present position I can still
harass the Admiralty and goad them into doing something before
it is too late. They have adopted a good many of my suggestions,
but alas, in a half-hearted way which spoils the whole thing.

I was tickled to death to read in the *Society News* that Sir J. J.
carried Lady J's *cash box* to the Albert Hall and was confronted
with his own identification disc. Ye Gods, what a burlesque, and
what time he has, and in the meantime I cannot get my letters
answered. . . .

We are out of luck at this end. We have had many hunts after
the S.M.s but have always, when it has come to the final blow,
just missed the shot — 5 in the last week — too sickening. They
have always been saved by a hair's breadth. But, our turn will
come. We have harassed them and have had only 2 ships
torpedoed out of 150 in the last fortnight, and these old merchant
craft are terrbily slow, and the days are getting very long.

226. *From his wife*

[BTY/18/30/37–44]   Hanover Lodge
                                                Saturday [12 May 1917]

*   *   *

I met Carson at Sally [?] Londonderry's last night. He came up
to me after dinner & said, How is the gallant Admiral? And I
said I had received a letter from you & that you seemed
depressed & expected your head would soon be on a charger.
And then I said, I hope you won't mind what I am going to say,
but he feels very much that he has not been consulted about all
the changes & he does not know what is going on at the Admiralty.

He said then, I am very glad you have told me. I have been telling them they must have daily communication with the C-in-C, & I will write him a long letter tomorrow. So, I don't think I have done any harm by saying what I did. We then sat down together & he said in his funny Irish way, Will you tell me what manner of man Burney is, a very nice old woman, I think, & why did J. get him there? He said, if you know, will you tell me. So then I told him the story. That you were arranging the appointments with Mr Balfour, that J. wanted Madden & you wanted Packs for the B.C.s & so it ended in Mr B. giving way about Burney as 2nd Sea Lord. Then he said, tell me in confidence about Madden, is he [—] wonderful man I am told he is? And I said, I did not think so. I said he had brain but no [—]. The poor old thing said, you know, it is very difficult for me to find out these things, but I am beginning to understand.

Pollen was there & after dinner had a good go at Carson about J, and Carson it seems, has seen his letter I sent you & I believe, quite agrees. I talked also to Pollen & he says, in another two months J. will go. Every week in *Land & Water* he is going to write about the battle of Jutland, making it a little stronger each week, & at the end of it he will go, he says. J. is already thinking about the Hamiltons' place at Rosyth.

Carson seems [?] very pleased at Sir E. Geddes going as Controller. He said, he is very clever and pushing. I do think all will come right in time, so cheer up. I sat next to Stamfordham & Sir E. Vincent, I can't remember their new names. Sir E. V. asked me why Jellicoe had not defeated the Germans at Jutland, and I said, ask me an easier question. He said he never believed he was a great man.

The American Admiral[1] was there. I only spoke to him a moment. I asked him if he was going up to see you, & he said he hoped to. He looked quite a nice man. Pollen had been putting him right about the battle of Jutland.

*   *   *

[1]Rear-Admiral W. S. Sims USN (1858–1936): commanding US Naval Forces Europe; a strong Anglophile; future President of US Naval War College; his *The Victory at Sea* (London, 1920) is valuable on convoy introduction.

227. *To his wife* [Aberdour House]

[BTY/17/41/24–6]   Grand Fleet
                                                       13.5.17

What a climate we live in, now enveloped in fog and my poor
old convoys are spread all over the North Sea. I don't know what
will come next.

Old Charlie B. was wrong. Duff does not leave the Admiralty
and Sinclair[1] does not go there, he has too much common sense
and refuses to move out of his cruiser squadron (don't repeat it).
I fear that those who will go there are no improvement on the
ones that go. Jellicoe is absolutely incapable of selecting good
men, because he dislikes men of character who have independent
views of their own. It is a fatal mistake that [?] and is
insurmountable.

                    *   *   *

I have a Bishop here now, a nice man, the Primus of Scotland,
Brechin is his title. . . . He is confirming a lot of sailors, quite an
extraordinary number, a lot of the old sinners. It's quaint the
effect the war is having on them.

                    *   *   *

228. *To his wife* [Aberdour House]

[BTY/17/41/28–30]   Grand Fleet
                                                       16.5.17

. . .

No, I have not heard from Carson, but I propose to send him
one which will cause a shake. They have triumphed about the
recent change at the Admiralty. The mountain has produced a
mouse. The changes are practically speaking only in change of
title and nothing else!!! They have introduced a civilian, presumably instead of old Francis Hopwood,[2] with much greater powers,

[1]Later Admiral Sir Edwyn Alexander-Sinclair (1865–1945): as Commodore
commanded 1st Cruiser Squadron under Beatty at Jutland; Rear-Admiral
commanding 6th Cruiser Squadron 1917.
[2]Francis Hopwood, later Lord Southborough (1860–1947): civil servant;
additional Civil Lord of Admiralty 1912–17, concerned with contracts.

and Halsey to help him. The latter was chosen because he is a complacent individual without much character or independent ideas. But the important question will be, who is going to be responsible for design and construction? Halsey has not the brains or the knowledge and Sir E. G. has not got the knowledge. Tothill[1] who takes Halsey's place is a worthy officer, without high qualifications. Jellicoe, Oliver, Duff are all what they were, with new names. Fisher,[2] one of my best captains, goes to assist. I grudge his departure because he was of the greatest assistance to me, but he will be a great addition to [?] the Admiralty and I hope will do good.

* * *

There was a charming article in the *National Review* called The Soul of England, which you must read; the right spirit and true. And when we turn to the other side and see the engineers striking it fairly makes one's blood boil, and nothing is done to them. Why not send them to the trenches? And they call Lloyd George a strong man. He is not, except when he knows it is popular, he [*sic*] a demagogue pure and simple.

In the meantime our gallant army is plugging away to some considerable effect on the Western Front and slaying Huns in large numbers. The enemy are using up their reserves and the day is dawning, is nearer, when we must arrive at some definite conclusion. Would that we could help, but we cannot at present, and must possess our souls in patience. Our time will come, as Madam Dubois says, and then we can fairly settle the thing once and for all. After that I am quite ready to go to the Admiralty, or anywhere else, if I am asked. . . .

---

[1] Later Admiral Sir Hugh Tothill (1865–1927): Rear Admiral and 4th Sea Lord (Supplies and Transport) May 1917—June 1919.

[2] Later Admiral Sir W. W. Fisher (1875–1937): entered RN 1880; Captain of battleship *St Vincent*; to Admiralty in succession to Duff as Director of Anti-Submarine Division May 1917 to end of war; COS Mediterranean 1919; Rear-Admiral 1922; 1st Battle Squadron 1922; DNI 1926; 4th Sea Lord 1927; DCNS & Vice-Admiral 1928; 1st Battle Squadron & 2nd-in-Command Mediterranean 1930; Admiral and CinC Mediterranean 1932; CinC Portsmouth 1936; died in office.

229. *To his wife* [Aberdour House]

[BTY/17/41/39–40]   Grand Fleet
                                                        22.5.17

. . .

We had some busy days at sea and some very interesting exercises and deployments. I am working some tactics which I think promise well, but our opportunities are so few and far between and the submarines are so numerous that it makes a great burden and responsibility taking the Fleet to sea purely for exercises. And yet if we don't practise them we shall do no good. I am rather disappointed with old Packs, (but don't think of saying a word to a soul), he does not seem to possess quite the right flair, or be quick enough in grasping the situation, and at high speeds it makes such a difference. But for the life of me I do not know a soul who would do it better. I can only go on instilling (or trying to) into him the right principles by which he must be governed. He had a glorious opportunity this time of doing a big thing in one exercise, if he had only been quick enough to realise it at the right moment. I suppose you have to be born with it.

*   *   *

I haven't heard from Carson, except a telegram asking for my views on a certain question. I have written him two letters of considerable length & importance lately and have received no reply to either. I will give him another 48 hours, and if I do not get an answer, I will send him a snorter. I expect the unfortunate man is thinking mostly about his pledges on the Ulster question and doesn't know which way to turn to get out of an awkward situation.

You ask me when I am coming down. I cannot tell at present, but should think about the 6th June, when there is a moon, possibly before, but depends upon events and how things go at the Admiralty. I should be able to bring the Battle Fleet down as soon as the anchorage has been made big enough to take it all. I fancy that will not be till July.

P.S. The King very kindly sent me a nice telegram, which I enclose [not included].

230.   *To his wife* [Aberdour House]

[BTY/17/41/41–3]   Grand Fleet
                                                                      24.5.17

. . .

I hear that the Admiralty is in a turmoil and they have all
been packing their portmanteaus [*sic*] with a view to taking their
departure. But as always happens, they still remain where they
are and the change is in name only.

Roger Keyes returned to the fold of the Grand Fleet yesterday,[1]
very pleased with himself at having been presented with a son.
You must get me a mug for him as he is another godson. I'll let
you know what his name is to be so that it can be inscribed upon
it. He was very full of you and Peter and all the good work you are
doing. He apparently had had a hard time with the Dardanelles
Commission, but no doubt he told you all about that.

I see in the *Land and Water* that Pollen has returned to the
attack. I am begining to ask myself what is the use of all these
attacks. They are not capable of achieving anything and they bring
the Navy into disrepute. I think I told you of the feeling that was
caused in the Fleet by old Custance's letter to *The Times* which
discredited the Navy and caused a feeling of unrest that we were
not doing our best or as much as we ought. Sturdee wrote to him
and told him how much it was felt in the Grand Fleet, and finished
up by saying that his letters were very disturbing, but were not
very helpful. He is a great supporter of mine now, Sturdee. I have
humoured the old beggar, and he is loyal and helpful, and we get
on very well. In fact all my admirals are splendid and help me
enormously to keep things going, and all our relations are
harmonious. Dear old John de Robeck is like a two year old, and
you wouldn't believe he is the same man as joined up 6 months
ago. He is 15 years younger and as cheerful & happy as a sandboy.

Six months I have commanded the Grand Fleet now and we
haven't met the enemy yet. How many months are we to wait? I
would not mind how many if I knew at the end we would get
them, but it is this haunting fear that we never shall and the
Grand Fleet will never be able to justify itself, that is the fly in
the ointment.

I have been asked by several officers of high degree if it is my

[1]To command 4th Battle Squadron.

intention to recognise or celebrate the 31st May. My answer is that that was one of the saddest days of my life, in which I lost many old and valued friends and trusted comrades, and the Navy missed one of the greatest opportunities of achieving the greatest and most glorious victory, and therefore it could not in any sense be considered a day for celebration. I like your idea of a Memorial Service and it must be that and nothing more.

I will send you dear old Packs and the battle-cruisers back in time unless something intervenes to prevent it.

You are quite right, dear heart, to be careful not to say anything about J. J. in the hearing of any naval people, and I should say as little as possible to any but those you can trust implicitly.

*   *   *

I heard from Carson, not very satisfactory. He says he will do what he can for Ryan, but do not mention it as he may be disappointed.

231.   *To his wife* [Aberdour House]

[BTY/17/41/45–7]   Grand Fleet
                                                    27.5.17

. . .

How did you manage to get hold of old Wyllie?[1] I hope he is making a successful picture of it for you, or rather skeleton to make it from.

I will get the battle-cruisers down to you if I possibly can by Thursday morning. I suppose you will have your service in the afternoon. They are doing their gunnery and owing to the weather being so misty they have not been able to finish, but they should do so by Wednesday at the latest and would then arrive Rosyth Thursday at daylight. . . .

Yes, there has been a reduction in the number of ships sunk, and we have been getting submarines, 3 up here last week. I think all fairly good and substantial cases. Yes, you are right, Carson is a politician first and a patriot 2nd. He wrote me that he was unable to write before because he had been so busy over the Irish question!!

[1] W. E. Wyllie RA (1851–1931): painter; a great admirer of the Navy; produced many wartime pictures, including one of *Lion* at Jutland.

*   *   *

Don't fuss your dear self about the destroyers and what people say. They are only mischievous busybodies. Like a great many other departments, the rascals were abominably careless and knocked their boats about in the most unpardonable ways, with the result that at one time nearly half of them were under repair, all caused by collisions etc, from pure carelessness. They are getting better. They know very well that I won't stand for that. But they also know very well that when they do well that it is recognised, and they are coming to hand now and are very much more efficient than they were. So, don't fuss, dear heart. Everything is going well with the fleet and all the captains tell me that we have made immense strides on the gunnery of the fleet. I know that, but it is a good sign when they come and tell me so, and I don't think I have made them unhappy or discontented. Tactically, we have made immense improvements and have worked out many problems, all to our advantage. Our exercises have borne good fruit and have been most valuable in every way.

*   *   *

232. *To his wife* [Aberdour House]

[BTY/17/41/54–6]   Grand Fleet
                                                     31.5.17

It hardly seems a year since that terrible day when we might have accomplished so much, and our failure to do so has cost us dear, when those great ships and gallant lives were lost. As time goes by one realises more clearly the opportunity that was missed, an opportunity that will never recur, and what would have been easy then will be infinitely more difficult in the future. Fate is not generous in the matter of giving opportunities, and if you miss one, you never get another. However, I console myself with the thought that the Battle-Cruiser Fleet did all that it could have done, and that the next time, if Fate is kind and gives us a next time, the Battle Fleet will have their chance.

The weary waiting is hard indeed, but the sailors are so extraordinarily happy and cheerful through it all, bless them, that they help me in the execution of my duties. We are never still all day, and every day, ships are firing away and manoeuvering about, and all acknowledge that we are advancing in efficiency day by day. They come [?], Admirals and Captains, and volunteer the statement from time to time, which is the greatest encouragement I could possibly have. One thought alone fills the mind of every soul, to keep on improving and improving until our great day comes to prove that it has not been all wasted effort. The fly in the ointment is the dread that that day may never come, and our efforts will have been all in vain. I never allow myself to think or speak of such a possibility, but at the back of my mind it is always there, like a nightmare.

Thank you, sweetheart, for your telegram. I hope that your service this afternoon was a success, which I am sure it was, as everything you do is well done. I am sorry that the other battle-cruisers did not get down on time, but they did not get their firing finished this afternoon, and I would not have sent the *Lion* & *Tiger* down with Packs if it had not been that you wanted them. Isn't that a terrible confession to make!!

*   *   *

I am not surprised to hear that Sir E. C. can realise what the defects at the Admiralty are, they are as plain as the nose on your face, but, if he is fussed over Ireland, he won't give much time to so little a thing as that!! These politicians are all alike, a disgusting breed without real patriotism.

*   *   *

233. *From his wife*

[BTY/18/31/2–6]   Aberdour
Friday [1 June 1917]

*   *   *

Captain Ryan tells me Commodore Hall paid him a visit yesterday & was very pleased with the Hydrophones. He said they were much better than he thought. It seems that the Board of Inventions always puts him off coming up & told him the things at Hawkcraig were no good. But why did he not come & see for himself? I should have thought he could have seen through them. They seem to have a wonderful hold on the Admiralty. He told Captain Ryan that until Jackson & Oliver are removed things will not improve at the Admiralty. They do what they like with Jellicoe. He is not strong enough & gives an order & they don't

carry it out, knowing J.J. will let it pass. It seems a strange state
of things.

*   *   *

234. *From Rear-Admiral Halsey* 3rd Sea Lord

[BTY/13/16/4]   26, Cheyne Walk,
[Holograph]   S. W.
                                                    Sunday June 17th 1917

My dear Sir David,
    An awful thought has struck me on arrival here this morning
that I promised Sir Edward Carson I would talk to you about the
possibility of using Invergordon again for the Ships' Companies
of the G. F. to visit for the purpose of recreation &c, and I quite
forgot to do so, as the various items that were discussed in your
cabin completely obliterated my promise from my head until after
I had left the ship — What I did want to say was this — In June
1915 when I became Capt of the Fleet I found that there was a
certain amount of feeling in the Fleet up at Scapa that they were
being rather cooped up & in comparison with the B.C.F. at Rosyth
both officers and men undoubtedly had a very poor time with no
relaxation of any sort outside their ships — and I am quite certain
that when the Squadrons began to visit Invergordon in turn it
made a very great difference to the general morale of the Fleet —
I am fully aware that the very high standard of morale still exists
in the Fleet, but from what I hear from several sources I cannot
help realising that there is a great sense of disappointment in the
Fleet now that the ships never get a spell away from Scapa except
for their refit, and I cannot help thinking that if it could possibly
be arranged for some ships to go there it would very materially
help to keep the officers and men in the happiest and best
condition of mind & temper — Of course this may be quite
impossible under the present conditions by lack of sufficient
destroyers, or because of the impossibility of keeping the channels
swept for immediate concentration, but I do hope you will not
resent my interference in telling you what I have heard and what
I actually realised myself was going on in 1915 when the ships had
been for 9 or 10 months at Scapa, as I am so certain that at that
time the value gained generally in the Fleet by the periodical visits

was enormous — The anticipation before ships actually went there was equal to the good results gained by the actual visits — As I said before I had promised Sir Edward to speak to you on this subject & this must be my only excuse for writing on a topic which does not affect me — I have given orders for the daily dkyd report to be sent to you & I will send you a copy of the information about the German Shipbuilding — The information was contained in the 1st copy of the appreciation of the naval situation which I think you said was not sent to you — The various other subjects discussed by you will be fully gone into and I will send you a report in due course.

I am wondering what your impressions are of the Controller — personally I feel sure that he will do a very great deal — he is a strong man with great driving power and he is all out for the country's good and not for his own glorification in any way — I have worked on & off with him for 4 months before he was asked to come to the Admiralty, as the transport work that I had to do as 4th S.L. was closely associated with his work in France & I can only say that I have formed a very high opinion of him in every way — Old Bruce[1] was perfectly splendid when he explained *his* Dockyard to Geddes yesterday, as I've no doubt Brand[2] has told you — The heat here in London is really terrific —

My very best wishes for the best of good luck and victory & my humble duty.

235. *Notes [by Halsey?] on Beatty's Views on Construction Policy. [Visit to Grand Fleet by Geddes and Halsey]*

[DEY/19]   18 June 1917
[copy]

In company with the Controller, I visited the Commander-in-Chief at Rosyth, and the following notes of our conversation are made out with a view to his wishes being known about the various subjects discussed.

The system of the re-organisation of the Controller's Department was explained at length to the Commander-in-Chief, and the various types of ships that it is proposed to build in the future,

[1]Commodore of the Dockyard, Rosyth.
[2]Later Admiral Sir Hubert Brand. Commodore Brand was Beatty's Captain of the Fleet (staff officer administration). He had been COS of Battle-Cruiser Fleet.

and the general acceleration of the present programme was also discussed at length.

The following points were urged by the Commander-in-Chief:-

(1) That consideration be given as to whether a less expensive form of destroyer cannot be designed for the purpose of submarine hunting and escorting. The Commander-in-Chief is of opinion that it is a waste of money and material to employ the destroyer whose real role is to attack the enemy's capital ships or the enemy destroyers, and which are necessarily very fast and as heavily armed, both with gun and torpedo, as is possible, for the purpose of escorting ships or hunting down submarines, as he contends that this can equally well be done by the same type of destroyer but with a reduced armament and greatly reduced horse-power. He thinks it may be possible to design some form of craft as the above, which can be turned out in far quicker time and far cheaper than the present design of destroyer. I told the Commander-in-Chief that this question has already been considered, and to a certain extent the reply is contained in the sloops and the 'P' boats, but that I would go into the question and inform the Board.

The Commander-in-Chief pointed out the urgent necessity of the earliest possible construction of as many light cruisers as possible. He pointed out that Germany had 18 light cruisers building, whereas we only have 16 projected, and he contends that in addition to the Zeppelins, which the German Fleet have as scouts, they have, or will shortly have, more light cruisers in their advanced line than the Grand Fleet can have.

As regards the 34 Convoy Sloops which have been approved to be built, the Commander-in-Chiefs asks:

(i) Cannot these Convoy Sloops be used for mine-sweeping in the same way as the First Sloop Flotilla is used at the Northern Base. I pointed out that these sloops were required for escort work in the Atlantic and Mediterranean. The Commander-in-Chief is of opinion that these sloops are not the best form of escort craft.

(ii) He suggests that these sloops, in addition to being used for mine-sweeping, might be fitted as mine-layers, and, if necessary, work in squadrons for either or both the above.

The Commander-in-Chief is very disturbed on the subject of the lack of efficient and fast seaplane carriers. I pointed out to him that the two projected seaplane carriers of the new design had not been laid down, as it was found that mine sweepers were so urgently required and that the building of these seaplane carriers would seriously affect their output; also that there would be no possible chance of these seaplane carriers being completed under 17–18 months at the very earliest. I suggested to him the possibility — provided the Board approved — of altering the first of the *Raleigh* class, namely, the *Cavendish*, and transforming her into a seaplane carrier.[1] This, if carried out now, would not delay her depreciably, and she should be completed by her contract date, namely February, unless her flying on deck was considered necessary, in which case she should be completed by April.

The Commander-in-Chief is very anxious that this should be approved, and I therefore bring it forward for consideration. In the meantime I am giving orders for the plans and drawings to be made. I had previously consulted the D.N.C.,[2] the D.C.D.S., and the Fifth Sea Lord,[3] all of whom concurred in the feasibility of the suggestion.

As regards the flying on deck, the Commander-in-Chief is going to inform me whether or not this is a necessity after consultation with his aerial advisers.

B.E. mine: The Commander-in-Chief enquired as to the policy with regard to the exisitng B.E. Mines, and I informed him that as far as I was aware they would continue to be laid until the H.2 mine was produced in sufficient numbers to employ the exisiting mine layers. He suggested that it would be worth consideration whether the B.E. mine could not be adapted for us as the mine for the Ryan ground mine. I told him I would make enquiries and inform him of the result.

The Commander-in-Chief asked that he might be informèd of the anticipated date of commencement of output of the H.2 mine and the rate at which they would be produced per month: also when the full rate of 10,000 per month would be attained.[4]

The question of repairs to the Fleet was discussed with a view to closer co-operation between the Admiralty and the Comman-

---

[1] The cruiser *Cavendish* was converted into a carrier, renamed *Vindictive*, in 1918.

[2] The Director of Naval Construction, Sir Eustace Tennyson d'Eyncourt (1868–1951). His papers are in NMM.

[3] In January 1917 the new post of 5th Sea Lord responsible for naval air duties was created; the first holder was Commodore Godfrey Paine, an experienced pilot. He sat on the Air Council, formed in 1918.

[4] The more effective H2 mine came into production in spring 1917 and available in numbers adequate for intensive anti-submarine use by the autumn. From 1916 Ryan had been experimenting with mines activated by hydrophones for the defence of Invergordon and Scapa Flow; Beatty as usual supported him (see Hackmann *Seek and Strike*, pp. 47–8).

der-in-Chief with regard to repairs to ships of the Grand Fleet. It was pointed out to the Commander-in-Chief that in many cases of late, repairs had been ordered by him and the Admiralty had not been informed, a dual control thus existing. The Commander-in-Chief fully realised how desirable it was that this should be avoided if possible, and every effort will be made for full information to be given to the Admiralty when it is necessary for urgent repairs to be effected by order of the Commander-in-Chief.

The Commander-in-Chief asked that he might be furnished with a copy of the daily state of important vessels in hand for repairs, in order that he might have first hand information of what was going on in the various Yards. I have given orders that his wishes shall be carried out.

The Commander-in-Chief asks whether there is any possibility of in any way accelerating the submarine construction and augmenting the projected submarine programme. He is firmly convinced that the only real reply to the submarine menace is that wherever a German submarine is, there must be also a British submarine, and he notes that whereas the Germans are probably turning out 15 submarines per month, our rate of construction will be very little over 4 per month.

The question of searchlights in light cruisers and destroyers was discussed, and the Commander-in-Chief entirely concurs with what has now been decided by the Admiralty, namely, that searchlights shall in no case be placed on director carrying masts in any ships, and the searchlights in destroyers should consist of two 10-inch on the bridge for signalling and navigation purposes, and one 24-inch on the torpedo tubes aft, manipulated from the bridge by Newitt's gear.

The Commander-in-Chief asks that where full speed trials are carried out after completion of a new ship, these should be carried out at deep draught, that is, with all fuel and fighting stores on board.

The question of the magnetic compass in the lower conning tower of the *Hood* class, and other ships which may have an interchange of magazine and shell room, was discussed, as there must be interference due to movable steel within the minimum distance. The Commander-in-Chief is of opinion that the magnetic compass should be retained with as great a directive force as is possible and that the fact of it being within minimum distance must be accepted.

Up to the present a salvage ship has always been retained in the vicinity of the Forth in order to cope with any accidents that may occur to the ships of the Grand Fleet. I consulted the Commander-in-Chief as to the advisability of using this salvage ship, when necessary, on the West Coast. He considered it inadvisable, and I concur in his opinion, although, of course, it means that our full effort is not being used for the salvage of ships that are already damaged or ashore, particularly round the coast of Ireland.

The question of the size and general arrangement in the bridges of all future destroyers was discussed, and the Commander-in-Chief entirely concurs in what has now been decided on. It was pointed out to the Commander-in-Chief how necessary it is for quick construction that everything as far as possible be standardised, and that as few alterations and additions be made as is possible whilst a ship is in course of construction. The Commander-in-Chief entirely concurred and has promised to discountenance any — except the most urgent — representations that may be made.

I consulted the Commander-in-Chief on the subject of his requirements for a Flotilla Leader for the 13th Submarine Flotilla as mentioned by him to Admiral Oliver. What the Commander-in-Chief requires is a destroyer which he proposes should be attached to the Flotilla for the use of the Captain S, who would at sea be on board this destroyer. He cannot afford a destroyer from the 13th Destroyer Flotilla for this duty, but pending an extra Destroyer being available, he is sending one of the destroyers of the 11th Submarine Flotilla to carry out this duty temporarily.

236. *From Halsey*

[BTY/13/16/5]   Admiralty
[Holograph]   June 18th 1917

Since writing to you yesterday I have found out about the output of H2 mines & it is substantially the same as I told you on Saturday, namely —

They commence this month with 400 & trials of the first 100 are going to take place from the *Princess Margaret* directly that ship is completed — we shall then anyhow know at last if we have or have not got a reliable mine.

The output of H mines will gradually increase until October when we should be turning out 7,000 per month — this is the original order for 40,000. A further order for 53,000 was placed with the Ministry of Munitions last April and these should begin to appear in November, after which our total uniform rate of production is to be 10,000 per month. As regards the adaptation of the B. E. & Service mine, the following is being done — The Service mines are being tried as the Ryan Ground mine and it is proposed to utilise the B. E. mines for deep defensive minefields round the coast and certain trade routes. I hope this will clear up the points you spoke of with regard to actual mines.

237. *To his wife* [Aberdour House]

[BTY/17/42/7–8]   Grand Fleet
                                                        19.6.17

*   *   *

I am in the middle of a big operation against enemy submarines which I pray may be successful. I have denuded myself of all destroyers, S. M.s, patrol vessels, seaplanes, airships etc. in the effort, so the fleet is immobilised for the time being. It's no use pecking at it and have taken the largest steps I can. No result to date, but I live in hope. It is time our luck turned, it has been dead out for a long time. Mercifully the weather helps us and it is not hard on our small craft which is something to be thankful for. . . .

I really do feel a hundred per cent better for my change of air and rest with you. It is such a peaceful spot, and you have made it so pretty and comfortable it is a joy to be there, out of the turmoil. And I feel now, that having had a glimpse of you, I can go on and wrestle with renewed vigour with the problems that beset me.

The Monarch arrives Thursday, he really is a nuisance and adds much to the labours, and is to remain until Monday. He is to be accompanied by Pressmen and cinematographers [*sic*]. It appears he is anxious that the world should know that he is doing something. But it does not help the war.

You will be glad to hear that they are going to make dear old Packs a vice-admiral. You need not say anything about it, except to him, until it comes, which will be at once.

238. *To his wife* [Aberdour House]

[BTY/17/43/2–3]   Grand Fleet
3.7.17

. . .

Only today I have found, in part, one of the causes of the visit from L. G. On reading the *Spectator* I find that Winston Churchill has been indulging the world with an article in the *Sunday Pictorial* of Sunday 24th June. Did you see it? In it, apparently having forgotten the article he wrote some months ago in which he pronounced the absolutely opposite opinion, he stated that the Navy was doing nothing and must become more aggressive. I don't mind all that, but apparently having been in close communion [?] with L. G. during the latter's Scottish visit, i.e. for 3 days, he had endeavoured to imbue him with his *new* ideas, hence a visit. I wish I had seen W. C.s article or heard of it before I had seen L. G., and I really would have given him something to think about. It is disgusting that a man who has been a Cabinet Minister and First Lord of the Admiralty should be allowed to write articles in a rag of a paper, belittling the officers and the great Service of which he was once the head. It is of course useless to expect a man such as he to do anything but intrigue and he has evidently made use of, or is attempting to make use of, a certain feeling that has been put about by some, that the Navy ought to be doing more, to make capital for himself & assist his intrigues to try and push himself into an office.

However I do not fuss myself about it. History is only repeating itself and it has always been the same, and there will always be dirty dogs in the world who endeavour to make capital of the difficulties of others.

*   *   *

I am *not* working too hard, but I have a great deal to do, principally of my own making, and are efforts to ginger other people up.

Am so glad to hear Ryan has had a success with his wireless boat. Tell him to send me a report as soon as he can.

239. *From his wife*

[BTY/18/32/16–18]   Aberdour
                                                Thursday [5 July 1917]

I have received your letter of the 3rd. I did not see Winston's letter in the *Pictorial* or have not heard of it. I should not think of it again. He is really a dead dog & people pay no attention to him. I dare say the P. M. thought there might be something in what he said to him & thought he would come & talk it over with you to see. But you may be quite certain he [–] it up afterwards & thought you were right and W. C. wrong. Winston is a disappointed blackguard, nothing more or less, & probably jealous of you. . . . I should not bother your head. In your position you are sure to be criticised, & you get it far less than others. So, don't you fret your dear self. . . . I don't think you have any reason to be really depressed & I do feel that all will come right & that people will no longer ask what the Navy is doing & believe they don't now.

I have telephoned your message to Captain Ryan about the wireless boat, & he says he will send a report at once.

*   *   *

240. *To his wife* [Aberdour House]

[BTY/17/43/8–9]   Grand Fleet
                                                          7.7.17

*   *   *

We are hunting hard as usual, but it is difficult to achieve success, and the result is very disappointing, but we must still go on. Our luck has been very bad. Every day we are within an ace of success, sometimes in two & even three places, but they can't quite pull it off. I am overhauling the scheme from another aspect now, and hope to improve, but it certainly does seem, over and over again, as if it was sheer bad luck which prevents us from reaping our reward. We have overcome the greatest difficulty of all now, and yet don't bring it off, so must probe deeper, but find the cause we will. It is a prodigious job, as it is like looking for a needle in a bundle of hay, and, when you have found it, trying to strike it with another needle. But we must stick to it, and I am sure the answer to the conundrum will be found, and also found quite a simple one. In the meantime it is very disheartening for everybody, who are as keen as mustard, and all do their best.

Sunday   At last the luck has turned and we have had a success. Please God it will lead to more. Anyway it is something and shows we are on the right tack. . . .

241.   *To his wife* [Aberdour House]

[BTY/17/43/11–12]   Grand Fleet
                                                       9.7.17

*   *   *

The news from the East, Russia, is very good and will cause the enemy immense trouble. The French are holding their own against very heavy and continuous attacks, which are costing the enemy heavy losses, and we are capable of moving forward when we are ready.

The role of the Navy is to keep its head and not be bounced into attempting impossible things by irresponsible and ignorant cranks. And we shall come out on top in the end. It is only a question of hanging on and not being forced. It may take many months, but we are winning now and all we have to do is to keep our heads and hold on. We are fighting today for much more than meets the eyes or the heart, and we cannot afford to take risks or gamble with the future. It is indeed for the freedom of the world, to save our children & our children's children from such a repetition of the wholesale sacrifices that are taking place daily.

In the meantime we are having a regatta, which takes the men's minds off the serious side of life & the weary waiting that they do so much of. The *Queen Elizabeth* has done extraordinary [*sic*] well and won most of the races, enthusiasm intense. Incidentally, they pulled me out to stroke the veterans' crew, and we won in a [–] trot, which gave much satisfaction to all except the losers. It's a great thing as it keeps them fit, 650 men we have pulling in the races, and unless they are physically and mentally fit we shall not do ourselves justice when our great day comes, and I cannot believe that it won't come. Indeed we would all lie down and turn up our toes if we thought for a moment there was a possibility of it being possible.

242. *To his wife* [Aberdour House]

[BTY/17/43/14–15]   Grand Fleet
                                                     11.7.17

A terrible calamity has befallen us and one of my fine battleships blew up at anchor at 11.30 PM, Monday night, the poor old *Vanguard* with over 1,000 men on board, in 25 seconds it was all over. The explosion was terrific, two men and one officer only were picked up, and the latter died soon after. Luckily 15 officers were out of the ship on board another ship at the time. A boat's crew was away and 3 officers & 50 odd men had been sent away on leave to make room for Admiral Sturdee and his staff who *were* going to her while his ship, the *Hercules*, was undergoing a re-fit. But fortunately for him & his staff I sent them on leave instead, or else he and all his staff would have been among the victims.[1]

It is an overwhelming blow and fairly stuns one to think about. One expects these things to happen when in the heat of battle, but when lying peacefully at anchor it is very much more terrible.

The cause is at present obscure, but I hope to be able to find out something. In any case it is as well for the present not to say too much about it, indeed I don't know, so it is of little use wasting time in idle conjecture.

Please do not say anything about it until it appears in the Papers. No mention is permitted at present in the newspapers yet, and all letters are heavily censored, but it will of course come out soon and I have advised the Admiralty to announce [*sic*].

Curiously enough only one officer in the ship was married and he was saved, that is, he was not on board at the time. It has of course been a shock to the Fleet and our business at present is to see that morale doesn't suffer. But it is uncanny to think of a ship going up like that in the dead of night without a second's warning and literally all to be over in 25 seconds, no more. That is the merciful side of the question.

                    *   *   *

[1]The battleship *Vanguard* blew up at Scapa on 9 July, probably due to defective cordite.

243. *To his wife* [Aberdour House]

[BTY/17/43/17–18]   Grand Fleet

13.7.17

I am a very bad correspondent, but am not so from inclination as it is always a joy to me to sit down and write to you. The trouble is, my time is so short. The days are not long enough and yet at times they are busy enough, and get rather wearisome. But we struggle on and, I hope, make headway.

We have had another success with the S.M.s. You can have no idea what filip it is to score even a small success in times like the present.

The poor old *Vanguard* incident is fading away. It is wonderful how the sailors put these things out of their mind almost immediately. We were under the shadow of a great calamity one minute, and it is almost forgotten the next. Such is life, and, God knows, I would not have it otherwise. The sailors are full of heart, but like children, forget at once.

For instance, today we had a great Boxing Carnival on the island. I thought of putting it off and then thought I wouldn't, as it would help to make them forget, and, bless them, they enjoyed themselves hugely for 9 solid hours, looking at men hammering themselves, 18,000 of them, an immense concourse. I went up for the Finals and presented the prizes, and took the opportunity of talking to them and telling them what fine fellows they were. They were a very sympathetic audience and one felt one could do anything with them, go anywhere and accomplish great things.

*   *   *

I hope to see you on Tuesday next. I have had to come down earlier than I expected, but it has just been fixed up, and not a soul knows it. . . .

244.   *To Hamilton*

[HTN/117]   Grand Fleet
                                                             14.7.17

I am sending Mr Hamnett from my office to be of any assistance he can in arranging for our advent. You will have received my wire to say that the Grand Fleet will be arriving at daylight Tuesday, and request to have the channel swept. It is I fear all very sudden but there is no harm in that, especially as secrecy means safety. He [?] is taking the berthing plan and our requirements as to fuelling. I hope you will be able to preserve the fact of our being expected a *Secret*. I hope to have the whole fleet anchored by 7 a.m.

Will you, if the weather is inclined to be thick, make to me by the 'I' method the visibility at May Island at intervals after 11 p.m. I hope to get the 1st Group at May Island at 1.45 a.m. and if it is very thick, we may have to turn round, or some Groups may have to. I shall preserve wireless silence after sailing from here.

We are a great Armada, including mine sweepers and will take a little fitting in the first time. So it is as well we should try early. Hope to see you Tuesday.

245.   *To his wife* [Aberdour House]

[BTY/17/44/4]   Grand Fleet
                                                             4.9.17

Isn't it rather a storm in a tea cup? Please don't think that I ever think you are *de trop*. I do not believe that you honestly think that, it seems to me to be utterly impossible. You must know that I am never quite happy when you are not with me.

I know, dear heart, that I am rather an impossible person, difficult to get on with, and moody and peevy at times. I know also that it has cost me a great deal, some change in your feelings towards me. But you must believe me when I say, as I have said again and again, that I just worship you today as I have ever done from the moment I first saw you.

Times are very difficult. Situations arise which are trying in the extreme. My burden is not a light one, though I try not to show it, or to think it harder than it really is. All of which tends no doubt to make me more unbearable than I was before, so, bear with me and don't imagine things which do not exist. You help me much when I can talk with you, but if you think of me as you said today, I shrivel up and can't talk about the things I should like to discuss.

246. *To his wife* [Aberdour House]

[BTY/17/44/8–9]
Grand Fleet
18.9.17

We had a busy day yesterday, exercises and movements [?] made much more exciting and complicated by the fact that we continuously were running into fog banks which reduced our visibility to nil. It was trying in the extreme, as we had something like 200 ships steaming at high speed in varying directions, and the risks of collision were added to those of the mine and the submarine. However no mishaps occurred and it was an interesting day. We had two American officers on board who were thrilled and said they had never thought of anything quite like it — were particularly astonished at the flexibility of the fleet, and the ease with which they were manoeuvred. They now know something of what we are capable of. I hope they are not German spies!!

* * *

I am wondering whether you have old Charlie B. with you. Tell him how sorry I was to have missed him, as I had much to talk to him about: I hope the condition of the sailors etc is going to be improved at once. I have been trying to do officially what he has been trying to do publicly for some time and I think we are going to win. All my time is spent fighting the Admiralty instead of the enemy, first on one thing and then on another. It was ever thus. He had exactly the same experience.

I hope old Packs will be of some assistance to you in helping to amuse the old man. . . .

247.   *To his wife* [Aberdour House]

[BTY/17/45/5–7]   Grand Fleet
                                                        3.10.17

. . .

Your letter of the 1st was very interesting and you seem to have had a successful engagement with the Jew Montague[1] and to have defeated him with great slaughter. Yes, he is appalling to look at, with that immense conceit and self confidence common to the Hebrew tribe, which gets him along, and, as he is clever, I suppose nothing will stop him. But how these politicians cling together. It was an outrageous statement of his saying that naval officers never liked the First Lord, implying a disloyalty to, I suppose, the most loyal Service in the world. I am glad you said that they liked them when they were gentlemen, which hits the nail on the head.

I am sorry to hear your opinion of old Packs. I hope he is not going to crack up. I really do not think he bears any malice against me because I took his light cruisers away. I haven't taken them away in the things that really matter, *i.e.* operations etc, and only in matters of administration, which had become too big for him to deal with, and required decentralising. He has only himself to blame. I cannot afford to allow all the mistakes that were made, to continue, because he couldn't manage it. After all, he must remember that I had a devil of a fight to get him the appointment at all, and I had to see that it was run efficiently which it is now, and is going very smoothly. I do not anticipate trouble with him, as after all, he is a gentleman and is not looking for reasons to have a row with me.

I am sorry to hear that they are all looking so sickly. Phillimore[2] and Dumaresq[3] are both inclined to be very yellow, and I dare

[1]Edwin Montagu (1879–1924): Liberal politician: Chancellor of the Duchy of Lancaster 1916; Minister of Munitions 1916; Secretary for India 1917–22.

[2]Later Admiral Sir Richard Phillimore (1864–1940): entered RN 1878; commanded *Inflexible* at Falklands and in Dardanelles; Rear-Admiral and headed naval mission to Russia 1915; commanding 1st Battle-Cruiser Squadron on *Repulse* 1916; Admiral Commanding Aircraft Carriers (a new post) March 1918 to end of war; Vice-Admiral 1920; Reserve Fleet 1920–2; CinC Plymouth 1923–6; Admiral 1924; retired 1929. See note 2 on page 453.

[3]Later Rear-Admiral John Dumaresq (1873–1922): Captain of the cruiser *Shannon* since 1913; Chairman of Grand Fleet post-Jutland Cruiser Committee; from 1917 served with Royal Australian Navy; see note 1 on page 224 for his gunnery control device.

say it was a cold day. It would perhaps be a good thing to have them all up here for a bit and give them some ozone, there is plenty to spare.

*   *   *

[P. S.]   If you can manage it at any time, ask Lady Brock to lunch. It will make things a lot easier for me if you can see a little of her.

248.   *To his wife* [Aberdour House]

[BTY/17/45/24–6]   Grand Fleet
13.10.17

*   *   *

Yes, the mutiny in the enemy Fleet is a sign of the times. They have no doubt stamped it out as it was over two months ago, but the fire is still smouldering and might break out again more violently at any moment.[1] I pray also that it will not touch us, but when we have to deal with a lot of weak-kneed politicians who pander to trade unions, and they are supported by a weak naval administration, one can never be quite sure what will happen. And there are signs that the feebleness of our Admiralty are [*sic*] encouraging ideas in their heads. . . .

You will have found old Burney installed in the seat of poor [?] Freddy Hamilton.[2] Geddes has been a dirty dog over the whole business, never asked my opinion, although I telegraphed and asked what names were being considered for the appointment. Wrote and apologised afterwards. It is a perfect scandal that our principal naval base should be commanded by a man who has no health or energy, and who has proved himself inefficient in his previous appointment. The war is not over yet and although he is there now and may stop there, there are other considerations which have to be taken into account. I hear Lady Burney is a nice old thing, but that won't help us to win the war. As a matter of fact Geddes is a darned funck[?]-stick and as weak as ditch water.

*   *   *

[1]Short-lived mutiny on German battleship *Prinzregent Luitpold*; put down with great severity, including ten death sentences, two of which were carried out. See Horn, *Mutiny on the High Seas*.

[2]Sir Frederick Hamilton, Flag Officer Scotland since 1 July 1916, died in office; replaced on 11 October by Sir Cecil Burney who had been succeeded as 2nd Sea Lord by Sir Leopold Heath on 27 September.

249.   *To his wife* [Hanover Lodge]

[BTY/17/45/32–4]   Grand Fleet
                                                         18.10.17

*   *   *

The enemy light cruisers have been more enterprising and been attacking our convoy in the North Sea and sank two of my poor destroyers at daylight yesterday. They dropped upon them (obviously with perfect information) just as it was getting light, and they, poor things, were not very bright, never expecting such a thing, they never having seen [?] one during the past 3 years, and became an easy prey. Having done that they sank 4 neutral ships and bolted for home.[1] I had light cruiser squadrons out, and they passed through them apparently in the dark and were never sighted, although they passed them twice, coming out and going home. It has been an anxious time and I don't know enough about it yet to say anything beyond the fact that our cruisers were well placed to stop them. Unfortunately we never heard about it until 11 hours after it happened, which gave them the dark hours to get back in, which made it just a matter of luck whether we saw them or not. Anyway luck was against us and we failed to stop them. It may have the effect of making them more enterprising, in which case we shall have our hands full very shortly. Don't say anything about it to anybody as I do not know enough at present to make out exactly what did happen, and it would not be fair to say anything until I know the facts.

250.   *To Rear-Admiral Richard Phillimore*[2]

[IWM/Phill]   Grand Fleet
[Holograph]   19.12.17

My Dear Phillimore,
    Set your mind at rest. I have no intention of permitting your departure from the Grand Fleet if I can help it.

---

[1]Marder, *From the Dreadnought* Vol. 4, pp. 294–9, states that nine not five neutrals were sunk.
[2]This shows Beatty's direct responsibility for the creation of the post of Flag Officer Aircraft Carriers to which Phillimore was appointed in March 1918. See note 2 on page 451.

What I want you to do is to take command of the Air Squadron of Ships [*sic*] which will be an integral and very important part of the Grand Fleet organisation, and, in command of which you will in all probability have more opportunity for sea service than in any other command.

When the opportunity occurs I should be glad if you would come over and see me.

Yours ever
DAVID BEATTY

251. *Notes on visit of Director of Intelligence Division to Beatty*

[BTY/7/9/5]   19th December 1917

In connection with the system by which intelligence is passed to the Commander-in-Chief, the D. I. D. explained that he is responsible for supplying the D. O. D. with information; the D. O. D. is responsible to the D. C. N. S.; the D. C. N. S. is responsible to the C. N. S. with whom rests the final decision as to how much of the information and in what manner it should be passed on to the Commander-in-Chief.[1] Under this system there may well be a delay of as much as three hours before important intelligence is passed on, and then it may well be in an incomplete form.

The Commander-in-Chief emphasised that in his opinion it was essential that the D.I.D. should transmit important intelligence direct.

The Commander-in-Chief explained to the D.I.D. that after the attack on the convoy on 12th December certain measures were taken to intercept enemy supporting forces, the presence of which were indicated by the Admiralty telegram stating that the *Emden* was in the neighbourhood of *Horns Reef*. Whilst these measures were being put into force, a telegram was received from the Admiralty placing the fleet at 1½ hours' notice. No reason for this notice was given, but in view of this the Commander-in-Chief

[1]DID, Rear-Admiral Sir Reginald Hall; DOD, Rear-Admiral Sir George Hope; DCNS, Rear-Admiral Sir Sydney Fremantle; CNS, Jellicoe had assumed this title on 14 May 1917.

recalled the 2nd Light Cruiser Squadron and destroyers which had put to sea from Scapa.

The D.I.D. could throw no light on the reason for placing the fleet at notice and so far as he is aware the situation in no way required it. Later the Admiralty telegraphed that the fleet might revert to the usual notice at the Commander-in-Chief's discretion. In view of the fact that the Commander-in-Chief had not been informed of the reason for the original notice, he was not in a position to say whether or not that notice should remain in force. Further, the fact of no reason being assigned for the notice and the consequent impression left on the Commander-in-Chief that the fleet was required to be kept concentrated to meet a probable move of the enemy, the dispositions contemplated for intercepting enemy supporting forces at sea were seriously interfered with.

The Commander-in-Chief informed the D.I.D. that he noted that early on the 16th December the W/T repeater was in *Graudenz*. Later on the 16th *Graudenz* turned over these duties to *Seydlitz* and shortly after this *Graudenz* ordered outposts to be on 'Kingsway'. This clearly indicated that *Graudenz* was going to move, but the Commander-in-Chief received no information of this until the receipt of the War Diary some days later. It is not understood why this information was not transmitted to the Commander-in-Chief at the same time as Admiralty telegram 855.

Although the enemy operations were later cancelled probably on account of the weather, this is no reason for not transmitting intelligence of vital importance to the Commander-in-Chief immediately on receipt.

In connection with the above, the intelligence received by the D.I.D. points to the probability of destroyers being used in support of barrier breakers which were being sent out on 'Kingsway'. The operation allowed for the forces going out something after four and getting back something after three (about 12–18 hours, that is, 6–9 hours out and 6–9 hours back). The appreciation of this is that as there is no sufficiently near objective for such an operation it is probable that the destroyers were to be used with the barrier breakers which would precede a force of heavy ships possibly going further out. The D.I.D. considered that as the first and second attacks have been by light cruisers and destroyers, so it was intended that the third attack should be by heavy ships in bad weather.

In intelligence transmitted prior to the attack on the convoy, it is noted that at 8.0 p.m. W/T restriction was placed on all waves until 2330 and on damped waves until 0800 next morning. The D.I.D. explained that this indicated the desire of the German Naval Staff to gain intelligence as to movements of forces which we had at sea. The Commander-in-Chief explained to the D.I.D. that he considered all such intelligence should be supplemented by a short appreciation, as the Commander-in-Chief's experience of various indications was necessarily limited as compared with that available at the Admiralty.

NOTE — The Officer Commanding, 2nd Torpedo Boat Division, ordered lights at 1000 at it was reasonable to assume the division was going out to escort something heavier than torpedo craft. As bad weather was prevalent, the probability was that battle-cruisers were to be employed.

252. *Selections from Grand Fleet Battle Instructions*[1]

[BTY/7/3/4]   *Queen Elizabeth*
                                                        1st January, 1918

GRAND FLEET BATTLE INSTRUCTIONS

The Grand Fleet Battle Instructions promulgated herewith give the guiding principles which are to be observed by all arms of the fleet when obtaining contact, and when in action, with the enemy.

2. Divisional Commanders and Commanding Officers are responsible that these guiding principles are brought to the notice of officers of the rank of Lieutenant and above, under their command, and of other officers whose duties require that they should be acquainted with the instructions.

David Beatty
Admiral,
Commander-in-Chief.

The Flag Officers, Commodores, and Officers in command of H. M. ships and destroyers of the Grand Fleet.

(Not issued to Fleet Minesweepers).
Copies to: —
   Admiralty;

[1]These extracts from GFBI from 1 Jan 1918 to 4 Dec 1918 show the development of Beatty's strategic and tactical concepts up to the end of the war.

Commander-in-Chief, Coast of Scotland;
Vice-Admiral Commanding, Orkneys and Shetlands;
Vice-Admiral Commanding, East Coast of England;
Commodore (S) *and Captain* (S.), *Harwich.*
Secret

1. GENERAL PRINCIPLES [January, 1918]

Enemy fleet reported at sea

1. On the enemy fleet being reported at sea the movements of the Grand Fleet will be guided by strategical considerations. It will be the endeavour to place the fleet between the enemy and his base.

Gaining touch with the enemy

2. When the British advanced light cruiser forces are in touch with the enemy, efforts will be directed to obtaining a favourable tactical position and to bringing the enemy to action.

With regard to the selection of position from which to fight the action, this will be governed by considerations of: —

(*a*) The general strategical position as indicated in *paragraph 1* above.

(*b*) *Light:* At dusk and dawn it is advantageous to have the enemy silhouetted against the sun; at other times it is advantageous to have the sun shining in the eyes of the enemy.

(*c*) *Wind:* To avoid smoke interference the leeward position is advantageous.

The relative importance of each of the above must vary with the particular circumstances, and must be decided at the time. No hard and fast rule can be laid down beforehand.

Tactical principles

3. The tactics will be governed by the following general principles: —

(*a*) The fleet to be deployed at right-angles to the bearing of the enemy's centre.

(*b*) Concentration of superior force on a portion of the enemy's fleet, the British battlefleet coming into action as a whole, and keeping together until the enemy's fleet has been disorganised and broken up.

(*c*) The range of action to be within gun range of the 12-inch gun ships, but outside the danger zone of 15,000 yard torpedoes fired from the enemy's battlefleet.

The general fighting principle is to bring to action the whole force of the enemy in order to annihilate him. The possibility of effecting this depends upon 'Time available.' When it is apparent that owing to failing light or the vicinity of minefields it will be impossible to annihilate the whole main force of the enemy, every endeavour will be made to annihilate a part of it rather than to continue to engage the whole. In such circumstances the signal will be made at the critical moment to concentrate the fire of the fleet on a part of the enemy, probably the rear, leaving the remaining enemy ships unfired at.

The Approach

4. The Commander-in-Chief will control the movements of the whole battlefleet during the approach and prior to deployment, when accurate station keeping is essential.

Position of fleet flagship

5. The fleet flagship will generally lead either the third or fourth division, depending on which of these two divisions is nearer the van of the battlefleet.

Deployment — High visibility

6. It is the intention in good visibility to move to a flank so as to open the 'A' arcs as soon as the longest range gun ships come into action, steering to close as quickly as possible.

The van ships should not close the gun range nearer than 16,000 yards, and if on reaching this range the signal to deploy has not been made, the Admiral commanding the van should lead away, maintaining the range and keeping just outside the torpedo danger zone of the enemy. Should the situation permit, the final deployment will be ordered by signal and will be at right angles to the line of bearing of the centre of the enemy.

Speed of the van

7. Should the enemy be fighting a retiring action and be in a position of advantage, the excess of speed of the van must be used with caution. The van must not be opened out to too great a distance from the centre and before the centre can come into gun range. Concentration on the enemy's rear is likely to provide the best results.

Disposition of the rear

8. If it is desired to adjust the rear of the line so as to bring the rear divisions nearer the enemy, the guides of the rear divisions will be stationed on a line of bearing from the guide of the divisions next ahead of them. Ships of the rear divisions should remain in line ahead, but the Commander of the rear division has

discretionary powers to form the ships of his division on a line of bearing.

Reports by the van and rear

9. During the initial stages of deployment the Flag Officers commanding the van and rear are to inform the Commander-in-Chief at frequent intervals of the gun range and bearing of the wing ships of the enemy's battlefleet.

Deployment — Low Visibility

10. In low visibility the commander of the column sighting the enemy is to report immediately to the Commander-in-Chief the bearing and distance. The commander of a wing column under these conditions has full authority to act without waiting for orders. He should decide and turn as necessary, forming his division or divisions on a line of bearing from the nearest division of the centre battle squadron and at right angles to the bearing of the enemy. Adjacent columns are to deploy or turn together to support.

In the case of deployment under conditions of visibility about equal to the gun range of the centre squadron, the British fleet will deploy immediately on sighting the enemy on a line of bearing at right angles to their centre.

Movements of Flag Officers when action is joined, etc.

11. When action is joined, the Flag Officers commanding battle squadrons and divisions of the battlefleet have full discretionary power to manœuvre their squadrons or divisions independently, whilst conforming generally to the movements of the Commander-in-Chief. The Commander-in-Chief will control the division in which the fleet flagship has taken station, and will make the necessary signals ordering the movements of the division which he may be leading. Such signal will convey the Commander-in-Chief's intentions to the Flag Officers of other squadrons or divisions, and they should conform to his movements as the situation demands.

Control by the Commander-in-Chief

12. Notwithstanding the decentralisation of command indicated above, the Commander-in-Chief will retain the power to order the movement of the whole fleet by a general signal. Such a movement may be necessary owing to information known only to him and in order to ensure decisive results.

Movements of Fifth Battle Squadron and Battle-Cruiser Force at the van

13. Failing instructions from the Commander-in-Chief, the

Admirals commanding the Fifth Battle Squadron and Battle-Cruiser Force must form their own judgment as to the flank of the battlefleet to proceed to during the approach, being guided by the general principles laid down in this section, and their knowledge of the order and course of the enemy, and moving so as to come into action at the same time as the main fleet. These forces are always to keep within supporting distance of each other and of the main fleet, and should not come under the fire of the enemy battlefleet before it is fully engaged by our battlefleet.

British main fleet to remain concentrated

14. As a general principle the British battlefleet will keep together until the defeat of the enemy has been ensured. Attacks by a division or squadron separately on a portion of the enemy should until then be avoided; nor should ships be detached from the battlefleet to deal with enemy disabled ships until the defeat of the enemy fleet is certain. Disabled ships are to be attacked by the British submarine flotillas following the battleline.

Action by rear if not in gun range and enemy ships fall out

15. An exception to the above may occur if the rear is not in gun range and the Admiral commanding considers it improbable that the general conditions will allow of his co-operating with the main body of the fleet. In this case, he may detail a portion of his squadron to deal with enemy ships which fall out. The detached force should not be stronger than is required for this duty. The remainder of the rear squadron is to press on and use every endeavour to get into gun range of the main body of the enemy.

Action when defeat of enemy is certain

16. When it is certain that the enemy is disorganised, and groups of disabled ships are falling out of the line, orders may be expected for dealing with the situation. Failing such orders, the Admiral commanding the rear has discretionary powers to detach the number of ships required.

Torpedo menace from the enemy main fleet

17. If the British fleet, owing to a turn away on the part of the enemy or other reason, finds itself in a position of torpedo disadvantage, provided visibility and other conditions admit, and the enemy can be kept under gunfire, it is the intention of the Commander-in-Chief to keep outside the line 15,000 yards from the enemy's course measured along the normal. If, however, this procedure would entail the loss of gunfire, the torpedo menace will be accepted, and the fleet turned towards the retiring enemy.

Circumstances may also arise during action in which the need for a rapid decision is imperative. Under these conditions the signal 'Engage the enemy more closely' may be expected, by which it is to be understood that the torpedo menace is to be disregarded and every effort made to close to decisive gun range.

Torpedo menace by enemy flotillas

18. The Commander-in-Chief relies on the offensive by the light cruiser squadrons and flotillas at the van, and on the anti-torpedo gun armament of all vessels, to break up and disorganise the enemy flotilla attacks before reaching the firing position. Should enemy flotillas reach the firing position and it is seen that torpedoes have been fired, the Flag Officers of divisions threatened are to take action to avoid the torpedoes by turning either towards or away, being guided in their action by the principle that the enemy fleet is to be kept engaged. Under normal conditions, a turn towards will be necessary since a turn away would rapidly run the divisions making it out of range. A turn either towards or away being decided on, one of a least 45° should be made, the original course being resumed at the earliest safe moment.

Initiative

19. Whenever Flag or Commanding Officers find themselves without special directions during an action, either from inability to make out or receive signals, or from unforeseen circumstances rendering previous orders inapplicable, they are to act as their judgement dictates in making every effort to damage the enemy. If, under these circumstances, vessels are detached from the main body owing to temporary disablement or other causes, they should usually attach themselves to some formed body of friendly ships rather than attempt individual action.

Disabled Ships

20. No ship is to be allowed to fall into the hands of the enemy. Commanding officers are held strictly responsible that ships which are abandoned in a sinking condition are absolutely incapable of being kept afloat, and are to ensure that any subsequent efforts on the part of the enemy to salve them will be ineffective.

2. INSTRUCTIONS FOR THE MAIN BATTLEFLEET
[1 January 1918]

(a) Fleet to be guided by movements of Commander-in-Chief

1. The main battlefleet is to be guided generally by the movements of the division led by the Commander-in-Chief, which should be considered as the rallying point.

The movements of the Commander-in-Chief must therefore be carefully watched, and his wishes, if possible, anticipated. Signals may be indistinguishable, and in any case the movement signalled may be commenced before the executive is made.

(b) Tactics if enemy turn away

2. The tactics to be followed by the British fleet if the enemy turn away are laid down in *paragraph 17 of Section 1, 'General Principles.'* These are based on the principle that the enemy must be kept under effective gunfire and the torpedo menace accepted. The British fleet may thereby be placed in a position of torpedo disadvantage. This disadvantage must be met by prompt avoiding action should torpedoes be met with. The enemy fleet on the other hand, if kept under effective gunfire will, it is hoped, become disorganised, its speed will be reduced, or units will become detached. Further turn away movements will thereby be frustrated, and the enemy will be forced to continue the engagement or surrender the detached units. The point to be emphasised is that only by keeping the enemy fleet engaged can the initiative remain with the British fleet and a decision be obtained.

If the enemy fleet makes use of a smoke screen the light cruisers and destroyers at the van and rear must keep the enemy fleet under observation and report all movements immediately. The British fleet will be moved so as to continue the engagement at the earliest moment.

(c) Turning

3. A bend created by the main battlefleet altering course in succession hampers mobility; a turn by squadrons, divisions or sub-divisions is preferable and will usually be adopted.

(d) Separate action

4. Separate action on the part of commanders of squadrons or divisions may be called for under the following circumstances: —

(a) Minelaying, or a threat of minelaying, ahead of the line of battle.

   The Flag Officer in the van may be in a position to see this whilst the Commander-in-Chief may not; the Flag Officer has full discretion to act.

(b) A movement of the Commander-in-Chief's division carried out without signal or before a signal has got through to all ships in the line.

(c) A movement of one of the enemy divisions necessitating a counter on our part, such as an attack on the rear, or an attempt to close for the purpose of firing torpedoes.

(e) Deployment

5. Action on approximately similar courses will be one of the underlying tactical objects since it is the form of action likely to give the most decisive results.

Should the fleets deploy in opposite directions, the decision as to whether we should stand on or not will depend on such considerations as: —

(a) The directions of sun and wind from a gunnery point of view.

(b) The probability of our inflicting serious damage whilst passing on opposite courses.

(c) The range at which deployment took place as affecting the desirability of making a 180° turn under fire.

The decision will be communicated by signal, and, in the event of our standing on, the Admiral at the van is not to circle the enemy's rear unless directed to do so.

Divisions turning in succession should do so without delay when the signal is made.

(f) Action if enemy fleet divides

6. If the German battlefleet divides after the deployment of the British fleet, and an attack on our rear is attempted, the Flag Officer in rear must deal with the attack failing orders from the Commander-in-Chief. The employment by the enemy of dummy battleships for an attack on the rear with a view to dividing our fleet is a possible, although not a probable, proceeding on his part.

(g) Engaging fast divisions

7. The enemy may employ a fast division to draw off a portion of our fleet from the action between the main bodies, so that, after accomplishing its object, the fast division may, by its superior speed, rejoin its own fleet leaving the ships engaged with it astern. When opposed to ships of much superior speed, caution is therefore necessary to avoid ruses of this nature.

(h) Speed

8. Subject to maintaining a good position, the speed of a column in line of battle should be less than the maximum, in order to facilitate station keeping, reduce smoke, and leave something in hand for emergency. Circumstances may, however, occur which necessitate a column proceeding at its utmost speed, at the expense of good station keeping; especially is this the case with the squadron in the van of the fleet when the Flag Officer commanding may find it necessary to order the ships of his

squadron to proceed at their utmost speed, in which case the slower ships are to allow the faster to pass.

(i) Helm

9. Small helm should be used in action, particularly at high speeds, otherwise good gunnery is impracticable.

(j) Report of flagship disabled

10. If, in the course of an action, any flagship is disabled and forced to quit the line, it is the duty of a ship near her (her next astern if able to do so), or one which is conveniently placed in the case of detached action, to inform the senior Flag Officer, unless such a report has already been passed by the injured ship herself.

(k) Fleet flagship disabled

11. Should the fleet flagship be disabled, this report is to be made as quickly as possible to the senior Flag Officer. If forced to quit the line, her destroyer tender,* or in her absence, the nearest attached cruiser, is at once to close her ready to embark the Commander-in-Chief and staff.

*NOTE — The destroyer tender is to take station two cables astern of the Commander-in-Chief's column during the 'approach' and about a mile on the disengaged beam of the fleet flagship, and near the repeating ship, after deployment.

3. INSTRUCTIONS FOR THE FIFTH AND SIXTH BATTLE SQUADRONS.
[1 January 1918]

(a) Stations when Cruising

1. The Fifth Battle Squadron will be stationed as shewn in the *Cruising Disposition Diagrams*, and will act in support of the advanced forces.

2. The Sixth Battle Squadron will be stationed as laid down in *Grand Fleet Manœuvring Orders*.

(b) Battle Stations

3. The Fifth and Sixth Battle Squadrons in action will act as fast divisions on the flank of the battlefleet. The Fifth Battle Squadron will usually be at the van, and the Sixth Battle Squadron at the rear of the main battle line as shewn in the *Diagram of Deployment*.

4. The Commander-in-Chief will endeavour to inform the Admirals commanding, Fifth and Sixth Battle Squadrons beforehand of the probable direction of deployment. Squadrons should

move to their respective flanks with a view to being in their required stations immediately after deployment.

Failing instructions from the Commander-in-Chief, the Admiral commanding, Fifth Battle Squadron must form his own judgment as to which flank of the battlefleet is going to become the van, being guided by the general principles laid down in *Section 1*, and his knowledge of the order and course of the enemy. In such an event the Admiral commanding, Sixth Battle Squadron, will be informed by the Commander-in-Chief as to the flank to which he should proceed.

If neither our own nor the enemy battle-cruisers are at the van, the duty of the battle squadron in the van is to attack the enemy ships from a commanding position, and to cover and support the light cruisers and flotillas at that end of the line.

If the enemy battle-cruisers are at the van of their fleet and ours are absent or at the rear, it becomes the primary duty of the battle squadron in the van to attack the enemy's battle-cruisers.

5. Under the conditions referred to in *paragraph 3* above, it may be desirable for the van squadron to draw further ahead to force in the enemy light craft and deny them a favourable position from which to attack our fleet; such action will ensure a favourable position for our light craft.

The Admiral commanding must be careful not to get isolated from the support of the main fleet. In the early stages, the van squadron should not as a rule close the range to less than that of the battle squadron in the van of the main battleline. The second ship of the battle squadron in the van of the main battleline is to inform the Admiral commanding, Fifth or Sixth Battle Squadron in the van of her range at intervals.

6. Should the enemy turn away and the British fleet be concentrating on the enemy rear, the duty of the battle squadron in the van is to act as a containing force for the enemy van, engaging the latter at long range and drawing sufficiently far ahead to be in a favourable position should the enemy attempt to turn back.

The duty of the squadron in the rear is to press in on the enemy rear. This squadron will necessarily come within torpedo range of the enemy and should therefore be in open order, ships being disposed on a line at right angles to the bearing of the enemy rear. The powerful secondary armament will probably be of value in breaking up enemy flotillas which may have attacked the main battleline and are retiring after that attack.

The squadrons must be prepared to turn at once without waiting orders from the Commander-in-Chief should a reversal of course by the enemy be observed. An enemy smoke screen hiding their rear ships is a possible indication of this movement. The Flag Officer at the rear of the main battleline and the Commander-in-Chief are to be informed as soon as possible of the change of course.

7. In reduced visibility the Fifth and Sixth Battle Squadrons are to remain in visual touch with the main battlefleet unless otherwise ordered.

8. Both before and after action has commenced, the Admirals commanding are to report at frequent intervals the bearing and distance of the enemy van and rear. If out of sight of the fleet flagship, the report should include the bearing and distance of the nearest unit of the main battlefleet. Early reports of enemy movements, such as alterations of course, should also be made.

4. INSTRUCTIONS FOR ATTACHED CRUISERS

1. The light cruisers attached to the battle squadrons are either stationed as shewn in the *Cruising Disposition Diagrams*, or may be ordered to act as links to maintain visual touch with the advanced squadrons.

2. During the approach as the advanced lines close the battlefleet, the attached cruisers should close in, keeping touch between the battlefleet and advanced forces until finally, before deployment, they attain a position one mile on the disengaged beam of the commanders of the second, third, and fifth divisions respectively. During the action, the light cruiser attached to the Fifth Battle Squadron should take station so as to repeat signals between the Fifth Battle Squadron and the main fleet. The remaining light cruisers are to act as repeating ships for the squadron to which they are attached.

If there are only two repeating ships, they are to divide the main battleline.

3. The duty of a repeating ship attached to a squadron is not only to repeat all signals made by the senior officer of the squadron, but also to make every endeavour to see that such signals are seen and understood. Repeating ships should, if necessary, leave their station for the purpose of getting signals through, but are to keep within effective visual signalling distance of the flagship to which they are attached.

4. Repeating ships are to report to the leading ship of the main

battle line if there are any gaps of over ten cables in the line, stating the positions. They are also to report to the Flag Officers adjacent any important movements which take place in the line, especially if any of our ships fall out of the line, when redistribution of gunfire may become necessary.

5. The attached cruisers are to keep a special look-out for enemy aircraft, and are to attack any aircraft which endeavour to attack the battle line.

5. INSTRUCTIONS FOR CRUISERS PRIOR TO DEPLOYMENT.
[1 January 1918]

(a) Duties of Advanced Light Cruisers

1. The light-cruisers on the advanced line are stationed in detached units, the object being to facilitate keeping in touch after sighting the enemy and to enable them to support one another when pressed. The ships of a unit are not intended to work in line ahead in daytime; their disposition should be that best suited for keeping a good look-out and for minimising danger from submarine attack. Provided their duties permit, the ships of a unit should work within visual signalling distance of one another and of the unit next to them, but in low visibility the width of the front must not be materially reduced from that ordered, as it is of importance that the fleet should be properly screened, and its flanks adequately protected.

2. When contact with the enemy is gained, it is the duty of the advanced light cruisers

(*a*) To maintain touch when the enemy is superior;

(*b*) To engage him when the enemy is equal or inferior.

The strength of the light cruisers should be economised, so that more ships do not concentrate at any one point than are necessary to accomplish their object. The light cruisers occupying the stations on the wings of the look-out line must avoid the temptation to close towards the centre to seek an action; their duties are primarily the important ones of protecting the flanks of the battlefleet, gaining information of the enemy's fleet, and, should they not be closely engaged, outflanking the enemy's screen. They are also to prevent minelaying in the probable path of the fleet.

(b) Duties of Fourth and Seventh Light Cruiser Squadron

3. The duties of the Fourth and Seventh Light Cruiser Squadrons are to support the advanced light cruisers if support is

needed, and, in the event of enemy's advanced forces becoming engaged with our Battle-Cruiser Force, to push on and gain touch with the enemy's battlefleet. The latter is to be considered a most important duty, in order that the Commander-in-Chief may receive accurate information before the battlefleets sight one another.

If the light cruisers of the Battle-Cruiser Force are not present, the Fourth and Seventh Light Cruiser Squadrons will constitute a screen for the battlefleet.

(c) Duties of First Cruiser Squadron

4. The duty of the First Cruiser Squadron is to support the advanced light cruisers, particularly if the German light cruiser force concentrates on the point of contact. On account of their thin armour and the large target they offer, they should be careful not to come under fire of enemy battle-cruisers or battleships at effective range.

(d) Duties of Battle-Cruisers

5. Battle-cruisers are to afford support to the British advanced forces, and assist in driving in the enemy scouting force, thus enabling the reconnaisance of the enemy main forces to be carried out by the lighter vessels. When the enemy main forces are located, battle-cruisers should be disposed to keep the enemy under observation, taking care not to be brought to action by superior force. The principles which govern the movements of our own main fleet as laid down in *Section 1* must be borne in mind in order that our battle-cruisers shall eventually attain their position at the van on deployment.

If the enemy battle-cruisers are supporting their light cruisers, and are at some distance from the enemy main fleet, they should be engaged closely and, if possible, prevented from rejoining their main force, our light cruisers at the same time pressing on with the object of locating the enemy main force. It is more probable, however, that enemy battle-cruisers will not be far from the enemy main force. This will necessitate great care on the part of our battle-cruiser squadrons which will then become solely an observation force.

*   *   *

(f) Reports

8. It is vital that the Commander-in-Chief should obtain reliable information of the bearing, distance and course of the enemy main force at the earliest moment; such information should also be passed simultaneously by visual to all adjacent ships. In order

that it may be plotted correctly relative to the position of the Commander-in-Chief, it should be based on the Commander-in-Chief's reference position which must therefore be passed out to all ships immediately on receipt.

To admit of information and reference positions being rapidly passed, advanced forces must be linked to the battlefleet by linking vessels which are in certain visual touch. This is allowed for in the *Cruising Disposition Diagrams*.

9. Any vessel having the enemy's battlefleet in sight is always to signal by visual on sighting the Commander-in-Chief, the course of the enemy's battlefleet and, if possible, the bearing of its van, centre and rear.

Light cruisers scouting ahead of, or in the vicinity of a unit of British submarines may have valuable information to give them concerning the enemy fleet. Such information should be given by visual.

The importance of all ships keeping a correct plot of the situation in order to facilitate accurate reporting is emphasised.

(g) Action on gaining touch

10. If, when in actual touch with the enemy, the senior officer or the captain of a ship acting singly, receives an order from a higher authority which it is evident may have been given in ignorance of the conditions of the moment, and which, if obeyed, would cause touch with the enemy to be lost, discretion must be exercised by the junior officer as to obeying the order and an early opportunity taken of representing the real facts; a signal made under such conditions is in the nature of an instruction.

11. When actual contact with the enemy is gained, the senior officer in touch must assume general control of all forces in the vicinity in order to ensure their co-operation.

12. If an enemy's or strange ship or ships are sighted, the vessels appointed to watch their motions are to use every endeavour to keep them in sight so as to give all information as to the enemy's class, numbers, order, position, course and speed; if there is any danger of the ships keeping touch being driven off by superior force, the Commander-in-Chief should be informed at once.

Vessels ordered to keep touch with the enemy for the purpose of giving information to the Commander-in-Chief are not to expose themselves to disablement, and consequent failure to perform their appointed duties, unless the circumstances require it and their orders cannot otherwise be carried out.

*   *   *

6. INSTRUCTIONS FOR CRUISERS IMMEDIATELY BEFORE AND AFTER DEPLOYMENT [1 January 1918]

(a) General

1. The British battle-cruisers, cruisers and light cruisers are responsible for the prevention of interference with the British battlefleet by enemy vessels of similar type, all of which possess the power to inflict damage if the opportunity is given to them.

This duty will best be achieved by attack, thus obtaining and retaining the initiative.

2. The senior officer in the vicinity should assume general control over squadrons and units adjacent, but orders will not be necessary unless there are signs of confusion or the situation obviously demands attention. Senior officers of squadrons are, in the absence of orders from the senior officer in the vicinity, to act on their own initiative guided by the principles laid down in *Section 1*.

3. Captains of single ships closing the fleet shortly before or after deployment should, if the situation admits, rejoin their squadrons. Otherwise they are to act on their own initiative, observing that more ships are required in the van than at the rear of the battlefleet.

4. When two or more vessels of similar class which have become detached from their squadrons are able to join one another, they should do so, the senior taking the junior under his orders.

5. A strict look-out must be kept at all times for enemy submarines. Cruisers should zig-zag constantly. It is important to drive in all enemy ships which might be employed in concealing the position of submarines, and to keep a specially good look-out on the flanks. The earlier a submarine is forced to dive, the more is her power for offensive action limited.

(b) Stations in Action

6. On the battlefleets closing one another, all units should endeavour to take up approximately the stations ordered for the deployment of the Grand Fleet. Flag and senior officers are to be careful to allow their squadrons and those next towards the battlefleet ample room, so that the battlefleet and other squadrons are not hampered; care will also be necessary on the part of the various squadrons to avoid overlapping and masking one another's fire. Any squadron which in the course of the preliminary action has crossed to the opposite flank, and is unlikely to attain its

assigned battle station without masking the battlefleet, is to remain on that flank.

(c) Duties of Battle-Cruisers

7. The primary function of the British battle-cruisers is the destruction of the enemy's battle-cruisers.

If the enemy has no battle-cruisers present, or after his battle-cruisers have been destroyed, the British battle-cruisers are to act as a fast division of the battlefleet and attack the van of the enemy if it is possible to attain a sufficiently commanding position. The ideal would be an attack by torpedoes on the enemy's battle line, and such strong offensive action against all enemy cruisers and torpedo craft at their van as to render such a position untenable.

(d) Duties of First Cruiser Squadron

8. Ships of the First Cruiser Squadron are required to make use of their high speed with the object of developing the maximum torpedo offensive and preventing possible minelaying ahead of the British fleet. In carrying out these duties they should move so as not to come under the gunfire of the enemy heavy ships without support.

It may be expected that the First Cruiser Squadron will be particularly favourably placed for observing movements of the enemy obscured from the main battleline by either a smoke screen or the smoke of battle. The utmost importance attaches to the immediate report by the First Cruiser Squadron of such movements.

(e) Duties of Light Cruisers in Action

9. Light cruisers on the flanks are in a good position to prevent mines being laid in the path or probable path of our fleet. In handling units in these positions this additional duty must be borne in mind and given due consideration.

Squadrons which find themselves in rear after deployment are to remain in rear so as to be available in the van if the fleet turns 180°; ships should take up positions which will enable them to watch the movements of the enemy fleet and enemy ships which might be suspected of laying mines, even at a considerable distance in rear of the German battlefleet. This is of particular importance in case the enemy deploys away from the direction of Heligoland with the possible object of reversing his course later and leading us over minefields, and also, in the other event, to prevent him from mining the routes to our bases astern of us.

Except as laid down above, and unless the opportunity presents itself of inflicting severe damage on enemy light cruisers or torpedo craft by independent action, the light cruisers of the. Battle-Cruiser Force are, once the enemy's battlefleet has been located, to use their utmost endeavour to take up their battle stations.

10. The duties of light cruisers during action include the following: —

Attack on the enemy's line of battle with torpedoes.

Attack on the enemy's light cruisers, torpedo craft and minelayers.

Support of our destroyers.

Reporting of enemy movements.

Note— These duties are not stated in the order of their importance, which must necessarily be governed by the circumstances exisiting at the time.

11. The rapidity with which the Germans divert their fire from one target to another, and the vulnerability of light cruisers to such fire must be borne in mind; light cruisers should screen themselves with smoke at once if they come under the fire of heavy ships.

It is important that the Fourth and Seventh Light Cruiser Squadrons should reach their battle stations as soon after deployment as possible, because the light cruiser squadrons of the Battle-Cruiser Force may be unable to close the battlefleet early in the action, and, in their absence, the destroyer flotillas will be without support by vessels of their own speed, whilst their numbers may be insufficient to deal unaided with the enemy flotillas; the armament and speed of the Fourth Light Cruiser Squadron supported by the Seventh Light Cruiser Squadron should enable enemy destroyers and light cruisers to be dealt with effectively.

12. The need for initiative on the part of Captains of light cruisers is to be encouraged to the utmost; the speed of these vessels, and their ability to gain favourable positions for attack, cannot be properly used if they are not given plenty of latitude by their senior officers.

Imprudence in taking the offensive is neither suggested nor required, and officers commanding light cruiser squadrons and flotillas are cautioned not to close the enemy battlefleet sufficiently to come under its fire until it is fully engaged; it would be disastrous to allow our light vessels to be defeated by the enemy's battlefleet before the latter became engaged with our own.

When both battlefleets are occupied with one another, the auxiliary forces of our fleet will be able to deal with those of the enemy without fear of encountering greatly superior force, and they must then take the offensive with all the means in their power.

(f) Reports during Action

13. Ships which are able to report movements of the enemy or result of our fire are to signal by searchlight if practicable, otherwise by W/T.

Reports of movements, provided they are made in good time, may be of great value, and any ship in a position to see clearly what is occurring, when it is probable that the Commander-in-Chief cannot, should not fail to make a report.

Signals for reporting the result of fire are provided in the signal books, but it must be remembered that with a number of ships engaged, such reports are of little value unless there is a decided tendency one way or the other, or the fall of shot of a ship can actually be recognised and reported to her.

If the enemy makes a smoke screen, it is essential for the Commander-in-Chief to receive reliable reports of the enemy's movements as soon as possible, either from ships in the van or rear of the battlefleet or from light cruisers stationed ahead or astern of the line, who may be able to see round the smoke screen, especially its weather side. The First Cruiser and Sixth Light Cruiser Squadrons will probably be in a good position for this purpose. If the situation admits, a special vessel should be detailed from each of these squadrons to take up positions as necessary, their primary duty being to observe and keep reporting any change in the movements or dispositions of the enemy. In such circumstances, kite balloons should be of value, and light-cruisers fitted with balloons should elevate them as high as possible.

(g) Duties of the Harwich Force

14. Three alternative positions are allotted to the Harwich Force in the *Diagram of Deployment*. The Force should take station approximately at 'R' (in the van) if possible, but if not able to attain this position, it should take station at 'S' or 'T' according to circumstances.

Should the enemy's battlefleet at first move away from Heligoland with the possible object of reversing course later to draw the British fleet over minefields or submarines, the Harwich Force, or a portion of it favourably placed, may be ordered to sweep twenty to thirty miles in rear of the enemy's fleet to counter this move and destroy the minelayers and submarines.

7. INSTRUCTIONS FOR DESTROYERS PRIOR TO DEPLOYMENT [1 January 1918]

(a) Screening

Destroyers screening the fleet on passage are to act in accordance with the instructions contained in the *Screening Diagrams* and the *Grand Fleet Signal Orders*.

Flotillas must at all times keep a good look-out on the battlefleet, particularly in the later stages of the approach and the early stages of deployment, in order that they may immediately conform to the movements of the battlefleet and occupy their assigned stations whilst avoiding any possibility of hampering the battlefleet.

During the approach, the fleet flagship destroyer tender is to take station two cables astern of the Commander-in-Chief's column.

(b) Action if a ship strikes a Mine

2. If the fleet, or a portion of the fleet, is cruising or making a passage and a ship strikes a mine or is torpedoed, two destroyers of the group screening are to be detached at once to its assistance. As a general rule, the two nearerst destroyers are to proceed on this duty without waiting for orders; they may be reinforced by signal later, but two are to act at once. In the case of a flank column, the two nearest destroyers on that flank are those to assist; in the case of a central column, the two nearest destroyers from the 'ahead' screen are to go.

3. If the ship has been mined, the destroyers are to stand by to give any assistance required; unless otherwise ordered, they will accompany her to the base to which she is ordered.

4. If the ship has been torpedoed, the destroyers are to take immediate steps to screen from further attack, taking up their positions according to the position of the ship with reference to the probable position of the attack and the speed the ship is able to maintain.

(c) Economy of Fuel

5. Fuel is to be economised to the utmost when on passage with the fleet; extravagance in expenditure may result in destroyers not being available at critical times, or in the curtailment of the operations.

8. INSTRUCTIONS FOR DESTROYERS AFTER DEPLOYMENT [1 January 1918]

(a) Attack on enemy

1. Detailed instructions for carrying out the torpedo attack on the enemy heavy ships are laid down in the *Torpedo Attack Memorandum*.

In high visibility, provided they are in a favourable position, British flotillas are to commence their attack as soon as the heavy ships are engaged. They should not attack earlier, or they will be driven off by the gunfire of the enemy fleet.

In low visibility, the attack should be made at the earliest possible moment. Under these conditions it may not be necessary to await the opening of gunfire by the main fleet.

2. If the advantage of torpedo position is with the enemy, British flotillas, except possibly those with and ahead of the battle-cruisers, will not be able to carry out an immediate attack. Under these disadvantagous circumstances, the efforts of such British flotillas must be concentrated on breaking up any enemy flotilla attacks which develop.

3. Should enemy flotillas attack first, British flotillas are to proceed to beat them off, and after meeting and engaging them are, if the situation is favourable, to press on and attack the enemy battle line with torpedoes in preference to turning back to re-engage the enemy flotillas, which should be dealt with by the supporting light cruiser squadrons and the secondary armaments of heavy ships.

4. The following guiding principles should be kept in view:—

(*a*)   Flotillas delivering a torpedo attack should avoid getting into positions which would allow enemy's destroyers to deliver a counter-attack without being engaged; and should therefore not as a rule get astern of the line joining the leading ships of the two fleets; it is desirable to turn in the direction of the British van to fire torpedoes.

(*b*)   If enemy flotillas do not counter-attack, British flotillas should return to their stations immediately after firing their torpedoes, so as to be ready for the enemy flotillas when they move.

(*c*)   Care must be taken not to pass within the destructive gun-range of the enemy line unless the enemy is heavily engaged.

(*d*)   In attacking enemy flotillas, destroyers should get close so that every projectile may hit; experience has shewn that it may take 20 to 30 hits to knock out a destroyer; maxims and pompoms must be used against personnel; destroyers must act quickly; not hesitating to use initiative since no orders are to be expected after general action has commenced.

5. Funnel smoke must be reduced to a minimum in order not to impede the fire or hamper the view of our ships.

If, after a destroyer action between the lines, the destroyers from the van cannot regain their station without masking the fire of the British fleet by smoke, they should go to the rear and make the best use they can of their guns and remaining torpedoes, joining one of the rear flotillas for preference or acting against disabled enemy vessels.

6. In proceeding to the attack against enemy heavy ships or light vessels, destroyers should not attempt to turn to attack close across the bows of a column of ships; a turn too early might seriously hamper the whole fleet, force a battleship off her steady course, or lead to a collision.

If attacking by divisions through a gap in the line between two columns, destroyers must be careful to keep close up to the rear of the leading column to avoid hampering the column astern.

7. If, before delivering the attack, and whilst still keeping station on our own fleet, destroyers should come under enemy fire, the half flotillas should be spread out at once so as to offer a less vulnerable target.

*　　*　　*

(f) Smoke screening destroyers

12. One destroyer will, on deployment, be attached to each squadron of the battlefleet, being stationed about one mile on the disengaged bow of the ship bearing the flag of the flag officer commanding the squadron. The duty of these destroyers in action is to screen disabled ships, or to attack disabled enemy ships if ordered to do so. They are to take station astern of the division of their respective flag officers on the approach.

When divisions turn in succession from the rear, these destroyers are at once to move out and smoke screen the turning points of their squadrons.

Note — The Rear-Admiral's division will not be screened.

(g) The fleet flagship destroyer tender

13. The fleet flagship destroyer tender is to take station about a mile on the disengaged beam of the fleet flagship and near the

repeating ship after deployment, and if the fleet flagship is disabled and forced to quit the line, is at once to close ready to embark the Commander-in-Chief and staff.

(h) Aircraft

14. Destroyers are to keep a good look-out for friendly aircraft alighting; if an aircraft carrier is not at hand, and circumstances permit, a destroyer in the vicinity should proceed to the assistance of a machine which has alighted.

9. TACTICAL EMPLOYMENT OF DESTROYERS BY THE ENEMY IN A FLEET ACTION [1 January 1918]

1. The maxim that only numbers can annihilate is held by the enemy to be particularly applicable to destroyer attacks. It may therefore be expected that, where possible, destroyers will attack in large numbers, and from two or more directions simultaneously.

2. If the number of light cruisers admits, one escorting cruiser is detailed to two flotillas to keep them informed of the course of the action and the range; also to assist in driving off our own light cruisers and destroyers.

3. The initial position of the enemy flotillas is believed to be about one mile on the disengaged beam of the line of battle, the foremost flotillas being abreast of the battle-cruisers, or slightly in advance of them if circumstances permit; the remaining flotillas are with the battlefleet, one pair being opposite the van division, one opposite the centre and one opposite the rear. As far as possible, destroyers with the longest range torpedoes are stationed at the van. The maximum known range of the torpedoes carried (19.7″) is 13,000 yards (about 25 knots), but it is reasonable to suppose that their latest weapons will be an improvement upon this and a range of 15,000 yards, 25 knots, is to be expected.

4. After action is commenced, the leading flotillas draw forward so as to be ready to attack from ahead immediately the time arrives, the flotillas in rear moving up into their places and attacking from ahead in their turn. If it is desired that all destroyers should attack as quickly as possible, they would do so by passing ahead of the battlefleet or breaking through the line. The most usual manœuvre is believed to be for the destroyers to pass between the battle-cruisers and the main battle line, but the 'break through' manœuvre is used if the fleets are closing one another quickly on similar courses, and opportunity is favourable for attack by large numbers in rapid succession. Pairs of flotillas

usually attack together. The guiding rule for the selection of the target is believed to be that ships to be attacked should bear initially about 135° from right ahead.

[30 April 1918]

5. The enemy destroyers will certainly endeavour to push their attack home to a point where their torpedoes cannot fail to reach our line, even should the battle line make a considerable turn away. Whilst flotillas are attacking, one or more escorting cruisers will probably proceed to positions where they can support them, other cruisers dropping astern to form a rallying point for flotillas returning.

6. For action against other destroyers, enemy destroyers are encouraged to set their torpedoes to run shallow. This is particularly the case at night when they are taught to fire at very close range.

7. The gunnery armament of enemy destroyers has been greatly strengthened, but the disposition of their guns is such as generally to render it tactically more advantageous for them to be pursued than to pursue. It is however desirable that at least a half-flotilla consisting of a leader and 8 destroyers should be used to meet the attack of one enemy flotilla which consists of 11 destroyers.

8. Enemy destroyers make much use of smoke screens both by day and night.

* * *

11. INSTRUCTIONS FOR GRAND FLEET SUBMARINES
[30 April 1918]

(a) Employment of Flotillas

1. The Tenth and Eleventh Flotillas will be employed in:—
(*a*) Detached operations as required.
(*b*) Defensive measures in case of a raid or invasion north of Flamborough Head.
(*c*) Co-operation with the fleet.

2. The Twelfth and Thirteenth Flotillas will proceed to sea with the fleet, taking part in any operations as units of the fleet; they will also be employed on detached operations as required.

3. Attention is called to *C. B. 01430 'Submarine Patrol Areas.'*

(b) Operations with the Fleet

4. Submarines from the Grand Fleet on patrol in the North Sea will be given, before sailing, the special fleet action patrol which

is to be taken up in accordance with *paras. 16 and 17 of C. B. 01430* should the signal be made.

5. Submarines of the Tenth and Eleventh Flotillas in harbour will receive orders either: —

(*a*) To take up positions on the special fleet action patrol lines or to proceed to a special rendezvous;

(*b*) To proceed direct to the Kattegat to cut off enemy ships met with; or

(*c*) To take up positions for the defence of the Newcastle, Blyth and Middlesborough areas.

The Twelfth and Thirteenth Submarine Flotillas will accompany the battlefleet and Battle-Cruiser Force respectively, and take up their allotted positions in the *Cruising Disposition Diagrams*.

6. If submarines are unable to keep station with the fleet on account of speed or weather, the Commander-in-Chief is to be so informed and orders will probably be given as to their movements. Failing instructions, all submarines unable to keep station are to follow the fleet. The light cruiser and leader of the Twelfth and Thirteenth Submarine Flotillas are to remain with the fleet so long as submarines from their flotillas are present. Should the whole flotilla be unable to keep up, the light cruiser or leader is to remain with the flotilla.

7. When the opposing light cruiser screens are in touch with each other (and wireless silence is no longer being maintained) the positions of our own and enemy ships must be plotted by the light cruiser or leader; a study of the movements of the various forces, combined with a thorough acquaintance with the *G.F.B.I.* and *G.F.M.O.* should give a good indication of the approximate time and direction of deployment.

The leaders are to remain in touch with their submarines, furnishing them with information as to the relative position of our own and enemy battlefleets as long as possible after which submarines are to act on their own initiative. Submarines may be spread by the Captain (S) as considered desirable during the approach to meet the particular situation.

8. Until the enemy heavy ships are sighted, it is important that the submarines of the Thirteenth Flotilla should keep in rear of the light cruiser screen, if necessary falling back on the battle-cruisers, in order that they shall not be forced to dive by enemy light craft, and thereby lose touch. As soon as the enemy heavy ships are reported, the submarines should press forward to the attack.

Submarines should dive at about five miles from the enemy fleet, but this distance will depend on the visibility. They should endeavour to avoid being sighted by enemy ships, more especially if situated on the side of the enemy which is away from the enemy's base as their known presence may cause the enemy to retreat, and thereby frustrate our fleet in the attempt to bring the enemy fleet to action.

9. It must be the main tactical endeavour of 'K' class submarines to place themselves between the enemy and his base, and, in certain cases, to attack the enemy on the reverse side from that on which our battlefleet will attack. For this purpose, in nearly all cases where the enemy is nearer to his base than the submarine force, the best procedure will be to steer a course more or less directly towards the enemy's base, units being spread about five miles apart and disposed at right aangles to the bearing of the enemy's base. The two following principles should be borne in mind: —

(a) Having passed the enemy's fleet, and whilst manoeuvring for position behind them, it is desirable that some portion of the fleet should be kept in sight; once lost the chances of sighting again are small.

(b) Although it is preferred that, in certain cases, submarines should manoeuvre for a position to attack later on instead of going in at the first opportunity, it should be understood that once the main fleets are engaged it will rarely be desirable to defer attacking.

(c) Duties of Submarines at the rear of the Battlefleet in a Fleet Action

10. All submarines at the rear of the battlefleet are to follow on the surface and move in readiness to attack the enemy fleet should it turn 180°; these submarines are also to deal with enemy disabled ships.

(d) General Orders for Fleet Action

11. Any submarines which lose contact during a fleet action owing to weather or other circumstances and still have torpedoes left, are, failing other instructions, to proceed to take up positions on the fleet action patrol lines (*vide C. B. 01430*) with a view to cutting off remaining enemy units. An endeavour will be made to inform the Captains (S) before the fleet sails of the patrol lines to be occupied and the order of their importance. This, however, may not be practicable, and the risk of encounter due to more than one submarine proceeding to a particular patrol line must

under the circumstances be accepted. It is to be realised that submarines on these patrols are placed with the object of attacking enemy ships. Submarines met with will probably be friendly and should not be attacked unless their enemy character is definitely established.

12. When all torpedoes have been expended, submarines are to return to their bases independently.

13. All minelayers working with the Grand Fleet will, if opportunity offers, be detached to lay mines on the enemy's line of retreat inside the submarine patrol lines; when so detached they will fly the black recognition sails (*vide S.F.O. 12*), although they may not at the time be in the presence of the enemy or British capital ships.

14. Once battle has been joined submarines are to act on their own initiative in accordance with the above instructions, and no further orders are to be expected.

12. INSTRUCTIONS FOR AIRCRAFT [25 November 1918]

(a) Heavier-than-air Machines — General
The present functions of aircraft working in conjunction with the fleet at sea are as follows: —

(*a*) *Reconnaissance.*
   (i)   Strategical — long distance scouting.
   (ii) Tactical — observation during the approach and action. Complementary to this is the prevention of reconnaissance by enemy aircraft.

(*b*) *Offence.*
   (i)   Destruction of enemy's air reconnaissance.
   (ii) Machine gun-fire on personnel of:—
      (*a*) Destroyers.
      (*b*) Capital ships.
      (*c*) Other vessels.
   (iii) Torpedo attack on capital ships. These functions, if successfully carried out, will produce results of great importance.

(*c*) *Assistance to Gun Control.* Observation, for individual units of our fleet, of alterations of course and inclination by the units of enemy fleet with which they are engaged, and of our fall of shot.

(*d*) *Defence.* The defence of our own ships and 'observing' aircraft from attack by the enemy's heavier-than-air machines.

2. The chief factor affecting the work of aircraft is visibility.

In reconnaissance, whilst under the best conditions it is possible for aircraft to have two fleets 100 miles apart simultaneously under observation, it must be recognised that under difficult conditions aircraft reports may not be received much in advance of those from light cruisers. Low clouds may hamper them very considerably, even in clear weather; rain or haze at once restricts their range of vision, and in fog or thick mist they are unable to operate.

3. In rough weather, the risks to aircraft flying over the open sea are considerable, but should a definite need for their use be apparent, in the presence or vicinity of the enemy, these risks must be accepted.

The question of whether the importance of the service to be carried out justifies the risk under the circumstances of the moment, must be decided by captains after hearing the reports of their flying officers.

4. All planes carried in ships other than those of the flying squadron must, if possible, be flown off prior to fire being opened, but flying off should be delayed as long as is practicable. Planes that cannot possibly be flown off from turrets and platforms prior to action should be thrown overboard to obviate the risk of fire, as they carry from 40 to 70 gallons of petrol.

(b) Allocation of Planes

5. Planes for the purposes outlined in *Paragraph 1* are distributed in the fleet as follows: —

(*a*)   *Reconnaissance*. In ships of the flying squadron.

(*b*)   *Offence*.

    (ii) In all squadrons.

    (ii) Mainly in *Argus* but a few in *Furious*.

(*c*)   *Gunnery*. In selected battleships, battle cruisers and cruisers.

(*d*)   *Defence*. In all squadrons.

(c) Stations of Flying Squadron

6. *Prior to Approach*. The stations of ships of the flying squadron are shown in the *Cruising Dispositon Diagrams*.

In low visibility *Furious* and *Vindictive* are to drop back to position 'U', proceeding to 5 miles ahead if visibility improves.

Owing to aircraft carriers having as a rule to turn when flying off, they cannot be expected always to keep in their assigned stations.

7. *Approach and Action*. First Division (*Furious* and *Vindictive*) is to keep in touch with the British advanced forces until general

action has commenced, and is then to take station ahead or on the disengaged side of the Fifth Battle Squadron. Full advantage is to be taken of these ships' high speed to utilise their torpedo armament.

Second Division (*Argus*) is to endeavour to attain during the approach, and maintain during action until all machines have been flown off, a position at a safe distance on the disengaged side of the van of the battlefleet, if necessary passing between the columns before deployment but taking care to be clear before fire is opened.

Third Division (*Pegasus* and *Nairana*) is to endeavour to attain a position at a safe distance on the disengaged side of the battle-fleet, and thereafter is to maintain touch as far as the speed and duties of the ships will permit, keeping on a safe bearing.

(d) Duties of the Flying Squadron and its Planes
First Division (*Furious* and *Vindictive*).

8. *Scouting Prior to Approach*. The 1st division will fly off reconnaissance planes to form an air-screen ahead of the fleet when ordered by the Commander-in-Chief. These planes are to be relieved by others as necessary. The number of planes flown will depend upon circumstances, but will usually not be less than two. Until otherwise ordered they are to maintain their fixed bearings from their carrier, at maximum visibility distance.

9. *Commencement of Approach*. On the advanced forces of the enemy being sighted, two further planes are immediately to be despatched by the 1st division so as to intercept the enemy's heavy forces and take up positions for observing their movements during the approach and action; the first plane making for the enemy's battlefleet, and the second for his battle cruisers. (These planes will be referred to as the Action Observation planes.)

Whilst the latter planes are on their way to their stations, both they and the scouting planes in position in the air-screen are to make all enemy reports possible.

The following is the relative order of importance of the items of their reports: —

(1) Composition and course
(2) Position
(3) Formation and disposition
(4) Amplification of above

For all forces sighted, priority being given to battle and battle cruiser squadrons.

10. *During Approach*. On the arrival of the Action Observation planes (*i.e.* on their reporting their objectives in sight) the original scouting planes of the screen are to be ordered to take up station

on the flanks of the enemy, one or more on each flank, as Action Lookout planes. From these positions they are to keep a wide lookout and search for and report the arrival and subsequent movements of all enemy light or auxiliary forces, the following being the relative order of importance: —

(*a*) Submarines.

(*b*) Minelayers, or widely detached light cruisers.

(*c*) Destroyer flotillas.

(*d*) Aircraft and aircraft carriers.

(*c*) Light cruisers close to enemy main forces or in touch with our own light cruisers.

11. *Action*. The duties laid down above, to be carried out during the approach phase, now merge into those that the planes will carry out as Action Observation and Action Lookout planes respectively; but, on the general deployment of the fleets for battle, the number of these planes up is, if possible, to be increased to 3 for the enemy heavy ships (2 over the battleships and 1 over the battle cruisers) and 4 for the wide lookout duty, (one pair, ahead and on the disengaged bow of the enemy; another pair, on similar bearings on our own fleet).

12. The duties of the above planes during action will be as follows:

(*a*) *Action Observation Planes*.

(i) Immediate reports of general alterations of course or formation by the enemy's battleships and battle cruisers.

N.B.—These reports are entirely distinct from those that will be made by gunnery planes, to units of our fleet, relative to alterations of course by units of the enemy's fleet on which they observing. They are for the information of the Commander-in-Chief, and should state whether alterations of course are made together or in succession, and by squadrons or as a whole.

(ii) Immediate information as to destroyer flotillas massing for attack, moving out for attack, and firing torpedoes.

(iii) The firing of torpedoes by any other unit of the enemy.

(iv) Other movements or events of importance in the enemy's line of battle.

(*b*) *Action Lookout Planes*. Reports of: —

(i) Submarines ahead of the fleet, or steering so as to approach for attack.

(ii) Mines in the water ahead of our fleet; minelayers or detached ships operating ahead, or steering so as to pass ahead of our fleet.

(iii) Electrically-controlled motor boats; torpedo-hydro-planes, &c.

(iv) The approach of additional ships or destroyers.

(v) Other movements by detached forces of the enemy (such as encircling movements by minelayers in anticipation of an alteration of course).

(vi) Aircraft and aircraft carriers.

13. The duty of the First Division during action is to keep in touch with their planes and to replace them or relieve them as necessary from time to time. (Planes when relieved should if possible fly on in *Argus*.)

The First Division will retain its fighting planes, and also any torpedo planes carried, for the later phases of the action, when the fighters flown from other ships have expended their fuel or ammunition and the main torpedo air-attacks have been delivered.

Second Division. (*Argus*)

14. *Argus* will maintain all available torpedo planes in constant readiness for attack. The order for attack will be given by the Commander-in-Chief, and may be expected at any moment from the commencement of the approach phase onwards. The attack ordered may be either a general one, by all available planes on the whole or any part of the enemy's line, or an attack by a definite number of units on a corresponding number of the enemy's ships.

(*Note* — *Argus* will normally carry five units of three machines each).

15. The two reconnaissance planes in *Argus* are not to be sent up unless ordered by the Commander-in-Chief or Admiral Commanding Aircraft. They are to be regarded as stand-by planes for the later phases of action or in the event of *Furious* or *Vindictive* being put out of action. In the latter case the functions laid down above for the machines of the First Division will at once devolve upon '*Argus*' reconnaissance planes (supplemented if necessary by seaplanes from *Pegasus* and *Nairana*), and *Argus* must therefore be in touch with the signals being made by the planes in the air.

16. The fighting planes of the Second Division of the Flying Squadron are to be retained for use later on in the action and none are to be flown off without orders, unless a very definite and unexpected need for them becomes apparent.

Third Division. (*Pegasus* and *Nairana*)

17. Should there appear to be a possibility of these ships losing touch with the fleet during action, their fighters are to be flown

off before this occurs; in such a case these planes are to take up a position over the British Battle Cruisers and await a favourable opportunity for attacking the massed destroyer flotillas at the head of the German line. Otherwise, the fighters of the Third Division are, like those of the First and Second Divisions, to be retained until later in the action.

18. Thereafter, until called upon to provide emergency seaplanes, the particular duty of the Third Division will be to form a base (the approximate position of which relative to our fleet may be generally known) to which planes may return; observing that the number of such planes may amount to more than 100 in a space of four hours.

19. On deployment, all destroyers detailed for screening the Flying Squadrons, with the exception of two (one each for the disengaged sides of the First and Second Divisions) are to take station with the Third Division for this duty. No attempt is to be made to salve planes, and occupants are to be picked up with all dispatch.

20. The seaplanes of the Third Division are to be retained as stand-by planes for the later phases of action or in the event of First Division or *Argus* being put out of action; in the latter case, the duties laid down above for reconnaissance planes devolve upon them, and touch must therefore be kept with the signals being made by planes in the air.

(e) Planes carried in other Squadrons of the Fleet

21. *Fighting Planes — Light Cruiser Squadrons*. Should a report of an enemy airship be received by W/T prior to gaining touch with the enemy, one fighter is at once to be despatched from each light cruiser squadron in the line A-K. If they fail to see the airship these planes are to proceed to maximum visibility distance ahead of their squadrons and continue to search for enemy reconnaissance, conforming to subsequent movements on the rough bearing on which they were despatched.

Should enemy aircraft be actually sighted from a squadron in the line A-K, it is at the discretion of the senior officer to fly off additional planes from his squadron.

22. On the enemy battle fleet coming in sight of planes flown as above, they should at once make for the leading ships of the enemy's columns (particularly those columns nearest the centre of the fleet) and deliver a vigorous attack on the personnel visible on their bridges. Planes may expend one half of their ammunition up to this phase, the remainder being reserved mainly for

destroyer flotillas after the deployment of the fleets.

23. Light cruiser planes not flown off prior to gaining touch with the enemy should, at the last moment, take station above their squadrons and await the opportunity indicated in *paragraph 22 above*.

24. On the deployment of the fleets, all light cruiser squadron fighters are to take station above that end of the enemy line to which their squadrons are opposite after deployment (in doubt, the head of the line) and there await favourable opportunities for atacking the enemy's destroyer flotillas (particularly the bridges of leaders) when massing for attack.

25. *Fighting Planes — Capital Ships.* The duties of fighters in all squadrons of heavy ships fall under two headings; the first, which is to be carried out by the planes from even numbered sub-divisions, is to patrol the area in the neighbourhood of their own squadron and search for and attack enemy heavier-than-air craft which during action might attempt observation work or the attack of our exposed personnel; the second, which is to be carried out by the planes from odd numbered sub-divisions, is to carry out similar duties over the enemy units with which their squadron is engaged, searching for enemy aircraft and protecting our action and gunnery observation planes in place of our capital ships.

26. Should there be no enemy aircraft present, or whenever a favourable opportunity arises, all fighters are to proceed to the attack of bridges and control positions and kite balloons of enemy capital ships, and the bridges and other exposed personnel of his destroyers. If electrically-controlled motor boats or torpedo-hydroplanes are seen approaching, they are to be attacked at once.

Fighters should make every endeavour to use this form of attack before their expenditure of fuel renders it necessary for them to land or leave the scene of action.

27. *Gunnery Observation Planes.* These planes are to proceed over units of the enemy forces as ordered by their Captains, according to the distribution of fire of the fleet, and carry out their assigned duties, keeping in touch with their squadrons and conforming to subsequent alterations in fire distribution.

The second or stand-by plane of each division should accompany and protect the machine actually observing, at the same time 'listening-in' and being prepared to take over.

28. A diagrammatic illustration of the instructions in this section is being promulgated in 'Tactics.'

(f) Kite balloons

29. When the Grand Fleet proceeds to sea kite balloons are to be flown from the following ships unless otherwise ordered: —
All light cruisers fitted with winches.
Courageous and *Glorious*.
Lion and *Repulse*.
Queen Elizabeth and *Barham*.
Two ships in each of the First, Second and Fourth Battle Squadrons.
Weather permitting, balloons are to be transferred to the above ships whenever the fleet is ordered to have steam for 2½ hours notice or less.

30. The balloons towed by cruisers and light cruisers are primarily intended for reconnaissance purposes, and should be flown as high as possible with the baskets manned during daylight hours in order to obtain early information of the enemy.

One balloon is to be flown at a high altitude for reconnaissance purposes by the battle-cruisers while cruising; the other is to be kept at a low altitude until action is joined.

The balloons towed by battleships are mainly for use in action to assist in observation of fire and to obtain information of the enemy's movements and as a constant torpedo look-out. These balloons should, therefore, be kept as low as possible until the two battlefleets are in sight of one another, but the fleet flagship may send her balloon up at an earlier stage to obtain information prior to deployment.

31. The visibility during action may possibly prevent balloons being of assistance to the towing ship, whilst they would form a convenient object for the enemy to range on. If such conditions prevail the balloon may be hauled down to a low altitude or cut adrift at the discretion of the Commanding Officer of the towing ship.

13. NIGHT FIGHTING INSTRUCTIONS [30 October 1918]

(a) General Remarks

1. The range of searchlights may at present, as a maximum, be considered as:
   5,000 yards for ships; 2,000 yards for destroyers.
2. Owing to the risk incurred from torpedo fire, it is undesirable for heavy ships to engage at night if it can be avoided. If, however, it is decided to engage, the general principle

to be followed is that searchlights are to be switched on, and the maximum volume of gun and torpedo fire opened simultaneously, ships turning away as necessary.

3. When it is decided to engage enemy ships, the searchlight is to be considered the primary means of illuminating them. Star shell are to be kept ready for firing but, generally, are only to be used for: —

(a) Examining a suspected area.

(b) Assisting gunfire when searchlights cannot be used.

4. Against an alert enemy it is unsafe to use star shell as a primary means of illumination. If, as may be expected, he switches on his searchlights simultaneously or in reply, the star shell effect is nullified. There would then be some loss of time in switching on and directing our searchlights and, in the meantime, our ships would be illuminated and seriously handicapped by the enemy's lights. It must be accepted that the result of a night action will depend on the first minute or so and that, if the most effective action is not taken immediately, it is unlikely that there will be time to recover.

5. As regards the procedure for heavy ships when in danger of torpedo attack, the first rule is concealment and evasion. This is the best protection against attack, and on no account should the position of a ship or division be given away by switching on searchlights and opening fire prematurely.

Star shell may be used effectively to point out enemy vessels to our destroyers.

6. When it is seen that enemy destroyers are delivering an attack which cannot be evaded, star shell are to be used to illuminate them as they do not disclose the movements of our own ships. When the enemy destroyers close to a dangerous range, searchlights are to be switched on by the leading ship to dazzle and confuse them.

7. When heavy ships are cruising in waters in which the enemy may be expected to be met with, the senior officers of units will as a rule be acquainted with the disposition of British ships and torpedo craft. Under such circumstances, captains of ships in the line are to be extremely careful in switching on searchlights and opening fire without signal from their respective flag officers. The case in which vessels are sighted coming up abaft the beam is one that will call for judgment on the part of the commanding officer of the rear ship of the line.

8.   In all cases of encountering enemy vessels at night, a ship is to report the fact to the Commander-in-Chief and senior officer of the squadron, ascertaining also that the signal has been received by other units immediately affected.

It will usually be sufficient if a 'first sighting of enemy' report is used combined with the signal giving the course steered, amplifying signals being made later if required. This is of importance in order that commanders of all units affected may receive this information as quickly as possible. In the case of several ships being in company, if the senior officer is disabled or for any reason does not make the signal within reasonable time, it is the duty of the next senior or some other ship to make certain that the signal is made.

9.   If a column is attacked or threatened by destroyers or submarines, the commander of the column is to manœuvre the column out of the danger area, using one of the following methods according to the situation at the time: —

(a)   Leading his column clear with or without signal.

(b)   Turning his column by flashing signal.

(c)   Turning his column together by means of the Fixed Light Manœuvring Signal.

The signal to alter course by the Fixed Light Manœuvring Signal may be made by the commander of the rear division of a squadron at his discretion, should the rear be attacked or threatened, in which case he is to make the executive also. When made under such circumstances, the signal is to apply only to the rear and is not to be repeated or acted on by ships of the division ahead.

(d)   Turning his column by the White Very's Light Signal.

10.   When destroyers are sighted within attacking distance at night it will probably be best to turn either away by the Fixed Light Manœuvring Signal, or towards by the Very's Light Signal. Although by both methods, especially the former, the position of the columns is shown to the enemy, this disadvantage must be accepted in view of the rapidity with which the manœuvre can be executed and the small target presented to the enemy's torpedoes. If destroyers are sighted outside attacking distance and it is considered that they have not seen the column of ships, it may be preferable to turn away in succession without signal. When the column consists of two divisions the rear division must always be ready to turn away even should the van division stand on.

11.   Whichever manœuvre is executed, the commander of the column concerned is to inform the commanders of other columns of the fact that he is engaged with the enemy craft, and the direction in which he is standing to avoid danger.

Normal helm is to be used for these turns. Speed is to be increased when turns are made in succession as laid down. No increase of speed is to be made when turns are made together (vide *G.F.M.O.S, paragraph 6*).

12.   It is probable that, on the receipt of the report that a column of the battlefleet has been attacked or has turned away to avoid attack, the Commander-in-Chief will order a general turn away of 90°, leaders together the rest in succession.

13.   The groups of destroyers screening the columns attacked or threatened should attack and keep touch with the enemy.

It is undesirable on a dark night that adjacent screening groups should detach themselves from the fleet to join the vessels engaged until the fleet is on the new course, and then only if ordered. In the event of light cruisers or destroyers being ordered to support vessels already engaged at night they should approach on a course which will not hamper the vessels they are supporting and should have fighting lights switched on.

The challenge procedure must be carried out before fire is opened and it must be borne in mind that vessels already in action may fail to reply to the V.B.S. and may have had their fighting lights shot away.

No item of recognition by appearance or pendants painted on the bow must be overlooked and under such circumstances fire should only be opened by the supporting vessels on a certain enemy.

(b) Challenge Procedure

14.   *General procedure on sighting a suspicious vessel or vessels* — Train guns and searchlights on the vessel; prepare to fire star shell; stand by to fire guns and torpedoes.

When in waters where the presence of enemy vessels is not expected: —

(*a*)   Make the challenge arc light and repeat once.

(*b*)   If the repetition is not answered in one minute, fire star shell to examine the vessel.

NOTE — Gunfire is not to be opened until the hostile character is established.

When in waters where the presence of enemy vessels is suspected, for example, on the night after a fleet action: —

(*a*) If the suspicious vessel makes a challenge other than the British, open fire.

(*b*) If the suspicious vessel makes no challenge and delay is inadvisible, fire the Very Brock Signal and make the challenge; if the former is not answered at once, open fire.

NOTE — A single ship should always endeavour to obtain a good torpedo position before challenging, and avoid the opposite.

(c) Attack and defence at night

15. *Battleship and battle-cruiser procedure.*

General Rules — (i) Searchlights must be used if the enemy uses them on you.

(ii) If searchlights are switched on, open fire simultaneously.

16. A division of battleships or battle-cruisers meeting enemy heavy ships: —

(*a*) Immediately the challenge procedure has been carried out, or sooner if the enemy character is unmistakable, switch on searchlights and open fire with guns and torpedoes.

(*b*) Ships ahead and astern of the one which has switched on are to fire star shell in order to make certain that no other enemy vessel is present.

(*c*) All enemy vessels are to be engaged, but no enemy vessel is to be illuminated by more than one of our ships.

(*d*) The division will be handled by its flag officer.

NOTE — If on an opposite course to the enemy, torpedoes are to be fired, and a turn away together of 90° made before coming on the enemy's beam, *i.e.*, before crossing the probable tracks of enemy torpedoes.

17. A division of heavy ships meeting destroyers: —

(*a*) Avoid attack by turning away without signal.

(*b*) If the attack cannot be avoided, the squadron will be handled by the flag officer, and turned as ordered. Fire is to be opened, star shell (only) being used to illuminate the enemy until they have closed to a dangerous range, when searchlights are to be switched on by the leading ship to dazzle them.

18. A single battleship or battle cruiser meeting enemy heavy vessels: —

(a) If engaging, switch on searchlights and open fire simultaneously.

(b) If not engaging, turn away, firing torpedoes.

   NOTE — If the ship is illuminated by enemy searchlights, switch on and open fire.

* * *

14. GENERAL INSTRUCTIONS AS TO ACTION TO BE TAKEN BY UNITS CONCERNED UNDER PARTICULAR CONDITIONS [20 May 1918]

(a) If mines are encountered

1. When the fleet is in ordinary cruising order, a vessel sighting a mine is to hoist the signal for 'Mine in sight.' Course is to be altered as necessary to avoid the mine, the customary syren sound signals for alteration of course being made. If possible, the mine should be sunk by rifle or light gun fire as it is passed, but heavy ships are not to stop or remain in the vicinity for the purpose.

During the approach, the same procedure as above is to be followed, but the syren is not to be sounded.

After deployment, a ship is to alter course to avoid the mine, and if possible, hoist the signal for 'Mine in sight' to indicate to the next astern the reason for the alteration of course; the syren is not to be sounded.

2. When in ordinary cruising order or during the approach, floating or Leon mines must be avoided by alteration of course. After deployment, the probability of the battlefleet encountering a line of mines of these types without previous warning should not be great: should they be met, however, commanders of divisions are to take the necessary steps to move their divisions clear of danger.

3. A cruiser or light cruiser observing enemy minelayers dropping mines should indicate the danger by dropping dan buoys marked as laid down in *Fleet Notice to Mariners No. 155 of 1916.* *NOTE* 500 — At night the buoys should be fitted with calcium lights.

Dan buoys with moorings should be dropped to mark moored mines, and buoys with cross-pieces, without moorings, used to denote drifting mines.

The information given by these mark buoys cannot be considered entirely reliable. It should be generally understood that such buoys indicate that a minelaying vessel has been observed in the vicinity of the buoy and on the reciprocal of the bearing indicated.

(b) Snaking the line when closely engaged, and procedure when being heavily hit.

4. When closely engaged, divisional commanders may alter course at their discretion 10° on either side of the mean course of the fleet, speed being increased at the same time. The remaining ships of the division are to follow the divisional commander in succession. In carrying out this procedure the lateral distance of guides from the mean course of the fleet is not to exceed 1,000 yards. The rear division of a squadron should conform generally to the movements of its leading division.

A single ship, when heavily hit, may alter the requisite number of degrees from the mean course of the division so as to shift her position laterally a distance of 500 yards. Such an alteration should be made with manœuvring helm, the number of degrees altered depending on the reserve of speed available. The fire of adjacent ships must not be blanketed.

If the leading ship of a pair which is concentrating on an enemy ship hauls out of the line, the rear ship is to conform, following in succession so as not to disturb the concentration.

If the rear ship of a pair concentrating on the enemy hauls out, the leader should edge over ahead in order to resume accurate fire concentration.

(c) Steps to be taken during action to reduce the torpedo menace

5. The officer commanding the rear of the main battleline has full discretion, when within the torpedo danger zone, either to open up the intervals to reduce the chance of torpedo hits, or to place the rear division on a line of bearing in open order towards the enemy, thus opening up the interval to enemy torpedoes approaching from before the beam. His decision in this respect must be guided by considerations of the general circumstances as affected by an extension of the line due to opening up the intervals and the movements of the van and centre.

6. It will be the endeavour to prevent enemy flotillas attaining a favourable torpedo position both by attacking with the British light forces at the van and by the use of the secondary armament of the fleet. It may also become necessary in the event of a heavy attack to deflect temporarily one or more turrets to disperse the enemy flotillas.

7. If enemy destroyer attacks are pressed home and destroyers attain the firing position, a tactical movement of either a turn

towards or away may be necessary to avoid torpedoes fired. The decision as to the action to be taken must be governed by the principle of keeping the enemy within gun-range. A turn towards causes the ship to present a narrow target and enables the track of the approaching torpedo to be seen more easily. Also gun-range is maintained.

A turn away would be made with the object of out-running the torpedo, but will seldom be possible since by such action ships will be taken outside gun-range.

A turn of at least 45° should normally be made. Less than 45° offers little safeguard.

8. Although it is desirable that the flag officers of divisions should direct divisions or sub-divisions to move as a whole when turning to avoid torpedoes, individual action may at any time be necessary, especially if the actual moment of firing is not observed; each ship must, therefore, have reliable and steady look-outs who are trained in submarine and torpedo track observation and who should be stationed both on the engaged and disengaged sides.

The correct procedure in each case of individual action must depend on the conditions, and no fixed rules can be laid down. Commanding officers, however, should study the plots of their ships' turning circles for the probable fleet speed with relation to the tracks of torpedoes approaching on various bearings, so as to be prepared to act when the emergency arises.

9. An investigation for a battleship, allowing a period of ten seconds between receiving the report of the bubbles and the order being given to the helmsman, and for speeds of ship of from 14 to 18 knots, gives the following rules for guidance: —

(*a*) Take immediate action if a torpedo is reported; use full helm.

(*b*) Bearings of bubbles from 0° to 70° turn towards; bearings of bubbles from 70° to 180° turn away. This is not to be considered a hard and fast rule, but indicates the probable best action. It should be noted in this connection that the objection to turning towards the engaged side is not so great as might be supposed. Experience has shewn that there is little risk of damaging our ships by firing over them at a distance of 2 to 3 cables when the enemy range is 12,000 yards or more.

(*c*) A turn of at least 45° should be made. Subsequent observations of the bearing and direction of the torpedo track must determine the time at which the ship should be steadied.

*   *   *

16. GUNNERY INSTRUCTIONS [25 June 1918]

(a) Fire Discipline

1. For Fire Discipline purposes each division is to be considered as a unit under its own Flag Officer and is to work under his immediate orders subject to the general control of the Admiral in command of the squadron.

2. Should circumstances require it the Commander-in-Chief will make the signal for fire to be opened generally.

3. It is improbable that the whole fleet will come into action simultaneously, and Divisional Commanders are not to await orders to open fire, but are to do so as soon as they consider desirable.

Divisional Commanders are to order the fire of their divisions as circumstances dictate, subject to the general instructions in Section (*b*). The fire of other divisions must not be interfered with.

4. Should only a part of the enemy's fleet be in sight or in range, the Commander-in-Chief, or senior officer of ships in sight of the enemy, if time permits will signal which divisions are to open fire (or cease fire) so as to prevent confusion and interference.

5. When the visibility is such that individual ships in the line sight the enemy before the Flag Officer of their division, ships are authorised to open fire without signal, provided they are certain the ship or ships sighted are hostile.

(b) Distribution of Fire

6. The distribution of the gun fire of the battlefleet will be directed by means of gyro compass bearings in accordance with the following principles.

7. The general bearing signalled by the fleet flagship will be the approximate direction of fire of those divisions of the fleet which are not concentrating their fire, and will be the bearing of the fleet flagship's target ship.

8. Before the enemy is in sight of the battlefleet, the Commander-in-Chief may make a preparative bearing as a warning to all ships. Turrets are then to be trained on this bearing.

9. Opening Fire. (*a*) *High Visibility* — The Commander-in-

Chief will make the general bearing to the fleet, followed by the executive. Admirals commanding the van and rear squadrons will then make by main W/T their divisional distribution signals for the information of all Divisional Commanders.

NOTE — This does not preclude any Divisional Commander opening fire before the above signals are made, as authorised in *paragraph 3*.

(*b*) *Low Visibility* — If the enemy is sighted first by the Admiral commanding the van or rear, he will make by main W/T his divisional distribution signal as a guide to the fleet; this will be confirmed if practicable by the Commander-in-Chief by means of a general bearing.

If the enemy is sighted first by one of the centre Divisional Commanders, he will make one of the divisional fire discipline signals to his division by Type 31 W/T, and by visual to adjacent Divisional Commanders. The latter, when opening fire, will signal similarly to the Divisional Commanders next towards the wing.

NOTES — (i)   The bearing signalled in this case is that of the Divisional Commander's target ship.

(ii)   In all cases the term 'Admiral commanding van or rear' refers to either the Admiral commanding the First or Fourth Battle Squadron according to the position of his squadron in the line.

10. Changing the Distribution of Fire of the Fleet— (*a*) Should the Commander-in-Chief wish to change the distribution, he will do so by making a new bearing followed after an interval by the executive; the former may be accompained by a 'Distribution of Gunfire Signal' addressed to certain divisions or squadrons.

(*b*) Should the Admiral commanding the van or rear squadron consider from information at his disposal, and which is not available to the Commander-in-Chief, that an alteration in the fire distribution is necessary, or that a heavier concentration on the van or rear is required, he will effect it by signal to his squadron and also to the Fifth or Sixth Battle Squadron if at his end of the line.

The signal is to be made both by main W/T and visual methods.

If the Commander-in-Chief considers it desirable, he will then shift the fire of the remaining divisions by means of a new general bearing so as to conform to this.

*   *   *

17. TORPEDO INSTRUCTIONS [4 December 1918]

Day Action — (a) General Remarks

In the attack on the enemy fleet with torpedoes, the maximum rate of torpedo fire is to be developed by all vessels as early as practicable. The number of enemy ships which will be damaged by torpedoes will chiefly depend on this rate of fire, and the importance of ensuring that no favourable opportunity of discharging torpedoes is missed cannot be too strongly emphasised.

2. To surprise the enemy and render an avoiding movement less likely to succeed is an important object to achieve in the torpedo attack. Surprise will be obtained by opening fire at a greater range than the enemy expects. The increase in the running range of torpedoes carried will effect this provided the secrecy of such increase is carefully safeguarded.

3. Commanders of divisions should order the attack on the enemy with torpedoes set to medium speed setting as soon as they consider the conditions admit, using the signals provided. It will usually not be possible to order the firing of torpedoes for more than a few minutes ahead, and therefore, when these signals are made, it is to be understood that as many torpedoes as possible are to be fired during the ensuing six minutes unless the number of torpedoes to be fired is specified.

The fact that these signals are not made, however, does not prohibit the fire of torpedoes set to medium speed setting from individual ships, who should take advantage of every favourable opportunity.

The signals should be made as often as necessary by Commanders of divisions, but the signal 'Cease firing torpedoes' will not usually be made.

NOTE — (i) The signal 'Open fire with torpedoes' is only to be used for opening fire with torpedoes set to the medium speed setting. When this signal is made all individual torpedo fire should cease until permission is given. The natural course of events, when once divisional control has commenced, would be for the signals to be repeated as necessary by the divisional commander.

(ii) If the signal is made by a divisional commander directing the division to fire torpedoes on a given bearing, ships should withold torpedo fire only if firing will endanger a friendly ship. Should the range be clear within the limits of visibility, torpedoes should be fired even though the objective of the divisional leader is not visible to each ship.

4. In order to assist the torpedo control officers, Commanders of divisions should signal to their divisions the course of the enemy torpedo target as estimated by reports received from aircraft, kite balloons and their own observations.

5. The depth adjustment for all torpedoes is to be 18 feet.

6. Precaution is to be taken that friendly ships are not endangered. A clear range indicator should always be used, but in calculating the danger to friendly ships, the risk from cold runs must be accepted, the danger zone being based on the supposition that torpedoes will run at a speed of one knot less than their stamped speed.

In connection with this it must be remembered that it may be necessary to alter course as much as 90° towards the enemy in the event of the latter making a decided turn away and that under these conditions friendly ships may be endangered by torpedoes fired from other friendly ships or squadrons unless the orders below are adhered to.

The fire from capital ships will not, however, be withheld for our own destroyers which foul the range, the depth adjustment being sufficient to take torpedoes under.

7. The E.R. setting is not to be used during a fleet action.

8. Torpedoes set to the medium speed setting may be fired by all ships subject to the following restrictions: —

(*a*) The main battlefleet, Fifth Battle Squadron and Second Battle Cruiser Squadron must only fire torpedoes to run outside the bearing of 60° from any capital ship.

(*b*) All other capital ships and light cruisers must only fire torpedoes adjusted to run between the bearings of 70° and 110° from the bearing of any capital ship except under conditions referred to in *para. 9* below.

NOTES—(i) The position of any friendly capital ship which may be broken down or out of action need not be considered.

(ii) If an individual ship hauls out of the line on the engaged side, say 200 yards, to avoid being hit, torpedoes may be fired over the same arc as if the ship was in the line. Ships in the line may also neglect the individual ship which has hauled out so far as their arcs of fire are concerned, provided their clear range indicator shows that the range is clear both with the present course and if a large alteration towards the enemy, proceeding at maximum speed,is made.

(iii) The senior officer present may make a signal cancelling the above restrictions if he considers the conditions are particularly favourable for torpedo attack. Such signal may either be addressed to all ships or to those squadrons referred to in (*a*) above only. The signal is to remain in force until negatived.

9. *Ships that are obviously so placed that their torpedo fire cannot endanger friendly ships, whatever their course, may disregard the restrictions laid down above. This would apply in the case of light cruiser squadrons which, when attacking with torpedoes or while supporting destroyer attacks, attain a position between the opposing lines.*

A table is issued in the *G. F. G. & T. O.* which gives the safe limit for torpedo fire acording to the distance of the firing ship from various classes of vessels. Ships which do not form part of the general battleline should be guided in their torpedo fire by this table.

10. After a large alteration of course by either of the opposing fleets, Commanders of divisions should make the signal to reopen fire as soon as the situation admits, but if no such signal is received, individual ships should open fire as soon as the position after the change of course is clear.

11. Torpedoes set to 18 feet depth will not pass under our light cruisers. Battle cruisers, Fifth Battle Squadron and divisions in the van must therefore cease torpedo fire *on forward bearings* when a light cruiser squadron is seen to be closing to attack with torpedoes or closing the enemy in support of destroyer attack.

(b) Altering course

12. The precautions given above for the firing of torpedoes on the medium speed setting will allow of free movement of the battlefleet in accordance with the Commander-in-Chief's intentions and without battleships being endangered by our own torpedo fire. All battle-cruisers and other fast units which are proceeding at greater speed than that of the torpedoes in use may,

however, be endangered by their own torpedo fire or that of other squadrons, should they make large alterations of course towards the enemy.

13. In order that senior officers of fast units may know the approximate position of torpedoes, it is desirable that (*a*) senior officers should retain control of the torpedo fire of their own squadrons (*b*) when possible, senior officers of squadrons should inform, by searchlight, any adjacent squadron seen to be altering course of the bearings on which torpedoes have just previously been fired, or that none have been fired.

The danger area of our own torpedoes can then be plotted. If the information from (*a*) and (*b*) above is not available, senior officers of fast units altering course must assume that adjacent squadrons are firing torpedoes in accordance with *paras. 8 and 11* above and must take precautions accordingly.

(c) Torpedo fire from units of the Fleet

14. Each division of the battlefleet and battle-cruisers should endeavour to effect a torpedo concentration on some part of the enemy's line, the natural torpedo errors and the different positions of the ships in the line ensuring a sufficient spread.

Light cruisers and destroyers stationed at the rear must be prepared for a turn of 180° by the enemy, and should be in immediate readiness for attacking the new enemy van in the event of this movement.

15. The development of the maximum torpedo offensive by the First Cruiser Squadron is a matter of first importance. These ships, by virtue of their speed, should be able to push well forward and ahead of the enemy to a position of torpedo advantage from which they will be able to concentrate torpedo fire on the enemy van from outside effective enemy gun range.

Submarines are to act in accordance with *Section 11*, the settings employed being at the discretion of commanding officers. The submarines at the rear of the British line are to attack any enemy ships disabled, and for this purpose should use their heavy warhead torpedoes first.

Night Action — (d) General remarks

16. Torpedoes are normally to be set to the high speed short range setting, and only under circumstances of specially high night visibility is the longer range setting to be used.

The E.R. setting is not to be used. The depth adjustment of torpedoes in heavy ships is to be 18 feet.

Torpedo fire from heavy ships is to be opened on any enemy

ship which may be within range, friendly ships being clear. No signals ordering this are to be expected.

Before opening torpedo fire at night, the proximity and movements of friendly vessels must be taken carefully into account. If the medium speed setting is used, the range counter should be adjusted to the maximum range likely to be required.

(e) Light Cruisers and Destroyers

17. Torpedoes are normally to be set to the high speed setting. The depth setting is to 12 feet in all cases.

18. Under circumstances of specially high night visibility, the medium range setting may be used, the proximity and probable movements of friendly vessels being taken carefully into account.

The E.R. setting is not to be used.

NOTE—Destroyers are not to fire torpedoes at enemy destroyers: —

> (*a*) When forming a submarine screen or in company with our own fleet.
>
> (*b*) When enemy's heavy ships may be met.

19. In attacks by light cruisers and destroyers, the larger the number of attacking boats the greater will be the enemy's difficulty in dealing with such attacks either by gunfire or by an avoiding movement. Surprise is an essential factor for success. The largest destroyer unit which can be handled effectively at night is a half-flotilla and the cruising disposition will therefore usually be with one half-flotilla from one to five miles astern of the other in readiness to support the latter. When committed to an attack, the divisions will follow each other rapidly; the attack is to be forced home, torpedo fire being withheld, generally speaking, until within 1,000 yards running range. It is undesirable, however, to close nearer than 500 yards running range, since the chances of the torpedo diving and running under the ship attacked are thereby increased. No signals are to be expected; although the half-flotilla will attack as a whole, individual boats must be prepared to act on their own initiative and fire their torpedoes as soon as the opportunity occurs.

20. Although the standard attack by destroyers at night will be close range, it may occur that a squadron of heavier ships is met with in bright moonlight or at early dawn. Under such circumstances, a 'browning' attack from a range of 3,000–5,000 yards, may offer greater chance of success. In these circumstances settings of torpedoes should be altered accordingly, the range the

torpedo will run being adjusted by the counter so as to ensure no danger to friendly ships which may be beyond the enemy.

21. Destroyers attacking in company at night should not do so at full speed, as this invariably disorganises the division and leads to general confusion.

NOTE—For definition of the terms 'E.R. setting,' 'medium speed setting' 'high speed setting' used in these instructions *vide G.F.O. & T.O.*

18. INSTRUCTIONS TO VARIOUS UNITS AFTER DAY ACTION [17 Sept. 1918]

(a) General Remarks

1. If time has not sufficed to defeat the enemy by nightfall, it is necessary to keep our forces concentrated with a view to an early renewal of the action. Ships of a class, therefore, which have become detached from their senior officer are to join the nearest flag or senior officer of similar vessels and are to work under his orders.

2. The main principle which should govern the action of all vessels is that the enemy must be pursued and the utmost damage inflicted on him. This does not imply individual pursuit but organised co-operation in shadowing and attacking the main force of the enemy.

3. The procedure to be adopted depends on: —

(*a*) The extent to which the enemy's forces have been defeated and disorganised.

(*b*) The position of the enemy with reference to his base.

(*c*) The weather.

(*d*) The operations of our submarines and minelayers.

(b) Attacks at Night

4. On darkness setting in, and failing instructions from the Commander-in-Chief, the Admiral Commanding Battle-Cruiser Force, if at the van, or if the Admiral Commanding, Battle-Cruiser Force is not in the van then the Flag Officer at the van of the main battlefleet, is to detail a light cruiser squadron, or squadrons to obtain and keep in touch with the enemy. If the enemy is towards the rear, the Flag Officer at the rear is to take similar action. In each case a report of the instructions given is to be made to the Commander-in-Chief.

Squadrons which may primarily be expected to be detailed for this duty are the First, Second, Fifth and Sixth Light Cruiser

Squadrons, and the senior officers of these squadrons should take action to anticipate these orders.

5. A force of destroyers to be referred to as the 'Attacking Force' will accompany the light cruisers with the object of attacking the enemy as soon as a favourable opportunity occurs.

6. The R.A., Harwich Force will, if possible, be placed in command of the night attack, the Commodore (F) remaining with the battlefleet unless otherwise directed, to reorganise the flotillas and submarine screen at daylight.

The attacking flotillas should be organised in half flotillas under a Captain (D), and should not separate into smaller units than divisions.

7. The selection of the flotillas to form the Attacking Force must depend on the positions of flotillas relative to the enemy at sunset and on the reports received as to readiness for further action.

Reports as to readiness for action should be made by destroyers to their respective leaders and half-leaders who should summarise and pass such reports to the R.A., Harwich Force and Commodore (F), or, should neither be on that flank of the battle line, to the senior Captain (D).

8. To form the Attacking Force a destroyer should have two or more torpedoes remaining, be able to steam 25 knots, have forebridge steering position serviceable, and preferably, but not of necessity, have efficient W/T. The amount of fuel necessary will depend on circumstances. The amount available can be judged by the average remaining in destroyers near.

9. As soon as the equivalent of two flotillas can be formed at each end of the line, the R.A. Harwich Force, and Commodore 'F', or the senior Captain (D) are to report to the Commander-in-Chief, the Admiral Commanding, Battle-Cruiser Force, and the Flag Officers at the van and rear of the main battle line stating the forces available and their positions.

10. If time permits, the Commander-in-Chief will issue instructions as to the composition of the Attacking Force.

If, however, it is seen that a favourable opportunity for carrying out the night attack may present itself and no instructions have been received from the Commander-in-Chief, the Admiral Commanding Battle-Cruiser Force if at the van, or, if the Admiral Commanding Battle-Cruiser Force is not at the van then the Flag Officer at the van of the main battlefleet has full discretion to direct an Attacking Force of destroyers to join the shadowing light cruiser squadron or squadrons, informing the Commander-in-Chief of the action taken. Should the rear of the battlefleet be in touch and not the van, the Flag Officer at the rear is to take similar action, having first satisfied himself that no attack has been ordered from the van. To avoid the confusion of encountering friendly forces at night, only one Attacking Force should usually be detailed unless specially ordered by the Commander-in-Chief. If the situation requires the employment of more than one Attacking Force during the night, the necessary instructions may be expected from the Commander-in-Chief, and every endeavour will be made to put the Attacking Forces in touch with each other before dark, and to give the various Attacking Forces full information regarding each other's proposed movements.

11. It is essential that the necessary information to enable the Attacking Force to be collected should be available to inform the flotillas before dark. In cases of urgency, and to assemble the Attacking Force rapidly, all destroyers (except leaders and half-leaders in the van) which are fit to form the Attacking Force may be ordered to concentrate on the ship denoted with all despatch. Similar orders may be given to all destroyers at the rear or on the flank.

12. Prior to the Attacking Force proceeding, it is important that information should be given to the senior officers as to the enemy position and probable movements; also any other intelligence which may affect the situation.

(c) Units not taking part in the Night Attack

13. The battlefleet will be guided by the movements and instructions of the Commander-in-Chief. If the enemy has still a large number of torpedo craft available, the battlefleet will probably not pursue on a direct course during the night.

The Battle-Cruiser Force will probably be required to act under the immediate orders of the Admiral Commanding, and be in position to support our Attacking Force at dawn.

A definite night cruising order can only be assumed if, when the action is discontinued, sufficient time remains to form up before dark. Directly darkness comes on, all ships are to proceed on the course and at the speed signalled, being careful not to close on friendly ships. Course will certainly be altered after dark again.

14. Destroyers which have not been detailed for the Attacking Force are to form half-flotillas as quickly as possible with the object of acting as a protection to the fleet against enemy torpedo

attacks during the night, and against submarine attack at daylight. Those unable to join their own flotillas are to form on the nearest leader or half-leader, the Commodóre (F) or Senior Captain (D) equalising the strength of half-flotillas. It is important that all destroyers should be attached to a leader or half-leader before dark, and that they should be given their reference position together with the course and speed of the fleet during the night.

253. *From Admiral Sir Rosslyn Wemyss*[1]

Admiralty
[BTY/13/39/5]   SECRET   28th January 1918

I have been thinking much of our squadron in the Swin,[2] and cannot myself feel that either its composition or its position is entirely satisfactory.

Taking into account the influence which the enemy Supreme Army Command has in dictating the general policy, there appears to me to be at least a possibility of a portion of the High Sea Fleet being used in combination with the forthcoming heavy attack on the Western Front; and I cannot help thinking that the German minefield which is being laid off the Dutch Coast has some bearing on the question, since it covers such a large area that it would seem to have some greater object than the mere interruption of the Dutch trade.

It is hardly to be expected that more than a portion of the German *Dreadnought* Fleet would be used for such a purpose; but if such action were to be taken, I conclude that it would take the form of a raid on the Straits by their light forces backed up by some of their heavy ships.

Is the force that we hold in the Swin sufficient to counter this? It appears to me that the presence of any of the *King Edwards* can be nothing but a source of weakness.

Any detachment sent to the Thames can, of course, only be such as will leave the Grand Fleet in such strength as you consider necessary to meet the High Sea Fleet, and will I suppose depend upon the reliance you place in the efficiency of the American ships. I know that Jellicoe's policy was to eventually bring down three of the *Superbs* and to attach them to the *Dreadnought*, but

[1]Wemyss became First Sea Lord on 27 December 1917.
[2]Squadron off Thames estuary composed of pre-*Dreadnought* battleships.

this he only contemplated doing when you considered that the 6th Battle Squadron was sufficiently proficient to take their place.[1]

I would be very much obliged if you would give me your ideas on the subject.

The destroyer question has been occupying me a good deal, and, although I have talked a lot to Heath[2] on the subject, I at present see no chance of ameliorating the situation for the present. The question of the training of young officers for the destroyers is, however, better than it was, and no steps which are possible will be left untaken to keep them up to the mark so far as the Admiralty is concerned.

The Inter-Allied Naval Council was on the whole a success. The First Lord is a past master at the art of conducting a meeting, and things went harmoniously.[3]

We are sending some officers out to Italy to try to get something better into the Otranto Barrage, and I do not despair of success.[4]

I am just off to Paris with the Prime Minister and will write to you on my return.[5]

254. *To his wife* [Aberdour House]

[BTY/17/48/4–5]

Grand Fleet
4.2.18

*   *   *

I am afraid that the Labour world is very upset and we are in for a lot of trouble. It causes me great anxiety as they will not finish my ships which are undergoing repair and refit. And we are getting behind hand and they are in consequence breaking down at the critical moment.

Germany settles her difficulties in the right way with a very heavy hand, and that ought to teach us something, but it won't.

[1]The 6th Battle Squadron;. the American Force under Rear-Admiral Hugh Rodman USN.

[2]Later Admiral Sir Leopold Heath (1861–1954): 2nd Sea Lord September 1917— 31 March 1918.

[3]Consisting of Navy Ministers and Chiefs of Naval Staff, first met in London 22 January 1918, its first task to work out command structure for the Mediterranean between Britain, France & Italy; Wemyss soon found it a waste of time and energy.

[4]Barrage of mines and nets across the Otranto Straits begun in October 1917, not completed until April 1918; its efficacy against U-boats is disputed.

[5]To attend Supreme War Council, established in November 1917 at Lloyd George's instigation to co-ordinate Allied strategy.

You see, our politicians only do things to retain popularity and votes. A man like Winston Churchill seems devoid of real patriotism and L. G.'s one desire is to keep in with everybody, except the Navy and Army, as they don't count in his political world.

* * *

255. *To his wife*[Aberdour House]

Grand Fleet
[BTY/17/48/7–9]   5.2.18

* * *

The American squadron enjoyed themselves greatly while we were out, and did very well, and will do better next time. I am sending old Rodman out on an operation of his own, which pleases him and gives them an idea that they are really taking part in the war. I trust they will come to no harm.

* * *

I see the Huns are settling their domestic difficulties in the only way possible, with the strong hand. It may be an object lesson to our weak-kneed politicians. But I fancy they haven't heard the last of it yet. When a police & military-ridden nation begins to kick hard, there is a great big charge of high explosive somewhere, and it will break out again sooner or later, it's a question of time, but the morale of the nation has suffered a severe blow. . . .

We have had some more successes and are rattling the Huns – this is for you only – but hope we can keep it up. Much depends on the weather.

256. *From Wemyss*

Admiralty
[BTY/13/39/7]   7th February 1918

I enclose you a tracing of the area off the Dutch Coast which shows the position in which the mines have been laid up to the present time as far as is known.[1] The fact that this minefield has been or is being laid does not in itself point to the fact that the enemy may be intending any operations on a large scale with their

---

[1] Not preserved in Beatty Papers.

fleet in these waters, but the fact that a minefield of considerably larger dimensions than is necessary for interference with the Dutch trade is being laid, leads one to suppose that there may be some larger object behind it. When the minefield has been extended to the North of the area, it appears possible that it may be the intention of the Germans to start the Dutch coal trade again and trust to this minefield to give their ships protection. This will be carefully watched. Under any circumstances the minefield would form a protection for the flank of a force operating down in that direction.

I quite see the point you make that whatever force we put in the Swin the enemy can bring a force superior to them, but there is another point of view – the stronger our force in the Swin, the larger force must the enemy risk in the narrow seas, and consequently the greater will be his reluctance to run the risk.

I am, of course, entirely in agreement with you that any dispersion which would leave the Grand Fleet without that superiority which you consider necessary would be unsound, and in my letter to you I laid this down as the basis of any detachment of forces. Under any circumstances, of course, the matter will have to stand over until you consider the American ships efficient.

I quite concur as to the Grand Fleet moving to Rosyth.

As I told you in my letter of yesterday, we have avoided putting details of the 0.2. scheme on paper more than is absolutely necessary, and I have asked Keyes to settle the matter privately with you.[1]

Your suggestions re a code being devised for 'route clear' or 'route foul', etc., is being taken into consideration and worked out, and you will be informed of the result later on.

A reply to your letter of the 27th January on the naval situation in home waters will be sent in a day or two: the reply has been delayed in order that all available information regarding the American mines can be given.

The *Goeben* getting away is perfectly damnable and has considerably upset me, since we at the Admiralty were under the happy delusion that there were sufficient brains and sufficient means out there to prevent it: of the latter there were; of the

---

[1]The plans for blockading Ostend and Zeebrugge.

former, apparently not. The whole things will, of course, be carefully gone into.[1]

My trip to Paris was fairly satisfactory inasmuch as no harm accrued from it, but I cannot say that much good was done: if any, it was of the negative sort, but the politicals succeeded in wasting two valuable days of my time. However, I amused myself in Paris, so that I have that much to the good at least!

I am under the impression that I have got on fairly good terms with the Prime Minister, but with these slippery gentlemen you never can tell what their real opinions are.

The First Lord has gone off for a trip to Rome and Egypt. At the latter place [sic] I think he will be of considerable use in helping to get the Italian authorities into line on the subject of the Otranto Barrage. The object of his visit to the latter place is really not naval at all but transportation.

I note all you say about the appointments to acting flag rank, and I feel pretty sure that the service need not be alarmed on the subject. The fact of the matter is that what I have done is to get a sympathetic attitude from the Members of the Board towards their undoubted power to do such a thing. It would never be done except when the actual necessity arose, and, as you know, I do foresee the possibilities of such a necessity arising, because of the state of the Rear-Admiral's list. I understand that the papers have been sent to you for information, and I think you will realise that the safeguards that have been taken are sufficient to ensure that no nepotism or undue favouritism will ever be exercised.

I know you will be glad to hear that the re-organisation of the Scandinavian Convoy has resulted in a saving of 40% of shipping, which I think is highly satisfactory and justifies the steps that were taken.

I should much like to have a yarn with you again, but whilst the First Lord is away I cannot very well leave London. It is a matter of conjecture as to when he will be back, but I do not think that at any rate it will be until the first week in March.

---

[1]*Goeben* and *Breslau* escaped through the Straits into Greek waters on 20 January 1918; both damaged by mines and *Breslau* sunk; *Goeben* returned to Straits where she was grounded; after unsuccessful air bombing she was towed to Constantinople, where she remained immobilised until the end of war.

257. *From King George V*

[BTY/15/4/7]   Buckingham Palace
[Holograph]   Feb. 10th 1918

. . .

I quite understand the anxiety which these convoys across the North Sea cause you. I think you are wise to insist on only one being at sea at a time. It is impossible to protect more & when a disaster occurs, all the press goes mad.

I was most distressed to hear of the deplorable accident which has just occurred to the 'K' boats, in which two were sunk & four others damaged, besides the loss of valuable trained officers & men. It is hard on you & the Grand Fleet as you have not too many of them.[1]

I am glad to hear that the United States Squadron are settling down & learning our ways. I expect they have a great deal to learn, but they will be a useful addition to your fleet . . .

I fear your weather this winter has been abominable, nothing but gales of wind & blizzards, & the poor small craft have suffered in consequence. The running on the rocks of those two destroyers in a snow storm was horrible, wonderful that there was one survivor.

I regret to say the U-boats are giving us a bad time again at the moment & they have sunk many large ships lately, especially in the Mediterranean, which we can ill afford to lose. Roger Keyes has begun well at Dover & has bagged several U-boats already. Bacon did well but was too theoretical.

I agree with you that the way Jellicoe was removed from Admiralty was unfortunate. The Prime Minister has had his knife into him for some time & wished for a change. I think Wemyss will do well & he has some first rate young brains to help him. He is full of sound common sense & does not go into details as much as J. did. I am sure there will be much more sympathy between the Admiralty & Grand Fleet than there was formerly.

*   *   *

[1] The 'K' class submarines were notably accident-prone. But two eminent submariners, Vice-Admiral Sir Arthur Hezlet in his *The Submarine and Seapower*, (London, 1967), p. 75, and Rear-Admiral Sir William Jameson in his *The Most Formidable Thing* (London, 1965), pp. 181, 258–9, think their weaknesses exaggerated. See note 1 on page 404.

258. *To his wife* [Aberdour House]

[BTY/17/48/21–3]

Grand Fleet
12.2.18

* * *

I am always glad to hear what you glean from other officers, especially Flag Officers or those who are sound in their views and know what they are talking about.

Yes, I am afraid old Packs is soft or weak or something, which prevents him from making firm decisions. For instance, he wrote me that the disaster to the *K*'s had had a very shaking effect on the officers & men in the other submarines, and suggested that they should all be given leave!! They want to be hardened, not softened, so I have sent one lot to sea and another shall follow at the earliest opportunity. Lack of sea experience is the cause of most of the disasters, and that I will correct.

* * *

Yes, I sent the 2nd Battle Squadron and 1st Battle Cruiser Squadron with the 4th Light Cruiser Squadron out for a special operation which was quite successful, and they will be back before you get this, *Deus Volens*.

I don't think I ever read such childish twaddle as that let loose by Jellicoe, in which he gives himself away painfully. Why will those who can't talk always give themselves away? It would appear that he was now endeavouring to curry favour with that old arch-ruffian Jacky Fisher!!

Now that Germany has made peace on her Eastern Front she will have a large number of troops available to reinforce her Western or Italian Fronts; ditto the Austrians. So we may expect some anxious weeks and months in front of us, and the end of the contest seems further off than ever. I never have believed that military achievement will bring the war to an end. It is a question now as to which can stand a war of exhaustion best, and there is no reason why that should last for many weary years yet. [*sic*] If we had twice the number of men on the Western Front we could never achieve such a military success as would bring the war to an end. It must depend upon what economic support the enemy can obtain from Russia, and that is a very doubtful question. If we are hard and firm we shall pull through, but not unless we are.

It is an interesting phase and we must see what will be forthcoming. Unless they achieve victories or improve their economic condition, and the former I have no doubt they will fail in, while the latter possibility is extremely doubtful, but unless they do one or the other, then I think there is a probability that they will crumple [?] up much more than we think at present is possible.

259. *To Wemyss*

[BTY/13/39/8]   *Queen Elizabeth*
[Copy]   13th February 1918

I have had long conversations with Carpenter and Chichester.[1] The latter left this morning and will be followed to-morrow by 5 Marine officers and 150 marines. He tells me that it will require a month's extensive training to fit them for the job – hence the haste.

As regards Carpenter, and his requirements, I have 200 Seamen including a complement of P. O.s and Leading Seamen, and 8 officers, making four units of 2 officers, 2 P. O.s, 2 Leading Seamen and 46 Seamen in each ready to go when and where required.

I will make arrangements to have 200 Stoker ratings including some P. O.s and E. R. A.s also ready to go when required.

Carpenter was unable to give me detailed information as to the scheme. From the general outline and the information he provided I would say that the operation is a practicable one, but to achieve success – and failure cannot be thought of – it is absolutely essential that the scheme should be worked out in the most minute detail, examined and re-examined. Those taking part must be exercised and practised until all possibility of mistake is eliminated. I should like to receive a copy of the final scheme in detail when it has been completed.

Carpenter informs me that it is proposed to carry out the operation between the 15th and 19th March. This does not seem possible in view of the absence, at the present time, of a detailed plan.

The impression I have is that there is a tendency to sketchiness.

[1]Officers detailed to get Beatty's help in the Zeebrugge operation. A. F. B. Carpenter (1881–1955), later to become Vice-Admiral, was Captain of *Vindictive* designated to put landing force on the mole; after the action he was awarded VC by ballot. Colonel Chichester Russell is mentioned by Wemyss in BTY13/39/6 of 6 February [not printed] as designated to command the Marine force.

Experience on the Western Front has shewn that all successes have been due to the most careful staff work and the most thorough training. Failures have been due to lack of preparation both in staff work and training.

Before I commit my gallant officers and men to a venture of the nature contemplated, I would like to be assured that no failure can be anticipated from either of these two factors. You will realise that the surrender of these picked officers and men involves some sacrifice of efficiency in the Fleet.

As regards the mining propositions for the Bight, I hope my telegram made the matter clear to you. I in no way wished to walk back on what I had previously agreed or the policy I had advocated.

I concur in the minefield proposed and it should be useful against enemy's submarines and surface vessels if the dummy minefield is discovered and deflects the latter over them. Otherwise I doubt whether surface vessels would proceed so far to the Westward, towards mine area I, before striking North or South of the proposed minefields.

As position R on Regent seems to be accurately fixed, there appears to be no obstacle in the way of enemy vessels passing out by that route to the North Dogger Bank Light Vessel – hence my suggestion to lay a minefield in the vicinity of that point.

260.   *To his wife* [Aberdour House]

Grand Fleet
[BTY/17/48/31–35]   Monday [18 February 1918]

*   *   *

I liked old Froude's[1] description of Ryan, which is almost identical with the description I gave of him to the 1st Sea Lord and 1st Lord (Jellicoe & Geddes) when I urged them to make more use of him, and not allow him to be hampered by others at the Admiralty and *Vernon*,[2] who were jealous of him. . . . I have had so many axes to sharpen, so many battles to fight and so many difficulties to overcome that I have not had the time or the oppor-

---

[1]See 263 below, which identifies Froude as the son of the Historian J. A. Froude (1818–1894). There were, however, two other Froudes one of whom (R. E.) had continued the experimental work on hull design begun by his father (William) and who, as Superintendent of the Admiralty Experimental Works at Haslar (1879–1919) carried out work on submarine hull design 1902–1914.

[2]*Vernon*: torpedo and mine establishment at Portsmouth.

tunity to ram home all my arguments. But you can rest assured that I realise as much as you do his good qualities, and the fact that enough use is not being made of them. There are others also who have many gifts and qualities which are not being made full use of, and I am continually in disagreement with the Admiralty at the way they disregard and make little use of the brains of those who could achieve much. I have made but little progress, but have some [?] and my very limited time prevents me from pursuing the questions as actively as I should like. But we are all human and only capable of a certain amount of work.

Yes, I like hearing what everybody says, not only Flag Officers, but I do prefer constructive criticism instead of destructive criticism. The latter is very easy to obtain, the former very difficult. If your young friends when they condemn everything wholesale would only provide me or you with some valuable suggestions as to how to improve matters, I should be eternally grateful. You must remember that destructive criticism carries with it no responsibility, whereas constructive criticism does. My one great difficulty is to get the younger officers to voice their views and ideas, and I think I can truthfully say that I have done my best to encourage it, and to make use of it. I have started them writing essays on every sort of subject. I have given prizes for the best and everybody in the Fleet knows quite well that if they send anything it will receive sympathetic treatment. I have received much, but not enough, and amazingly little of any real value. I don't tell them that, but ask them to try again. The result is that I have a very poor opinion of the brains, if any, old or young. I am always being told young so and so is so clever, and can do this and that. And I catch hold of them and try and get something out, but the bubble always bursts, and I generally find they have earned their reputation by having a caustic tongue and a gift of criticising all that is done, and being tried [sic] destructively, they can knock down, but they can't build up again. The old gentlemen can't either, but they have learnt a little wisdom and do not indulge so freely in denouncing [?] everything and everybody.

I see in the telegrams that Robertson has succumbed to the Press and Downing Street intrigue. God knows where we shall all end. It will be a race now which they get rid of first, Haig or myself.

*   *   *

261. *From Wemyss*

[BTY/13/39/10]   Admiralty
                                           Feb 20th [1918]

The incident of the other night when we thought that an enemy
Battle Squadron might be going to make a dash on the northern
convoy, has set me thinking. And, under the full understanding
that you know a great deal more of the situation than I do, and
that you are in a much better position to form a correct judgement
of the possibilities than I am, I venture to give you my thoughts
on paper.

The routes and dates of sailing of this convoy can, within certain
limits, be estimated by the enemy with a fair approach to accuracy.
We may also assume the possibility that the enemy has become
aware of the fact that the strength of the covering force is pretty
uniform, *viz*, a light cruiser squadron with either a division of the
battle fleet or a battle-cruiser squadron; and when the escorting
force consists of the 12″ *Dreadnought*s, or of the 2nd Battle-
Cruiser Squadron its strength is insufficient to meet the whole of
the enemy's battle-cruiser force.

If we do receive information tending to make us anticipate that
the enemy proposes to raid a convoy with heavy ships, it is easy
for us to send out the whole of our battle-cruiser force, or even
the whole of the Grand Fleet. If we do *not* receive such information we cannot rely on securing the safety of the convoy, as
the enemy would be as likely as not to send out all his battle
cruisers or a battle squadron. I would therefore ask you to take
into account whether the use of a battle division or of a battle-
cruiser squadron as a matter of routine, is altogether advisable.
Whether the strength of the supporting force should not be
raised — taking of course into consideration such intelligence as
the Admiralty are able to provide you with, and whether indeed,
on occasions, no heavy forces should be sent out.

I hope my rather feeble English is sufficient to give you an idea
of the drift of my thought. I hope Fremantle may be coming up
to you very shortly, when perhaps you could talk the matter over
with him.

Absence of First Lord gives me a bit more work, so I am pretty
busy, but I am not over-burdened.

London much agitated all this last week by the Lloyd George-

Versailles row.[1] The fall of the former was even confidently predicted by many, but they just [?] have wriggled out of the tight place into which their foolishness and bad methods of conducting business placed them. Old Robertson has behaved like the single minded brick that he is.

What about coming to Rosyth 1st week in March when I could come up & meet you?

262. *To Wemyss*

[BTY/13/39/11]   Grand Fleet
[Incomplete draft] [Holograph]   [22] February 1918

And I state emphatically that if Captain Ryan's talents were fully utilised their value to the State would be incalculable.[2] To this end I make to you the following suggestions.

(1) He should remain the head of the Hydrophone service which he has created but should be entirely relieved of all routine work conncected with it.

(2) He should be consulted and kept fully informed on all matters connected with new developments of Hydrophones found in enemy submarines.

(3) He should be allowed to work in his own way and given such facilities as he asks for. These will not be found to be excessive or unreasonable.

(4) If he makes a definite recommendation it should be adopted if possible and not referred for the opinion of others who know less about the subject than he has forgotten.

I have just heard that the B.I.R. are now exerting themselves to interfere with the fitting of hydrophones in submarines, making suggestions and advocating changes without any reference to Captain Ryan. As he was responsible for the initiation of these listening appliances in S.M.s and has hitherto always dealt with all matters relating to them, it is rather astounding that the B.I.R. Committee should have dealt with the matter without any refer-

[1]Over Lloyd George's proposal to establish a committee to control the allocation of Allied army reserves in France; seen by Robertson, CIGS and Haig as derogatory to their authority.
[2]For Ryan's achievements see note 1 on page 390.

ence to him. It provides a good example of the methods which deal with the general hydrophone question & indicate the overlapping & duplication of work that exists, and matters of vital importance get thrown into a chaotic state.

Many instances have occurred in the past where the opinions of Captain Ryan have been at variance with those of the B.I.R. as regards the suitability of scientific apparatus under *seagoing conditions*, in which subsequent experience has shown Ryan to have been right and the B.I.R. to be wrong.

I would most strongly urge that Hawkcraig should be officially recognised as the experimental station and training school for S. M.s under Commodore (S). The establishment is fully capable of undertaking the work as Ryan himself has a full knowledge of the various systems involved and has experimented with them at Hawkcraig.

I am quite sure that the Commodore (S) has no wish that his existing arrangements should be interfered with.

I have given you a devil of a dosing [?] over a subsidiary question, but it is important that we should advance and not have the wheels clogged by the continual differences of opinion of technical experts. So, read it and turn it over to your D.A.S.D. who deals with that department. He has an immense asset in Ryan if he would only use him in the right way.

The most reliable test of the work he has done is a comparison of the practical results obtained by his instruments and systems with those of other scientific advisers.

I hope to see you in the course of the next week or ten days after conversations with your D.C.N.S.

263.   *To Wemyss*

[BTY/13/39/11]   *Queen Elizabeth*
[Office Copy]   22 February, 1918

I note with some surprise and concern that in the Report of the Experimental Work of the Anti-Submarine Division for December it is stated that no mention is made of the work down at Hawkcraig 'because it is not connected with anti-submarine work'. Now, on page 3 of the Anti-submarine Report for November it states definitely that 'Up to the present the only apparatus which can be applied practically to the detection of submarines has been the hydrophone'.

Now, the introduction of the hydrophone as an anti-submarine device was first originated by Ryan in October or November, 1914. After overcoming an immense amount of opposition, it was gradually recognised as a valuable asset and addition to harbour defences. The opposition with which it was received, however, delayed its general adoption for over a year. The principal original obstructions were, I am right in saying, the *Vernon* and the technical experts at the Admiralty. How the hydrophone has developed since is a matter of common knowledge – improved, built up and expanded by Ryan, who has trained practically all the hydrophone observers serving at the present time.

Ryan then produced the hydrophone for fitting in submarines, again meeting with the greatest opposition; and it was not until an enemy submarine was salved off Havre and found to be fitted with a type of microphone very inferior to Ryan's that it was considered there was anything of value in the idea, although Ryan had demonstrated its value over and over again. Even then it was obstructed by Commodore (S) to such an extent that it was not until last year, 1917, after a furious interchange of telegrams, that we were able to get our submarines fitted.

Again, Ryan produced in 1916 a device for equipping a mine with a microphone attachment. This was actually at the Admiralty for a matter of months before anything was done – sat on by somebody – and it was not until April, 1917, when I called the attention of the First Sea Lord (Jellicoe) to its value, that anything was done. Then every sort of trouble ensued, every sort of mine was produced by various artists, trials long and wearisome took place, and everybody was ready to cut everybody else's throat, till eventually, after more delays extending over months, they came back to Ryan's mine grudgingly and hesitatingly.

What are the deductions to be drawn from this? — That jealousy and rancour are clogging the wheels of efficiency and development, and there is not the 'pull together' which alone will help us to win the War.

I attach an analysis of Ryan, which has come into my hand, made by an elderly gentleman, Ashey A. Froude, who has been connected with him for three years. He is a son of the historian Froude, and is exceptionally shrewd and observant, broad in his knowledge of human nature, and, having been associated with many men of high intellectual attainments, is well able to make an accurate estimate in this case. His estimate is one with which I entirely agree; indeed, it is almost identical with what I told Jellicoe of his gifts and capabilities.

264. *From Wemyss*

[BTY/13/39/14]

Admiralty
26th March, 1918

The general situation is anxious, but in my judgment not as bad as may be judged from general information. There is no doubt that we are having a bad time on the Western Front, but I gather that the position there is by no means lost or even irretrievable.[1]

To go into the military state of affairs would take too much detail and too long.

The disquieting part to me appears to be the fact that our military intelligence is unable to form a correct opinion of the numbers of the enemy's reserves. The War Office assure me that they do not think an attack in the Northern sector likely, but if I am correct in thinking that their estimate of numbers is wrong, they may be also wrong in this direction.

This leads one straight to the question of naval co-operation on the enemy's part, and the question which I have always had in my mind therefore immediately arises — Are we close to a raid on the Channel?

Our mining policy has been, I believe, more successful even than we expected it to be. There are signs that the enemy is thoroughly disgruntled inside the Bight, and is not quite sure how or when he can get out. This, of course, is all to our good, but at the same time we know that it is possible for him to get out so far as mining is concerned, and that there is nothing to stop him getting into the Straits.

We are, therefore, seriously contemplating bringing the Fleet down to Rosyth. At the moment of this letter leaving we have not decided to do so, since there does not appear to be an actual immediate necessity for such a step, but I do think that it may arise at any moment.

I am reinforced in my idea of there being no immediate

---

[1] See note 1 on page 517.

necessity for the Grand Fleet to come South by the fact that three of the enemy's *Dreadnoughts* are still in the Baltic.

We have also to contemplate the possibility of the enemy succeeding in cutting through our lines. If he does do this and our counter attacks are not successful, it will probably result in our swinging our right flank back and holding the Northern Coast of France. The soldiers are of opinion that this can be done.

If we succeeded in getting into such a position, the situation from a naval point of view should not be materially changed, but the enemy may think that it will be and may be induced to try more active measures afloat.

What the action of the enemy in France could be it is, of course, impossible to tell. The situation would be, I suppose, that he would get to Paris and would be between us on the North and the French armies on the South — not a very pleasant situation for him, I should think.

At a meeting of the Cabinet this morning, although no actual decision as to our armies holding the Northern Coast with their backs to the sea was arrived at, I do not think they will decide otherwise when the time comes to take the decision.

I pointed out to them as simply as I could the absolute necessity of their so doing from a naval point of view, and, as it coincided with the military point of view, I think there is no doubt that that will be the policy which will be adopted if the situation so arises.

I am putting this all before you as simply as possible in order that you may know our ideas on the situation, and I hope that it may be of assistance to you.

Very many thanks for your letter of the 24th.

With regard to Richmond's[1] appointment, I am very well aware of his good qualities and also of his drawbacks, and it is the latter which have made me up to now hesitate in having him here. I am in entire agreement with Evan-Thomas, Napier, Goodenough,

[1] Later Admiral Sir Herbert Richmond (1871–1946): Captain of battleship *Conqueror* in Grand Fleet; entered RN 1885; Director of Training and Staff Duties, a new division of Naval Staff, April 1918; his views were thought too controversial and he was posted to battleship *Erin* 1919; Rear-Admiral and President of re-established Naval War College 1920; CinC East Indies 1923; Vice-Admiral 1925; first Commandant of Imperial Defence College 1926; Admiral 1929; retired at his own request, having been formally reprimanded for expressing his unorthodox opinions, 1931; Professor of Imperial and Naval History, Cambridge 1933; Master of Downing College, Cambridge, 1935; the most stringent critic of Admiralty policy of the era and a distinguished naval historian; his most notable book is *Statesmen and Sea Power* (Oxford, 1946); his papers are in the NMM. See also Arthur Marder, *Portrait of an Admiral* (London, 1952).

Sinclair, Bentinck and Brand on the subject of his disqualifications as regards education; and as I know something about it and have strong opinions myself, I shall be on the look out and shall not let him run off the rails. This will be all the easier as I intend him to work directly under me. Now that I have withdrawn all opposition and got him here, I realise that there are many things in which he will be of the greatest value in helping us.

I have just returned from a visit to Queenstown, where I have been discussing that damnable Irish Sea situation with Bayly.[1]

I think that all steps that are possible will be taken to ameliorate the situation there; but it is an infernal place, because of the ability of the submarines to lie on the bottom and frustrate all our bloodhounds.

We are going through some rather difficult times just at present owing to the difficulties of the situation caused by the D.N.O. question. I very fully realise the confidence of everybody that Dreyer possesses, and I most sincerely hope that we shall be able to come to some satisfactory solution of what is an extremely difficult problem.[2]

Directly you come South I shall certainly arrange a meeting with you. I find that these talks are of the greatest assistance and help one very much.

It is difficult to believe that the war can go on at this pace, and if the enemy does not bring off a brilliant success on the Western Front now, I hope and really believe that he will fall down exhausted.

What the naval situation would be under such circumstances is difficult to imagine.

All good luck to you.

[1] Admiral Sir Lewis Bayly; commanding ASW operations in Western Approaches; see note 1 on page 57.
[2] Later Admiral Sir Frederick Dreyer (1878–1956): entered RN 1891; outstanding performance both on *Britannia* and sub-Lieutenants' courses; gunnery specialist; in DNO's department co-operated with A. H. Pollen in an aim-corrector device 1907; Flag Commander to CinC Atlantic (Jellicoe); Captain 1913; Flag Captain to Jellicoe 1915; DNO 1916; in June 1918 appointed to new post of Director of Naval Artillery and Torpedoes, acting as chief weapons adviser to Naval Staff; the DNO was in future to concentrate on supply. For his contribution to gunnery improvements and their relation to Pollen's achievements; see note 1 on page 241.

265. *From Wemyss*

[BTY/13/39/15]

Admiralty
30th March, 1918

It has been decided to do away with the ships which are at present in the mouth of the Thames, since it is unanimously agreed that they can be of no possible use and are merely locking up men.

At the same time, you know my ideas on the subject and how anxious I am, if possible, to have a sufficient force there. By 'sufficient' I mean 4 *Dreadnought*s, and I ask you most earnestly to take into consideration the possibility of releasing 3 of the *Superb*s to join the *Dreadnought* and form a squadron there. As explained to you before, however, I would not think of pressing you to reduce your own force to anything smaller than you think is absolutely necessary.

It is, of course, a great disappointment that the Americans are not coming along quickly enough. Do you think that, when they have arrived at a certain state of efficiency, it would be a good thing to get over four more and train them in the same way that you have trained this squadron.

I am sure you will understand my anxiety about the force in the Thames. There are so many possible circumstances in which a mobile force would be of such enormous value.

I am going to keep the *Dreadnought* in commission but pay off the other two ships, and in the meantime will keep the *Dreadnought* where she is until I hear from you, when, if you find you cannot release three *Superb*s, I will send her up to join you, if you wish.

I had a regular stand-up fight against the politicians and the army at the War Cabinet yesterday. You will hardly believe it, but they actually suggested — nay, almost demanded — that the ships of the Grand Fleet should be reduced in the number of Marines, in order to strengthen some of the battalions abroad.

I flatly refused to countenance any such suggestion, and I think they were rather surprised, and even hurt, at the non-possumus position which I took up. The soldiers actually put on a sort of aggrieved air as though we were not playing the game!

However, after the Cabinet I got Wilson[1] to come over and see

---

[1] Sir Henry Wilson, CIGS.

me and we talked the matter out quietly, and I believe that I made him see reason and that we shall have no more attacks from the soldiers; though with the politicians and their ignorance of affairs naval and their short-sightedness as to events of the future, one can never tell what they may do.

Geddes is perfectly straight and allright on the subject and will back me up to the last. On this question, however, I do not require backing up, because it is a subject on which I will hear nothing more; and should they — which, of course, they cannot — insist on it, they will have to do without me.

It is difficult ramming into the heads of ignorant people the knowledge which to us is A.B.C. and has been sucked in with one's mother's milk, so to speak.

To-day as I write, matters seem to be less bad than they were, though naturally the position is very critical. Should the Germans get to Amiens, or even into such a position as to be able to shell it, our position will be very uncomfortable, since it is, as you know, the centre of a vast railway organisation.

As I told you before, the military intelligence do not seem to know what reserves the Germans have; and it is that which makes me somewhat uncomfortable.

If we defeat them heavily now, which does not seem impossible, I do not see that it will be otherwise than sitting opposite each other again for some months, with always the possibility of a big attack elsewhere if we have miscalculated their reserves.

The general idea is that the enemy hoped to be making his last attack, and that his internal position would not allow of his going on, and I think there might have been something in this had we been able to hold him in our battle position; but they have made so great an advance, that I am afraid it may have the effect of bucking up his people, thereby enabling him to go on with the war in the hope, perhaps, of knocking out Italy later on.

All there is, however, merely speculative, because there is only one thing that is certain, and that is that we do not know enough of his internal condition.

In the meantime our policy in the Bight seems to be fairly successful and to be doing what we wanted to do.

The enemy seems fairly rattled here. The bag has been decidedly good. Have just sent you off a wire re. the 3rd Battle Squadron, also one proposing send Fisher to you [sic] to consult about anti-submarine measures in North Sea.

[This last paragraph a hand written addition to typed letter]

266.   *To Wemyss*

[BTY/13/39/16]   *Queen Elizabeth*
[Copy]   1.4.18

Yours of the 30th re forming a Squadron of 4 battleships to be stationed at the mouth of the Thames. I cannot see my way to altering my views on the subject of reducing the Grand Fleet to meet this.

At present we frequently have a Division of battleships, i.e. 4 ships, or squadron of battleships, i.e. 8 ships, in support of convoy.

These cannot be relied upon to make concentration at all times. 4 battleships are continuously undergoing refit.

To deflect 3 to the Thames Squadron would entail the possible reduction of the Grand Fleet by 11 ships on the critical day. A reduction of force which would militate against obtaining decisive results.

A further reduction of our force is to be expected by losses due to mines and submarines intelligently used by the enemy with whom the initiative lies, before we can bring him to action.

The combined reductions might well cause the Grand Fleet to be inferior in numbers of ships capable of lying in the line.

Under these circumstances I am sure you will agree that concentration of force should be aimed at instead of dispersion.

I am not clear as to the object of 4 battleships which are modern and fast being placed in the Swin or mouth of the Thames. Any large operation of the enemy in those restricted waters would be preceded by the mining in of such a force as you require.

Originally it was a political object, but that at this stage must give way to essentials, and could be met by the 2 *King Edward* class you proposed to place there.

For the defence of the narrow waters reliance must be placed generally on minelaying and submarines. If at any time it was considered that the danger from enemy heavy vessels was very great, the Grand Fleet as a whole must be brought to Rosyth and if circumstances permitted at the time, consideration might be given to the stationing of a strong advanced force at the Humber.

But even this I would not advocate at present on account of the practical difficulty of concentrating which would result.

I shall be glad to see Fisher and discuss the anti S.M. measures. This deep mine field is a source of considerable anxiety.

Before I agreed to the d–d thing going down they assured me

THE BEATTY PAPERS

it would be perfectly safe for heavy draught vessels to pass over it. After recent experience this seems more than doubtful.

The navigational difficulties of making this place are sufficiently great after 3 or 4 days in the North Sea in a fog without adding to them.

For instance John de Robeck under just these circumstances was out 20 miles in his D.R. last night and passed over the Eastern end of the line laid. Mercifully he struck nothing or his P. V.s saved him.

The original advantage of this place was that directly you were clear of the Pentland Skerries you could steer any course between Coppinsay and Kinnaird Head.

The enemy curtailed it in the South with the Moray Firth minefield and now we have curtailed it in the North producing a situation somewhat similar to the much abused funnel at the Firth of Forth.

I hope to come Rosyth [sic] in the course of this next fortnight, when I hope to have the opportunity of another talk. If you cannot come up I will come down, but feel that we ought to meet.

Heligoland Bight mining policy is bearing fruit, which is a good thing. We must keep it up, and in the Skaggerack and many other places.

[Last 2 paragraphs a handwritten addition]

267.   *To his wife* [Aberdour House]

Grand Fleet
7.4.18

All news is good in that we are holding our own and making the Hun pay heavily. If he can keep up his attacks and we can continue to take toll of him at the present rate, without further loss of our positions, we can hardly ask for anything better. From all accounts his losses have been terrific and can hardly be exaggerated.

We get news through private letters from brothers and relations of our fellows at the Front and they all say the same. So if it only continues, German morale will break and our turn will come. . . .

It seems to me there are two possibilities. If he succeeds in breaking through and forces the British to wheel back for the defence of our Channel Ports, it may be well worth his while to have a combined naval and military offensive on them, using his ships to destroy our communications across the Channel, even at the risk of being intercepted. If he fails, and fails badly, in sheer desperation he may be tempted to try a last *coup* against the British coast. It really does look as if he were determined to force an issue one way or another.[1]

The internal situation of Germany is really an unknown quality and, if it is as bad as the most optimistic state it to be, then he must achieve a great success on the Western Front, or against us, or be discredited. We must always remember that he is ruled by a great military party who count risks and losses as nothing, who may make the same mistake as Napoleon did, and gamble upon obtaining a naval victory.

With such in my mind one cannot afford to run the shadow of a risk, as an indecisive action on the sea with the main fleets, would amount to a German victory. Therefore, at all costs we must aim at annihilation. To obtain this is indeed a difficult problem. The North Sea is so small and the spread of ships so great, that in a few hours the beggars can retire behind minefields and submarine screens in their own waters. I often wonder what Nelson would have thought of it. His high spirit would have chafed him to death by this time.

*   *   *

268. *To Wemyss*

[BTY/13/39/22]   *Queen Elizabeth*
[Draft]   31/5/18

Thank you for your telegram and your letter. I am relieved to hear that you are not contemplating a return to inspectorship of target practice.

I never thought for a moment that you ever had any idea of Admiralty officials interfering with the gunnery training of the Grand Fleet.

---

[1]During March–June 1918 Germany launched her final offensive; this was repulsed with great losses on both sides; German reserves were exhausted and their retreat began in July; a succinct account is given in Llewellyn Woodward, *Britain and the War of 1914–18* (London, 1967), pp 379–96.

I quite sympathise with your natural desire to be acquainted with gunnery progress, whether officially or unofficially, and am prepared to keep you fully informed in all respects as to our progress and endeavours etc.

The return you called for, as I stated in my previous letter contains no information of any real value.

I am not quite clear as to what a Gunnery Division on the War Staff is going to do for you. Gunnery problems are so very complex and technical nowadays, that unless one is in constant touch one gets out of step. For instance the problems today are quite different to what they were when Dreyer was Flag Captain to late C-in-C, and I am quite sure that even he is not up to date in the questions under trial and consideration in the Fleet today.

I do not like the idea of creating a Director of Gunnery, that is a very high sounding title, and if it is not entirely a misnomer, he is going to be a very important person, governing all questions relating to gunnery i.e. training and personnel now dealt with by *Excellent*, material now dealt with by D.N.O. and usage of Artillery or practical work which deals with all Fleet Gunnery problems now dealt with by C-in-C G. F.

In fact I am the Director of Gunnery of the Grand Fleet and will surely clash with any gentleman appointed as Director of Gunnery at the Admiralty, where there is no practical gunnery and where they cannot be up to date in gunnery problems which can only be worked out in the Fleet at sea. The C-in-C must be and is responsible for the efficiency of the Grand Fleet and could not possibly consider interference. If he fails clear him out; or if it is thought possible he might fail it would indicate that the right man has not been selected for the job. The same applies to the outlying Fleets!! If there is any reason to be disatisfied with their efficiency the only remedy in war time is to change the C-in-C, but in war time you must trust the man in charge.

As this step you have in contemplation is a very important one and may have far reaching effects I think it would be as well if we could have a talk about it before you do anything.

Apparently it has got about in the Fleet and is causing considerable comment which does not conduce to the smooth working of the big machine which has during the last 18 months worked wonderfully smoothly, although many changes and innovations have been introduced: and I need not say, that I am sure the last thing you would dream of, would be doing anything that would interfere with the smooth progress that is being made with the multitudinous gunnery problems we have in hand.

I am very sorry to hear you are contemplating relieving Dreyer from his most important duties as D.N.O. You may remember that I renounced any idea of taking him in *Warspite* so that he should *not be* disturbed in continuing his very considerable service in the position of D.N.O. We have suffered so much in the past from the fact that the office of D.N.O. was not adequately filled that I dread any changes there. Our position at sea would be very different today if we had had a real No. 1 man as D.N.O. since the beginning of the war.

Today is the anniversary of the saddest day in my life and I speak and write with considerable feeling and definitely state that if the battle-cruisers on 31st May '16 had been provided with the shell which were capable of doing what was expected of them the result would have been vastly different and the whole course of the war would have been changed and improved.

Is it therefore unreasonable that I should view any changes in that important office with misgiving and more especially when Dreyer is going to be employed in an appointment which might reasonably be occupied by a Gunnery Commander i.e. to keep you conversant with gunnery progress!

Indeed a Commander (G), except to advise the Naval Staff, is unnecessary, because I as the Director of Gunnery of the Grand Fleet can give you all the information you require.

[This paragraph deleted in original]

Indeed except to advise Naval Staff [*sic*] he would only be an interpreter to you of the information which I, as the Director of Gunnery of the G. F., will keep you provided [*sic*] as you require.

[This paragraph a hand written addition.]

269. *From Wemyss*

[BTY/13/39/23]

Admiralty
3rd June, 1918

I have just returned from Paris, where I have been tussling with various elements who do not seem to have any ideas beyond that line which runs from the North Sea to Switzerland — a line which unfortunately does not seem too strong at the present moment. C.I.G.S. is the man whom it appears to be most difficult to get to see more than three or four days ahead. Haig and Foch are both much more perspicuous, and we shall I believe get our naval way, unless they leave matters too long and are forced into other ways by the enemy.

I did not return with any very great feelings of confidence, and I must confess that I think the situation is grave, though I believe that we have got over graver ones before now. Still, the enemy is very unpleasantly close to Paris.

I also was under the impression that I had come away from Paris with the Mediterranean question settled entirely to our satisfaction; but on my return I received a telegram from the First Lord, who had remained behind, to say that after all our Italian friends had 'ratted'. What that actually means I do not know, but at any rate further difficulties have been deliberately placed in our way.

On my return I received your letter on the subject of gunnery. The question is, of course, still in embryo, and I hope before it materialises further to have conversations with you on the subject. Under any circumstances I will write to you to-morrow or the next day to give you further details; but of one thing you may rest assured, and that is that there will be no interference with the gunnery policy or gunnery training of the Grand Fleet or of the Harwich and Dover Forces. With these there is no question and no difficulty, but there are great difficulties with regard to the squadrons abroad, and I cannot, I am sorry to say, think that the situations there are entirely satisfactory. Whilst you are going ahead by leaps and bounds, I have every reason to believe that the others are deteriorating, and to take the step that you suggest, namely, to relieve the various Commanders-in-Chief, is quite impracticable.

With regard to the Director of Gunnery, or whatever his designation may be, I cannot agree with you that a Gunnery Commander would sufficiently fill the bill. The fact of the matter is that I have not sufficient technical gunnery knowledge or experience to feel myself in touch with the whole question, and even were the man who sits in my chair a greater technical expert than myself, from the force of circumstances I feel pretty well persuaded that he should have more up-to-date knowledge than a man of his years and seniority can be expected to be in possession of.

As a matter of fact the D.N.O., as such, has not the proper status for giving that advice which it appears to me it is essential that the Naval Staff should have. In Dreyer, of course, we have a most exceptional man, and my object is to make use of his exceptional abilities to a greater extent than is now done to relieve him from certain of the less important work now done by the D.N.O., and to keep the whole thing under his eye.

I feel sure that this is the right line to pursue so long as we do not make a mess of the distribution of duties, and this will be studied most carefully before anything is done.

The way in which routine work and pure drudgery has increased in all these materiel departments is beyond the conception of any person who has not actually had experience of it. The output of material [sic] has so vastly increased, the difficulties of co-ordination of work in the various materiel [sic] branches has grown so much as to make the question one of ever increasing difficulty to deal with; and organisation and re-distrubution of work seem to be the only solution of the case.

I can perfectly well understand your anxieties on the subject and most thoroughly do I sympathise with you, especially when I take into consideration the date on which your letter was written; and it is because I realise and sympathise that I am struggling to get the matter on a more firm foundation.

The fact of your renouncing Dreyer in the Grand Fleet gave me to think furiously, and no doubt led my thoughts into the way of trying to make the best possible use of his exceptional qualities. If I can be assured, as I think I shall be able to be, that the good that he has done, and is doing, as D.N.O. will not suffer, and that the time which has hitherto been given by him to certain details can be taken over by other men and devoted to more important work, the proposal cannot but be a good one.

I know you will agree that the establishment of a proper staff at the Admiralty has done nothing but good and is in fact the only way in which we can get along, but the very fact of its establishment teaches us as we go along how the distribution of work can be bettered and carries with it inevitable changes. I have learnt more in this direction during the last six months than I would have thought possible. *Experientia docet.*

You with your experience of the Grand Fleet have arrived at the conclusion that you and your officers are the only people who can satisfactorily and properly develop their gunnery. In this I fully concur. I, with my gradually increasing experience of the Admiralty, believe that the steps which I am proposing are the ones which will get the best results and the closest liaison (which

I know you agree with me is so necessary) between the Admiralty
and the Sea Service.

270. *From Rear-Admiral Phillimore* (Admiral
Commanding Aircraft)

[BTY/13/30/1]   *Furious*[1]
[Holograph]   22 June 1918

I understand that the Lieutenant who was taken in the seaplane
couldn't speak much English and that therefore the two pilots
from this ship who were also on board the *Valentine*[2] didn't get
very much out of him.

He didn't know how the athletic sports at Sylt would get on
without him as he was organising them, & he wanted his mother
to know he was safe — as he is the only son left. He'd only been
relieved from patrol at 1 a.m. & was sent out again when the two
machines who sighted us first returned, & reported they had been
chased by land machines. Two of *Furious*'s pilots attacked one of
them, but only, it appears, shot off one man's finger. On the other
hand the Hun shot away a control wire from the Lewis gun from
one of ours, the pilot being a 'star-turn' D.S.C. man from the
Western front.

The first pair carried small bombs & were only patrolling, the
next lot were sent out with orders to bomb the ship.

The seaplane was a fine-looking machine & I should have liked
to have brought her in, but only *Furious* could have done so.

The captured pilot had photographed *Furious* but destroyed his
plates before they got him.

This ship's anti-aircraft fire was very bad the first time, but
improved afterwards. Now she has one of *Royal Oak*'s 3″ mounted
right aft, she will be less vulnerable. Nicholson is mounting a
Lewis gun forward and drawing some more from the R.A.F. as
they'll go for this ship in future.

Heath, the youngster who brought down the seaplane was only
taken out from Turnhouse to complete the number of pilots,

---

[1]*Furious*: light battle-cruiser converted to aircraft carrier 1917; attacked by two
enemy seaplanes which she repulsed, shooting down one, June 1918; her Sopwith
Camels attacked Zeppelin sheds at Tondern on 19 July 1918.
[2]*Valentine*: a destroyer flotilla leader.

as the 'bombing flight' were left behind. (He entered as a boy domestic.)

I am afraid people are beginning to talk about the next operation, but am on the track of one officer & if I can get evidence, I will bring him forward for a Court Martial. Of course the bombing practice excites comment, and as the machines only have a 2¾ to 2½ hours fuel capacity, the choice of objectives is very limited, and Germany cannot be very wide of the mark.

[P.S.]   Groves was here the other day & flew from *Australia*'s turret in a single seater. Certainly the first time that a Captain (or Brigadier-General) has done so.[1]

271.   *To his wife* [Aberdour House]

[BTY/17/52/2–4]

Grand Fleet
2.7.18

I see in the telegrams that London is flooded with the Flu and also in many parts of the country it is rampant. . . . It is a most infernal bug and has laid hold of my staff properly. . . . so we are working rather short handed. It does not last very long but takes it out of them and leaves them limp and reduced.[2]

* * *

The delay in commencing the next attack on the part of the Hun is somewhat difficult to understand. No doubt he gains strength by waiting, but so do we, in much greater proportion. . . .

As to the Navy, that is a closed book and no amount of conjecture will lead you to the right spot. Our only role is to safeguard our weak points and harass him in his own waters all we can, and this we are doing, tempt him if possible, but at a considerable risk. Sooner or later he may make a false move. He has made two and may make a third. In the meantime we must exercise that patience which is so terribly hard and unsatisfactory. But we must remember that the same problem obtained in the old wars. There is a parallel for nearly every case, and they in the end reaped their reward, and so I believe we shall reap ours. But vigilance can't for a moment be relaxed and we must be always

---

[1]Captain Robert M. Groves: Assistant Secretary to the Air Council.
[2]A serious influenza epidemic throughout Britain in 1918–19 killed some 150,000 people.

ready to take advantage of it when the opportunity occurs. The submarine is still a thorn, a very unpleasant one too, but he is not the danger he was, and the country is better off for food today than it has been for 1½ years, and the American troops are pouring in uninterruptedly and in ever growing numbers. So on the whole we have much to be thankful for.

*   *   *

272. *To Wemyss*

[BTY/13/39/33]   *Queen Elizabeth*
[Copy]   10th August 1918

The substance of your letter of 6th August has naturally been the subject of my earnest consideration since the Report appeared in the Newspapers of the changes in the Higher Command of the High Sea Fleet, and at the German Admiralty.[1]

Such changes cannot make any alteration to our view of the naval situation. The danger points which existed previously are still the same and can again be summarised as being:—

1. Atlantic Convoy.
2. North Sea Convoy.
    (a). While crossing the North Sea and in close proximity to Norwegian coast
    (b) While voyaging along the coast between the Thames and the Firth, more especially between Humber and Farn Islands.
3. Attack on Dover Patrol or raid on Channel Ports.
4. Raids on East coast.

What may be expected and anticipated is greater activity, and this will require greater vigilance on our part. To this end I have given orders that all Submarines on the permanent patrols, i.e. T, R, Z48, Z49, Y1 and Y2, i.e. Utsire Light, are to be relieved on patrol

Mining by surface vessels in the vicinity of our main bases must be more seriously considered as the nights get longer. I think at present we have good safeguards in our distant submarine Patrol, our two KS Patrols and the Special Patrol

[1]Scheer succeeded Holtzendorff as Chief of the Naval Staff & Hipper became CinC High Seas Fleet on 11 August 1918.

There is also the possibility that the enemy may display greater enterprise in attempting to bring to action our Light Cruiser Squadrons when on distant sweeps, and also to interfere with our minelaying excursions in the North and their attendant supports.

In the past we baited the trap with forces varying from a battle squadron to a light cruiser squadron, the traps being the convoy. We took considerable risks with our eyes open in the hope of achieving a great success, and as you know, we all but brought it off on the 25th April 1918.

With the laying of the barrage and the convoy passing to the North of it, the same trap does not exist; but the laying of the Barrage itself provides the trap, and the supporting force the bait. You can realise therefore that the strength and composition of the supporting force provides me with plenty of anxious moments. The new German command may deal more actively with the problem, and we have anxious times in front.

Anxiety will, however, be well repaid, if when a chance comes, our Intelligence Department can tell us a little more than last time, and our outposts, i.e. the submarines on patrol, do not again fail us.

Re propaganda. I fully understand the situation and am quite ready to put my own views in the background, and fall in with anything you suggest. I indeed wrote to the Admiralty on the subject of visits of journalists and writers only the other day asking to have the matter put on a more correct basis.

The situation as regards the American mines and Northern barrage is a very serious one: as I understand it the Admiralty allowed the Americans to jump us with their mine and accepted it on their own statements without taking sufficient steps to satisfy themselves as to whether it could or would do all that was claimed for it. That would have been justifiable if they were to be used in mining American waters, but certainly not when they plant the infernal things in our waters, for which the Grand Fleet is responsible.

From the reports of explosions that have been received from every kind of craft a large percentage of them have blown up. The latest fiasco is such that the Americans themselves gave up and went home after laying one line, which apparently blew up as it was laid. The mines that are still remaining are of no value against enemy submarines on the surface and there is no reason for them to dive in those waters. So all we have done is to waste valuable vessels, time and material, in planting the North Sea with stuff which debars us from using it and can do no harm to the enemy. When the winter gales come along they will turn the North Sea into a place in which it will be extremely dangerous to cruise at all.

I was glad to get the paper on the naval defence of the Empire, unfortunately it arrived twenty-four hours after the Dominion representatives had gone away.

The draft on the duties of D.N.A.T. which you sent up puts the matter quite satisfactorily and I thank you for your consideration.

I saw Fisher at Hawkcraig who told me that you had had a satisfactory demonstration. I pray hard that Ryan's Porpoise will prove of value. The failure of the Nash Fish has been very disappointing, and the large forces that have been allocated to developing the hunt with it, during all these fine weather months, might have been more usefully employed: but we live and learn. I am sure you are on the right track if you stick to Ryan's advice, I am a great believer in him.[1]

273.   *From Wemyss*

[BTY/13/39/38]

Admiralty
August 15th, 1918

Many thanks for your letter of the 10th August. I agree with you that the changes in the German Admiralty and in the High Sea Fleet cannot alter our views on the position and of the Naval situation generally.

Von Scheer, when interviewed last year, was made to state that he was a firm believer in the submarine campaign, but he was careful not to prophesy when the submarines were likely to achieve definite results.

With reference to the points you mention:-

(1) *Atlantic Barrage*. It is, of course, always possible that the enemy may think it worth his while to send battleships to assist in the submarine campaign, but the situation would appear to be changing in our favour owing to the exit from the North Sea being restricted by the Northern barrage.

---

[1]Porpoise: experimental directional hydrophone, in production at end of war; in trials Ryan's model was more effective than the one produced by G. H. Nash, a civilian working for General Electric; see Hackmann, *Seek and Strike*, pp. 45–52, 60–2.

It has been reported that two submarines that attempted to cross the mine barrage were damaged. The enemy are, therefore, aware that mines have actually been laid, and that the declaration of the area is not a bluff. It does not seem likely, therefore, that surface craft would attempt to cross it.

The alternatives are to use the passage through Norwegian territorial waters, the navigation of which is admittedly difficult, or to pass within easy reach of our bases with the increased possibility of being brought to action. The chances of intercepting raiders on their return would also appear to be greater than before the barrage was laid.

Taking the above facts, which are well known to the enemy, into consideration, I think that the laying of the Northern Barrage has, to a certain extent, reduced the danger to the Atlantic Convoys.

(2) *North Sea Convoy*. The foregoing remarks on the Northern barrage and its effect on the Atlantic convoy applies also, but to a much greater extent, to the Scandinavian convoy whilst passing between the Orkneys and Norway.

It is, of course, possible that a raid on the convoy, when in the vicinity of the Norwegian Coast, may be attempted by destroyers, but it does not seem to me to be likely that larger ships would be used.

The situation as regards protection of the convoy when coasting between the Thames and the Firth of Forth would also appear to be changing in our favour with the laying of the East Coast Minefields, but I agree with you that a raid of this nature is always a possibility.

(3) *Attack on Dover patrol or raid on Channel ports*. It is supposed that relations between the German Navy and the German Army are strained owing to the failure of the former to seriously interrupt the Channel communications and to prevent the American troops from reaching Europe, and I am not sure but that the recent changes in the German Admiralty reflect this.

That the High Sea Fleet may be forced by the military leaders to attempt a raid on the Channel may well seem to be within the range of possibility, though it is not seen how the enemy can hope for more than a temporary dislocation of our communications.

In connection with this, I have to-day had a long talk with the C.I.G.S. who tells me that in his judgment there is now but little chance, if any, of any attack being made on the North of the Western front, so that if I am right in my supposition that a raid on the Channel would be carried out in conjunction with such an operation there seems little chance of a raid on the Channel at present.

(4) *Raids on the East coast.* The material damage which the enemy can hope for in such a raid is small, and he knows it; but, of course, there is still the chance, as there always has been, of such a raid being carried out with the idea of causing troops to be retained in England. The laying of the East coast minefield, when *extended northwards*, will act as a protection to the munition producing area in the vicinity of the Tyne and Tees.

I agree with you that mining by surface vessels is the most likely form of any greater activity, and unless we can get early information from our submarines, the chance of bringing vessels like the *Brummer* and *Bremse* to action is a very remote one.[1]

I am not inclined to anticipate that the enemy will make an effort to intercept the minelayers working on the Northern barrage, since he will have nothing like the same chance of obtaining information of their movements as he has in the case of the Scandinavian convoys; the speed of the minelayers is much greater, and he will probably imagine that the laying of the fields commenced at the Southern limits and that to reach the minelayers he would have to pass over mines already laid. The question of intelligence was carefully gone into after the events of the 28th April, and though the organisation has been improved in minor respects since then, we must not anticipate that any greater degree of warning can be relied on.

In the past, it has been hoped that any unusual disposition of Zeppelins for reconnaissance would give warning of intended movements, but it was clearly shown on the 28th April that under certain conditions the enemy are prepared to do without reconnaissance by airships.

I sympathise with your feeling about the American mines, but I think it should be remembered that the decision was arrived at at a time when the submarine campaign overshadowed everything, and that drastic measures necessitating the whole-hearted operations of the Americans were required, and this, I believe, it was only possible to obtain by agreeing to the use of their mines.

In spite of all their faults, the American mines have caused the submarines to avoid the notified area and pass through waters

---

[1] *Brumme* and *Bremse*: German mine-laying cruisers which carried out an attack on a Scandinavian convoy on 17 October 1917.

through which our patrols might have dealt effectively with them had the Fish hydrophone done all that we expected of it.

I have not yet given up hope that the Fish hydrophone will eventually kill submarines, since probable cases of success with them have already been reported from the Mediterranean and the Southern Patrol.

I also hope that the 'Porpoise' may come up to expectations, in which case we shall have to find and equip a hunting flotilla of destroyers to work it with.

On the other hand, should the 'Porpoise' not come up to expectations, the question of completing Area 'B' of the Northern barrage with surface and deep minefields will have to be carefully re-considered, as we cannot allow the submarines to pass unmolested out of the North Sea.

Such a step as this would, I know, create some difficulties as regards the convoy, but if Area 'B' were extended so as to reach the coasts of the Orkneys, I do not see why the Westray Channel should not be used.

I am sure you will have been interested to notice the excitement caused in the Bight by the Harwich force and the C.M.B.s.

The German communique puts our force down as 21 ships of the line, and consequently his air reconnaissance must either have been very much at fault, or he has some ulterior motive in wishing it to be believed that we had a strong force present.

I think there is little doubt but that since the Zeebrugge and Ostende operations the enemy have been very nervous of an attack of this description on their coast, and our activity may have led them to believe that something of this kind was being attempted.

I meant to have sent this letter off yesterday but my time has been so occupied with Colonials, War Cabinets, etc. that I could not manage it.

274. *Balfour[1] to Robert Cecil[2]*

[BTY/14/2/3]   22 August 1918
Very Private

Norway And The Mine Barrage

I visited the Commander-in-Chief of the Grand Fleet yesterday, Wednesday 21 August, with no desire to talk politics. But after luncheon the conversation turned on Norway and the anti-submarine barrage; and I found to my surprise a very sharp distinction between the views of the Admiralty and the views of the Commander-in-Chief.

I summarise in this paper the opinions expressed by the latter.

(1) The whole scheme of the barrage is American, and the Admiralty have allowed themselves to be rushed into it without sufficient experimental knowledge.

(2) The minefield marked A in the diagrammatic map consists of mines laid at all depths. It is a proclaimed area, but in the Commander-in-Chief's opinion, if the enemy chose to risk it, they could traverse it with a loss of about one in ten.

(3) The minefield marked B originally consisted only of deep laid mines of American construction. It was supposed to be safe for surface vessels. The idea was to patrol it sedulously: thus either catching the submarines before they dived or forcing them to submerge into the minefield.

(4) As soon as this was laid, the Commander-in-Chief sent a surface vessel into area B. It was promptly blown up and the greater part of the crew were lost. Thereupon the Commander-in-Chief insisted that the whole Area B should be swept. It is now therefore without mines.

(5) If the barrage is to be effective it must evidently be re-mined. But: (a) In the Commander-in-Chief's view it must be mined from top to bottom like Area A, and (b) though it may all

[1]Balfour as Foreign Secretary was concerned about Admiralty pressure to mine Norwegian territorial waters to prevent passage of enemy shipping and submarines; Beatty was ordered to do this but was strongly opposed to it without Norway's consent; Cabinet accepted this and consent was obtained on 29 September; mining was never carried out because of the approach of the end of war.

[2]Lord Robert Cecil, later Viscount Cecil of Chelwood (1864–1958), 3rd son of 3rd Marquess of Salisbury, former Conservative Prime Minister; Minister of Blockade 1916–18; a post-war advocate and founder of the League of Nations. Balfour's mother was the daughter of the 2nd Marquess.

be 'proclaimed', there must *in fact* be a free passage ten miles wide left at its Orkney or Western end.

(6) This is not to let convoys through. These must go through the difficult channel between the islands. The object of the Commander-in-Chief is to have a short and safe passage for his own ships, so as to enable him to cut off any enemy raiders who should force the barrage for the purpose of attacking Norwegian convoys.

(7) When asked whether this ten mile passage could be kept clear of submarines by patrolling, the answer was that it could be made very difficult for them. When asked whether the Norwegians could not do as much for their three mile passage, the answer was that they could if they would, and if they had a sufficient force of destroyers.

(8) The Commander-in-Chief is evidently most anxious not to drive things to an extremity with Norway. His main reasons are:

(a) That, however striking was our show of superior force, an untoward accident might easily occur — a Norwegian destroyer might fire a shot in defence of the integrity of Norwegian waters, she might be sunk, and irreparable injury thus be done to the good relations of two friendly navies and two friendly countries;

(b) The operation of forcibly laying mines within the three mile limit could only be carried out by daylight and in clear weather: it would therefore be provocative on the face of it;

(c) The lead between the islands and the Norwegian coast would of course be left open to merchant ships. But what, in these circumstances, is to prevent the German submarines using it for their own purposes? Are *we* to patrol it, and fight the submarines when we find them? If so, the insult to Norway's independence is flagrant and continuous. On the other hand, it is unreasonable to think that the Norwegians would patrol it, after we had flagrantly forced their hand;

(d) If we violate Norwegian neutrality, Germany will certainly do the same. In that event all the coastwise traffic which now goes round the South of Norway and gets made up into convoys at Bergen would be interrupted. The Commander-in-Chief thought this might prove most serious to our interests.

(9) The general effect of the Commander-in-Chief's talk was to shew that he disliked the whole business, and had the gravest misgivings as to its results. His resolve to keep open an unacknowledged channel ten miles wide at the western end of the barrage was never admitted to us by the Admiralty; but it accounts for

DIAGRAMMATIC MAP

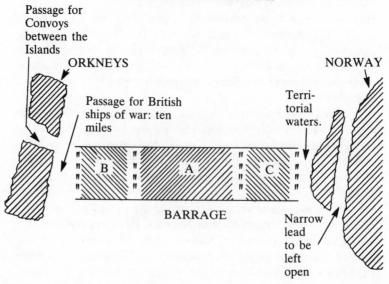

[Handwritten note by Balfour.]

This diagram is an incorrect rendering of what I intended to convey, since [?] the Orkney passage is represented as coming North of the Barrage. But the error is not material to the main argument.

AJB

the ambiguous and hesitating answers which they gave us when we pressed them on the point. In my opinion we shall find ourselves in a most embarrassing position, if and when it is discovered that we have compelled the Norwegians by force to submit to a three mile patrolled channel being mined, on the ground that nothing but mining is effective, while we insist on keeping *un*mined a ten mile patrolled channel at the other end of the barrage!

The Commander-in-Chief begged us not to be precipitate.

I told him in reply that, from a Foreign Office point of view, the whole operation of violating the rights (even if they were but technical rights) of a small and friendly Power was odious: but that the strongly pressed policy of the Admiralty might drive the Government to take this course in the interests not merely of the associated belligerents, but of Neutrals themselves.

275. *From Wemyss*
[Handwritten marginal notes by Beatty are shown in square brackets in the text]

Admiralty
[BTY/13/39/38]   SECRET   August 23rd 1918

My dear Commander-in-Chief,

Your desire to leave a 10 mile passage between the mine barrage and the Orkneys has raised a very serious and critical position between ourselves and the Americans. Admiral Sims holds very strong views on the subject [*So do I and I have to command the sea, not Admiral Sims.], which may be summarised as follows:-

The American Government desire to complete the Northern barrage from land to land, and nothing short of this will satisfy them [*I agree when the rest of the barrage shows that it is of real value.]; their views being that any gate in the barrage, however small, renders it ineffectual. If it is ineffectual, they consider that the whole of their great efforts and large expenditure is thrown away, and Admiral Sims would, under those circumstances, recommend his Government to stop work on the whole business. [*Most of this expenditure has been thrown away already by faulty mines and lack of experimental work.]

Now such a state of affairs will have a very much more disastrous effect on our relations with the United States [*Cannot believe this.] than it would have on the actual material position. It would inevitably lead to the recall of Admiral Sims. [*All this is beside the question.] He has explained to me more than once how intrigues on 'the other side' are going on with the idea of getting him out of this billet. For us to lose Admiral Sims would be a very serious matter. His loyalty and co-operation with us has been extraordinary, and I very much doubt whether any other United States Naval Officer would have achieved the same results as he has. He has suppressed self and a good deal of American *amour propre* to obtain this satisfactory state of affairs and has shown himself to be very broad-minded and thoroughly loyal to the Allies. [*As regards those with the G.F. it is mainly due to Admiral Rodman.] The manner in which the United States Naval Forces cooperate with ours, the way in which their Officers consider themselves part of our forces, are facts which I believe to be mainly due to him, and under such circumstances, you can well imagine with what disquietude I view any possibility of his removal.

The question of the actual efficiency of the mines of the Northern barrage is one upon which there can be, and indeed is, diversity of opinion. Admiral Sims believes them to be more materially efficient than we do. I, on the other hand, believe them to be more morally effective than, probably, you do. If the enemy is going to be hampered in any way by the barrage, I think that the moral side of the question is nearly as important as the material side (especially where surface craft are concerned).

If the barrage is completed, the situation will be that the enemy will have to order his submarines to pass twice over a minefield, however effectual or ineffectual it actually may be, and the moral consequences on the crews of such procedure should not be left out of account when balancing the pros and cons.

One of my chief aims ever since I have been C.N.S. has been to ensure, as far as it is possible for me to do so, that when you go to sea with the Grand Fleet, there shall be no misgivings in your mind as to the general, as apart from the tactical or strategical, situation, and that there shall, if possible, be nothing to hinder you from giving your whole and undivided attention to the problem of defeating the High Sea Fleet as quickly and as effectually as possible directly it puts to sea. You can understand, therefore, how anxious I am that, in coming to any decision on the subject of the barrage, there should be universal agreement on the subject.

Taking all these circumstances into consideration, I would ask you to re-consider the question of the 10 mile passage.

It would indeed be a calamity if the Americans were now to chuck their hand in over the Northern barrage. The enemy would know it, and, moreover, it would surely lead to that friction and want of sympathy between the United States and ourselves which has heretofore been so conspicuous by its absence.

There is one other aspect of the subject. [*The question can be reconsidered when the territorial waters of Norway are mined.] To leave this 10 mile passage would be inconsistent, since we are making such strenuous efforts to make the Norwegians *mine* their territorial waters, the only possible effectual way of stopping enemy submarines from getting through them. The fact that mining is the only efficacious way of dealing with the submarine is a point which we have impressed upon all the Allies, and one with which they are in entire agreement, and are consequently backing us up in our protestations to Norway.

To enable us, therefore, to decide upon and pursue a consistent and logical policy, we should proceed on the hypothesis that the Northern barrage is effective. As a whole, the policy of the Northern barrage is the result of careful consideration of all the aspects of the Anti-Submarine War. It is the keystone of our offensive anti-submarine policy, and we must deal with it as such.

We have immense resources available wherewith to reinforce it and render it even more and more effective.

No doubt, as with any other great measure, failures in detail must occur, but such failures can be rectified by the use of these resources.

If this hypothesis of the effectiveness of the barrage is taken, the necessity of the Grand Fleet affording protection to the convoy (North of the barrage) disappears, and although, as practical men, we must envisage the possibility of its non-effectiveness, it would not be logical to allow provision for such eventuality to interfere with the carrying out of a large policy by all the means in our power.

276. *From Wemyss*

[BTY/13/39/40]

Admiralty
30th August, 1918.

The First Lord had meant coming up to see you by to-night's mail, but since the situation is such as it is he has thought it better to leave you quite clear and to defer his visit. What he wanted to see you about is your conversation with Mr. Balfour. It appears that Mr. Balfour wrote to Lord Robert Cecil giving him a resume of his conversation with you, and this was the cause of the First Lord's telegram to you yesterday your reply to which very clearly cleared up the situation on one point.

Mr. Balfour's letter, whether meant or not, certainly implied that there were grave differences of opinion between you and the Admiralty on the large question of the barrage and Norwegian territorial waters, upon which he apparently inferred that you had been appealing to him. This of course I know to be all nonsense, but unfortunately it is one of those matters which, going beyond the actual people concerned, casues confusion of thought and perhaps disagreeables.

A direct result has been the postponement of the Norwegian question for a week or more.

I should have liked to come myself, but with Fremantle away I cannot leave the Admiralty. I am quite sure that an interview between the First Lord and yourself will clear matters up in a manner which no writing or telegraphing will do.

I am sending this letter up by special messenger.

277. *To Wemyss*

[BTY/13/39/42]   Queen Elizabeth
[Copy]   Sunday (1st September 1918)

I am at a loss to understand what the fuss is all about. The Admiralty are fully aware of my views on the subject of the Northern barrage and I have nothing to add to what I have said and written on quite a number of occasions.

I have said nothing to Mr Balfour that I have not also said to the Admiralty. So you can gauge exactly what the differences are that exist between our views on that question. No other question was mentioned in our conversation.

The First Lord asked me to write him fully my views on the Northern barrage and I replied I have nothing to add to what I have already said. So as letters generally appear to lead to more misunderstanding I think very strongly that a personal conversation is the only thing that can clear it up. That there have been differences of opinion as to the whole question is apparent. But I should not altogether call them differences of policy, but rather differences of detail.

For instance I agreed to the original policy on the stipulation that all technical difficulties should be overcome before committing ourselves to planting mines which might become a source of considerable danger to our ships. Apparently no experiments were carried out to obtain certain information until after they were laid instead of before.

Thus my stipulations were ignored and we were within an ace of suffering from a serious disaster.

Again there was a strong effort on the part of, presumably the Americans, to force us to mine up to Orkney coast, with which as you know, I cannot agree at this juncture and until I know where we are as regards the whole.

Again my orders from Admiralty to mine Norwegian territorial waters implied that Norwegian Government would not be informed and opposition might be expected. I have stated emphatically that as regards the policy of doing this the Norwegian Government must be informed beforehand.

Since, I have received more recent orders stating that they will be informed.

I do not think I have been difficult or ambiguous about my views and have acceded to Admiralty wishes in practically every respect.

But you will allow I have to look at it from the G.F. point of view and I dread to think what the North Sea will be like after winter gales with mines floating about with fathoms of wire attached which will catch our P.V.s, and the deep switches failing to operate.

I was wanting to take the Fleet North before the Minelaying operation in Area 'B', which would mean sailing from here Tuesday. We ought to get on with our Quarters firing. Will you let me know as to whether the situation will permit.

I would of course hang on if you thought it desirable to have this vexed question thrashed out at an interview. Send me a wire as soon as you can decide, as I want to do some exercises en route and the first part of the Force would have to sail Tuesday morning.

I could of course postpone until after the mining operation, say Monday 9th. It would make it a little later in the quarter to complete but that is not very important. All things being equal I should like to go on Tuesday next, so will leave it at that.

It was unfortunate that the 1st Minelaying Squadron could not have got the minefield down off the Tyne while they have been waiting for the next stunt up North.

278.   *From Wemyss*

[BTY/13/39/43]   Admiralty
Private   September 2nd, 1918

The general situation I have dealt with in a separate and semi-official letter, and this contained my reasons for wanting you to remain where you are until the 9th, so that you see that the situation created by A.J.B.'s letter has nothing to do with it. However, I am persuading the First Lord to take advantage of your remaining where you are to go up and pay you a visit; because, like you, I feel convinced that a few words passed between you will clear up the somewhat ambiguous state of affairs as they exist at present. To my mind, there is no ambiguity, and I do not see that there would have been in anyone else's had it not been for this letter which A.J.B. wrote to Robert Cecil. I agree with your views that, on the whole, there is no difference between us on the question of policy, though, of course, there is in detail, and after all, it is one of my jobs to try and get over these differences of detail and to marry all opinions together, if possible.

Of course, our American friends, not having the responsibility that we have, do not look upon it from the same point of view as we do, and I am rather inclined to think that Sims is of opinion that all these matters are so simple that they can be settled by us here sitting round at a table, without reference to you. You and I know very differently, but what I know better than you is how difficult it is to get these Americans into a sane, clear and sound state of thinking. They have much to learn, and, honestly, I think they are learning quickly, but it takes a long time for them to pick up the three, I may say four, years of experience that they are behind us.

As you know, I had hoped that the First Lord would have gone up to see you on Friday night, but I thought that it was not fair that you should be worried by such matters whilst we were in a state of uncertainty as to possibilities arising from enemy's action, and, therefore, it was decided that he should not go, and our two letters were the result. Now, however, I hope that one day this week he will go up and meet you, and talk the matter over.

Between ourselves, I think that A.J.B's letter (quite unintentionally, I have no doubt) gave a wrong impression to Robert Cecil, and Robert Cecil, being the true son of his father, was unable to deal straightly with it, and instead of coming to the Admiralty and having the matter cleared up, sat on it for several days, thereby by no means improving the situation. With all this writing and all this roundabout, you will realise how easy it is to raise a false atmosphere which I think can be best dispelled by a personal interview.

The First Lord agrees with me — I have shown him all the letters which have passed between us on the subject, and he sees as clearly as I do that such differences as do exist are those of detail and not of policy; but when this information came to him from the Foreign Office he was a little alarmed, because he realised that even if there was no difference of policy A.J.B.'s letter intimated at least that there might be.

279. *Extract from Secret Fleet Orders on Scandinavian Convoys*

[BTY/7/4/3]   [4 September 1918]

*   *   *

2. Humber – Tyne – Methil – Scandinavian Convoys

(*a*) *Detailed information*

The convoy system in the North Sea is under the general direction of the Commander-in-Chief, Coast of Scotland and the arrangements are described in detail in *Rosyth Secret Memorandum No. 057/19* of 15 February 1918.

(*b*) *Protection of Convoys*

2. Orders as regards the protection of convoys, so far as the convoy leader and escort forces are concerned, have been issued by the Commander-in-Chief, Coast of Scotland.

In the event of attack by surface craft, the general procedure is that the armed boarding steamer and auxiliary patrol vessels will endeavour to lead the convoy out of danger and towards support under cover of a smoke screen. The escorting destroyers will concentrate as rapidly as possible, and in face of superior forces, will retire at once and at speed, making full use of a defensive smoke screen, on to the supporting force, reporting the composition of the enemy force and the position of attack. Should the enemy retire, the utmost endeavour is to be made to keep in touch and report movements. The senior officer of the supporting force will take general charge of subsequent operations, and will inform the convoy leader and escorting destroyers of his position, course, and speed immediately on receiving information of the attack.

3. It is undesirable to attempt to lay down detailed instructions as to the action to be taken by the senior officer of the supporting force in the event of an attack on the convoy by enemy surface craft. Senior officers must be guided by circumstances, and the information they have of the movements of any other units of the Grand Fleet.

The primary duty of the supporting force is to protect the

convoy. It must be borne in mind that the enemy's force is likely to be superior in speed and care must therefore be taken that supporting forces are not drawn away, thus leaving the convoy open to attack by enemy light forces which will probably have been detailed for the purpose, and which may not have been located by our light cruisers. The light cruisers should be kept concentrated and in touch with the battleships or battle-cruisers; the whole force should be manoeuvred in proximity to the convoy and proceed to any threatened portion of it.

4. Either a light cruiser squadron only, or a light cruiser squadron with a subdivision, division, or two divisions of heavy ships, will usually be detailed to support the 'OZ' and 'HZ' convoys. The supporting force is to make the challenge to the escort force on sighting the convoy for the first time.

The light cruiser squadron is to gain visual touch with the convoy, and during daylight hours the supporting force is to steer as necessary along the convoy route, maintaining touch and making wide zig-zags. The nature of the zig-zag must depend on the speed of advance of the convoy, but, weather permitting, the speed through the water of the supporting force should not be less than 16.5 knots by day and 15 knots at night.

5. If heavy ships and light cruisers form the supporting force, the light cruisers are, during daylight, to be spread ahead and on each bow of the heavy ships at visibility distance with the object of giving warning of the approach of enemy vessels. Light cruisers spread are to be at visibility distance from each other. The convoy should be sighted by one or more units of the supporting force, as directed by the senior officer, every hour.

Whilst the 'HZ' convoy is being collected by the escort force off the Norwegian coast, supporting forces are, as a general rule, to cruise to the southward outside territorial waters, keeping within supporting distance.

6. During dark hours, the supporting force should cruise with its light cruisers stationed on the beam of and to the southward of the heavy ships, the whole supporting force turning at pre-arranged times and gaining visual touch with the convoy at daylight, care being taken that the supporting force keeps within effective distance of the convoy. It may be desirable, more especially on moonlight nights, to station a light cruiser as a connecting link between the convoy and the supporting force.

7. The employment of strong supporting forces with the Scandinavian convoy will offer the enemy increased opportunities

for submarine attack. Squadrons should cruise in line abreast during daylight hours whether screened by destroyers or not. This formation affords the maximum protection against submarine attack, and, with ships in open order, is both flexible and safe.

8. The supporting force is generally to maintain the 'Second degree of readiness' during daylight, and the 'Third degree of readiness' during dark hours. Special precautions are necessary against enemy attack at dawn.

9. In the event of early warning regarding enemy movements being received from the Admiralty, or Commander-in-Chief, Grand Fleet, the senior officer of the supporting force is to give the necessary orders to the convoy leader for the diversion of the convoy to a safe route.

10. Should the weather conditions render it undesirable for screening destroyers to remain in company with supporting forces, destroyers are, circumstances permitting, to proceed along the convoy route at slow speed in the same direction as the convoy or, if necessary, lie to. They should rejoin at a rendezvous given by the senior officer of the supporting force concerned as soon as the weather permits.

11. Airships will scout thirty miles to the eastward of convoys when south of latitude 58° N. during daylight hours, weather permitting, and may sometimes accompany the convoy.

280.   *To Eugénie Godfrey-Faussett*

[CCG/SLGF/14/1/A]   The Grand Fleet
[Copy]   6.9.18.

Carissima Mia, I note your remarks as to posting of my letters and therefore this will go Sunday morning and not tomorrow, indeed it is tomorrow, Saturday, already and the date at the top is wrong. I love your philosophy as contained in your last and I too try to live up to that same standard. I admit to you it is not always easy and I'll tell you why. One day this week (I had been having a particularly trying and anxious time) I was talking about the burden of the responsibility and stated that I wished there would be some relaxation as I was tired of continually having to make decisions all of which involved considerable responsibility. Although it appeared that confidences had been invited and that my audience was in a sympathetic mood, I was met by the rejoinder, 'Oh, if you feel the burden too great, I should give it up, or not talk about it'!! My dear, out of your great wisdom and wonderful understanding, what would you make of that. To me it appeared somewhat brutal. I could only reply 'that no doubt I had exaggerated it, I was only seeking sympathy'. I added that even the great Nelson wrote to Emma that 'he was inflicted with *too heavy* a burden' — also unfortunately there was no record of what Emma's reply was, but I doubted her having retorted 'He had better give it up or not talk about it'. I doubted whether his burden was anything approaching mine. But what I really lacked was a sympathetic Emma!! Having got that little dig in, I felt better. But, my golden-haired houri, what manner of mood must a human being be in (who has been so much to me in the past) who can realise so little my responsibilities and the strain involved that would make a response of that nature. She did not mean to be unkind but I presume was bored at my talking about it all. You see, I like sympathy, I like to talk to somebody who is sympathetic who can look at things from my point of view, and who can help me with a little flattering encouragement. I am sure that it would help me to do better, as I have told you, I am terribly human and liked to be believed in and would yield and be soothed by a little — only a little — gentle stroking and understanding.

Am I asking too much or am I too exacting. You can answer perfectly truthfully and I couldn't be hurt by anything you would say. For four years I have lived among my staff and with them it is impossible to be despondent or to groan or open my heart. I have to keep them up, to carry them along on the top of the wave of hope, cheerfulness, confidence etc. and cannot indulge in despondency or grumblings so dear to the heart of every Britisher. Not that I am despondent in the least. As I finished my conversation by saying that she need not be alarmed, if I could not bear the burden. I am quite certain nobody else could. That was swank, as David calls it — But I was shrivelled up — you say she is unhappy with tempestuous scenes followed by reconciliations. But why? I am all for her being perfectly happy and anything that would add to that, I am ready to subscribe to. They are not on my account. One of these days the worm will turn, it hasn't time at present, and I don't like being thought a worm. You said he thought we had had a row and there was no harm (that was putting it in a low standard, I find you can't help it when it comes) but having seen one of my letters, he had thought different.

Doesn't that provide the cause for the tempestuous scenes? And it's a bit thick when my letters are handed over to the other side — Not that I am entering into any competition. I haven't the time or the opportunity and if I cannot hold my own under the circumstances, then it is not worth fighting for.

You see, adorata mia, I have taken you very literally when you said lay your small problems before me and you would try to unravel them.

I think I should like to meet your sister-in-law, she is a philosopher after my own heart. I was greatly amused at her acceptance of the inevitable.

The Hun is terribly restless and has been raging backwards and forwards in his inner waters, which may portend many things and it behoves us to be very much on the qui vive and we spend much of our time at short notice. Having many craft at sea, they provide vulnerable points, all susceptible to attack which makes the situation anxious. Anything might come out of it but I fear nothing will, but one never knows and all we can do is to safeguard the weak spots and be ready to strike.

It is heavenly to think that I was with you in your dreams, that at least is something to be grateful for, but they are unsatisfactory things at the best as one is always so disappointed when one wakes up. Tata goes down with David on Tuesday. I would that I were coming too. I started to go North last Monday but the situation was too uncertain. I shall go on Monday next if it clears sufficiently but that also is uncertain and in that case I shall be here until something more definite turns up. If so, what a pity you cannot be at Aberdour to play tennis and give us tea while Tata is away.

I just loved my little Red Lion pretending to be asleep which he isn't. It is a beautiful little model and he is winking at me as I write and reminds me of you looking at me across the table with those divine blue eyes that I just love to kiss.

Now, my comrade of dreamland, do not get into that glorious head of yours that I am unhappy and make yourself unhappy thinking about it. I am only in an analytical mood and like to know the ways and wherefores of things. And as long as I know there is a prospect of seeing you in the near future I do not care a damn for anything else. What a blessed feeling that is, that there is somebody one wants to see and who wants to be seen, even if it does not come off, it is comforting. For Heaven's sake stave off the postman's strike, that would be a disaster of the first magnitude to me. I haven't seen anything of it in the papers. My dear, don't give way to bad fits, as you call them, they don't help any and are so bad for you. You must bring that dear logical brain of yours to bear on the situation and they will disappear.

281. *To his wife* [Aberdour House]

[BTY/17/52/18–19]   Grand Fleet
                                              Sunday [22 September 1918]

*   *   *

The Arch-Fiends will lose in morale greatly, more especially as they are being pushed back from the sea to the Ardennes and are losing thousands of prisoners daily. The question always uppermost in my mind is what effect will it have on their sea policy. I cannot imagine that the morale of the submarine crews can be maintained against the heavy losses they sustain, when they hear on their return that the war is being lost on land. We hear that there has been considerable discontent showing itself in the Navy at Kiel, necessitating the presence of the Emperor to talk to them. Well, there are two ways of looking at that. If there is real discontent the best way to kill it is to send them to sea. On the other hand, if there is no discontent, the advent of the Kaiser may be the preliminary to an undertaking by the naval forces. It might be said to portend the advent of the High Sea Fleet. But now we have a crumpling of the enemy's allies, who might thereby see the 'writing on the wall' and therefore be seriously considering the necessity of truly fixing his peace terms. We know that of all things he is desirous of regaining his colonies, and the latter without a navy are of no value, therefore if he thinks there is any chance of securing his colonies in the peace terms, he is not likely to risk the destruction of his navy.

On the other hand, if he recognises that he has no chance of recovering his colonies after the war, then he may consider the possibility of attempting some great blow with the High Sea Fleet. But, generally speaking, our prospects are poor. It is terrible to think that it is possible after all these weary months of waiting, we shall not have an opportunity of striking a blow. But events are moving so rapidly that anything might happen.

*   *   *

282. *To Wemyss*

[BTY/13/40/2]   *Queen Elizabeth*
                                                      4th October 1918

Thank you for your letter. I am sorry I shall not have the opportunity of discussing the situation with you or the D.C.N.S. There are many new features of considerable importance brought about by our recent victories on land which will require consideration.

I am afraid I cannot agree with you that there is no change in the situation in the North Sea. The fact that three flotillas have been moved from Flanders to the North Sea constitutes, to my mind, a very considerable change.

Also, I cannot agree that the Grand Fleet is not concerned with the situation in the southern part of the North Sea. This is not the policy that has been accepted hitherto.

One of the reasons for moving the Grand Fleet to the southern base was to enable some of its units to be utilised in the southern waters if there was a possiblity of the enemy evacuating the Flanders Ports. Evacuation was to be expected if our advance into Belgium met with sufficient success.

The moving of three flotillas from Flanders to North Sea Ports was certainly an operation to be interfered with if possible.

Undoubtedly it was a difficult enough task, but not altogether impossible if sufficient Forces had been used. Our opportunities in the sea are so few that it is necessary to snatch at any and every one that presents itself.

It is a matter of very great regret that we have not been able to take advantage at sea of the successes that have been gained so gallantly and so thoroughly by the Allied Forces on shore. There can be but little doubt that part of the enemy flotillas did actually pass through waters in which they might have been intercepted.

The question now arises, which I am sure you will agree requires consideration, as to the redistribution of our light forces now in southern waters in view of the accession of strength to the enemy's North sea flotillas and the corresponding reduction of their forces in Flanders.

I will urge on you the necessity of consideration in good time. Events are moving very fast and with the winter coming on with all its depressing effect upon the enemy coming on the top of the severe hammering he has had, it behoves us to be prepared *now* for any eventuality.

Fortunately we have been able to carry out most of our firings with exception of 5th and 6th Battle Squadrons, and as soon as I feel more sure of the situation I will send them North one at a time to do it.

I cannot believe at the present juncture that it would be wise to keep the Fleet North, and I believe you are of the same opinion.

283. *To Wemyss*

[BTY/13/40/8] 18 October 1918

Copy Of Personal Letter From Commander-In-Chief To The First Sea Lord Forwarded With H. F. 0022/174 Of 18th October 1918

I enclose you the letter containing points on the situation as regards enemy submarines as they appear to me [not printed]. What we have to guard against is a sudden change of policy (in the use of his submarines) on the part of the enemy.

What we may have to face is a concentration of the submarines off the Firth of Forth. We are not at present well prepared for such a change, which seems to me a highly probable move on his part.

That he would accept the terms of the Armistice is unthinkable, but some change must take place in his naval policy.

He has a formidable weapon in his submarines if he concentrates them on his legitimate objective, i.e. the Grand Fleet, and we shall *have* losses to contend with, so I urge upon you the necessity of consideration and collaboration on this subject at *an early date*, or we shall be again too late.

284.   *From Wemyss*

[BTY/13/40/11]   Admiralty
                                                         October 19th, 1918.

I sincerely hope that you will be able to respond to my telegram which I have just sent you by coming up to London.

I hope that my letter of yesterday made clear to you how up and down is the situation, how very undefined, and how difficult it is to come to any resolution. I have, however, this morning been speaking to the Prime Minister, and he is holding this conference on Monday at which Douglas Haig will be present, and I sincerely hope you also. You will then be able to gauge the whole atmosphere, naval, military and political.

I have just this minute received your letter of the 18th on reconcentration of submarines. It is a question which is always in our minds and constantly being discussed, indeed, I have always considered a possible banking up of them with a view to their being used otherwise as one of the possible indications of further movements of the High Sea Fleet. As you know, we are always ready to take steps of the sort indicated in your letter, but the time for doing so certainly has not yet arisen. We have had the same position more than once before, namely, a comparatively small number of submarines out after there have been a large number operating. The situation is perpetually being watched, and so far, at any rate, there is no indication that this occasion is different from others.

We are living in moving times, and I understand that the Government are expecting some sort of reply on behalf of the enemy to the President's last message within the next few hours. Monday, therefore, will probably be a most important day, and I most sincerely hope that you will be able to come.

As I told you in my telegram, we will, of course, make any arrangements for you that you like in the way of special trains, etc. In the event of your coming, will you come straight from the station to the Mall House where I shall be delighted to give you bath, breakfast, etc., and we could have a talk before we go to Downing Street.

Of course, I will send to meet you at the station.

285. *From Rear-Admiral Sir Sydney Fremantle* (DCNS)

[BTY/13/12/3]

Admiralty
29/10/18

The plot has thickened appreciably since I wrote on Sunday, and it seems now absolutely clear that the enemy wishes you to come out to the Southward, over a submarine trap.

The 3 submarines off Rattray Head seem to be placed with the intention of intercepting ships joining you at Rosyth from Invergordon and Scapa. EXP, the last one to be stationed, cannot get there for 3 days at least, which is interesting evidence that the enemy has not timed himself to a definitely-timed sortie.

There is no evidence whatever of any intention to send out raiders, nor do I think the political situation makes that likely. If raiders do get out, we are fairly well prepared to deal with them by our arrangements for diverting convoys and by the U.S. battleships.

Hall favours the idea of an attack on the defences of Rosyth, possibly by net-breakers with submarines to follow them. Such an operation offers such a small chance of success that I cannot think it probable, and the net, gun, and patrol defences are so complete that one almost hopes the enemy might try it. It is unlikely that such an operation would be supported by heavy ships, as they would have to pass through the enemy's own mine-field.

My idea is that the enemy's most probable line of action is to come outside his mine-fields, make W/T signals for a few hours, and then return. In such an event, the only way we can get even with him is to play his game with the submarines. It is for this reason that we have established two more submarine patrols from the Harwich Force and it is I think worth your consideration whether Q and Z 57 should not be established.

As to the Bight mining policy, our idea is to hamper his arrangements generally, and to improve our chances of getting information of his exit. He found our A.68 last night, and probably a submarine being taken out went back with her escort.

I do not suppose that any mine-field would prevent him coming out in force if he meant to come, but these mine-fields on the routes impose on him the necessity for mine-sweeping — which helps to give us warning of his intentions — and if some ship were mined when he goes out, there would be signals which would give us information.

For these reasons we are laying another 20th Flotilla line to-night.

I had hoped that Fisher[1] would have been able to report some results before now, but the attempts to kill submarines by hunting processes are a constant series of disappointments. I do not attach much importance to the directionals placing so many submarines outside area X, as they probably go outside to make their signals and then return.

No news has come from Versailles, nor is any likely to, so I have repeated your telegram to the 1st Lord.

Calthorpe was negotiating all day yesterday and hopes to get all our demands, subject to a few small concessions.

Goodbye, and the best of luck on 'the day'.

286. *From Wemyss*

[BTY/13/40/17]

Admiralty
November 5th, 1918

The state of affairs in the High Seas Fleet is not very clear, but at least one thing seems certain, and that is, that the crews of some of the ships or of some of the shore establishments have mutinied, and are under the control of the 'Soldiers' Council', whatever that may be.[2] I do not think that we have as yet enough information to get a good and clear appreciation of the situation, but we may look forward to one of two possibilities,

(1) Such events as have happened forcing the High Seas Fleet out as a desperate action,

(2) The disintegration being so great that they cannot possibly come out.

In the case of (1), if it is to happen at all, it would probably happen as soon as ever the 3rd Battle Squadron could come through from Kiel to Wilhelmshaven, and here again we are confronted with the fact that if there really is a revolution and there are 'Soldiers' Councils' in charge, it might be impossible for them to get through the Canal.

---

[1]Captain W. W. Fisher: see note 2 on page 431.

[2]On 22 October Hipper ordered to sail and bring Grand Fleet to action; a sortie planned for 30 October, but as fleet assembled, mutiny spread and the move was cancelled, and Sailors' Councils were established. See Horn, *Mutiny on the High Seas*, pp. 203ff, Herwig, *The German Naval Officer Corps*, Chapters 9–11.

You will remember that the last trouble in the Fleet began in the minesweepers. If this is the case now, I do not see how they are going to sweep themselves out although it is conceivable that they might risk it and come out without their minesweepers and barrier breakers.

The next question that arises is, could they rely on their submarines acting with them? It seems likely to think that those submarines which are based on Kiel will probably be disaffected and they might not get any move on them.

As regards (2) the question arises, can we attack them in any way? The only answer that I can see is by torpedo aeroplane. Groves[1] tells me that so far as he knows such an attack might be brought off in the course of the next week or ten days, weather, of course, always permitting. I do not see how we can get at them in any other way.

The Supreme War Council have decided that the terms of armistice shall be – the surrender of 160 submarines and the internment of the ships mentioned by you in a neutral port with their ammunition out and only nucleus crews on board, with the exception of the *Baden* which they absolutely refuse to include in the terms of armistice.[2] I had an assurance from the Prime Minister given me in the presence of the War Cabinet that he and all the others were determined that *none* of these ships should be given back to the Germans. In a way I was pleased with these terms as I believed that directly the Germans heard them they would refuse and would come out and fight, in which case we should have got all we wanted; but if the Fleet is disintegrated as we believe it may be the whole situation is altered, and God knows what may happen.

You will see how complicated is the situation and how many possibilities there are, and I hope you will as soon as possible give us your views on the subject.

I am going back to Paris tomorrow as it appears that they expect a flag of truce within the next few days. I wish that it were you who were going to meet them, but I feel that it would not be right

---

[1]Groves: see note 1 on page 533.
[2]The complexities of the negotiations on Armistice terms are detailed in Marder, *From the Dreadnought*, Vol. 5, pp 175–8. The Admiralty had wanted all German surface ships to be surrendered, but the Supreme War Council settled for ten battleships & six battle-cruisers, and smaller craft only; Beatty unsuccessfully argued for the surrender of Heligoland. There was also an inter-Allied dispute as to the exact fate of the surrendered ships; Allied Naval Council decided on Scapa Flow internment on 13 November.

for you to leave the Grand Fleet at this moment, neither would you care to do so. Should there be any question of surrender quite apart from terms of armistice, we will hope that such will happen on the quarter-deck of the *Queen Elizabeth* in whatever place you may select.

If by any chance the terms of armistice are accepted, which I doubt, or rather, which I doubted a few hours ago, perhaps you will consider what you think proper to do in the way of escorting the German Fleet to the neutral port, which will probably have to be Vigo or Arosa Bay, and of leaving there a squadron of supervision.

The latest signal to such enemy submarines as remain in the Mediterranean indicate that for the present, at any rate, the campaign against merchant shipping is at an end. We must, however, always remember that the enemy can put it into force again at very short notice. Under these circumstances, we are all considering the advisability of sending more destroyers from escorting work to the North Sea. Such destroyers would, of course, be of no use to you either for screening your battleships or for battle, since they are untrained for Fleet work, so that should any such be concentrated in the North Sea, they will only be of use in purely anti-submarine work. You will understand a natural desire on our part not to reduce the escorts further than they have already been reduced until it is absolutely necessary to do so. Anything further in this way means reducing the escorts to the merest skeleton, which one is naturally reluctant to do while there is a chance of the war on merchant shipping being renewed. In any case, no reduction of escort in the case of troop convoys can be considered for the present, at any rate.

Will you please communicate direct with Fremantle during my absence? I shall be on the end of a telephone wire.

PS. Internment of ships is to be under British surveyance; no ammunition on board. In event of revolution at Kiel not having affected the Fleet, it is within the bounds of possibility that ships in Baltic might join remainder of H. S. Fleet in North Sea via Belt and Kattegat.

Fisher will come to see you on Thursday morning to talk about plans. Probably by time you receive this letter the whole picture may have altered!!

287. *Procedure regarding carrying out of naval terms of armistice* [Typed copy with marginal notes* by Beatty]

[BTY/7/10/5]   [November 1918]

Agenda paper giving points for discussion with Rear Admiral Hugo Meurer acting as Plenipotentiary for the German High Naval Command.[1]
NOTE: – All times are given in Greenwich Mean Time.

Article XX

Information as to location and movements of German ships.	Rear Admiral Meurer is requested to give this information, furnishing a list of ships with their present whereabouts. (This is to include submarines.)
Notification to Neutrals as to freedom of navigation in all Territorial waters.	Information is also requested as to whether notification has been promulgated.

Article XXI

Naval prisoners.	This article is being dealt with direct by the British and German Governments.

Article XXII

Handing over to the Allies and United States of all submarines. *Commission wd be reqd to see that there no SMs left in German ports: *or* to make necessary arrangements to ensure that they either leave German Ports at earliest possible moment or are totally destroyed before the Date of Armistice expires, i.e. 17th Dec[r]	Information is requested as to— (a) number of submarines ready to put to sea by 8.0 a.m. Monday 18th November 1918. (b) number, additional to those referred to in (a), which will be ready to put to sea between Monday 18th November and 8.0 a.m. Monday 25th November 1918.

[1]Rear-Admiral H. Meurer, Hipper's representative, arrived on 15 November in the light cruiser, *Königsberg*.

Rear Admiral Meurer is informed as follows:—

2. The German submarines should sail in flotillas of approximately 20 boats on dates which will be communicated by the British Naval Command to the German Naval Command.

The rendezvous to which they are to proceed is –

Latitude 52°.05′ North
Longitude 2°.05′ East

at 0730 G. M. T. on the day selected.

3. A Transport flying the German Flag should accompany the submarines to take their crews back to Germany.

4. A force of light cruisers and destroyers will meet and escort the submarines to their anchorage.

5. The German Flotilla is to be formed in 4 divisions of 5 submarines each, the divisions being in single line ahead and led by the transport.

6. The transport will be led independently of the submarines to her anchorage by a light cruiser distinguished by a Blue Ensign at the Foremast Head. Speed 15 knots. She should be directed to follow the motions of the light cruiser accurately. Two destroyers will follow the transport.

*10 knots

7. Four destroyers, each distinguished by a Blue Ensign at the foremast head, will each lead a division of 5 submarines. Speed 12 knots. The Commanding Officers of the submarines should be directed to follow the destroyer leading them accurately at 2 cables (400 yards) apart, a space of 4 cables dividing each division of submarines.

*9 knots

Signals to stop engines and to anchor will be made by the escorting vessels to their respective divisions by International Code.

8. The Commanding Officer of each German submarine will, on the arrival of the British Officer, hand over a signed declaration that he has complied with the demands laid down as follows: —
That the submarine is in the following condition: —
(1) Batteries fully charged up.
(2) Full complement of torpedoes on board, launched back clear of torpedo tubes and without warheads.
(3) That no explosives of any sort are on board.
(4) That the submarine is in running condition, fully blown.
(5) That all periscopes are in place and in working and efficient condition.
(6) That all sea valves are closed and watertight doors

left in efficient condition;
W/T apparatus left in
working order.
(7) That no infernal machines
or booby traps of any sort
are on board.
(9) Each Commanding
Officer is, in addition, to
present a list of the names of
all officers and men in his
ship.
10. On arrival of the British
crews, the German crews,
except those actually
attending machinery are to
be paraded together on the
forecastle in charge of an
officer, and are to leave their
vessels when ordered to do
so.
11. The German
Commanding Officer of each
submarine will be required to
personally conduct the
British Officer taking over
and give him the details of
his vessel, and every facility
for taking over.
12. When the operation has
been completed, the German
officers and men will take
their places in the boat
provided and will be taken to
the transport or vessel
detailed to take them back to
Germany.
13. When all the crews are on
board the transports and all
on the submarines have
arrived in Harwich Harbour,
the transport will be ordered
to weigh and will follow the

escort provided to Position in Latitude 52°.05′ North, Longitude 2°.10′ East and will then be permitted to return to Germany.

Article XXIII
German surface warships to be interned.
*Agreed

Rear Admiral Meurer is informed as follows: —
(a) It is necessary the ships should first proceed to an anchorage in the Firth of Forth but outside the precincts of the port. This is to allow for examination and for embarkation of the British Navigating parties who are required in order to ensure the vessels being safely passed through the British mine fields, en route to Port of Internment.

*Agreed

*24 hours notice

(b) It is proposed that the German ships to be interned should rendezvous in a position 50 miles 90° from May Island, the leading ship being in that position at 8.0 a.m. on the prescribed date.

*Noted

(c) The route from the German base will be given after receipt of information as to German mine fields in the Heligoland Bight.
(d) German ships are to approach the rendezvous on a course 270°, speed 15 knots, and are to be formed up as follows: —
(i) Heavy ships in single line ahead in close order 3 cables apart with the battle-cruisers leading.

(ii) Light cruisers in single line ahead, 3 cables apart, the leading light cruiser 3 miles astern of the rear battleship.

(iii) Destroyers to be in five groups 3 miles astern of the rear light cruiser.

*Noted

(e) Guns are to be in the securing position, trained fore and aft.

*Noted

(f) A sufficient force will meet the German ships and escort them to the anchorage.

(g) Three light cruisers each flying a blue ensign at the mast-head will be detailed to

*Noted

proceed ahead of the German heavy ships, German light cruisers and German destroyers respectively and lead them to the anchorage.

(h) A plan of the anchorage is attached.

Rear Admiral Meurer's opinion is requested as to whether the German ships could proceed direct to the anchoring berths shown on the plan. Failing this their engines should be stopped and anchors let go by international signal made by the light cruiser which leads the vessels in. Arrangements would be made to shift them to their correct berths later.

Other German warships
*i.e. List of Battleships
Lt. Cruisers
TBDs
Fleet Auxiliaries

Rear Admiral Meurer is requested to furnish a list of those surface warships of the German Navy, including river craft and auxiliary

*List of river craft & other auxiliaries to be provided later. The R A's advice as to what ports are capable of being used as anchorages (safe) for these disarmed vessels.

vessels, not specified for internment.
It is the intention that these surface warships should be divided amongst the various German bases and not concentrated all at any particular base.
Rear Admiral Meurer is requested to state his proposals for giving effect to this.

Article XXIV
Right of Allies to sweep up German Mine-fields

Information is requested from Rear Admiral Meurer as to the position of German mine-fields outside territorial waters.

Article XXV
Freedom of Allies to and from Baltic
*Commission will be reqd to draw up the details of what they consider necessary to disarm & render ineffective the German forts etc. What subsequent supervision will be necessary to ensure they are complied with.

Information is required as to steps Germany proposes to take to allow of safe access of all classes of vessels to the Baltic and whether the German Navy intends to sweep up the German mine-fields laid.
It is pointed out that if the Allied Navies and the United States Navy have to sweep up the German mine-fields in order to obtain access to the Baltic, then it will be necessary for the Allies and the United States to occupy the ports in the entrance.
If, on the other hand, the German Navy undertakes to sweep these minefields, commencing forthwith and completing the work as soon as possible, and undertakes

to report immediately this work is complete, and always provided that the forts, fortifications, batteries and defence works are demobilised and rendered ineffective to the satisfaction of the Allies and the United States Naval Commission, then the Allies and the United States are prepared to refrain for the present from exercising the right granted by this article of occupying the forts, fortifications, batteries and defence works.

Article XXVI
Blockade

Rear Admiral Meurer is informed that the provisioning of Germany must depend upon the rapidity and good will with which these Armistice terms are put into effect.

Article XXVII
Naval Aircraft
*Commission will be reqd to inspect the aircraft & check the no's assembled at the German bases specified –

Rear Admiral Meurer is requested to furnish a list of the Naval Aircraft involved, and to state his proposals for carrying out the terms of this Article.

Article XXX
Merchant ships belonging to Allied and Associated Powers now in German hands.

Rear Admiral Meurer is requested to furnish a list of these and the ports at which they are at present. The ports to which they are to be restored will be specified later.

288. *Address delivered by*
Admiral Sir David Beatty, G.C.B., G.C.V.O., D.S.O., on
board H.M.S. Lion, on 24th November 1918, to the
Officers and Men of Lion and First Battle-Cruiser
Squadron.

[KEL/106]   24. Nov. 1918

Officers and Men of the First Battle Cruiser Squadron,
    You are going away to-day to perform a final duty, and I could
not let you go without visiting a part of my old command, and
more especially my old flagship, to say a few words. First of all
to thank you for all that you have done during the past four and
a half years to enable us to achieve a triumph, which you
witnessed, and which has surpassed anything that has ever
occurred before. I thank you for maintaining cheerfulness through
the long weary years of war, for having maintained an efficiency
which has created a prestige in the minds of the enemy, and has
brought about his downfall. England owes the Grand Fleet a
great, great debt. The world owes the Grand Fleet a great debt.
It has been said before, and it will be said many times again, that
the war, which is now on the threshold of coming to an end, has
been won by sea-power. You are the representatives of sea-power.
Military successes have been great. Military victories have been
achieved under circumstances which have produced difficulties,
all of which have been overcome by the greatest gallantry, devotion to duty and sacrifice. But all that would have been of no
value without the sea-power of England. On you lies the great
burden, and to you is due great credit.
    I have always said in the past that the High Sea Fleet would
have to come out and meet the Grand Fleet. I was not a false
prophet; they are out (*laughter*), and they are now in. (*Loud
laughter.*) They are in our pockets, and the 1st Battle-Cruiser
Squadron is going to look after them. The 1st Battle-Cruiser
Squadron, in fact the Battle-Cruiser Force, has a more intimate
acquaintance with the enemy than any other force of the Grand
Fleet. It has been their great fortune to have cast their eye upon
them on several occasions, and generally with very good effect.
But we never expected that the last time we should see them as
a great force would be when they were being shepherded, like a
flock of sheep, by the Grand Fleet. It was a pitiable sight, in fact
I should say it was a horrible sight, to see these great ships that

we have been looking forward so long to seeing, expecting them to have the same courage that we expect from men whose work lies upon great waters — we did expect them to do something for the honour of their country — and I think it was a pitiable sight to see them come in, led by a British light cruiser, with their old antagonists, the battle-cruisers, gazing at them. I am sure that the sides of this gallant old ship, which have been well hammered in the past, must have ached — as I ached, as all ached — to give them another dose of what we had intended for them. But I will say this, that their humiliating end was a suitable end and a proper end for a foe so lacking in chivalry and in what we look for from an honourable foe. From the beginning his strategy, his tactics and his behaviour have been beneath contempt, and worthy of a nation which has waged war in the manner in which the enemy has waged war.

They are now going to be taken away and placed under the guardianship of the Grand Fleet at Scapa, where they will enjoy (*laughter*), as we have enjoyed, the pleasures of Scapa. (*Laughter*.) But they have nothing to look forward to as we had. That which kept up our spirits, kept up our efficiency. They have nothing to look forward to except degradation. The 1st Battle-Cruiser Squadron has been selected, because it is the 1st Battle-Cruiser Squadron, to take them there. And I consider it, and I am sure that you consider it, a great honour to have the guarding and shepherding of the enemy to their last resting place, until it is decided what shall be done with them; and I am sure that you will look after them, and see there is no skipping about on Flotta, better than anybody else can.

I want to touch on one other topic, and that is, that any of you who have dealings with representatives of the High Sea Fleet will remember what they have done in the past — no clapping them on the back, giving them a cigarette, and calling them 'old chap.' As I have said in my memorandum, you have to treat them with courtesy, cold courtesy. Every time you feel sorry for them, remember what they have done in the past. Don't ever forget it; it would be the greatest mistake in the world. The British sailor is very sympathetic. We know that he has a very large heart, and sometimes a very short memory. In this case just contract your heart and lengthen your memory, and remember that the enemy that you are looking after is despicable, nothing more nor less. He is not worthy of the sacrifice of one blue-jacket in the Grand Fleet. And that is the one bright spot in the fact that he did not give us what we hoped for — a good stand-up fight. He would not be worthy of the loss of one life in the Grand Fleet; he is too far beneath us.

When you have got him safely housed at Scapa, you will be relieved by other ships who will take over the duty of looking after him. I daresay there is one question in your minds (*laughter*) which I had better say before you say it, 'What about a bit of leave?' (*Loud laughter.*) That will not be forgotten. I think you can trust to me that as soon as the moment comes when it is possible to give leave you shall have leave. (*Cheers.*)

289. *To Eugénie Godfrey-Faussett*

[CCC/SLGF/14/1/B]   The Grand Fleet
[Copy[1]]   26.11.18

My dear, dear comrade, I was so glad to get your pathetic little note, it took a great weight off my mind to know that though serious it was not dangerous. I have been aching to write to you for days but I simply haven't a moment. I hardly leave the ship, 2 hours is the most I've done for a long time and even that has been rare . . . You poor dear, I am so terribly sorry for you just now and it seems cruel hard but, please God, they'll find out the cause of all your troubles and put you right. You are so brave about it all that it seems to make it worse — that sounds silly, doesn't it. I won't bother you with silly reflections but you know that my thoughts are with you all the time and I do know that you will be alright again and your own, indomitable self before long.

I am beginning to wish we were still at war, this peace business makes me tired, all hopes destroyed, all ideas of glorious achievement gone by the board, nothing but an immense drudgery and masses of problems which there seems to be great difficulty in solving.

It all began with the advent of Admiral Meurer. You wd. have loved that, it was dramatic and tragic to a high degree.

He arrived onboard at 7.p.m., pitch dark aided by a thick fog,

[1]Roskill, *Admiral of the Fleet*, p. 276 and note, states that he was unable to check this copy with the original which has been lost and that full accuracy cannot be guaranteed.

in which he could see nothing and had no idea he was surrounded by the greatest fleet in the world. I arranged a most beautiful setting, my dramatic sense was highly developed at the moment. When he marched up the gangway he was met by a blaze of light from groups of the strongest electric sunlights which lighted the gangway and the path to be trod from there to my hatchway, outside the path everything was inky black and perfect stillness. Actually on the edge of the path of light, half in and half out, was a line of the fattest marine sentries, about 2 paces apart with fixed bayonets upon which the light gleamed, wherever he looked he met a bayonet. He was met by Tommy Brand and Chatfield who were frigidity itself. The wretch nearly collapsed on the Quarter Deck, and his party were led to my cabin where I met him supported by my 2nd-in-Command (I wish he hadn't a beard, I nearly asked him to take it off, it spoilt the scene), O.de B., Tyrwhitt and several members of my staff.

I wouldn't accept him as being what he said he was until he produced documentary evidence in support of his statement and identified his staff. Having 'Pray be seated', I read him my prepared instructions and refused to discuss them but said they must be thought over and answered on the morrow. They were greatly depressed, overwhelmingly so, and I kept on feeling sorry for them but kept going on by repeating to myself, *Lusitania*, Belgian atrocities, Belgian prince, British prisoners, and I won in a trot. So much so that Meurer in a voice like lead, with an ashen grey face, said, I do not think the Commander-in-Chief is aware of the condition of Germany, and then in dull heavy tones, began to retail the effect of the blockades. It had brought revolution in the North which had spread to the South, then to East and finally to the West, that anarchy was rampant, the seed was sown, it remained for the harvest of human lives to be reaped in the interior of Germany as well as on the frontiers. Men, women and children under six were non-existent, that Germany was destroyed utterly, the latter with a wail in his voice. It had no effect, I only said to myself thank God for the British Navy. This is your work, without it no victory on land would have availed or even been possible. I told them to return with their answers in the morning. He then informed me he had 3 delegates of the Sailors' & Work-man's Council onboard who were anxious to take part in the conversations. I naturally said I knew them not and did not intend to know them better, which was the one source of relief to the stricken party. And they stepped out into the darkness and fog to do the 12 miles back to their ship.

I retired and was nearly sick.

They returned the next day, still in the thickest fog I've seen in the F. of F., it was a fine achievement on the part of the *Oak* in getting them through but very late, and they brought their replies.

Generally speaking, they would agree to anything, they raised points here and there which were firmly squashed. They prated about the honour of their submarine crews being possibly assailed, which nearly lifted me out of my chair. However, I scathingly replied that their personal safety wd. be assured, which wd. doubtless satisfy their honour. In any case, it was different to ours and we couldn't waste time over it. I had them onboard until after midnight and Woodley overfed them, I fear. When it came to signing the documents, I thought he would collapse, he took two shots at it, putting his pen down twice, but we got him over it and they retired into the fog in grim silence. If I could draw, I could make a glorious picture but it would require a Leonardo de Vinci to do it well, it was very poignant all the time and rather wearing. It was curious, all the time he was in the Firth of Forth it was the thickest fog imaginable, he never knew that he passed through lines of the finest ships in the world, they were just out of sight, I think the Bon Dieu was kind to him in that —

The next act in the drama I must keep for another letter, you will have read most of it in the papers, there were rather bad accounts that I saw and it was a Wonderful Day.

*   *   *

LIST OF DOCUMENTS

Collections used:

BTY: The Papers of Admiral of the Fleet Earl Beatty, National Maritime Museum.

CCC/DRAX: The Papers of Admiral Sir Reginald P.-E.-E. Drax, Churchill College, Cambridge.

CCC/SLGF: The Papers of Sir Shane Leslie and Captain Sir Bryan Godfrey Faussett, Churchill College, Cambridge.

DEY: The Papers of Sir Eustace Tennyson d'Eyncourt, National Maritime Museum.

HTN: The Papers of Admiral Sir Frederick Hamilton, National Maritime Museum.

IWM/GWYNNE: The Papers of H. A. Gwynne, Imperial War Museum.

IWM/PHILL: The Papers of Admiral Sir Richard Phillimore, Imperial War Museum.

KEL: The Papers of Admiral of the Fleet Sir John Kelly, National Maritime Museum.

LAR: The Papers of Captain Dennis Larking, National Maritime Museum.

PART I

1.	To his wife	22–27 Aug 1902	BTY/17/8/20–21
2.	To his wife	29 Aug–2 Sep 1902	BTY/17/8/43–51
3.	To his wife	18 Sep 1902	BTY/17/9/73–78
4.	To his wife	20 Sep 1902	BTY/17/9/88–93
5.	To his wife	21 Sep 1902	BTY/17/9/95–98
6.	To his wife	3 Oct 1902	BTY/17/10/11–15
7.	From his wife	16 Apr 1905	BTY/18/2/30–37
8.	From his wife	27 July 1905	BTY/18/4/33–40
9.	From his wife	13 Mar 1908	BTY/18/17/61–67
10.	To his wife	16 Feb 1909	BTY/17/12/64–69
11.	To his wife	20 Feb 1909	BTY/17/12/85–89
12.	To his wife	6 Apr 1909	BTY/17/13/35–40

13.	To his wife	13 Apr 1909	BTY/17/13/68–71
14.	To his wife	16 Apr 1909	BTY/17/13/76–82
15.	To his wife	2–4 July 1909	BTY/17/15/8–19
16.	To his wife	13–14 July 1909	BTY/17/15/62–68
17.	To his wife	6 Dec 1909	BTY/17/18/27–30
18.	To his wife	10 Dec 1909	BTY/17/18/46–53
19.	To his wife	29 Dec 1909	BTY/17/18/88–93
20.	From Captain E. C. Troubridge	5 July 1911	BTY/2/2/1
21.	To Reginald McKenna	24 July 1911	BTY/2/2/4
22.	From Troubridge	26 July 1911	BTY/2/2/2
23.	To Troubridge	26 July 1911	BTY/2/2/6
24.	To his wife	4 Feb 1912	BTY/17/20/9
25.	To his wife	24 Mar 1912	BTY/17/20/11–12
26.	Beatty's paper for Winston Churchill on naval dispositions in a war against Germany	7 Apr 1912	BTY/2/3/6
27.	To his wife	24 May 1912	BTY/17/20/38–39
28.	To his wife	27 May 1912	BTY/17/20/44–45
29.	To his wife	1 June 1912	BTY/17/21/1–2
30.	To his wife	10 July 1912	BTY/17/21/6–7
31.	To his wife	14 July 1912	BTY/17/21/12–15
32.	To his wife	23 July 1912	BTY/17/21/18–19

PART II

33.	From Admiralty	1 Feb 1913	BTY/2/4/1
34.	Filson Young, 'The Things that Matter' Pall Mall Gazette	3 Mar 1913	BTY/2/4/2
35.	To his wife	1 Apr 1913	BTY/17/22/15
36.	Beatty's 'Functions of a Battle-Cruiser Squadron'	5 Apr 1913	BTY/2/4/3
37.	To his wife	5 Apr 1913	BTY/17/23/15–16
38.	To his wife	9 Apr 1913	BTY/17/23/22–23
39.	To his wife	11 Apr 1913	BTY/17/23/25–26
40.	To his wife	11 Apr 1913	BTY/17/23/28
41.	To his wife	8 May 1913	BTY/17/24/17–19
42.	To CinC Home Fleets	4 June 1913	CCC/DRAX /4/1

PART III

74.	To his wife	29 Sep 1914	BTY/17/29/37–40
75.	To his wife	11 Oct 1914	BTY/17/30/14–16
76.	To Churchill	17 Oct 1914	CCC/SLGF/3/3
77.	To his wife	20 Oct 1914	BTY/17/30/33–35
78.	To his wife	23 Oct 1914	BTY/17/30/37–39
79.	To his wife	30 Oct 1914	BTY/17/30 56–57
80.	To Fisher	6 Nov 1914	BTY/3/2/1
81.	To his wife	2 Nov 1914	BTY/17/31/2–5
82.	To his wife	3–4 Nov 1914	BTY/17/31/7–10
83.	To his wife	5 Nov 1914	BTY/17/31/12–13
84.	To his wife	6 Nov 1914	BTY/17/31/15–16
85.	To his wife	7 Nov 1914	BTY/17/31/18–20
86.	To his wife	10 Nov 1914	BTY/17/31/22–24
87.	To his wife	12 Nov 1914	BTY/17/31/29–30
88.	To his wife	13–14 Nov 1914	BTY/17/31/32–33
89.	To Jellicoe	13 Nov 1914	BTY/13/21/3
90.	To Jellicoe	14 Nov 1914	BTY/13/21/3
91.	To his wife	16 Nov 1914	BTY/17/31/35–37
92.	To his wife	21 Nov 1914	BTY/17/31/42–43
93.	From Churchill	22 Nov 1914	BTY/3/2/2
94.	To Churchill	Nov 1914	BTY/3/2/3
95.	To his wife	26 Nov 1914	BTY/17/31/47–49
96.	From Churchill	30 Nov 1914	BTY/14/4/1
97.	To his wife	2 Dec 1914	BTY/17/32/5–7
98.	From his wife	3 Dec 1914	BTY/17/32/9–11
99.	To his wife	4 Dec 1914	BTY/17/32/13–14
100.	To his wife	10 Dec 1914	BTY/17/32/23–26
101.	To his wife	11 Dec 1914	BTY/17/32/28–29
102.	From Goodenough	18 Dec 1914	BTY/3/3/1
103.	To Warrender	19 Dec 1914	BTY/3/3/14
104.	To Jellicoe	19 Dec 1914	BTY/3/3/16–17
105.	Goodenough to Jellicoe	20 Dec 1914	BTY/3/3/3
106.	Goodenough to Jellicoe	20 Dec 1914	BTY/3/3/3
107.	Signal Copies after Scarborough Raid	17–20 Dec 1914	BTY/3/3/4–13
108.	Jellicoe to Goodenough	23 Dec 1914	BTY/3/3/19
109.	Beatty Memorandum to Commanding Officers and the Engineer Captain, 1st BCS	28 Dec 1914	HTN/ 17

110.	Jellicoe to Flag Officers and Commodores	30 Dec 1914	BTY/3/3/20
111.	To Admiralty	26 Feb 1915	BTY/3/3/24

PART IV

112.	From Rear-Admiral Moore	25 Jan 1915	BTY/4/6/7
113.	From Goodenough	25 Jan 1915	BTY/4/6/7
114.	From Chatfield	27 Jan 1915	BTY/4/6/7
115.	From Captain Pelly	31 Jan 1915	BTY/4/6/7
116.	To Jellicoe	2 Feb 1915	BTY/4/6/7
117.	From Moore	7 Feb 1915	BTY/4/2
118.	To Admiralty	9 Feb 1915	BTY/4/6/7
119.	Signal Notes	Undated	BTY/4/6/7
120.	Notes re lessons learned from action on January 24, 1915	Undated	BTY/4/6/7
121.	From Moore	29 Jan 1915	BTY/4/6/7
122.	From Chatfield	2 Feb 1915	BTY/4/6/7
123.	From Pelly	25 Jan 1915	BTY/4/6/7
124.	Jellicoe to Admiralty	10 Feb 1915	BTY/4/1/1
125.	To Pelly	11 Feb 1915	BTY/4/5/1
126.	From Moore	13 Feb 1915	BTY/4/2
127.	To Admiral Sir Frederick Hamilton	17 Feb 1915	HTN/117
128.	Revision of BCF Orders	18 Feb 1915	CCC/DRAX/1/3
129.	To Hamilton	21 Feb 1915	HTN/117
130.	From Chatfield	2 Mar 1915	BTY/4/5/6
131.	From Jellicoe	3 Mar 1915	BTY/4/5/1
132.	To his wife	15 Mar 1915	BTY/17/33/14–15
133.	To his wife	19 Mar 1915	BTY/17/33/17–18
134.	To his wife	20 Mar 1915	BTY/17/33/19–20
135.	From his wife	1 May 1915	BTY/18/23/1–7
136.	To his wife	2 May 1915	BTY/17/33/23–25
137.	From his wife	3 May 1915	BTY/18/23/17–22
138.	To his wife	4 May 1915	BTY/17/33/28–29
139.	To his wife	21 May 1915	BTY/17/33/33–35
140.	To his wife	29 June 1915	BTY/17/34/10–11
141.	To Hamilton	21 July 1915	HTN/117
142.	To his wife	30 July 1915	BTY/17/34/13–15
143.	To Jellicoe	12 Aug 1915	BTY/13/21/22
144.	To Hamilton	25 Aug 1915	HTN/117

145.	To Asquith	3 Feb 1916	BTY/5/2/2
146.	From Rear-Admiral Brock	18 Feb 1916	BTY/5/2/3
147.	From Rear-Admiral Pakenham	19 Feb 1916	BTY/5/2/3
148.	To Jellicoe	21 Feb 1916	BTY/5/2/3
149.	From Jellicoe	24 Feb 1916	BTY/5/2/3
150.	To Jellicoe	3 Mar 1916	BTY/5/2/3
151.	From Jellicoe	6 Mar 1916	BTY/5/2/3
152.	Jellicoe to Admiralty	10 Mar 1916	BTY/5/2/3
153.	From Jellicoe	13 Mar 1916	BTY/5/2/3
154.	From Jellicoe	11 Apr 1916	BTY/13/22/8
155.	To Jellicoe	14 Apr 1916	BTY/13/22/10
156.	To Jellicoe	7 May 1916	BTY/13/22/12
157.	To his wife	7 May 1916	BTY/17/35/11
158.	Jellicoe to Admiralty	11 May 1916	BTY/5/2/4

PART V

159.	To Admiralty	3 June 1916	HTN/122/B
160.	From Jellicoe	4 June 1916	BTY/13/22/13
161.	To Dennis Larking	5 June 1916	LAR/1/24
162.	Admiralty to Commanders-in-Chief and Other Officers	5 June 1916	HTN/122/B
163.	From Hamilton's Journal	7 June 1916	HTN/106
164.	To Jellicoe	12 June 1916	BTY/6/1/3
165.	From Jellicoe	13 June 1916	BTY/13/22/14
166.	To H. A. Gwynne Editor *Morning Post*	18 June 1916	IWM/GWYNNE MSS
167.	To A. J. Balfour	21 June 1916	BTY/6/3/15
168.	Lessons from Battle of 31 May 1916 (notes from Vice-Admiral Sturdee to Beatty)	21 June 1916	BTY/6/17/8
169.	Advance report of Gunnery Committee	22 June 1916	BTY/6/17/5
170.	Private H. Willons RMLI	31 May–1 June 1916	BTY/6/14/1

171.	Petty Officer Dan Sheppard (director Layer)	31 May–1 June 1916	BTY/6/14/2
172.	Interim Report of Committee on Construction to Vice-Admiral Commanding BCF	23 June 1916	BTY/6/17/4
173.	Additional Report of Gunnery Committee	24 June 1916	BTY/6/17/7
174.	Notes by Beatty	26 June 1916	BTY/6/3/16
175.	Lady Beatty to Larking	10 July 1916	LAR/2
176.	Addition to Battle-Cruiser Orders	3 Aug 1916	CCC/DRAX/1/3

PART VI

177.	From Balfour	22 Nov 1916	BTY/7/1/1
178.	To Balfour	22 Nov 1916	BTY/7/1/1
179.	To Balfour	27 Nov 1916	BTY/7/1/2
180.	From Balfour	27 Nov 1916	BTY/7/1/2
181.	From Admiralty	27 Nov 1916	BTY/7/1/5
182.	To Admiralty	28 Nov 1916	BTY/7/1/6
183.	From King George V	3 Dec 1916	BTY/15/4/2
184.	To his wife	4 Dec 1916	BTY/17/36/17–18
185.	From his wife	13 Dec 1916	BTY/18/25/46–51
186.	To his wife	15 Dec 1916	BTY/17/36/29–30
187.	From his wife	15 Dec 1916	BTY/18/25/53–60
188.	To his wife	21 Dec 1916	BTY/17/36/41–43
189.	To Hamilton	26 Dec 1916	HTN/117
190.	To his wife	30 Dec 1916	BTY/17/36/56–57
191.	To Hamilton	20 Jan 1917	HTN/117
192.	To his wife	25 Jan 1917	BTY/17/37/22–23
193.	To Hamilton	28 Jan 1917	HTN/117
194.	To his wife	30 Jan 1917	BTY/17/37/28–30
195.	To Admiralty	31 Jan 1917	BTY/7/9/[1]
196.	To his wife	1 Feb 1917	BTY/17/38/2–3
197.	To his wife	3 Feb 1917	BTY/17/38/5–6
198.	To his wife	5 Feb 1917	BTY/17/38/7–8
199.	To his wife	6 Feb 1917	BTY/17/38/10–13
200.	To his wife	9 Feb 1917	BTY/17/38/19–21
201.	From Rear-Admiral Halsey (4th Sea Lord)	14 Feb 1917	BTY/13/16/3

202.	Notes on tactical exercises carried out on 24 February 1917	24 Feb 1917	BTY/7/2/8
203.	To his wife	28 Feb 1917	BTY/17/38/31–32
204.	To his wife	1 Mar 1917	BTY/17/39/2–4
205.	To his wife	12 Mar 1917	BTY/17/39/16–18
206.	To his wife	14 Mar 1917	BTY/17/39/20–22
207.	From his wife	17 Mar 1917	BTY/18/28/68–71
208.	To his wife	18 Mar 1917	BTY/17/39/26–27
209.	To his wife	28 Mar 1917	BTY/17/39/38–39
210.	To his wife	30 Mar 1917	BTY/17/39/41–43
211.	To his wife	1 Apr 1917	BTY/17/40/2–3
212.	To his wife	15 Apr 1917	BTY/17/40/8
213.	To his wife	21 Apr 1917	BTY/17/40/10–11
214.	To his wife	25 Apr 1917	BTY/17/40/16–17
215.	From King George V	26 Apr 1917	BTY/15/4/5
216.	To his wife	27 Apr 1917	BTY/17/40/19–21
217.	To his wife	1 May 1917	BTY/17/41/2
218.	To his wife	2 May 1917	BTY/17/41/4–5
219.	To his wife	3 May 1917	BTY/17/41/7–9
220.	From his wife	7 May 1917	BTY/18/30/7–13
221.	To Admiralty	8 May 1917	BTY/22/5
222.	To his wife	8 May 1917	BTY/17/41/14–15
223.	To his wife	10 May 1917	BTY/17/41/17–19
224.	To Eugénie Godfrey-Faussett	10 May 1917	CCC/SLGF/14/1/A
225.	To his wife	11 May 1917	BTY/17/41/21–22
226.	From his wife	12 May 1917	BTY/18/30/37–44
227.	To his wife	13 May 1917	BTY/17/41/24–26
228.	To his wife	16 May 1917	BTY/17/41/28–30
229.	To his wife	22 May 1917	BTY/17/41/39–40
230.	To his wife	24 May 1917	BTY/17/41/42–43
231.	To his wife	27 May 1917	BTY/17/41/45–47
232.	To his wife	31 May 1917	BTY/17/41/54–56
233.	From his wife	1 June 1917	BTY/18/31/2–6
234.	From Rear-Admiral Halsey (3rd Sea Lord)	17 June 1917	BTY/13/16/4
235.	Notes on Beatty's views on construction policy	18 June 1917	DEY/19
236.	From Halsey	18 June 1917	BTY/13/16/5
237.	To his wife	19 June 1917	BTY/17/42/7–8

238.	To his wife	3 July 1917	BTY/17/43/2–3
239.	From his wife	5 July 1917	BTY/18/32/16–18
240.	To his wife	7 July 1917	BTY/17/43/8–9
241.	To his wife	9 July 1917	BTY/17/43/11–12
242.	To his wife	11 July 1917	BTY/17/43/14–15
243.	To his wife	13 July 1917	BTY/17/43/17–18
244.	To Hamilton	14 July 1917	HTN/117
245.	To his wife	4 Sep 1917	BTY/17/44/4
246.	To his wife	18 Sep 1917	BTY/17/44/8–9
247.	To his wife	3 Oct 1917	BTY/17/45/5–7
248.	To his wife	13 Oct 1917	BTY/17/45/24–26
249.	To his wife	18 Oct 1917	BTY/17/45/32–34
250.	To Rear Admiral Richard Phillimore	19 Dec 1917	IWM/PHILL
251.	Notes on visit of DID to Beatty	19 Dec 1917	BTY/7/9/5
252.	Selections from Grand Fleet Battle Instructions	1 Jan 1918	BTY/7/3/4
253.	From Admiral Sir Rosslyn Wemyss	27 Jan 1918	BTY/13/39/5
254.	To his wife	4 Feb 1918	BTY/17/48/4–5
255.	To his wife	5 Feb 1918	BTY/17/48/7–9
256.	From Wemyss	7 Feb 1918	BTY/13/39/7
257.	From King George V	10 Feb 1918	BTY/15/4/7
258.	To his wife	12 Feb 1918	BTY/17/48/21–23
259.	To Wemyss	13 Feb 1918	BTY/13/39/8
260.	To his wife	18 Feb 1918	BTY 17/48/31–35
261.	From Wemyss	20 Feb 1918	BTY/13/39/10
262.	To Wemyss	22 Feb 1918	BTY/13/39/11
263.	To Wemyss	22 Feb 1918	BTY/13/39/11
264.	From Wemyss	26 Mar 1918	BTY/13/39/14
265.	From Wemyss	30 Mar 1918	BTY/13/39/15
266.	To Wemyss	1 Apr 1918	BTY/13/39/16
267.	To his wife	7 Apr 1918	BTY/17/50/14–15
268.	To Wemyss	31 May 1918	BTY/13/39/22
269.	From Wemyss	3 June 1918	BTY/13/39/23
270.	From Rear Admiral Phillimore	22 June 1918	BTY/13/30/1
271.	To his wife	2 July 1918	BTY/17/52/2–4
272.	To Wemyss	10 Aug 1918	BTY/13/39/33
273.	From Wemyss	15 Aug 1918	BTY/13/39/38
274.	Balfour to Robert Cecil	22 Aug 1918	BTY/14/2/3

275.	From Wemyss	23 Aug 1918	BTY/13/39/38
276.	From Wemyss	30 Aug 1918	BTY/13/39/40
277.	To Wemyss	1 Sep 1918	BTY/13/39/42
278.	From Wemyss	2 Sep 1918	BTY/13/39/43
279.	Extract from secret Fleet Orders on Scandinavian Convoys	4 Sep 1918	BTY/7/4/3
280.	To Eugénie Godfrey-Faussett	6 Sep 1918	CCC/SLGF/14/1/A
281.	To his wife	22 Sep 1918	BTY/17/52/18–19
282.	To Wemyss	4 Oct 1918	BTY/13/40/2
283.	To Wemyss	18 Oct 1918	BTY/13/40/8
284.	From Wemyss	19 Oct 1918	BTY/13/40/11
285.	From Rear-Admiral Sir Sydney Fremantle (DCNS)	29 Oct 1918	BTY/13/12/3
286.	From Wemyss	5 Nov 1918	BTY/13/40/17
287.	Procedure regarding Carrying out of naval terms of armistice	Nov 1918	BTY/7/10/5
288.	Address delivered by Beatty on board HMS *Lion* to ships' companies of *Lion* and 1st BCS	24 Nov 1918	KEL/106
289.	To Eugénie Godfrey-Faussett	26 Nov 1918	CCC/SLGF/1/B

INDEX

[Ranks are those then held. Distinguished careers are outlined in the footnotes.]

Navy Records Society
(Founded 1893)

The Navy Records Society was established for the purpose of printing unpublished manuscripts and rare works of naval interest. The Society is open to all who are interested in naval history, and any person wishing to become a member should apply to the Hon. Secretary, c/o the Public Record Office, Chancery Lane, London WC2A 1LR. The annual subscription is £15, which entitles the member to receive one free copy of each work issued by the Society in that year, and to buy earlier issues at much reduced prices.

The prices to members and non-members respectively are given after each volume, and orders should be sent, enclosing no money, to the Hon. Treasurer, Binder Hamlyn, 8 St. Bride Street, London EC4A 4DA. Those marked 'TS' and 'SP' are published for the Society by Temple Smith and Scolar Press, and available to non-members only from the Gower Publishing Group, Gower House, Croft Road, Aldershot, Hampshire GU11 3HR. Those marked 'A & U' are published by George Allen & Unwin, and available to non-members only through bookshops.

The Society has already published:

Vols. 1 and 2. *State Papers relating to the Defeat of the Spanish Armada, Anno 1588* Vols I & II, ed. Professor J. K. Laughton. (£12.00 ea./£40.00 set TS)

Vol. 3. *Letters of Lord Hood, 1781–82*, ed. David Hannay. (*Out of Print*)

Vol. 4. *Index to James's Naval History*, ed. Hon. T. Brassey. (*Out of Print*)

Vol. 5. *Life of Captain Stephen Martin, 1666–1740*, ed. Sir Clements R. Markham. (*Out of Print*)

Vol. 6. *Journal of Rear-Admiral Bartholomew James,*

593

1725–1828, ed. Professor J. K. Laughton and Commander J. Y. F. Sulivan. (*Out of Print*)

Vol. 7. *Hollond's Discourses of the Navy, 1638 & 1658*, ed. J. R. Tanner. (*Out of Print*)

Vol. 8. *Naval Accounts and Inventories in the Reign of Henry VII*, ed. M. Oppenheim. (*Out of Print*)

Vol. 9. *Journal of Sir George Rooke*, ed. Oscar Browning. (*Out of Print*)

Vol. 10. *Letters and Papers relating to the War with France, 1512–13*, ed. Alfred Spont. (*Out of Print*)

Vol. 11. *Papers relating to the Spanish War, 1585–87*, ed. Julian S. Corbett. (£15.00/£35.00 TS)

Vol. 12. *Journals and Letters of Admiral of the Fleet Sir Thomas Byam Martin, 1773–1854*, Vol, II, ed. Admiral Sir R. Vesey Hamilton. (*Out of Print*)

Vol. 13. *Papers relating to the First Dutch War, 1652–54*, Vol. I, ed. Dr S. R. Gardiner. (*Out of Print*)

Vol. 14. *Papers relating to the Blockade of Brest, 1803–5*, Vol. I, ed. J. Leyland. (*Out of Print*)

Vol. 15. *History of the Russian Fleet during the Reign of Peter the Great, by a Contemporary Englishman*, ed. Admiral Sir Cyprian Bridge. (*Out of Print*)

Vol. 16. *Logs of the Great Sea Fights, 1794–1805*, Vol. I, ed. Vice-Admiral Sir T. Sturges Jackson. (£12.00/£20.00)

Vol. 17. *Papers relating to the First Dutch War, 1652–54*, Vol. II, ed. Dr S. R. Gardiner. (*Out of Print*)

Vol. 18. *Logs of the Great Sea Fights, 1794–1805*, Vol. II, ed. Vice-Admiral Sir T. Sturges Jackson. (£12.00/£20.00)

Vol. 19. *Journals and Letters of Admiral of the Fleet Sir Thomas Byam Martin, 1773–1854*, Vol. III, ed. Admiral Sir R. Vesey Hamilton. (*Out of Print*)

Vol. 20. *The Naval Miscellany*, Vol. I, ed. Professor J. K. Laughton. (£15.00/£20.00)

Vol. 21. *Papers relating to the Blockade of Brest, 1803–5*, Vol. II, ed. J. Leyland. (*Out of Print*)

Vols. 22 and 23. *The Naval Tracts of Sir William Monson*, Vols I & II, ed. M. Oppenheim (*Out of Print*)

Vol. 24. *Journals and Letters of Admiral of the Fleet Sir Thomas Byam Martin, 1773–1854*, Vol. I ed. Admiral Sir R. Vesey Hamilton. (*Out of Print*)

Vol. 25. *Nelson and the Neapolitan Jacobins*, ed. H. C. Gutteridge. (*Out of Print*)

Vol 26. *A Descriptive Catalogue of the Naval Manuscripts in the Pepysian Library*, Vol I, ed. J. R. Tanner. (*Out of Print*)

Vol. 27. *A Descriptive Catalogue of the Naval Manuscripts in the Pepysian Library*, Vol. II, ed. J. R. Tanner (*Out of Print*)

Vol. 28. *The Correspondence of Admiral John Markham, 1801–7*, ed. Sir Clements R. Markham. (*Out of Print*)

Vol. 29. *Fighting Instructions, 1530–1816*, ed. Julian S. Corbett. (*Out of Print*)

Vol. 30. *Papers relating to the First Dutch War, 1652–54*, Vol. III, ed. Dr S. R. Gardiner. (*Out of Print*)

Vol. 31. *The Recollections of Commander James Anthony Gardner, 1775–1814*, ed. Admiral Sir R. Vesey Hamilton and Professor J. K. Laughton. (*£15.00/£20.00*)

Vol. 32. *Letters and Papers of Charles, Lord Barham, 1758–1813*, Vol. I, ed. Sir J. K. Laughton. (*£15.00/£20.00*)

Vol. 33. *Naval Songs and Ballads*, ed. Professor C. H. Firth. (*Out of Print*)

Vol. 34. *Views of the Battles of the Third Dutch War*, ed. Julian S. Corbett. (*Out of Print*)

Vol. 35. *Signals and Instructions, 1776–1794*, ed. Julian S. Corbett. (*Out of Print*)

Vol. 36. *A Descriptive Catalogue of the Naval Manuscripts in the Pepysian Library*, Vol. III, ed. J. R. Tanner. (*Out of Print*)

Vol. 37. *Papers relating to the First Dutch War, 1652–54*, Vol. IV, ed. C. T. Atkinson. (*Out of Print*)

Vol. 38. *Letters and Papers of Charles, Lord Barham, 1758–1813*, Vol. II, ed. Sir J. K. Laughton. (*£15.00/£20.00*)

Vol. 39. *Letters and Papers of Charles, Lord Barham, 1758–1813*, Vol. III, ed. Sir J. K. Laughton. (*£15.00/£20.00*)

Vol. 40. *The Naval Miscellany*, Vol. II, ed. Sir J. K. Laughton. (*£15.00/£20.00*)

Vol. 41. *Papers relating to the First Dutch War, 1652–54*, Vol. V, ed. C. T. Atkinson. (*£8.00/£20.00*)

Vol. 42. *Papers relating to the Loss of Minorca in 1756*, ed. Captain H. W. Richmond. (*£8.00/£20.00*)

Vol. 43. *The Naval Tracts of Sir William Monson*, Vol. III, ed. M. Oppenheim. (*£8.00/£20.00*)

Vol. 44. *The Old Scots Navy, 1689–1710*, ed. James Grant. (*Out of Print*)

Vol. 45. *The Naval Tracts of Sir William Monson*, Vol. IV, ed. M. Oppenheim. (*£8.00/£20.00*)

Vol. 46. *The Private Papers of George, Second Earl Spencer*,

Vol. I, ed. Julian S. Corbett (*£8.00/£20.00*)

Vol. 47. *The Naval Tracts of Sir William Monson*, Vol. V, ed. M. Oppenheim. (*£8.00/£20.00*)

Vol. 48. *The Private Papers of George, Second Earl Spencer*, Vol. II, ed. Julian S. Corbett. (*Out of Print*)

Vol. 49. *Documents relating to Law and Custom of the Sea*, Vol. I, ed. R. G. Marsden. (*£8.00/£20.00*)

Vol. 50. *Documents relating to Law and Custom of the Sea*, Vol. II, ed. R. G. Marsden. (*£8.00/£20.00*)

Vol. 51. *Autobiography of Phineas Pett*, ed. W. G. Perrin. (*Out of Print*)

Vol. 52. *The Life of Admiral Sir John Leake*, Vol. I, ed. G. A. R. Callender. (*£8.00/£20.00*)

Vol. 53. *The Life of Admiral Sir John Leake*, Vol. II, ed. G. A. R. Callender. (*£8.00/£20.00*)

Vol. 54. *The Life and Works of Sir Henry Mainwaring*, Vol. I, ed. G. E. Manwaring. (*£8.00/£20.00*)

Vol. 55. *The Letters of Lord St. Vincent, 1801–1804*, Vol. I, ed. D. B. Smith. (*Out of Print*)

Vol. 56. *The Life and Works of Sir Henry Mainwaring*, Vol. II, ed. G. E. Manwaring and W. G. Perrin. (*Out of Print*)

Vol. 57. *A descriptive Catalogue of the Naval Manuscripts in the Pepysian Library*, Vol. IV, ed. Dr J. R. Tanner. (*Out of Print*)

Vol. 58 *The Private Papers of George, Second Earl Spencer*, Vol. III, ed. Rear-Admiral H. W. Richmond. (*Out of Print*)

Vol. 59. *The Private Papers of George, Second Earl Spencer*, Vol. IV, ed. Rear-Admiral H. W. Richmond. (*Out of Print*)

Vol. 60 *Samuel Pepys's Naval Minutes*, ed. Dr. J. R. Tanner. (*£15.00/£20.00*)

Vol. 61. *The Letters of Lord St. Vincent, 1801–1804*, Vol. II, ed. D. B. Smith. (*Out of Print*)

Vol. 62. *Letters and Papers of Admiral Viscount Keith*, Vol. I, ed. W. G. Perrin. (*Out of Print*)

Vol. 63. *The Naval Miscellany*, Vol. III, ed. W. G. Perrin. (*Out of Print*)

Vol. 64. *The Journal of the First Earl of Sandwich*, ed. R. C. Anderson. (*Out of Print*)

Vol. 65. *Boteler's Dialogues*, ed. W. G. Perrin. (*£8.00/£20.00*)

Vol. 66. *Papers relating to the First Dutch War, 1652–54*, Vol. VI, ed. C. T. Atkinson. (*£8.00/£20.00*)

Vol. 67. *The Byng Papers*, Vol. I, ed. W. C. B. Tunstall (*£8.00/£20.00*)

Vol. 68. *The Byng Papers*, Vol. II, ed. W. C. B. Tunstall. (*£8.00/£20.00*)

Vol. 69. *The Private Papers of John, Earl of Sandwich*, Vol. I, ed. G. R. Barnes & Lt Cdr J. H. Owen. (*£8.00/£20.00*)

Corrigenda to *Papers relating to the First Dutch War, 1652–54*, ed. Captain A. C. Dewar. (*Free*)

Vol. 70. *The Byng Papers*, Vol. III, ed. W. C. B. Tunstall. (*£8.00/£20.00*)

Vol. 71. *The Private Papers of John, Earl of Sandwich*, Vol. II, ed. G. R. Barnes and Lt Cdr J. H. Owen. (*£8.00/£20.00*)

Vol. 72. *Piracy in the Levant, 1827–8*, ed. Lt Cdr C. G. Pitcairn Jones. (*£8.00/£20.00*)

Vol. 73. *The Tangier Papers of Samuel Pepys*, ed. Edwin Chappell. (*£15.00/£20.00*)

Vol. 74. *The Tomlinson Papers*, ed. J. G. Bullocke. (*£8.00/£20.00*)

Vol. 75. *The Private Papers of John, Earl of Sandwich*, Vol. III, ed. G. R. Barnes and Lt Cdr J. H. Owen. (*Out of Print*)

Vol. 76. *The Letters of Robert Blake*, ed. Rev. J. R. Powell. (*Out of Print*)

Vol. 77. *Letters and Papers of Admiral the Hon. Samuel Barrington*, Vol. I, ed. D. Bonner-Smith. (*£8.00/£20.00*)

Vol. 78. *The Private Papers of John, Earl of Sandwich*, Vol. IV, ed. G. R. Barnes and Lt Cdr J. H. Owen. (*Out of Print*)

Vol. 79. *The Journals of Sir Thomas Allin, 1660–1678*, Vol. I, ed. R. C. Anderson. (*£8.00/£20.00*)

Vol. 80. *The Journals of Sir Thomas Allin, 1660–1678*, Vol. II, ed. R. C. Anderson. (*£8.00/£20.00*)

Vol. 81. *Letters and Papers of Admiral the Hon. Samuel Barrington*, Vol. II, ed. D. Bonner-Smith. (*Out of Print*)

Vol. 82. *Captain Boteler's Recollections, 1808–1830*, ed. D. Bonner-Smith (*Out of Print*)

Vol. 83. *Russian War, 1854, Baltic and Black Sea: Official Correspondence*, ed. D. Bonner-Smith and Captain A. C. Dewar. (*Out of Print*)

Vol. 84. *Russian War, 1855, Baltic: Official Correspondence*, ed. D. Bonner-Smith (*Out of Print*)

Vol. 85. *Russian War, 1855, Black Sea: Official Correspondence*, ed. Captain A. C. Dewar. (*Out of Print*)

Vol. 86. *Journals and Narratives of the Third Dutch War*, ed. R. C. Anderson. (*Out of Print*)

Vol. 87. *The Naval Brigades in the Indian Mutiny, 1857–58*, ed.

Cdr W. B. Rowbotham. (*Out of Print*)

Vol. 88. *Patee Byng's Journal*, ed. J. L. Cranmer-Byng. (*Out of Print*)

Vol. 89. *The Sergison Papers, 1688–1702*, ed. Cdr R. D. Merriman. (*£8.00/£20.00*)

Vol. 90. *The Keith Papers*, Vol. II, ed. C. C. Lloyd. (*Out of Print*)

Vol. 91. *Five Naval Journals, 1789–1817*, ed. Rear-Admiral H. G. Thursfield. (*Out of Print*)

Vol. 92. *The Naval Miscellany*, Vol. IV, ed. C. C. Lloyd. (*Out of Print*)

Vol. 93. *Sir William Dillon's Narrative of Professional Adventures, 1790–1839*, Vol. I, ed. Professor Michael A. Lewis. (*Out of Print*)

Vol. 94. *The Walker Expedition to Quebec, 1711*, ed. Professor Gerald S. Graham. (*Out of Print*)

Vol. 95. *The Second China War, 1856–60*, ed. D. Bonner-Smith and E. W. R. Lumby. (*Out of Print*)

Vol. 96. *The Keith Papers*, Vol. III, ed. C. C. Lloyd. (*£8.00/£20.00*)

Vol. 97. *Sir William Dillon's Narrative of Professional Adventures, 1790–1839*, Vol. II, ed. Professor Michael A. Lewis. (*Out of Print*)

Vol. 98. *The Private Correspondence of Admiral Lord Collingwood*, ed. Professor Edward Hughes. (*Out of Print*)

Vol. 99. *The Vernon Papers, 1739–1745*, ed. B. McL. Ranft (*Out of Print*)

Vol. 100. *Nelson's Letters to his Wife and other Documents*, ed. Lt Cdr G. P. B. Naish. (*£8.00/£20.00*)

Vol. 101. *A Memoir of James Trevenen, 1760–1790*, ed. Professor C. C. Lloyd and Dr R. C. Anderson. (*Out of Print*)

Vol. 102. *The Papers of Admiral Sir John Fisher*, Vol. I, ed. Lt Cdr P. K. Kemp. (*Out of Print*)

Vol. 103. *Queen Anne's Navy*, ed. Cdr R. D. Merriman. (*Out of Print*)

Vol. 104. *The Navy and South America, 1807–1823*, ed. Professor G. S. Graham and Professor R. A. Humphreys. (*£8.00/£20.00*)

Vol. 105. *Documents relating to the Civil War, 1642–1648*, ed. Rev. J. R. Powell and E. K. Timings. (*Out of Print*)

Vol. 106. *The Papers of Admiral Sir John Fisher*, Vol. II, ed. Lt Cdr P. K. Kemp. (*Out of Print*)

Vol. 107. *The Health of Seamen*, ed. Professor C. C. Lloyd. (*£8.00/£20.00*)

Vol. 108. *The Jellicoe Papers*, Vol. I, ed. A. Temple Patterson. (*£8.00/£20.00*)

Vol. 109. *Documents relating to Anson's Voyage round the World, 1740–1744*, ed. Dr Glyndwr Williams. (*£8.00/£20.00*)

Vol. 110. *The Saumarez Papers: The Baltic, 1808–1812*, ed. A. N. Ryan. (*£8.00/£20.00*)

Vol. 111. *The Jellicoe Papers*, Vol. II, ed. A. Temple Patterson. (*£8.00/£20.00*)

Vol. 112. *The Rupert and Monck Letterbook, 1666*, ed. Rev. J. R. Powell and E. K. Timings. (*£8.00/£20.00*)

Vol. 113. *Documents relating to the Royal Naval Air Service*, Vol. I., ed. Captain S. W. Roskill. (*£8.00/£20.00*)

Vol. 114. *The Siege and Capture of Havana, 1762*, ed. Professor David Syrett. (*£8.00/£20.00*)

Vol. 115. *Policy and Operations in the Mediterranean, 1912–14*, ed. E. W. R. Lumby. (*£8.00/£20.00*)

Vol. 116. *The Jacobean Commissions of Enquiry, 1608 & 1618*, ed. Dr. A. P. McGowan. (*£8.00/£20.00*)

Vol. 117. *The Keyes Papers*, Vol. I, ed. Dr Paul G. Halpern. (*£8.00/£20.00*)

Vol. 118. *The Royal Navy and North America: The Warren Papers, 1736–1752*, ed. Dr Julian Gwyn. (*£8.00/£20.00*)

Vol. 119. *The Manning of the Royal Navy: Selected Public Pamphlets 1693–1873*, ed. Professor J. S. Bromley. (*£8.00/£20.00*)

Vol. 120. *Naval Administration, 1715–1750*, ed. Professor D. A. Baugh. (*£8.00/£20.00*)

Vol. 121. *The Keyes Papers*, Vol. II, ed. Dr Paul G. Halpern. (*£8.00/£20.00*)

Vol. 122. *The Keyes Papers*, Vol. III, ed. Dr Paul G. Halpern. (*£8.00/£20.00*)

Vol. 123. *The Navy of the Lancastrian Kings: Accounts and Inventories of William Soper, Keeper of the King's Ships 1422–1427*, ed. Dr Susan Rose. (*£8.00/£20.00*)

Vol. 124. *The Pollen Papers: The Privately Circulated Printed Works of Arthur Hungerford Pollen, 1901–1916*, ed. Dr Jon T. Sumida. (*£8.00/£20.00 A & U*)

Vol. 125. *The Naval Miscellany*, Vol. V, ed. N. A. M. Rodger. (*£8.00/£30.00 A & U*)

Vol. 126. *The Royal Navy in the Mediterranean, 1915–1918*, ed. Professor Paul G. Halpern. (*£8.00/£35.00 TS*)

Vol. 127. *The Expedition of Sir John Norris and Sir Francis Drake to Spain and Portugal, 1589*, ed. Professor R. B. Wernham. (*£8.00/£35.00 TS*)

Vol. 128. *The Beatty Papers*, Vol. I, 1902–1918, ed. B. McL. Ranft (£8.00/c. £40.00 SP)